THE SNOW GODS

They are as towering as the mountains they rule.

ELIZABETH CHANDLER the imperious New Englander whose passion for **ANTON** astonishes her.

DIGGER PRINCE cheated by war of an Olympic gold, who finds a private war among Tito's partisans high in the mountains of Yugoslavia.

MARTA whose attempts to reunite the family exacerbate the conflict and through whose eyes we tour Vienna in the gay, doomed days before the Nazis seize power.

KELLY PRINCE Digger's son, the greatest skier of them all, who must choose between his own dream and his father's.

D1313400

Bring me men to match my mountains . . .

FOSS

THE SNOW GODS

Herbert Burkholz

A STAR BOOK
published by
the Paperback Division of
W H Allen & Co. Plc

A Star Book
Published in 1987
by the Paperback Division of
W H Allen & Co. Plc
44 Hill Street, London W1X 8LB

First published in Great Britain in two volumes by
W H Allen & Co. Plc in 1986

Copyright © Herbert Burkholz, 1985

Printed and bound in Great Britain by
Anchor Brendon Ltd, Tiptree, Essex

ISBN 0 352 32004 4

This book is dedicated to
PHILIP D. FAGANS, JR.,
and to the memory of
HELEN SUE FAGANS

Volume 1

BOOK ONE

ANTON

Chapter One

They call it Alpine skiing, and it's a simple sport. You go up to the top of the mountain and then you come down again. Up and down, it's as simple as that, and there are three ways to do it.

You can race down at sixty miles an hour, skiing flat out through the drops and over the moguls, skittering past the pine trees and the blur of faces streaking by. Skis bucketing over washboard hidden in tree shade that fades as the trees fall away before the long run down the ravine, straight and white, and then the hill falls away again down around the shoulder that leads to the final, painful, pushing schuss, and the banner at the finish below. You can do it that way and they call it downhill racing.

You can do it that way, or you can come down weaving through a complex set of gates with exquisite precision, a tight-rope walker at thirty miles an hour, a ballet master dancing on knives, a measure of grace plus speed as you shift your edges, clickety-clack, in the knee-bending, shoulder-bobbing rhythm that takes you once again to that banner at the finish below. You can do it that way and they call it a slalom.

You can do it either of those two ways, or you can combine the two and come down the mountain at almost the speed of the downhill, manoeuvring gates with almost the precision of the slalom, in an exhausting hybrid called the giant slalom, and that's Alpine skiing, too. It's all Alpine skiing when you go up the mountain and then come down again. It's as simple as that, which means that it isn't simple at all, but it's what my family has been doing with competence for over seventy years, and for most of my life it has been all that really matters.

I say this less in pride than in sadness. It isn't much to be proud of at the age of twenty-four, and right now I'm not sure that I have even that. There was a time when I did not count myself as being fully alive unless I was smoking down a thirty-degree slope, but not any more. Not since that day at Piz d'Rel when something snapped. Something made of neither meat nor bone, but it snapped just as surely as a tibia or a tendon, and ever since then I haven't been sure of anything.

Which is why I now inhabit a tiny, sunbaked clamshell of an island in the Mediterranean, sitting here surrounded by stacks of old letters and diaries, albums filled with cracked and browning photos, leather bound record books, and enough cups and medals and trophies to fill a hardware store. The memorabilia of my family, seventy years' worth and all mine now. Much too suddenly, all mine to sift through and muse upon as I try to stitch together the pieces of my life, reconstruct it back to where it was before something snapped. That day at Piz d'Rel I took off my skis, leaned them against the wall of the church, and went inside to where the bodies of those I had loved lay dripping on a makeshift altar. I sat with the bodies through the night, and in the morning I knew that I would never put those skis on again until I understood what had snapped, and why. That was only months ago, and now, as I write this in the summer of 1983, there are four unanswered letters on my desk from the U.S. Ski Team, all of them asking what my plans will be for this coming Olympic year. The letters deserve to be answered, and I know that in order to do that I first must come to an understanding of myself, and of this gifted, obsessed, charitable, greedy, murderous, kindhearted family of mine.

And what a strange place this is in which to contemplate the antics of the family. Our name has always been linked with skis, snow, and mountains, and this island hasn't seen real snow since the Ice Age. Outside my window the orange trees march down the valley in orderly rows, the fig trees curl close to the ground, and the pods of the dry *algarobas* clack together in the breeze like busy gossips. Chickens scratch, a dog barks, the hot and heavy air is spiced by an African offshoot, and across the valley, heard with startling clarity, a farmer berates his mule. A wedge of the sea, turned pearl by the bounce of the early-morning sun, shows through a notch in the hills, and shows me as well a world far removed from those mountains which have always been home to me. Sea level, lowlands, the weight of a sun almost tropical, no speed down here at all. Everything crawls here, the perfect pace for me now, and the perfect place in which to begin this chronicle, to play with these family memories the way a child might play in a graveyard: beating bones on headstones, making merry.

Bones as dry as these family relics that surround me, letters, diaries, photographs, and on top of the pile five charcoal sketches dated in the year 1913. Impressions of the Prinz family made by an itinerant artist passing through St. Anton am Arlberg in the Austrian Tirol. The work is of indifferent quality, but the pictures are forceful in their crudity and the faces leap from the paper.

The first is of my great-grandfather, Sepp Prinz, farmer and carpenter, but here he is drawn as a biblical patriarch in robes, holding the crook of a shepherd. Full-bearded, stern, a lined face with righteous eyes, a man who would slaughter his son on the altar unassailed by doubts.

Next, his wife, Hanna, sketched in her farmhouse kitchen, a soup ladle in her hand, a pot on the stove, a flush to her cheeks. A smiling, maternal woman, but underneath that smile the sketcher has caught a glimpse of the Germanic steel that insists on, and enforces, order in the home.

Otto next, the older son, twenty-four that year and a reserve officer in the imperial army, but here he is limned as a medieval knight in armour, the visor of the helmet open to reveal the face. That face, so much like his father's: the same clamped determination, the same righteous eyes, but within those eyes an ambition that his father lacks. An overwhelming desire to achieve . . . what? Anything. Anything at all, anyplace in the world. Just to be something more than what he is right now: the son of a Tirolean farmer.

After that a cavalier in the style of Hals, plumed hat cocked rakishly over laughing eyes, curled moustaches, a mocking smile. The younger son, Anton, at twenty, and my paternal grandfather. Within my limited range of the family, he is the founder and the source of strength. Whatever I am now, part of me is derived from him, and as I rummage through these family bones, I must get to know him better.

The final picture is that of Marta, the baby sister of fifteen, posing as if she were already the toast of the Vienna Hofopera, her beauty and her presence blooming. In a moment of prescience the artist has sketched her in the costume of Madama

11

Butterfly, a role she will one day make her own. Perhaps as he sketched she sang to him.

Thus, Sepp and Hanna Prinz, and their three children; and there ought to be one of Lili Wangenmann as well. Lili of the *vollschlank* figure, full but slim; sleepy-eyed and knowing. There should be one of Lili because she was part of it all back in 1914 when Otto and Anton split the family in two. That's the way the family dates events. To the rest of the world, 1914 was the year of the Archduke Franz Ferdinand and the assassination at Sarajevo, the year of armies mustered up and on the move, of brass bands and banners, and a giant step taken away from an age of innocence. But not to us. The way we reckon things, that was the year that Anton and Otto fought in the barnyard over Lili Wangenmann and split the family in two. The tremors that shook the rest of the world were only offstage rumbles.

They started fighting just after dawn, the two brothers slugging away at each other under a sky barely lit by a hazy sun. Below them the valley was filled with a fog that masked the roofs and spires of St. Anton am Arlberg, and above them the peaks were lost in masses of clouds that dribbled wet, unwelcome snow. Fruit trees, stripped by the season to bare and ugly sticks, were sheathed in slick ice, and darker ice lined the eaves that overhung the barn. The brothers circled each other warily, dragging their booted feet through the slush and the cow dung that mired the ground behind the barn. Otto's nose leaked blood, and Anton's lip was split. Their clothes were caked with mud, and their arms hung heavily as they circled. It was a brutal, senseless fight, but they had been fighting all their lives, ever since each had been old enough to raise an arm and clench a fist. Neither of them noticed their father standing in the shadowed doorway of the barn, watching and waiting for one of them to fall.

The fight ended suddenly. Anton caught his brother high on the cheek, and Otto replied with a kick to the groin that missed and hit a shin instead. Anton grunted with pain and charged, grappling. He got an ear between his teeth and bit hard. Otto screamed, but he didn't stop punching. Anton took a fist deep in the belly, slipped, flailed his arms, and went down. He tried to get up, but Otto's boot was in his ribs, knocking him down again. He stared up at his brother. Blood dripped from Otto's

12

nose, and he smiled thinly as he drew back his foot to use the boot again.

'Enough, no more,' said Sepp Prinz, and then he was in between his two sons. He pushed Otto back and said mildly, 'Enough, before you kill each other. What started it this time?'

Otto looked at the ground and did not answer.

'I asked you a question.' Sepp's voice was still mild. 'I expect an answer.'

Otto looked up. 'I'm sorry, Papa. No disrespect, but it isn't something I can talk about.'

Sepp grunted and glanced down at Anton. 'It looks as if you lost.'

'I slipped,' Anton protested, grinning up at his father.

'No, you lost.' He put down a hand to help Anton up, and then his two sons were standing before him, still fighting mad and ready to leap at each other, but restrained by his stern authority. The sternness showed in the hard lines of his face, but his eyes were sad and the sight of that sadness restrained them as well. He waited for a moment before he spoke, waiting for the heavy breathing, the blood, and the tempers to subside. He shook his head, wagging it slowly from side to side the way farmers do in the mountains when faced with a natural disaster that cannot be controlled: a flood, an avalanche, a blighted crop. Sepp's sons were his natural disasters, and so he wagged his head slowly.

'All right, now I'm asking both of you,' he said. 'What started it?'

Otto shook his head stubbornly. 'I'm sorry, but it's not something that a gentleman can discuss. It involves a lady.'

'You don't know any ladies,' Sepp pointed out, 'and you're not a gentleman.'

Otto's eyes narrowed, and he drew himself up. 'I hold a commission in the imperial army, and that makes me a gentleman by anybody's standards.'

'One of God's miracles,' Sepp said sourly. 'A simple farmer like me has a gentleman for a son.' He turned to Anton. 'So now I'm asking you. What started it?'

'No disrespect, Papa, but I think Otto is right. It's nothing to talk about.'

Sepp made a face of pretended astonishment. 'You mean that you agree with your brother?'

13

Anton grinned, ignoring the pain from his split lip. 'Just this once.'

'So now you're a gentleman, too?'

'No, Papa, you know I'm not. I'm a *Bergbauer* just like you and I don't know any fine ladies. But there's a woman involved, and even if she isn't a lady she deserves to be treated like one.'

Sepp grunted his approval of the answer, but his head was wagging again. 'So . . . I can't force you to tell me, but this constant fighting, how is it going to end?'

Neither son responded. They had been through this too many times to think that an answer was needed. These parental lectures followed a predictable pattern. Next would come the part about brotherly love, about the sacred ties that bind a family together, and the need for a team of horses to pull evenly in the harness. After that would come a reference to the Deity, an equally pious invocation of the name of the Emperor Franz Josef, an allusion to the grief they were causing their mother, and then the stern commandment to forget all this foolishness and get back to work.

But Sepp said none of these things. He wasn't even looking at them. His eyes were directed up the slope of the mountainside, and his sons turned their heads to see what he was staring at. A lone skier was working his way downhill towards the farm, turning in long and awkward arcs.

'Joachim Wangenmann,' said Sepp.

'Damn,' said Anton. Otto smiled grimly.

Sepp rubbed his nose and shook his head. 'What the devil does he want at this time of the day?'

Anton and Otto did not answer, but they each had an excellent idea of what Lili Wangenmann's father wanted.

That's the way it began, according to the family legend. Part myth and part memory, the legend has been passed down to be minced and remoulded according to the needs of each generation until now, seventy years later, the authorized version is the one you choose to believe. Mostly, it depends on which side of the family you belong to.

On my side of it, my grandfather Anton is represented as a warmhearted, fun-loving, hardworking mountain man, an accomplished carpenter who built his own skis, and an expert climber and skier. Otto is pictured as narrow, humourless, and

14

snobbish, an indifferent carpenter and a man not to be trusted on the mountain. At twenty-four, in that year of 1914, he had never been known to romp with a girl at haying time, sneak a drink, play a game of cards, or indulge in any of the other casual vices which, for the young men of the valley, made life barely tolerable. Luck and determination had got him an appointment into the Imperial Academy at Märisch-Weisskirchen as a one-year volunteer, and at the end of that year he had returned home with a commission in the artillery reserve, a vocabulary of Viennese slang that fell strangely on Arlberg ears, and the unshakeable conviction that he was made of finer stuff than his fellows.

The other side of the family sees things differently. To them, Otto embodied the Germanic virtues of obedience, loyalty, and orderliness; a soldier with an honourable war record. Anton, to them, was frivolous and irresponsible, a scoundrel who avoided military service, and who showed what kind of a man he was by trying, unsuccessfully, *Gott sei danke*, to rape his brother's sweetheart. That's the way they see it on that side of the family.

As for my own opinion, I can't pretend to be neutral. The writing of history belongs to the survivors, which means that I get to tell this story my way.

Chapter Two

In the autumn of 1913 all the traditional signs pointed to an early winter in the Austrian Arlberg, and a heavy one. Spotted weasels were found in the forests, migrating birds were massed against the skies, and knowing farmers noted that their horses were growing a thick and rough-haired undercoat. Other signs appeared: meteor showers, crimson sunsets, and in the woods below Steuben a reliable man saw the silver unicorn at night, an unfailing herald of the coldest and the deepest snows. Early in the autumn the farmers responded to the signs. This year there was no waiting on ceremony to bring the cattle down from the high Alpine pastures with their horns decorated with boughs of spruce and pine, garlanded with ribbons. The precious animals, grey-brown and glossy, were herded down early, and after that the hay harvest was brought in with the same haste. Only when the cattle were safely under cover and the winter's fodder stored in dry places did the farmers dare to look at the sky, to wait and to wonder.

They did not have long to wait, for that year the signs were right. Winter came down on the Arlberg before the leaves on the trees were fully turned, and it came with the force of an angry fist. The temperature dropped in October and stayed where it had fallen, moving water froze, and then the snows came: first the dustings to powder the peaks of Mattunjoch and Valluga, and then the steady, daily fall that covered the floors of the valleys, the slopes, and the rising ridges. By November the Arlberg was white, by January it was bleak, and for much of the time it was still. Outside the towns not even sleighs could move in such weather, horses foundered in belly-high snow, and if a farmer was forced to leave the warmth of his kitchen *Heizbank,* for whatever reason, he did it on skis, gliding the downhill slopes and when he had to climb, wrapping the boards with moleskins to give him purchase. The men of the Arlberg had always lived with snow the way fishermen live with the tides, but that winter the snow was a curse that lay over the mountains. Hundreds of miles away in Vienna, where Franz Josef still ruled over a chocolate empire, the snow was a seasonal diversion that fell to amuse a pirouetting people and provide the proper setting for a winter's *Wienerwalzer*. In Vienna everyone knew, with the simple delight of children, that snow was really powdered sugar and that the Alps were crowned with *Schlagobers*. Wintertime was fun time in Vienna, but in the Austrian Arlberg that winter was dark and brutal. The days were spent under low and leaden skies, and if at night the wind whipped up to clear away the clouds, the stars that were revealed shone cold, and distant and unfriendly.

On one of those wind-whipped nights in January of 1914, twenty-year-old Anton Prinz climbed the ridge above and behind his father's house, edging his skis carefully against the slope of the hill. It was after midnight, and above him the loom of the mountain was a darker patch of darkness, while in the valley below the village of St. Anton was a smudge that was marked by a speckle of lights. He climbed in darkness with only the moon to show him where to place his skis, but he could have made the climb just as easily if there had been no moon

16

at all. The terrain beneath him was, in gentler seasons, the communal pasture that lay between his father's farm and that of Joachim Wangenmann farther up the mountain and it was ground that he had roamed since boyhood. Now the pasture was covered with a layer of snow so thick and so fresh that without his skis he would have sunk beneath the surface, but he made his moves easily, swinging his poles and shuffling uphill in the jerky rhythm of the experienced climber. His progress was steady and silent, and the only sound that he made in the night was an occasional chuckle as he thought of Lili Wangenmann waiting for him in her second-storey bedroom. His chuckle was answered by a rumble in the night from higher up the slope as the mountain shrugged and shifted its load of snow.

'Be quiet,' he muttered to the mountain. 'People are sleeping.'

He spoke to the mountain naturally, as if to a person, and he did not think it an odd thing to do. Everyone he knew did the same, although not all of them admitted it. To the *Bergbauern,* those who farmed in the high places, the mountain was a real and living presence to be respected and feared, and if possible, to be loved. Anton was one of those who added love to his fear and respect, although three times in his young lifetime he had seen the *Lawine* come roaring down, the slab-avalanche destroying everything in its path, levelling houses, snapping trees like sticks, burying cattle and snatching lives. Like all mountain people he lived enveloped in a never-ending *Leu-Sorg,* a dread of the avalanche, but still he loved his mountain, and in a highly personal way. A lowlander can love a particular piece of earth simply because he owns it, but a mountain man loves terrain the way he might love a fascinating, but difficult, woman.

The mountain was quiet as he topped the ridge and the Wangenmann farmhouse came into sight. The house was dark and silent, as any respectable home would have been at that hour, with Papa and Mama Wangenmann fast asleep. Not even a dog growled a warning as he approached; it was a night for a dog to curl up close to the kitchen stove. Skis over his shoulder now, he flitted across the hard-packed snow of the yard, dodging from one snowbank to another, keeping clear of the patches of moonlight, and then he was safe within the shadowed angle where the back of the house joined the mountainside. Like most of the other homes on the mountain, the Wangenmann house

17

was built into the side of the hill. To those who farmed the mountain slopes a piece of level land was a luxury to be used for the site of a barn, for a stand of fruit trees or a vegetable patch. After those uses there was rarely level land left over for a house, and besides, the local wisdom decreed that a house built into the mountainside was the best protection against the terrors of the avalanche. That these homes were regularly swept away when the *Lawine* came rumbling down in no way lessened the custom.

Anton glanced up at the second storey of the house and the window of Lili's bedroom, shuttered against the night. He grinned to himself, knowing that the shutter would be unlatched, and grinned again at the sight of the hand and foot holds neatly cut into the ice that sheathed the side of the building. They led directly to Lili's window, and Anton, along with six of his closest friends, climbed that icy ladder regularly. Winter life was hard in the Arlberg and relaxations were numbered: a game of skat at Friedrich's Tavern, a swig of cider in the back of the barn, and for a special few a midnight visit to Lili Wangenmann. It was an open question as to whether or not her parents knew that their daughter entertained visitors nightly. It seemed impossible that they could have slept unaware through all those bumpings and scrapings up the east wall and then the subsequent muffled thuds and creaks from the second-floor bedroom; but Papa Wangenmann had never once risen from his bed to repel an intruder, and none of the boys seemed to worry that he might.

Least of all Anton. Hippity-hop, like a monkey on a stick, he scrambled up the side of the house, flipped the shutter open, and in the same motion gripped the window ledge and pulled himself over it. The room was dark, no candle lit, and he could just make out the bed against the far wall.

'Lili,' he called softly.

'Who is it?' asked her sleepy voice from a mound of blankets in the middle of the bed.

'Anton.'

'Ah, Anton.' It was said with a burble of affection, for she was still half asleep. Then she was suddenly awake. She sat up in bed and the blankets fell away. 'Anton? *Ach du meine Gott,* what are you doing here?'

'That's a stupid question,' he said, throwing his cap and his

18

gloves on the floor and starting to unbutton his jacket. 'It's Wednesday, isn't it? Faithful Anton, every Wednesday.'

'But didn't they tell you?'

'They? Tell me what?' His jacket was off now, and he leaned against the wall to unlace his boots.

'Oh, God, they didn't. Listen, you can't stay, you have to get out of here.'

'That's not only stupid, it's crazy. Do you know how cold it is out there?' One boot off, he went to work on the frozen laces of the other.

'Don't do that,' she said, her voice rising anxiously. 'Stop taking your clothes off, you have to go.'

'And I will,' he assured her, tugging at the boot. 'About an hour from now.'

'No, now, right this minute.'

'What the devil is the matter with you?' The boot came off in his hand and he stood holding it, peering across the room. 'This isn't like you, Lili.'

'They were supposed to tell you.' Her voice was a muted wail. 'I told Karl, and I told Dolf, and I told Peter. I told all the other fellows and I told them to tell you, too.'

'For God's sake, tell me what?'

'I'm not doing it any more, Anton. Not for anybody.'

'Not funny, Lili.'

'I mean it. They were supposed to tell you.'

'Nobody told me anything.' He padded across the icy floor to the bed and looked down at her. He could not see her face clearly, but he could smell the delightful yeasty aroma that rose up from her bed-warmed body: fresh-baked bread with just a hint of cinnamon. The odour, as always, aroused him, and he reached for her, but she twisted away.

'No,' she said, 'don't touch me.'

'Jesus, you really mean it, don't you?'

'I told you.'

He eased down to sit on the bed, careful not to startle her. He fumbled for matches, lit the candle on the table, and turned to her. He was startled by what he saw. He had expected the sight of bare and bouncing flesh, unbound hair that fell below the waist, and loose lips stretched in a welcoming grin. Instead, her face was pale in the wavering light: round, smooth, and sad-eyed. Her hair was coiled in braids, her arms were folded across

19

her breasts, and her simple woollen nightdress, long-sleeved and buttoned to the throat, completed a picture of disturbed innocence.

He reached out a hand and touched her gently on the shoulder, and said, '*Also*, Lili, what's this all about?'

She shook her head. 'I just don't want to do it anymore.'

'Not even with me? I thought I was your favourite.' He said it jokingly, for she had no favourites, all of her men were special to her.

'Not with anybody. I told the others to tell you that.'

'I haven't been off the farm for a week.' Then, pointedly, 'Not since the last time I was here. Things were a little different then.'

She shrugged. 'Things change.'

'Of course they do. Things change and you don't want to do it anymore. Well, I can understand that.'

'Good. Will you go now, please?'

'But how come you still leave the shutter unlatched?'

She looked away.

'So you *are* doing it with somebody.'

'No.'

'Then why the shutter? Expecting a visitor?'

'It's not what you think.' She still would not look at him.

'What am I supposed to think? It's too late for the Three Kings to come calling.'

She turned to him, her face screwed tight with concern. 'All right, I'm expecting someone, any minute now. That's why you have to go.'

'Not fair, Lili, not fair. You can't give it to one of the boys and cut the rest of us off.'

She flared suddenly. 'Anton, I'm begging you. It isn't one of the other boys, it's somebody new, and he doesn't know about me. I mean, about you and all the others. He's . . . serious. He respects me, he says that he loves me, and I think . . . I think he wants to marry me.'

Anton whistled softly in amazement, then realized what he had done, and said, 'I'm sorry.'

'That's all right, I know what I am, but don't you see? This is my chance and I don't want to lose it. That's why I told the other boys that I'm not doing it anymore and that's why I'm begging you to get out of here. Now, and quick, before he gets here.'

'Marriage, by God. Really?'

'I think so,' she said slowly. 'I think he's leading up to it. The way he talks sometimes . . .'

'I hope he does more than just talk.'

Her chin tilted up. 'I told you, he respects me. We talk, and he kisses me, but mostly we talk. And that's all.'

'What do you talk about?' he asked, intrigued.

'Life. And art. And poetry.'

'Jesus, you're committing a sin, do you know that? The best piece of ass in the Tirol and all you do is talk about life with this poetry lover?'

'That's the way he wants it.'

'Then he deserves what he gets,' Anton said in disgust. 'My God, what a waste. And this talking lover, this great orator, does he have a name?'

She hesitated, then shook her head.

'Come on, Lili, you can tell me. You won't be able to keep it a secret forever.'

She looked down at her folded hands. 'No, you'll laugh.'

'You mean I know him? Now you have to tell me. I won't laugh, I promise you. Marriage is nothing to laugh about.'

She sighed and said, 'I guess you're right, it won't be a secret for long.' She looked up and stared at him directly. 'It's your brother, Otto.'

He laughed.

'You promised,' she protested.

'But Otto?' He was laughing so hard that he could barely say the words. 'That's impossible.'

'It's very possible.' Her face was pained. 'And I'm asking you again, please don't laugh.'

Anton held his breath for a moment, struggled, and managed to control himself. 'But Otto doesn't even look at girls. He's saving himself for the woman he marries.'

'That's right. That's me.'

He shook his head in wonder. 'Are you sure he doesn't know? About me and all the others?'

'I'm sure.' Her face cleared, and she smiled easily. 'I could tell if he did. Otto's different, he's a romantic, very gallant. He believes all that business about eternal love, ladies and gentlemen, kissing the hand. He even reads Goethe and Schiller to me. Right now he's reading *The Sorrows of Werther*.'

'Christ, that's just like him, courting a girl with Goethe. Doesn't he ever read you love poetry? Von Arnim or Brentano?'

'It doesn't make any difference, I don't pay much attention to the words,' she admitted. 'It just makes me feel good. Look, you're not going to spoil it for me, are you? You won't tell him about us?'

Anton touched her cheek tenderly with a single finger, remembering all the romps and the giggles, the fierce excitements, the warm enfoldings, and all the soft places in which he had hidden. She had been an honest and open woman to them all, open to each of them equally and honestly lustful in her enjoyment of them. He shook his head, wise enough to feel sad over what he was losing.

'Don't worry about that,' he said. 'Nobody is going to tell Otto anything, not me and not anybody else. I'll make sure of that.'

'It could be my last chance.'

'I told you, don't worry. Worry more about Otto. You're not getting very much, you know.'

'Don't tell me that. I know what I'm getting, and it's more than you would ever give me. Would you even dream of marrying me?'

He looked away, searching for his boots.

'Or Karl, or Eugen, or any of the others? Would they?'

He did not answer.

'So don't tell me what I'm getting, because I'm glad to get it. Otto may have some funny ideas but he'll make a good husband.'

'The funny thing is, he will.' Anton pulled at his boots, lacing them quickly. 'You'll get your fill of Goethe every night.'

'After we're married I'll teach him the other things.'

'I bet you will.' He shrugged himself into his jacket and jammed his knitted cap down over his ears. 'For your sake I hope he learns quick.'

She smiled sadly. 'You'll go now, yes?'

'I'm gone,' he said, swinging over the windowsill. '*Glück*.'

'*Glück,* Anton.'

He went down the side of the building as nimbly as he had gone up, still a monkey on a stick but now with a definable

22

ache in his groin and an indefinable sadness in his soul. He manoeuvred the few feet of the ice ladder, dropped away from the side of the building, turned in midair, and to his astonishment landed squarely in front of his brother, Otto, who had been watching his descent with an open mouth and unbelieving eyes. The moon was still up, the skies still clear, and the expression on Otto's face was easy to read: confusion mixed with a slowly growing rage.

In his parade-ground voice, he bellowed, 'What the devil are you doing here?'

'Collecting,' was Anton's brisk reply. 'Herr Wangenmann was very generous, he gave me two kronen for the church organ fund. I'm in charge of this district.'

'Organ? Fund?'

'If you went to church more often you'd know that the organ sounds like a dying cow these days.'

'I go as much as you do, maybe more.'

'Then you've been sleeping through mass. Look, Otto, fifty kreuze from every soul in the valley and we'll have the organ fixed in no time at all. Now, that isn't much to ask, is it?'

'No, that sounds fair.'

'Of course it's fair. A man has a right to be proud of his organ, and if we all get together and push we can have the finest instrument in the Tirol. So how about fifty from you?'

'Forget the money for a minute. I want to know what you were – '

'I can't forget, I'm in charge of collection. Somebody has to do the dirty work.' Edging his way around Otto as he spoke, making for the snowbank where his skis were propped, he kept up the chatter. 'Look, Otto, everybody knows how tight you are with money, but this is different, this is a question of town pride. Now let's have the fifty.'

'I wouldn't give you a dry piece of dung, much less a copper.'

'I was afraid you'd say that.' Reaching the skis, he laid them out flat on the packed snow, slammed his boots into the toe irons, and quickly adjusted the straps. 'It isn't as if you can't afford it. You got twenty kronen when you sold your heifer.'

'It was fifteen and I had to give Papa half. Now what I want to know – '

'All right, keep your money till the day you die, you miser.' Anton plucked his poles from the snowbank. He shuffled his skis to rid the bottoms of any ice that might have formed. 'I'll pay your fifty myself, but only because you're my brother and I don't want shame on the family.'

'Shame? Now wait a minute – '

'Can't wait, have to be going. I have three more homes to visit tonight. It's long, hard work, this collecting.'

'Don't move, you little louse. Before you go I want to know exactly what you were doing up there.'

'Me? Where?'

'There.' Otto pointed up at the window. 'In Lili's bedroom.'

'Oh, there.' Anton gave his brother an angelic smile. 'Just collecting.'

He slammed his poles into the snow and exploded out of a standing start, taking four quick skating steps to build some speed, and then he was out of the Wangenmann yard, dropping over the ridge and down the steep incline of the mountainside, his skis running smoothly along the moonlit slope. A quick glance over his shoulder told him that there would be no pursuit: Otto was already scaling the side of the Wangenmann house, reaching for the unlatched shutters.

'Lili, you've got problems,' he muttered, 'and come to think of it, so do I.'

He ran the side of the mountain swinging in giant loops across the slope, rotating his heavy skis firmly through each turn. Push, pull, and turn, he swung downhill in the easy rhythm, losing himself in the soar of the glide, and at the same time putting aside all thoughts of Otto and Lili. The icy air struck at his cheeks and his slitted eyes, frosted his lips and crackled the hairs inside his nose, but he did not feel it. It was always that way when he skied. He was alone with the mountain and nothing else mattered.

The euphoria ended as he topped the ridge above the Prinz farm and came to a stop behind the barn. Stacking his skis inside the wall, he debated going to his room and decided against it. There was trouble coming, and his room was the first place where Otto would go looking for him. He walked quietly down the dirt-packed aisle between the rows of stalls, making soft and soothing greetings to the drowsy cows, and dug himself a hole in the stack of hay near the rear door. He pushed himself in firmly, burying himself in the hay, and settled in for the night. It was not the first time he had slept that way.

I'm sorry, Lili, I stayed too long, he thought, I really spoiled it for you, didn't I?

That was his last thought as he slid into sleep, and his first when he awoke was that someone was dancing a polka on his chest, someone wearing sharp-cleated Alpine boots. When he opened his eyes the barn was still dark, but Otto's face floated over him. Something sharp and heavy pressed against his chest. He reached up slowly and felt the cold tines of the pitchfork there. The points had pierced his clothing and lay against his skin. In the stillness he could hear Otto's forced, uneven breathing.

'Take that thing away,' he said, pleased that his voice sounded calm.

'You bastard.'

'You're holding the pitchfork so you get to call the names.'

'You're a pig and a bastard.'

'Look, Otto, if you're angry about the fifty kreuze we can forget about it. I'll put your name on the list anyway.'

'Church fund . . . organ . . . and all the time you . . . ' He stopped. His shoulders were shaking.

'Brother, have I done something to make you unhappy?'

'You know what you did, you unspeakable swine. Oh yes, you know.'

'Unspeakable swine? God, sometimes you talk like a bad operetta.' Anton gasped as Otto increased the pressure on the pitchfork. 'Take that damn thing away – are you trying to kill me?'

'I should. That's what you deserve, you perverted sex fiend.'

'Please, I may be a sex fiend but there's nothing perverted about it.'

'No? Nothing perverted about abusing that poor little girl last night?'

'I beg your pardon? Would you mind telling me which poor little girl this was? I abuse so many, you know.'

'I won't mention her name in your filthy presence, but you know who I mean. The fine, sweet, innocent girl you tried to seduce.'

'Operetta words again. Where do you get them from? People like us don't seduce girls, we roll them in the hay.'

'You're right, "seduce" is too soft a word for it. "Rape" is more like it. Thank God she was able to fight you off.'

'Oh-ho.'

'What was that?'

'Nothing, just the dawn breaking. Are you by any chance referring to Lili Wangenmann?'

'Don't mention her name with your stinking mouth.' Otto's voice was a throttled scream. 'My God, Anton, how could you do something like that? That lovely child was still in tears when I left her.'

'And she told you that I . . . ?'

'She told me everything. How you stole into her room, tried to make love to her, and when she fought back how you tried to . . . to force her.'

'She said that?'

'Do you deny it?'

Ah, my clever Lili, how quick you are. Otto comes scrambling in through the window demanding an explanation and the oldest instinct in the world takes over. Tears flow from those soft eyes, that incredible bosom heaves, and the finger gets pointed straight at Anton. Rape, is it? How do you rape the Simplon Tunnel?

'Otto, take that pitchfork away and let's talk.'

'You talk. I'm waiting to hear what you have to say.'

'I have nothing to say.'

'Then you admit it?'

'Admit what? That I tried to rape her? For God's sake, Otto, Lili Wangenmann is . . .'

He stopped, unable to go on. There were all those nights of warmth and wonderment shared, and if she had never been his alone she had always been his when he needed her. She had never asked him for anything and he had never thought of himself as being in her debt, but now he knew that the least he owed her was silence.

Otto prodded with the pitchfork. 'Go ahead.'

'Lili is a fine young woman. Serious, virtuous, that sort of thing. She'll make some man a wonderful wife.'

'Quite right, and that man is me. The lady has consented to become my wife.'

That language again. It's the poetry, he thought, but he said, 'My congratulations, Otto. Seriously.'

'I don't want them, not from you. Not after what you tried to do to her.'

'Yes, I can understand that. I don't blame you at all.' He said it as humbly as he could, fighting to keep his face straight. He was about to get his head knocked off for the sake of the honour of Lili Wangenmann, and that was laughable even with a pitchfork up against his chest.

'So, it's true.'

Anton nodded, searching for words that would satisfy his brother's romantic turn of mind, and came up with, 'I don't know what came óver me, Otto. It was a moment of madness.'

'That's all I wanted to hear.'

Otto flung the pitchfork aside, and Anton jumped to his feet. Otto swung and missed. Anton swung and connected, and then they were hammering away at each other, up and down the aisles between the rows of uncaring cows and then out of the barn and into the watery dawn. They battled that way until Anton went down, and Sepp stepped between them, and Lili's father came skiing down the mountain. Joachim Wangenmann skimmed into the barnyard, stomped free of his boards, and nodded briefly to his neighbour. He strode over to Otto and folded him into a rough embrace, then turned to Anton and hit him in the face with his fist. Anton took the blow without moving.

Wangenmann turned to Sepp and said, 'Let's go inside. We have things to talk about.'

The collective fate of Anton, Otto, and Lili was determined before the day was out. At breakfast that morning Lili had confided the fictional story of the attempted rape to her mother, being careful to add that Otto had driven away the intruder and then had proposed marriage to her. Her mother did not believe the rape part of the story for a moment. Frieda Wangenmann had a fairly good idea of what had been going on at night in Lili's bedroom, but she shared her daughter's sense of opportunity. Otto Prinz was too good a catch to let get away, and she reacted on two levels almost simultaneously. First she gave her daughter a healthy smack across the face for lying, and then she advised her to stick to the story without deviation of any kind, particularly when discussing the matter with her father, who was, by default, the most innocent member of the family.

Within hours, through the chemistry peculiar to small towns, the story of the attempted rape spread from the mountainside and into the village, hopping from house to house and shop to shop, making the full cycle from the rectory of the parish church to the back room of Friedrich's Tavern. The tale grew as it travelled, taking on colourful details. Lili was confined to bed, in shock. Her eyes were blackened and her jaw was broken, not to forget the rope marks on her wrists where Anton had tied her to the bedposts. Other details, too delicate to mention, were only hinted at, and heads wagged knowingly.

Most of those wagging heads were grey, for it was the older generation of St. Anton that was scandalized. The younger people laughed at the thought of such an unlikely assault, but they did their laughing privately. They lived in a world ruled by their elders, and they had no voice in the scandal market. The elders were cooking up a soup, Anton was in it, and they had no desire to join him in the pot. With no one to tell his side of the story, Anton was converted within hours from a likeable farmboy to a pariah.

Joachim Wangenmann and Sepp Prinz stepped into the family carpentry shop for their private conversation, and minutes later a red-faced Sepp emerged looking about wildly for his younger son. When Anton could not be found, Sepp called for his daughter, Marta, and dispatched her down into town to fetch the parish priest. Father Klaus was an old man, but he made the climb up from the valley with Herr Bürgermeister Schlicter supporting him on one side and Herr Doktor Stolz on the other. When Julius Beckman, the postmaster and thus the sole representative of imperial authority in St. Anton, arrived to join the others in the carpentry shop the concentration of local power was complete. There, amid the odours of rich tobacco, fresh-cut shavings, and potato schnapps, Anton was accused, tried *in absentia,* and condemned.

While the village elders were solemnly deciding his fate, Anton sat in the back room of Friedrich's Tavern warming his hands near the metal plates of the wood-burning stove, a glass of cider beside him. Around the large table usually reserved for the skat players sat six of his friends, all of them regular visitors to Lili's bedroom. These were the sports of the town, always ready for a drink or a laugh. Now their glasses were full but their faces were glum as they listened to Anton tell the story of the night before. When he was finished there were low whistles, and sighs and the shaking of heads.

'Bad luck,' said Peter Ickle. 'Just pure bad luck. One of us should have told you to stay away from her, but you weren't around all week.'

'Not your fault,' Anton told him.

'More bad luck, your brother showing up. He really doesn't know about her?'

Anton shook his head. 'He's in love. The real thing, poetry and all. He's going to marry her.'

'A miracle. He'll be canonized for sure.'

'That doesn't help Anton,' Eugen Schwimmer pointed out. 'You're in it up to your ass, my friend.'

'I know.'

'What a joke, raping Lili Wangenmann.'

'I've been trying to laugh, but nothing happens.'

'The dirty bitch.'

'No, none of that,' Anton said quickly. 'Lili's a friend. She just did what she had to do.' He held no resentment against the girl, for as Peter had said, it was just bad luck. Trapped, she had pointed a finger, and that finger had started a snowball rolling downhill which now had grown to the size of an avalanche.

And heading straight for me, he thought. Aloud, he said, 'How is it here in town? What are the people saying?'

He was looking at Karl Lang, his closest friend among the six, an amiable, freckle-faced butcher's helper with an open smile and an insatiable appetite for Karl May's novels about the American wild west.

'Well, pardner,' he drawled, 'they're saying around town that you're a sex maniac, that's what they're saying.'

'I never denied it,' Anton muttered.

'They're also saying that you're a menace to the fair women of St. Anton.'

'Some menace. There are maybe five that I'd look at twice.'

'You'd better start taking this seriously,' Karl warned him. 'These people are talking lynch law. They're getting up a posse right now.'

Anton grimaced and swallowed some cider. 'My friend, I'm in the soup and there's nothing I can do about it.'

'Nonsense.' Karl dropped the cowboy accent and said briskly, 'Of course there's something you can do. You can marry the girl.'

Anton smiled thinly and shook his head.

29

'You think it's funny?'

'Not really. I was expecting you to say something like that.'

'Well, what's wrong with the idea? Forget what she said about marrying Otto. You know damn well that if you asked her the right way Lili would marry you like a shot off a shovel. Then presto, just like magic, the attempted rape becomes just another lovers' quarrel. The whole town laughs and your problems are over. You see what I mean?'

'I see it all right. I saw it before you did, but I don't like it very much.'

'Anton, I'm talking to you like you were my own brother – '

'No thanks, the one I've got is enough.'

'You know what I mean. Of course you don't want to marry her. Who would? But it's your only way out, *Mensch*, you're in deep trouble. You could wind up in front of the *Bürgermeister*, and even if you don't, how are you going to live here after this? The old poops in this town will make mincemeat out of you. The men won't do business with you and the women will cut you dead. Isn't that so?' He looked around the table for support.

'He's right,' said Dolf Mathies, and the others murmured their agreement.

'Marrying her is logical,' said Eugen. 'You have to admit that.'

'And we're all great believers in logic, aren't we?' Anton stirred in his chair. He had been listening carefully, but with his eyes half closed and his fingers laced behind his head. 'And that's the best advice you can give me? Marry the girl?'

Again the nods and murmurs all around the table.

'Nobody has any other ideas?'

'What else can you do?' asked Peter.

'It isn't what I can do, it's what you can do.' He finished the last of his cider, rolling it on his tongue before he swallowed. 'I'm a little disappointed with my loyal comrades. I had the feeling that you might come up with something better than that. Something more . . . helpful.'

It was Karl Lang who saw it coming, and said, 'Now wait a minute, Anton . . . '

'Wait for what?' Anton's fist hit the table, and glasses jumped. 'I've been sitting here waiting and nobody has had the guts to say it. We've all been screwing that girl, not just me. Night after night, for over a year.'

'Look, you can't ask us to – '

30

'I'm not asking, I'm waiting. I'm waiting for someone to say, "Anton old boy, we'll stick with you, we'll back you up. We'll stand up and tell the whole town what's been going on and then they can shove their rape case where it belongs." That's what I'm waiting for.' There was silence in the room. He looked around the table. 'So now I'm asking. Who's going to do that? How many?'

Seconds ticked by. He looked at each of them directly, eye to eye, one by one, and their eyes turned away from his. Peter Ickle broke the silence.

'I've got work to do,' he said. He pushed himself away from the table and went out the back door. Eugen Schwimmer muttered something deep in his throat and got up to follow. One by one the others went, flinging on caps and scarves, until only Karl was left at the table with Anton. The perpetual grin was still on his face, and his eyes were lively.

'Well,' Anton asked him, 'what's keeping you?'

'You asked for a volunteer. Here I am.'

'You'd do that for me?'

'I'm offering, but I don't think I'm risking anything. You'd never do that to Lili. I know it, and you know it, so I think I'm pretty safe.'

'You are. I could never do it.'

'So why the masquerade just now?'

'Maybe I wanted to find out who my friends are.'

'Well, now you know.'

'Yes.' He stood up, pulled on his mittens, and stuffed his cap over his ears. 'Thanks for the offer. I know you weren't risking much, but I'm glad you did it.'

He started for the door, but Karl stopped him with a hand on his arm. Sprawled in the chair, he put on the mock cowboy drawl and said, 'Do yourself a favour, pardner. Marry the girl. It's your only way out.'

Anton gripped the hand on his arm and squeezed. 'Thanks Karl, but I could never marry her. It would be too degrading.'

'You'd get over it after a while.'

Anton smiled gently. 'I meant for Lili, not for me.'

As he went out the back door he lowered his head against the sharp edge of the wind, bracing himself for the long climb home. It was almost dark when he arrived there, striding into the barnyard with his skis over his shoulder. He never made it into the house. The door opened and his father came out carrying bundles, Otto close behind him. The door closed. His father placed the bundles on the snow. There was a suitcase with all of his clothing in it. There was a paper parcel of bread, cheese, and sausage. There was a small leather purse filled with silver coins. His father stepped back and folded his arms across his chest. Otto, behind him, lounged against the door, one corner of his lips twisted in quiet contentment. All this was done in a silence more eloquent than angry words could ever be.

Anton broke the silence first. 'You mean now? Right now? Just like this?'

'This very minute,' said Sepp. His voice was low and the words came slowly, pulled from him with pain. 'You don't sleep in this house tonight.'

'Papa, please . . . '

'Don't call me that. After what you did, I'm not your father any more.'

'Don't I get a chance to explain?'

The massive head wagged slowly. 'There aren't any words to explain what you did. I want you to go now. There's money in that purse, enough to take you far away. I don't care where you go, but go this minute. And don't come back.'

'Without coming into the house? What about Mama? Marta? Can't I speak to them?'

Again the head wagged. 'You have cut yourself off from the women of this house. Just go.'

Anton stared at the darkened house, sure that behind those blind windows his mother and sister were watching the scene. The moment of weakness came then. In that moment he wanted to fling himself forward into his father's arms, plead, beg, tell the truth, and get himself out from under the weight of this imagined sin. Then the moment passed. He stiffened himself and fixed his father's face in his mind with a final look.

'All right, Papa,' he said softly. 'I'm going.'

He picked up the purse, bounced it once in his hand, and slipped it into his pocket. The parcel of food went into another pocket, and he strapped the suitcase to his back like a knapsack. Burdened that way, he knelt to strap on his skis, and when he rose to his feet he was smiling. One last look at his father and brother, and then the smile turned into a laugh. He threw back his head and let the laughter roll out of him. The sound of it

32

rang, it bounced from the barn to the house and rattled the windows. It was a wild laugh, bitter but free. He was still laughing as he jumped lightly and skied away, still laughing as he reached the slope and started down the mountain, still laughing as he gathered speed and in the dusk became another spot of darkness disappearing.

He slept that night in the back room of Friedrich's Tavern and the next morning he began the journey which would, after two months of travel, bring him to the village of Sedgewick Falls in rural Vermont just in time for the maple sugar season.

Chapter Three

Harley Swenson didn't count for much in the social order of Sedgewick Falls, Vermont. Harley was a failure in every way but one. Small in size, long in years, short on cash, he was a foul-mouthed drunkard, an acidulous wit, an undependable worker, and a constant profaner of the Sabbath; but he was also the only man in Sedgewick Falls who could announce with unerring accuracy when the day had come to tap the sugar maples. It was always towards the end of March after the first comparatively warm days had set the sap flowing in the trees. Warm, sunny days followed by freezing nights; the swing in the temperature moved the sap up from the roots and into the trunk like a cosmic suction pump until the maple was bursting with juice and it was time to tap the flow. Trouble was that if you tapped it too soon you discouraged the tree from producing, and if you tapped it too late you were likely to find that the sap was already on the ebb. There were any number of theories as to when to start the tap. Some people went by the phases of the moon, others by the severity of the temperature swing, still others by the depth of the slowly melting snow; but most people just waited for Harley Swenson to set the day. Nobody knew how he did it, but Harley was never wrong, and in the spring of 1914 the date that he chose was Thursday, the twenty-sixth of March.

'Tomorrow?' said Ethan Morris. 'Damnation, you know that for certain?'

'Course I do,' said Jesse Prescott. 'Tomorrow's the day.'

'Well of all the all-fired unholy luck.'

They stood in front of the woodshed that jutted out from the sugar-house where Ethan had been quartering logs when the sound of Jesse's sleigh bells had come to him over the snow meadows, the harness bells tinkling in time to the gait of the horse as the sleigh came into sight down on Brush Hollow Road and then turned up into the driveway. It was the worst time of the year for moving about, with the roads still too deep in snow for wheels but not really right for runners, either. But Jesse Prescott was not the sort of man to keep good news to himself, and so he had hitched up and set out on a circuit of the outlying farms to pass the word along. He had thought that the news was good, but Ethan seemed anything but pleased to hear it.

Ethan prodded, 'You sure he said tomorrow?'

'Doggone it, I already said it twice. More'n I'd do for most folks.'

'God damn son of a bitch.' Ethan swung the axe over his head and sank it viciously into a log. 'That tears it, that tears it for good.'

'You got somethin' against Thursdays? Get bit by one once?'

'By God, are you blind, Jesse Prescott? Just take a look around you.'

He waved angrily at the area in front of the woodshed and the sugar-house, which was stacked high with mountains of uncut logs. When sugaring time came it took a heap of firewood to fuel the flames under the evaporating pans, wood that had to be cut into quarter-log chunks.

'Looks like you left her a bit late,' Jesse observed.

'Do tell,' Ethan said tartly, and then he eased off. 'I was figurin' on a couple-a-three more days to get the wood in. Seems to me a few more ice-cold nights is what she needs to get the sap up.'

'That ain't the way Harley figures it.' Jesse gave a good sharp look at the stacked logs and then at the cordwood piled in the shed. 'Still, you don't have that much to go. A good afternoon's work and you'll have enough.'

'Enough for my own sugarbush, but I got the Chandler trees to do as well.'

Jesse nodded his understanding. Ethan farmed two short sections of rocky land that barely provided for his wife and

34

himself, his horse, and his dog. What kept him just this side of penury were the untended lands of the Chandler family that abutted on his own: one hundred and twenty acres of maple, birch, and elm which had never been cleared and never been farmed. The Chandler land ran from Brush Hollow Road down to where Long Brook Pond milled around before hooking up with the Pebble River, and the only building on it, or the wreck of one, was what once had been a sawmill on the bank of the pond. No one had worked the mill for decades, and no one had worked the land at all except for its trees. Now it all belonged to Elizabeth Chandler, who lived in town and who paid Ethan the only hard cash he saw all year long for tapping the maples at sugaring time, clearing away the second-growth timber, and posting the land against hunters.

'Firewood,' Jesse said understandingly. 'And no one around to help you cut it.'

'Not with Harley making his godforsaken, preordained proclamation from the top of Mount Sinai. Every soul in Sedgewick Falls'll be cutting wood today against tomorrow.'

'Including me,' Jesse was careful to say.

'Drat that man if he couldn't have waited a few more days before getting up on his hind legs and howling sugar. Does the same thing every year, he does. Knows darn well it takes a man a full five days to set up the trees, but did you ever hear of Harley calling for sugar at the beginning of the week? Hell no, not Harley. It's always Thursday, or Friday, or summat like that just so's the old buzzard can watch his churchgoing neighbours a-working on the Sabbath. Well, damn his hide for the pleasure he gets from it.'

'My, my. 'Tweren't Harley who didn't get his wood in on time, not the way I see it.'

'He don't *have* any wood, and he don't have any trees, neither. All he has is a big mouth.'

'Which is a lucky thing for us, I have to say. Mighty lucky he was even able to get the word out this year, seeing where he is.'

'Which is where?'

'Which is in the lockup.'

'Harley in jail?'

'Drunk and a public nuisance, as usual. But he got the word out through Mrs. Gardner, what brings in the meals. Judge

35

riding circuit over from Burlington put him in three days ago. Funniest sight you ever saw. This Judge Peckerwood or whatever his name is, being from Burlington he don't know the folks here, and so he takes one look at Harley and he says, "You're charged with being drunk in a public place. Where do you live?" And Harley says, 'Sedgewick Falls." "All your life?" asks the judge, and Harley says, "Not yet." Almost bust my britches laughing.'

'Yep, that sounds like our Harley.'

'Judge didn't think it was funny. Give him ten days or ten dollars. Guess you know which Harley took.'

'So he's been in the lockup for three days now.' Ethan rubbed at his bristly chin. 'Should be all sobered up, I reckon.'

'Eah-yuh.'

'And a-thirsty for cider.'

'Eah-yuh.'

'And seven more days to go before he sees any.'

'Eah-yuh. Unless some soul pays his fine.' Jesse's lips cracked into a thin smile. 'I reckon you've got yourself a woodcutter after all.'

'A dollar a day, and found. Five days' work and I pay your fine to boot. Take it or leave it.'

'Got caught short with yer wood, did ye?' Harley Swenson spat on the straw that covered the floor of the cell.

'Do you want it or don't you?'

''Gainst the constitution of the state of Vermont, that's what it is. Outlaws slavery, ye know.'

Ethan sighed, and waited. Behind him the town selectman, Seth Cobb, shifted his feet impatiently, the jail keys jangling in his fist. The lockup in Sedgewick Falls was not a proper jailhouse but only a room at the back of the livery stable with bars on the windows and door. The room was dank and only dimly lit with a single lantern hanging from the roof beam. It was, however, warmed by a stove glowing cherry-red in the corner; but the stove was a mixed blessing. With no proper sanitary facilities and straw that was rarely changed, the warmth from the store magnified the stench of horses and humans until it was enough to stagger a man coming in from the clean outside air. Seth Cobb's aristocratic nose was creased into what looked like a permanent wrinkle.

36

'Make up your mind, Harley,' he said. 'Can't wait on you all day.'

Harley ignored the selectman. 'Ye said a dollar a day and found. That include cidey?'

'In moderation.'

Harley grunted; he had his own definition of the word. Still, he got to his feet, brushing straw from his trousers, and held out his hand. 'All right, ye got yerself five days' worth of slavery, Vermont-style. Let's get at it.'

As the two men slapped hands to seal the deal a voice from a darkened corner of the cell said, 'Hey, Mr Boss, you need another man, maybe?'

'Well, I'll be whipped, someone else in here?' Ethan swung round to the sound. As his eyes adjusted to the dimness beyond the glow of the lamp he made out the forms of two men sitting on the floor with their backs against the wall, their arms around their knees. 'Looks like Harley threw hisself a litter of pups in here. Who are they, Seth?'

'One is a Canuck,' the selectman said. 'In for drunk just like Harley.'

'T'other?'

'Can't rightly say. He isn't any prisoner, just a wandering boy looking for a job. No money, no food, no place to stay, don't speak more'n a few words of English. Couldn't let him starve or freeze, so the selectmen decided to let him stay here, leastwise till the weather eases. Christian charity, couldn't do anything else but.'

'Christian charity.' The words left much unsaid.

'Now, Ethan, what did you expect us to do, put him up at the inn? You'd be doing the town a favour if you took him off our hands. The Canuck, too.'

'Let's take a look at 'em.'

Ethan unhooked the lantern from the roof beam and took it over to the corner as the two men jumped to their feet. He held the lantern high to see their faces. They were both big men, but in different ways. The Canuck was tall and broad, with a full black beard and a stocking cap perched on the top of his head. The other was shorter, rounder, but sheathed with solid muscle like a hard rubber ball. He looked as if he wanted to smile, and his eyes were bright and curious. Both men looked as if they could chop wood all day and then square-dance till morning.

37

Ethan peered sharply at the Canuck and said, 'I know you. Johnny summat. Stonemason, ain't ya?'

The big man grinned. 'Jean-Pierre Alimont, *monsieur*. Best God damn mason in town, only no work now. You give me an axe and I chop you plenty wood, by God.'

Ethan turned to the other one. 'What about you? You a Canuck too?'

The shorter man grinned, but did not answer. He clearly had not understood the words. Jean-Pierre said quickly, 'No, he's no Canuck, he's some kind of a German fella called Anton. Don't speak no English, but he do good work, I betcha.'

'How do you talk to him if you can't talk to him?'

'Oh, we talk okay. A few words French, a few words *allemand,* a few words English like salt in the stew.' Jean-Pierre's black beard split in a grin again. 'And we talk with the hands. With the hands it's easy. How about it? We go work the sugar with you?'

Ethan hesitated. Like most Yankees he had a deep-rooted suspicion of the French Canadians who came south of the border in search of jobs in Vermont and New Hampshire. They were foreign, they were Roman Catholics, and they were strange in their ways, a combination designed to set a Yankee tooth on edge. Most of them congregated in the quarry towns and in Burlington proper, but every village in northern Vermont had its share of them. They talked too loudly, argued fiercely, and drank wine instead of decent cider, but they could work like horses, he knew. As for the other fellow, he seemed amiable enough, and capable. Besides, in Ethan's small world people were either Green Mountain natives, popish Canucks, or bastards from over in York State. By those limited standards this Anton was just another Canuck who happened not to speak French, which made him just as employable as Jean-Pierre.

'All right, come along, the two of you,' he said in sudden decision, and he made for the door and the clean, cold air outside. His three new employees, tugging down caps and scarves, followed quickly behind.

'Here now, what about the fines?' the selectman called after him.

'Don't you worrit yourself about that. Miz Chandler, she'll stop by to pay you.'

*

38

The next morning Elizabeth Chandler was up early to get ready for the sugaring. She rose before dawn, bathed from a basin, dressed herself in warm wools and sturdy tweeds, and ate a simple breakfast of toasted cornbread, tea, and unfermented apple juice. She did all this in a state of high excitement. Sugaring time had always been a treat for her as a child, and it remained one now. The pungency of burning birchwood mixed with the aroma of boiling sap was a memory that she carried forward from year to year, renewing it each spring as part of her faith in the cycle of life. She had read Sir James Frazer and she knew enough about fertility symbols to adopt the maple tree, unblushingly, as her own. Each year the sap rose in the trees as the earth revived itself, and clever men tapped the fountains of sweetness. It was a particularly Vermont-like way of doing things, taking back a bit from the earth while the tree wasn't looking, and she far preferred it to the legends of sacrificed kings and virgins. This way, not even the tree got hurt, despite what Mr Howells had to say. She had read William Dean Howells as well, and although she admired the man as a novelist and a critic, she knew that he was mistaken when he attributed the gnarled appearance of the maple tree to excessive tappings for sap.

Mr Howells is full of baloney, she decided as she rinsed her teacup under the kitchen pump. Only a fraction of the sap gets tapped; most of it reaches the branches. Besides, the man is from Ohio, so what does he know about Vermont maples?

She moved about the house preparing herself for a day out of doors, collecting scarves, gloves, and a woollen cap which she knew did not become her but would warm her ears in any weather. Then she gave instructions for the day to the hired girl, had the hired man hitch up the sleigh, and set out for the Chandler lands out beyond Brush Hollow Road, alone and not displeased to be that way.

Elizabeth was that anomaly of her times, a young and single woman who lived alone and liked it. She had been alone for three years now since the death of her parents in the influenza sweep of 1911, and at twenty-two she was still unmarried and determined to stay that way. There had been no lack of suitors, for although she was far from being a beauty she was well built and fair-skinned, with clear grey eyes and a capable cast to her features. Those capable features gave a hint as to why she had firmly rejected every man who had pursued her. She was capable and she knew it. She was also highly intelligent, and she knew full well there was not a mind in Sedgewick Falls, male or female, that could match her own.

Four years at the Priam Academy at Bennington had seen to that. An unusual institution for the times, the Priam operated on the assumption that women could think. It taught them Logic and Literature, French and German, Philosophy and Religion, and in the case of Elizabeth Chandler it instilled in her a lifelong passion for the poetry of George Noel Gordon, Lord Byron. Returning to Sedgewick Falls after those years at Priam, Elizabeth knew that she could never mate with a man who was not her intellectual equal, although her female friends warned her that such an uppity attitude was a direct invitation to spinsterhood.

'The word does not frighten me,' she told them. 'What horrifies me is the thought of spending a lifetime with a man who thinks that a syllogism is a tool for bending horseshoes and that Henry James is the governor of Massachusetts.'

Her friends, both married and single, pointed out that the comment was unfair; Sedgewick Falls had its educated men. George Wheelwright, who had been her most ardent suitor before he grew weary and married elsewhere, had been to Dartmouth College and could define the difference between the disjunctive and the categorical syllogism without peeking in the book; while Harrison Cobb, her current beau and a graduate of the Law School at Yale, had read *The Ambassadors* twice, although neither time all the way through.

'Unfair,' Elizabeth agreed, 'but accurate enough in a general sense. It isn't a lack of education that I deplore, it's a total lack of intellectual curiosity in this town.'

Her young and married lady friends observed, with a certain amount of tittering and odd glances, that there was a good deal more to marriage than intellectual curiosity.

Elizabeth met these smirks head-on; as usual, she had a line from Byron that applied. 'Maidens, like moths, are ever caught by glare. Thank you very much, but I prefer to avoid the candle. That way, at least, I won't be calving once a year like some young ladies I know.'

In the parochial setting of Sedgewick Falls this attitude was a challenge to an established order, and any other female in her place would have felt the weight of society's disapproval. But not Elizabeth Chandler, not with her name and her money. There had been Chandlers in that part of Vermont going back to the pre-Revolutionary days of the Hampshire Grants, and there had been Chandlers with Ethan Allen at Fort Ticonderoga. Chandlers had battled the rocky soil of Sedgewick County for generations. Some had flourished, some had failed, but always honourably; and Elizabeth's father, the last of his line, had been before his death a town selectman, a trustee of the Sedgewick National Bank, a deacon of the First Congregational Church, and the proprietor of the largest feed and grain store in the county. What he left her was not a fortune as the world counts wealth, but it was considerable for Sedgewick Falls. There was the house on Crown Street where she lived, free and clear; her parents' home and now her own. There was a controlling interest in Chandler's Feed and Grain, now under the managership of her former suitor, George Wheelwright. There were the proceeds of the sale of three-quarters of the business, now carefully invested with a Boston broker. And finally there was, as bedrock to all this, the one hundred and twenty acres of prime timberland that was her untouchable reserve. With assets such as these Elizabeth could compare maidens and moths and mock the glare of the candle, and Sedgewick Falls could only listen and smile weakly.

It was out to those acres that she now took herself, riding behind a smoothly striding cob, the runners of the phaeton ticking at occasional stones. Outside the town the skies just after dawn were grey, but fair with promise, and out along Brush Hollow Road the meadows of snow were marred by signs of spring: melting islands of earth, and rock and bushes bare and glistening. In her mind she smelled the woodsmoke and the syrup of the years that stretched back to her childhood, and she leaned forward eagerly, both fists steady on the reins, ready to renew her contact with the cycle, to witness once again the rising and the tapping of the sap. What she did not know was that just like any other maiden, and any other moth, she was riding directly into the glare of the candle.

Anton Prinz awoke at about the same time that Elizabeth did, but his bed had been the packed-dirt floor of Ethan Morris's sugarhouse, his pillow had been a quarter-cut log, and he had

41

slept for less than six hours. Ethan had taken his trio of conscripted labourers directly from the jailhouse to the farm and had set them at once to chopping. They had worked straight through a clear and icy afternoon, stopped at six o'clock for a supper of cold beans wrapped in a pancake, and had gone on to chop until almost midnight by the light of coal-oil lamps hung from rafters and trees. Coffee then, steaming tin mugs of it, and a jar of cider for Harley, before bedding down in the fire-warmed sugarhouse. The sleep had been deep and good, and now Anton stretched as he wakened, wincing at the pull of sore muscles. The pale light seeping in through the chinks in the walls told him that it was time to be moving. When he looked around he saw that Harley and Jean-Pierre were already gone, and he hurried outside. Morning ablutions were quick and simple. A dash behind a tree to relieve the burden of the night, a handful of snow to wash with, and an icicle snapped from the sugarhouse eaves to rub against his gums and crunch between his teeth.

'Hey there, come and get it.' It was Ethan calling to him from the back porch, waving an arm. The words meant nothing to him, but the invitation was clear.

'*Ich komme,*' he shouted in reply, and then forced himself to say slowly, 'Eye yam cumming.'

The business of language oppressed him. You grow up with a language, slowly becoming conversant, then fluent, and at time positively dazzling in the use of it, and then you take a few steps away from home and find yourself cut off at the roots. He calculated that it was now almost three months since he had left the Tirol, and for half of that time he had heard no German spoken at all. In the beginning it had been hard enough to travel frozen roads among frozen people, but there had been the consolation and the convenience of the language. From St. Anton to Bregenz, to Munich, and all the way north to Hamburg he had bumped along in his innocent way without a thought of what would happen once he had landed on a foreign shore. Even aboard the steamship *Bremen* the other passengers in the steerage section had been mostly German-speaking, although their flinty northern accents had grated on his ears. Fourteen days in crossing, fourteen stormy days in the North Atlantic which had both thrilled and sickened him, but at least it was in German that they had comforted each other. And then the shock of Boston and the blank stares of incomprehension which were the only answers that he got to his questions. Of course, he had managed. Of course, you always manage. There was a German-speaking customs official who had helped, and a teamster from Alsace who had driven him out of town on a load of bricks and had pointed him north; and failing people like that you could always jump up and down flapping your arms, clucking loudly and holding a hand under your tail to show that you wanted an egg, not a pork chop, and so you managed. You also managed to make a perfect fool out of yourself, and after a while the helplessness robs you of spirit. For the past few weeks he had trudged the roads of New England blindly travelling north in search of he knew not what, and each day of blank stares and silence, of suspicious farmers and tight-lipped housewives who shook their heads and turned away, had sunk him lower and lower. The lowest point had been the foul-smelling, pest-ridden lockup in town, but he was out of that now, and a day's worth of work with a double-bitted axe had given him a sense of value again.

Still, I will have to learn this language, he told himself. A word is a piece of silver, a word is a sword, a word is the way of a man with a maid, at least in the beginning. Without the words I'm nothing.

He hurried into the house for a breakfast of hot beans, coffee, and bread, a silent meal to be shovelled down without ceremony. Jean-Pierre smiled at him sleepily, dozing over his plate, while Harley picked at the food without enthusiasm and Ethan drummed his fingers on the table, anxious to get going. Anton ate as much as he could of the bread and beans that birdlike Martha Morris set in front of him, washed it down with a swig of coffee so hot that it scalded his tongue, and nodded to Ethan to show that he was ready.

'Let's get a-goin' then,' said the farmer. 'That sugar won't wait on us forever.'

Outside in the barnyard the horse was hitched to a heavy sledge that was filled with the paraphernalia of sugar-making: stacks of buckets, whittled wooden taps, a set of braces with bits, and dozens of pieces of tin, each bent into the shape of a tiny tent. The procedure seemed simple enough. You drilled into the maple with the brace and bit, plugged the hole with the tap, and hung a bucket onto the end of it to collect the seeping sap. The purpose of the little tents puzzled him until Jean-Pierre explained that they fitted over the bucket and tap to prevent loose snow from falling in and diluting the product. What puzzled him even more was how they were going to work across the snow meadows and into the stands of maple trees. The snow was still waist-high in places, and although the horse and sledge could manoeuvre it safely, the men would be floundering within a dozen steps. Ethan answered that question by going into the barn and coming out with a stack of cross-laced snowshoes, each as wide as the wings of a bat and tapering off to a point behind. He threw them on the ground.

'Only three pair,' he announced. 'Some soul has to ride the sledge lessen he wants to risk his neck with those godforsaken sticks over there.'

Anton followed his pointing finger, and when he realized that he was looking at a pair of skis leaning against the wall of the barn he took a deep breath and said softly, '*Heilige Maria.*'

They were roughly formed and badly finished, much too short and with ridiculous upcurves at the front and rear. They were warped out of shape and had only the simplest of leather toe and heel straps, but they were skis, all right, and he was startled to feel his eyes begin to water at the sight of them. He stopped himself just this side of disgrace and examined them fondly. It was like holding a piece of his home in his hands, a slab of his mother's *Kuchen* or his father's favourite pipe. He knew that the others were looking at him strangely, and he grinned at them.

'*Ich möchte diese,*' he said '*Gehen wir!*' He dropped the skis onto the snow, slipped his boots into the straps, and reached for the rickety poles.

'Hey there, hold your horses,' Ethan shouted. 'I don't want you breaking your dang-fool head afore we get any work done.'

But Anton was gone before the words were said, slipping down the gentle grade and out of the barnyard. He followed the natural slope of the land, testing the skis that carried him. They pulled and they snagged and they didn't turn true, but he forced them into line with his ankles and knees. Muscles unused for three months creaked, but he laughed at the ache, and laughed again as he thought of the last time he had skied over snow. The night he had left home, laughing that time too, racing down to St Anton trailing bubbles of bitter laughter in his wake.

It was a different sort of laughter now, bitter-free and it made him realize how profoundly sad the last three months had been. He lifted his head, his eyes moving over the melting fields and the tops of the snow-shouldered pines to the sugarloaf shape of Mount Wellington looming through the wisps of high mist. It was country he had never seen before, but it was country that he knew. He had a belly full of beans, skis on his boots, and the promise of a day's pay ahead of him. It was enough to make his spirits soar, and his body soared as well as he came up out of his crouch to jump this time just for the joy of it, and turned in the air to land facing back the way he had come. The others still stood in the barnyard gaping at him. Jean-Pierre took off his stocking cap and waved it wildly round his head in a salute to the acrobatics.

Maybe, Anton thought, just maybe it's time to be happy again.

'*Gehen wir,*' he yelled to the others, '*los, los,*' and when they did not move he thought the words out carefully in English. 'Come . . . on . . . let's . . . go,' he yelled again, and as the sledge started up he turned to lead the way to the nearest stand of maples.

Chapter Four

From the Journals of Elizabeth Chandler

Friday, 27 March 1914

This will be difficult. I have not yet begun, and already the pen in my hand trembles. God give me the strength to set this record down tonight. For the past nine years I have been a faithful keeper of this journal, never faltering, and I am determined that this day must prove no exception. I will record the happenings of the past forty-eight hours, and I will do it without tears. I loathe weeping women, and as I have told myself more than once today, I have nothing about which to weep. Nothing evil has befallen me, unless confusion be construed as evil.

I admit to being confused, but who would not be so in my place? I do not know very much about the carnal side of life, but if I am ignorant of life I am not a ninny, either. I know very well what makes a woman tick. Lord knows, I've heard my own clock ticking long enough. Every woman knows that sound, and also knows that experience is only the confirmation of instinct.

But when you get right down to it, all I really know is myself . . . and that is all I want to know. Me, what happens inside of me, not anybody else. I have never been in harmony with my peers and do not wish to be so. What I have is peculiar to me, and only to me: a warm and passionate desire to be anything I wish to be, and if that should include the right to be cold and dispassionate, so be it. That is all I have ever wanted, that right, and now – God help me – I am not so sure. Foolishly, I had thought that I had constructed an edifice of values within which I could dwell for the rest of my life and now at the age of only twenty-two I find that the building has been shaken to its foundations, still standing but no longer the fortress I had thought it to be. Shaken not by a concept, not by a vision that came in the night, not by a categorical truth or a burning bush . . . but only by a man. Only a man, Mr Anton Prinz, newly arrived in these parts.

Yes, the confession, reluctantly penned. This maiden, like the moth, has flown directly into the glare of the candle. Having reserved myself for nothing less than excellence, I find myself conquered by the most ordinary of men.

But yet, how unfair to name him that. (My damnable intellectual snobbery again.) He has so many qualities that I am tempted to describe them here – the thrust of that jaw and those cold, knowing eyes – but I shall put that aside, for I see that I am rambling. Clearly, I hesitate to get into the essentials of this entry, mooning over jawbones. A description of the gentleman may come later, but now is a time for honest reflection and a sober recitation of events. If one muse has sustained me in these pages through the years it has been Clio, not Erato, and now is not the time to change allegiances. We all know what Mr Lincoln said about swapping horses when crossing a stream.

To begin then, not *in medias res,* as I was taught it at Priam, but in simple chronological fashion, I arrived at the Morris farmhouse yesterday morning much vexed to find that Ethan and his hired hands had already left to go sugaring without waiting for my arrival. I had planned, as always, to go with the men to help with the tapping, and this left me 'high and dry', for they had taken the sledge and all of the snowshoes. I was so unsettled by this display of masculine indifference, and so disappointed, that I was tempted to take off after them, snowshoes or no, but little Martha Morris rightly pointed out that my skirts would founder me for sure. It must have been a man who first chained women into skirts, and may the devil roast him for it. With a proper pair of trews I would have risked it, but as it was I found myself imprisoned in the kitchen until such time as the men returned for the midday meal.

And it was just as well that I was. Martha Morris is a good soul and a fine Christian woman, but she is not my idea of a proper housekeeper. The crock of beans she was about to pop into the oven had been rinsed through only once and was thick with stems and unwanted greenery. The dough for her bread, 'rye and injun,' was poorly kneaded and in want of more rising, and the side of bacon she was about to cut into was encrusted with unscraped mould. Further, the breakfast dishes had not been done, the lids on the Glenwood stove were still to be sanded, and there were half a dozen other chores around the house that needed attention. Thus I found myself well occupied yesterday morning performing those disagreeable tasks which in my own home are the province of a hired woman; but there was nothing for it. I simply cannot bear the sight of sloth, and so I rolled up my sleeves, borrowed an apron, and set to work side by side with Martha, Vermont-style. And was repaid for my efforts by the woman's unceasing chatter. Lord deliver me from a voluble female, but nothing could deter this one from describing in detail the two hired men who were working that day with her husband. (Harley Swenson, being local, she dismissed with a sniff.) I had to hear all about their roughness of dress (as if our men wear silk when they work), the way they ate their beans (as if there are more ways than one), the way they cooled their coffee (as if we scalded our throats with our own), and, as might be expected, an essay on the oddness of the languages they spoke.

'One's Canuck, but not t'other,' she said in that scratchy voice of hers, and I use the offensive word *Canuck* only to quote her exactly. I prefer to say 'French-Canadian,' considering the extra syllables well spent.

Then I asked her what nationality the other man might be and she allowed as how she did not know, saying only that he was 'some sort of furriner,' and adding that he had a sly and charming smile and was obviously the type that you couldn't trust farther than you could sling a dead cat for all that he might sneak up on a soul at night with unspeakable horrors in mind. Thus do our parochial manners betray us, and, needless to say, the mention of those horrors was truncated by a gasp of apology as she pretended to remember my maiden condition. The woman is truly impossible.

Nevertheless, I stuck it out in the kitchen, for if there is any female I dislike more than the one who slavishly accepts the bonds of matrimony and housekeeping it is the one who, having accepted them, fails to do the job properly. So between this and that it was close on to noontime before I was able to take my apron off, make myself a cup of tea (after inspecting said cup carefully), and go outside onto the front porch to await the return of the men for their meal.

The sky was clear and so was the air, the earlier promise of the day fulfilled, and I could easily see across the meadows to where the stands of birch and maple covered the rise of Knobby Hill from top to bottom, the trees against the snow as sharp as pencil strokes. Beyond the hill the land rose up again in the first of the steps that it takes as it leaps to the feet of Mount Wellington, and off to the west I could see the river and the thick groves there along both banks. It was from out of those trees that I saw the horse-drawn sledge emerge accompanied by three black dots which I knew to be the men on snowshoes. Only three? There ought to have been another, and just then I saw him. Instead of following the river he had climbed to the top of Knobby Hill and now he was descending on skis, weaving his way in and out of the trees as he rushed downhill. It was quite a sight. We don't use skis much in these parts, only the trappers who go to the mountains in search of the civet, the bobcat, and the occasional 'painter,' and they use them mostly to keep from sinking into the snow, slipping and sliding gracelessly. Not like Mr Anton Prinz, for it was he. He came downhill like the wind itself, twisting and turning in an exhibition of speed and grace that left me breathless as he sped across the meadows, lightly jumped a buried fence, and skimmed into the barnyard to come to a stop in a shimmering arc of high-flung snow and ice. An impressive performance.

A pause now for a cup of tea, and to rest these fingers.

Rereading the above, what rubbish I have written! Had I

presented such a paper during my Priam days it would have been returned to me slashed with red pencil. Such language. An impressive performance . . . speed and grace . . . shimmering arcs . . . all that trash and not one true word about how I really felt when I saw that godlike form descending. Not a single word about the knot that formed within me then, so tight that I thought I must choke, nor of the sudden, helpless melting at the core, uncontrolled . . .

I cannot write this. I do not have the words, or if I do they are impoverished and, like Byron, I must let them describe the undescribable. It is not my way to use such words, nor is it the way of my people. Byron again, who must have known. *The cold in clime are cold in blood. Their love can scarce deserve the name.* I hesitate to speak of love, but in truth we are frozen folk with ice where our feelings should be and a cool disdain for those who choose to display their emotions. That is the way we are, and it is a proper way to be. Imagine how much work would get done if we all went about like a pack of Italians or Frenchmen clutching our bosoms and howling to the moon whenever . . . whenever . . . whenever we felt like it?

Tarnation, but that's no way to be.

Except that I still can see the line of his jaw and his eyes as he gazed at me. Resting on his ski poles after his exertions, he saw me on the porch, and he slowly straightened, one hand going to his cap. He took it off, less as a salute than to make himself at home, and his eyes were on mine so cold and knowing as if he could feel the knot within me, as if he could sense the melting.

'Good morning,' I said, and in great understatement added, 'You ski very well.'

'*Grüss Gott.*' He smiled, but shook his head. '*Es tut mir leid, meine Dame. Ich spreche nicht englisch.*'

So he was German; one mystery solved. At Priam my knowledge of German was second to my French, but an elastic memory is the mark of a first-class mind. In his own language, I said, 'Very well then, we shall speak in German. I was admiring your skiing.'

'*Um Himmelswillen!*' A smile of uncontained delight spread over his face. 'Are you German then?'

'No, American. I learned the language at school.' I was tempted to add that I had chosen to learn it because a knowledge of German is essential to the study of medicine, and at that time of my girlhood I had toyed with the thought of a medical career. It seemed a bit much to say so, however, and I asked, 'Where are you from in Germany?'

'Austria, the Tirol,' he corrected. He looked as if he wanted to put his heels together, but of course that was impossible wearing skis. 'Anton Prinz, *gnädige Frau*.'

'*Fräulein*,' I corrected in turn, wondering what to say next. He was clearly waiting for me to speak, a mark of respect, I suppose. Without realizing it I had risen from my seat and now stood at the railing of the porch gazing down on him. I must have looked a proper fool that way, struck dumb and staring, and with that ridiculous woollen cap pulled down over my ears. I wanted desperately to snatch it off despite the cold, but I controlled the impulse. Once again he seemed to know what I was thinking as he stood there resting easily on his ski poles, his eyes merry and the beginnings of a smile on his lips. I felt my cheeks grow warm (although I *never* blush) and knew that I should have to retreat inside the house, when I was spared this embarrassment by the arrival of the sledge and the men on snowshoes.

'Excuse me, *Fräulein*, I must tend the fires.' He said it reluctantly, but he kicked off the skis and loped away towards the sugarhouse as the sledge slid into the yard loaded down with brimming buckets of sap.

I watched him go for as long as I dared, and then turned my attention to Ethan Morris, who stood at the side of the sledge bawling instructions to his helpers for all the world like an army sergeant on the parade ground. I suppose that it was done for my benefit, but after all, it was only old Harley Swenson and a French-Canadian chap of impressive proportions (although I privately decided that Mr Prinz was equally muscular in his own way). Well, I felt agitated enough to need a goat to whip, and I'm afraid that poor Ethan was elected. I purely gave him 'Hail Columbia' for sneaking off without me that morning, and in his usual hangdog way he mumbled something about the sugarbush waiting for no man nor beast. Of course we both knew that he meant no woman, and that he had gone off early to avoid being burdened with my presence.

But burden or no, he could not object to my helping to unload the buckets from the sledge and taking them down to the sugarhouse to be emptied into the evaporation tank. Anton Prinz already had a roaring fire going under the tank, dancing around it like a merry devil, pitching in chunks of hardwood and gauging the flames as if he had been sugaring off all his life. He give me the flash of a grin as I came in lugging my bucket of sap, but there was no time for words, not then.

Making sugar calls for constant labour and precise timing. The sap must be brought to the boil and kept at that heat as it filters through the long maze of baffles in the tank. When it reaches the end of the tank it must have achieved just the right consistency (eleven pounds to the gallon for syrup, more for sugar) and just the right temperature, or else the batch is ruined. This means constant woodcutting and fuelling of the fire as the process goes on around the clock. I figure that it takes five or six healthy maple trees to produce forty gallons of sap, which will then throw off just one gallon of syrup. It is a wearisome process with little profit in it, and I sometimes wonder why we continue to do it. Tradition, I suppose, and the lure of childhood memories.

Once all the sap had been emptied into the tank and the fire had been brought to the proper pitch (as judged by Ethan with Solomonlike solemnity), we were able to go to our dinner, for it would be some time before the boiling began. In the crowded kitchen I confess that I contrived to seat myself next to Mr Prinz, although that was really nothing more than simple hospitality, since I was the only person there with whom he could converse.

Converse? It was more like opening up a floodgate. The poor man had not heard his own language spoken in weeks, and having no other he had been living in a linguistic limbo. Now it all came pouring out as he 'tucked into' the dish of bacon and beans before him, eating in a hearty, two-fisted fashion which some might find coarse, but which to me seemed only healthy and natural. Breaking off chunks of bread and gulping his coffee, he told me of how he had left his home in the Tirol after a family dispute (some *mittel*-Europa melodrama, no doubt), and had made his way north through Germany to the port of Hamburg determined to – which trite phrase to use? Seek his fortune on foreign shores? Exchange the Old World for the New? Shake the dust of Europe from his boots? Choose any of

51

the above, but the end result was that he took ship for Boston, landed there, and headed directly north in search of mountains.

'I am a mountain man,' he explained to me. 'I was born in the high places and that is where I must live. There was this Bavarian fellow on the docks in Boston, at the *Zollinspektion*, you know, and I asked him where the mountains are in America. He says to me, "There are two ways you can go. All the way out west where the Indians live, or straight north where the Yankees live. The Yankees live closer."' He shrugged. 'I didn't know what a Yankee was but it sounded better than the Indians, so I took the short road and here I am.'

There he was, and there I was, as well, drinking in every word he was saying, neglecting my food, and trying not to notice the looks on the faces of the others at the table. Harley was paying me no mind, just wolfing his beans and swigging his cider, but the others, well, you'd think that I was a trained seal juggling a ball on my nose just because I was carrying on a conversation in a foreign tongue. Martha Morris kept giving me quick pecking glances like a suspicious chicken, and Ethan's frowning face showed clear disapproval. Jean-Pierre smiled at me indulgently, but even his was the look of a patronizing adult for a child. I ignored them. I was fascinated by the story being told, fascinated with the teller of the tale, and I was working as well at trying to understand the unfamiliar Austrian accent, which bounced like a grasshopper from word to word. By the time the story had progressed to the lockup in Sedgewick Falls, however, I had got the hang of it and was even up to modifying my own *hochdeutsch* in response.

All this took place during the mere twenty minutes that could be allowed for the meal, and when that time was up it was my firm intention to continue the conversation, no matter how. I accomplished this, not very subtly, by suggesting to Ethan that he and the other two men return to the sugarbush to continue tapping while Mr Prinz and I stayed at the sugarhouse, he to replenish the fuel supply and I to keep an eye on the sugaring process. Ethan didn't like that very much but there was little he could do about it. After all, they are my trees.

I wish now that I could remember in detail what we spoke of during that afternoon in the sugarhouse, but the subsequent events of the night have, I fear, washed them from my mind. A pity, because in general I recall it as one of those rare times in my life when I was wholly relaxed in the presence of another. Normally I am too much on my guard with people, and somewhat fearful . . . but that is neither here nor there. Sitting in the sugarhouse with Mr Prinz, tending to the sap while he chopped the wood in the effortless and economical fashion of the born outdoorsman, I felt . . . at home. For the first time in three years, since my beloved parents were taken from me, I felt myself in the presence of one who could do me only good. The words came easily then.

I remember that he spoke of mountains. He seems obsessed by them, convinced that people who live in high places constitute a breed far superior to anything that the lowlands can produce. His is the world of Alpine meadows and snowy passes, crags, and tors and peaks. He has only contempt for merchants and other men of affairs, reserving his respect for those who deal in elemental forces. The mountains claim his first allegiance, together with this business of skiing, which is his other passion. His language tells the story. When he speaks of skiing he will generally use the conventional word *skilaufen*, but at other times he will refer to it in Germanic combinations which translate as 'ski-flying', and 'ski-soaring', and even 'ski-dancing'. It is obviously something more than just a means of transportation for him.

I shall have to learn how.

At one point he said, 'These mountains of yours, what are they called?'

'The nearest is Mount Wellington, the one to the north is Mount Mansfield. Taken all together the chain is called the Green Mountains.'

'And are they truly green?'

'Indeed they are, once the snow is gone.'

'They are different from my mountains.' He rested for a moment, leaning on the handle of the axe. 'My mountains are higher, of course, and . . .' He searched for the word and came up with *grausam* '..crueller. Yours seem more rounded. Not exactly gentle, but friendly.'

'Is it a bad thing for a mountain to be friendly?'

He considered the concept before answering. 'A mountain must be a challenge,' he said finally, 'but there is such a thing as a friendly challenge. I would like to ski your mountains sometime.'

'You may find them something less than friendly if you do.'

By this time I knew that I was smitten with the man, but I wasn't about to let him run down Vermont's most prominent aspect.

He smiled at the tartness in my voice, and said, 'Perhaps.' He applied himself to the wood, and when he spoke again he did not look at me, saying the words as he swung the axe. 'These Green Mountains, this place, it could be a home for me if I could find a way to make a living here.'

The effect of these words on me can be imagined. I said firmly, 'There is always a way for a man who is willing to work hard.'

He grunted as the axe bit into a log. 'Not so easy for a man with no money.'

'There is always a way,' I repeated.

He accepted this piece of homespun philosophy silently, working away with his axe flashing silver, then copper as it reflected the glow of the flames beneath the tank. The sap was boiling now, and throwing off that best-remembered of childhood odours. I kept the viscous liquid moving with the paddle, stirring now here and now there to keep it flowing evenly through the baffles. It was a time of quiet contentment with the thud of the axe and the sweet smell of the sugar providing a homey setting.

'This land, you own it all?' He was taking another breather, wiping his brow with a kerchief which I fear was none too clean. 'The land and the trees, too?'

'All of it.' I managed to keep pride from inflecting my tone.

'Then why don't you use it? Why do you let it stand idle?'

'You mean cut down the trees?'

'Only the ones that are ready to be cut. You have a fortune in timber here. You even have a mill you could use.'

'I have no need for a fortune,' I said, trying hard not to appear the *grande dame*, 'and I prefer to keep the trees as they are.'

He shook his head. 'Such a waste.'

'Perhaps, but that is the way that I wish it.'

He saw that the subject was closed and he went back to making the chips fly.

Oh-ho, young feller, I thought, so that's what's on your mind. Not that what he said came as a surprise. Others have been after me to cut and clear the Chandler timber: Seth Cobb for one, and Mr Oates at the bank. It amused me that this brash stranger should make the same observation 'on the spot,' as it were. He was clearly a bright young man, and ambitious. It was also clear that when he spoke of my timber he was including himself in those plans. Strangely, I did not object to this forwardness, considering it instead as a positive quality, a sign of 'get up and go.' (Yes, I know. The candle was fairly blazing and the moth was blind.)

Just before sunset the men came in from the fields with the sledge once again laden with buckets of sap, and now the labours of the night began. The fresh, cold sap had to be introduced into the tank at the far end so as not to bring the mass below a boil, and the fire had to be kept a-blazing. Oh, we worked, all right: Mr Prinz and the amiable Jean-Pierre chopping and fuelling while Ethan emptied buckets and I wielded the paddle briskly. Only useless Harley Swenson failed to carry his share of the load, leaning insolently against the wall of the sugarhouse with a jar of cider in his hand, not his first of the day and not his fifth, either. In truth, the man was fairly muddled with drink. I gave him several hard looks which did no good at all, but I hesitated to speak out, since that was properly Ethan's job and I did not wish to lower him before the others.

Oh, how I wish now that I had. Never again will I place a rational notion second to a man's vanity.

There was no time to stop for supper. At about six o'clock Martha brought in a pot of squirrel stew, which she handed around with slabs of bread. It was a touch too gamy for my taste, and so I contented myself with dipping the bread in the gravy and then performing the childhood trick of pouring a spiral of newly made syrup onto a patch of clean snow, thus treating myself to a piece of taffy for dessert with a bite of sour pickle after to cut the sweetness. The men, however, seemed to enjoy the stew, all of them eating heartily with the exception of Harley, who took only his favourite liquid refreshment. Coffee did for the rest of us, and then our labours continued into the night.

Ruddy fire devils dancing on the sugarhouse walls, and Ethan calling, 'Wood, lads, wood. Let's have some more wood.'

'*Voyons*, Anton, we give him wood, *hein*? We chop like h – .' The massive Jean-Pierre grinning a challenge through his curly beard, Mr Prinz with a flash of teeth in reply, and then the two

55

of them are slashing away lickety-split, metal flashing, each determined to outdo the other. Chunks fly, the fire roars, the syrup bubbles, and my heart lifts up at such a merry sight. Would that it could have stopped there, caught as in a painting to hang on the wall. What a brave tableau it would have made: 'Sugaring Time,' or some such title, by Winslow Homer, or even Mr Eakins.

But I ramble again, wishing no doubt to stay put in the past, afraid to go on. But there is no past for me now, and no painting to hang on the wall. The firelight flickered and the picture came apart.

Dark, and warm and sugar-sweet cosy, a little girl's nest in the night. That was the shelf at the end of the sugarhouse, away from the glare and the roar of the flames but nigh enough to be heated by them, and that was where I would tumble at last when my eyes would refuse to stay open. Oh, what big eyes I had way back then, wanting to see it all, touch it all, taste it all at sugaring time, and I would stay up all night to be part of it under licence from the most indulgent of papas. All night, that is, until excitement and fatigue joined forces to tug at my eyelids and bubble up yawns, and then it was time to tumble home onto the sugarhouse shelf and sleep until dawn.

Was the maple sweeter then, did the birch smoke sting more smartly? It seems so now in memory . . . ah yes, I know, 'The good old times – all times when old are good.' But still, there was the little girl's nest on the sugarhouse shelf, and waking in the night to feel my father's arms around me as he joined me in rest, holding me safe as we slept. One eye open sleepily to peek at the flames and at the shadowy figure dancing round the fire, then shut again as I snuggled in close to the warmth of Papa's coat, burying myself there in the odours of wool and tobacco, the faint tang of cider. Everything seemed so safe.

Enough of childhood. Childhood is done, and nothing is safe any more. Get on with it, girl.

I worked with the others until midnight, stirring, heating, drawing off syrup, and then took my rest on the sugarhouse shelf, cloaked in the gloom at the end of the shed, part of the process but private from it. I slept, and slept well, woke as in childhood to peek at the flames and closed my eyes contentedly, leaning back within the comfort of the arms that enclosed me and the reassuring odours of the male animal. And then woke again sharply, truly awake this time and jolted out of childhood's memory. I was awake in the here and now, with the arms of a sleeping man around me.

Mr Prinz was asleep, make no mistake about that. I will not assign blame where none belongs. I realize now that he had crawled up onto the shelf, just as I had, to snatch forty winks from a long day of grinding toil, and once asleep had turned towards me and burrowed in close the way a puppy or a kitten will, seeking comfort in company. Now he lay on his side behind me, his arms around me and his chin tucked into the warmth of my shoulder. He was asleep, I am sure of it, and in his sleep he murmured names and places strange to me. He was asleep, I am certain, but his hands moved lightly over me. He was asleep, but he was doing exactly what I wanted him to do. Just as in *Childe Harold,* I felt those 'hands promiscuously applied, round the slight waist or down the glowing side.' I had wakened from one dream into another.

Then I froze, not in fear of those hands but afraid that the others might see. My eyes were fully open now, and I could see them round the tank: Ethan taking a turn with my paddle, Jean-Pierre slumped against the wall at his ease, and Harley pitching chunks of wood on the fire, his jar of cider at rest on the floor. I realized that although I could see them I was safe from their eyes behind a curtain drawn by the shadows. Knowing that, I turned within the circle of those arms to face Mr Prinz and press myself close to him. I did this without any conscious decision, as if it were the most natural thing in the world. As indeed it was. The moth was turning to face the flame.

When he felt me close to him he opened his eyes, at once awake. His face showed surprise, then amusement, then a sudden alarm. He whispered, 'Forgive me, *Fräulein,* I was asleep, I didn't know what I was doing.'

'You were asleep,' I agreed. 'No harm was done.' I said it bravely enough, but I own that I was trembling.

Perhaps he mistook that tremor for fear; he began to edge away from me. 'I meant nothing. I'll go now.'

'Do you really wish to go?' More bravado.

He stopped moving. He was silent for a moment, his eyes on mine, the hint of a smile again on his lips. 'No,' he said softly,

'I don't want to go, but I am a stranger here. I don't know the customs and I don't want to get into any trouble.'

'The only trouble will come if I scream for help.'

The smile was broader now. 'Are you going to scream?'

'No. At least, not yet.'

His arms around me tightened, holding me closer still, and our lips were almost touching. Then he hesitated. 'The others . . . ?'

'They cannot see.' I raised my face to his.

Still he did not move, muttering. 'This is crazy.'

'How so?'

'You are a lady.'

'I should hope so.'

'And I am no gentleman.'

'Perhaps, but I hope that you know how to act like one. You are embarrassing me, Mr Prinz. Are you going to kiss me, or not?'

He inclined his head and kissed me full on the lips. I returned the kiss. Heartily, I hope, but with some anxiety, having done this sort of spooning only with one of my suitors, and not very much of it at that. I was not at all sure that I was doing it properly, but apparently my fears were groundless.

His eyes alive, he asked, 'Is that how a gentleman acts?'

'I think so. At least, it was very nice.' And then I admitted, 'I really don't know. I've never done anything quite like this before.'

'I didn't think you had.'

It was meant as a compliment, but it piqued me. 'Oh, are you disappointed?'

He put a finger to my lips. 'Stop talking like that. I've been wanting to do it all day long.'

'Have you?' I could not conceal my delight. 'I must admit that I was hoping you would.'

'Not a very ladylike thing to say.'

That gave me pause, but it was time to throw the bonnet over the windmill. 'Perhaps not, but it is something that a woman says if she means it. When she speaks like that she speaks from her heart. Ladies do, too.'

He looked at me strangely. These were not the sort of words he had expected to hear. No doubt he was accustomed to trading kisses and banter casually. For a moment I feared that I had alarmed him with my frankness, then he put his finger to my lips again, stroking gently, saying, 'I like it when you speak from your heart. And I'm glad that you wanted me to kiss you.'

'I did from the first moment I saw you.' The bonnet was fairly soaring now, over the windmill and far away. 'When you came flying down that hill you looked so happy and so free – '

My words stopped there, not for a lack of them but because he was kissing me again, warmer and wilder this time. The roar of the fire rose up in my ears, my eyes were closed and my lips were sealed. The world was somewhere else, and I was content to be beyond it. Then time caught me up and took me away, swinging me sweetly from its pendulum.

In the popular novels the author now would say that it is time to draw the veil of modesty over the two lovers. And so we shall. Words of passion? None from me. Byron was able to rhyme 'possess'd' with 'bless'd,' but that's a poet's trick and I'll leave it to them. I will say only that the pendulum swung, and in that time some fine and gentle things were done to me. I was the happiest of women in that time, and then the time ran out.

'Wood,' yelled Ethan, cracking a dream. 'Dagnab it, who's been watching the fire? Wood on the far end, lots of it. Frenchman, Harley, get t'chopping. Where the devil is that Anton fella?'

At Ethan's words my lover cursed gently, and drew away. A smile of rueful apology, a kiss, a rapid rearrangement of his style, and then he bounded from the shelf. I watched him go fondly as he strode to the woodpile. I saw . . .

Write firmly now, steel nib pressed to paper, the pen a surgical tool to describe what happened next in spare, unsparing strokes.

Jean-Pierre, axe in hand, began at once to attack a massive log.

Harley tossed off the last of his cider, pitched the jar away, and took up his tool.

Anton's axe was sunk into a log, and he reached for it.

Drunken, bleary-eyed, staggering Harley Swenson raised his blade high over his head, his back to my lover, about to swing on a log. He swung, and as he did he stumbled, half falling and turning in a circle.

Jean-Pierre's mouth opened wide to shout an alarm that was never sounded.

Harley's axe came down as Anton reached for his own across

the log. The blade bit into his wrist and cut clear through, thudding into the wood. The hand was severed completely, it fell to the floor.

Silence. Dead silence as blood gushed forth from the stump in a river, and within that silence another tableau, not nearly so merry as the first. Jean-Pierre already in motion to aid, half a step taken. Harley dazed and unbelieving. Ethan round-eyed and useless. Anton staring as his life poured out at the wrist, not yet feeling pain. All this in a flick of time, and then the tableau broke as Anton moved. He knew exactly what he had to do.

He was three long steps from the evaporation tank, and he took the first in a stride, the second in a lurch, and the third in a stagger that fetched him up close against the metal flank of the vat. Then he raised his left arm high and shoved the shattered stump of his wrist deep into the boiling, sizzling, bubbling sap. A tick of time, another, and then he finally screamed. Just once, and then the scream was cut short as he fell to the floor, unconscious.

It is sunset now, the day after the one I have described, and I have been sitting here at the escritoire for hours setting down the events of yesterday at Ethan's farm. During those hours the shadows have lengthened, the room has grown chill, and my fingers have stiffened so that I am scarcely able to grasp the pen. But grasp it I will, and would even if it were a nettle, for I must complete this entry. I was not raised into the habit of leaving jobs unfinished.

I have just come from looking in on him. He sleeps deeply in the spare room upstairs, on my linen, in my home. The house is quiet, Crown Street being broad and lined with trees, and few are the sleighs and the wagons that pass by. Motorcars, too, are rare in this part of town, and I am spared their din except for those occasions when Harrison Cobb comes calling in his Oldsmobile or the McClures in their new little Oakland. The hired help have been ordered to step like mice, and so the house is quiet and he sleeps. He mutters and tosses, but he does not wake, for he is deep under the influence of morphine. Dr Cornelius says that he will keep him that way for as long as possible, certainly through this night, but the time will come when he will have to wake and face the pain. And the loss. But for the moment he sleeps, and I am grateful for that much. Dr Cornelius would have kept him in his surgery, but I insisted that he be brought here. He is mine now in every way, and it is my duty to care for him.

The doctor calls it a miracle, or rather a combination of circumstances which only Divine Providence could have supplied. His words, as best I remember them:

'Amazing that he had the courage to do it. Even more amazing that he knew what to do, considering his condition. He must have been in a state of total shock, yet something inside the man figured out the one course of action that could save his life. And figured it out in seconds. When he plunged his wrist into that vat of sizzling syrup he sealed off every gushing blood vessel and laid down a protective coat that was better than any bandage. If he hadn't done it he would have been dead within minutes. As it is he stands a good chance for a full recovery, minus his left hand of course.'

Yet all of that would have gone for naught if the Frenchman had not taken charge. It was he who leaped forward to catch Mr Prinz as he fell, who strapped on his belt as a rough tourniquet, and who drove my sleigh in a wild ride back to town with only the cold edge of a quarter-moon to show us the way. And it was he who grabbed up a jug of spirits to put in the sleigh.

'You keep him dosed up good with that,' he instructed me as we started off. 'You don't want him waking up.'

I did as I was bidden, pouring it into the man straight from the jug despite the sputters and gasps, and the primitive anaesthetic did its work. By the time we arrived at the surgery, Mr Prinz was blessedly unconscious. I must find a way to reward the Frenchman.

The sun has set and the dusk brought with it a visitor, the Reverend Dr James O. Walmsley, pastor of the First Congregational Church. He has just left. When I was told he was here I felt an easing on my heart.

How kind, I thought. He has heard of the accident and has come to offer spiritual comfort.

I was mistaken. The good divine came only in response to the rumours now rife in town, and to warn me of the impropriety of . . . ahem . . . a maiden lady harbouring an unknown man under her roof considering the . . . ahem . . . unchaperoned circumstances.

I sent him packing with a flea in his ear.

Midnight, and now I sit beside his bed to pen these final lines of the day. I shall stay here through the night until he wakens; he must see me when first he opens his eyes. His face is calm in sleep, although terribly pale, and his breathing is easy, no doubt the result of the last of the morphine. I touch a finger to his cheek and wonder that no words have passed between us, no pledges and no vows, and yet I know that our lives are inextricably entwined.

Heavenly Father who comes to comfort us in the night, hear my prayer for this young man stricken in adversity. He is a good man, Father, strong and honest, but soon he will awaken to a world which he is ill prepared to face. He will awaken to pain, and he will bear that pain. He will awaken to fear, and he will conquer that fear. But he will also awaken incomplete of his God-given limbs, and I do not know how he will manage to bear that. He is a man of the flesh, not the mind, a young man powerful and confident in the use of his body, and now a part of that body has been taken from him. Help him, Father, to find the strength to live with one hand as other men live with two. Help him to find the strength to excel, as he must excel, despite this handicap. And should he falter, Father, then help me to find the strength to give him comfort and courage, and to set him on the road again.

For I have chosen this man to love, Father, and he must not fail.

I ask this of You in the name of Your only begotten son, Christ Jesus.

Amen.

Mark those words: *I have chosen him.* Has my *hubris* been rewarded in advance? Ah, well, I cannot change, nor should I. It is a very special thing to be a woman.

Yesterday my world was firm, today it's topsy-turvy and nothing will ever be the same. Never again will I go 'a-sugaring' among the maple trees at springtime, and there's another sadness for you.

Chapter Five

Otto Prinz and Lili Wangenmann were married in the spring of 1914, and in the summer of that year he went off to war. They were wed on the first day of May in the parish church of St Anton, where the bride glowed, the groom preened, the priest droned, and the unrepaired and unrepentant organ supplied the obligatory burst of Lohengrin. In contrast to the wheezey Lohengrin was the set of Schubert *Lieder* sung by the groom's sister, young Marta Prinz, in a voice both delicate and affecting. Marta, in fact, came close to eclipsing the bride that day. Her youthful beauty, like a freshly stamped coin, and the emotion evoked by her singing charmed everyone who saw and heard her. After the ceremony Sepp and Hanna accepted congratulations both on the marriage of their son and the singing of their daughter. Herr Rapp, the choirmaster and music teacher, who had provided the piano accompaniment, also came in for his share of compliments. These he was careful to deflect in the direction of his pupil.

'A unique voice,' he told those who crowded around him outside the church. 'The child has a natural ability – she sings the way the rest of us breathe. Lord knows what will become of her, though. A voice like that one deserves to be trained in Munich or Vienna. I've done as much as I can for her.' He shot a contemptuous glance at Sepp and Hanna standing with the wedding party. 'But just try to convince certain people of that. Certain people whose horizons are bounded by their pigpens.'

But if Lili was outshone that day by her younger sister-in-law, she did not show any resentment over it, nor did she feel any. The simple fact that she was marrying Otto Prinz was enough to glorify the day for her, and ahead lay the wedding trip to Innsbruck, seven full days of big-city wonderment before returning to St Anton and the routine of life on the farm. There Lili slipped into her assigned role as the younger matron of the Prinz household, cheerfully assuming her full share of the domestic burdens. She scrubbed, she milked, she fed the chickens and the pigs, and if her strudel still had a long way to go her mother-in-law was forced to admit that she showed a deft enough hand with the barley soup and the *Gugelhupf*. During those first months of her marriage she cemented her position in the family by honouring her husband's father, deferring to his mother, charming his little sister, and dazing the man himself with a fierce sensuality that was far beyond any dream or expectation.

It was a time of contentment for Lili, for God had been good to her. Only a few months before she had despaired of ever finding a husband. Today she was not only a respectable married woman but the wife of a reserve officer in the imperial army, which placed her a cut above any other girl in town of her age. A baby or two (there was already a sign that one was on the way) and her contentment would be complete. This was happiness, she decided, this contentment which was so much more substantial than love. Contentment had a weight of its own, like a purse full of silver coins that swung solidly against your thigh. Love, when you thought about it carefully, weighed very little.

By all accounts that spring and summer were the fairest within memory, and not just in the Tirol. In later years it would seem that those last few months before the war were lived within a golden haze that extended from Great Britain to the Urals, and in retrospect everyone would have a story to tell of cattle never plumper and cream never thicker, of lush grass and luminescent skies, of lazy days and dripping honeycombs, perfumed nights and streams that ran thick with fat trout. It was as if, after the fact, the last European summer of peace and innocence deserved to be invested with a glory that never was, and thus would never be again.

The golden summer, and Lili's contentment, ended early and abruptly with the assassination of the Archduke Franz Ferdinand, heir to the throne of the Austro-Hungarian Empire. The killing in Sarajevo signalled the coming of autumn in June, followed quickly by winter in July as the Old Gentleman in Vienna called for a general mobilization of the army and issued a declaration of war. On the twenty-fifth of July, Otto shook the camphor balls out of his beloved uniform and proudly put on the light blue tunic and dark blue trousers of the *kaiserlich und königliche* Austrian army while Lili sewed the two gold stars of an Oberleutnant onto his collar. Her hands shook as she worked the needle and she pricked her fingers often. One Serbian bullet, she knew, could easily empty her purse of contentment and leave her a beggar again.

'You *will* be careful?' she asked, a beggar in advance. 'You'll come back safely to me?'

It was the ancient question which women must ask and men must frown at silently. That afternoon they walked through Alpine meadows under a sun both soft and strong, lazily herding the cattle before them. Theirs was only a pretence of labour, for even old Sepp recognized that with Otto leaving the next day the young couple deserved some private time together. They walked with twined fingers, plucking stems of rich grass to crack between their teeth, and after a while they found a spot of shade to use as both a tent and a table. They ate a simple meal, sipped wine from a skin, and Lili repeated her plea.

'You will be careful, won't you?'

Again, he did not answer. He sat beside her with his long legs drawn up to his chest, his arms around his knees, and stared broodingly at the grass between his feet. In her few months of marriage Lili had learned to recognize this mood of her husband's, this time when the devils of his discontent gripped him firmly by the throat and rattled his bones. She sighed inwardly. He wanted so much for himself, and there was so little that she could do for him that way. She knew something about men, after all. For two years she had juggled the lives of seven of them, keeping each one in his turn both proud and content; but those had been men of a basic contentment, not like this demon-driven husband of hers who longed for showers of glory and the smiles of princes. She sighed again and forced a smile of her own, cuddling closer.

'Look, sweetheart,' she said lightly, 'all I'm asking is that you don't do anything foolish. Don't play soldier too seriously.'

He turned slowly to look at her. 'You laugh at my dreams, don't you?'

'No.'

'Yes, you do, but I understand. I am an easy person to laugh at, me and my dreams.'

'I'm not laughing,' she said carefully. 'There's nothing wrong with dreaming, just as long as you don't confuse the dream with the real thing.'

He shook his head. 'You've got it upside down. The ordinary man is content to dream. Men like me must turn their dreams into reality. Do you have any idea what I would do to make a name for myself? To get away from this life of cowshit and pigshit? Just to *be* somebody?'

'You are somebody. You're my husband, and that's enough for me.'

'But not for me. You see, I would do anything.' His words came in a hoarse whisper. 'Anything at all. Name it, name the foulest thing in the world, and I'd do it. Go ahead, name something.'

'I . . . I can't.'

'What do I have to do? Kill a priest? Strangle a nun? Burn down a church? I'd do it, believe me. I'd pay the devil himself to do it for me.'

'Otto!' Lili sketched a quick cross with her thumb.

'I mean it, Lili. Anything. You understand?'

'I understand,' she said dully, thinking: He's hopeless. He lives in this storybook world, and me, God help me, I'm stuck there with him. Tomorrow he goes off to war like a little toy soldier and he's going to do something incredibly stupid, I know he is, a cavalry charge or something like that. Volunteers? *Jawohl,* Herr General, Oberleutnant Prinz at your service and ready to ride. Never fear, sir, my men will follow me into hell. Good man, Prinz, the Emperor will hear of this. And off he goes to get himself killed, except that they don't have horses in the mountain artillery, not the kind you charge with. Anyway, something insane like that and there I am, the young widow Prinz, and doesn't she look lovely in black? What a joke. God, if Anton were here, how he'd laugh.

While Lili and Otto were saying their farewells in the pasture, Marta was on her way down to the village for her weekly music lessons with Herr Rapp, a market basket on her arm. The basket was not meant for shopping; it contained several operatic scores that she had borrowed the week before from her teacher. She lived in a world of opera. Singing *Lieder* was both enjoyable and rewarding, but she knew in her heart that her future lay on the operatic stage. She tried each week to borrow something new from Herr Rapp, another role to be studied and, if possible, committed to memory. This week it had been Zerlina, and as

66

she walked lightly down the mountain path, she sang to herself, *'Batti, batti, o bel Masetto, la tua povera Zerlina...'*

Her voice died away as she saw her brother and sister-in-law sitting under the shade trees near the pasture, and she took care to avoid their seeing her. Marta did not dislike Lili, and Otto was, after all, her elder brother, but as a couple the sight of them offended her. Like most of the other young people in the village, she knew how badly her brother Anton had been treated in the supposed scandal, and the resentment still rankled.

We all behaved badly, she thought. There was never any rape. Surely Mama, as a woman, should have seen that. She could have been more loving and less outraged. And Papa didn't have to act like the patriarch in *La Juive*, so fierce and hard. And me? No excuses for me, either. There I was, the untouched Zerlina, and he was my jolly brother, the one who always laughed away my tears and bandaged my bruises, and treated me like a lady, not a child. And what did I do that terrible night? Did I reach my hand out to him? No, I stayed inside the house while Papa and Otto sent him away, Otto standing there with his thumbs hooked into his belt like an insolent Scarpia. And Anton, who was he in that family scene? Tannhäuser, perhaps, pale and unhappy, about to begin his pilgrimage to Rome. Is that where he is now, in Italy? Or did he go to Spain to be a barber in Seville? Soldiering in Egypt as the Captain of the Guard? Perhaps in the Golden West in that new thing by Puccini. Well, wherever he is, he is out of this terrible war, I trust. I suppose it is all right for people like Otto who enjoy dressing up in uniforms and dashing about giving orders, but Anton would have hated it. And all his friends called up to the army, too. Peter, Eugen, Karl, and the rest of them. All the young men are gone, nobody left to flirt with. It isn't fair at all.

Thoughts of young men reminded her of her music lesson with Herr Rapp, and she moved more rapidly down the path. Herr Rapp was not a young man, but there were times when he thought he was, times when music lessons in the choir loft became quite breathless. Nothing truly improper ever came to pass, but if the young Zerlina was still untouched she was certainly not unpinched. There were parts of her body that Marta could not see, but that she was sure turned black and blue after every weekly lesson. She hurried down to the village, the valley stretched out at her feet. It was an inspiring sight, no matter that she saw it every day. She knew that she lived in a place of great natural beauty, in a secure home, and with loving parents. She also knew that what she had was not enough for her, would never be, and not for the first time she wondered when some man would come to take her away from a life that so far had centred on pigpens, chicken coops, and pinches in the choir loft.

'Wien, Wien, city of my dreams,' she sang, as she hurried on down the hill.

Otto reported to the depot of the Fifth Regiment of Mountain Artillery at Landeck, where he was ordered out of his dress uniform and into the pike-grey tunic, knee breeches, woollen stockings, and climbing boots of the mountain troops. All Tiroleans were automatically enrolled in mountain units, and because of this many of the young men of St Anton were also assigned to the Fifth Regiment, but as private soldiers. Within the regimental organization, six of them had the questionable luck to be posted to Otto's battery: Peter Ickle, Eugen Schwimmer, Cowboy Karl Lang, Dolf Mathies, Willi Gebaur, and Gunther Rapp. They were all close friends of Anton Prinz's, and all were members of the Lili Wangenmann social circle.

In the week that followed the mobilization order the Fifth Mountain depot was a model of confusion as the regiment struggled to transform itself from a peacetime fraternity of chocolate soldiers into a wartime fighting unit. Men who had been civilians only days before struggled with unfamiliar equipment, ordnance officers with worried faces checked and rechecked ammunition supplies, and the three battalion kitchens improvised the feeding of a full-strength regiment using equipment designed for the bare bones of the peacetime cadre.

The confusion was compounded by a political situation that changed daily as the nations of Europe flung about declarations of war as freely as drunken hussars challenging each other under the code duello. First Austria slapped the Serbian face, then their German partners flung the gauntlet at the Russians and the French. The British came in on the Allied side, the Austrians declared against the Tsar, while Italy, in violation of the Triple Alliance, abandoned both Austria and Germany by declaring its neutrality.

The Austro-Hungarian general staff had two strategic plans,

one based on a war with Serbia alone, and the other on a war with both Serbia and Russia. As the crisis of confusion mounted the general staff, pressed to make a decision, came up with a truly Viennese solution to the situation by putting both plans into operation at once. Thus regiments on the Russian front were transported halfway across the empire to Serbia while units in the south were entrained for the east. Orders were followed by counter-orders, and by the end of the first week of war the depot of the Fifth Regiment of Mountain Artillery was a boiling pot of rumours and confusion.

Through all the chaos strode the reassuring figure of Kranski, the Feuerwerker, as the sergeant-major of an artillery regiment was called. Kranski was not a Tirolean but a veteran of an old-line *Kaiserjäger* outfit seconded to the Fifth Mountain on mobilization day, and he knew that his most pressing job was to get to know his officers. The men he could leave to the junior NCOs for the moment, and the problems of food and ordnance could be handled by the specialists, but he had to know which of his officers could be counted on. Some of them he knew from previous service, some by reputation only, and some not at all. One of those latter was the new commander of the Eighth Battery, Oberleutnant Prinz, and the Feuerwerker did what any other senior NCO would have done in his place: He checked out the new officer with the lads from his hometown.

'He's a shit, *Mensch,* that's what he is,' Karl Lang told him. 'An absolute disaster.'

'Don't call me that again,' the sergeant-major said mildly. It was, after all, the first day. 'You call me Herr Feuerwerker.'

'*Jawohl,* Herr Feuerwerker, but with respect, he's still a shit.'

'That doesn't tell me anything. Most officers are shits, but some are decent shits. What's wrong with this one?'

'Wrong? He's going to get us all killed, that's what's wrong.'

'That's part of his job, getting you killed, and it still doesn't tell me what's wrong with the man.'

The Feuerwerker waited for an explanation. The men were gathered in a corner of the depot next to the rows of 100mm mountain howitzers lined up spade to muzzle. The bronze Skodas gleamed in peacetime perfection, and the air was heavy with the acrid odours of polish and oil. The corner was an island of calm in the chaotic yard as mules brayed, hoof-beats thundered, sergeants swore, and messengers dashed about blindly.

The echoing screech of unoiled iron wheels provided a crazy obbligato to the racket.

Under the barrage of all this noise the six St Anton boys looked around at each other, waiting for someone to speak. None of them wanted to voice what was on all of their minds: that for a year they had all been enjoying the woman who, by a trick of fate, was now their officer's wife. And that somehow he might find out about it. Karl Lang shook his head imperceptibly, a warning to keep such thoughts silent.

Finally the Feuerwerker said, 'This is strictly between us, you have my word on it.'

Karl said slowly, 'The problem is, we're all from peasant families in the Arlberg . . .'

'So what? Do I look like a city boy to you?'

'With respect, Herr Feuerwerker, you don't understand. When I say that we're all peasants I mean that Otto is, too. Oberleutnant Prinz, that is.'

Kranski let his surprise show with a long whistle. 'A peasant and an officer. I never heard of such a thing. How the devil did he get a commission?'

'He was at Märisch-Weisskirchen. He's an ambitious man, and he doesn't want to tend cattle for the rest of his life. This war is a blessing for Otto – it's his ticket off the farm.'

Dolf Mathies, the quiet one, nodded his agreement. 'Otto is a peasant like us, but he wants to get ahead. Herr Feuerwerker, you are a soldier, so you know what that means. He is going to get ahead over our dead bodies if he has to.'

'Artillerymen die in bed,' quoted Kranski. 'Even in the mountain artillery. You boys are worrying about nothing.'

'Herr Feuerwerker,' said Karl, 'I have known Otto Prinz all my life, and he scares me. He never scared me at home, but here in the army he scares me out of my mind.'

'I see. What is your name . . . Lang? Let me tell you something, Lang. First of all, you scare too easily. Second of all, you're letting the wrong man scare you. Let me show you who you should worry about. Do you know what second call sounds like on the bugle?'

'Yes, sir. Like a bullfrog belching.'

'Quite so. Now, this afternoon when you hear the bullfrog belch, I want you to come looking for me, you hear? And when you find me, you and I are going to see how long it takes for one man to load and unload the caisson of one of these bronze Skodas. Ten times running, blindfolded. Who knows, Lang, you may set a new regimental record. Understood?'

'*Jawohl,*' barked Karl, but his eyes were filled with dismay.

Kranski turned and strode across the hard-packed floor of the depot. His twisted lips suppressed a grin, but what he had heard about Prinz bothered him. A peasant officer, by God. The situation would have made a merry plot for an operetta, but if those lads were right it could be serious. He had seen what messy affairs could result from officers merely raised out of the petty bourgeoisie, but for a farm boy to be commissioned into the aristocratic officer corps of the Austro-Hungarian army was unheard of. He thought of having a word with the battery NCOs, the Zugsführer and the Korporal, but he decided against it. He wanted them loyal to their officer, not confused by gossip.

I'll have to keep an eye on him myself, he thought as he hurried on to the next battery.

Within a week the Feuerwerker's worst fears about the Eighth Battery were confirmed. A careful reading of the regimental daily reports showed the problem clearly. *Eighth Battery, Special Duty Assignment. Latrine digging: Lang, Schwimmer, Ickle, Mathies, Gebaur, Rapp. Detail for mule shoeing: Schwimmer, Mathies, Ickle, Lang, Rapp, Gebaur. Extra sentry duty: Lang, Mathies, Rapp. Extra stable duty: Schwimmer, Ickle, Gebaur.* It went on that way daily. There were eighteen men in the battery, but whenever there was a dirty detail to be done the six men from St Anton were assigned to it by the chum of their childhood, Oberleutnant Prinz. Not one to jump to conclusions, the Feuerwerker had a quiet chat with the battery Zugsführer and the Korporal. Were these six acting up? Were they drawing these details as punishment? The Zug was an old-timer, too old in fact for field duty, and the Korporal was a time-server concerned only with protecting his stripe, but they answered honestly. No, nothing like that, they assured Kranski. The six were no better, or worse, than any of the other recruits in the battery. They just seemed to draw the dirty end of the stick every time the Oberleutnant issued orders.

The Feuerwerker was debating in his mind what to do about the situation when he was saved the trouble by the regimental commander, Colonel Max von Moltitz. The colonel also read the daily reports carefully, and he was soldier enough to know who really ran the regiment on a day-to-day basis. After the first week at Landeck he called his trusted Feuerwerker into his office and asked him pointedly what the hell was going on in the Eighth Battery.

'Six men drawing all the nasty details,' he said. 'Something like that can ruin a battery. Is it a disciplinary problem?'

'Do I have the colonel's permission to speak freely?'

'Of course. Sit down, Kranski. Have a schnapps.'

The colonel's idea of a schnapps was a pony of cognac. Kranski took one careful sip and set it aside, at the same time setting aside the formality of the third-person address due to an officer. 'There's nothing wrong with those men, colonel, it's the Oberleutnant.'

The colonel's muttonchop whiskers waggled sadly. 'I know, the man should never have been commissioned. It's a strange army these days. A peasant for an officer, by God. Are you saying that he doesn't know how to run his battery?'

'I wouldn't say that,' was Kranski's cautious reply. 'From what I hear he's a number-one mountain man and he'll make a good officer someday.'

'A good officer doesn't ride six of his men into the ground.'

'Those six are from his own hometown, sir. They all were children together, playmates, and now he's their officer.'

'Mother of God.' Von Moltitz downed his cognac in one swig, something the Feuerwerker had not dared to do, and now regretted. 'So this Prinz is showing his old chums who the boss is.'

'Yes, sir.'

'Nothing more complicated? Some sort of feud? Those mountain people can keep a good hate going for generations over a stolen cow.'

'I think not, sir. It's just a difficult situation for both the Oberleutnant and the men. I was hoping that you would have a word with him, man to man.'

'Man to man? And what language do I speak to him?'

The Feuerwerker stared uncomprehendingly.

'What do I have in common with the man? Can I appeal to his sense of duty? Loyalty to his class? He wouldn't know what I was talking about.'

'Yes, sir.'

'No, Kranski, he's one of yours, not mine.' He looked at the

Feuerwerker keenly. 'No offence, you understand. You're the man to keep a close eye on him, and on the battery as well. I want that battery cleaned up, and I'm making it your personal responsibility.'

The colonel sat back with the air of a man who has put his brain to work and solved a difficult problem. Kranski, who knew that nothing at all had been solved, sprang to his feet.

'It will be as the colonel orders,' he said crisply. He cast a regretful glance at the pony of cognac, still almost full, before he saluted and left the room.

Although Italy had declared her neutrality, a neutral Italy was a potential enemy to Austria, and so on the seventh of August the Fifth Mountain Regiment entrained in fifty-four boxcars filled with howitzers and mortars, horses, mules, and men, heading into the south Tirol to augment the forces guarding the Italian frontier. The trip took three days, during which time the regiment, and its livestock, lived, ate, and slept in the unventilated boxcars that rolled slowly over the Tirolean countryside, jerking to a stop every few minutes and then inching on again. The heat in the cars was oppressive, the stench unbearable even to farm boys, and the only break in the hellish days came when the train was halted to water the animals and exchange the foul straw for fresh. The food was terrible, as well, but no one had an appetite anyway.

Cowboy Karl Lang, always on the lookout for an edge, found himself a niche in the corner of his car where two broken wooden slats provided enough of an airhole to project a warm breeze onto his sweating face and neck. During the first day of the journey he never moved from his corner, disembarking only at the watering hour to stride up and down beside the silent train, smoking cigarettes in furious succession, until it was time to board again. For the rest of that day he sat quietly by his airhole, sipped water from his canteen, and read and reread a letter received from Anton Prinz.

Hey Cowboy:

I'm in a town called Sedgewick Falls, in the province of Vermont, in the United States of America. Keep that to yourself.

Here in the envelope is a postal order for one hundred American dollars, all I can spare right now. Use it to get your fat ass up to Hamburg and by that time I should have another hundred dollars waiting for you at the *poste restante* there. That will not be enough for the passage to Boston, so you'll have to beg, borrow, or steal the rest, but do it. Get over here as quick as you can. This place is God's country, Karl. Maybe not so pretty as the Tirol, but fine country, good mountains, and a man can make something out of himself here, not like the old country.

I'm telling you, Karl, getting kicked out of St Anton was the best thing that ever happened to me. Already I am learning to speak English, I'm living in a big house with two servants, I have started in the timber business, and I have a wonderful woman who is going to be my wife. This is no load of cowshit, I mean it. I don't care how you do it, just get here. I'll have a job waiting for you in my new sawmill, so don't worry about making a living here. No excuses, Karl, just do it. You'll never regret it, unless you want to spend the rest of your life sawing bones and hacking meat for old Lobermacher.

Your friend,
Anton

P.S.   Remember when we were kids and I always said I could lick you with one hand tied behind my back? Well, when you get here I'll prove it to you.

Karl shook his head sadly, folded the letter, and put it back in the envelope. Also in the envelope was the American postal order, uncashed. The letter had arrived on the twenty-fourth of July, the day before the general mobilization that had swept him into the army. For perhaps the hundredth time he told himself that the letter was a joke, a silly piece of bragging, and for the hundred-and-first time he felt the quiver in his gut that told him it was no joke at all. The money order proved that. He didn't know how much one hundred American dollars were worth but it had to be a lot of money. Too much for a joke. He swore softly and slammed his fist against the boxcar wall. Then he reached into his pocket for a square of paper and the nub of a pencil, and began to write with the paper on his knee and his head bent to the light.

Anton, you always were a lucky son of a bitch, and I guess I'm still dipped in shit. I got your letter and the money one day, one stinking day, before the army grabbed me, and now I'm in it up to my neck. So thanks for the money (I haven't cashed the postal) and thanks for thinking of me over there in God's country, but it looks like I'm stuck here until the fucking war is finished. Everybody says that it can't go on past Christmas, and then the Cowboy will make his move, so be on the lookout for me, pardner. Just find me the same kind of soft berth that you found for yourself and you won't hear me complaining.

Some of the boys from home – Eugen, Peter, Dolf, Willi, and Gunther – are here with me in the same regiment, same battery, but I haven't told them anything about your letter. You said to keep it quiet, and you know me, chum. Never a word. But I'm glad the boys are here. It's good to have some friends in this pisspot of an army. It's bad enough just being here, but as a punishment for our sins we've got your brother Otto for our officer, and knowing how you feel about him I know you won't mind it if I say that he's turning out to be a perfect prick. To make it short and sweet, he's got it in for the six of us from home and he's doing his best to make our lives miserable. We get every dirty job in the battery. This isn't just soldier talk, complaining, you know? It's almost as if he gets offended by the sight of us, like we remind him that he may be an officer but he'll never be a gentleman. Whenever that happens it's off to dig ditches for us all, or something else charming like that. You know how I am, Anton, I try to take things pretty much the way they come, but if things keep up this way your brother and I are going to have some accounts to settle once the uniforms come off.

Like I said, I try to take things easy, but some of the other boys are getting edgy about it. Willi and Eugen, you know how they can get, and they started it. Jesus, it scares me silly just to think about it, but they figure that Otto knows about us and Lili. About *all* of us and Lili. They figure he *has* to know, because why else would we be getting this special treatment? First it was just Willi and Eugen, but now they've got the others worried, too. I'm the only one who doesn't see it that way. Your brother was always a bastard and he hasn't changed, that's all. That's what I told the lads, and besides, how could he know? Gebaur says that I'm full of shit, that a lot of people in town had a good idea what was going on, and that somebody must have told him, but I don't believe it. That isn't Otto's way. You know how he is. If he really knew he would have come after us with a pistol, or something like that, but not what he's doing now. Not this silly army shit.

That's what I tell the boys, but I tell you this, Anton, there are times when I think, what if he really does know? Those are the times when I can't sleep at night.

So that's what I've got on my plate right now, not very much like Mama's home cooking, and you're on the other side of the world sucking the rich tit. That's all right with me. You know how I am, chum, I don't get jealous. I just want a bit of the same, and one of these days I'll get it. You can count on that. So keep my job open at the sawmill and I'll be coming down the road as soon as I can.

I don't know how I'm going to get this letter to you, but there has to be a way and I'll find it. You know the way I am, chum. The Cowboy always finds a way.

> **Good luck until I see you,**
> **Karl**

After three days in transit the regiment gratefully disembarked at the town of Villach and began the march south through Slovenia, crossing over the pass at Wurzen and into the compact and densely forested terrain of the Julian Alps. The long regimental column of marching men, wagon trains, limbered guns, and caissons snaked through the Alpine valleys following the contours of the Italian border until it reached the foothills surrounding Mount Krn, where it came under the command of General Oskar Potiorek's Fifth Army. There the troops took up positions on the western face of the mountain overlooking the border, and with the regiment in place the men settled in for what was actually little more than a spell of peacetime soldiering. Far away in France the first great battles of the war were being fought; to the north in East Prussia the armies of von Prittwitz were engaged with the Russians under Samsonov; and closer by on the Serbian border Potiorek had launched an invasion over the Jadar River. But Italy still remained neutral, and for the men of the Fifth the war was a safe, if wearying, round of training formations, inspections, and patrols. To most of the officers and men this assignment away from the actual fighting seemed like a delightful gift, but as soon as the regiment was settled in, Otto Prinz applied to his colonel for an immediate transfer to a fighting front. The request was denied, and a disgruntled Otto Prinz went back to his troops to resume the facsimile that passed for war on the Italian front, convinced that once again he had been cheated out of a chance for glory. The next morning, as the mists lifted, he stood gloomily beside his guns and exercised the crews by sighting in on the Isonzo River below, and beyond the river on the roads and fortifications that ringed the sleepy little Italian town of Caporetto.

Chapter Six

From the Journals of Elizabeth Chandler

Monday, 6 April 1914
I wonder at the origin of the phrase 'one-horse town'. Is it meant to signify a place so small that it can support only one horse? Or is the meaning metaphysical, denoting a part of the world so limited in scope that only one of anything can exist there: one set of ideas, one way of doing things, one standard of morality . . . and one horse? Probably the former, although I should prefer to think the latter. I have lived in Sedgewick Falls all of my life and I intend to die here. Big cities repel me, I shun the mass, and I have done very nicely so far without the so-called intellectual stimulation that is said to be provided in places such as Boston and New York. But for narrow-minded, bigoted, vicious, gossipy, sheer social cussedness you purely cannot beat a one-horse town in Vermont. It is two weeks now since the day of the accident, and in all that time the only caller at this house has been Dr Cornelius, and he in a professional capacity only. Where are the friends of my girlhood, the confidantes and intimates? Where are the men who once claimed they adored me? Where are the older, sober counsellors of my youth? The snows of yesteryear, indeed. It seems I am being ostracized for having a man under my roof. The fools.

On a more encouraging note, Mr Prinz continues to improve, although the pain is still with him. Dr Cornelius says that we must expect that for some time to come, and that an occasional fever should not surprise me. Nothing would surprise me; I have no time for being surprised. Nursing a man back to health is a full day's work, and I fall into bed each night exhausted.

Wednesday, 8 April 1914
I have condemned my fellows too quickly. If the Lord would have spared Sodom for the sake of ten righteous men will not one man and one woman suffice for Sedgewick Falls?

Which is to say that Jack and Portia McClure came calling this afternoon, explaining that they had heard of the accident and had waited this long only to allow my household time to resume its normal aspect. (As if it will ever be normal again.) They asked after the progress of 'your young friend,' commiserated with me over his circumstances, and agreed that keeping him here to recover in my home was the only sensible and Christian course of action to take. They also asked to meet Mr Prinz, but when I explained the gravity of his condition they agreed to a postponement of that pleasure. They stayed for an hour, took tea, and left, leaving behind them a sense of goodwill and encouragement. What fine friends they are. Jack McClure may be a cynic, a pseudosophisticate, and a bit of a tippler, but he is made of solid stuff. Besides, such vices suit well to a journalist.

Wednesday, 22 April 1914
One month today since the accident, and Dr Cornelius is pleased with the progress made. The stump is healing nicely, there are no more fevers, and the pain is only occasional. The patient, however, continues in a despondent frame of mind, which is only to be expected. He is, however, anxious to be up and about – a promising sign. I must think of things to kindle his interest.

There is also the question of Jean-Pierre, who has virtually made his home in the carriage house. I have no objections to this since his visits to the upstairs bedroom clearly have a salubrious effect on Mr Prinz. I leave them alone and they get on like a house afire, chattering away in a jumble of German, French, vulgar English, and sign language. Mr Prinz is always more relaxed afterwards, and so I am grateful for the Frenchman's presence, but I must think of something for him to do. I have no room for idle hands here.

There is also Mr Prinz's future to consider, and now is the time for the spadework to be done. 'Waste not an hour,' said

Nelson. Waste not a minute, say I. In my heart of hearts I am confident that my patient will make a full and effective recovery, but he still will be a one-handed man in search of a vocation. It was he who first mentioned the timber business to me, and that might be an answer. Perhaps it is time for those trees of mine to turn a profit for me . . . for us. I have it in mind to consult with Mr Oates at the bank today and make the first inquiries.

Later:

Clarence Oates comes close to being the most exasperating man I have ever known. Ever since the death of my beloved parents he has been urging me to put my timberland to work, offering the services of the bank to underwrite the scheme and manage it. Today when I proposed doing something quite similar and asked him for an estimate of the costs, he hemmed and hawed and but-but-butted. Apparently it was a good idea when the bank stood to make a share of the profits, but not nearly so good if I were to run it myself. He finally put it into words.

'Seems sort of risky to me, Lizzy.' (He knows that I loathe that name.) 'What do you know about the timber business?'

'Enough to know that I don't know enough,' I told him tartly. 'I have it in mind to take in a partner.'

'Partner, is it? And who might that be?'

'That's my business for the minute.'

'Eh-yup, so it is. And telling me that is as good as telling me his name.'

'You don't know his name.'

'No, I don't, and neither does anybody else in town. Leastwise his second name. Now you listen to me, missy – '

'I did not come here for a lecture, Mr Oates.'

'Well, you're going to get one anyways. Your daddy and I did business together for thirty-some years, and that gives me some rights. I'm not going to stand by and watch Sam Chandler's daughter make a fool out of herself going into business with some foreigner who nobody knows from Adam's off ox. Your private life is your own affair, although I must say that I don't hold with the way you're conducting yourself these days. But now you're talking business . . . finance . . . and I'd be lacking in my duty to your father's memory if I let you go through with something like this.'

79

'I don't see that there's anything you can do to stop me,' I said coolly.

He thought about that for a moment. 'Don't suppose I can, at that. Nobody can when a woman's got the bit in her teeth. But I don't have to be a part of it. You can go to Hades in a handbasket if it suits you, Lizzy, but you'll get no help from me in this venture.'

I stood up, preparing for a sweep from the room. 'That's as may be, Clarence Oates, but bear this in mind. I expect to have an estimate of cost on this venture from you within the next three weeks. If I do not have it I will not find it inconvenient to transfer my custom to the Boston Trust over in Gainesville. All of my custom, mind you. Shares, bonds, and savings, and all the accounts of Chandler's Feed and Grain.'

The man's face went pasty. 'The devil you will.'

'Invoke whom you wish. I am of age and the money is mine to do with as I see fit. Now put that in your Yankee pipe and smoke it.'

I swept.

Friday, 24 April 1914

The McClures continue to be the only ones in town to recognize my existence. They make a point of stopping by every few days to demonstrate their loyalty, but they stand alone, poor dears.

Life continues on, of course. I am treated civilly enough in the shops, milk and bread and eggs are delivered to my door, and the daily commerce of life goes uninterrupted. But socially I am the outcast. It is a truly deplorable situation, and only Jack McClure, with his dubious sense of humour, seems to find it amusing.

'You're going to have to marry him, Liz' is the refrain he sings. 'Marry your little German boy and make an honest man out of him.'

My reply is a sniff of disdain. (It isn't, really, but I wish that it were. I have seen the phrase used in books but have never understood how it is done.)

Sunday, 26 April 1914

So much for the First Congregational Church of Sedgewick Falls. Today was the first Sunday since the accident when I felt that I could gather the strength to attend, and I was looking forward to the spiritual solace which our simple service has always provided for me. More fool, I.

Our revered pastor, Dr James O. Walmsley, took his text from First Corinthians, 15:33: 'Be not deceived: evil communications corrupt good manners.' This he interpreted to mean that communion with the bad corrupts the character of the good, which he further extrapolated into a rousing appeal to the godly to cut themselves off from the evil which flourishes within the community. This 'evil,' the old windbag made clear, was none other than that scarlet-lettered hussy Elizabeth Chandler, although he did not mention me by name. Didn't dare to, the ninny, knew I'd sue the pants off him if he did. But he made it clear enough, all right, and after the service there wasn't a single soul who came up to greet me, wish on me the blessings of the Sabbath, or simply smile in passing. People I have known all my life. People I have called friend, and comrade.

George and Amanda Wheelwright
Harrison Cobb
Lucy Powdermaker
Sarah Dalton, and others
Just like Koko, I've got a little list.

Monday, 27 April 1914
What bothers me most is what all these tarnation fools think must be going on in this house. If they had half the brains they were born with they would realize that I am nursing an injured man back to health, a man who has barely the strength to stretch his legs, much less . . .

I say nothing of this to Mr Prinz, of course. I have started him on his English lessons, and he seems a willing student. There is, however, most definitely going to be a problem of accent.

Tuesday, 5 May 1914
A banner day, for today Mr Prinz went out of doors for the first time, if only to sit in front of the carriage house with Jean-Pierre and chat, smoke a pipe, and enjoy the sun. I watched them from the window, being reluctant to intrude on their male companionship, but later I asked what they had talked about. The answer came first in German, but our rule now is 'English only,' and he said, 'Der hand. He iss machen der hand.'

So Jean-Pierre is true to his promise. He is actually carving a wooden hand which eventually will fit by an arrangement of straps to the lower left arm. Mr Prinz does not think much of the project, saying, 'I got only vun hand now. Vot's der sense I make it look like two?' He is, however, intrigued by another idea of Jean-Pierre's, a second hand, but this one in the form of a fist with a hole bored through to aid in the holding of tools. Or a ski pole. 'Dot makes sense,' he says.

Monday, 11 May 1914
I heard today from Mr Oates at the bank. Apparently his sense of business acumen is sharper than his nose for scandal. As my papa used to say, there are nine ways to skin a cat, but the easiest way to skin a banker is to squeeze his pocket.

I must admit that the man can do good work when he is forced to it. He presented me with a carefully prepared analysis of the Brush Hollow Road property showing the amount of timber (in board feet) that could be cut economically each year, the anticipated net return on the sale of such timber if hauled to Burlington for milling, and the cost of refurbishing the old mill on Long Brook Pond should I decide to do the milling here. The cost of entering into the venture, even should I fix up the mill, is surprisingly small. Five thousand dollars will do for initial expenses, and the investment should be returned threefold within two years. I ought to have done this ages ago, and to think that I never would have done it at all had it not been for Mr Prinz's circumstances. How mysterious are the ways of the Lord! Out of suffering comes profit.

Thursday, 14 May 1914
Mr Prinz gains strength daily in every way. He is a truly amazing man with a resiliency of body and spirit that can only be admired. He now is able to do almost everything for himself, including the lacing of his boots and the cutting of his meat, through the use of Jean-Pierre's ingenious substitute. He cannot as yet shave himself, but the Frenchman has taken over the function of barber as well as factotum, performing this service daily. He has left Mr Prinz with a brave moustache that flatters him greatly.

My own nursing skills have gone into desuetude now that there is no longer a dressing to be changed, and my only service is to help him in his bathing. He has recently objected to this on the grounds of modesty, but I quickly pointed out that

(1) During the early days of his convalescence I bathed him in a fashion as intimately as that of a mother bathing her child, and

(2) Whether or not he chooses to remember it, we were lovers once for a moment, and I, for one, intend that we be so again.

I am afraid that I embarrassed the dear man.

Sunday, 16 May 1914

. . . Mr Prinz gains strength daily. . . .

Friday, 22 May 1914

Mr Prinz has an astonishing appetite. He will, in truth, eat anything and lots of it, but it occurred to me that he might be homesick for some of the dishes of his native land. This has led to a suspension of the 'English-only' rule in the area of the kitchen as he attempts to instruct me in the art of creating dishes such as *Wiener Schnitzel, Gröstl,* and *Apfelstrudel.* It has also led to a certain amount of discontent for Hetty, who tends to think of the kitchen as her personal domain, and who has had to be reminded of the basic facts of employment.

The *Schnitzel,* of course, is just a scallop of veal, and the *Gröstl* nothing more than a 'fry-up' of cooked beef, potatoes, and onions, but the *Strudel* calls for a delicate touch in the rolling out of the dough. Mr Prinz tells me that in the Tirol the dough is considered to be thin enough only when a newspaper can be read through it. I have not yet attained this state of perfection, but I am aiming for it and I generally get what I aim for.

In every way, Mr Prinz continues to gain strength.

Monday, 1 June 1914

For some time now I have referred to the fact that Mr Prinz has been slowly, but steadily, regaining his health and strength. I shall now confide, to these pages only, that in a certain sense his recovery is complete, for I no longer can rail in my mind at the fools in this town who think that illicit love is flourishing under my roof. It flourishes, indeed, and merrily. Enough said on that subject.

83

Thursday, 4 June 1914

. . . I call him Anton now. The names by which he calls me I
will not confide even to these pages. . . .

Friday, 5 June 1914

I suppose I have known the way it would have to be for some
time now, but have refused to allow myself to think about it.
For almost three months it has been enough to nurse him back
to health, to restore the strength of both body and soul, and to
love him mightily without a thought for the future. But the
future is now, and I know what I must do. Or rather, what I
must not do.

This because clear to me this evening when the McClures
called and met Anton for the first time. He was nervous, of
course, but he handled himself beautifully. As usual we took
tea together, with Anton manoeuvring his cup smoothly, and I
could see that both Jack and Portia were taken with him. How
could they not be? There is something endearing about him that
is almost childlike, but just as you are about to settle for that
definition of the man you glimpse the rock of strength inside
him.

The conversation was difficult for him; his English still has a
long way to go. Jack did his best to put him at his ease by asking
about the state of affairs in the Austro-Hungarian Empire. (Jack
is convinced that a war is coming to Europe.) My poor darling,
what does he know about the affairs of empire? He knows his
mountains and his valleys, and that is all he knows, but he
managed to speak quite to the point about the various national
groups that are pulling the empire apart, and about the great
respect still held for the Old Gentleman in Vienna. Jack, God
bless him, listened as he would to the imperial ambassador.

While this was going on, Portia and I escaped to the kitchen
to refresh the teapot, and once we were alone she gave me a
knowing look, and said, 'I'm so happy for you, Elizabeth. He's
a fine young man.'

Her emphasis on the word 'young' got her a prompt reply.
'He is two years younger than I am, if that's what you are fishing
for.'

My tartness drew only a smile from her; she knows my manner
too well. 'I was curious,' she admitted, 'but two years is nothing

84

at all between a man and a woman. I have known happy marriages, where the woman is five years older, and more.'

'Do tell. And who was speaking of marriage?'

'Why, we were . . . weren't we?'

'I don't recall using the word.'

Her smile faded and her lips grew thin. 'What's all this, then?'

I shrugged. Prettily, I hope.

She put her hands on my shoulders and shook me lightly. 'What's going on inside of that topsy-turvy head of yours?'

I smiled. Enigmatically, I hope.

She leaned close, our faces almost touching. Her voice was low and hard. 'You're planning some mischief, aren't you?'

I did not answer.

'Elizabeth Chandler, I love you dearly, but there are times when you are a perverse and wilful woman. Now you tell me this minute, and in plain English: Do you and Anton plan to marry?'

I temporized by saying lightly, 'Actually, he hasn't asked me yet.'

'Stuff, plain stuff.' She shook her head impatiently. 'If he hasn't it's only because he assumes that you will. Just the way he looks at you . . . almost indecent, I'd call it. I'm not talking about his plans, I'm talking about yours. Are you going to marry him?'

I stared at her silently, but it was answer enough.

'You fool,' she said slowly, and drew back. 'It's the town, isn't it?'

I nodded.

'You won't give them the satisfaction.'

I nodded again. 'I will not do it, Portia.'

'You have to do it. Either that, or give him up.'

'I will do neither.' I realized that all this time I had been holding the empty kettle in my hand, and I set it on the stove. 'Don't you see? I was made an outcast because I committed an act of Christian charity.'

'Asses abound in this world.'

'And does that mean that I must live by the rules of the asses? Portia, to marry now would be to admit that I had done something wrong, and now wish to do right . . . but I have done no wrong. To marry now would be to conform myself to the standards of an ignorant and narrow-minded society . . . but I conform to no standards but my own. To marry would be to go down on my knees before Sedgewick Falls and beg for forgiveness . . . but I go on my knees before the Lord God and Anton Prinz, no one else. Therefore, my decision.'

'The decision of your stiff-necked pride,' she said in disgust.

'My pride, indeed,' I agreed. 'I don't contest that. If Pope was right and pride is the vice of fools, then I am the most foolish woman who ever walked this earth. But Pope was wrong. His vice is my virtue, the only one, perhaps, which still is left to me. I have my pride, and I know what I must do. What I must *not* do. I will not marry him. We shall go on as we are, together but unwed.'

Her face was a mask of sorrow. 'And does he know that yet?'

I shook my head and turned to fill the kettle.

I reproduce this here the way it happened, the words the way they were said. So stilted. I do not reproduce my own sadness, or the tortuous process that led to my decision.

Saturday, 6 June 1914

For better or for worse we are now in the timber business. This morning Anton and I drove out to the woodlot with Jean-Pierre handling the reins as we drove through town looking straight ahead to avoid giving gawkers on the sidewalks the satisfaction of a stare. Then we were out of town and bowling along Brush Hollow Road with Blazer stepping out smartly under the lash. And well she might, for this was her first true outing in weeks. It was a fair day today, and fine with a butter-coloured sun, the fields green around us, and in the ditches alongside the road a flourish of wildflowers: laurel, and burdock, and Queen Anne's lace. The air was filled with summer scents, and I clung to Anton's arm as we jolted over a stone. When he felt my hand he looked down at me and smiled. He is smiling more often now, and when he does it is a glory.

We stopped first at the Morris farm, paid perfunctory respects to Ethan and Martha, and set out over the fields. As we approached the sugarhouse I glanced at Anton to see if he would turn his head when we passed the spot. He did not, and so I too marched straight ahead, ignoring the place. Only Jean-Pierre scowled at the sight of it.

We spent the better part of two hours tramping through the

stands of birch and pine, maple and elm, while the two men marked in their minds the first sections to be cleared, second growth cut away, and avenues formed down which to haul the logs. Their voices rang loudly in the woods, the happy voices of men at work again. Clearly they will do well together with Anton in general charge and Jean-Pierre the boss in the field. I, of course, will control the purse.

It was down to the pond then to inspect the ruins of the mill. While the men clambered over the crumbled walls and poked around inside. I spread a cloth on the bank above where the water runs dark and fast near the shore, and laid out the picnic lunch. A roast chicken, the butt of a ham, bread, cheese, pickles, and a crock of buttermilk. A quick check for ants, and I called the men to their food.

The conversation while we ate was 'shop talk' filled with words and phrases strange to me: gang saw, and flume, and pressure head. The language they used was the usual jumble of French, German, and a variety of English which, while picturesque, was vulgar enough to call for a muttered ''scuse me' tossed in my direction after almost every sentence. I am not one of those women who thinks, affectionately, of men as being nothing more than grown-up boys. Men are men, and boys are boys. But there is something boyish about a man who enjoys his work, and so it was with these two. As for the coarseness of language, I shall have to lead my Anton away from that, but for the moment it is a means of communication which he needs. It is surely only a matter of convenience, for his German shows no sign of vulgarity.

The subject under discussion was the mill and whether or not it could be put back into working order – a question of rebuilding the flume to provide sufficient water pressure to run the saws. Anton was sure that it could be done, while Jean-Pierre had his doubts. As they argued, however, it became clear that they had adopted roles to suit the needs of their relationship: Anton as the enthusiastic optimist, and Jean-Pierre the somewhat older and conservative 'devil's advocate.' In the end it was agreed to try to rebuild the flume, the decision coming as the last of the chicken disappeared and the buttermilk crock was emptied. Jean-Pierre insisted on helping me to rinse off the dishes in the stream and repack the basket, and then announced that he was off for a walk in the aid of digestion. He made the statement in that serious voice which the French reserve for anything to do with the production, preparation, or consumption of food, but he obviously wanted to leave us alone for a while in that pastoral setting.

Then it was time for me to curl myself up within the curve of Anton's arm and lie with my eyes closed and my cheek against his chest. (The curve of his left arm. He seems to prefer it that way, to hold me with his injured arm, reserving the one with the hand for caresses.) The sun was hot and insects buzzed, but the breeze from off the pond was a balm to the brow. A peaceful time, a contented time, the contentment of a well-fed child with nothing to fear, about to slip into a languorous doze when his voice, half-choked, spoke my name.

'Lizbet, I got something to say.'

'Say on,' I murmured.

'I can't, not in English.'

'You know the rules.' I was definitely drowsy.

'Ya, sure I know, but this makes too G – d – important, 'scuse me. Please, Liz, this I gotta say in Cherman.'

I moved away from him, sat up and composed myself, and nodded. 'Go ahead.'

'Thank you,' he said, and then in German, 'Lizbet, I want you to know that there are certain things I understand, things that you haven't told me. About the people in this town, the way they've been treating you. Because of me.'

'How do you know?' I asked, and then realized the obvious answer. 'Has Jean-Pierre . . .'

He held up his hand. 'Yes, he's told me a few things, but I had a pretty good idea of what was happening anyway. Nobody comes to the house except the McClures, and you never go out to see people. It was obvious. You should have told me.'

'I didn't want you upset,' I said faintly. 'These people . . .'

'I know all about these people and I know about small towns.' He grinned. 'I come from the smallest town in the world. So I understand, and I also understand why you are doing this business with the timber.'

I felt the need to defend my position. 'This is a business venture, purely business, and I expect to show a profit from it. I did not do it just for you.'

'Not just, but partly.'

'Yes, partly,' I admitted. 'It's exactly the sort of thing you

88

should be doing, but it isn't philanthropy, anything but. These trees are made of gold.'

He nodded his agreement. 'It's going to be a good business, yes. This time next year you'll have an operating mill producing lumber. The year after that you'll be shipping it as far as Burlington, and after that . . . well, I have plans for after that.'

'What sort of plans?'

'Why stop at raw lumber? After all, my father trained me to be a carpenter. After a while I want to see a carpentry shop next to the mill. Cabinets, tables, chairs, shelving . . .'

'Skis?'

'Right, skis. I can build anything like that, I have already. Get me the right kind of workers and we'll have a second business, maybe bigger than the first.'

'You make it sound very grand,' I said, and reached out a hand to hold his. 'You're half a Yankee already.'

He laughed at the way the word 'Yankee' came out of my German-speaking mouth. 'It's more than grand, Lizbet. It lets me say things now that I couldn't say before.' He was suddenly solemn, and the words he spoke next, although they came from the heart, had the texture of words well rehearsed.

'Just a couple of months ago I was a kid from the Tirol in a strange country, without a word of English and without a penny in my pocket. Today I can sit here with you and plan a future without any limit. All this because of you.'

'It certainly is not. You are the one who is going to make our future happen.'

'Please,' he said gently. 'I know what you mean, but please listen. Because of you I am suddenly a man with a future, a man of substance, which means that now I can say things that I couldn't say before.'

He paused, and I waited, dreading what was coming next. A child could see what was coming next.

'A penniless kid with one hand and no job. I couldn't ask you then to be my wife. How could I? But now I can, and I'm asking.'

He stopped and waited. I said nothing.

'It's about time, isn't it, Lizbet? Isn't it time we got married?'

I remained silent, and he was puzzled. 'Am I doing this wrong? Maybe I should have talked about love first, but you

89

know that I love you and I know how you feel about me. Am I right?'

'Yes, of course you are.'

'Then what is it? Did I forget to say something? After all, I don't know the customs here. What does a Yankee say when he asks a woman to be his wife?'

In a small voice, I replied,'He says exactly what you've said.'

'Good, I'm glad I didn't make any mistakes. And I'm still asking. Will you marry me, Lizbet?'

I took a deep breath, and said, 'No, Anton. No, my darling, I will not.' And then I told him exactly why not.

Hans Secker, concierge of the Post Hotel in St Anton, flipped idly through the pages of the reservations ledger on his desk and shook his head sadly. In normal years the months of December through March formed the busy season, with the hotel full to capacity and a waiting list several pages long. Ever since the establishment of the Hannes Schneider Ski School at the hotel several years before the war, the first snows of the season had brought with them flocks of would-be skiers eager to learn the latest turns and try out their skills on the mountains. This new interest in skiing as a sport, rather than a simple means of mountain transportation, had brought a measure of prosperity to the village, and hotels such as the Post and the Schwartzer Adler down the road had come to count on the revenue it brought each year.

But this first winter of the war was part of no normal year. All the young men were gone, even Hannes Schneider was serving with a mountain regiment, and the tourist trade had dwindled to a trickle. No English, of course, and no French; they were the enemy now. The Germans were busy with their own battles, while the wealthy sportsmen from Vienna, those not on active service, preferred to avoid the mountain resorts for fear of being thought frivolous in wartime. As if a Viennese could ever be thought frivolous!

Secker shook his head again and turned to the page for today: 20 January 1915. Three arrivals due on the Vienna Express. The Baron Dieter von Ulm, Herr Franz Harz, and Fräulein Francesca Simonetti who was actually Frau Harz, but who performed at the Vienna Opera under her professional name. Three reservations when there should have been a dozen, but at least they were old customers, people of title and prominence. Even had they not been patrons of long standing they would have been familiar to a concierge such as Secker, who prided himself on keeping current with the world of fashionable Vienna by reading the illustrated papers daily. As his eyes ran over the names he rapidly flipped through his mental file on them.

Baron Dieter von Ulm, a tall, almost reedy gentleman in his mid-thirties, with a beaky Hapsburg nose jutting out over his moustache. A little bit of this, a little bit of that, and nothing much of anything. An amateur painter, dilettante poet, patron of the musical arts . . . hmmm, yes, and according to the less respectable periodicals a patron as well to several of the ballerinas in the *corps de ballet* of the Vienna Opera. From a Silesian family, yes, supposed to be heir to some coal and iron mines there, but now he's a Viennese as a *Sachertorte*. He's the only one of the three who will do any skiing, but half of the time he'll be chasing the chambermaids round the rooms. And catching them, worse luck.

Franz Harz, short and stocky, strong jaw, looks like a lion with that mane of greying hair. Not yet forty, but one of the leading impresarios of musical Vienna, whose productions of Mozart and Wagner have filled both the Burgtheater and the Hofopera. An authentic genius with a flaming temper and an obsession for perfection. At least he won't be chasing chambermaids, no little girls from the *corps de ballet* for this one. The difference between talent and genius. Franz Harz reaches high, plucks stars, and tucks them into his waistcoat pocket. He'll do no skiing. He will sit in front of the fire all day, play skat or whist at night, complain about the food, the wine, the weather, the war, the state of the Viennese theatre, and end up provoking an argument with someone, anyone, that will end with broken glasses on the floor.

La Simonetti, Italian-born and for the past seven years one of the leading sopranos of the Vienna Opera, cast in the traditional mould: tall, deep-bosomed, and blonde. Getting a bit long in the tooth now and, according to the papers, a touch short in the wind. Nonetheless, she is still a beauty, the sort one would expect Herr Harz to choose for a wife, and still an imposing Brünnhilde. But, like her husband, impossible to satisfy, and never truly happy away from Vienna. If we had any guests to speak of here she would irritate them to distraction with her

91

morning vocalizing, dominate the use of the piano in the lounge, and protest twice hourly about the draughts that sneak under the doors. In the old days one could keep her happy with a young and powerful ski instructor, but all those are away in the army now. No, she won't last long this time. After exactly five days of sulking and complaining she will develop an overnight case of laryngitis and leave the next morning to consult with her physician in Vienna, leaving her husband to drink too much cognac and argue into the night, and the baron to chase his chambermaids. *My* chambermaids. With any luck her voice will go on the third day, not the fifth.

Three butterflies from Vienna, thought Secker, but one must not complain. The way things are we could use a few more like them.

He looked up from the register as the sound of a train whistle echoed down the valley. A glance at the clock on the wall showed that the Vienna Express was on time, and a snap of his fingers sent four idling porters scurrying off to the station to help the new arrivals with their luggage.

Some time later the trio from Vienna swept into the hotel on a wave of cold air, chirping as happily as little birds to feel the warmth of the lobby, while behind them came the porters bent double under a load of leather cases, hat boxes, skis, and one small steamer trunk. The impresario Harz led the way, brandishing his cane theatrically, followed by his wife with her head held regally high, her eyes disdainful, with a diffident von Ulm bringing up the rear.

'Secker, old fellow, how very good to see you again,' said Harz. 'What delicious weather you're having. Air with a snap to it, a tang, a brilliance. Not at all like what we get in town.'

Secker made the appropriate bows and murmured the appropriate phrases. 'A pleasure to have you in our house again, *mein Herren*. I trust your trip was comfortable?'

'It was not,' said La Simonetti. 'It was cold and damp, and three times we were switched off the line to let other trains pass. Once we waited over an hour.'

'Troop trains,' explained her husband.

'Ah, the war, madam, the war.' Secker spread his hands expressively. 'Who can control the war?'

'Secker, what goes here?' Von Ulm's eyes swept around the empty lobby. 'Where is everybody?'

'Again, the war, Herr Baron. It has been a very quiet season so far. And how does it go in Vienna?'

Von Ulm laughed shortly. 'Did you hear what Karl Kraus said about that the other day? No, you wouldn't, not out here. He said that in Berlin conditions are serious but not hopeless, while in Vienna conditions are hopeless but not serious.'

Secker laughed dutifully, but Harz twisted his lips into a sour smile. 'Vienna survives. Vienna always survives. They'll be waltzing at Sacher's on Armageddon day.'

'And why not?' asked his wife. 'Some people are born to dance and sing, and others are born to fight. Let the Germans do the fighting. They're good at it.'

'The snow, Secker, more important, how is the snow?' said von Ulm, rubbing his hands together.

'That we have plenty of, Herr Baron. That's one thing even the war cannot change.'

As befitted their station, Secker personally escorted his guests to their suites of rooms on the second floor, gave instructions to the chambermaids, made sure that the tiled stoves were drawing well, and then returned to his desk to stare once again at the empty lobby. He thought of what the woman had said – that some people are born to sing and dance, and others to fight – and he shook his head sadly. The gesture was almost a habit by now. He had a son and two nephews in the army.

Three Vienna butterflies, he thought, but what would we do without them?

As Secker had predicted, von Ulm was the only one of the three to do any skiing. Francesca read the illustrated papers every morning, shopped for antique pots and homemade scarves, vocalized twice daily, and justified Secker's faith in her by complaining about the soup, the meat, *and* the wine on the very first night. Her husband, despite his delight with the tangy mountain air, scared himself up a skat game with two other guests equally bored and rarely left the card table near the fireplace in the lounge. But von Ulm skied. Early the first morning he was out at the ski school behind the hotel, and in the afternoon he climbed with a guide a good third of the way up Gampen before skiing down with more enthusiasm than style. He did the same the second day, and on the third announced that he would like to try another mountain for variety.

93

'You could go up on Rendel,' suggested his guide, who was growing bored with the floundering amateur and who, at any rate, was being paid by the week. 'You won't need me for that one; it's an easy hill. Do you good to get off by yourself, gain some confidence.'

It was snowing lightly the next morning when von Ulm started up on Rendel, his skis over his shoulder and one of his poles acting as an alpenstock. The snowfall increased as he climbed, but he kept his head down and his feet moving. After half an hour he noticed that the snow was drifting up to his knees and that the wind was picking up steadily, but he was not concerned. Looking downhill, he still could see the shapes of the houses and the point of the church spire in the village below. He turned to resume his climb, and as he did the world turned white. The snow, coming down in sheets now, blinded him completely, and he gasped as a fresh gust of wind whipping down the mountainside punched the air from his lungs. He stopped, stood still, and brushed the clumps of wet snow from his eyes as he tried to regain his sense of direction, but it was hopeless. He could tell uphill from downhill, but that was all. He was wrapped in a white cocoon, unable to see as far as his hands and barely able to breathe. In a matter of minutes the snow had changed from a picturesque decoration to a frightening menace.

Von Ulm was soaked through to his skin and his face and hands were blue with cold when he stumbled up to the kitchen door of Sepp and Hanna Prinz. The plump, motherly, fiftyish peasant woman who opened the door to his frantic knocking took one look at him, clucked sympathetically, and swept him inside without a word. She sat him in front of the kitchen fire, called to someone named Marta to bring blankets quickly, called to someone named Lili to bring more wood, and had a bowl of hot soup and a slab of bread in front of him before his frigid mind could register what was happening.

'First you get that soup inside of you,' she said in a friendly, garrulous way, 'and then we get you dried off. You have another pair of pants with you? No, of course not, where would you be hiding them? All right, so you take the clothes off and wrap yourself up in the blankets while they dry. Marta, *Liebchen,* where are those blankets? Lili, the fire, poke it up. My God, man, what were you thinking of, climbing up here in such weather?'

'It came on so swiftly,' he said through chattering teeth. 'Suddenly everything was white.'

'That's the way it happens in these mountains. You were very lucky, Herr . . . ?'

'Von Ulm,' he managed to say.

'Herr von Ulm,' Hanna said respectfully. She had never before met a man with a von in front of his name.

'Baron, actually. I am indebted to you, madam, for taking me in this way.'

'No, no, it is nothing.' A von and a baron as well. Embarrassed at being addressed as madam, she raised her voice sharply to call, 'Marta! Lili! Where are you?'

The daughter of the house, who appeared with a stack of coarse brown blankets, peeked shyly at von Ulm as she set down her burden. Even with frozen fingers and teeth that refused to stay still he could see that she was a young woman of extraordinary loveliness with a heart-shaped face and glossy blonde braids. Another, somewhat older woman came in with an armload of wood to lay on the fire, but she stared at him frankly without the shyness of the younger one. She was taller, with a touch of coarseness to her features, and he noted that she was far gone in pregnancy before his attention was reclaimed by the bowl of soup in front of him.

'If the Herr Baron will take another swallow, and then off with those clothes,' said Hanna. 'Marta and Lili and I will turn our backs while you do it. And remember every stitch off and hung up to dry.'

Von Ulm smiled weakly. He had idolized his own mother during her lifetime, and so it did not seem odd to him to be ordered about by a peasant woman in such a motherly fashion. He stripped down to the skin, hung his clothes neatly on the backs of chairs, and wrapped himself in the blankets, saying, 'I am finished now, thank you.'

Hanna turned and gave a nod of approval. 'Good, now attend to your soup. Marta, give those potatoes a stir. Lili, is the table set? Papa will be in soon.'

Von Ulm obediently spooned up soup, hunching his shoulders under the blanket and shivering in the warmth of the fire. He realized now that the woman of the house had been right. He had been out of his depth in luck to stumble across this house in the storm. The floundering, icy trip up the mountainside had exhausted him, and with the hot soup inside of him and the fire toasting his toes he felt himself slipping off into a languorous doze. It was a delightful feeling, and he did not try to fight it. His chin dropped onto his chest and he was soon asleep.

He was still asleep when Sepp Prinz came in from the carpentry shop for his midday meal. Hanna explained the stranger's presence to her husband while he snorted over the washbasin and scrubbed his fingers.

'The man is a fool,' said Sepp, drying his hands. 'One of those sportsmen from Vienna, is he?'

'His name is von Ulm, a baron,' Hanna said shyly. 'He called me madam.'

'Did he, now?' Sepp tried to keep his voice gruff, but pleasure showed. 'Well, why shouldn't he?'

'His voice is soft,' was Lili's contribution. 'And his hands look soft as well.'

Sepp was unimpressed with these details. 'Soft hands and a soft head, no doubt.'

Marta chirped, 'You should have seen him when he came in, Papa. His moustache was frozen solid.'

'He's lucky it was only his moustache.' Sepp patted his daughter's head absently. 'Well, wake him up and we'll eat.'

Hanna shook her head. 'Better to let him sleep. He had some soup and bread before.'

'Which is more than I've had. I'm starving.' Sepp slipped into his seat at the table and bowed his head. 'God in heaven, we thank You for the food on our table, and we ask Your blessing on this house. Amen.'

His left hand speared a bratwurst from the platter as he pronounced the grace, and without further ceremony he and the three women piled spicy sausages bursting with juice and mounds of fluffy potatoes onto their plates while the stranger slept on. He was still asleep when dinner was finished and the family went back to the routines that filled their winter afternoons: Sepp to the carpentry shop, Hanna to her endless rounds of cleaning, Lili to her sewing basket, and Marta to the dishes followed by her music practice.

It was the middle of the afternoon before the blanketed figure in front of the hearth finally stirred, wakened by the sound somewhere in the house of a piano and a young voice singing. Still half asleep, he listened to the music dreamily, wondering where he was. The Hofopera? Franz's house? A rehearsal? *Non mi toccò la punta delle dita*. The music was Mozart, of course, *Giovanni*, but the voice was unfamiliar. It certainly wasn't Francesca, not the way she was singing these days, not with such dramatic depth and colour in the midrange. Besides, Francesca hadn't sung Zerlina in ages, too thick for it now. Five years ago, perhaps, but not today. Then who could . . . ?

'*Batti, batti, o bel Masetto, la tua povera Zerlina...*'

'Good God,' he muttered, and sat up abruptly, his eyes open now to see that the kitchen was empty and the fire was low.

' . . . *le tue botte ad aspettar...*'

Who the devil was singing? Da Ponte's words, spun into a silvery sweetness, rang through the house. He felt a clutching in his midsection and a shiver round his shoulders, a direct reaction to the sound of that voice. For some people the sound of an extraordinary voice produced goose bumps of the flesh and palpitations of the heart; for Dieter von Ulm it was this fist in his gut and the shivering shoulders. The sensation was not strange to him, he had felt it in opera houses all over Europe, but never on a peasant farm in the Tirol. The voice continued to weave its magic, and the knot in his belly grew tighter.

'One thing,' he said to himself. 'Dear God, just one thing. Let it be the young girl, not the pregnant one.'

He dressed quickly in his dry clothing and followed the sound of the music to the front parlour. He paused in the doorway, unseen, vastly pleased to see that it was Marta who sat at the piano, accompanying herself as she sang. ' . . . *notte e dí vogliam passar.*' At the end of Zerlina's aria she rested for a moment staring pensively at the sheet music on the rack. Then she turned several pages, struck a chord, and sang, '*Voi che sapete – che cos' é amor.*' More Mozart, Figaro this time, and again the same richness of tone that flowed in a pure legato. He shook his head in disbelief. Truly, God gives golden larynxes to stableboys and milkmaids. This voice of remarkable purity and range was as fine as he had ever heard. Untrained, of course, an imperfect conception of tempo, a tendency towards a rubato which could be destructive unless it were corrected. But how could it be any other way? He doubted that she had ever seen the inside of an opera house, much less heard an actual performance. Training would cure such imperfections, but first, always first, there was the voice. That voice had now left Mozart behind, turning to

Brünnhilde's warning to her father, '*Dir rat ich, Vater, rüste dich selbst*,' and he marvelled at the ease with which the transition was made: Mozart to Wagner, silk forged into steel without apparent strain.

She's a natural, he thought. *Sui generis*. I've found myself a natural in the mountains of the Tirol.

The excitement welled up in him, and in that moment he knew that he had found his future. At the age of thirty-three von Ulm had no illusions about himself. He knew that he was a useless member of an equally useless society: a dilettante in the arts, a dabbler in verse, a dauber of paints, and an indifferent performer on the piano. But one thing he knew well, and that was music and musicians. The Vienna Hofopera was his second home, and he was never happier than when he was waiting for the curtain to go up sitting under the frescoed ceiling lit by glowing chandeliers now dimming; among the white-shouldered ladies and uniformed men, the Emperor in his imperial box and the students in the claque at the top of the house. This was his world, the golden world that Mahler had created and peopled with such superlative singers as Slezak, and Demuth, and Weidman; Lucie Weidt, Selma Kurz, Anna von Mildenburg, and Francesca Simonetti. Those were the gods of his golden world, and standing in the doorway of that farmhouse parlour he knew that now his purpose in life was to make this young girl a part of it.

It was a pivotal moment, and many years later, when Marta was his wife and Franz Harz was her lover, he was to recall it, and say to Harz, 'I never experienced anything like it, before or after. Listening to her sing changed my entire life. In that one moment I knew that if I never did anything else in the world I had to bring that young girl to Vienna and make her the prima donna at the Hofopera. It was the first and only goal I ever set for myself, and I accomplished it.'

And Harz was to say with a sour smile, 'You accomplished shit. What did you ever do for her besides marry her?'

'Unfair, Franz. I discovered her.'

'And who haggled with that cunning father of hers? Who paid him off to let her go with us to Vienna?'

'You did, Franz.' *With my money*...a thought unspoken.

'Who took her into his own home and treated her like a daughter?'

'You did, Franz.' *Some treatment . . . some daughter. At least I married her.*

'Who found her the best voice coach in Vienna?'

'You did, Franz.' *And took a rakeoff on the fees I paid.*

'Who managed her début? Who mounted a special perform-ance of *Così* just to present her to Vienna?'

'You did, Franz.' *And made a small fortune out of it.*

'Who worked with her, drove her, cursed her, moulded her into what she is today? Did you do any of that?'

'No, Franz, you did.' To argue with your wife's lover was not the Viennese way. 'You did all that, but I discovered her.'

'Yes, I'll give you that much. You discovered her, the way a pig noses up a truffle. But never forget that I created her.'

But that was years into the future, and now as von Ulm stepped into the parlour his boots squeaked on the hardwood floor, and Marta looked up. At the sight of him her voice died away and her fingers slipped from the keys. She stared at him wordlessly, as tensed as a bird about to take flight.

He smiled at her easily. 'Relax, little one, I'm not going to eat you. I have something very important to say to you, and then I must have a long talk with your father and mother.'

Chapter Seven

The fifth regiment of Mountain Artillery, the Eighth Battery of which was commanded by Oberleutnant Otto Prinz, was emplaced high on a mountainside above the town of Caporetto. That was the name in Italian; in Slovenian it was called Kobarid, and the mountain was known variously as Mount Krn, or Krnberg, or Montagna Nera. It was all the same piece of real estate, the language depending on the occupying power at the time. The regiment was bivouacked in caves along the ridge, one battery to a cave, enlisted men only. The officers had a cave of their own, as did the regimental headquarters. Without the caves the position could not have been held, for tenting out was impossible in the wintertime. The caves, however, were dry and could be warmed by fires if one didn't mind the smoke.

From the ridge the troops could see the town below and the

Isonzo River, which then was the border between Italy and the Austro-Hungarian Empire. Italy was still neutral, but the regiment's guns were sighted in on the roads and the bridges, ready to open fire if the situation changed. Also below the ridge, but to the right, was an indentation in the hillside almost a mile across, a punchbowl with steep and icy slopes, and on the far side of it the north face rose up to form the dark and towering peak which gave the mountain its name. It was there that the trouble started.

The trouble was that the Fifth Artillery was the only Austrian unit on the mountain and they had to be located precisely there on that ridge to maintain a field of fire on the river. With no support or covering troops this left them open to flanking attacks up the other faces of the mountain. Everyone knew that eventually Italy would be coming into the war on the side of the Allies, the only question was when, and Colonel von Moltitz was determined not to be caught by surprise. He organized a system of patrols on his flanks, which in practical terms meant skiing an arc halfway around the punchbowl, climbing to the peak for observations, and then skiing back again. It was not a difficult job for a regiment made up of mountain men, and from the colonel's point of view it served more than one purpose.

Von Moltitz was an aristocrat and a confirmed believer in the natural order of things, which meant the natural superiority of his caste, and he didn't give two raps about the emotional well-being of his troops. They were all peasants, and they weren't supposed to have finer feelings. It was enough that they were kept fed, shod, dry, and ready to fight. But von Moltitz was also an old-line officer, and he knew how quickly the rust of inactivity could clog the efficiency of a body of men. That was a peacetime problem, because war scoured rust before it could take hold, but the Fifth Artillery was caught up in what was essentially a peacetime condition. To the north in Russia, and to the southwest in Serbia, other Austrian troops were in constant combat, but the Fifth sat perched on its mountain overlooking neutral Italy waiting for something to happen and accumulating rust. The men needed an active diversion, and von Moltitz provided it by turning the daily perimeter patrol into a form of skiing competition.

The standard patrol routine was to leave the regimental lines just after sunrise, ski the arc of the ridge around the punchbowl as far as the base of the mountain's peak, a tilted face of black basalt perpetually windswept and free of snow. Then the drill was to stack the skis and climb, roped for safety, clutching at outcroppings and hammering pitons home, until the top was reached. Eight separate observation reports covering the approaches to Krnberg were then made and entered in the log by the officer in charge, times and compass bearings noted, before the troops could scramble down the rock face to regain their skis and head for home. But not along the arc of the ridge this time. The last leg home was down into the punchbowl, schussing the slopes flat out as if they were boys again back home on a Sunday afternoon. Into the bowl with enough speed to carry them partway up the other side, and then a herringbone clamber to the lip of the ridge and a desperate poling to the regimental lines, the last man over always breathless and floundering. Time marked as that last man crossed the line, entered in the operational day book, and the battery with the best time of the week received the regimental colours on Sunday after church service. It was an exercise designed to eliminate military rust, and von Moltitz was proud of the condition of his troops achieved over the months at a cost of only sprains and bruises, and one broken leg.

The man with the broken leg was Korporal Emil Platt of the Eighth Battery, and his injury came to him not during one of the perimeter patrols but as the result of an argument with a runaway gun carriage. The day that Platt was packed off down the mountain on a mule litter, Herr Feuerwerker Kranski popped his head into the cave occupied by the Eighth Battery and looked around for Cowboy Karl Lang. The cave, as always, was dimly lit and filled with smoke and the acrid odours of unwashed men, mules, cabbage soup, and damp wool drying. It was the time of the midday meal, and Kranski spotted his target stirring a giant kettle over a fire near the front of the cave. The regiment messed by batteries, each unit drawing raw supplies from the quartermaster and cooking its own meals, invariably a soup of cabbage, potatoes, and scraps of meat. The position of cook was supposed to pass in rotation, but Lang was the battery favourite because of his civilian occupation as a butcher's apprentice. He, at least, knew meat, and could be depended upon to come back to the cave with something more than gristle and bones. Now, ignoring the smoke and the heat of the fire, he carefully stirred the soup kettle with a long wooden paddle, his face intent as he bent to the task.

From out of the nearby gloom the voice of Eugen Schwimmer said, 'No wonder the soup always tastes like sawdust. Who ever heard of stirring soup with a wooden paddle?'

'Your mama stirs soup with a wooden spoon,' Peter Ickle pointed out.

'Don't mention my mama's soup in the same breath with this swill. Besides, her spoon is hard, polished wood. That paddle has splinters in it. They fall off in the pot.'

'Did you ever find a splinter of wood in your soup?'

'I thought I did once,' said Gunther Rapp, 'but it turned out to be a piece of meat. Chewed on it for half an hour before I could tell the difference.'

There was laughter, and the Cowboy looked up, adding his grin, but his mind was busy with calculations. There was soup in the pot for the eighteen men in the battery, but Platt was on his way down the mountain with his broken leg and the Zugsführer was fast asleep. Bound to stay that way through the midday meal and content himself later with a chunk of bread and the slivovitz in his canteen. That left two extra portions for his boys.

In a quiet voice he said to the St Anton men gathered near the fire, 'There's a little extra today. When I ladle it out, eat fast, then hand me back your bowl and I'll top it off again.'

His friends grinned up their thanks at him, and he shook his head. 'I'm not doing you any favours, you're going to need it. We've got the duty this afternoon, the six of us again.'

The grins changed to groans, and Schwimmer said angrily, 'Jesus, what is it this time?'

'Repacking ammo,' Karl told him, and the groans deepened. It was a filthy job. 'Our Oberleutnant volunteered us.'

'Fucking Otto. The St Anton Six gets it again.'

'The bastard, I'd like to see him dirty his hands, just once.'

'He's trying to kill us, that's what it is.'

'He really is,' Willi said despondently. He looked around at his friends, and said in a whisper, 'He knows. I'm telling you he knows.'

'Shut your face,' Karl said sharply. 'I don't want to hear that kind of talk. He doesn't know a damn thing.'

'Then why . . . ?'

102

'It's just another dirty detail like the rest of them.' He bent over until his face was close to Gebaur's, their noses almost touching. 'So keep your mouth shut and stop making us nervous. That's all it is, you hear me?'

Gebaur nodded and looked away, unconvinced.

'*Achtung!*' Someone finally saw Kranski standing in the gloom near the mouth of the cave and shouted the word, but the Feuerwerker ignored the formality. 'Lang,' he called. 'Outside, double time.'

Karl looked up and nodded casually. Double time was standard time for Kranski, and the phrase had no more meaning than a sergeant's curse. Pulling on his heavy coat, he handed the paddle to Eugen with instructions for a slow and steady stir, and ducked out of the cave and into the frosty air. Along the line of the ridge the other caves belched gouts of smoke, each one laden with the odour of boiling cabbage.

'We're safe as long as the wind holds,' he said thoughtfully. 'If the Italians ever attack they'll never get past our poison gas.'

The Feuerwerker ignored the comment. Over the months he had come to his own accommodation with Lang. The man was totally lacking in military courtesy and respect, but when it was time to work he put in a solid day's worth of soldiering. Kranski was willing to accept a certain amount of irreverence in exchange for that.

'Cowboy,' he said, 'I'm putting you up for Platt's stripe. You're the Korporal now.'

Karl looked up at the grey sky leaking flakes of wet snow. 'Herr Feuerwerker, tell me, can you see the sun?'

Kranski looked up, puzzled. 'No, of course not.'

'Neither can I, but I think you've been standing out in it for too long.'

'You don't want the job?'

'Sure I do. I could use the extra pennies.'

'Then what?'

'The Oberleutnant, that's what. He'll never approve it.'

'I've already spoken to him. He says the job is yours.'

Karl hid his surprise with a grimace. 'Makes no difference. You know what I think of him. Can you see me taking orders from that shit?'

'Easy with the language,' Kranski said automatically. 'Look, you take orders from him now.'

'No, I don't. The Zugsführer takes the orders, passes them on to the Korporal, and he tells me what to do. That way I have nothing to do with Otto, and that's the way I want to keep it.'

'You'd still have the Zugsführer in between.'

'Our Zug is past it and you know it. Worthless, should never be in the field. No, *Mensch*, it would all fall on me and it would just lead to trouble.'

'Are you refusing the promotion?'

'That's it.'

Kranski took time to chew on the lower ends of his moustache before exploding. 'God damn it in hell, man, what is it with you and this lieutenant?'

'I told you back in Landeck. He's going to get us killed one of these days.'

'It's got to be something more than that.' Kranski remembered the colonel's observation about mountain feuds. 'Did he ever take something from you? Steal your girl, or something like that?'

Karl's face was impassive, thinking: Did he? Maybe he did, but not the way this old one means it. He laughed without any humour. 'I don't own anything that the Oberleutnant would want. In fact, I don't own anything at all.'

'No bad blood between your families?'

'We don't go in for feuds where I come from, no matter what people say.'

'No bad blood, but you're taking a lot of shit from him, you and your friends.'

'Glad to see that somebody noticed.'

'If you take the stripe you'll be in a better position to keep him off your backs.'

Karl considered the point – it was a good one – but he shook his head. 'I'll take care of my boys my own way.'

Kranski grunted his approval. It was an attitude he appreciated, but his personal feelings had no place here. The battery needed an NCO, and Lang was the man for the job. 'I'm sorry, Cowboy, but you're the new corporal whether you like it or not. That's an order.'

Karl drew himself up into a formal salute. '*Jawohl,* Herr Feuerwerker.'

'Tell your Zugsführer that I said so. The actual order will come from the colonel later today.'

104

'Right now our dear Zuggy is fast asleep. Some of these older NCOs need an afternoon nap.'

'And some of them can still soldier you into the ground. All right, corporal, tell him when he wakes up.' The Feuerwerker turned to go, then added, 'Look, I have no choice here, it has to be this way. You're the best I've got in the battery.'

'It's a mistake,' Karl said flatly. He went back into the cave to serve the soup.

Anyone who spends time on the sides and the tops of mountains knows that they have to be humoured and treated like individuals, for no two mountains are the same. There are angry mountains and smiling hills, savage crags, mischievous tors, and peaks as aloof as an eremite. There are mountains that snore and grumble at night, and others that sleep as soundly as a dog in front of a fire. They are a symbol of constancy, but they are in every way capricious, defying a man's understanding and demanding of his patience. No sane man fights with a mountain for the simple reason that a mountain fights back. There never yet has been a man built as big as a mountain.

Mount Krn, like any other mountain, felt free to break its own rules. Most years the heavy snows lingered there well into May, but in the winter of 1915 the mountain yawned, the thaw started early, and in the middle of March the slopes began to come apart. The snow was still skiable, just barely, but the new conditions changed the rules for the perimeter patrols. Each battery drawing the duty still skied the rim of the punchbowl as far as the basalt tower, climbed to the top, made its observations, and then returned to camp. But with the thaw coming early there was no longer the joyful schuss down into the punchbowl and the climb up the other side. The bottom of the punchbowl was a mess, with much of the snow washed away and deep ravines cut between the rocks. Only a few bridges of snow remained intact over those ravines. Because of this the patrols were now ordered to retrace the path along the rim, taking the long way home. The new orders, in effect, put an end to the competition within the regiment, leaving the Third Battery as the undisputed recordholder with a time of two hours and fifty-five minutes. It was a record that Otto envied the way a farmer covets a neighbour's prize yearling.

On Wednesday, 24 March 1915, the Eighth Battery was assigned to perimeter patrol in accordance with standing orders.

0700: The battery prepares to move out. The Zugsführer has reported ill the past three days and it is Korporal Karl Lang who inspects the men's equipment, tugging a strap here, a binding there, moving from man to man checking weapons, haversacks, skis, and boots. He does his work intently, unsmiling, ordering two of the men to change into fresh, dry stockings, and another to replace a missing screw in a heel plate. No one has seen the new Korporal smile since he put on his stripe. At 0720 he reports to the Oberleutnant that the battery is assembled and ready.

Otto says good-naturedly, 'I hope so, Karl. We're moving fast today.'

Karl stares blankly. It is the first time that Otto has called him by his Christian name since they both put on the uniform.

0725: Eighth Battery moves out in a column of twos with Otto at the head and Karl bringing up the rear. They shuffle out of camp like sleep-walkers on skis, each staring dully at the back of the man in front of him. Once they are out of the lee of the ridge they pick up a waking wind, and without any formal order they lengthen their pace to the stride of the *Langlaufer,* skis skimming and poles stabbing smoothly. They are skiing on the flat, but every once in a while a variance in the terrain allows them a downhill drop to pick up speed and ease the burden of the poling. They are not yet fully awake, but they ski instinctively, the way a sleepy sailor walks a tilted deck.

0745: A watery sun appears and Otto, on the point, picks up the pace. When the skiers directly behind him lag back he calls over his shoulder to close up the column. The men begin to sweat, stretching their legs and bending into the rhythm of the stride. At the rear of the column Karl wonders why Otto is pushing so hard so early. There are no more records to set.

0816: The tower is in sight and the pace has not slackened. Every so often Otto pumps his left fist skyward, calling for more speed, and the men respond. Some of them grumble, but no one falls back. Some of the others begin to realize how fast a pace they are setting, and like Karl they wonder why.

0831: The patrol arrives at the base of the tower, and while the men strip off and stack their skis and poles, Otto checks his timepiece. Sixty-six minutes to the tower, excellent time.

Without orders the men form into climbing parties, ready to rope up for the ascent, but Otto stops them.

'The Korporal and I are going up alone,' he says, and points to Peter Ickle. 'You're in charge here until we come down.'

Peter nods slowly, confused. This is clearly outside of the standing orders. His confusion grows when the Oberleutnant takes him aside and says quietly, 'Let the men rest. I want them fresh for the trip back. Get them on their feet when you see us start down. By the time I reach the bottom I want them with their skis on and ready to move.' He hesitates, then adds, 'I know I can count on you, Peter.'

He motions to Karl, and they rope up for the climb. Karl's mind is stretching as he checks his knots. *Peter*? Otto never used Ickle's first name even at home. What kind of a routine patrol is this?

0834: Otto and Karl work their way up the face of the tower with Otto leading on the rope. It is a tiring climb, but not a difficult one. There are plenty of hand and footholds in the fissured surface, and pitons that were hammered into the rock months before. Otto takes a belay on the rope, bracing as Karl follows him up. For a moment they are nose to nose on the face of the cliff, joined by rope, rock and sweat. It is a communal moment, and Otto grins boyishly. Karl, caught by surprise, almost grins back.

0851: Atop the tower, a flat section, slightly inclined, that provides an overview of the three faces of the mountain. The morning fog has lifted, and below them the town, the river, and the bridges are in clear sight. Otto makes his observations quickly, using compass and binoculars, calling out the bearings to Karl, who marks them in a notebook. All observations are negative, no movement in the town or on any of the approaches to the mountain. Otto packs away his glasses. He and Karl are lying flat on their bellies, side by side. He rolls over and sits up, resting on his hip.

'Cowboy,' he says, 'how would you like to break the record on the way back to camp?'

'Record?'

'The patrol record. Two hours and fifty-five minutes. We're ahead of it now and we can beat it.'

The meaning of the words barely registers. First Otto calls him by name and now he employs the *du* of their childhood.

Then the words sink in. The record? What the hell is going on here? There's only one way to set a new record, and that way is impossible.

'What are you talking about?' he says slowly, and without realizing it he also uses the *du*.

'We're going back through the punchbowl.'

'You're crazy.' Then six months of army life catch up with him. 'I'm sorry. With respect, Herr Oberleutnant.'

'Forget about that.' Otto is grinning again. 'Up here, all alone, we're just two boys from St Anton.'

The hell we are, Karl thinks, but he doesn't say it. 'You want to cross the punchbowl? It can't be done.'

'It can. There are three snow bridges left, all of them solid.'

'It's against orders.'

'The hell with orders.' Otto is positively exuberant now. 'Since when did you turn into a little tin soldier?'

'All right, to hell with orders, but we're not going into the punchbowl. It isn't safe.'

'I'm telling you it is. Look, Karl, we may not be friends, but you know you can trust me when it comes to the mountain. Those bridges are safe, and I want that record.'

Karl thinks: All right, here it is. What I've been afraid of from the start. I knew that it would come sooner or later, but I figured it would come with the guns going off, not for some stupid regimental record. But here it is, and sooner than I thought. The son of a bitch is going to get us all killed.

'If you want the record that bad,' he says, 'go and get it yourself.'

Otto shakes his head impatiently, 'Don't talk nonsense. It has to be the entire battery.'

Karl is on his feet and standing at rigid attention. 'Are you ordering me into the punchbowl, Herr Oberleutnant?'

'Ach, Karl, don't be that way.'

'Because you'll have to make it a direct order.'

Otto pushes himself up and stands facing his Korporal. He hooks his thumbs into the web of his belt and rocks back on his heels. 'What if I could convince you that the middle bridge is safe?'

'There's no way you can do that.'

'But there is.' A hint of a smile on Otto's lips. 'I know it's safe because I crossed over it last night.'

Disbelief in Karl's eyes. 'Alone? At night?'

'I had to be sure. I want that record, and I want it bad. I tried the bridge last night, both ways. It's as solid as a rock.'

The disbelief is replaced by a reluctant admiration. 'Christ, Otto, you could have been killed.'

'No, I knew it was safe, I just had to be sure. Well, what do you say? Are you with me?'

The temptation is there, the urge to kick caution in the ass, to be a kid again flying downhill in reckless abandon with his heart pumping fear and excitement in equal doses. The temptation, but just for the moment. That's Otto's game, not his. He shakes his head.

'I don't care if you crossed an elephant over that bridge last night,' he says. 'It isn't worth the risk.'

Otto's lips thin out into a frown. 'Very well, I'm making it an order.'

'*Jawohl*, Herr Oberleutnant.'

'When we reach the base you will form the battery into squads. First squad takes the lead with me, second squad follows with you at the rear.'

'*Jawohl*, Herr Oberleutnant.' The St Anton Six, he thinks bitterly. Last in line, on the hot spot again.

'Any questions?'

'Only one. What the hell is so important about this God damn record?'

Otto starts to say something, hesitates, then shakes his head. 'I could never explain it to you, never in a million years. You have your orders, Korporal. Let's go.'

0917: Otto and Karl descend to the base of the tower, where Peter has the troops skied-up and ready to roll. Karl gives them the word about the punchbowl and sets the order of march. He is disgusted to see no fear on the faces of the men, hear no grumbling from the ranks; disgusted because it means they trust him. If the Cowboy says that we're going into the punchbowl, hell, let's go. We'll be back in camp in time for the soup. Some of the fools even give a low cheer.

But the Cowboy isn't cheering. There is a deep pool of ice inside of him as the troops form up in a column of twos and move out with the St Anton Six at the rear. Another temptation comes to him, the pressing desire to jam his poles into the snow and refuse to go any farther, because if anything happens to that bridge it will be the last in line who will get the chop. But this urge lasts no longer than the other did. He bows his head and moves after his men, gliding up to the lip of the punchbowl. With the rest of the troops he stares down into it, and at the middle of the three snow bridges that span the rocks and the ravines.

Otto gives the order, forearm thrown forward, and the column of men drops over the lip to go streaking down into the bowl over a strip of snow less than fifty metres wide. They are a third of the way down when the bridge begins to come apart.

In that moment when the snow bridge at Krn began to unravel, Otto Prinz reached deep within himself and became as one with the mountain. He made a split-second deal with the hill, and he kept his part of the bargain. He became, in that existential moment, a flat-out skier racing for his life, and those of his men. The moment was his alone, a speck of time in which he was transformed into the authentic skier he would never be again. Never mind that he should not have been there in the first place. Never mind that he had recklessly jeopardized the lives of his men for an empty honour. He did not panic, he did not put on the brakes, he did not try to scramble back the way he had come. He made the only move possible, shrieking, 'Forward,' at the top of his voice, stretching out over his skis and dropping down the hill in wild abandon, his men strung out behind him. He shifted and he dodged as whole sections of the bridge fell away; jumping, twisting in midair to avoid a knot of ice exploding under pressure. More explosions up and down the span, a bombardment of them as if the battery were under fire from enemy artillery, gouts of snow and ice shooting up all around them. They sped across the bridge in a sinuous line, each man racing for his life. Skis chattered, grasping for purchase. Otto led them on the fastest downhill line, never checking. He lifted up over a rift and each of them followed, landed, and stayed in his tracks as he cut left to avoid another chasm forming. Right, left again with the end of the bridge just ahead, and then they tucked down low in the final schuss to safety. It was Otto's moment. It was impossible for him to move wrong. For the first and last time in his life he was an integral part of the mountain, and he could not fail.

It was over in minutes. The battery reached the comparative

safety of the bottom of the bowl and clustered there silently, staring back up the hill. It looked like a battlefield. The bridge was gone, tumbled into powder on the rocks of the ravine, and the rumble of its passing echoed in their ears. Someone made a quick count of the men and announced that they were short six.

Otto, still staring uphill, snapped, 'Korporal, form the men into squads and get the names of the missing.'

Silence, not the customary 'Jawohl.'

'Korporal Lang?'

'The Cowboy isn't here. That's him up there.'

High up on the side of the punchbowl was the figure of a single man clinging to the icy slope.

When Karl heard the first sharp *crack* and felt the tremor under his skis, he knew what he had bought. What was safe for one man crossing in the middle of a freezing night was about to fall apart under the weight of an entire battery in the milder air of the day. He heard Otto's shriek, saw him start his race for the bottom, and knew instinctively that the move was right for the men up front. He also knew that the move was wrong for the men in the rear. Dead wrong.

'Second squad back,' he shouted.

That was all he had time for. The snow in front of him erupted with a roar, shook him, and threw him uphill. Flat on his back, he stabbed with his poles to keep from slipping forward and watched, stunned as the bridge below him opened up in a yawning gap tht swallowed up one, then another, then all five of the men in front of him. They went in silently, falling far to the floor of the ravine along with the tons of ice and snow that buried them there. He saw them go and knew exactly who they were. Beyond the gap the rest of the troops went speeding down the hill.

He crawled as close to the edge of the gap as he dared, and looked down. There was nothing to see except snow and ice below, but he had expected nothing. Dolf, Peter, Eugen, Gunther, Willi . . . all gone. Without realizing it he began to sob, his chest heaving and his throat closed tight. There were tears on his face, but he did not feel them.

'Jesus, Willi, you were right,' he said through the sobs, his chin still pressed to the snow. 'The bastard knew all along, and he tried to kill us. All of us, at the end of the line. He *knew*.'

He might have stayed there longer, staring down into the burial pit of the men he knew best, but the sharp blasts of a whistle raised his head. Somebody below was trying to get his attention, waving now, signalling him to climb out of the bowl and circle the rim back to camp. Only officers used whistles that way.

'*Jawohl*, Herr Oberleutnant,' he muttered. 'I'm coming. Be patient, I'll be there as soon as I can.'

It took him almost two hours to make the climb and ski wearily back to camp. He knew that he was weary from the way his skis dragged, but his mind was clear. He felt strangely light-headed, but nothing worse than that. He knew exactly what he was going to do. When he saw the columns of oily smoke that marked the campsite he stopped, unslung his rifle, fed a cartridge into the chamber, moved on again. Once in camp he took off his skis and went directly to the cave that housed the regimental headquarters. He marched into the cave as casually as if he were coming home to dinner in his mother's kitchen, and stopped just within the entranceway.

There were six men in the cave. Colonel von Moltitz and three of his officers sat at a table with Otto seated across from them, his head in his hands. The only other person present was Feuerwerker Kranski standing a respectful three paces behind his colonel. At the sound of Karl's entrance they all looked up. Relief showed on the faces of the colonel and his aides. Otto stared dully. Only Kranski sensed something, and frowned. He took a step towards the entrance.

'No,' said Karl. He unslung his rifle and worked the bolt.

'Put it down, son,' said the Feuerwerker, taking another step.

'In a minute.' He raised the rifle and aimed it at Otto. 'He killed them, Kranski.'

'Put it down. It's bad enough. Don't make it worse.'

'He murdered them.' Karl's voice was calm, almost conversational.

'It was an accident, Cowboy.'

The officers at the table sat stiffly, as if they were embarrassed by the intrusion. They kept their hands carefully on the table. Otto simply stared, his eyes unfocused. Von Moltitz said, 'Feuerwerker, disarm that man.'

'Don't try it,' said Karl without rancour. 'It wasn't an accident, he planned it that way. We were screwing his wife, you know.

All six of us. Seven if you include his brother, Anton. We screwed her for over a year before they were married.'

Kranski pleaded, 'Damn it, Cowboy, shut your mouth.'

'Six of us, the five he killed and me. We thought he didn't know, but he did. Willi said that he knew, but I didn't listen to him. Poor little Willi, he was right and now he's dead. They're all dead.'

Von Moltitz said sharply, 'Feuerwerker, I gave you an order.'

Kranski raised his open hands and shrugged. 'Cowboy, you heard the colonel. I have to take it away from you. So make it easy for me, will you? Lay it down and then we'll talk some more.'

'There's nothing to talk about. I should have listened to Willi.' He raised his head away from the sights to look directly at Otto. 'She wasn't worth it, you murdering son of a bitch. A good piece of ass, but she wasn't worth the lives of five men.' He knew that the tears and the sobs were going to start again soon, and he fought to control them. 'God damn it, Otto, all the girls in St Anton and you had to marry the town pump.'

Otto's eyes were wide and his head was up now, his neck arched stiffly. He choked out the words, 'All of you?'

Karl jerked the rifle impatiently. 'How did you find out?'

'Anton too?'

'Who told you?'

'No one told me. I . . . I didn't know.'

'You knew.'

'You're wrong, soldier,' von Moltitz observed. 'Your officer didn't know, he just found out. You just told him.'

'He knew,' Karl repeated stubbornly.

'Nonsense. Look at his face, look at the horror on it. No, you're wrong. He didn't know, and he didn't kill your friends.'

Kranski made his move then, leaping. His fingers touched the barrel of the rifle as Karl fired, brushing it lightly, but just enough. The bullet hit Otto in the left knee and knocked him to the ground. Then the rifle was on the dirt floor of the cave and Kranski's arms were locked around Karl and holding him motionless. Karl did not try to move. He rested in Kranski's arms.

'God damn it, boy, God damn it,' said the Feuerwerker. He said it over and over.

Two of the colonel's aides knelt over Otto while the third

went runing for medical attention. A low and vibrating wail filled the cave, the cry of an animal in pain. The animal was Otto, but the pain did not come from his knee. It was too soon for that.

The colonel looked curiously from Karl to Otto, and back again. His lips thinned in distaste, his worst fears about the wartime army confirmed. Two peasants brawling over some slut, and one of them an officer. It could never have happened in the old regiment.

'He really didn't know,' he said absently, 'but he certainly knows now.'

Otto Prinz was discharged from active service because of a wound suffered in the line of duty. He returned home to St Anton as a hero two weeks after the birth of his son, Hannes. He spoke to no one for a month; not his wife, not his parents, not his few friends. At the end of that time he chose a night when Sepp and Hanna were visiting neighbours and systematically beat his wife into insensibility. He came close to killing her. No charges were ever filed against him, and Lili made no complaint. Wife-beating was not that uncommon in the Tirol, and there was always the war to blame.

Karl Lang was tried before a military court and sentenced to twenty years at hard labour at Landeck Prison in the Tirol.

Chapter Eight

From the Journals of Elizabeth Chandler

Saturday, 1 January 1916
Now for my accounting of the past twelve months as time wheels round on its pivot and a new year begins. This is a comfortable tradition within the family. My father taught me early in life that we are all accountable for our actions, and just as each Sunday we present an accounting to the Lord, even so each year we owe ourselves a similar summary. Like so many others my father chose the first day of the year as his time for reckoning up, and out of filial respect I have continued the custom. It is,

of course, an arbitrary and meaningless distinction to make. No planets cojoin each January first, nor do the heavens reform themselves then for our convenience, but as a date it is as good as any other. Thus, to business.

In general summary the Chandler Lumber Company last year cut, finished, and produced a total of 467,282 board feet of hardwood. Of this amount fifty-two percent was shipped to Sharples Brothers in Burlington, eleven percent to other yards, and the balance retained for the use of Prinz Carpentries. The depletion of stock amounted to an estimated three percent of the woodlot, all maple, ash, and oak from the West 60 section, and replacement seeding will begin in the spring. The overall profit has been enough to return my original investment to me six months earlier than anticipated, and prospects for the coming year are encouraging, as the war in Europe, which shows no sign of a conclusion, increases the demand for American hardwoods. Once again I thank the Lord that Mr Wilson, Democrat though he may be, has kept us out of war for another year.

During this same period Prinz Carpentries made some strides forward, although it has yet to show a proft. Anton is concerned about this and I try to reassure him, pointing out that the carpentry business, by its very nature, will take a while to establish. More important than immediate profit is the steady accumulation of orders for tables, chairs, and cabinetry, enough to keep three men busy under his direction. Profit-making will come in time, but my beloved is concerned that he is not 'pulling his weight' in our joint ventures, and in a sense he is not. I would never reproach him with the fact, but he is truly no businessman. He does not have the head for it, nor the desire to apply himself in trade for all the grandness of his plans. He would much rather climb up a hill than march down a column of figures, and during the winter months it is almost impossible to keep him in the workshop and away from his beloved mountains and his skis. He has been in these parts less than two years now, but I am certain that no native Vermonter is as familiar as he is with the slopes, the forests, and the peaks of Mounts Wellington and Mansfield. Because of this I find more and more of the daily business routine being pressed upon me, but I make no complaints. Anton and I are partners in every way, and I am certainly capable of coping with such matters.

Indeed, this is small enough coin to pay for the love and

companionship that I share with this man, the most ideal of partners, and the odd thought strikes me that without him at my side I should not be able to bear up under the weight of public disapproval that continues to surround me. Odd because without him at my side there would be no such censure from the apes and asses of this village. But there it is, and I would not have it any other way. Anton knows this and he respects my feelings on the subject of marriage, although I regret that his own position is not nearly so firm. I fear that he sees my stand as being one more of obstinacy than of principle, and he continues to suggest that we wed. 'Suggest' is too mild a term, for he is after me constantly, choosing those occasions when he thinks me to be the most pliable. He is wasting his time. As easily move Mount Mansfield as move me in matters where my pride is touched.

Saturday, 7 April 1917
Well, we are in it now, the fat in the fire. Mr Wilson, who told us loud and clear last year how he had kept us out of war, has finally showed his true Democrat colours, and a spineless Congress has followed along as meekly as lambs to the slaughter, voting us into a European war. Lambs to the slaughter, indeed, and soon, no doubt, there will be another monument raised on the village green alongside the one of our Civil War dead, another obscene pile of cannonballs, and another generation of weeping widows. Thank the good Lord that my Anton is out of it, they won't come looking for one-handed soldiers, although the dear fool is as patriotic as any tub-thumper in town. A regular fire-eater, he is, breathing defiance at what he charmingly calls 'doze****Chermans' in the Teutonic accent which I fear he will never lose. A clear case of the newly converted becoming more Catholic than the Pope, meaning that only as an expression, of course. My Anton is red, white, and blue clear through, no matter that his homeland lies on the other side of the trenches. To hear him talk you would think that every evil in the world had its roots somewhere east of the Rhine, and that the destruction of the German-speaking race is part and parcel of mankind's salvation. My Cato calls for the destruction of Carthage, and as the ultimate idiocy he is even talking of changing his name to Prince, although no one here in town has yet to express an anti-German sentiment towards him. (Afraid

116

to, is my thought. They know they'd have me to reckon with.) Still, he speaks of doing it, a shining example of the darn fool tricks that a man can get up to when infected with a patriotic pride.

For all of that, the war should expand our activities considerably.

Tuesday, 22 May 1917

He has gone and done it, filed it by deed poll. He is Mr Anton Prince now, and the ninnies of the town have made a local hero out of him over it, as much as if he'd gone and captured Kaiser Bill all by himself. Sheer nonsense, but I could not dissuade him from the action. As might be expected, the change of his name has brought him round once again to the changing of my name, as well. I delivered the usual reply to that suggestion.

Tuesday, 1 January 1918

Now for my accounting of the last twelve months as time wheels around on its pivot and a new year begins. In general summary, the Chandler Lumber Company last year cut, finished, and produced 1,784,037 board feet of hardwood. Of this, seventy-eight percent was sold to the U.S. Navy Shipyards in Portsmouth, eleven percent to Sharples Brothers, nine percent to other yards, and the balance retained for the making of skis. It should be noted that we now number among our assets $25,000 worth of these new-fangled Liberty Bonds. Mighty nice business the government is in, profit in the guise of patriotism. Wish I could borrow money at those rates. I'd treble my activities in no time at all if I could.

Tuesday, 12 November 1918

It's over now. Finally, after that most disheartening false alarm, the war is truly over, and now the stay-at-home heroes who never risked a drop of blood will have their day. *Americanus victorius.* The flags will fly even higher, the eagle will scream, and the peaceful cannons now will bray that asinine acknowledgment which only manhood gives to man. There will be a perfect orgy of self-congratulation, all in praise of folly, but I suppose one can live with that. At least, it's over. The little boys have put their toys away at last.

This will doubtless mean a certain retrenchment in our lumber

117

activities, but we cannot complain. We have come out of it all quite nicely, and now with the war over people are bound to have more time for recreation. Which means that our ski business should increase. Everyone says that Anton makes the finest skis in New England. So far we've limited ourselves to five hundred pair a year, but there is no reason why we cannot produce more if the market is there for the product.

Friday, 27 June 1919
The indications are now unmistakable. After all these years I am at last with child. For this I give thanks to a generous Deity, but must also wonder why, in His mysterious fashion, He took so long to get around to it. Nevertheless, a mother I shall be, one of the world's blessed.

Shall I elaborate? Shall I bare my feelings further? Shall I churn my soul to bring forth on these pages the curds and whey of impending motherhood? I shall not. I am pleased by this circumstance, pleased beyond measure, but exaltation escapes me. Let other women seek fulfilment in this process; my star shines elsewhere. Still, I am pleased. I have long wished for the opportunity to rear a daughter in the modern manner, free of superstitious rubbish, and of the restraints which have ever bound our sex. I welcome the challenge.

Of course, it will not be easy. This cursed town will now have another supply of stony words to fling at me. No doubt they will think of some pippins. I welcome that challenge, as well.

Tomorrow being Saturday and thus a half-holiday, I shall take the opportunity to present this news to A.

Saturday, 28 June 1919
With a calmness of spirit, and with the firmness of intention that has ever been the essence of my character, I shall now record the events of the day. If my hand should tremble or my pen should shake it will be both understandable and forgivable, for never have I been so humbled and humiliated.

I told Anton the happy news this afternoon following the midday meal, and his initial response was predictable. He gawked, he beamed, he gushed. He embraced me, roughly at first, and then gingerly. He urged me to care for myself, and ran for a cushion to place at my back. He knelt beside my chair,

118

expressed the appropriate sentiments, and then astonished me by asking when we would be wed.

'What is this?' I exclaimed. 'You know my feelings on the subject.'

'But this changes everything.' He was quite excited.

'It certainly does not. I am perfectly willing to bear this child out of wedlock.'

'What's that?'

'No wedding,' I explained. 'We shall have this child proudly, and I shall raise her in the light of my feminist convictions, and of those two pioneering women Alice Paul and Lucy Burns.'

'Bloomer girls!'

'That is a barbaric thing to say.'

'And what if this girl is a boy?'

'I have the unshakeable conviction that she will not be. Mothers have such feelings.'

'But what if?'

'I would welcome the challenge to raise a male with feminist convictions.'

'And no marriage?'

'No, sir, there will be none.'

The poor man was puzzled. 'But aren't you ashamed to have a baby with no marriage?'

'Certainly not. Having a baby is a perfectly natural female function. Marriage, on the other hand, is an artificial convention imposed by society. I see no connection between the two, and I see no occasion for shame. To marry now would be an insult to everything I believe in.'

He looked at me strangely, 'Thank God I don't insult so easy, but it's good to know you're not ashamed.' Then he rose, and in one motion picked me up in his arms and made for the front door.

I am sure that I did not squeal, but I cried, 'What are you doing? Put me down.'

He did not answer. He carried me out of the door and across the front lawn, heading for the street. When he came to the carriage house he stopped, as if thinking to hitch up the buggy, but he knew full well that if he set me down I would run back to the house and lock myself in. So on he went, left on Crown Street and up to Main with me clutched in his arms, my fists beating on his chest and my angry voice a menace in his ear.

Worse luck, it was a fine day with people out of doors, and we attracted considerable attention as he carried me the length of Main Street past the hardware store, Cain's Grocery, the Sawyers' Bank, the Civil War monument with its pyramid of cannonballs, Glenn's Pharmacy, Chandler's Feed and Grain, and beyond the Town Hall, all the time holding me lightly but firmly in those blacksmith's arms of his, ignoring my cries and pleas and greeting the dumbstruck people on the street with a casual 'Hi, there,' as if he were carrying nothing more than a pig to market. The inevitable pack of small boys formed up behind us, hooting and whistling, while more sedate citizens, although equally curious, followed at a respectable distance. By the time we reached the white clapboard façade of the First Congregational Church we had an impressive group in attendance.

He paused there, and someone worked up the courage to call out, 'Hey, Anton, where are you taking her?'

He turned to face the crowd, turning me with him. 'What does it look like? We're going to get married.'

'We are not,' I shouted, my fists at his face.

Some wit called out, 'Don't seem like the lady has the same idea,' and there was laughter.

'She's just shy,' Anton explained.

'Liz Chandler was never shy a day in her life. If she's so all-fired willing, how come you have to carry her?'

His arms tightened around me, and he grinned like an oafish boy. 'That's just so she don't have to walk so far. You see, she's going to have a baby.'

I confess that I covered my face with my hands.

As if he hadn't done enough, he repeated it to the suddenly silent crowd. 'A baby, and she isn't ashamed of it, by God.'

Then he turned and strode up the driveway to the rectory, the residence of that spineless hypocrite the Reverend James O. Walmsley. A light kick on the door took the place of a knock, and once we were inside he set me on my feet and instructed the Reverend Dr Worm to marry us on the spot. Well, Walmsley is a ditherer at best, and he looked as if he wanted to go through the floor. Dither he did, mumbling about the intricacies of the posting of the banns and the desirability of a long engagement period.

Anton cut him off brusquely. 'We've been engaged too God damn long already, excuse the language. You marry us now.'

'But why the haste?' the Worm said fluttering. 'Surely you can wait.'

'I can, but she can't. She's going to have a baby.'

'My goodness, how very . . . fortunate for you.'

'You bet, so now we get married. A baby is for marriage, and a marriage for babies, right?'

'Well, yes, that's generally the way it works. Elizabeth, don't you have anything to say about this?'

I took my hands from my face. My cheeks may have been pink, but my chin was up. 'Would it make any difference if I did? I've just been hauled through the streets like a sack of wheat and shamed before the town.'

Anton protested, 'Hey, you said no shame.'

'You're a fool,' I snapped at him. 'There is a world of difference between being privately proud and publicly humiliated.'

The Worm cleared his throat. 'But my dear . . . what he says . . . is it true?'

'You're a bigger fool than he is. Of course it's true.'

'Then you wish to be married?'

'I certainly do not.'

'But if you are . . . in a family way . . . don't you think it would be wise to . . .'

'What for? To legitimize my baby? No church on this earth has the power to legitimize the fruit of my body, and no government either.'

Anton interjected, 'Your body? You making this baby by yourself?'

I ignored him. 'Or perhaps you think I should marry just to satisfy that crowd of yahoos out there. Did you hear them catcalling? They haven't had a treat like this since the last time Harley Swenson got drunk and fell through the ice.'

'But if you will not marry . . . think of the stigma that the child will bear.'

'Let society wear the brand.' I was speaking wildly by now. 'My daughter will bear none. I will not wed, and that is final.'

'The hell it is,' said Anton. 'Lizbet, you're a fine woman and you're a lot smarter than me, but sometimes you got no more brains than a horse's hind end. All this talk about society, and government and churches . . . all you're saying is that you're

121

too God damn proud, excuse the language, to do things the way everybody else does 'em.'

'I refuse to bow to the dictates of convention.'

'You mean you got to be different.'

'I *am* different.' I was close to stamping my foot. 'That's the whole point, don't you see?'

'I'll tell you what I see,' he said. 'For five years now I've been asking you to marry me and you say no. Everything else, okay. You cook my food, you run the house, you make love with me, excuse me, reverend, but that's how we got into this trouble . . . you do everything that a wife should do, but you won't be a wife. And for five years I don't push you. I understand why you do it. This town, these people, the way they treat you, they're like pigs. So I don't argue with you because I respect your feelings. But now, this is something different. You think I'm going to live like this the rest of my life? You think I'm going to watch my kid grow up and people call him a bastard? No, Lizbet, not me. You always say how you can take care of yourself, and you say how you're going to raise the baby. Okay, good, you do it. Because I'm telling you right now, unless we get married, I'm finished.'

'Finished?'

'Finished. I pack up and I leave Sedgewick Falls. And I don't come back. I don't ever come back.'

'You'd do this to me?'

'You're doing it to yourself. It's up to you.'

I looked at him carefully, and saw that he meant it. There was no sign of my amiable, easygoing Anton. This was the resolute man who had thrust his shattered wrist into the boiling sugar vat. For the first time in five years he was placing the rock of his will against my own, and I felt a sadness deep within me as I realized what I was going to have to do. I thought of the life I was carrying. I thought of the teachings of Alice Paul and Lucy Burns. I thought of all my good intentions, all the resolutions I had made and kept, and now this one which would have to be broken. I thought of all that, balanced my world on my scales, and then said quietly, 'Very well, Anton, I will marry you.'

A broad grin broke across his face. 'You will?'

'I have said it, and I will do it.'

The Worm said, 'My dear, you are making a very wise decision.'

'I'm pleased that you think so,' I said coolly. 'Reverend, according to my calculations my daughter will be born sometime next January. You may make plans for a wedding to take place exactly four weeks after the birth of the child.'

'Good Lord.'

'Four weeks. Four weeks *after*,' I repeated, and turned to Anton. 'And now, Mr Prince, I think we might go home. You need not carry me this time. Walking is healthy for a woman in my condition.'

Thursday, 8 January 1920

John Joseph Prince was born this day weighing eight pounds and eleven ounces. The Lord moves in mysterious ways indeed. For all the trouble that he took he might have given me the baby girl I wanted.

Wednesday, 11 February 1920

The wedding was held in the rectory. The town has had its victory. I now sign myself Mrs Anton Prince.

Chapter Nine

The house at 72 Hadikgasse, in Vienna's suburban Penzing district, was a massive two-storey villa of more than thirty rooms, surrounded by acres of ornamental gardens. Stone statuary adorned its outer walls, fir trees provided a protective shade, and a tower higher than the trees rose over the entranceway. This was no ordinary house. It had been the temporary home of Richard Wagner, on loan from a Baron Rochow, during the composition of *Die Meistersinger,* and in a musical city such as Vienna this historical connection had been enough to ensure that each succeeding occupant had kept the villa shining as brightly as a jewel in a velvet box. Eleven servants were needed to maintain this lustre, three alone for the gardens, and the kitchen could provide a seven-course dinner for three dozen people on half a day's notice. In the poverty-stricken Austria of 1925, it seemed a miracle that anyone could still afford to live in such a fashion, but in November of that year the occupants of 72 Hadikgasse were the Baron Dieter von Ulm, his wife, who was the celebrated soprano Marta Prinz, and their twin children, Willi and Mimi.

On one of those November mornings Marta von Ulm came up from sleep like a lazy fish circling towards a sunlit surface. She slept between scented silk sheets, and the first sensation that reached her each morning was the aroma of lavender, and after that the softness of the silk against her skin. It was a delightful way in which to wake, better than any other she knew save for the slow slide of her lover's thigh nestling close; but Marta always woke alone with her silk and her lavender. Her husband slept in his own bedroom down the hall, and her lover slept just about anywhere.

Nose pressed to the pillow, Marta broke through the surface of her sleep with her eyes still closed and with two thoughts fully formed in her mind. The first was that she had no performance that day. Each of her days was ruled by whether or not she was scheduled to sing that night on the stage of the Vienna State Opera, and a performance day was like no other. It was a day of silence and seclusion with her voice never raised above a whisper, but today she was free to laugh and shout and enjoy whatever pleasures came her way.

That pleasure was diminished by her second thought: that today was the day to settle things with Franz about his latest infatuation. The Polish soprano Alma Cymrowitz was nineteen, winsomely attractive, and reportedly willing to do anything at all to succeed on the musical stage in Vienna. The only bar to her ambitions appeared to be a voice that faltered distressingly in the upper register, and according to the coffee-house gossip she had been accepted into the company of the Staatsopera only as a concession to Franz. The same gossip had her sharing his bed, but this came as no surprise to musical Vienna. Every manager promoted his favourites, and Franz Harz had never been known to be overly concerned with vocal perfection when he was on the trail of a new conquest.

For all he cares the bitch could squeal like a stuck pig, thought Marta, just so long as she does her squealing in his bed. But not after today. Either he gives her up, or we're finished.

She sighed and buried her head in the pillow, wondering how

many times over the past years she had made that same vow to herself. Either she goes or I go, Franz, and that's final. But there was never anything final about it. The girl always went, and a few months later there was always another. She wondered whether it was worth all the effort, and decided that it was. Franz was her first and lifelong love, and they both knew that her threats were idle. Separating him from his little girlfriends was now nothing more than a housewifely chore that had to be performed: dirty, disagreeable, but necessary. Like scrubbing stockings in a bucket in the wintertime. It had been ten years since she had last put her hands into a pail of cold, soapy water, but she remembered the sensation and decided that with little Miss Cymrowitz singing Octavian tonight, today might just be the day to do a little scrubbing.

Occupied with these thoughts, and with her eyes still closed, she heard a rustling noise and for the first time realized that she was not alone in her bedroom. She sighed again, wishing that Dieter would find some other way of paying his attentions to her. He did not feel the urge very often, but whenever he did he chose to come padding down the hallway from his own bedroom to sit in the chair by her window and watch her as she came awake. It was touching in a way, but so typical of her ineffectual husband. If he wanted her why didn't he simply say so and take her instead of creeping into her room this way? She tried to bury her irritation. Dieter had faults as a husband, but he was the truest friend she had, and she treasured him for that. She opened her eyes and smiled in pretended surprise at the sight of him sitting quietly in the window chair, his long and elegant legs cased in royal-blue pyjamas, the belt of his dressing gown carefully knotted.

'*Morgen*,' she said lazily, stretching.

'*Morgen*, darling.' He rose, and came to the bed to stand over her. He looked down questioningly. 'I thought that perhaps . . .'

She raised her arms in answer and kicked away the sheets. Moments later it was all over, the stickiness between her thighs the only sign of what had passed between them. No heaving bosom, no sweaty skin, no racing pulse. One of Dieter's many virtues was that when he was moved to passion he performed so quickly that there was never any time for her to become excited, much less frustrated. It made the transaction simple and satisfactory to them both. Now he sat on the edge of the

125

bed, the belt of his gown once again precisely knotted, while they chatted about the coming day.

Marta's day was a full one. A morning session with her *répétiteur,* Herr Kluger, a light lunch in her dressing room at the opera house, afternoon rehearsal for next week's *Figaro,* and then home for an hour with the children. Dinner, and then back to the opera to hear Jeritza in *Der Rosenkavalier.*

'Will you be coming tonight?' she asked her husband.

'Today is Thursday,' he reminded her. 'Cards at the Malakoffs.'

'Oh dear, we mustn't miss our Thursday-night cards,' she said affectionately.

'My only vice,' he said, shrugging.

'You really should come to hear Maria tonight. If she can sing Tosca lying flat on the stage perhaps she'll do the Marschallin standing on her head.'

Dieter clicked his tongue reprovingly. 'Come, come, you know you adore her.'

'Darling, I do, she's magnificent.' Marta's voice was a birdlike trill. 'It's the tricks that irritate me.'

'She says that lying down relaxes her.'

'Perhaps I'll try it in my *Figaro.* I'll sing Susanna hanging by my heels.' She arched her back and kicked her legs up in the air, singing softly, *'Venite, inginocchiatevi, resate fermo lì.* What do you think?'

'I approve.' He pulled her legs down. 'You'll be the sensation of Vienna with your heels in the air and your skirts down around your ears. I can hear the bravas now.'

'I hadn't thought about that part of it,' Marta said, giggling. 'All right, play cards tonight if you must. You'll be missing the Cymrowitz as well.'

'No great loss. I hear she screeches.'

'A spinto really shouldn't sing Octavian anyway.'

'You sing Octavian delightfully. For a spinto.'

'Me? Oh well, that's something else again.'

Dieter looked amused. 'You have plans for this young lady, don't you?'

'I wouldn't waste my time with the bitch.'

'As you wish,' Dieter said politely.

'Oh damn, I suppose I have. I can't sit still, I have to do

something.' With the pretence dropped, her eyes filled with sadness. 'Dieter, I haven't seen him in ten days, ten whole days.'

'Darling, you know how busy Franz gets.'

'Yes, he's terribly, terribly busy. He's never in the studio when I call, and when I send him notes he sends them back with some excuse. That's always the way when he's got something new.'

'You've been through this with him before,' Dieter observed. 'It doesn't last forever, you know.'

'I know, but it's hell while it does. The bastard, why does he do these things to me?'

'It isn't you, he's always been this way.'

'Well, I can't take any more of it. It's time for me to do something.'

'Be careful, *Schatz.*' Her husband put a soothing arm around her. 'You can't keep a man like Franz on a rope, you have to give him some room.'

'That's not all I'm going to give him,' she said in a fierce, tiny voice.

'Marta, please don't do anything crazy. Remember, no matter what else, the man loves you. You know how much he loves you.'

'You love me too, but you don't go chasing after every slut in Vienna.'

'Me? Oh well, to use your own words, that's something else again.' They laughed together, somewhat sadly, and then Dieter said, 'Perhaps I'll come tonight after all. I should hear this screeching marvel.'

'Good, I wish you would. Is your day very busy?'

'Nothing much. A few appointments in town. Just business.'

Marta nodded blankly, as she always did when business was mentioned. She had no idea what sort of business her husband was engaged in, save that it dealt with his family's coal mines in Silesia. She had never bothered to inquire further than that, partly out of indifference and partly because she intuitively knew that her questions would not be welcome. She was content in her ignorance. Whatever it was that Dieter did, he obviously did it superbly. During all of the economic ups and downs of postwar Austria, when a suitcase full of banknotes bought a kilo of potatoes, the von Ulm household had continued in a style that was almost indecent for the times. The villa in Penzing, the

Gräf & Stift and the Opel in the converted carriage house, and the parade of contented tradesmen who were paid each month in gold, not paper, all testified to Dieter's financial wizardry.

'Will you be home for dinner?' she asked him.

'Of course.'

'Try to be early, would you? You should spend more time with the children.'

'Yes, we both should.'

They looked at each other uncomfortably. The problem was not that they ignored their children, but that the twins showed little desire to spend any time with their parents. They were strange, secretive beings who seemed to live only within their twinhood, without the need for any other human contact. Like most twins they were inseparable, but Willi and Mimi had gone far beyond that. They clearly resented the intrusions of the outside world, feeding off each other in a strange symbiosis. By the time they were three years old they had developed a language all their own – a mixture of nursery German, inflected grunts, clicks, and buzzes – which only they could understand and which they used as a shield for their privacy. They were polite to their parents, but reserved, apparently unmoved by the kisses and endearments that most children accept as a currency of exchange. They were slim, short, dark-haired beauties who insisted on being dressed in the same stark blacks and whites, the line of difference between them blurred by identical haircuts and clothing. Now, at the age of four, they were like adorable aliens transplanted from another planet, awesome to their parents and absolutely frightening to their Scottish nanny.

Marta and Dieter looked away from each other, reluctant to speak. It was always that way these days when the children were mentioned. Then Dieter kissed her again, and was gone.

Moments later there was a single knock on the door, and Helga slipped into the room with a muttered greeting. Marta stretched herself out of bed, peeled off her nightgown, and let it drop to the carpet as the girl went to the bathroom to fill the tub. Somehow she always seemed to know the mornings when Dieter would visit, and she discreetly stayed away until he was gone.

I wonder if he pays her to do that, Marta thought. I wouldn't

128

put it past him, he's such a gentleman. Imagine, tipping the maid when you want to *shtup* your wife. Only in Vienna.

While the tub filled with steaming, aromatic water, she stood naked in front of the full-length bathroom mirror as she did every morning, examining her body for imaginary flaws. She drew back her lips and peered closely at her teeth, her nose, the curve of her shoulder, the taper of her waist. Turning sideways, she tucked in her belly and cupped her breasts in her hands, searching for a nonexistent sag, then bent over to run her fingertips over silky-smooth thighs and calves. Finally convinced that she had not aged into a crone overnight, she pinned up her hair, ready for the bath, but she continued to stare into the mirror. What she saw was a well-formed twenty-six-year-old woman, the mother of two children, the Baroness von Ulm, and Die Prinz in the fashion that Vienna used to designate the stars of its musical stage. She was ten years away from the Tirol and a life which she now could only barely remember.

Did I really wash stockings in a bucket? she wondered. Did I really haul slops for the pigs? And did I really get on that train, an innocent, frightened girl with nothing but a voice and a face, and come to Vienna with Dieter and Franz? And Die Simonetti, not to forget her, that hysterical bitch.

The first two years in Vienna had been like going to school all over again, but a school infinitely more complex than the one-room affair in St Anton. There were voice lessons, first with Gustafson, and then after Franz had fought with him over the Garcia system, with Herr Kluger. There were language lessons, first Italian, then French, then English, then of all things German to correct a certain accent as it was delicately put. There were acting lessons with a coach from the Burgtheater, dancing lessons with a retired ballerina, fencing lessons for grace, and even lessons in the simple art of sitting at a table and eating a meal properly. So much to learn, with the ultimate lesson under the tutelage of Professor Franz Harz himself, who nightly presided over the transformation of an untouched peasant girl into a passionate and sophisticated lover. Short, arrogant, stubborn, and abusive, Franz possessed none of the qualities she once had dreamed of in a man, but she had been totally his from the very first day she came under his roof. And

129

she still was, although she was now Die Prinz, and the Baroness von Ulm.

It was Franz who had made her a baroness. After two years of living *chez* Harz, with Franz slipping into her room every night and the hateful Simonetti erupting in tantrum fits of jealousy as regularly as Stromboli, the situation had finally become intolerable. Marriage had seemed the only avenue of escape, and Franz himself had suggested von Ulm.

'Marry the man, it's the perfect answer,' he had said. 'He's a decent sort, and he adores you.'

'How do you know he adores me?'

'You can see it in his eyes. Besides, I had a little chat with him.'

'You didn't!'

'Somebody has to arrange these things. Don't be a fool, Marta, he's got money to burn and it won't make any difference between us. We'll still be able to see each other.'

'Did you arrange that too?'

'Don't ask so many questions. Marry the man, and let's settle down to a normal life, Vienna-style.'

She had fought the idea at first, but in the end she had done as Franz suggested. In those days she had always done as Franz suggested, from the choice of a gown to the choice of a role. And had never regretted it. He was unerring in his choices for her, and he did not fail in his choice of her husband. There was no one in the world with whom she could speak as openly and as intimately as she could with Dieter. He was the perfect partner for her, if not the perfect lover. He was a considerate husband, a trustworthy friend, and in eight years of marriage he had never once reproached her for her continuing romance with the man who had brought them together.

She came out of her bath to the odours of coffee and fresh croissants, her table set next to the window overlooking what, in a different season, would have been a flower garden bordered by luxuriant hedges. On this grey morning, however, the garden was red, raw earth, the hedges were sticks, and only the fir trees gave life to the scene. Dots of rain rattled the window, and she shivered without reason as she sipped her coffee and turned to the morning mail.

She made a pile of the letters concerning future engagements; they would be sent on to Franz for his attention. She made a

130

second pile of requests for photographs, autographs, and charitable appearances; those would be handled by the office of Herr Schalk at the opera house. A third pile was usually for personal mail, but this morning there was only one such letter, and she frowned as she recognized the awkward, untrained handwriting of her mother. She scanned the letter quickly.

. . . not for us, you understand, for Otto and Lili, and only if it is a loan. You know the way Otto is, so much pride. He has a little business now, a tiny store in the village where he sells the skis that he makes in the carpentry shop. Poor soul, he cannot go up on the mountains with his bad knee and he cannot work on the farm, so he puts his hands to work to make a living. How unfair it is that a boy should be crippled for the Fatherland and then be thrown aside like that. If we still had the Emperor he would never allow it. Everyone says that Otto makes the finest skis, but business is bad and there are all the bills to pay. Papa and I try to help from the money that you send us but there is never enough, and you know the way Otto gets when things go bad for him. First a few drinks, then a few bad names, and then the beating starts and poor Lili is in for it again. I try to get Papa to do something about it, but he will not stand between husband and wife.

Little Marta, I cannot tell you how bad that part of it is. Otto does not use his hands the way another man would, he uses a stick, and he marks her terribly. Whenever he does it she is black and blue for a week, and she never tries to stop him. She just stands there with her head down like a cow under the hammer, and takes the blows. But the worst is not the beatings, it is the names that he calls her, filthiness about what she did before they were married. Such words I could never repeat. I don't know, it was different when I was young, but whatever she did she does not deserve to be beaten this way. Not forever, not for the rest of her life. I was hoping that when little Kurt was born things would be better, but nothing changes. Hannes and Kurt grow up like animals, afraid of their father but with no respect for him, and they roam the mountains where he cannot follow them, as wild as wolves. That is what worries me most, the children, and that is why I am writing. Perhaps when Otto is out of debt and does not have to worry things will change for all of them. I dislike so much having to ask, but . . .

*

Marta made a note to stop in at her bankers, shaking her head at the thought of Lili meekly accepting the beatings, and wondering at the same time what sort of life she herself would have had if she had stayed in the mountains. She shuddered at the thought and tried to picture Dieter raising his fist to her. The notion made her smile. And Franz? No, Franz had no need to use his hands. He had other ways of bruising her.

A glance at the ormolu clock near her bed told her she was late. She dressed quickly, with the unconcern of a woman who knows that she is at all times in fashion, but she hesitated over her jewellery. She rejected several rings, then picked up one set with a giant topaz. It was a gift from Franz, and had become a talisman, for she usually wore it only on the nights when she performed. On impulse, she slipped it on, took a last look in the mirror, and hurried down the hall to the nursery.

Peeking in, she saw the twins seated at a low table, their sleek, dark heads bent over a sketching pad. Today they were dressed in matching black trousers and white middy blouses, which meant that tomorrow they would wear ankle-length, full-sleeved robes of a black-and-white domino design. It was trousers one day and robes the next, alternating the male and female impression, and should the pattern be broken the twins were capable of refusing to dress at all and spending the day romping naked in the nursery. The first time this had happened their governess, Mrs McCan, whose concepts of nursery conduct were rooted in the better homes of London, had come close to hysteria while chasing the slim, bare bodies round the room in a vain attempt to clothe them. It had taken all of Marta's charm and tact to calm the Scotswoman, and ever since then the appropriate wardrobes had always been available.

'Good morning, darlings, good morning.'

'Good morning, Mama.' Two heads turned and two voices piped together as Marta swept into the room on a cloud of kisses, bending over to peck and to hug the twins, who suffered the caresses with polite smiles. One of them said, 'You look very pretty, Mama,' and the other nodded agreement.

'Thank you, darlings, but I can't stay long, just time enough for a kiss, and then I must trot away fast as a pony to do you-know-what.'

'Dress up in funny clothes,' said Willi, and Mimi added, 'And sing silly songs to silly people.' It was an old joke between them.

'Yes, that's exactly what I must do. Good morning, Mrs McCan.'

'Good morning, madam,' said the nanny. Her German was precise, but the burr of her accent made it sound comical. She was a short and bony woman whose face had long ago collapsed into a pudding of disappointment. She was clearing away the remains of a nursery breakfast.

'And did we have a happy breakfast?' Marta asked meaningfully. She said it in English.

Mrs McCan replied in the same language, 'That we did not, madam. Most of it left on the plates as usual. I don't know how these children stay alive, eating the way they do.'

'Darlings, how bad of you,' Marta told the twins. 'You know you must finish.'

Willi made a deep sound in his throat that sounded like *threeeeep,* followed by two clicks. Mimi nodded, and made a buzzing noise in her nose.

'Do stop that,' said Marta. 'You know how it bothers me.'

'You speak English to her,' Mimi pointed out, 'and we don't understand.'

'That's quite different. What did you say?'

'It was oatmeal again, and it was lumpy.'

'But we drank all the chocolate,' said Willi.

'Oh dear, I see.' Hesitantly, she said, 'Mrs McCan, don't you think they might have something lighter for breakfast? A piece of fruit or a croissant?'

The nanny's sniff was audible. 'No child was ever hurt by a bowl of hot oaties in the morning. I must say, madam, that I don't hold with spoiling children with fancy fruits and such.'

'There's nothing terribly exotic about a pear,' said Marta, who had never seen such a thing until she was a grown woman. 'Please see that they have something light and nourishing at lunchtime. An omelette, perhaps.'

'Cook is planning liver.'

'An omelette,' Marta said firmly.

Willi made the threeping noise again, and Mimi laughed.

'Children, stop,' Marta said absently. She crouched down between them to look at the sketch blocks. 'And what have we been drawing?'

'A cat,' said Mimi, holding up a sheet of paper for examination.

'Indeed, it is, and a very fine tabby. Willi, where is yours?'

'That *is* mine. We do it together.'

'Oh, you take turns. How nice.'

'No, not turns,' said Mimi. 'Like this.'

She put the paper on the table and picked up a pencil with her left hand. Willi, sitting beside her, covered her left hand with his right so that they both were grasping the pencil. He made the buzzing noise in his nose, and with no apparent effort the pencil began to move over the paper, skimming lightly and touching down to fill in the black of the cat's button nose, then moving on to draw the curlicues of sprouting whiskers. The two little heads bent over the paper in deep and silent concentration, but the hands on the pencil moved as one.

Marta looked up at Mrs McCan, and the nanny nodded grimly. 'Aye, they've been doing it that way for some time now.'

'How . . . how very clever,' Marta said faintly.

'As clever as the devil, some would say.'

'Yes . . . well.' She looked down again. The joined hands now were sketching the curve of a tail. Her head felt light, but she forced her voice to sound gay. 'I must be off now, darlings. Time for me to put on my funny clothes and sing my silly songs.'

Intent on what they were doing, the twins did not respond. She waited a moment, then kissed the tops of their heads and left the nursery quickly.

Chapter Ten

After it was all over Franz knew that he should have seen it coming. What happened at the Staatsopera that night contained all the dramatic ingredients that Vienna loved both onstage and off. There was a fiasco and a triumph, a lover lost and a lover regained, high theatrics, intrigue, beautiful music, and laughter laced with tears. It was Viennese kitsch at its best and its worst, and a seasoned observer of the musical scene should have been able to write the script for the evening in advance. It would have made a naughty operetta, Franz decided later, and he would have called it *The Topaz*.

THE TOPAZ

Act One; Scene One

The time: *The morning of 8 November 1925.*
The place: *The Café Opern on the Ringstrasse.*

The setting: The Opern Café is one of Franz Harz's three residences, but his only real home. His legal residence is a narrow building on the Schönlaterngasse, but everyone knows that only his estranged wife, La Simonetti, lives there in solitary bitterness. His studio apartment in the Heinrichshof, directly across from the operà house, has a more proper claim as his residence, but in truth it is nothing more than a place to sleep. The third residence, and his only true home, is the Opern Café across the Ringstrasse from the studio and nestled comfortably close to the Renaissance columns and arcades of the Staatsopera. The café is both his living room and his business office. He entertains there, closes deals there, and answers his mail on café stationery. He is there every morning from ten o'clock on, a cup of *grosser Brauner* in front of him, conducting his affairs and greeting his friends in the unhurried atmosphere of the Vienna coffeehouse.

This morning he sits deep in conversation with Franz Schalk, director of the Staatsopera. Schalk is a veteran of the house on the Opernstrasse. He was brought there as *Kapellmeister* by the legendary Gustav Mahler, and since that day he has been witness to all the dramatic upheavals, the plots and the counterplots, which have made the Vienna Opera the most controversial musical theatre in Europe. He saw the genius of Mahler spat upon by mediocrities, and the genius himself sent packing into exile. He lived through the short reign of the aristocratic Felix von Weingartner, and saw the city turn against him as well. Along with all the other musicians in the house he suffered under the money-grubbing policies of Hans Gregor, the first of the businessmen directors. For five years, he himself shared the directorship with Richard Strauss until Vienna once again displayed its mediocrity by ousting the greatest composer of the times. Now he rules alone, a short, thin man with a beard and a pince-nez, who looks more like a university professor than a musician. The Staatsopera is his life, and anyone who threatens the stability of the company is his enemy. Now he has such an enemy in mind and he bangs angrily on the table with his fist. Coffee cups bounce.

SCHALK: I won't have it, Franz. I can't let people use my opera house to settle their personal feuds. Marta Prinz is going around saying the most terrible things about the Cymrowitz girl.

FRANZ: What can she possibly say? Alma is just a child, a talented lovely child. How can one criticize a child?

SCHALK: If she's a child, my friend, then you've been sleeping with children. Do you know what happens to people who sleep with children? They get pissed on, that's what, and you're right in the line of fire.

FRANZ: Me? Why me?

SCHALK: Because it's all your fault. You manage them both and you sleep with them both. You should be able to control them both.

FRANZ: Alma isn't giving you any trouble, it's just Marta up to her usual tricks. What's she been saying?

SCHALK: All sorts of nonsense. That the girl is nothing more than a talented amateur, that she'll never be a professional, that she'll crack the first time the crowd gets on to her. (*He hesitates.*) And then there's her upper register. That part isn't nonsense, I'm afraid.

FRANZ: A matter of training, nothing more. It will come in time.

SCHALK: Franz, she's only secure to a high A, maybe a B-flat. After that . . . ?

FRANZ: All in good time. As I said, she's only a child.

SCHALK: I wish you'd stop using that word. You make her sound like a schoolgirl in a blue uniform. She's a grown woman with a shaky tessitura, and I wish I'd never signed her.

136

FRANZ: We made an agreement; one hand washes the other. I took care of your little friend in Prague, didn't I?

SCHALK: I know, I know, we all have these little pots to boil, but this one is boiling over. I'm holding you responsible, Franz. Either you get rid of your new girlfriend, or you get the old one to shut her mouth. She's upsetting the company, and I won't have it.

FRANZ: Look, you can count on it, I'll have a talk with her. Christ, but she gives me a headache. (*He rubs his forehead and grimaces.*) She's too much of a professional to act this way.

SCHALK: I wish you would send the other one packing. That would solve everything. (*He gets up to leave.*)

FRANZ: Shit, that bastard de la Torre is looking at us. As soon as you leave he'll be over here twisting my ear. He wants me to get him a Rodolfo.

SCHALK: Insane. The man has a fine, natural leggiero voice, but he doesn't have the timbre for a dramatic tenor.

FRANZ: You try telling him that. He wants to sing *Bohème*.

SCHALK: Von Bülow was right, tenors are a disease. These singers are our cross to bear.

FRANZ: True, but we couldn't live without them.

SCHALK: I know, but wouldn't it be wonderful? Imagine, Franz, an opera house without singers. What heaven that would be. (*Schalk exits. He is barely out the door when the Spanish tenor Manuel de la Torre slips into his seat. At the same time a waiter approaches the table with a note in his hand.*)

MANUEL: Did you speak to the director? Did you ask him?

FRANZ: Please, Manuel, I think I'm getting a headache.

MANUEL: But you promised you'd speak to him.

WAITER: (*He hands Franz the note.*) A messenger is waiting outside for an answer.

FRANZ: Excuse me, Manuel. (*Franz unfolds the note, and reads it. As he does, Alma's disembodied voice is heard.*)

ALMA'S VOICE: I'm shaking all over. Die Prinz has invited me to lunch in her dressing room. She says that she wants to talk to me about my Octavian, but who knows? What do I do? Much love, Alma.

FRANZ: Sweet Jesus, what is that woman up to now?

MANUEL: (*Trying to peek at the note*) Trouble?

FRANZ: Is there anything else these days? (*He scribbles on the bottom of the note, and as he does his disembodied voice is heard.*)

FRANZ'S VOICE: You go, you eat, you act polite, and you listen carefully. You might just learn something from this great artist. She's sung more Octavians than you've eaten *Sachertorten*, and that's going some. Meet me in the green-room at two and tell me all about it. Franz.

FRANZ: (*He hands the note to the waiter and turns back to Manuel.*) Listen, Manuel *mio*, listen carefully. I'm talking to you not as your manager, not just a friend, but like an *aficionado*, someone who adores to hear you sing. When you talk this way I have to think, What is this man doing to himself? Why is he throwing away God's natural gift? I think of your Almaviva, your Nemorino, your Don Ottavio . . . gems, every one of them. I think of your Fenton, the way you sing it so soft like a flower, tiny petals opening up one by one. When I hear you sing Fenton, I cry. The truth. Me, Franz Harz, I cry. You have the exquisite tones of a tenore leggiero, and this you want to throw away . . .

MANUEL: Not throw away, just extend myself a little further.

FRANZ: Throw away. You think you can play with your voice the way a child plays with a whistle? Sure, you want to sing Rodolfo, you want to sing Alfredo, you want to sing Des Grieux . . . who doesn't? But what's going to happen to your voice if you do this? You push a voice on one end and something has to give on the other . . . Oh, Christ and all the holy angels, not now.

MANUEL: What? What have I done?

FRANZ: No, not you. (*His distress is caused by the sight of the von Ulm chauffeur in royal-blue livery threading his way between the tables, a brown paper bag under one arm and an envelope in his hand.*) I'm going to have to change my café – they find me too easily here. Good morning, Felix.

FELIX: (*Touching his cap and handing over the envelope*) Good morning, *mein Herr*. I was told to wait for an answer.

FRANZ: Yes, yes, they all want answers. (*Franz opens the envelope and reads the note, shading it from Manuel's curious eyes. As he reads it we hear Marta's disembodied voice.*)

MARTA'S VOICE: My darling, it has been ten long days. How much longer will you continue to avoid me? I will be at the house tonight to hear Jeritza. Will you meet me after the performance, the usual place at the bottom of the grand staircase? I promise you, darling, no tears, no angry words, just the love for you that never dies. Your own, Marta. (*Franz looks away. The scene is frozen in tableau, and we hear Franz's disembodied voice.*)

FRANZ'S VOICE: No tears, no angry words, which means that she knows. Damn this town for a gossiping sewer. And if I meet her, what happens? Plenty of tears, plenty of angry words, and a flaming row before the night is over. No, I won't put myself through that again. Besides, I promised Alma a late supper. Oh, Christ, my poor head. (*The tableau breaks, and Franz writes on the back of the note.*) My darling, impossible to meet you tonight; pressing business prevents it. Patience, we will be together soon. As always, Franz.

FRANZ: (*He returns the note to Felix.*) The baroness is entertaining at lunch today?

FELIX: Yes, *mein Herr,* two ladies. (*He taps the parcel under his arm.*) I bought the lunch myself.

FRANZ: (*Aside*) Two ladies? Damn it, who's the other one? (*To Felix*) What did you get, and where did you get it?

FELIX: Black Forest ham, breast of capon, Liptauer cheese, bread and wine, all from Sacher. Oh yes, and *Cremeschnitten.*

FRANZ: The *Cremeschnitten* from Sacher, too?

FELIX: (*He manages to look both pompous and horrified.*) Certainly not, *mein Herr.* From Demel, of course.

FRANZ: Of course. (*Felix exits, and Franz lets the smile slide from his face. Manuel notices, and his own lips curve gleefully.*)

MANUEL: So, Die Prinz found out about the new one, did she?

FRANZ: Who mentioned any names?

MANUEL: Who has to?

FRANZ: God damn this town.

MANUEL: (*Laughing*) Forget it, Vienna is full of beautiful women. Getting back to the *Bohème,* Franz, it's really just a matter of voice projection. After all, the range is the same—

FRANZ: (*Snarling*) Forget *Bohème,* you've got as much chance of singing Rodolfo as I have of screwing Dietrich. Your voice isn't up to it. You're a chicken tenor, a *tenore bianco,* and that's all there is to it.

MANUEL: Son of a bitch, that's nice and blunt. Anyway, it's better than the other shit you were handing me. (*He looks downcast, but then he brightens.*) You mean you haven't?

140

FRANZ: What?

MANUEL: Screwed Dietrich.

FRANZ: Manuel, my head is splitting. Be quiet for a while and let me think.

CURTAIN

Act One; Scene Two

The time: *Moments later.*
The place: *The studio of Alois Kluger, Marta's singing coach.*

The setting: Kluger's studio is in the Heinrichschof, directly across from the opera house. It is one long garretlike room. Marta stands at the window looking out over the rainswept Ringstrasse. Kluger sits at the piano making pencil markings on a score. The walls of the studio are lined with books, and there is a merry fire in the grate.

There is a knock at the door, and Felix enters. He gives Marta Franz's answer. She reads it, nodding as if she had expected nothing else, and tosses the paper into the fire.

MARTA: Take the food to my dressing room and have the table set for three. Then go and find Joseph Schostal for me. He'll be under the arcade in this rain, or if he isn't there, try the Café Walch. Tell him I must see him at once, something most important. Have him wait for me in the dressing room.

FELIX: Yes, baroness. (*Felix exits. Kluger, at the piano, strikes a chord, and then another as a suggestion that there is work to be done, but Marta ignores the hint and returns to look out the window.*)

MARTA: These little games we play. The luncheon, the note to Franz, his transparent excuse . . . all moves in a game we've played so many times before. Like two little windup toys, we have to play the game over and over. Little toy Franz has to snatch at the sugarplums, and little toy Marta has to slap his wrist every time. All the moves, formalized and inevitable in a game that I win every time.

(*She sighs.*)

So far, but the last move will always be his. Time will take care of that. Time works for men, not for women. Time lets us win the battles, but they always win the wars. The time will come, and then the game will be over . . . the first wrinkle, the first grey hair, the first extra pinch of flesh, and Franz will have won his war. But until then we keep on playing the game, and I wish I could stop it right now. How grand it would be to stop it in real life the way the Marschallin does it on the stage, getting up in the dead of night to stop all the clocks, stopping all of our time that way.

(*She sings.*)
Manchmal steh'ich auf mitten in der Nacht, und lass die Uhren alle, alle stehn.
(*Kluger plays the last few notes of the Marschallin's music along with her, and she turns to face him, trying to smile.*)

KLUGER: Were you thinking of singing the Marschallin tonight? Is there something the matter with Madam Jeritza?

MARTA: No, no. I was just thinking how nice it would be.

KLUGER: To stop all the clocks?

MARTA: Every one.

KLUGER: What a sad thought for a beautiful young woman.

MARTA: No one stays young forever, Alois. Except on the stage.

KLUGER: Yes, on the stage the Marschallin is always thirty-two and Octavian is always seventeen.

MARTA: And she always loses him to Sophie. That never changes either.

KLUGER: Nor should it. On the stage we must live in an orderly world.

MARTA: There's Vienna for you. Order on the stage and chaos in the streets.

KLUGER: Better than the other way around. (*He closes the score on the rack.*) You don't want to continue, do you?

MARTA: I don't much feel like a young and gay Susanna.

KLUGER: Then we'll stop. You really don't need coaching in the part. How many Susannas have you done?

MARTA: Twenty-six. One for every year of my life.

KLUGER: Oh dear, that sounds terribly depressing. A cup of tea will put a stop to that.

MARTA: (*Laughing*) Just like my mother, a good cup of tea fixes everything. And you know, most of the time she was right.

KLUGER: A little homesick, perhaps?

MARTA: (*She shakes her head, then changes her mind.*)
Perhaps, I don't know. Just this morning I was thinking how dreadful it would have been if I had stayed in the Tirol, but now I'm not so sure. It was a simple life there, and a good one. There were people I could talk to.

KLUGER: You have people here.

MARTA: Forgive me, Alois, I didn't mean you, but it's not the same. Your own kind, you know? There was a brother once . . . if I could talk to him today . . . (*Her voice trails off. Then, in a different tone:*) She's beautiful, isn't she?

KLUGER: Alma Cymrowitz? Well, a highly attractive young lady.

MARTA: And only nineteen years old.

KLUGER: But not forever.

MARTA: No, there's that. I'm giving her lunch today, telling her all my tricks.

KLUGER: Very magnanimous of you.

MARTA: One of the lessons I first learned in Vienna. Act like a lady even if it hurts. Tell me the truth, what do you think of her voice?

KLUGER: (*After a pause*) It's a clean, serviceable voice. Plenty of power and expressing in the lower notes, more than enough, but it has no top. No C at all, no B-natural, not even a good B-flat. The A is firm, but the B-flat has to be scooped. Actually, it's very sad, like a lovely Greek statue with the head knocked off.

MARTA: Can you do anything about it?

KLUGER: Franz seems to think so, but . . . forgive me . . . Franz isn't thinking with his head these days.

MARTA: Yes, we both know what he's using instead of his brain.

KLUGER: He should know better. How do you train a voice for a note that was never there, and never will be?

MARTA: You're right, it's sad.

KLUGER: So, have I answered your question? You have nothing to fear from her vocally.

MARTA: No, not vocally. I was never really concerned about that part of it.

KLUGER: It's the only part where my advice is any good. I coach voices, not hearts. The rest you have to take care of yourself.

MARTA: (*Looking at the clock*) Yes, and it's time for me to do just that.

KLUGER: Your luncheon, of course. Forgive an old man's curiosity, but I'm shameless. You told Felix to set the table for three?

MARTA: (*She is suddenly busy collecting purse, gloves, and coat. She does not look at him.*) Yes, I've invited Kitty Lehr as well.

KLUGER: (*Surprised*) The one who is singing Marianne tonight?

MARTA: The same. (*A pause. She finally looks at him.*) She's also understudy for the Cymrowitz.

KLUGER: The Octavian and the understudy, too. Very generous, indeed. And you sent your man to get Josef Scholstal?

(*He waits for her to say something, but she only stares at him defiantly. He chuckles, and shakes his head, laughing.*) Always the lady? Even when it hurts?

(*His laughter grows into a roar as she exits with the* CURTAIN.)

Act Two; Scene One

The time: *Moments later.*
The place: *Outside Kluger's studio.*

The setting: Marta comes out of the building. It is raining heavily, and the Ringstrasse looks more like a river than a boulevard. She looks around helplessly, wondering how she will cross, but the problem is quickly solved. In the musical city of Vienna, where cabdrivers come to blows over coloraturas and barbers know *Lohengrin* backward, the face of a prima donna is as familiar as the tower of Stephansturm. As soon as she puts one hesitant foot onto the pavement she is recognized by the commissionaire standing under the awning in front of the Café Heinrichshof, who covers her at once with his umbrella. Two men passing by take in the situation and volunteer their services. They lock hands to form a seat for Marta, who rests there gracefully, her own hands lightly touching their shoulders. Three more men are recruited from the café to run out onto the boulevard and stop traffic, and Marta is whisked across the Ringstrasse while the orchestra plays Von Suppé's *Light Cavalry Overture.* There she is deposited under the arcade of the opera

145

house, safe and dry and laughing. The two men who have carried her watch her go inside.

FIRST MAN: (*Looking at his right hand*) By God, I'll never wash this again.

SECOND MAN: (*Looking at his left*) I'm thinking of cutting mine off and having it bronzed.

CURTAIN

Act Two; Scene Two

The time: *Moments later.*
The place: *Marta's dressing room.*

The setting: It is a small but lavishly furnished room with the conventional screens, chairs, and sofas. A makeup table runs along one wall, and against the other is an oval table set for a meal. Helga, the dresser, fusses at the closet with a costume, while Felix, in a white jacket now, attends the table. Josef Schostal stands waiting patiently in a corner. The *chef du claque* of the Vienna Opera is a large, bulky man. He has not removed his overcoat, which is dripping with rain, nor has he presumed to seat himself. Marta enters, still laughing.

MARTA: Oh, what a ride that was. Why, Herr Schostal, just look at you. You should have made yourself comfortable.

SCHOSTAL: Thank you, baroness, but I think I know my place in the scheme of things.

MARTA: Nonsense, you are much too modest. Singers and conductors come and go, but where would we all be without the claque? Felix, take his coat at once. Helga, a chair and some wine. (*Schostal allows his coat to be removed and settles heavily into a chair, accepting a glass of wine. Marta sits opposite him, perched on the edge of her seat.*)

SCHOSTAL: Very kind, thank you, very kind. Unfortunately, too many artists think of the claque as nothing but a bunch of paid applauders.

146

MARTA: (*Hotly*) Then those are ignorant people. It's the claque that makes the opera grand.

SCHOSTAL: Yes, we have our uses. The audience is an ignorant beast that never knows when to show appreciation. It is the task of the claque to correct such ignorance.

MARTA: And you do, you do. Look what you did for my *Aida* last week.

SCHOSTAL: Indeed. God only knows why Verdi left no room for applause after the Nile aria, but a voice such as yours must be properly complimented. Believe me, it isn't easy applauding directly into the music, but sometimes, it has to be done. The timing must be perfect – it has to strike like lightning or the effect is lost.

MARTA: You made the evening for me, but the outsiders wouldn't know that.

SCHOSTAL: Well, there you are. I sometimes think it would be better if the audience were forbidden to applaud. Let them pay their way in and enjoy the music, but leave the applause to the claque. How many times have you heard ignorant people applaud Don José after he sings '*La fleur que tu m'avais jetée?*' And why? Because he ends on a high B, and so it seems like the time to clap. We in the claque, of course, know that he still must sing '*Carmen, je t'aime,*' and so we hold back.

MARTA: The ignorance of audiences today is appalling.

SCHOSTAL: Which is why the artist must depend on the claque. I think I may safely say that under my direction our claque has become a precise instrument of musical timing and psychological skill that brings pace, warmth, and a sense of well-being to every performance.

(*He pauses.*)
Unfortunately, the occupation is not well paid.

MARTA: (*Snapping her fingers*) Felix, Helga, outside.

(*They exit, and Marta leans close to Schostal.*)
A propos of that, I have a small favour that needs to be done.

SCHOSTAL: Command me, diva.

(*Their heads come closer. Orchestral music swells in the background, a waltz from Der Rosenkavalier that masks their conversation. Schostal nods his understanding.*)

MARTA: Then you'll do it?

SCHOSTAL: Remember that I am known as a man of principles.

MARTA: I wouldn't dream of trying to tempt you. (*She hands him a wad of banknotes.*)

SCHOSTAL: The whole world knows that Josef Schostal cannot be paid to applaud a bad singer, and he cannot be paid to hiss at a good one. (*He slips the money into his pocket.*) But that's as far as my principles go.

CURTAIN

Act Two; Scene Three

The time: *Two hours later.*
The place: *The greenroom of the Vienna Opera.*

The setting: A large room used as a salon, for receptions and for minor auditions. Franz and Alma are discovered embracing next to the piano.

ALMA: (*Kissing him*) More, more.

FRANZ: (*He gently pushes her away, then wipes his lips.*) You've been eating Liptauer cheese. Enough with the kisses, tell me about the lunch.

ALMA: (*Excitedly*) It was nothing like what I expected. She was charming, absolutely charming.

FRANZ: Those charm lessons cost me a fortune. She's plotting something, but I'll be damned if I can see it.

ALMA: At first I didn't know what to think. I was afraid she was going to bite my head off, you know, because of us, but I felt pretty safe with Kitty there.

FRANZ: That's another thing I don't understand. What the hell does she want with Kitty Lehr?

ALMA: You're being too hard on her. She wanted to give us some tips about playing Octavian, that's all. I like her, Franz, she was very kind.

FRANZ: Marta gives away nothing for free, but I'm glad to see that the charm lessons weren't wasted.

ALMA: It wasn't that way at all, she was just trying to be helpful. After a while it was fun, like a picnic. The food was delicious, everything from Sacher.

FRANZ: The pastry was from Demel. Tell me what you talked about. Tell me everything exactly.

ALMA: Well, let's see now. First we talked about how difficult it is to play Octavian. I mean, a woman playing the part of a man who plays the part of a woman. Marta said that —

FRANZ: Marta? Is it Marta now?

ALMA: She said to call her that. She said that first you have to learn how to walk and hold yourself like a man. The trouble comes when you put on the woman's clothes and you're tempted to act like yourself, just be a woman. Marta says you must never do that. She says you must keep on thinking like a man, but a man who is wearing skirts. Otherwise the aspect of the role is destroyed.

FRANZ: (*Doubtfully*) She's right, of course, but is that all you talked about? Skirts and trousers?

ALMA: Oh no, there were lots of other things, little things like the tempo and the beat. (*Pause*) Like in the finale when the orchestra plays in three-four? Sophie and Octavian are also singing in three-four, but the Marschallin is singing in four-four at the same time. It can drive you crazy unless the conductor takes the beat in one, so do you know what Marta does?

FRANZ: Yes, she closes her eyes. I taught her to do that.

ALMA: You did? I thought it was her idea. Anyway, she says that's one time when you don't want to see the beat, so she closes her eyes as if she's overcome with passion. She says it's simpler that way, but the conductors don't like you to do it. Did you really teach her that?

FRANZ: I did, and now that she's told you every bitch in Vienna is going to sing the last act blindfolded. What else did you talk about?

ALMA: Just things like that. Really, we didn't talk about anything personal. At least, I didn't. It was different with Kitty.

FRANZ: (*Pouncing*) What about Kitty?

ALMA: Well, you know, she's going nowhere in all these *comprimario* roles. A maid here, a duenna there, an orphan girl. Marta said she would try to get her something better.

FRANZ: She did, did she? And what did she want in return?

ALMA: Really, Franz, that isn't fair.

FRANZ: What else did they talk about?

ALMA: I really couldn't say. I had to leave then.

FRANZ: Leave? You mean you left them alone?

ALMA: Don't snap at me, I had to. You told me to meet you here at two, so I just excused myself and slipped away. I don't know what they talked about after I left. (*Franz grimaces, and touches his temples gingerly.*) What is it, did I do something wrong?

FRANZ: No, of course not. It's just that I have the feeling that I'm missing something. It's this damn headache of mine. I can't think straight. (*He takes her arm and they walk to the door together. He kisses her lightly.*)

ALMA: She's a lovely lady, you know. What bastards you men can be.

FRANZ: What's that supposed to mean?

ALMA: You really could be nicer to her.

FRANZ: You too? My God, those charm le sons were worth every penny.
(*They exit with the CURTAIN.*)

Act Two; Scene Four

The time: *A few minutes later.*
The place: *The stage and the wings of the Vienna Opera.*

The setting: Franz stands in the gloom of the OP wing watching as an assistant conductor, Herr Molden, puts the cast through the rehearsal of *Figaro*. The singers are all veterans who clearly consider this a formality. They are working on the first act with Marta, as Susanna, walking through the scene with Cherubino. She sings her lines mezzo voce, barely singing at all. She laughs and she postures, bending her lithe body gracefully, and even in rehearsal clothes she looks delightful.

SUSANNA: (*Singing*) *Povero Cherubin, siete voi pazzo?*

FRANZ: (*As if in response*) No, he isn't crazy, my sweet, but you're beginning to drive me nuts. Damn it, don't you see that you're st ll the only one who can move me right down to the core? If you would only stop hounding me you could have me forever.

CHERUBINO: (*Singing*) . . . *ogni donna mi fa palpitar...*

FRANZ: (*As if in response*) Me too, kid. Every woman makes my heart beat faster, and that's how I got into this mess.

151

CHERUBINO: (*Singing*) . . . *E se non ho chi m'oda, parlo d'amor con me.*

FRANZ: I've often wondered if that means what it sounds like. Well, I haven't got that desperate yet.

(*Onstage the Cherubino has run behind the chair to hide from the arrival of the Count. The chair, a temporary prop, is much too small, and Cherubino's head sticks out over the top. Marta, as Susanna, sees this and shoves the head down, leaning on it with her elbow. She lounges against the chair that way with a look of assumed innocence. The Count, making his entrance, breaks into laughter at the sight, and the rest of the company follows. Molden, at the harpsichord, smiles. He takes his fingers from the keyboard.*)

MOLDEN: Very well, baroness, you've made your point. We'll need a larger chair. Shall we continue? From the letter D, please.

COUNT: *Susanna, tu mi sembri* . . .

(*As the music begins again, Schalk appears in the wings next to Franz. He nods contentedly towards the stage.*)

SCHALK: Look how relaxed she is. Quite a difference from the past few weeks. I have you to thank for that.

FRANZ: I'll take the thanks in cash. What are you thanking me for?

SCHALK: You said you would talk to her, and you obviously did. Everyone has heard about her luncheon with the Cymrowitz.

FRANZ: Damn this town.

SCHALK: The lunch was a nice touch.

FRANZ: I'm a specialist in nice touches, but I had nothing to do with that one. To tell you the truth I don't know what the hell is going on around here any more. Why is she singing mezzo voce?

SCHALK: It's the rain. She's afraid of a sore throat and she doesn't want to push her voice.

FRANZ: That's wise. (*Franz's eyes are on the stage watching Marta parry the advances of the Count. Her eyes, in turn, sweep stage right and meet with his. She gives him a dazzling smile. He turns away, looking uncomfortable. Schalk has noticed the exchange.*)

SCHALK: Franz, how about a word of advice from an old friend?

FRANZ: How about minding your own business?

SCHALK: This company is my business.

FRANZ: What are you complaining about now? You wanted peace, and you got it.

SCHALK: But for how long? Look, you've already plucked this Polish daisy, so why keep it up? You're not in love with her, are you?

FRANZ: Don't be absurd.

SCHALK: Then get rid of her. (*He nods towards the stage.*) They don't come any better than that lady out there.

FRANZ: You think I don't know that?

SCHALK: You don't act like it.

FRANZ: (*In a low, controlled roar*) That's because nobody tells me what to do. A lot of people have tried, but it doesn't work. I run my own life.

SCHALK: Yes, and you're not doing very well at it, are you?

FRANZ: Probably not, but it's the best I can do. (*He turns to leave.*) I'm getting out of here before you all drive me crazy.

COUNT: (*Singing*) Ah, no Susanna . . . *tu ben sai quanto io t'amo* . . .

FRANZ: (*Shouting over his shoulder*) You too? Well, I wish you luck. As far as I'm concerned, if you want her that bad you can have her. (*He rushes out as the* CURTAIN *falls.*)

Act Three; Scene One

The time: *The evening of the same day.*
The place: *The lobby of the Vienna Opera, the foot of the grand staircase.*

The setting: It is just before curtain time, and the audience is filing into the hall. The end of the Empire has transformed the opera audience. The knowledgeable music lovers – the students, the musicians, the claque – still inhabit the upper, cheaper regions, and the traditional middle classes have retained their middle-level boxes, but the orchestra seats now are occupied by the swindlers and the speculators, the easy-money boys, and the black marketeers. They know a few catch phrases and some of the current favourites, but few can tell *Aida* from *Rigoletto* without a programme. When the curtain is up they tend to gather in groups to gossip, play cards, drink beer, wolf down sausages, and scan the house with opera glasses in search of celebrities.

Franz and Dieter stand at the bottom of the staircase, and the crowd flows around them. They are dressed for the evening, and finishing the last of their cigars. They see each other and come together, nodding gravely.

DIETER: I was hoping to run into you. I think we have something to say to each other.

FRANZ: Please don't start with me, Dieter. There's nothing I can say about the situation at the moment.

DIETER: I'm disappointed with you, my friend. I gave you my most precious possession. The least you could do is treat my gift with respect.

154

FRANZ: Your gift? You old hypocrite, she was mine long before she was yours to give.

DIETER: (*With dignity*) That may be true, but I'm still her husband, and that counts for something, even in Vienna.

FRANZ: It gives you the right to suffer silently, and that's all.

DIETER: When I suffer it isn't because of anything that you and Marta do. I suffer only when she is unhappy.

FRANZ: How noble.

DIETER: It goes with the title. Look, old man, let's talk frankly. Can't you get rid of your little friend?

FRANZ: Those things aren't done so easily.

DIETER: Of course they are, it's done every day. If you don't have the stomach for it, I'll do it for you.

FRANZ: (*Laughing*) I'd like to see that. You're a good fellow, Dieter, but you'd be out of your depth. It's a job for a sinner, not a saint. Besides, I haven't said that I want to be rid of her.

DIETER: I hope you do. You're making a wonderful woman perfectly miserable. (*Marta comes up to them on that line, having worked her way through the crowd. She smiles with genuine warmth, kisses Dieter's cheek, and extends her hand to Franz. At the same time two pages start to circulate through the lobby, one of them sounding a gong.*)

MARTA: My two favourite men. You both look eminently presentable.

FRANZ: And you . . . lovelier than ever. (*Franz bends to sketch a kiss over her hand, and freezes in that position when he sees that she is wearing the topaz ring. He straightens up and looks at her questioningly.*)

155

MARTA: (*Ignoring his look*) I've just come from Maria's dressing room. It's going to be a glorious evening.

FIRST PAGE: (*Sounding the gong*) Curtain time, please . . .

SECOND PAGE: The management wishes to announce that . . .

FRANZ: That ring?

MARTA: Do you like it? Oh, of course, you gave it to me. I thought it might go well tonight.

FRANZ: But you never wear it except –

FIRST PAGE: Curtain, please, curtain . . .

SECOND PAGE: . . . the part of Marianne will be sung by . . .

DIETER: I think we should get to our seats.

MARTA: (*Taking his arm*) Of course, darling. Coming up, Franz?

FRANZ: What the hell is going on here?

MARTA: (*Sweetly*) What the hell do you think, my love?

FIRST PAGE: Curtain, curtain . . . (*Marta and Dieter turn to ascend the staircase, leaving Franz staring after them.*)

SECOND PAGE: . . . tonight by Fraülein Paula Spengle . . .

FRANZ: (*To himself*) But she never wears it except when she's going to sing.

SECOND PAGE: (*Passing close by*) The management announces that due to the indisposition of Fraülein Kitty Lehr the part of Marianne will be sung tonight by Fraülein Paula Spengle. The management . . .

(*Franz stands motionless, as if struck. The lobby empties quickly, and now he is alone there with the two pages. We hear a wave*

156

of applause from the hall as Schalk, the conductor, takes his place, and then the statement of the French horn announcing the first theme of the orchestral introduction. As the introduction continues, Franz slowly lowers himself until he is sitting on the steps, a bewildered look on his face. The pages stare at him curiously.

FRANZ: (*Muttering to himself with the music in the background. He holds up a finger as he makes each point.*) She has lunch with Alma and charms her out of her boots. That's one. She sings mezzo voce this afternoon because she doesn't want to strain her voice. That's two. She's wearing the topaz ring. That's three. For some reason Kitty isn't singing tonight, which means that there's no understudy for Alma. That's four.

(*The witty and romantic introduction draws to its close, a parody of an impassioned climax. There is a moment of silence as the curtain goes up, and then Alma's voice is heard in the lobby as she sings Octavian's opening lines.*)

OCTAVIAN: *Wie du warst! Wie du bist! Das weiss niemand, das ahnt keiner!*

JERITZA as the MARSCHALLIN: *Beklagt Er sich über das, Quinquin? Möcht' Er, dass viele das wüssten?*

OCTAVIAN: *Engel! Nein! Selig bin ich . . .*

(*Alma's voice falters.*) *. . . was heisst das Du?*

(*She falters again, badly this time, Franz's head is up and he is listening intently when the explosion comes in a series of catcalls by booming voices.*)

FIRST VOICE: What kind of singing do you call that?

SECOND VOICE: Assassin, you're murdering the music.

THIRD VOICE: Is that a voice or a steam whistle?

FOURTH VOICE: Not good enough for Vienna, lady.

FIFTH VOICE: *Raus, raus,* get off the stage. (*Alma continues to sing shakily, but she is drowned out by a barrage of jeers, hoots, and whistles.*)

MANY VOICES: Back to Warsaw! Off the stage! That's no voice! An insult to Strauss! An insult to Vienna! Get her off!

FRANZ: The bitch, the merciless bitch. (*He jumps to his feet and rushes up the grand staircase.*)

Act Three; Scene Two

The time: *Immediately after.*
The place: *The main hall of the Vienna Opera House, showing the stage and a slice of the house from top to bottom with two first-tier boxes in the foreground. Dieter and Marta occupy one box. The second is empty.*

The setting: The house is in an uproar, with the claque, led by Josef Schostal, booing and hurling insults at the stage. The mob in the orchestra seats, ignorant but willing to be led, has joined in the jeering. Alma, in the male clothing of Octavian, has retreated upstage from the footlights and cowers against the backdrop. The orchestra is silent, and Alma has stopped singing. One of her arms is raised across her face as if to ward off the insults. Schalk, in the pit, signals for the singers to begin again, but he cannot get Alma's attention. She is frozen in place by fear, a bird under the eye of the snake. Jeritza, lolling on the bed, looks bored. Dieter and Marta sit silently in their box; they could be carved from stone. Franz dashes into the empty box beside them, looks down on the chaotic scene, and cups his hands around his mouth.

FRANZ: (*Shouting*) Alma, start again, start again. Damn it, girl, don't let them beat you. (*Aside*) She has to sing, she can't just quit. (*Shouting*) Alma, *da capo, da capo.* Watch the conductor. (*Aside*) Shit, she isn't going to make it. (*Alma suddenly covers her face with her hands and runs offstage. The triumphant audience roars, and Schalk reluctantly signals the curtain down. The noise begins to fade as the scene on the stage is mercifully obliterated. Schalk disappears from the podium.*)

158

FRANZ: (*Calling to Marta*) That's a nice piece of work you did tonight. Are you proud of yourself.

MARTA: Proud, no. Content, yes. (*Franz pounds his fist into his palm in frustration and runs out of the box.*)

MARTA: (*To Dieter, casually.*) Do you remember the night I was booed in Bologna?

DIETER: (*Equally calm*) *Butterfly,* wasn't it?

MARTA: I was very bad that night, as bad as I've ever been.

DIETER: They boo everybody in Bologna; they booed Caruso there. They'd boo the Pope if he had any kind of a voice.

MARTA: No, I was really bad. They must have been on me for ten minutes, but I never let them get me. I just kept on singing. Nobody could hear me, I couldn't even hear myself, but they knew I was singing.

DIETER: I remember. You were magnificent. And when they finally quieted down you gave them the *cornuto.* (*He raises his hand with two fingers extended as horns.*) That really got them going again.

MARTA: Another five minutes, at least, but they never got to me. You must never let them get to you. Do you see what I mean about her now?

DIETER: It was very cruel.

MARTA: Yes, but you see? She's not a professional, and she never will be. She had to find out sometime.

DIETER: Yes, I suppose so, but I hate to see something like that. (*On this line Schalk enters from the back of the box. He looks shaken, and he mops his brow constantly.*)

SCHALK: Animals, nothing better than animals. Baroness . . . ?

159

MARTA: Herr Schalk.

SCHALK: You see the situation?

MARTA: Can she return?

SCHALK: Impossible. She is totally hysterical, locked herself in her dressing room.

MARTA: The understudy?

SCHALK: (*He grimaces.*) As you may have heard, there is none tonight.

MARTA: Is there anyone else in the house?

SCHALK: Only you. Is it possible to ask . . . ?

MARTA: Of course I'll go on. There's no question of that.

SCHALK: Thank God.

MARTA: (*To Dieter*) Will you excuse me, darling?

DIETER: Naturally.

MARTA: (*Rising, suddenly brisk*) I'll need ten minutes to dress and the wardrobe mistress to dress me.

SCHALK: Anything else? The score?

MARTA: Not for Octavian. I could sing it in my sleep.

SCHALK: Please don't, not tonight. One fiasco is enough.

MARTA: Stop worrying. (*She laughs, and links her arm in his.*) Come, Herr Schalk, off we go to save the evening. (*All over the house the opera glasses have been focused on the box, and on the conversation between Marta and Schalk. The audience draws the correct conclusion and, led by the claque, they begin to chant.*)

MANY VOICES: Die PRINZ . . . Die PRINZ . . . Die PRINZ . . . Die PRINZ . . . Die PRINZ . . . Die PRINZ . . .

MARTA: You see, there's nothing to worry about. I have them in my hand already. (*She exits with Schalk as the chant continues.*)

CURTAIN

Act Three; Scene Three

The time: *One hour after the final curtain of* Der Rosenkavalier.
The place: *Marta's dressing room.*

The setting: The same as Act Two; Scene Two, but now the room is crowded with elegantly dressed men and women shrieking their congratulations to Marta on her superlative performance. Marta, still dressed in Octavian's breeches and doublet, rests on the sofa, bouquets of flowers surrounding her. Dieter stands on one side of her and Schalk on the other. At times they make ineffectual efforts to clear the room, but no one wants to leave the ambience of triumph. Then a hush falls over the room as Jeritza enters. A path is made for her, and she comes directly to Marta, bending over to kiss her cheek.

JERITZA: I couldn't leave the house without stopping by. You were magnificent, darling. You saved us all.

MARTA: (*With a weak wave of her hand*) One more Octavian, nothing special.

JERITZA: No, it was very special indeed. Aside from everything else, you were never better. (*Jeritza kisses her again, then looks around the room indignantly.*) Why are you all abusing this child? Can't you let her relax? Come now, all of you, out of here. You haven't even given her a chance to change. Out, out, give her some privacy. (*The imperious diva begins to shoo people out of the room. Dieter and Schalk join in to help, and soon the room is cleared. Schalk is the last to leave, blowing an affectionate kiss. Dieter and Marta are left alone; even the wardrobe mistress is gone.*)

161

(*While Dieter busies himself with a cigar, Marta rises wearily from the couch and crosses to behind the screen. There she begins to undress, and as she removes each piece of male attire she hurls it over the screen. Dieter watches this with amusement.*

DIETER: I haven't given my personal congratulations. That was quite a performance, darling.

MARTA: Just another Octavian.

DIETER: I wasn't referring to that performance.

MARTA: Oh, the other business. That's the Prinz in me. We all tend to do things rather thoroughly.

DIETER: Still, all that energy expended just to crush a flea.

MARTA: They are never fleas, my dear. They may bite like fleas, but potentially they are as dangerous as a sabre-toothed tiger.

DIETER: What love it must take to face such tigers.

MARTA: What nonsense it seems, now that it's over.

DIETER: Is it over?

MARTA: As far as I'm concerned it is. If she isn't destroyed, if she can rise up out of these ashes, then she deserves him.

DIETER: Then it's over. She isn't any phoenix, just a vulnerable young girl. (*Marta appears from behind the screen. She is wearing the same gown she wore earlier. Her face shows her weariness, but her voice is light.*)

MARTA: Darling, that's touching. If I didn't know you better I'd think you were trying to make me feel guilty.

DIETER: Impossible. (*Marta looks at him doubtfully, not quite sure what he means. He takes her arm.*)

DIETER: Come, time to go. (*They walk to the dressing-room door. Dieter starts to turn right down the corridor, but Marta stops him, turning left.*)

MARTA: I'd like to go out through the front of the house.

CURTAIN
Act Three; Scene Four

The time: *Immediately after.*
The place: *The lobby of the Vienna Opera, the same as* Act Three; *Scene One.*

The setting: Dieter and Marta enter arm in arm. The lobby is deserted, save for Franz, who stands at the foot of the grand staircase, exactly the rendezvous that Marta had suggested in her note. His normally immaculate hair is rumpled and his evening dress dishevelled. He nods a grave greeting as they come together, then bends over Marta's hand.

FRANZ: Shall I congratulate you, or turn you over my knee?

MARTA: How is she, Franz?

FRANZ: (*He shrugs*). About as you'd expect. (*He makes a show of consulting his watch.*) On her way back to Warsaw by now. The midnight express.

MARTA: (*A pause*) I'm sorry.

FRANZ: Yes, I'm sure you are.

MARTA: No, I mean it. I think in my heart I was hoping she would be able to stand up to it.

FRANZ: You don't really mean that.

MARTA: No, I suppose I don't. But if she had, I would have saluted her.

FRANZ: Well, she didn't, and that's that. (*He makes a washing motion with his hands. Then, to Dieter:*) What did you think of your wife tonight? Proud?

DIETER: As always. That never changes.

163

FRANZ: Even that night in Bologna? Remember how they booed her then? (*He shakes his head.*) But not tonight, not tonight. I thought we might make a little celebration out of it. Some champagne at Sacher's, just the three of us, just like old times.

DIETER: (*It is his turn to consult his watch.*) That's very kind, but I'm afraid I have an appointment with a deck of cards. There's still time for me to play a few rubbers at the Malakoffs'. (*To Marta:*) Will you excuse me, darling?

MARTA: (*She smiles gently.*) Of course I will. (*Then, softly*) Thank you.

FRANZ: Good night then, old man. Good luck with the cards.

DIETER: Good night, and thank you, but that's one thing I never need. I always have luck with the cards.

(*They leave then, separating as Dieter turns off to the side entrance of the lobby, while Marta and Franz, her head resting against his shoulder, cross to the high front doors.*)

(*The musicians should all have gone home by now, but some must have stayed behind, because somewhere some strings are playing 'The Merry Widow Waltz.'*)

Josef Schostal, large and bulky in an ancient dinner jacket, walks down the grand staircase with his hands extended in front of him. He is doing what he does best. He is applauding.)

CURTAIN

Chapter Eleven

Digger Prince, son of Anton and Elizabeth, learned to crawl, walk, and ski in that order, and one action followed quickly upon the other. At the age of two he was fully at home on skis, scooting around his backyard on the miniature pair fashioned

164

by his father. A year later he was skimming down small hills, and by the time he was five, under Anton's benevolent eye, he could ski anywhere that his sturdy little body could take him. No one ever taught him how to ski; there was never any need. He was a natural skier in the same way that some children are natural swimmers, or riders of horses. He simply strapped on his skis and went, moving easily and fluidly over the snow, the boards on his feet an extension of his body. He had been baptized John, but no one called him that. From earliest days he had been known as Digger because of the fierce and determined way that he dug his skis into the snow as he carved out his turns. He no longer dug his skis that way but the name had stuck. Only his mother had objected to it. She had fought against it, banned its use in her home, and finally, reluctantly, had learned to live with it. The boy was Digger Prince to all of Sedgewick Falls.

On a Saturday in November of 1927, Anton and the seven-year-old Digger came skiing down through a stand of timber partway up the side of Mount Wellington, weaving in and out among the trees. Once out on the open slope they came to a stop at the top of a steep incline, their skis edged in against the fall line. Below them the snowfields dropped directly to the foothills of the mountain, and beyond those hills they could see the stretch of chequered meadows, the black curve of Pebble River, and the bulge in the curve that was Long Brook Pond. At the edge of that pond, although they could not see it, was the sawmill and factory of the Prince Carpentry Company. From where they stood, however, they could see no sign of human habitation. They were alone on the mountain, surrounded by silence. They had been up since early morning, climbing and skiing, had lunched on chocolate and apples, and now the position of the sun told them that it was time to be heading home.

Close to three o'clock, Anton thought, and I was supposed to be back by two. Well, Mr Wallace Avery will have to wait. Elizabeth will keep him company, fill him full of tea and cookies until it comes out of his ears.

His appointment to see Avery at home was part of his manner of doing business. Although he had a small office at the factory, he hated to be confined to it, preferring to conduct his affairs and make his decisions either in the open air or in the privacy of his parlour. The decision that he faced with Avery today was of major importance, and Anton knew enough about himself to recognize that he had stayed late on the mountain in order to put off that moment of decision. Avery was the proprietor of a chain of sporting goods shops in Boston, Providence, and New York, and over the past two years he had been Anton's largest single customer for skis and poles. Now he wanted to triple his purchase orders. He saw skiing, particularly in New England, as a burgeoning sport and a future industry, and he was about to back his vision with ten additional stores in the mountain areas. Anton agreed with the man's foresight, but turning out that many skis each year would mean curtailing his production of such staples as cabinets, tables and chairs. It would mean, in effect, going full-time into the ski business. It was a gamble he was willing to take, but still he hesitated over the final decision.

Beside him, his son shuffled his skis impatiently, waiting for the word to start downhill again. Mountains, for Digger, existed to be run as rapidly as possible. The slope below them was one they skied regularly and they had their own names for the various features of the hill: the Dog's Nose, the Sheep's Head, the Camelback. They had skied the area earlier in the day, and their tracks still showed on the snow: a straight schuss with a jump.

'Papa, can we go now?' asked Digger.

'In a minute. How are you going to run it?'

The boy looked at him in surprise. 'The same as we did this morning. Down to the Sheep's Head, jump it, and keep on going.'

Anton shook his head. The boy was a natural skier, but he still had a lot to learn about snow. He had to learn that the mountain wore many faces, and that the mask changed quickly during the course of the day. He had to learn the difference between sun crust and rain crust on the surface of the snow. He had to learn that the crust that is crisp and crunchy in the morning can be soggy at noon and close to freezing at the end of the day. He had to learn to take nothing on the mountain for granted.

'We go down now, but this way,' he said, pointing out the course he wanted with the ski pole in his right hand. The other pole was gripped in a wooden fist. 'And we go slow.'

They skied down slowly to what they called the Sheep's Head,

166

a sharp, snow-covered projection from the hillside caused by a bump in the terrain. Anton led the way around it, and down the side of it. He stopped when his head was below the level of the projection. He pointed to the edge of the Sheep's Head where the snow had drifted up since the morning into a cornice that extended the projection by several feet. He knocked the cornice with his pole and it crumbled away.

'That can happen when the weather is dry and the wind is up,' he explained. 'If you tried to jump that you would go right through.'

Digger nodded seriously, his eyes narrowed as they measured how much the snow had drifted. Then he said, 'Papa, I don't want to sound like a wise guy, but I wouldn't have jumped from there. I would have pre-jumped from further back where the snow is solid. I'm not saying that I knew about the cornice, 'cause I didn't, but I never would have been on it.'

'That's right,' Anton agreed, 'but what if your pre-jump is bad and you come down short? Then you come down right on the cornice and you go through.'

'That wouldn't happen, Papa, not the way I do it,' said the boy, and added hastily, 'but it *could* happen, I can see that. Thank you for showing me.'

Anton nodded, satisfied. He knew that the boy would remember. It was rare that he had to be told something twice if that something had to do with skiing or mountains. 'Time to go down now,' he said.

'Can I climb back up and ski the Sheep's Head first?'

He smiled at his son's enthusiasm, but shook his head. 'No, I have an appointment, and I'm late already.'

'Okay, last one down is . . .' Without waiting to say what the last one down would be, Digger turned and dropped down the fall line straight as a string, standing on his skis as casually as if he were leaning against a wall and not speeding down a mountainside. Anton watched him go pridefully.

Another couple of years and he can ski anywhere, he thought. If I was still living in Austria I'd have people banging on my door trying to make a racer out of him. Well, who knows, even in America.

He took off after his son, who was fast disappearing down the hill.

While Anton was heading for home, Elizabeth was there in

167

the parlour doing her best to entertain Mr Wallace Avery. The merchant was a short, portly Bostonian with a reputation for sharp, but fair, trading. He had been sitting on the sofa for over an hour now, sipping tea and nibbling at biscuits, and trying without success to conceal his impatience. In his world of business, tardiness was close to being a cardinal sin, and what made Anton's lateness all the more sinful was that he was keeping a buyer waiting, not a seller. Nobody kept a buyer waiting.

Aware of his impatience, Elizabeth dratted her husband and dratted the boy as well for staying on the mountain so long. She knew very well what Anton's answer to Avery was going to be. He was going to say yes, he was going to supply the product, he was going to devote ninety percent of the company to the manufacture of skis and poles. This they had discussed as husband and wife, and she thoroughly approved of the move. She was tempted to tell this to Avery, tempted to tell him that the forms were all prepared and that a few signatures were all that were needed to complete the transaction. But she said nothing. She knew that the proper Bostonian would be shocked by the very idea of a woman talking business to him, and so she continued to make small talk, silently dratting her husband, and listen with half an ear to what Avery was saying about some ski race being organized in Europe by a man named Lunn. Her relief was intense when she heard the sound of Anton's Marmon turning into the driveway, and then the slam of the back door as he came into the house.

A moment later Anton poked his head into the parlour, greeted Avery, and excused himself while he changed out of his boots. 'Boots in the parlour is *verboten*,' he explained with a wink. 'I'll be right back.'

Elizabeth compressed her lips, but said nothing. Wet ski boots were *verboten* anywhere in the house, and her husband knew it. He should have got rid of them on the back porch. He returned quickly, however, wearing carpet slippers. He shook hands with Avery, kissed his wife's cheek, and settled into his easy chair. He lit his pipe, scratching the match on the back of his wooden hand, and looked around brightly.

'Well, first I got to apologize for keeping you waiting,' he said. 'It's a terrible thing when I get on the mountain, I forget about time. And my boy is even worse. He wants to run every trail twice.'

168

'Quite all right,' said Avery, 'so long as you're here now. Your charming wife has been most entertaining.'

'Where is the boy?' asked Elizabeth.

'In the kitchen, having cocoa.' He saw the look on his wife's face. 'Yes, yes, he took his boots off. He's not a slob like his papa, he left his out on the porch.' He turned to Avery. 'So, I don't keep you waiting any longer, I tell you right now we got a deal.'

Avery's expression brightened. 'You'll do it, then?'

'My word on it. We'll ship five hundred pair, skis and poles, by the first of the month, and five hundred more before Christmas. The rest in January and February.'

'Excellent. The terms as agreed?'

'Like we said. I don't change a deal in the middle.'

'All charges FOB Sedgewick Falls?'

'That's right.' Anton worked at getting his pipe going. 'I got the order forms ready to sign in my desk.'

'We haven't discussed the insurance yet.'

'I got that in my desk, too.'

Anton started to rise heavily from his chair. Elizabeth waved him down and went to the desk for the papers. She handed them to her husband. She knew that it was time to remove herself while the men talked business.

She said, 'If you gentlemen will excuse me . . . ?' Both men nodded absently as she left.

She went looking for her son in the kitchen, but he wasn't there. Mrs Mulloy, the housekeeper, shook her head in mock irritation when Elizabeth asked where the boy was.

'Too late, missus,' she said. 'He drank his chocolate like a streak, changed his shoes, and went racing out of here like a house afire. Said something about going down to the school to play ball in the gymnasium.'

'Mrs Mulloy, really, you should have stopped him. You know that he's supposed to study on Saturday afternoons.'

'Missus, you try holding that boy down. It's more than I can do.'

Elizabeth came close to slamming the kitchen door in vexation as she left. The boy was impossible about his studies. It seemed that anything was preferable to opening a book. And Anton was no help, either. He thought it only natural for a seven-year-old, almost eight, to shy away from schoolwork.

When I was his age, she thought, I was reading Milton and loving it. Didn't understand half of it, but that made no difference. It was the adventure of it all.

She wasted time around the house until it seemed appropriate to return to the parlour. As soon as she entered the room she knew that something was wrong. Nothing overt, but she could tell by the look on Anton's face that he was upset. When he saw her in the doorway, he said, almost reluctantly, 'Come in, Lizbet. You should maybe hear this.'

Wallace Avery turned a face full of enthusiasm to her. 'Yes, I started to tell Mrs Prince earlier about this man Lunn's idea. Arnold Lunn, an Englishman. He intends to hold the first international ski race this winter, actually two races, a downhill and a slalom, with the prize going to the man with the best combined score. And not just the men, there will be races for the ladies as well. He's got a good deal of backing for the project, even talked the Englishman Lord Roberts of Kandahar into donating the trophy. It's a humdinger of an idea.'

'It sounds fascinating,' Elizabeth murmured, wondering why such news should upset her husband.

'More than fascinating,' Avery exclaimed. 'Something like this, if the idea catches on, could prove to be a blessing to your business. Give it time and you'll be selling skis like hotcakes. Frankly, I was just telling Mr Prince here that a really go-ahead businessman would make a point of being at those races to show off his product. Take a few samples along, let the racers try them out. That's the way to do business these days.'

Elizabeth looked at her husband curiously. She could see nothing wrong with what Avery was saying. It sounded quite sensible. Hesitantly, she asked, 'Anton, what do you think?'

'I don't know, Lisbet. A trip like that would be a big expense, all the way to Austria.'

'Austria!'

'Well, sure,' said Avery. 'You didn't think they were going to hold it in Vermont, did you? I say hang the expense, you can't make money without spending money. Prince, if I were you I'd make that trip, and I'd take my family with me, too. Make a holiday out of it. Why, man, it's the chance of a lifetime to see Europe and do some business at the same time.'

'I already saw Europe,' Anton said glumly. 'Too much of it. I like it here.'

170

Elizabeth asked, 'Exactly where in Austria are these races being held?'

'That's the best part of it,' Avery crowed. 'This fellow Lunn looked over all the prime locations in the Alps and decided that the best place to have the races was your husband's hometown, St Anton in the Arlberg.'

'I see,' she said. She was beginning to.

Anton twisted uncomfortably. 'They've even got Hannes Schneider in on it. He runs the ski school at the Post Hotel. They're calling it the Arlberg-Kandahar race.'

Elizabeth said thoughtfully, 'Mr Avery, do you really think it would be worth our while to go there? For business purposes, that is.'

'Absolutely, Mrs Prince, and not just for business. It would be a homecoming, too, for your husband. Now what do you think about that?'

'I don't know what Lizbet thinks,' said Anton, 'but when I left the Arlberg I swore that I'd never go back, and I won't. Not for all the ski business in the world.'

We'll see about that, thought Elizabeth, and after Avery had left, the order forms signed and the deal accomplished, she sat down opposite her husband and said, 'My dear, I think that we must have a talk.'

'Not if it's about St Anton.'

'It is, and I think that we must. I have known you for almost fourteen years now, and I have never asked you the circumstances under which you left your home. Obviously there was some family unpleasantness, but I have respected your feelings and have kept my curiosity to myself. Now I think the time has come for you to tell me.'

'I don't want to,' he said miserably, looking away. 'Please don't ask.'

'But I am asking, and you must tell me. We are partners and we share everything. Now we must share this. You cannot say no to me.'

He looked up at her and took her hands. 'All right, I got to tell you. Because of love, because of trust. I just hope to God you understand.'

He told her then exactly what had happened. He hid nothing. He told her about the seven boys from St Anton, about the

171

weekly visits to Lili Wangenmann's bedroom, about the accusation of rape and how he was forced to leave town.

'That's how I came to Vermont,' he said, 'and that's the God's honest truth.' He had not let go of her hands during the telling. He did now. 'You believe me, don't you?'

'Of course I do,' she said briskly. 'The idea of you assaulting someone is just plain ludicrous. I must say that I don't think much of your behaviour, you and your friends, but I suppose I'd have to chalk that up to boys will be boys. Apparently the young lady was willing enough. And she later married your brother?'

'Yes. I got a letter from a friend.'

Elizabeth drummed her fingers on the arms of her chair. She was aware of an anger growing within her, a sense of outrage. 'And the town simply judged you and condemned you on the basis of an unsupported statement?'

'You know what a small town is like. You saw what they did to you here.'

'Indeed, I do know. And would no one stand up for you?'

'One friend, the one who wrote the letter, he wanted to. I wouldn't let him do it.'

'And your family?'

'They threw me out.'

'Damn them.' She beat a fist on the chair.

He spread his hands. 'So now you see why I can't go back. It would be a scandal all over again.'

'I'm not at all sure about that.' Elizabeth was silent for a long while, thinking. Then she said, 'By thunder, nothing riles me more than people telling me what I can do and what I can't. Where I can go and where I can't. I think that you should go, Anton. I think we all should go, you, me, and the boy. We'll show them our family, and if the people there don't like it, they can lump it. We'll rub their noses in it.' She smiled at him brilliantly. 'I say that we should do it, and I say that we should do it in style.'

They did it in a style that left the village of St Anton am Arlberg buzzing. First came a letter from the dimly remembered Anton Prinz to the Post Hotel, reserving the best suite of rooms available during the week of the Arlberg-Kandahar race. Next came a letter from the same Herr Prinz, who now spelled his name somewhat differently, to the *Bürgermeister* of the village

172

enclosing an international money order in the amount of one thousand American dollars as a contribution to the Fund for the Needy. On the same day the parish priest received a similar letter enclosing the same amount for the Children's Christmas Collection. Elizabeth's concept of style began to have its effect when the *Bürgermeister* and the priest met in the bank, compared money orders, checked the exchange rates, and found that two thousand dollars was more than four times the yearly wage of an Austrian workingman. Nothing could have been better calculated to whet the interest of the village in the return of the one-time pariah.

The Prince family arrived by way of Zurich in a chauffeur-driven Daimler, father and son in stiff new suits and Elizabeth dressed in a fashion that even Vienna would not see for another year. The chauffeur was instructed to drive the length of the main street twice before parking in front of the Post Hotel. There the luggage was unloaded together with a packing crate containing the samples of skis. The concierge who came out to greet them was the younger Hans Secker, a contemporary of Anton's. His greeting was respectful, and without a trace of the intimacy to which he was entitled.

'Your rooms are prepared, *mein Herren,*' he said. 'Your luggage will be taken up at once.'

'Not the crate,' Anton told him. 'That must be stored below.'

'In the shed, *mein Herr,* of course.'

'And don't send the luggage up just yet,' said Elizabeth, confusing the man with her precise *hochdeutsch*. 'We shall want to inspect the rooms first.'

After that, Secker was not surprised when the first suite of rooms shown was arbitrarily rejected, the second dismissed with contempt, and the third found barely adequate. He was congratulating himself on that accomplishment when Elizabeth said, 'I notice that there is a small sitting room in the lobby, adjoining the larger one.'

'Yes, madam, the writing room.'

'Excellent. We shall want it for our use in the evenings.'

Secker started to protest, and thought better of it. Something in the woman's voice prompted him to bow and say simply, 'As madam wishes.'

When Secker left, Anton breathed deeply. He was dying to

173

undo his collar, but he did not dare. He asked his wife wearily, 'All right, what do we do now?'

'I shall supervise the unpacking,' she told him, 'while you go down and make sure that the chauffeur is properly settled.' She turned to her son. 'And you will open a book, any book, but preferably a German grammar, and read for an hour.'

'I already speak German,' said the boy.

'You speak nothing close to it. The book, please, and try to keep your shirt cuffs clean.'

'And after that?' Anton asked.

'After that we shall dine, and then we shall go to our sitting room, and sit.'

'Just sit?'

'Just so.'

After dinner they sat in regal isolation in the quondam writing room, Elizabeth with an untouched cup of coffee by her side, Anton with his pipe, and Digger chained to his German grammar. They sat undisturbed, but well aware of the glances of passersby directed at them through the open doorway. All of St Anton apparently knew that Anton Prinz, now a millionaire at least, had returned with an American wife and child, and everyone wanted a glimpse of this unlikely Croesus.

It was a difficult time for Anton as he sat there showing only a calm exterior. Actually, he was half dazed. One whole set of emotions urged him to run out of the hotel and climb the familiar mountain path to the house where he had been born. Other emotions would have had him out on the streets and in familiar haunts searching for old comrades. A third emotion, deeply sprung, told him that he had made a mistake in coming, and commanded an immediate retreat. Fortunately, Elizabeth had anticipated all of these feelings, and so, carefully briefed by his wife, Anton gave in to none of them. He simply sat and waited. So far things were going the way his wife had said that they would back in Sedgewick Falls. Before they had embarked on the journey she had predicted the course of events.

'You must avoid any signs of eagerness,' she had told him then. 'You must make them all come to you. There will be no problem with the mayor and the priest. They are professionals in the use of money and power, and their entire lives have been spent either bowing to those who are over them or kicking those who are under them. They will know when it is time to bow. It

174

will be different with your parents. They are simple people and they will be confused, but they will follow the lead of the priest and the mayor. They will put on their Sunday best and they will come to you. That leaves your brother, and frankly I don't know what he will do. It depends, I suppose, on whether his greed outweighs his jealousy. As for his wife, however, I can guarantee that we will see neither hide nor hair of her. She will not appear.' At this point Elizabeth's voice had softened. 'Let me warn you of one more thing. Do not be surprised at the appearance of your parents. They will be older and less formidable than you remember them. And do not be surprised by the feelings that you find you have for them. Those feelings, too, may be quite different from what you expect.'

As Elizabeth had anticipated, the first visitors to enter the room were the *Bürgermeister* and the parish priest, one with his hat in his hand and the other clearly wishing that convention might allow him to do the same. They were, to Anton's surprise, the same men who had occupied those offices fourteen years before: Father Klaus even older and drier; Herr Schlicter's jowls now pendulous and his tiny eyes buried in fat. Behind them appeared Sepp and Hanna. At first only their heads showed peering cautiously into the room, fear on their wizened faces that they had stumbled into the wrong place. They took in the sight of the mature man in the foreign clothes casually smoking his pipe, the fashionably dressed and imperious woman, the young boy with the arrogant lift to his chin, and their eyes grew round. Then, slowly, they recognized their son and they willed their feet to enter the room. Behind them came their other son, Otto, limping noticeably and followed by his own two boys. Step by step the group approached the table where the Princes sat . . . courtiers advancing on royalty. They stopped a few feet from the table as Anton rose to greet them. His mother started forward, her eyes filled with tears and her arms extended to embrace her son, but she was stopped by a sharp word from the *Bürgermeister*.

'Please, Frau Prinz,' he said. 'First must come the official speech of welcome.' He cleared his throat noisily, his hands gripping the brim of his hat. 'Herr Prinz, it is my great honour as *Bürgermeister* of St Anton am Arlberg to welcome you back to the village of your birth. You are a son of this soil and there will always be a place for you here. Not many of our young men

175

go forth to find their fortunes in the world beyond our mountains. You are one of the few, and we honour you for it. Welcome home, Anton Prinz. Welcome, welcome, welcome.'

Herr Schlicter bowed sharply, and took a step back. Anton inclined his head. Again his mother started forward, but this time it was Father Klaus who stopped her. He raised his hand in benediction.

'In the name of the Holy Mother Church,' he intoned, 'I welcome back into our midst a son of St Anton, Anton Prinz, who has returned from a faraway place to the bosom of his family. May the blessings of the Lord be showered upon this reunion. Welcome home, Anton Prinz. Welcome, welcome, welcome.'

'Now?' asked Hanna in a loud voice. 'Now am I allowed to kiss my baby son?'

Without waiting for an answer she rushed forward and threw her arms around Anton. Sepp, too, came up to give an embrace, a broad grin on his face.

'My boy, my boy,' he said, pounding Anton on the back.

'Let me look at you,' said Hanna, sobbing. 'Oh, you've got so big and so handsome.'

'It's a miracle,' said his father, still pounding. 'A blessing from God. We thought we'd never see you again.'

'All these years,' said his mother, a hint of a whine in her voice, 'and never once did we hear from you. Not even a letter to say you were alive.'

Otto came forward, dragging a leg, a fixed grin on his face. 'Welcome home, brother, it's good to see you again.' He patted Anton lightly on the shoulder.

'He was always a good boy,' Sepp was telling the priest. 'A little mischief, maybe, just like any other boy.'

'Heaven is filled with mischievous boys,' the priest assured him. 'Those are the ones who grow up to be successful men.'

Anton stood still and let himself be kissed and pounded and squeezed without responding. He was trying to sort out his thoughts. So far no one had said anything about Lili or the supposed rape, and it was clear that no one was going to. He was being treated like a local hero, someone who had willingly left his home to seek his fortune across the ocean, and not as an object of loathing who had been cast out of society. The

176

twisted logic of these people was transparent. If he was guilty of nothing, then neither were they.

He had been warned by his wife to expect conflicting emotions, but no warning could have prepared him for what he felt now. He had expected to feel a filial devotion to the parents who had given him birth and life. He had expected to feel some shred of brotherly affection for Otto, and some curious instinct of blood towards his nephews. He had expected, for better or worse, a sense of a family reunited.

He felt none of this. He felt exactly the same as he had felt on that other winter night when he had been thrust away from the family hearth and kicked out into the cold to live or die as he might. He felt anger. He felt outrage. He felt the sweet pleasure of pure hatred. The feeling was so strong that his body began to shake.

Elizabeth, who had anticipated all of this, now touched his sleeve lightly, and in English said the one word 'Steady'.

The one word was enough. He was suddenly calm as he observed this fragment of his family. He saw them clearly now. He saw his father as a sly and avaricious peasant suddenly presented with a vision of riches. He saw his mother as a vacuous woman whose only positive function in his life had been to give him birth with the same care as a cow dropping a calf. He saw the mask of greed on his brother's face that barely concealed a corrosive envy. He saw his older nephew, Hannes, at the age of thirteen, sizing him up with the calculating eyes of a petty thief. He saw the eyes of his younger nephew, Kurt, as well. The boy was about the age of his own son, but he paid no attention to him. If he had, he would have seen a warm and friendly curiosity in those eyes, but in that moment his interest did not extend to warm and friendly children. He was too busy hating.

Ignoring his doting relatives, he turned to Elizabeth and said in English, 'Well, what do you think of my family? Did you ever see such a bunch of scoundrels in your life? If I gave them a chance they'd pick my pocket right here and now.'

Elizabeth smiled. 'Are you sure they speak no English?'

'Pretty sure, and to tell you the truth I don't care if they do. Do you see how they've changed it all around? Now I'm the local boy who went to America to make good. Nothing about what really happened, nothing about what they did to me.'

177

'They may actually remember it that way now. What are you going to do about it?'

'I'd like to tell them all to go to hell.'

Elizabeth raised an eyebrow, but said nothing. The others in the room had fallen silent during this exchange in English, their faces puzzled. Anton turned to his son, who was perched on the edge of his chair. He looked alert and concerned.

'Digger, do you understand what's going on here?'

The boy's eyes narrowed. 'I can understand some of the German, but not all of it. Are these people really my grandma and grandpa?'

'They are, and the other man is my brother.'

'Don't you love them? It sounds like you're mad at them.'

'Well, I am, and I'll tell you why. Maybe you'll learn something from it. A long time ago these people threw me out of this town. I was accused of a terrible crime, something I didn't do, but I was convicted without a trial and told to leave this place forever. These people did this to me. My father forced me out of my own home. My mother did nothing to protect me. My brother plotted against me and was happy to see me go. These other two, the priest and the mayor, were just as bad. Now I come back here with my pockets full of money and they want to forget what happened. They want to love me again. They want to put their hands in my pockets. Now, what do you think of that?'

'Papa, are you really asking me a question?'

'I am. I'm hoping you'll learn something from this.'

'Then I'd do what you said. I'd tell them all to go to hell.'

Anton threw back his head and roared with laughter. His parents and his brother, not understanding, laughed along nervously. The priest and the *Bürgermeister* gave polite smiles.

Elizabeth said, 'Language, please.'

'I'm sorry, Mama, but that's what Papa said.'

'He may say it, you may not.' She looked at her husband keenly. 'And is that what you are going to do?'

'Are you testing me, Lizbet? You know I won't. And Digger, this is another lesson to learn. Sometimes a man does something that he doesn't feel like doing, not because it's right but because it's better. So I'm not going to tell them to go you know where. I'm going to give them big hugs and kisses and tell them that I love them. I'm going to let them think they fooled me. I'm

178

going to give them some money, not a lot but enough to buy a cow or a couple of pigs, and that way nobody gets hurt and everybody is happy. And do you know why I'm going to do that?'

'No, Papa.' They were on the mountain again, and he was watching his father break away a dangerous cornice of snow.

'Because a man has only one family, boy, and this one, God help me, is mine.' He smiled affectionately at his wife. 'Is that okay with you, Lizbet?'

She returned the smile. 'Completely. I expected nothing else.'

Anton turned back to the strained faces watching him. Although they had not understood the words they had known they were being discussed. He looked at them grimly, letting them dwell with their concern for a moment longer, then let a smile break over his face. In quick succession he bent to kiss his mother's cheek, grasped his father's shoulders lightly, and held out his hand to his brother. The relief in the room was palpable.

'So here I am,' he said in a booming voice. 'Your son has come back from across the sea. This is my wife, and this is my son, and we're all happy to be here. It's good to be home again.'

'Of course it is,' said his mother, her head bobbing happily. 'There's no place like home. It was really very naughty of you to stay away for so long.'

Chapter Twelve

Two days later Anton sat relaxed in the parlour of his father's home, surrounded by familiar sights and smells. Nothing had changed in the room in the years he had been away. Marta's piano still stood against the wall, and the multicoloured lamp that had so fascinated him as a child still hung above the table. There was still the glass-fronted cabinet filled with untouchable china figurines, the equally untouchable fowling pieces pegged to the wall, and the faded portrait of Franz Josef preserved as if against a second coming. There was the characteristic odour of the place as well, compounded of woodsmoke and shavings, wool, tobacco, cinnamon, and orange peel; and over it all the

179

aroma of *Tafelspitz* that came from the kitchen, where his mother was preparing the midday meal. He winced inwardly at the thought of that meal: the meat and dumplings in heavy gravy, the leeks in cream sauce, and the stupefying array of cakes that was sure to follow. It was a festive meal that Mama Prinz was preparing, a homecoming meal, but Anton's stomach was no longer accustomed to such heavy foods, and he knew that he would suffer for it later.

Still, he was able to relax. Across the room his father sat in amiable, if slightly strained, conversation with Elizabeth, the old man still unsure of how to treat this American woman who spoke German like a princess from Berlin. In front of the hearth, Otto poked moodily at the fire, his older son, Hannes, crouched beside him like a faithful field dog. Anton allowed himself a grim smile at his brother's obvious discomfort. Lili had yet to make an appearance. Otto had told them with regrets that she was ill with a grippe, and Anton and Elizabeth had received the information with grave concern and a knowing exchange of looks between themselves. They did not expect a quick recovery. Childish shrieks from outside the house accounted for the other two members of the family. Digger Prince and Kurt Prinz, eight and nine years old respectively, had taken to each other at once, and now they were cavorting on their skis somewhere up the mountainside. Anton sighed. There was still one member of the family missing, and although he had been told it over and over again he found it hard to believe that his little sister was now a baroness and a leading favourite in the opera in Vienna.

My own fault for not knowing about it, he thought. *I'll bet her name has been in the papers back home, but I never bother with things like that. Maybe when we're finished here we'll go on to Vienna for a couple of days. I'd trade in this whole bunch for just five minutes with Marta.*

There were others missing as well, not family but in some ways closer than any family could have been. He had spent the day before wandering through the town refreshing faded memories, and at the same time asking after old friends. Bit by bit he had accumulated the sad news. Peter Ickle, Eugen Schwimmer, Dolf Mathies, Willi Gebaur, Gunther Rapp, Karl Lang: all of them killed in the war. Unbelievable that Karl was dead; he had seemed indestructible. It was at Friedrich's Tavern

180

that Anton had finally got the story from the bottle-nosed proprietor.

'The way I heard it, they all got it in the same battle,' Friedrich had told him. 'Somewhere on the Italian front. It was a terrible business in the town when the families were notified, so many from one small place. At first we thought it was only five of them, but after a month another notice came that said that the Lang boy was dead too. All your old gang, right? Lucky thing for you that you got out when you did.'

'How did it happen?' Anton had asked wonderingly.

A shrug from Friedrich. 'Who knows? They never said much in those notices. Your brother might know. He was an officer in that regiment and he was wounded just around that time. Ask him.'

But Anton had asked no questions so far. He had spent the rest of the day looking up the racers who were already in town, chatting with them about skiing and mountains, and then turning the conversation to his own product. No obligation and no charge, he had explained, just try the skis and see if you like them. If they feel good, then use them in the race if you want to. So far two men, Walter Rüegg and Karl Beuner, had agreed to give them a try, and there would be more racers coming into town in the next two days. The idea was working out well so far despite confusion about the name. Prince Skis, so close to the Prinz Skis made by Otto here in St Anton. Apparently, Otto's skis were well thought of by the racers, and several had expressed a preference for them. 'A Prinz ski has a good heavy feel to it,' was the way one of them had put it. 'You know that you've got a piece of lumber on your foot, not a toothpick.'

And what, thought Anton, is so wonderful about skiing with two trees strapped to your feet? The lighter the better, but some of these people will never learn. Strange that we both should wind up making skis. Although not so strange when you figure that the old man used to make the best ski in the Arlberg. I wonder what it's like for Otto, not being able to ski any more. What a place for a skier to be wounded. Or is there a good place?

Displaying the results of that wound, Otto left the fire to come limping across the room. He slid crabwise onto the chair next to Anton, and Hannes at once moved over to sit on the floor beside him. Otto smiled companionably at his brother.

'I hear that you've been handing out samples of your skis,' he said. 'Walter Rüegg showed me a pair. Is that how you do business in America, you give them away?'

Anton laughed. 'No, I couldn't make any money that way. It's just an idea to get the name known.'

'A damn good idea. I should have thought of that myself.'

Anton thought: What's this, compliments from Otto? 'What did you think of the ski?'

'A little on the light side.'

'That's the way I make them. Easier to turn.'

'Around here they like a ski that takes a man to push it. Have you seen any of mine?'

'Not yet.'

Otto turned to his son. 'Hannes, get a ski from the porch.'

The boy went out and came back with a long brown ski that he gave to his father, who handed it over to Anton. Manipulating it with one hand, Anton examined the ski curiously, then looked up and asked, 'Ash?'

'Of course.'

'You'd be better off with hickory. More flexibility, more resilience. That's what I use.'

'I'd have to import it. There is no native hickory in Austria.'

'I know that, I was born here.' Anton examined the ski again. 'This is made from a solid piece of wood. You'd do better to laminate. Use the hard wood inside and laminate the cheaper wood over it. It costs less to make that way, and it gives you a better ride.'

'In the Arlberg we have always carved skis out of a single piece of wood.'

'I know. Like I said, I was born here. I'm just saying you could do it better.'

Otto flushed angrily. 'That's only your opinion. That's a fine ski, nothing wrong with it.'

Anton said soothingly, 'I didn't say there was. Actually, it's a good piece of craftsmanship, I couldn't do it better myself.' He lowered his voice. 'But this ski is ten years behind the times. Papa could have made it. You're not using the best materials and you're not using the best designs. You don't even have metal edges on it.'

'A good mountain man doesn't need metal edges on his skis.'

Anton tried not to show his exasperation. 'The idea is to

182

make it easier for people to ski, not harder. Just because you and I learned to ski without metal edges doesn't mean that other people have to. I wouldn't dream of skiing without an edge these days.'

'There's nothing wrong with making skis the old way.'

'Go ahead, I'm not stopping you. With competition like yours I could make a fortune here.'

'I wouldn't be too sure about that. There are plenty of people around here who don't like the idea of a foreigner coming in and telling us our business.'

Their voices had risen, and across the room both Sepp and Elizabeth turned to look at them. Elizabeth frowned at her husband, and he at once lowered his voice and took a different tone.

'Otto, let's not argue,' he said. 'We argued enough and look what it got us. You make skis your way and I'll make them my way.'

'Your way isn't very popular around here,' Otto retorted, unwilling to let it go, and he might have said more, but Mama Prinz came in then to say that dinner was almost ready and that it was time to get the children in.

Otto told Hannes, 'Go find them and bring them in. They can't be far away.'

Digger and Kurt were playing uphill, laughing and chattering as if they had known each other for years, not hours. The younger Prinz boy was short and chubby, and had brown eyes that sparkled. He skied the hill adeptly, bouncing around the slopes like a good-natured rubber ball. When he was near either his father or his brother he seemed subdued, almost apprehensive, but once away from them he bubbled with enthusiasm and laughter. When the two boys had been sent out to play by their elders, Digger had instinctively turned his skis downhill, but Kurt had dragged him the other way, climbing uphill to a natural projection sticking out of the slope. There, under Kurt's direction, they had spent an hour packing snow until they had a natural ski jump from which they could soar. Now they took turns racing down the chute, flying through the air, and landing with arms spread out wide and legs bent in a telemark position. Every once in a while they paused to repack the chute with fresh snow, lying sprawled on the hillside on their bellies.

'Pack it down hard,' said Kurt as he swept snow onto the

track with his arms. His face was flaming red from the cold, but the grin was still there. 'Is this the way you do it where you live?'

'Sometimes.' Digger had to choose his German words carefully; he did not have too many of them. His knowledge of the language came from hearing his father speak it, and he knew that his mother was right. He needed to study. 'Most of the time we just ski down the mountain.'

'No jumping?'

Digger played with the words in his head. He wanted to say that he did plenty of jumping. Whenever something got in his way he jumped it: a rock, or a tree limb, or the Sheep's Head on Mount Wellington. But he did not jump just for the fun of it. Skiing was for racing down, not jumping off. He wanted to say that to Kurt, but he could not put the words together in German. All he could say was, 'Sometimes I jump, and sometimes I do not jump.'

Kurt understood at once. 'You don't speak much German, do you?'

'No, but I'm studying.'

'I don't speak any English.' The words were offered as a consolation.

'Maybe I could teach you English and you could teach me German.'

Kurt's face lit up. 'That would be fun.'

'But there wouldn't be time. We're leaving here after the races.'

Kurt's face fell at that, but he brightened again. 'Maybe I could come sometime to where you live. Then we could teach each other.'

Excitedly, Digger said, 'That would be . . .' He wanted to say 'terrific,' but settled for one of his father's favourite words, ' . . . *wunderbar*. And when you come I could show you our mountains.'

'Are they very high?'

'They're the highest in the world.'

Kurt knew that wasn't so. He knew that the Alps were the highest, and he was about to say so when he heard his brother's voice calling.

'*Halloo, up there.*' The words came bouncing in the still air. '*Come on down, it's time to eat.*'

184

Kurt's face changed at the sound of his brother's voice. The smile was gone as he scrambled to his feet. 'Let's go – that's Hannes calling.'

Digger got up too, brushing snow from his front. 'One more jump and then we'll go down.'

'No, come now.' Kurt pulled his arm. 'We have to go now.'

'We have time for one more.'

'Not when Hannes calls.' There was actual fear on Kurt's face. 'Please, let's go.'

'One more and then I'll race you down to the house.'

'*All right, you little bastards, I can see you up there. Come on down.*'

'Digger, please. You don't want to make Hannes angry.'

'I'm not making him angry, I just want another jump.' He turned and started to climb back up the hill.

'I'm going down.'

'Go ahead.'

'*Last chance, you two. Get down here.*'

Digger kept on climbing. He did not know what was being yelled at him, but he knew that he was being yelled at, and he didn't like it. No one in Sedgewick Falls used that tone of voice with him. Behind him he heard the sound of Kurt's skis heading downhill, but he kept on climbing.

'*All right, now you're going to get it.*'

He assumed that the words were aimed at Kurt. He turned to see what was happening, and stared in amazement. Hannes was climbing uphill on skis. He had never seen anyone climb so fast. The older boy simply set his skis in a herringbone position and ran uphill as if he were running up a ladder. He passed Kurt, who was skiing down, and kept on coming. He was on top of Digger in a flash. His face was twisted with anger. His hand shot out and he grabbed Digger by the shoulder.

'Got you, you little shit,' he said. 'Who do you think you are? When I call you, you come.'

'Let go of me,' Digger said in English. All his German had fled. He tried to twist away, but Hannes's grip was too strong.

' "Let go. Let go." ' Hannes imitated the English words mockingly. 'Speak German, why don't you?' He gripped Digger's other shoulder and began to shake him with both hands.

'Stop it, you're hurting me.'

Hannes did not understand the words, but he recognized the tone of voice. He heard weakness, and his instinct was to react to weakness with force. 'Maybe you need a lesson,' he grunted. 'Maybe you need to learn to come when somebody calls.' He twisted Digger's body, forcing him over onto his side, and onto the snow.

Digger was frightened. He felt his face grow hot and his knees sag. He had played his share of rough-and-tumble games at home, and had taken his share of lumps and bruises, but he had never before been attacked by someone who deliberately wanted to harm him. He felt his skis slip out from under him, and then he was lying on the snow with Hannes bending over him.

'When I whistle, the dogs dance,' Hannes said in his ear. 'Understand?'

Digger understood that much. He struck out in a spasm of panic. It was a wild swing and it missed, but he had forgotten that he was carrying a ski pole in that hand. The pole came around and caught Hannes across the face. It was less a blow than a stinging slap, but Hannes howled in anger. He shifted his grip from Digger's shoulders to his head and pushed his face into the snow. Digger shut his eyes. The snow was in his nose and he could not open his mouth to breathe. He tried to push up, but the pressure on his head was relentless. Then the pressure was suddenly gone.

He came up gasping, clearing his eyes. He heard heavy breathing and a grunt of pain above him. He looked up and saw Hannes with his head jerked back. Kurt was riding on his brother's shoulders, one hand under his jaw and the other yanking at his hair. In the stillness of the moment he had time to realize that Kurt must have climbed all the way back up the hill to help him.

'Run, Digger,' Kurt was yelling.

He did not run. He jumped at Hannes, and then the three boys were rolling over and over in the snow, swinging wildly, their skis clashing together. Hannes fought back, hampered by Kurt's grip on his head. It was a dogfight between two puppies and a mastiff until Digger lowered his head and launched himself at Hannes's belly, ramming him there. The breath ran out of Hannes with a deep sigh and he doubled over, gasping.

'Now run,' said Kurt, and they both ran, taking off downhill as fast as their skis could carry them. They skied straight down the fall line without looking back, heading for the safety of the house. Digger skied blindly. The fear was gone, replaced by anger, and he could feel the heat of it. Beside him, Kurt crouched over his skis, a grim look on his face, and Digger knew that his cousin would have to pay for what he had done. They skied into the barnyard and coasted to the back porch before they dared to look uphill for Hannes. They saw him coming down, skiing slowly and shaking his head. They took off their skis and racked them on the porch.

'Digger, listen,' said Kurt. 'You don't say anything inside, you understand?'

'But he hit me. He tried to . . .' His German was back, but he was so angry that the words would not come. 'If you hadn't come back . . .'

'I know, but it wouldn't do any good to say anything. It's better for me if you don't. Please?'

'He's going to get you for this, isn't he?'

'That's between Hannes and me. That's the way it always is. So you will be quiet, yes?'

'Yes. I didn't say thank you. For helping.'

'That's all right,' Kurt's grin was back for a moment, then gone again. 'No talk inside, much better that way. Now quick, let's go in before he gets here.'

Kurt hurried into the house, stamping his feet on the doormat first. As he opened the door the heavy aroma of roasting meat swept out from the kitchen. The smell reminded Digger of how hungry he was, but he stayed outside on the porch for a moment, struggling with his anger. Now that it was over the anger was directed at himself, not at Hannes. He was angry at himself for the words he had been unable to speak, and he was angry at himself for the panicky fear he had felt. He told himself that he must never let those weaknesses beat him again. Then he went inside to wash up for dinner.

After a while it stopped being fun for Anton. At first there had been joys rediscovered. He skied familiar mountains, and his heart lifted up at the sight of the peaks of his childhood. He ran along familiar ridges, often with his son at his side, and there was an abiding pleasure in passing on the lore of these mountains to the boy, unveiling fresh slopes for him, and watching the awe that came into his eyes as the grandeur of the

Alps unfolded before him. For Digger's sake alone he now was glad that he had made the trip, but there were other pleasures as well. There was the secret delight of speaking his native language daily as he walked around the town accepting the greetings of citizens barely remembered. He was Herr Anton Prince now, a man of substance and respect, and he was human enough to enjoy the attentions of those who once had condemned him. There was the simple pleasure of reawakening certain sights, and sounds and smells, for even the toll of the church bell was particular to St Anton, and the aroma of the smoke that curled from each chimney was peculiar to the place. It snowed each day, and the snow that fell, it seemed to him, differed in style from New England's crisp white blankets. Everything that he saw or touched or sniffed was illumined by the lights of his childhood, and at first there was pleasure enough in just that.

But in the end it wasn't enough, and it all turned sour. He had hoped that his feelings about his parents would change, but he could not fool himself into thinking that they were any more than what they were. He had hoped to be able to see Lili, to greet her as nothing more than an old friend, but Otto continued to keep her out of sight. He had hoped to come to some sort of an accommodation with the past, but the past persisted, turning things sour. As the days of the races approached he found himself yearning for the softer hills of home, the rising ridges of the mountains of Vermont.

But before he could go home there was business to attend to. During the week before the races he circulated among those who had come to compete. Most of them were Austrian, but there were Swiss and Germans, Italians and Englishmen as well. This was a new breed of skier, men and women to whom skis were more than a means of transportation, more than a source of recreation; they were a passport into a world of daring. These people spoke a jargon all their own, guarded the secrets of their waxes jealously, and lived only for the days at the end of the week when they could match themselves against the mountains. All of them were excited about this new Arlberg-Kandahar race, and Hannes Schneider's sponsorship of it. Schneider was the preeminent ski instructor and technician in the world. Born in nearby Steuben, he had come to the Post Hotel as an instructor in 1907, and he had been there ever since, except for the war years when he had fought in the same mountain troops as had Otto Prinz. After the war he had put together an all-star teaching staff that quickly made the Hannes Schneider Ski School world-famous and introduced the Arlberg technique of instruction that would dominate the sport for decades. It was mainly due to Hannes Schneider that European interest in skiing was so great. The racers knew this, and knew that his sponsorship of the Arlberg-Kandahar was a stamp of legitimacy on their efforts.

It was to these racers that Anton showed his skis and offered them for trial. He had thought that the offer would be taken up quickly – who would say no to a free pair of skis? – and he was surprised at the amount of resistance that he met. Many of the racers were simply not interested. One of the reluctant ones was Walter Kusche, a downhiller with an international reputation.

'I've been using Austrian skis all my life,' he explained. 'I wouldn't want to start with something foreign.'

'Foreign?' exclaimed Anton. 'I was born right here in town. What's foreign about that?'

'Maybe you were born here, but you make those skis in America, don't you? What does an American know about making skis?'

'Look, Kusche, I'm not asking you to buy them, I'm just asking you to try them. If you don't like them then you give them back. What could be fairer than that?'

Kusche handled one of the samples suspiciously. 'It looks all right, but I understand it's not a solid piece of wood. Just little broken-up pieces glued together inside.'

Anton patiently explained how the process of lamination worked, and how it actually strengthened the construction of the ski. Kusche nodded as if he understood, but he still was dubious.

'And what happens if I scrape a rock or put too much pressure on the ski?' he asked, and then answered his own question. 'Those little pieces come apart, the ski goes bust and so do I.'

'That could never happen.' Once again Anton explained the construction, pointing out how light and safe the ski really was, and eventually Kusche agreed, reluctantly, to try out a pair in practice before the downhill race began.

It went the same way with the other racers. Nobody wanted to try something new, particularly something made in so unlikely a place as America, but Anton's patient explanations won some

189

of them over, and in the end he was able to dispose of the dozen pair of skis he had brought with him. Having done that, he was then able to turn his attention to a personal matter.

He found Karl Lang's mother living in a small, chilly room in a house on the edge of town. Her husband was dead and her only income was a small pension and the money she made as a laundress. Birdlike, and wrapped in black, she stared at Anton through red and rheumy eyes when he came to call, unable to place him at first. Then she nodded her head rapidly.

'Yes, yes, Anton Prinz, the bad boy who went away to America. I heard you were back. Are you still a bad boy?'

'No, Mother, I'm a good boy now,' he said gently. 'I learned to be a good boy in America. I first heard about Karl and I came by to see how you are.'

'Ah, Karl. That seems so long ago, that terrible war. So many boys killed.' She was suddenly spiteful. 'But not you. You went away.'

'That's right, I did.'

'What's that?' She pointed to his wooden hand. 'Is that from the war?'

'No, an accident.'

'Again, you were lucky.'

'That's right, Mother, I was lucky. I came by to see if you needed anything.' He looked around the room: a bed, a table, a chair, a cold hearth. 'Things don't look too good here.'

'How should they look? Who cares about an old widow without a son to work for her?'

'Things will be different now. I've put some money in the bank for you, and I've made arrangements with Herr Schlaet. All you have to do is go down to the bank every Friday and Schlaet will give you money to live on for the week. Do you understand that?'

She stared at him for so long that he thought she had not heard him. Then she said, 'Of course I understand. I'm not an idiot, I'm just old. But why would you do this?'

'Karl was my friend.'

'That's right, he was. Thick as thieves, the two of you. You and those other boys, doing the business every night with Lili Wangenmann.'

He wasn't sure he had heard her right. 'You mean, you knew?'

190

'A lot of people knew. You boys weren't as clever as you thought you were.'

'But why didn't you say something?'

'What for? And get my own boy in trouble?' She peered at him through running eyes. 'Why would I want to do that?'

Why, indeed? Anton thought. She took care of her own. Which was more than mine did.

He stood up, patted the woman on the shoulder, and put some money on the table.

'What's that for?' she asked. 'You already told me about the bank.'

'Go out and buy some firewood now. Buy some bread and some schnapps, keep yourself warm tonight. You're a good mother.'

She gathered in the silver. 'And you turned out to be a good boy, after all.'

'I always was, Mother. We were all good boys.'

He walked back to the centre of town and stopped at his brother's shop. He found Otto in a small office in the rear, relaxed in a deep chair and with a demijohn on the desk in front of him. As Anton came through the door he raised a glass in salute.

'Good morning, brother,' he said. 'Come sit and have a drink.'

'No thanks, too early for me.'

'Suit yourself. Have you got rid of all your skis?'

'Yes, finally. It wasn't easy.'

'Well, you know the way people are around here. They don't take to new ideas too quickly.'

'Some of them are living in the last century.'

'Oh, they're all right. I sell a lot of skis to those people. They appreciate good old-fashioned workmanship.'

'Let's not start that again.'

'No, no arguments. I just think I make a better ski than you do. Tell you what, how about a bet on whose ski comes in first? I'm betting that a pair of mine finishes ahead of a pair of yours. What do you say?'

'You want to bet on the skis, not the skier? That's crazy.'

'Not at all. Let's make it for a bottle of schnapps.'

'Otto, I didn't come here to talk about skis. I came to ask about Karl Lang.'

Otto's eyes narrowed. 'Lang? The Cowboy? What about him?'

'I want to know how he died. You were in the same outfit – you should know.'

'My God, Anton, that was a long time ago.'

'He was my friend, and I'd like to know. You mean you don't remember?'

'I'm trying to. Lang, let me see now. Lang.'

'And the rest of my friends, Peter, Willi, the others. They were all in your regiment, weren't they?'

Otto nodded soberly. 'All of them, and they were fine boys, too. They were all wiped out around the same time. One of the first battles on that front. We lost a lot of men that day.'

'And Karl?'

'Afraid I can't help you there. He bought it after I got this.' Otto tapped his knee. 'I was in the hospital for a month after I was wounded. I heard that Karl was killed a few weeks later. A sniper, I think it was. That's all I remember. I'm sorry, but it was so long ago.'

'I see. Thank you. I know this is ancient history to you, but it's all new to me. All those boys . . . gone.'

'It was a bad time for all of us.'

'Yes, you too. How did it happen to you?'

Otto filled his glass from the demijohn. He held it up to the light, then drank off half of it. 'Brother, let me tell you something about old soldiers. There are two kinds, those who talk about the war and those who don't. I'm the second kind. I did what I had to do for my country and my Emperor. That's all I have to say about it.' He finished what was left in his glass, and said more brightly, 'Now, how about that bet? My skis against yours for a bottle of schnapps.'

'Whatever you say,' Anton said absently. 'All right, for a bottle of schnapps.'

They ran the downhill race on Saturday with the slalom to come on Sunday. Saturday morning was clear and cold, without the flurries that had fallen during the week. The snow on the course was fresh, and it sparkled. Anton was out on the hill early with the racers, who were warming up by skiing the lower part of the mountain before climbing up to the starting gate at the twenty-three-hundred-metre level. He had a list of the twelve

192

men to whom he had given his skis, and one by one he searched them out to see what they thought of his product. He was pleased, but not surprised, by the answers they gave him. All twelve spoke highly of the lighter, more manoeuvrable skis, and all intended to use them in the race.

'She goes like velvet,' said Walter Kusche. 'I admit it, I was wrong. I tried it out just to humour you, but it's a damn fine ski. Tell you the truth, I still don't like the idea of all those bits of wood inside, but she goes like lightning and that's what counts.'

'Don't be afraid to push it,' Anton told him. 'The ski can take all the strain you give it.'

'I hope so, because I'm going to give it plenty today. I'm going to take this mountain apart.'

'You do that. I've got a bottle of schnapps riding on those skis.' He told Kusche about the bet with Otto.

The racer leaned on his poles to bring his head closer to Anton. 'Listen, Prince, about your brother.' He hesitated. 'He isn't doing you any good by the things he's saying about your skis.'

'What is he saying?'

'The same that everybody else has been thinking. That the ski is too light and it won't stand the strain. I know better, I've tried it out, but a lot of people are listening to what he's saying.'

'Well, Otto is in the business himself. I guess he feels he has to defend his own product.'

'Maybe so, but still, he's your brother. You should have a word with him.'

'Thanks, Kusche, don't you worry about it. Good luck.'

When the racers began their climb to the top, Anton skied down to the bottom to take up a position near the finish line. He stuck his skis into a snowbank and jumped up and down, swinging his arms across his chest. The air was dry, but the cold was so piercing that standing still soon became painful. Some of the spectators had started a bonfire, and he went over to get close to it. Otto was standing near the flames with a tall man dressed in city clothing. They both had their hands to the fire, rubbing them briskly. Otto waved him over.

'Good morning, brother,' he said. 'Did you bring the schnapps?'

'The race hasn't even started yet. Don't worry, if you win you'll get your bottle.'

'Oh, I'll win all right.' He turned to the man standing next to him. 'Let me introduce you to Herr Fritsch from Munich.'

Fritsch put out his hand. He was a man in his fifties with dead-white skin. 'A pleasure, Herr Prinz. Your brother has been telling me about you. It's not often that I get a chance to meet a big businessman from America.'

'Not so big. Are you in the ski business too, or did you come just to enjoy the races?'

Fritsch and Otto looked at each other, and an understanding passed between them. Otto nodded.

'I'm just visiting,' Fritsch said. 'I'm not in business.'

'Herr Fritsch is an official of the National Socialist Party in Germany,' said Otto. He was unable to keep the pride out of his voice. 'A very high official.'

'National Socialists?' Anton shuffled his feet closer to the fire. 'That's the Nazis, right? That rabble-rouser Hitler who went to jail.'

Otto opened his mouth to protest, but Fritsch said mildly, 'Is that how they see us in America? Actually, we have got quite respectable, you know. Over a hundred thousand members in Germany alone, and growing every day. We even have respectable businessmen like your brother in the party.'

Anton glanced at Otto in surprise. 'Here in Austria? I thought the Nazis were a German movement.'

'Which shows how much you know,' said Otto.

Fritsch looked at him reprovingly. 'In that case we should educate your brother. Herr Prinz, the concern of the party is the concern of every German-speaking person. In addition to our thirty-four districts in the Fatherland we have seven additional *Gaue* for Austria, Danzig, the Saar and the Sudetenland. Each *Gau* is divided into *Kreise,* with a local *Kreisleiter* in charge. In this area that happens to be your brother. We are very proud to have him with us.'

Otto bowed his head modestly, but it was clear that Fritsch's words were like a tonic to him. He straightened his back and his legs, and his chin came up.

'It sounds like an important position,' said Anton, but he spoke without conviction. He couldn't imagine any legitimate

194

organization entrusting real power to his brother. 'I didn't know that you were interested in politics, Otto.'

'There's a lot that you don't know about me.'

Fritsch said, 'You might take the time to find out about us yourself. After all, you are one of us.'

'No,' Anton said politely. 'I'm an American.'

Fritsch dismissed that with a wave of his hand. 'You are a member of the greater German-speaking nation. Our politics are your politics.'

'No, permit me to disagree again. Back home in Vermont I vote the straight Republican ticket. That's all I know about politics, and that's all I want to know. You'll excuse me now. The race should be starting soon, and I have to get back to the finish line.'

Elizabeth joined him just before the race began. She had Digger and Kurt in tow. The two boys had been inseparable since the day at the ski jump, and they now announced that they were going up the hill to watch the race from beside the *Känguruh-sprung*. Anton nodded his permission and they were off, climbing up beside the *piste* like monkeys on skis. Elizabeth watched them with approval.

'That's a fine child,' she said. 'It's nice to know that there's one decent Prinz.'

'He'll grow out of it,' Anton said sourly. 'The only decent one is my sister, unless she's changed too.'

'Do you still want to go on to Vienna?'

'Just as soon as these races are over.'

'*Achtung, Achtung.*' The blare came from a loudspeaker horn that was nailed to a tree. 'The first skier is on the course. Gottfried Scheer, from Zurich.'

It was over a minute before they could see the racer coming down the mountain, then he flashed off the *Känguruh-sprung*, soared through the air and landed on the *Zielschuss* to make the dash for the finish. After a moment his time was announced, and then the fact that the second racer was on the course. And the third, and the fourth. Anton consulted his list. Walter Kusche was due to start next.

Beside him, Elizabeth said, 'I know that we make our living from this, but I must say that watching a ski race is just about the dullest way to spend an afternoon that I can imagine. There's nothing to see. Just a flash and the racer is over the line.'

195

Anton nodded absently. His eyes were fixed on the *Känguruh* where Kusche would first appear. He saw a flash of colour, and Kusche was in the air, floating downhill, his skis adjusted to the angle of the slope, ready to land. He hit with his skis in a perfect telemark, one ahead of the other and his knees bent deeply. Then, as the crowd gasped, the snow exploded. Kusche pitched forward, hit, bounced high in the air, hit again, and lay still on the slope. Officials from the side of the *piste* rushed out to him.

Elizabeth clutched Anton's arm. 'What happened?'

'I don't know. It looked like a perfect landing.'

'Is he hurt?'

'It doesn't look good.'

The officials were clustered about Kusche, and one of them was signalling for a sled to be brought out. From below, Anton and Elizabeth watched as the skis were detached from the racer's boots and he was gently rolled onto the sled. He was strapped in place and the descent began, one official controlling the sled and two others following behind. When they got to the bottom a crowd closed in around the sled. Anton and Elizabeth pushed to get through. Around them they heard the murmur, *broken leg, broken leg.*

'Out of the way, out of the way,' the officials called. 'We have to get this man to a doctor.'

Anton managed to bull his way through to the sled. He knelt beside it. Kusche's face was twisted in pain.

'Kusche, what happened?'

'Your God damn ski, that's what happened,' the man said disgustedly. 'Christ, what a mess.'

'What do you mean, the ski?'

'It snapped, that's what I mean. It couldn't take the pressure. As soon as I hit on the landing the tip blew off. Oh, Jesus, that hurts.'

One of the officials tapped Anton on the shoulder. 'Step back, please, we have to move him.'

'Just one minute,' Anton said frantically. 'Kusche, listen, that's impossible. It couldn't have happened.'

'Couldn't, my ass, it did. Damn it, Prince, you could have killed me. You almost did. My own fault I guess. All those bits of wood inside. Should never have trusted it.'

'That's enough – you'll have to step back now.' As Anton rose the official shouldered him out of the way, pushing the sled through the crowd. As he passed by he handed Anton a ski. 'Here, I thought you might want this.'

Anton stared at the ski he had made. The tip was gone, cut off as if struck by an axe. Without the tip the ski had nose-dived into the snow, spilling the skier and twisting his leg in the grip of the beartrap binding. The result had to be a broken leg. Anton looked up. The eyes of the crowd were on him, some sympathetic, some condemning. He shouldered the ski and walked over to where Elizabeth was waiting.

In the breath of a whisper, she asked, 'What is it?'

'Look.' He pointed to the broken end of the ski. It was a clean break, straight across. 'It couldn't happen, but if it did, one chance in a million, it would never look like that. It would be shredded and twisted, not clean. That ski didn't break by accident.'

'Someone . . . ?'

'Sure, it's been weakened, then painted over. Easy enough, if you know what you're doing. I could do it myself if I had the equipment here.'

'But who?'

His voice was low and controlled, but the words came spilling out. 'God damn son of a bitch, woman, do you have to ask me that?'

She stared at him, speechless.

'I'm sorry, Lizbet. Forgive me.'

'Certainly,' she said calmly. 'You're quite right, I should have seen it at once. Someone who knows skis, and someone with a shop here in town. What a truly vile person he is.'

'We don't have any proof. We never will have.'

'But there must be something . . .' She broke off. 'Anton, what about the others?'

'I know, I've been thinking. There's nothing we can do.'

'But they have to be warned.'

'How can I do that? I can't stop the whole race. Besides, we don't know how many he did. Maybe just this one, maybe all of them. We have to wait and see.'

'Hey, brother,' Otto called. He stood beside the bonfire, his face slick and bright from the flames. 'You'd better go buy that bottle of schnapps. You'll never win a bet with broken skis.'

Anton stared at him, his face showing nothing. Elizabeth said tightly, 'If I were a man, I would kill him now.'

'No, you wouldn't. Control yourself. We have to wait.'

They waited through the afternoon while the racers ran the course. Four other Prince skis broke during the race, the tip snapping off, but there were no other serious accidents. There were spills and bruises, but no broken bones. Four disgusted racers walked down the mountain and threw their broken skis at Anton's feet. He said nothing to them. The crowd around the bonfire, led by Otto, jeered each time it happened, but Anton said nothing to them either. When the last of the twelve was safely down, Anton gathered up the broken skis, carried them over to the fire, and dumped them into the heart of it. The crowd cheered.

'You see, brother?' Otto shouted. 'Maybe I can't ski any more, but I know how to make them so they don't break.'

Anton stared at him silently. He stared for so long that Otto licked his lips nervously and began to edge away. Anton took a paper-wrapped bottle out of his pocket. He tossed it to Otto, who fumbled it and then held on.

'You see, Otto, I had it ready all the time.'

He went back to where Elizabeth waited. She said, 'You should have struck him.'

'A cripple?'

'Even so.'

He shivered in the cold. 'Go back to the hotel and start the packing. We won't wait for the slalom, we'll leave in the morning. Tell the driver to be ready. I'll wait here until the boys come down.'

'Which way will we be going? To Vienna?'

'No, back to Zurich. I want to go home. I should never have come back here. I should never have left Vermont.'

BOOK TWO

DIGGER

Chapter Thirteen

The Mediterranean island of Ibiza, in this summer of 1983, provides a most unlikely training camp for me. This is the first summer in seven years that I have not trained with the US Ski Team, but the regimen continues on my own. Each morning I run the ten kilometres up to San Carlos and back, do my hundreds by the side of the road, skip rope, charge up hills, and finish with a one-mile round-trip swim to Rat Island. The routine is an exercise in futility, and I don't know why I keep it up. I tell myself that I have to stay in shape, but I can't tell myself why. I'm going nowhere; the team goes on without me. The World Cup racing season will begin in December with a slalom at Kranjska Gora, and I won't be there. There's a downhill at Schladming the following week, and I won't be there. I won't be at Val d'Isère the week after that, or at Courmayeur, or Val Gardena, and when they raise the Olympic flag at Sarajevo, I won't be there either. Still, every morning at five-thirty I'm out on the road getting loose, staying in shape, preparing myself for some unraceable race, some uncontestable contest somewhere down the line. It's sad enough to laugh about. Kelly Prince, the skier with no place to ski.

I spend the rest of each day in the room in which I write these words. The room is long and low, an ell of the house in which I live, with thick masonry walls and a tiled floor to keep out the worst of the summer heat. My desk is a table by the window, and other tables run around three walls. On those tables are the memorabilia of the Princes and Prinzes, the treasure trove into which I dip daily as I try to come up with an understanding of myself, and of what snapped inside me last winter at Piz d'Rel. On one table are the journals of my grandmother, Elizabeth Chandler Prince: sixty-three volumes, all with the same hand-tooled leather bindings, the same powder-blue paper, the same precise script. On the next table are the corporate records

201

of the Prince Carpentry Company (later the Prince Ski Company), the fire-blackened files of Prinz Skis (courtesy of my Uncle Kurt), and a stack of financial statements for the Royal Ski Company (about which, more later). Around the wall on the next table are folders filled with newspaper clippings, some from sports sections and some from the news of the real world; and beside them a stack of books: *Digger Prince, Soldier on Skis*, by Harold Overton (Masterson & Clark); *The Yugoslav Experience*, by J. Linhart (Oxford University Press); *The War in Slovenia*, by Russel Bowers (Macmillan); and many more. Next, the trophies, a full table of them, and after that the table where I can lose myself for hours flipping through the folders and the albums of old photographs, some faded, some clear, all of them trying to tell me something.

So go my days, and my search, a journey of discovery seeking some nexus to bind me first to my father, Digger, and then to his father, Anton; and at times I have the feeling that I'm looking in the wrong places. I'm after a definition of fear, the essence and the why of it, and that won't be found in dusty archives. I'll find it only in myself, I fear, but still I wander each day down the line of tables picking up a morsel here and there to hold, to muse upon, to conjure up the past.

This photograph, for example, taken in Lake Placid, New York, at the Winter Olympics of 1932. Remarkable when you think that only four years before, Anton had left his hometown for the second time in his life with the jeers of his brother ringing in his ears, determined once again to divorce himself from his Austrian connection. Now, here he is posing in a group portrait with Otto, and Marta and the rest of the family, and one has to wonder why.

The reason was Marta's bright idea. At least, she thought it was bright. Actually, it was a terrible idea, and it didn't have a hope in hell of working. She was singing at the Metropolitan Opera that season when she heard that both Anton and Otto would be at Lake Placid for the Olympics. A well-meaning meddler in other people's affairs (perhaps because she handled her own so poorly) she at once blew a hole in her schedule at the Met and entrained for Lake Placid with her bright idea in hand, determined to heal the family breach. Only she could have engineered such an unlikely reunion, and only she could have persuaded her brothers to pose for this photographic

202

portrait taken in front of the Stevens House Hotel in a winterset of snowbanks etched with sharp shadows and icicles dripping from overloaded eaves, the adults grouped on the hotel porch and the children on the steps below. Examine the picture as they all compose themselves in the instant before the camera clicks.

Marta stands in the centre between her brothers, dwarfed by them despite the inches added to her height by a towering caracul hat. She gives the camera a smile that is heartfelt as well as professional. This reunion is wholly her creation and she is pleased with herself. Gatti had a fit when he heard that she would miss two performances, and there will be penalties to pay, no doubt, but it will be worth it if she can pull off her bright idea. After all, who else could have charmed Anton and Otto into staying at the same hotel with her? And who else could have blasted Franz out of his comfortable suite in New York and onto the Lake Placid train? Impossible man, the darling. Although the true darling, as usual, is Dieter, who has been an absolute lamb since the bright idea first struck her. So Marta has every right to be pleased with herself, and her smile is dazzling.

Beside her, Anton's face is set in a rigid frown. He's still trying to figure out how he got talked into this by his baby sister. He's in Lake Placid to sell skis to the Olympic athletes, and for no other reason. Certainly not to meet with that bastard Otto. Over the past few years he has got to know his sister again, and he trusts her motives, but still he's on his guard.

On Marta's other side, Otto's face is a study in divided feelings as he absently fingers the tiny gold swastika in his lapel. He too is here to sell skis, but right now his thoughts are on his wife, standing close by. So far, Anton and Lili have treated each other as childhood friends, nothing more, and he intends to see that it stays that way. He stopped caring about Lili long ago, she's just a piece of meat to him, but she's *his* piece of meat and all the world had better know it.

Elizabeth Chandler Prince stands grim and forbidding at her husband's side. Marta may have been able to charm Anton into this meeting, but she hasn't been able to convince his wife that any good can come out of it. Elizabeth remembers the day of the first Arlberg-Kandahar too clearly, and she has little patience with the Austrian branch of the family. Of them all, only Lili

203

attracts her interest. Any woman, poorly used, has always enlisted her sympathy, and she would like to snatch this one out of the life she leads and show her a better world. Besides, she feels a sneaking admiration for Lili's reputation of so long ago. Seven men dangling from a single apron string! Some secret genius must lie buried there.

Of the other three adults on the porch, Dieter looks bored, Franz's face is composed in contentment, and Lili stares stoically at the camera. Dieter is bored because he is always bored when he is away from Vienna's round of card games, coffeehouses, and gossiping anterooms. Franz is content because he has found a willing chambermaid on the second floor of the hotel with whom he has an appointment in the laundry room after lunch. Also, he likes being in America and he likes doing business with Americans, several of whom have made him interesting offers. To accept would be to leave Vienna, and God only knows how Marta would react to that, but the offers are appealing. Lili's stoic stare is that of a joyless woman with the spirit beaten out of her. Not that Otto often beats her any more; the only time he takes his stick to her is when he wants her body afterwards. It helps his mood, and in a perverse way she is pleased that her flesh can still serve such a function.

The children are ranged on the steps below the porch, and Hannes, the eldest, has taken the centre position. He is a tall seventeen with his father's lankiness and the same pinched, suspicious eyes over a probing nose, the same slash of lips, the same tiny swastika pinned to his sweater. His brother, Kurt, crouches on the steps beside him, a chubby, friendly puppy dog to whom each day brings new delights. Off to the side are the twins, Willi and Mimi, dressed identically in black ski pants, white parkas, and chequered woollen caps. Indistinguishable one from the other, their immaculate features are composed and incurious as they observe an alien world. And leaning easily against a rail is the boy who will be my father one day. At the age of twelve Digger is already a natural mountain man, but if he is his father's son on the hill he is his mother's son as well. He has Elizabeth's height and her clear, grey eyes, her fair hair, and the same assured self-confidence that is only a step away from arrogance. He looks impatient, most likely because he is wasting time that could have been spent skiing.

Posed now, and composed as they ever will be, the Princes

and Prinzes and those who attend them wait for the click of the camera.

The newly coined Winter Olympics came to Lake Placid in 1932 and promptly transformed the town. Main Street bustled, room rents tripled, and bearlike athletes with furry accents paraded the village streets. The home-team Americans did well. Irving Jaffee, the kid from the streets of New York, won two gold medals in speed skating, John Shea won two of his own, the bobsled team took gold as well, and the hockey team settled for silver. But in the skiing the winners were all Scandinavian: Sven Utterstrom, Veli Saarinen and Birger Ruud. This was not Alpine skiing, no downhill or slalom; that would not come to the Olympics for another four years. This was skiing Nordic-style: jumping from a ninety-metre hill, or slogging over the flat snow-fields in punishing cross-country races. It was far removed from the sport of the Alps, but the athletes wore skis and Anton and Otto, and a score of other manufacturers, were there to promote their products. What neither one of the brothers realized was that the other one would be there, and that their sister would seize the opportunity to bring them all together.

Marta presented her bright idea the day after she arrived in Lake Placid. That evening she invited her brothers to postpran-dial coffee and cognac in a private room on the second floor of the Stevens House. No other members of the family were invited; it was only for the children of Sepp and Hanna. Marta poured the coffee for her brothers with her own hands, made sure that their glasses were charged and the cognac bottle handy, and then settled back to lecture them.

'This has to do with business,' she said, 'and before you two start asking yourselves what your sister knows about business, let me tell you something about my husband. A lot of people think that Dieter is just a social butterfly, and maybe he is, but he is also a lot more than that. He's a man who knows the right people, and he's a man whom people trust. This means that he can get the answers to just about any questions I want to ask. All he has to do is make a few discreet calls to his banker friends, the ones he plays cards with. Well, I asked my questions and I got my answers. About the two of you.'

Both Anton and Otto murmured unhappily, but she ignored them, going on. 'The situation in this family is ridiculous. You're

205

both in the business of making skis, you're both doing well, but you both could be doing much better.'

She turned to Anton. 'Let me tell you what I know about you. You are one of the biggest manufacturers of skiing equipment in America today. You've doubled your gross sales every year for the past three years. You make what is considered to be an excellent product, but you have a major problem. You do all right here in America, but you can't sell to Europeans. They refuse to believe that a first-class ski can be made in America. They won't buy it, and if you can't sell in Europe you'll never grow any larger. How is that for a description of your situation?'

Anton said nothing. He looked at his sister silently. After a while he nodded slowly.

Marta turned to Otto. 'Now for you. From what I hear, you have a good business too. Your growth rate is just about the same as Anton's, and the two of you are probably grossing within ten percent of each other. But you have a problem as well. People aren't buying your skis the way they used to. You haven't kept up with the times; you haven't made a change in your design in years. People don't want what you're making any more. They want a more comfortable ski, and unless you give it to them you're going to see your sales go down. From what I hear, they already have, and if you don't do something about it quickly you're going to be in big trouble. Now tell me, how far wrong am I in that?'

Otto smiled at her pleasantly. 'This is not the sort of thing I talk about,' he said, 'not even to my darling sister. But let me ask a question of my own. Which one of those bloodsucking Jew bankers in Vienna gave your husband this information about me? I'd like to know his name.'

'We're not going to get anywhere if you talk like that. Please try to be sensible, Otto. I have something in mind, and I'd like you to hear it.'

Anton said, 'All right, Marta, you've been building up to it long enough. What is it?'

Marta raised a practised eyebrow. 'You mean it isn't obvious? Anton, you make a modern, efficient ski, but you can't sell it in Europe because it's made in America. Otto, you need a new product and you need it quickly. The two of you need each other. If Otto manufactures the Prince ski back in Austria it becomes a European product that you both can sell all over the world. Anton, all you have to do is give Otto the licence to make your ski, and then the two of you divide the profits. It's very simple, isn't it?'

Anton stared at her. 'You mean you want me to go into business with him? With that . . . that . . .'

'With your brother. It's the most logical thing in the world.'

'Logical? It's crazy. I'd rather go into business with the devil. You know what he did to me at the Arlberg-Kandahar. He sabotaged my skis, that's what he did.'

'That is a lie,' Otto shouted. He was up out of his chair. 'You've been saying that for years, and I won't have it any more. I had nothing to do with those skis' breaking. They were just bad skis.'

Anton, too, was up and shouting. 'They're better skis than you ever made. You filed them down and painted them over, that's what you did. Sure I've been saying it for years, and I'll keep on saying it, you saboteur.'

'Do you hear the way he talks?' Otto screamed at Marta. 'How did you think I could ever be associated with someone like that? I'm surprised at you. He can't even make a decent ski without its falling apart.'

'If you ever touch another one of my skis I'll break your neck.'

'Then keep your filthy skis where they belong, here in America. Austrians don't want anything to do with them.'

'Enough,' said Marta, and it was the voice of the Baroness von Ulm, commanding. Both men fell silent. 'The two of you are ridiculous, truly you are. It's just like the old days – you can't have a simple conversation without fighting. Do you realize how absurd you look? A one-legged man and a one-handed man about to start swinging at each other. What a sight that would be.'

Anton let the breath go out of him, and a faint smile touched the corner of his lips. Otto's lips were also twitching in something close to a grin.

'Quite a sight, indeed,' said Anton. 'It would be something to see.'

'We could sell tickets for it,' Otto agreed. 'The people would die laughing.'

'It seems that we finally agree on something.'

'On more than one thing. The idea is impossible.'

207

'Totally.' Anton went over to Marta and cupped her chin gently in his hand. 'A good try, little one, but you see how it is. It could never work.'

She shook her head angrily, and her whole body quivered. 'It's just that it makes me so mad, the two of you fighting this way. It's not the way a family should be.'

'It's the way this family has always been, and nothing is going to change that, Marta. Nothing.'

'What a foolish thought,' Elizabeth said. 'Imagine, the nerve of the woman, suggesting a thing like that.'

'Not nerve,' said Anton, who had had time to cool off and reflect. 'She's just trying to help. Actually, it's not such a bad idea.'

'You're not seriously considering it, are you?' It was late that night and they were preparing for bed, Elizabeth seated in front of the vanity mirror brushing her hair relentlessly. 'I won't have it. I won't let you do it.'

'I said it was a good idea, and it is. It would solve some problems. But not with Otto. Never with Otto.'

'Then I can sleep well tonight.'

Later, when they were in bed and close to sleep, Elizabeth murmured, 'Anton, something else. It's so obvious the way you and Lili avoid each other. You don't say a word to her, and if you come into a room she makes some excuse to go out. It shouldn't be that way. It looks worse than if you really had something to hide.'

Anton shifted his weight, and the bedsprings creaked. Hesitantly, he said, 'It's hard to know what to do. We were just kids when we were lovers. So what do you say to someone like that?' He sighed in the darkness. 'It's too confusing for me, so I don't say anything at all.'

'But you should. It was so long ago, and now she's your brother's wife. You should treat her that way. Be nice to her, Anton, say a few words. I feel sorry for her.'

'Yes, you would. I do too.'

'He beats her, doesn't he?'

'I don't know. I think maybe he does.'

'A wifebeater. You're not doing business with him. You're not.'

'I'm not.' Anton yawned.

208

'And say the first word to Lili. She needs some kindness in her life.'

But it was Lili who said the first word. The next day the cutter from the Stevens House, a huge sleigh capable of carrying twenty people, left the hotel for Mount Van Hoevenberg and the trials of the bobsled run. Of all the members of the Prinz reunion only Dieter and Anton and Lili were aboard, with the others occupied elsewhere. It was a brave and colourful outing with plumes fixed to the harnesses of the four-horse team and pennants snapping overhead, but the trip was cut short. They were barely out of the town of Lake Placid travelling south on the firmly packed snow when they saw the stream of sleighs coming towards them from the mountain. The driver of the first one, while he was still far off, cracked his whip several times, popping like gunfire, to get their attention, and as he passed, yelled out, 'Go back, go back, no bobs today.'

'Too hot on the mountain,' called someone from another sled. 'The ice is melting.'

A groan from the occupants of the cutter as their driver pulled up his horses and laboriously turned them around to head back to town. Once returned to the Stevens House, the driver pulled into the large shed which acted as a garage and the hotel guests descended, grumbling to each other for this was the third straight day on which the bobsled runs had been cancelled because of the weather. Anton sat stiffly in one of the back seats, waiting for the others to leave. Across the aisle Lili sat in a similar position, staring down at her hands folded in her lap. Dieter was one of the last off the cutter, nodding to Anton, tipping his hat to Lili, and then he was gone. The two of them were alone in the shed except for the driver, who was busy unhitching the horses.

'Stay as long as ye like,' he called to them in a York State version of Yankee asperity. 'Don't cost nothin' extry.'

It was dim and cold in the shed, and it was foolish to sit there that way, staring straight ahead, the two of them ignoring each other but reluctant to leave. Anton shook himself and was ready to move when Lili turned and said the first words.

'This is silly,' she said, looking at him directly. 'We can't keep on pretending that we're strangers.'

'I know,' Anton said heavily.

'We should talk.'

'That's not so easy.'

'Because of what I did to you? Is that why?'

'No, I never held that against you. You did what you had to do.'

'Then we should talk,' she said with a sudden and surprising firmness. 'There's nothing wrong with us talking.'

'I guess not.'

'But not now. Otto will be looking for me.' She looked at him speculatively, and her face was as lively as a young girl's. 'Will you meet me here tonight before dinner? We can talk then.'

'Here?'

'Right here in the sleigh. No one will bother us here. One hour before dinner?'

He swallowed hard, and nodded.

Later, in the night, they sat in the dark under piled-up lap robes, close but not touching. The words came slowly at first, for neither wanted to open old wounds. They spoke of family instead.

'Your wife . . . such a lady . . . and your son, a fine young man.'

'Your boys . . .'

'Yes, I know. Kurt is a good boy, but Hannes . . . like a wild animal sometimes. I can't believe he came from me.'

'Kids are kids. They change.'

'Marta's children, so strange.'

'Nothing from Vienna surprises me.'

'They make me nervous. Did you see them skating yesterday? Round and around on the ice together, not even holding hands, but moving exactly the same, like one person. So scarey, it made me shiver.'

'That happens with twins sometimes,' said Anton. 'What about this man Harz? What is he to her?'

'Her manager.'

'That's all?'

'And her lover.'

'Oh.' He shook his head in the darkness. 'My baby sister. Ah well, things like that happen in Vienna.'

Lili giggled. 'Anton, things like that happen all over the world, or have you forgotten?'

He felt the old familiar warmth of her then, the warmth

of Lili Wangenmann composed in equal parts of friendship, affection, and passion; and at the same time smelled for the first time in years the aroma of freshly baked bread and cinnamon that was so particularly hers. It was the aroma that stirred him most. He was a happily married man within the conventions of his marriage. He made love to his wife regularly and ardently, and he was not above savouring strange flesh on his occasional trips to Boston and New York. But this was something different. This was the flesh of his youth that he smelled, the aromas of his childhood as familiar to him as his mother's baking or his father's pipe. He felt his stomach turn over within him, and he clenched his one hand into a fist.

Lili giggled again. 'Anton, do you know what day it is today?'

'What day?' he repeated, confused. 'It's Wednesday.'

'Good, you remembered. Or did you?'

'What?'

'Faithful Anton, every Wednesday. Remember?'

'By God, you're right. Wednesday was my day.' Memories of the long and icy trek up Rendle washed over him, the chilling climb to her window and the warmth that waited inside. Wonderingly, he repeated, 'Wednesday was my day.'

'It still is,' she said softly.

He took her to him then, and after that first embrace there was all the fuss and bother of fumbling underneath the robes, snaps, and hooks and buttons, and then she was helping him as she realized that his one hand could not do it all. Cold and dark underneath the robes, and the seat of the cutter was hard, but they were laughing softly together now, living memories, and unaware of discomfort. Only once did she flinch from the touch of the stump of his wrist, the first time it touched her, and she was hit in the heart by the thought that if it had not been for her . . . and then the thought was gone, all thought was gone, and they were back again in time at their youthful revels as the springs of the cutter bucked and squeaked.

When it was over and they had fumbled again to set their clothing right, Anton sat back, breathing hard, and said, 'By God, that was Wednesday, all right. Can't fool me about Wednesdays. I'm an expert.'

'You are,' said Lili, snuggling close. 'You always were an expert.'

'Not what I meant, but thank you. It's been a long time since

211

I did it in the back seat of a cutter. Thank you again, Lili. Thank you for a piece of my youth.'

'Mmmm,' Lili murmured, her face buried in his shoulder. 'My youth too. I had forgotten what it was like to be young.'

They rested together in companionable silence until it was time for them to reappear, by separate routes, at the Stevens House for dinner. They looked each other over carefully, searching for signs of the remnants of passion, and then, satisfied that their secret was safe, they made their way in the dimness out of the shed and up the path to the hotel.

Digger was bored stiff at Lake Placid. The skating and the bobsled and all the other winter sports were of no interest to him, and ski jumping seemed like a waste of good snow that could better be used for downhill racing. But there was no downhill racing at this Olympics, and the recreational skiing was limited because the Olympic committee had preempted the best sites on Whiteface Mountain for its own use. When he heard that the local Snobird Club had organized its own downhill, he rushed to his father to ask if he could enter.

'Sure you can,' said Anton, 'if you can grow three years by tomorrow. It says on the bulletin board that you have to be fifteen.'

Digger thought about that, then said quietly, 'Papa, I could pass for fifteen. Everybody says I look older.'

'But I would have to say so.'

'Would you?'

'Are you asking me to lie for you, boy?'

Digger's face fell. 'No, of course not. I'm sorry. I didn't think of it that way.'

'But that's what it would be.'

'I know. It's just that I could win it, I know I could. Have you seen the kids around here ski? They're not very much.'

'There's your cousin Hannes. I hear he's entering.'

'I could beat him too.'

'He's seventeen, and he's a strong boy.'

Digger made a face. 'Makes no difference, I could beat him. He skis wild, out of control half the time.'

'That's what makes a good downhiller, taking chances.' Anton put his arm around his son's shoulders. 'I'm sorry, but I can't lie for you, and it's just as well. You're too young for a race like that anyway.'

During that time at Lake Placid the one bright spot for Digger was his cousin Kurt. By this time Digger's German was fluent, and Kurt's English was rapidly approaching that point. Over the past few years they had tried corresponding, but neither was a natural letter writer, and the exchange had languished. Now, with an entire week at their disposal, they threw themselves back into the friendship and spent as much time as they could together. They skied together, played together, ate together, and kept up a nonstop conversation. The only subject they never discussed was the enmity between their fathers.

On the morning of the race they took their skis and hiked down the road around to the far side of Whiteface Mountain. There they climbed with their skis on their backs until they were high above the starting hut where the racers were gathered. They crouched down on their heels and waited, watching what was going on below. Digger took a bar of chocolate out of his pocket, broke it in two, and passed half over to his cousin.

'Thanks,' said Kurt. 'I have an apple. Do you want it?'

Digger shook his head. 'I'm not hungry. The chocolate is for energy.'

'Do you know how you're going to do it?'

'Wait until it's almost over, then ski down and say that I want to race.'

'They won't let you.'

'We'll see.'

'There's a two-dollar entrance fee. Do you have two dollars?'

'No.'

After a moment, Kurt said, 'My mother gave me a dollar to spend. I still have it if you want it.'

Digger grinned at him. 'No thanks, I'll figure something out.'

Kurt pointed downhill. 'There's Hannes.'

Hannes was crouched in the snow near the starting hut, spreading a layer of wax on his skis. He wore a bib with the number eight on it. When he was finished waxing he stood up and loosened his muscles by kicking his legs in the air. With each kick his ski boot went higher than his head. Digger remembered him climbing uphill as if he were climbing a ladder. He knew how strong those legs were.

'How good is he back home?' he asked Kurt.

213

'The best. Not the best of the men, but the best of the boys. A real *Kanone*.'

'Not on this mountain. I'm going to whip his ass today.'

Down at the bottom, Anton and Otto stood together at the finish line as the racers began to come down the course. Anton had come alone and would have preferred to stay that way, but Otto had joined him. He was full of enthusiasm about his son's skiing, and he wanted to talk about it.

'Wait till you see him,' he said. 'He's better than I ever was. He skis like he was shot out of a gun. Straight ahead.'

'That's the way to do it if you want to win races,' Anton conceded.

'Back home he's the ski leader of the Hitler Youth, and they are the best in the district.'

'You're still mixed up with those gangsters?'

Otto pointed to the swastika on his lapel. 'What does this look like? You've been listening to the Jews over here. The international bankers have no love for Adolf Hitler, believe me.'

'I don't know any international bankers and I only know one or two Jews. But I know that the Nazis can only bring trouble to Germany. God help Austria if they get into power up north.'

'You don't know what you're talking about,' Otto said impatiently. 'You didn't go through the war with us. It was the Jews in Berlin and Vienna who sold us out. If you had stayed at home you would know that.'

'Let me remind you that I didn't have any choice about staying at home.'

'That old business, why bring that up? You could have stayed in Austria, you didn't have to go all the way to America. If you had stayed at home, if you had been in the army, if you had been wounded the way I was, then you wouldn't talk this way.'

A man called to the crowd through a megaphone: *'On the course now, number eight, Hannes Prinz.'*

'Here comes your boy.'

Up at the top, Hannes heard the starter say, 'Go,' and he took off downhill poling furiously until he had built up speed, and then tucked himself low over his skis as he dropped down the steep incline. The course swung to the left in a tight turn, then back again, the surface of the snow hard and slick. He followed the tracks of the racers who had gone before him into

214

a stand of fir trees laden with snow. The branches whipped at him, showering powder, as he passed by. Out of the trees and along a ridge marked with flags, still following tracks that showed the fastest line, he leaned into the next turn pressing hard, and then he was skidding down a shoulder in bright sunlight. The trail was narrow here, the snow was chopped by skis, and to the right the shoulder fell away in a precipitous drop to a chasm below. Up ahead a tangle of brush lay across the trail. Pass it on the right or the left? The left was the uphill side, and longer, but to pass on the right meant to ski on the very edge of the shoulder with that drop only inches away. Split-second decision. All the tracks led to the left, and he followed them, up and around the brush and down into an icy chute that cut off the sun, then out again and pressing for the banner at the finish line. He crossed the line low and extended, to a scatter of shouts and applause. His legs were aching as he stood up and pushed back his goggles.

'That was number eight, Hannes Prinz, finishing, folks. His time . . . two minutes and three seconds, exactly. Best time so far.'

Up at the starter's hut Digger approached the official in charge, a lantern-jawed man with a stubble of beard, and asked if it was too late to enter the race. Lantern-jaw looked him over carefully and twanged, 'How old ye be, sonny?'

'Fifteen and a half. Sixteen soon.'

'Where ye from?'

'Over Vermont way. Sedgewick Falls.'

'Pretty puny fer fifteen, ain't ya? Grow 'em small over thataway.'

York State bastard, the boy thought, but he just grinned. 'I'm big enough to ski it, mister, really I am.'

'Cost ye two dollars entrance fee. Ye got two dollars, boy?'

'Don't have it on me, but my daddy has it down below. He'll pay it, don't worry.'

'Don't worrit me none. He'll pay, or it'll come outta yer hide.' Lantern-jaw passed over a bib with a number on it. 'Put this on. We're almost finished, so ye go off next.'

'Who has the fastest time so far?'

Lantern-jaw scratched his chin. 'Number eight. Some German kid.'

'Austrian,' said Digger, and when the man looked at him, 'Never mind.'

He set himself in the starting gate, his eyes fixed on the trail below. He said to himself softly, 'Straight ahead. All the way. No checks.'

'*Go*!'

He launched himself out of the starting gate, booming down the fall line with his body low, his head down, and his arms forward, skittering over the rutted tracks of the earlier skiers. He took the high line round the first curve and into the trees, his eyes in slits behind the goggles, the trees a blur whipping by. Another blur of the flags on the ridge and the glare of the sun came off the snow in diamond points as the trail narrowed down along the shoulder. Running free here, hard and smooth, and he felt his heart lift up inside as it always did when the hill was right, and the snow was right and the speed was just the way it ought to be: throwing him out, and down and far; and up ahead the tangle of brush that lay across the trail. Part of him saw that all the tracks led left around the brush, but that part never registered. Without a conscious thought his legs elected the lower, faster way, running along the rim beside the drop. He felt the lurch as his right ski slid and went off into space, nothing below it, and he felt the lurch in his belly as well. He teetered, left ski gripping, edging hard, right ski up in the air, and now he felt the empty space beneath him all the way up to the back of his neck. He ran along the rim that way, canted over on the edge of one ski in a stretch of time that went on and on, the muscles in his left leg screaming until the mountain moved out from under him and gave him room again. Solid snow beneath both skis, his right leg slammed down and he was whirling into the chute of ice, in and out of the sun, and tucked into the final, aching schuss that stretched him down the mountainside and over the line between the flags, down the hill, and home.

He came to a stop with a flourish that threw up a curtain of snow and ice. The first face he saw was that of his father, and that face was angry as Anton came towards him over the snow. He stood still on his skis and waited. His father towered over him.

'How did you get in this race?' Anton asked.

'I told the man on top that I was fifteen.'

216

'Is that how I taught you?'

'No, Papa. It was wrong to lie. I'm sorry, but I had to run this race.'

'Get your skis off,' Anton said grimly. 'We're going back to the hotel.'

'The time on the last runner,' called the man with the megaphone, *'was one minute fifty-nine and two-fifths. That makes him the winner, folks, whoever he is. He was a late entrant and we don't have his name.'*

Anton's head jerked up. 'Does he mean you?'

'Yep,' said Digger calmly.

'You won?'

'That's what he says. I was pretty sure I would.'

'You won.' Anton's voice jumped with excitement. 'You beat them all. The hell with that, you beat Otto's boy.'

'What was his time?'

'Two minutes three. God damn, you beat him.'

'Will that last runner give us his name? We need the name of the winner, please.'

Anton whipped around and called across the snow, 'His name is John Prince. That's my son, John Prince.'

'Digger, Papa, please,' the boy prompted.

'Digger Prince,' Anton yelled, 'and he's the best God damn skier in Vermont except for me, and maybe York State too.'

'Digger Prince the winner, folks. Digger Prince.'

Digger nodded, a grin on his face. It was the first time he had ever heard his name called out in public that way, and it sounded good. Digger Prince, the winner. The first time, but not the last time, he promised himself. He tried to stand as tall and as straight as he could as he looked around at the people applauding politely. It was a good feeling, but it suddenly stopped being good when he saw Hannes. His cousin wasn't applauding. He was staring at Digger with eyes so full of hate that the emotion was a living thing between them, stretching out over the snow. He had never seen naked hate before. He stared back as hard as he could, knowing that he had to match the hate with something. He didn't know what that something was, but he kept his eyes fixed and he did not move. Someone came between them, blocking the view, and when the way was clear again Hannes had gone. Digger realized that he had been

217

holding his breath, and he let it out. Only then did he remember to tell his father that they owed the man at the top two dollars.

Chapter Fourteen

Nineteen thirty-four was a year of turmoil in Austria. The year opened in an atmosphere of tension and suspicion as the Socialist Party organized its private army, the Schutzbund, in opposition to the private army of the right, the Heimwehr. The breach between the left and the right was total, although each side knew that unless there was a united front against the Nazis the country was lost. With Hitler in power in Germany, and with the Austrian Nazi Party now a legal movement, there were constant rumblings from across the border for an *Anschluss,* or union, between the two German-speaking states. Few, if any, Austrians had any illusions about what that would mean; it would certainly not be a union of two equal partners. Despite this, the right and left of Austrian politics refused to work with each other, with Chancellor Dollfuss of the Christian Socials refusing even to negotiate with the Socialists.

By February the atmosphere was explosive, and the fuse was lit when the Socialists of Vienna called a general strike, which resulted in the total loss of gas, electricity, and public transportation. Dollfuss, by chance, was in Budapest at the time, but his deputy, Major Emil Fey, saw the strike as an opportunity to stamp out the Socialists once and for all. He mobilized the Vienna section of the Heimwehr, flung it into battle against the Socialist Schutzbund, and civil war broke out in the city. Late in the day the government moved field artillery into town and succeeded in driving the Socialists into the northern part of the city, where they took refuge in a series of modern concrete tenement blocks that were as strong as fortresses. Despite this, the Socialists were forced to surrender after twenty-four hours of intensive artillery bombardment. Some of the Schutzbund held out longer in Floridsdorf across the Danube, but in two days it was all over. The Socialist leaders fled to Czechoslovakia, the mayor of Vienna was imprisoned, and the Socialist Municipality of Vienna, which had lasted for sixteen years, was ended.

It was a victory for the right, but the only true winners were the Nazis.

By June of that year life in Vienna was gayer than at any time since the end of the war. It seemed that the menace of a civil war had passed, and at the same time negotiations with Hitler had produced a statement from the German Chancellor that he recognized total Austrian independence and was determined to respect it. Bolstered by such fragile assurance, Vienna was its former self again. The old imperial uniforms reappeared, dusty and faded, but still impressive. The brilliant Opera Ball was revived, trade was good, the currency was stable, and even the chronic unemployment seemed to be easing. It was a time for optimism, but it was only an illusion. By July the familiar Nazi rumblings could be heard again from across the frontier, and rumours circulated in Vienna of an impending putsch against the government. Details of the plot leaked out, but the warnings reached the government in an inaccurate form, and much too late.

On the twenty-fifth of July, twenty men gathered in a tram-line carbarn situated not far from the Chancellery in Vienna. They were all members of the Austrian Nazi Party, drawn from every part of the country, and with the exception of the leader they were unknown to each other. This anonymity was deliberate, and they had been instructed to address each other only by number. The leader was Number One, and so on down the line. The man known as Number Seven in the group was Hannes Prinz. At nineteen, Otto's son was fully grown into a tall, broad, athletic man with a ruthless determination to achieve his goals, and a blind and driving obedience to the Nazi Party. His assignment to this special squad had come as a direct result of these attributes.

In the carbarn the twenty men quickly changed into uniforms of the Austrian army, complete with sidearms, and then piled into three automobiles which were waiting outside. It was a short drive to the Chancellery, where they disembarked and formed into a squad with Number One acting as the officer. Barking orders, he marched them onto the Chancellery grounds and up to the front door of the building, which was guarded by two soldiers. Number One halted the squad and said simply, 'Four and Six. Now.' Those two men jumped forward and subdued the guards while the rest of the squad poured in through the door and into the ornate lobby still decorated in the style of the *Kaiserstaat*. They pounded up the great staircase to the office of the Chancellor and threw open the doors. Dollfuss, his deputy Major Fey, and three other men looked up from paper-laden desks with expressions of dismay on their faces.

'No firing,' said Number One, but his order was intended only for his men, not for himself. He drew his pistol and shot Dollfuss three times in the chest. The Chancellor slumped forward over his desk, his blood leaking over immaculate government documents. Then the weight of his body pulled him sideways, and he slid from his chair to the floor. He lay there unmoving.

In the shocked silence that followed the shooting, Number One pointed his pistol at Major Fey and said, 'You're staying here. The others can leave.'

As the three aides hurried from the room, the men of the squad took up positions at the windows and doors. Hannes, as Number Seven, had the post at the window directly behind the Chancellor's desk and his feet were only inches from Dollfuss's outstretched hand. From across the room Number Three called out from his window, 'Troops forming up in the courtyard below, sir.'

'That was anticipated,' Number One said calmly. He motioned for Major Fey to be seated at his desk. The man who had massacred the Socialists in February was totally unnerved, and barely managed to totter to his chair.

'What do you want from me?' he croaked.

'You're going to get us out of here,' Number One told him, 'but for the moment you are going to sit there quietly.'

'More troops out in front,' Number Three called out from his window. 'Looks like they have police with them, too.'

'That also was anticipated,' said Number One. 'Everyone stay calm.'

From his post at the window Hannes could see the government troops forming up in the courtyard, and for the first time he began to have doubts about the organization of this venture. He did not question that the assassination of Dollfuss was vital to the interests of the Nazi Party, but he had not volunteered for a suicide mission and he did not see how they were going to get out of the Chancellery alive. He was wondering about this when he heard a faint moan and looked down at his feet. Dollfuss's eyes were open and his lips were moving.

220

'Number One,' Hannes called sharply, 'this man isn't dead.'

Number One came across the room quickly and knelt over the fallen Chancellor. 'Amazing,' he said. 'I put three good ones in him and he's still breathing.'

Hannes drew his pistol. 'Shall I finish him off?'

Number One hesitated. He looked down at Dollfuss, then out the window at the troops in the courtyard. 'No,' he said, 'not yet. Just let him lie there.'

Dollfuss moaned again and moved his lips, trying to say something. The word came out in a series of stutters.

'What's he saying?' Number One asked.

Hannes knelt over the dying man and listened. He looked up at his leader. 'He's saying, "Priest." He wants to confess.'

Number One threw back his head and laughed. 'The old villain. They all call for a priest when it comes to the end, don't they?'

The telephone rang then. Number One's head came up and he called to his men. 'That's what we've been waiting for. Keep your eyes open and call out if there's any movement down below.' He hurried across to the desk where Fey was sitting and pointed to the ringing telephone. 'You're going to answer that and you're going to get us out of here. It's your neck if you can't do it. Safe conduct to the German border is what we're asking for, and you're the hostage, Major Fey. If you can get it for us, you live. If you can't . . .' He shrugged. 'Pick it up and start negotiating.'

Fey looked at the instrument as if it were a live animal about to strike at him. He asked, 'What if they ask about the Chancellor?'

'You say nothing about what has happened here. If they ask, you simply say that the Chancellor is alive but that you have been appointed to negotiate. Now go to it.'

The negotiations took four hours while Fey argued and pleaded with the commander of the troops in the courtyard, and with the President of the Austrian Republic, who had been tied into the telephone line from his holiday retreat in Carinthia. During those four hours Dollfuss grew weaker and weaker as he vainly called for a priest, and Hannes grew more and more doubtful that any of them was going to get out of the situation alive. It was stupid, just plain idiotic, to try to pretend that the Chancellor was alive and well. He was barely alive, and not for

221

long, a fact that would be made painfully clear once a safe conduct was granted and troops were allowed to enter the office. The whole affair had been botched from the beginning and they were all going to be lined up against the wall and shot.

Hannes, my boy, this is a fuck-up, he told himself, and it's time for you to get out.

Turning from the window, he called out, 'Number Seven requests permission to leave post.'

When Number One nodded his permission he crossed the room and whispered in his leader's ear. Number One scowled and said, 'Certainly not. Piss against the wall if you have to.'

Hannes put a pained look on his face. 'It's not a piss that I have to take.'

Still scowling, Number One waved his hand in permission. 'Go ahead then, but make it quick. There's a place down the hall.'

Hannes hurried out of the room and down the deserted corridors towards the rear of the building. As he had expected, he found a back staircase designed for the use of tradesmen and porters, and quickly scampered down the stairs past the ground floor to the basement. He climbed up on a box and peered out one of the basement windows set high above the floor and just above ground level. He found himself staring at the back of a row of uniform-clad legs standing at attention. It was the work of a moment to prise open the window, hoist himself through it, and wiggle out onto the flagstones of the courtyard. He got to his feet quickly, looking around to see if he had been observed, but all heads were facing the main entrance of the building. Taking a military pace, he strode without hesitation to the rear of the nearest body of troops and took up a position directly behind the last rank of men. Dressed as he was in the uniform of a sergeant of infantry, he looked exactly as if he belonged there.

Hannes stood at attention in the sweltering heat of the July afternoon until the unit he had attached himself to was temporarily relieved. At the command of the officer in charge he marched out of the Chancellery grounds at the rear of the formation, keeping perfect step, and once past the gates he quickly lost himself in the crowd that had gathered there. Less than two hours later he was back in civilian clothing and seated in a compartment on the Innsbruck Express, heading west. The railroad station had been boiling with gossip. The rumour was that Major Fey had finally secured an agreement for safe conduct to the border, but only on the condition that no blood had been shed. This condition he had wisely kept to himself, and when government troops had entered the office and found Dollfuss dead the conspirators had been promptly arrested. According to the gossip they were sure to be hanged.

Hannes looked out the window at the countryside passing by. He smiled at his reflection in the glass. The party had been looking for martyrs, and it had got nineteen of them. The twentieth was heading home to the Tirol for a while. It was time to lie low and wait for better days.

Against this background of civil unrest and menace from the north the institution of the Vienna Opera continued on unperturbed, as did the life and the career of Marta von Ulm, Die Prinz. Unperturbed, but not without change. As she moved into her mid-thirties her voice became softer and richer, allowing her to extend her range of roles and bringing new triumphs her way. Age, and time, also served to bring into focus her relationships with the two men in her life. Not even occasionally now did Dieter come padding into her bedroom in the early morning. The days of their passion, sputtering as it had been, were over, and they lived together now as the most congenial of friends. With Franz the situation also took on an institutional aspect. Regularly, once each year, he could be counted on to find himself an ambitious young singer or actress and overwhelm her for a week, or two, or three. Then would come the inevitable flare-up and Marta would shake her lover loose from sticky female fingers and reclaim him for her own. But most important of all, the passing of time gave Marta the mixed pleasure of watching her children grow.

Willi and Mimi matured rapidly in the hothouse atmosphere of Vienna in the Thirties, witnesses to the sensuality and corruption all around them, and as they entered their teenage years they took on the look of angelic choristers with knowing eyes. Despite this look they exuded an aura of asexuality. Clearly male and female now, at thirteen their alien airs and their removal from the world around them made them seem more like dissociated observers of the human condition than like ordinary mortals subject to the Fall. They were always together, had no

223

friends of any age, and spent their leisure time reading from a single book, painting pictures with a single brush, or lying on the drawing-room floor and listening to music on the gramophone with an intensity that bordered on a hypnotic state. Each winter when they went with their mother to St Anton for the skiing they kept themselves aloof from their Prinz connections, skiing the high passes of the mountains for days at a time, sheltering at night in the climbers' cabins and coming down to the valley only when they were thoroughly sated with life at the top. The mountain people there, who occasionally caught glimpses of them skiing through the stands of pine and fir or working along a faraway ridgeline, called them 'the gnomes' and thought them to be cursed.

It was after one of these winter vacations that Marta returned to Vienna with the children to find that Dieter had engaged a new chauffeur. Jacques, who had served them so well for so many years, was to be pensioned off.

'It was unavoidable,' Dieter told her. 'I don't know whether it was the years or the schnapps, but he was getting absolutely shaky behind the wheel. The final straw came last week. Imagine, driving the new Mercedes directly into the milk wagon down the street. Thank God no one was hurt. He *claims* that the horse reared and startled him, but frankly I think he was half asleep. I'm sorry, darling, I know how much you like the old chap, but he had to go. Full pension, of course.'

'The children will miss him,' mused Marta. The old driver was the only one of the servants whom the twins would favour with a smile.

'I know, but there was nothing else I could do.'

'What is the new man like?'

'His name is Martin, a clean-cut sort of chap. About forty, I'd say. Seems to know about motors.'

It was not until the next morning that Marta met the new chauffeur. She appraised him carefully as he held the door of the Mercedes open for her, and she followed him with her eyes as he came around to slide into the driver's seat. Through the speaking tube, he asked, 'The Opera House, baroness?'

'Yes, Martin.'

A solidly built man, she thought, perhaps more than forty with all the grey hair, but why does he seem so familiar to me?

She studied the back of his head as they drove into town,

wishing that she could ask him to turn around so that she could see his face again. His features nagged at her memory, but she could not place them. Also his voice . . . something about his voice. He had spoken only a few words but . . . yes, of course, those broad o's . . . just the way the people spoke back home . . . just the way she herself once had spoken. And then suddenly she knew. She picked up the speaking tube.

'Martin, stop the car, please.'

'Here, baroness? Right here?'

'Right here. Stop at the side of the road.'

He brought the car to a smooth stop on the grassy verge of the road and sat without moving, his eyes facing forward.

'Martin,' she said, 'please turn around and face me.'

Slowly, reluctantly, his head turned until she could see his face in profile. 'Farther, please,' she ordered.

He shifted his body so that he could look directly into the back seat through the glass partition. Marta's eyes met his and locked there. She studied his features silently. Finally, she said, 'Your name isn't Martin at all. You're Karl Lang from St Anton, aren't you?'

His eyes narrowed, and he said, 'Baroness, please . . .'

'Aren't you?'

He nodded slowly.

'Good, I thought so. Now, start the car and go down the road about a hundred metres to the next right turning. Follow the turn and you will come to a small dairy shop at the end of the street. That's where we're going. We're going to have ourselves some fresh coffee with *Schlag,* and you are going to tell me what this is all about.'

'Madam, I couldn't do that.' He seemed horrified. 'I couldn't sit down in a public place with you. It would be scandalous.'

'On the contrary. In Vienna it would be considered affected, but nothing more. Now go.'

Once they were seated at a small table in the back of the dairy, Marta pulled off her gloves, tapped the marble tabletop with a fingernail, and said, 'Now, what's this all about? You're supposed to be dead. Killed in action on the Italian front was the way I heard it when I was a girl. That was twenty years ago. When did you come back to life?'

Karl twisted nervously in his seat, his cap in his hands and his coffee untouched before him. 'Baroness, really, I can't sit here with you this way.'

'Let's start by doing away with the "baroness". That's not what you used to call me when you let me ride on your back like a horsey.'

For the first time Karl's features relaxed into a smile. 'You remember that, do you?'

'Of course I do. You were my brother's best friend, weren't you? You called me Marta then, and that's what you call me now. At least, when we are alone. Now let me hear you say it.'

'All right, Marta, all right, but it isn't easy to call the famous diva, Die Prinz, by her first name. Of course, I knew it was you when the agency sent me to apply for the job. I shouldn't have gone, but I was hoping you wouldn't remember, and . . .' He stopped and looked away.

'I know. Jobs are hard to find these days. Particularly for a man who has been dead twenty years, I should think.'

He shook his head grimly. 'No, I was never dead. That's the choice that the army gives you when they send you to prison. If you want them to, they send home word that you've been killed. No shame for the family that way.'

'Prison,' Marta said faintly.

'I was sentenced to twenty years.'

'You mean you've been there all this time?'

The smile came back to his face. 'No, the end of the war meant the end of my prison. When the Emperor abdicated there was a general amnesty for people like me. Altogether, I was inside just short of four years. Of course, once I got out I couldn't very well go home.'

'Of course not,' Marta murmured. 'You were supposed to be dead. How terrible for you. And for your family.'

Karl shrugged. 'Probably better that way.'

Marta hesitated. 'Karl, is it improper to ask what you . . . I mean, why you were sent to prison?'

He regarded her silently. 'Of course, if you thought I was dead you wouldn't know. So Otto never said anything. I didn't think he would.'

'Otto? My brother? What's he got to do with this?'

'Marta, little Marta.' He shook his head, laughing silently. 'All these years you didn't know. I was court-martialled and

226

sent to jail for shooting your brother. I tried to kill the son of a bitch, but I only got him in the knee.'

He told her all about it then. He tried to skim over the relationship of the seven young men to Lili Wangenmann, but she waved her hand impatiently to indicate that that part, at least, was known. She urged him on, listening intently as he described his army days, the St Anton Six, the last patrol, and the death of his five friends. She put her face in her hands when he told her about the long trek back to camp, the scene in the cave, and the shot that only wounded Otto. When he lapsed into silence she shook her head slowly, looked up, then took some coins from her purse and put them on the table.

'Let's walk,' she said. 'I can't absorb all this sitting here.'

The dairy shop was set at the edge of a tiny forest, and they walked silently among the trees and over a rutted path, Marta with her eyes on the ground and a blade of grass between her teeth. She sucked on it thoughtfully, but she did not speak. The earth was soft and muddy from the recent rain and soon her boots were filthy, but she walked on. Karl dropped back a discreet pace to leave her alone with her thoughts, and they crossed through the woods that way, circling back until they came again to the dead-end street where the dairy stood. As they came out of the trees, Marta turned to face him.

'This is all true?' she asked quietly. 'On the head of your mother?'

'I don't even know if my mother is still alive.'

'I don't know either,' Marta admitted. 'I don't keep up with things back home any more. But you know what I mean. Is it true?'

'Yes, little Marta, all of it. On the head of my mother, wherever she is.'

'And that's how my heroic brother got his battle wound?'

'Is that the story he tells? Battle wound?'

'They gave him a medal for it.'

'Well, why not? If they can make me dead they can make him a hero. It really doesn't matter any more.'

'Tell me, one thing I must know. Do you still think he killed your friends? Eugen and Dolf and the others?'

'No, not any more. I thought so then. I think I went a little crazy. More than a little. I was sure he had planned it that way. But not any more. Not that it makes any difference. He killed

227

them accidentally just to break that stupid record. He killed them just as surely as if he had shot them each in the head. He's just as guilty.'

'Yes,' she said softly, 'I see that. And they gave him a medal for it.' She started to put a hand on his arm, thought better of it, and drew it back. 'Karl, you realize that I have to tell my husband about all this. I keep nothing from him.'

'I thought you might say that. It's all right, there are other jobs.'

'Oh no, I didn't mean that. You'll stay on with us, I'll insist on that. But I have to tell him.'

'As you wish, little Marta, as you wish. Just don't tell him that you used to ride horsey on my back. You were only five years old, but I don't think he would appreciate that.'

Marta smiled faintly and walked to the car. Karl followed quickly and opened the door for her. The smile disappeared as she looked at him.

'We'll have to hurry, Martin,' she said. 'I'm already late for rehearsal.'

The new chauffeur inclined his head slightly. 'Yes, baroness, at your orders.'

The only positive result of Marta's bright idea at Lake Placid was Anton's growing conviction that the only way to crack the Austrian market was by a massive frontal assault. There would be no more begging distributors to handle his product, no more scrambling to place an order for a hundred pair of skis here and there. Instead, he entered into correspondence with a Viennese importer named Pilnik, and made arrangements to ship eight thousand pair at a price that was dangerously close to his own cost. Even if Pilnik managed to sell every ski, Anton would barely break even, but his name would be established in the prime Austrian market. If the skis did not sell the loss would be substantial, but it was a gamble that Anton was willing to take.

The skis were shipped early in 1935, and two months later Anton received a notice from the Customs Bureau in Vienna stating that the shipment was being held in bond pending the filing of further documentation. The notice appeared to be nothing more than a broad strip of bureaucratic red tape, and it was sent to Pilnik with instructions to clear the shipment as quickly as possible. Pilnik's reply followed.

'4 April. I have filed the required forms with the Customs Bureau and have been advised that the shipment will be released within the next two weeks.'

And then, '27 May. I regret to report that the shipment still has not been released. Further forms are now required; however, they are unobtainable since they have not yet been printed. I am told that they will be available shortly.'

'7 July. I confess my embarrassment in the matter of your shipment. Having filed all the necessary documents, I am now told by Customs that there will be an additional charge for the storage of the skis from the date of their receipt until the present. I enclose the Customs invoice and await your instructions.'

'24 July. Receipt of your payment is acknowledged. The funds have been transferred to the proper authorities.'

'12 September. I can understand the sharp tone of your last letter, but you must understand that I am exerting every effort to secure the release of your shipment. In thirty years of doing business I have never encountered such a situation. It seems impossible to move your skis through Customs. I have offered the usual persuasions, which have been accepted but which have produced no results. This, in itself, is outside my experience, since our Customs officials are known to be venal, but trustworthy. I am continuing my efforts.'

'15 November. I have nothing new to report. Every effort that I make to clear your shipment is met by another wall of bureaucratic delay. The situation is impossible. If you wish to replace me in this matter I will understand.'

Early in January of 1936, Anton and Elizabeth sailed from Boston harbour on board the *Bremen* bound for the Winter Olympics to be held in Garmisch-Partenkirchen, Germany. Although the Games were their eventual destination they went first to Vienna to see what could be done about releasing the shipment of skis. They travelled without Digger. The boy's schoolwork, Elizabeth had decided, was too poor to allow for time off, and he had been left, sullen and rebellious, in the care of the housekeeper, Mrs Mulloy. He would miss not only the Olympics, but a chance to see Kurt. Both losses hurt.

Anton and Elizabeth arrived in Vienna and the next day Anton moved against the Viennese bureaucracy. At ten in the morning he presented himself at the main hall of the Customs Bureau, displayed his documents, and was asked to wait. After an hour he was received by a junior official who studied his papers and passed him on to someone higher. This higher someone notified Anton that he was in the wrong department, accompanied him across the hall, and turned him over to someone still more senior. This august person kept him waiting only fifteen minutes, and the shipping papers were examined for the fourth time that morning.

'You will want to see Herr Becker about this,' he was told. 'Herr Becker is in charge of all special cases.'

Herr Becker was an enormously fat man with a shining pink face and a jolly smile. He sat Anton down, offered him coffee, and beamed at him with his hands folded over his belly. Anton presented his papers yet another time, but Becker waved them away cheerfully.

'No need for that, I'm familiar with the case,' he said. 'No doubt you want your shipment released.'

'That's what I'm here for,' Anton said patiently. 'You've had those skis in bond for almost a year. What do I have to do to get them out?'

'Nothing simpler, my dear fellow. Just pay the impost.'

'Another charge? What is it this time?'

Herr Becker tut-tutted with cupid-bow lips. 'Most neglectful of your man Pilnik. He should have kept you informed of the new regulations.'

'Which new regulations are those?'

'Why, the luxury surtax. It applies to all manufactured imports in categories C through G. Sporting goods fall under category F. Let me see now, I should have your schedule somewhere here.' Becker rummaged over his desk and came up with a typewritten list. 'Here you are. The figure at the bottom is the total surcharge.'

Anton read the figures carefully, then read them again. The total charge was more than twice the value of the skis themselves. He looked up and said, 'This is impossible.'

'I thought you might say that.'

'I won't pay it.'

'That's up to you.'

'I'll ship those skis back to America before I'll let you squeeze me like this.'

'No, you won't.'

'Who is going to stop me?'

'I am. Those skis go nowhere until you pay the charge. The impost is to get them out of bond, and it doesn't matter what direction they're going in. Into the country or out, you still have to pay it.'

'Robbery.'

'Now, now. It's the law.'

'And when did this new law take effect?'

'I'm not sure. Last week? Last month? It really doesn't matter, does it? Look here, why don't you take the schedule with you and think it over? Let me know what you decide to do. I assure you that it's a matter of indifference to me. For all I care your skis can stay in the warehouse forever.'

That afternoon Anton sat with Dieter von Ulm in the Café Walch on the Ringstrasse and told his brother-in-law of his conversation with Herr Becker. When he was finished he stared moodily at the whipped-cream confection in front of him that passed for an honest cup of coffee in Vienna.

'I was willing to gamble,' he said, 'but I didn't know that the dice were going to be loaded.'

'Very curious,' said Dieter. He ran a finger over his immaculate moustache and crossed one knife edge of a trouser leg over the other. He was at home in the Café Walch; it was his regular afternoon stop. 'One becomes accustomed to corruption, but this seems to be something else entirely. It's as if they don't want you to get the skis out ever.'

'It looks that way, doesn't it? It isn't worth it to me to get them out of bond. I might as well leave them there and swallow the loss.'

'Will it be a large one?'

'Large enough. It won't break me, but it's going to hurt.'

'I see. But who would want to do this to you? Who would profit from it?'

'No one. That's what bothers me. It's a puzzle without an answer.'

'Permit me to doubt that. It has been my experience that the more bizarre the puzzle, the simpler the solution once you find it.'

Anton absorbed that without comment, wondering what

experience Dieter was referring to. From what he knew, the man did nothing but sit in cafés and play cards day and night.

'I wonder,' Dieter said mildly, 'if you would mind if I inquired into this matter. Most discreetly, of course. I just might be able to turn up something helpful.'

'What did you have in mind?'

'Then I may?' Dieter looked around the room, his eyes darting from table to table. They fastened on a slight, elderly man sitting in a far corner playing single-handed chess. Dieter murmured, 'Hallstein, of course.' He unfolded himself gracefully, and stood up. 'Forgive me if I leave you alone at the table. I shan't be but a moment.'

'Certainly.'

Anton watched as Dieter went over to the chess player's table, said a few words, and sat down. Some conversation followed, and then the chess player snapped his fingers for a waiter, who was dispatched to summon a gentleman sitting near the door who had the look of a diplomat gone to seed. Three heads conferred, and then the waiter was sent again, this time to request the presence of a man in a bowler hat who was eating a knockwurst. For a while there were four heads bent close together, and then the conference disbanded. The chess player returned to his board, the bowler hat to his sausage, Dieter to his own table, while the diplomat left the café and disappeared out onto the Ringstrasse.

'You don't think much of that coffee, do you?' said Dieter, seating himself. 'Let me get you something else.'

'What was that all about?'

'A congress of ideas, nothing more.'

'Who are those people?'

'One meets a variety of types in the course of a day. Helpful, perhaps. We shall see. One of them has gone on an errand. He shouldn't be too long.'

The diplomat was gone for over an hour. During that time Dieter tried to keep his guest amused with a running commentary on the patrons of the café, the latest scandals around town, and the gossip from the opera. Anton listened absently, occupied with his own thoughts and planning the words he would use to explain to Elizabeth what had happened. He was so deep in thought that he did not at first notice the return of the diplomat, who appeared beside Dieter, bent to whisper something in his ear, and then handed over a buff-coloured envelope. Dieter nodded his thanks and said something too soft for Anton to hear. The diplomat shook his head emphatically, made a silent farewell, and went back to his table. On the way he had a word with the bowler hat and exchanged a nod with the chess player.

Dieter opened the envelope, took out a single sheet of paper, and read the handwritten message. He read it again, nodding to himself. He looked up, and said, 'A simple solution to a bizarre situation. You were never intended to receive those skis, that was the reason for that ridiculous surcharge. They knew that you would never pay it.'

'I don't understand.'

'Apparently, under the current customs law a shipment that remains in bond for more than a year without the charges being paid on it is subject to seizure by the Customs Bureau. The bureau may then dispose of the merchandise to whomever it pleases, and at whatever price it sees fit to charge.'

'They could steal my skis that way?'

'Perfectly legally.'

'One year? But it isn't a year yet.'

Dieter glanced at the note. 'Not for another seventeen days, fortunately. You have plenty of time.'

'To do what? I can't afford to pay those charges.'

'You won't have to.' Dieter tapped the sheet of paper with a fingertip. 'This note is from someone who is somewhat superior to Herr Becker. He suggests that you present yourself to Becker tomorrow morning. Your clearance papers will be ready. There will be no charge.'

'But how?'

'Becker already has his instructions.'

'How did you do this?'

'Please, it was a minor accommodation, nothing more.' Dieter looked distressed, as if fending off thanks in advance. 'The gentleman who wrote this note is under a slight obligation to me, a matter of cards. I have been patient with him, and he is happy to show his appreciation. That so-called surcharge will be waived. It was strictly Becker's doing.'

'And the skis are mine?'

'You need only present the papers.'

'I don't know how to thank you. Those other men . . .' He looked over at the chess player's table. 'What did they . . . ?'

'They were good enough to suggest an approach to the situation. They have certain experience in these matters.'

Anton sat back in his seat, bewildered. Without thought, he picked up his cup of coffee and drained it. The coffee was cold, but he barely noticed that. There was a piece of the puzzle still unsolved. He saw that Dieter was looking at him thoughtfully, as if waiting for the inevitable question.

'I have to ask,' he said. 'Who was going to get the skis?'

'I was hoping to avoid that.'

'Who is it? Do you know?'

'I'm afraid that I do.'

'Otto?'

'Of course.'

'Damn.'

'I imagine that he made his deal with Becker quite some time ago. Once the year was up the bureau would have sold him the skis for a moderate price and Becker would have got his cut.'

'And Otto would have got eight thousand pair of first-class Prince skis. Just sand off the name, paint on his own, and there would be nothing I could do about it.'

'I suppose he intended something like that,' Dieter said languidly. He seemed to have lost interest in the matter. 'He has an ingenious mind, doesn't he? If only he would apply it properly.'

'I'm still trying to think of some way to thank you.'

'Please, please, there's no need for that.' He was distinctly embarrassed now. 'You're dining with us tonight, of course?'

'Yes.'

'Good, we're looking forward to it. Marta and I are planning a little surprise for you after dinner.'

'I don't think I can take another one today.'

'You'll simply have to manage. This one has been planned for quite some time.'

Dinner that evening at 72 Hadikgasse had the makings of a festive occasion. Anton and Elizabeth were riding the crest of an elation brought about by their victory over the Customs Bureau, and Dieter was comfortably relaxed in the role of guardian angel. The meal was a masterpiece to match their moods. The soup was a Germiny à l'Oseille, the fish was blue trout, and the roast a crown of veal. Dom Pérignon was served throughout the meal, but despite the surface gaiety there was an air of strain in the room that hampered the conversation. Marta was uncommonly silent and preoccupied, while Dieter did his best to keep his guests amused. At first Anton and Elizabeth thought that they might be witnessing the aftermath of a family quarrel, but the source of the strain became clear when Anton asked after Franz Harz.

'How is the old bear?' he asked. 'I'll want to see him before we go to Garmisch.'

There was silence. Marta looked down at her plate, her lips pressed tight. After a moment, Dieter cleared his throat and said, 'Franz is no longer in Vienna. He left several weeks ago for California.'

'Hollywood?'

'Yes. Several people have been after him for some time to go out there and work with them. Our Franzie finally gave in, and I can't say that I blame him. There is a great deal of money involved.'

'But what does Franz know about films?'

'He's doing the same thing there that he was doing here. Working with artists. They say he has a brilliant future in Hollywood.'

Marta looked up and forced a smile to her lips. 'Darling, what an absurd thing to say. You make it sound as if Franz is going to stay there forever.'

'Marta, we don't know exactly . . .'

'He said that it was just for one project and then he would be back.'

'He didn't quite say that, my dear.'

'I mean, what would he do in a place like California? Can you imagine Franz without the Café Opern? Impossible.'

Dieter said nothing. He patted his moustache nervously.

Marta's voice rode high and her smile began to come apart. 'He'll be back in three months, four at the most. He told me so.'

'Marta, please, you can't count on . . .'

'But he did, he promised me. He wouldn't lie to me, would he?'

Again there was no answer from Dieter and an embarrassed silence in the room until Elizabeth broke it with her no-nonsense tone of voice, saying, 'I'm told that California is a barbaric place, and Franz is certainly no barbarian. No doubt he will be back when he said he would.'

Marta looked at her gratefully, and Anton quickly turned the conversation to a recounting of his morning at the Customs Bureau. He described Herr Becker in detail, the incredible bulk of him, the rosebud lips, the skin as shiny as a sausage casing, and he managed to lighten the mood at the table. It wasn't enough to make his sister smile, but it got them all through the meal without any further strain. Finally, Dieter said:

'Anton, I promised you a surprise after dinner.'

That brought Marta's first smile of the evening. 'Oh yes, it's time for that.'

Anton pretended to groan. 'Time for what? I'm not up to anything exciting.'

'There's someone here who wants to talk to you. He's waiting now in Dieter's study.'

'Not another tax collector?'

'Nothing like that,' said Dieter. 'Follow me, I'll show you the way.'

It took a moment after Dieter closed the door behind him for Anton's eyes to adjust to the dim light in the study. There was only the glow of one Tiffany lamp on the desk, enough to splash a yellow pool for several feet before it was engulfed in the surrounding darkness of oak and wool and leather-bound books. After that moment he was able to make out the figure of the man standing at the side of the desk, just within the light, not sitting behind it where one might expect him to be. Anton peered at the vaguely familiar form.

'You wanted to speak to me?' he asked.

'Herr Prinz?'

'Prince, if you don't mind.'

'Herr *Anton* Prince from St. Anton am Arlberg?'

'Yes, yes. What is all this?'

'Just checking, old buddy, just checking,' said the man in a mock drawl of the American West. 'A man's got to be sure who he's riding the trail with these days. Set yourself down and we'll have a little pow-wow.'

'Good God in heaven.' And then with growing realization, 'It can't be, can it? Is it you, Cowboy? Really you?'

'It's me, pardner,' said Karl, stepping fully into the light. 'Or what's left of me after twenty years.'

236

Anton roared something inarticulate and charged across the room with his arms spread wide. Karl braced to meet him, and the two collided in the middle of the room, wrestling in bear hugs, pounding each other's backs, growling their pleasure. Then they stopped and stood back to appraise each other.

Anton spoke first. 'You're supposed to be dead.'

'So you heard that, did you? Well, I'm not.'

'I know. It wasn't a ghost who just pounded me on the back. Well, tell me. How did you rise from the dead?'

'In a minute. Let me look at you. Christ, you haven't changed, not much anyway. Still built like a bull, maybe a little more around the middle . . . hey, what happened to your hand?'

'What?' Anton shook his head. 'Oh, that. So long ago I sometimes forget about it.'

'So that's what you meant,' Karl said, suddenly thoughtful. ' "I always said I could lick you with one hand tied behind my back – well, when you get here I'll prove it to you." That's what you said.'

'When did I say that?'

'In the letter that you wrote to me. Just after you got to America.'

Anton snapped his fingers. 'That's right, I did. What a memory you have.'

'Not really. I read that letter over and over, every day for four years. They don't give you books in Landeck Prison, and it was the only thing I had to read. Do you wonder that I remember it word for word?'

'Prison?' For the first time Anton noticed that Karl was wearing the von Ulm livery. 'There's a lot I don't understand here, Cowboy.'

'Like I said, pardner, sit down and let's start the pow-wow.'

The story that Karl told Anton was fuller in detail and more pungent in expression than the one he had told Marta in their walk through the forest, but in essence it was the same tale. By the time he was finished Anton's cheeks were wet and his neck was bowed.

'That's the way they died?' he said haltingly. 'Eugen, Dolf, Willi . . . all of them?'

'Yes.'

'Otto killed them.' It was a statement, not a question.

'Yes.'

'And nobody knows this?'

'Nobody back home. The army takes care of its own.'

'My brother. My own brother.'

'Are you surprised? You knew the way he was.'

'Yes, but still he has to pay for this.'

'No, Anton.' Karl held out a hand. 'That's not why I told you all this, not for revenge. It's too long ago, it doesn't matter any more. Besides, I had my chance at him and I missed. That's enough revenge for both of us.'

'And what have you been doing all these years?'

'A little of this, a little of that. A cook in a restaurant for a couple of years, then mostly with engines after that. You know me, Anton. The Cowboy always gets along.'

'You could have come to me in America. I told you in that letter there would always be a job for you there.'

Karl looked away, for the first time embarrassed. 'It never seemed like the right time. And then, there was the question of money.'

'I sent you some, not much, but some.'

'That money order, that was the first thing that got stolen in Landeck Prison.' Karl laughed shortly. 'Besides, it wouldn't have got me very far.'

'You could have written to me.'

'I know, I know.' His voice trailed away, and he repeated without conviction, 'It never seemed like the right time.'

'Well, it's the right time now,' Anton said firmly. 'My wife and I are going to Garmisch for the Olympic Games, and after that to Hamburg, where we sail for home. And this time you're coming with me, Cowboy. Twenty years late, but you're coming along.'

Karl shook his head sadly. 'No, old buddy. It's a fine gesture, just what I'd expect you to say, but it wouldn't work. Think about it and you'll see that I'm right. Maybe back then, but not now. What would I do in America now? I don't speak the language, I don't know the ropes, and I'm too old to start learning. No, Anton, it will never be the right time for me now.'

'But you always wanted to go there. To see the cowboys and the Indians.' It was hard to keep his voice steady.

'Kid stuff.' Karl waved it away. 'No, I'm better off where I am now, right here. Your sister and her husband, they treat me right, and I give them a good day's work. I'm happy here, really

I am. Tell you what. When you get back home you send me some of those postal cards, the ones with the pictures of the cowboys and the Indians on them. Send me a load of them and I'll put them up all over my room. I have a very nice room here over the garage. You send me those pictures, Anton. I'd like that, really I would.'

'Damn it, Karl.' Anton's hand reached out and grabbed the Cowboy's arm, and squeezed. 'God damn it all.'

'Come on, old buddy. It's really all right.'

After that there did not seem much to say, but the two old friends sat for a while longer in silence before Anton finally rose to join the others in the salon, and Karl made his way through the back hallways to his very nice room over the garage.

Chapter Fifteen

From the Journals of Elizabeth Chandler Prince

Saturday, 14 November 1936
It is 'Boom Time' in New England, no doubt about it. People aren't making much money, but prices are low and in this neck of the woods there are few men looking for jobs. None of this Blue Eagle or WPA for us, and even though there is a CCC camp over north of Burlington, you won't find many Vermont boys in there digging ditches and cutting timber. Those are York State boys, and downstate boys and city boys wearing the khaki and taking Uncle Sam's dollar because they can't find work back home. Our own young fellows have plenty to do, thank the merciful Lord, and a lot of it is because of the skiing. When a man is right, he's right, and my Anton trumpeted loud and long that skiing would be the salvation of us all. Now just look at those weekend ski trains coming up from Boston and New York filled with flocks of people looking for a few days of sun and snow. No, nobody argues about skiing with Anton any more, not with seven new hotels within a fifty-mile radius of town, and more to come. First the hotels, and now there is work for the men carving out ski trails all over the mountainsides.

With all of that it is no surprise that the sales of our skis have tripled in two years, and the end is not in sight. The carpentry operation is now totally involved in the making of skis, and from what Anton says this new idea of a towing rope is going to make the sport even bigger. They started using the first one over at Woodstock, and just imagine not having to trudge up the hill. Dawn of a new age, says Anton, and I believe it. Soon you'll have every Tom, Dick, and Harry out on the slopes, not just your outdoor types who are willing to climb the mountains. Time was when it took a real man to go skiing, but now with these rope tows it's going to be a different story, and that story is going to mean money in the bank.

The fact that this rope-tow contraption is the brainchild of one Mr Bunny Bertram has Digger all puffed up. It seems that Mr Bertram is the former captain of the Dartmouth College ski team, and anything to do with that institution sets my boy's ears a-perking. He knows the names of every member of the ski team and the football team, and one could only wish that he would concentrate as much time and energy on his studies. Which do not go well at all. I have spoken to his teachers at the high school, and the consensus of opinion, I regret to say, is that he simply is not a natural student. Plenty of brain power, but he lacks the drive and determination that produce good grades. Like his father, he would rather be up and about, tramping over the mountains, than sit before the fire with a book in his hands. It seems that the only way I can stimulate him into studying is with the bald threat that unless his grades improve he will not be accepted at Dartmouth. The Dartmouth skiers – Rideout, Litchfield, Hunter, and Durrance – are part of his personal pantheon, and so far the threat has been effective. A cheap device to use on the boy, but I have no qualms about that. He *will* go to Dartmouth, and he *will* study law, and he *will* live up to his God-given abilities. Anton, I know, would prefer to see him in the family business, but I'll have no part of that. I created that business for my own good man, solely as a focus for his energies. I have no intention of passing it down to succeeding generations as a means of fostering idleness.

By his senior year in high school Digger knew exactly what he wanted to do with the rest of his life, and his plans were nothing like those of his mother. Dartmouth was less important to him that Elizabeth thought. If not Dartmouth, then the smaller

240

Quincy College with its equally fine ski team coached by the German Martin Gregorius, would be just as acceptable, and after that the 1940 Winter Olympics and a gold medal. College and an Olympic gold were the immediate goals, and after that he wanted nothing more than the chance to ski every day, screw as many girls as possible, and make a lot of money. During those Depression years when there were twenty million Americans out of work, his high school friends spoke convincingly of professional careers even though they secretly knew that they would wind up clerking in the family store or farming the same pieces of land over which their fathers had laboured. Digger skipped that phase of self-delusion. After college and the Olympics his plans were to go to work for Prince Skis and eventually take over the running of the firm. The business would give him the money, and the money would give him the freedom to ski and to chase after girls. Those were his only goals, and the only person who stood in his way was his mother.

For some time now he had stopped trying to figure out his feelings for her. At seventeen he was without illusions, doubting and disrespectful of all that he saw around him, hard-eyed and hard-nosed, although there was no good reason why he should have been that way. His parents were conventional enough to conform to most of the myths that people create in order to soften their lives, and no vagabond cynic had passed through Sedgewick Falls to inject him with a sense of calculating realism. Nonetheless, that realism distinguished him from his peers, and he grew up unencumbered by the burdens of piety, charity, and the romantic tradition. He was sure that he once had loved his mother in the way of a clinging child, but it was years since he had clung, and now all he felt was the fragile grip of an obligation. A son was obliged to his mother, no matter what. It was part of a social contract that he was willing to honour. Up to a point, and the point was reached on the day he was graduated from high school. That day should have been a time of quiet excitement for the family as a layer of the future was slowly peeled away like wrapping paper on a Christmas gift, but instead Digger would always remember it as the day he first saw his mother weep bitterly.

He had never before seen her tears because it was part of the Chandler code not to give way before others . . . any others, even a son. Still, on the day of the high school commencement

241

exercises Elizabeth wept openly, shielded, perhaps, by all the other tear-streaked faces in the audience that day. Mothers were meant to cry at such times, and more than one father was seen to gulp and set his chin firmly as the school orchestra pumped out *Pomp and Circumstance* and the file of adults-to-be paraded down the aisle and up onto the stage to receive the ritual handshake and sheepskin. There were plenty of tears flowing that day, but Elizabeth Prince was the only parent present whose tears were the product not of joy but of rage and frustration. Only her husband and her son knew that she was angry enough to bite tenpenny nails. In the pages of the Sedgewick Falls High School yearbook Digger was listed among the graduating seniors as: *Class President, Captain of the Ski Team, Captain of the Basketball Team, Glee Club President, Deputy Editor of the* Clarion, *and Man Most Likely to Succeed*. This collection of triumphs was meaningless to Elizabeth. The magic initials, HS, for Honour Society, were missing, and next to the entry *College of choice* was listed the damning word *Quincy*. He had not been graduated with honours and he had not been admitted to Dartmouth – a mediocre academic average of 77.5 had seen to that – and so Elizabeth wept into a wadded handkerchief during the ceremony, and again as she and Anton walked with their son on the high school lawn among other parents and graduates strolling in family knots. The Kodaks were out and clicking under the splendid sun of early June and Anton had brought his along, but Elizabeth waved away the suggestion and averted her face.

'Don't,' she said. 'I have no need for a memento of this occasion.'

'Lizbet, please,' said Anton. It was both a warning and a plea. As long as she confined herself to tears she could be mistaken for just another misty-eyed mother, but once she started with words she could embarrass them all. A few paces ahead of them Digger ambled over the grass with his thumbs hooked into his pockets, his head high as he greeted his friends with a wink or a nod. He kept his lips fixed in an easy grin. He knew what was going on behind him, but he kept the knowledge from showing on his face.

He heard his mother say, 'Besides, I must look a sight with my eyes all red. I'd break the camera, the way I look.'

'You got no reason to cry,' Anton said doggedly. 'It's a happy day.'

'By your standards, perhaps, not mine.'

'The boy did good.'

'Parsons do good,' came the inevitable correction. 'The boy did well.'

'So?'

'A cow does well when she gives milk. A pig does well when he eats swill. We don't give them medals for it.' The murmur of her voice grew sharper. 'The boy did as well as he had to, and no more.'

The tears started again. Walking ahead, Digger could not see them, but he heard the sobs muffled by the handkerchief, and then the words that poured out high and tight. He wasn't supposed to hear them, but he did.

'All my plans wasted. I tried my best and I failed. All his life I've tried to instil in him a sense of quest, a thirst for excellence, a need to learn and to know. And I failed. He simply does not have a first-class mind, and I might as well admit it. He has plenty of charm, I'll give him that. I doubt that there's an adolescent female in this town who hasn't felt the touch of that charm. It makes things too easy for him, that and his God-given body. The body of a young god, but where's the *mens sana* to go with the *corpore sano*? I wanted Dartmouth for him so badly, and what did I get? Quincy.' She spat the word. 'Quincy, where all he'll do is ski and use his charm to his damnation. And there's nothing I can do about it now, I've done my best and it wasn't enough.' Her voice rose in pitch, shrill now, and piercing. 'All my dreams for him, gone. All that energy, wasted. All that time invested in a second-rate – '

'Lizbet, enough,' his father said sharply, and cut her off in midflight. 'This isn't fair to the boy, and besides, people are starting to look. I think maybe it's better you go home now.'

'We had all best go home.'

'No, it's his day. It's only right that he should be here with his friends. But you go now, go ahead. We'll be home after a while and you try and make it nice, yes? You do that.'

Digger did not hear his mother's reply. He turned in time to see her hurrying away across the lawn, her head bent over and the sodden handkerchief pressed against her face. His father's unhappy eyes met his.

'It's only that she wants so much for you,' Anton said slowly. 'She wants you to be the best.'

Just as slowly, Digger said, 'I am the best. In some things.'

'Not the things she wants for you.'

'Makes no difference. I graduated from high school today, and she should have said something. Even if she didn't mean it she could have said something nice. I'm not ashamed of what I did here.'

'No, you shouldn't be. You did fine, and you shouldn't let this spoil the day for you. It's just that she's upset. She's still your mother, and she still loves you.'

'No, she doesn't.'

'Don't talk that way.'

'Pop, it's true and you know it.'

'She's a good wife and a good mother.'

'I know she is. I was talking about love.'

'That too.'

'No. She loves herself and she loves you, but nobody else. That's all she's got room for.'

Anton looked away, staring across the lawn and down the street to the distant figure of his wife hurrying home. When he turned back to his son his eyes were moist. He had no bar against showing emotion in public. Haltingly, he said, 'Some people are like that. There just isn't enough room. It's not their fault.'

Digger put his hand on his father's arm and squeezed. 'It's all right. It doesn't make any difference any more.'

He looked around him at the groups of people on the lawn, the girls in linen dresses and the boys stiff in jackets and ties, the parents quietly proud. He saw smiles everywhere, heard ripples of laughter, and wanted to be somewhere else.

'Come on, let's go home,' he said to his father. 'There's nothing else going to happen around here.'

Anton took off his hat and fanned his face with it. 'You sure you want to go?'

'Yes.'

'Okay, but we take the long way home. Give your mother a chance to . . . you know?'

'Sure,' said Digger, 'anything you say.' After that day he stopped wondering about whether or not he loved his mother. It didn't seem to matter much any more.

Digger entered Quincy College in the autumn of 1937, and if Quincy wasn't Dartmouth it was good enough for him. It did not bother him at all that Quincy lacked the Ivy League veneer of the older New Hampshire institution, that it was somewhat inferior academically, or that its football team was a regional joke. The school was just old enough, its buildings just weathered enough, its ivy just leafy enough to provide the proper collegiate aura, but more important than any aura were the two delightful facts that Quincy was coeducational, and that its ski team was one of the best in New England. Years later he would look back on his freshman year at Quincy as a time of delight, and the three people he would remember most from that year would be Martin Gregorius, Elena Montejo, and his cousin, Kurt Prinz.

Gregorius was the coach of the ski team, a refugee from Nazi Germany whose assaults on the English language were unrelenting and memorable. Short, stocky, and with an unruly mass of hair, he was a firm believer in skiing under strict control at all times, and he opened every season by taking his team to the top of Mount Van Buren and pointing down the precipitous slope studded with rocks and blue ice. His speech to the skiers was always short and vivid.

'Dot, chentlemen, iss vot ve shki today, und remembering pliss, it iss not dot ve vin der race, inschted dot ve shki good. Shki, no fall, dot's der most important dink of der dinks.'

On this opening day of the 1937 season he sent the established members of the squad down the hill and then turned to the group of applicants waiting to try out for the team. He did not address them as 'chentlemen.'

'You poys listen good, pliss. If you vant to be on dis shki team, vun dink you gotta undershtood. Here ve got no shtars. Ve take der shteep shtuff shtraight, but ve are shkiing all der time under control. No fancy shtuff, no falling down, no show-offing. Control, control, control. Undershtood? Okay you, der first vun, show me your shtuff.'

One by one each applicant shuffled up to the edge and on a signal from Gregorius launched himself forward and down the slope, negotiating the steep terrain conservatively without risking a fall. Digger was the last in line, and as he took his place the coach looked at him keenly.

'Dot's Prinz, der name, no?'

'Prince.'

'Dot's vot I'm saying. I'm hearing about you, Prinz. Pretty hot shtuff, dot's vot I'm hearing.'

Digger kept his eyes fixed on the downhill slope.

'New England junior champion, issn't it?'

Digger shrugged, but did not answer.

'Okay, so show me. *Los!*'

Digger dropped down the side of the mountain like an elevator with its cable cut, like a stone hurled down a well, like an earthbound pheasant shot out of the sky. He careered down Mount Van Buren without a semblance of control, taking the shortest distance between the top and the bottom by skimming the ice, jumping the rocks, and skidding his turns at impossible speeds. He was full seconds faster than anyone else on the hill. Later, recounting the scene, Gregorius would say, 'I told him to go und he vent. Vun minute he's shtanding dere at der top und der neggest dink I know he's down by der bottom. Right avay I know I've got a vinner. I also know dot vun day he's goink to kill himself shkiing dot vay.'

Gregorius skied down to the bottom of the hill with a storm on his face. He ignored the others and went directly to Digger, who stood waiting, resting on his poles and knowing what was coming.

'You call dot control, vot you chust did?'

'It was fast.'

'Und it vas ugly.'

Digger shifted awkwardly on his skis. 'Coach, I can ski pretty or I can ski fast, but I can't do both at the same time. Not when I'm racing downhill. If you want to see me ski pretty just set up some slalom poles.'

'I vant to see control.'

'Coach, a downhill racer is always halfway out of control. He has to be if he's going to win.'

'Dot's some fine philosophy. Who taught you dot?'

'My father.'

'Ah, yah, Anton Prinz, der shkimacher. Vell, ve don't do dinks like dot around here.'

Digger looked at him levelly. 'It's the only way I know how to ski. It's the only way I want to ski.'

'Den you don't shki mit me. On dis here team you shki it my vay, mit control. Vill you do dot?'

'I'll try.'

'Vill you *do* it?' Gregorius insisted.

Digger hesitated, and then said, 'Yes.'

The coach peered at him. 'Are you lying by me?'

'Yes.'

'Dot's vot I thought.' Gregorius turned away.

'Am I on the team?'

'Of course you're on der team,' Gregorius roared over his shoulder. 'You're der best dink dot I see around here in years. Crazy, but der best. You're on der team until you break der neck. Den you're off der team.'

Most of the traditions at Quincy were borrowed from other institutions. Its Winter Carnival was copied from Dartmouth's, its *alma mater* came from Cornell, and its various residency 'colleges,' which took the place of Greek-letter fraternities, were named after counterparts at Oxford and Cambridge. Thus, Digger had been rushed by, and accepted into, Balliol House, the most prestigious on campus, although as a freshman his room there was tiny and tucked away on the top floor. That night he sat in his room and wrote to his father, telling him the news about the team and at the same time mentioning that the members provided their own skis, most of which were old and battered. The following Saturday afternoon Anton arrived at school with a long box strapped to the top of the Packard, a blanket under it to protect the roof of the car. Digger was not surprised to see that his father had come alone. Anton asked where he could find Gregorius, and Digger gave him directions out to the ski hut at the mountain.

'I'll be back in an hour,' Anton told him. 'We'll have supper together?'

'They call it dinner here.'

'Whatever they call it.'

'Sure. I've got a date but I'll break it.'

'With a girl?'

'Jeez, Pop, what else?'

'Don't go breaking your date. You'll both have supper with me and then I'll start for home.'

Anton found Gregorius in the waxing room of the ski hut, labouring over an old pair of boards with a hot iron. He smiled at the *germütlich* atmosphere of the room: the familiar odours of hot wax, wet wool, and rough-cut tobacco, the skis hung from brightly coloured pegs, and the Ski Heil talisman on the wall made of broken tips nailed together. He introduced himself, and after hearing a few sentences of the coach's English he interrupted him in German, saying, 'I think it would be better if we spoke in the mother tongue.'

Gregorius bridled, and said, 'There's nothing wrong with my English,' but he said it in German.

'Of course not,' Anton lied blandly, 'but it would make it easier for me. I've been in America twenty years but I still can't get the hang of the language.'

'Well, in that case . . . what can I do for you?'

'I've got a heavy wooden box on top of my car. You can help me bring it in here.'

The two men lugged the crate into the hut, and Anton prised the lid open with a tyre iron. Inside were a dozen pair of brand-new Prince skis still glossy with factory paint and wax. Gregorius picked one out and examined it.

'Nice work,' he said, putting it back. 'Unfortunately I'm not in the market to buy any skis. I don't have the budget for it.'

'Who said anything about buying? These are for the team, no charge.'

The coach's eyebrows went up. 'That's very good of you.'

'The team should have the best.'

'Very generous. And good advertising for you.'

'You can always paint over the names,' Anton said stiffly.

'No, no, I didn't mean it that way. I thought I was paying you a compliment. Really, don't take offence. This calls for a drink. I don't have any schnapps but I have some first-class cider in a keg.'

'I don't drink cider.' Anton held up his artificial hand. 'Cider got me this.'

'Then some *Glühwein*? I've got some cinnamon and I could heat the wine on the stove.' Gregorius seemed anxious to atone for the remark. 'Please, it will just take a minute.'

Anton nodded his agreement, and after a flurry of preparations the two men sat themselves close to the glowing stove, each with a mug of steaming, aromatic wine close at hand. Gregorius took a sip, smacked his lips, and reached in a pocket for pipe and tobacco. Anton lit a cigar and eased back in the rickety chair.

'So,' he said. 'Tell me about my son.'

Gregorius fussed with his pipe, got it going, and pointed the stem at his visitor. 'Your son is crazy, but he's the best skier I've ever had here. Right now, in America, only Dick Durrance is better, and one of these days your boy will beat him too. That's how good he is.'

Anton nodded contentedly. 'I trained him myself, he should be. So you think he has a chance for 1940?'

'The Olympics? Definitely, unless he kills himself first.'

Anton frowned. 'He skis hard, that's all. That's the way I taught him.'

'Look, Prinz, I don't want to get into a battle with you over this. How you taught your boy is your business, but I work for the college and I have a responsibility to these young men. So I teach them safe skiing, control skiing. My job is to keep them all in one piece.'

'That's no way to win races.'

'Have you looked at my record?'

'All right, you win your share,' Anton conceded. 'More than your share. I should have put it differently. It's no way to train champions, and that's what my boy is going to be.'

'If he lives that long. Your boy is crazy, he's got his brains in his feet.'

Unperturbed, Anton said, 'Only when he's on the mountain. Take the skis off him and he's a perfectly normal young man. Actually, the best ones have to be a little crazy on the hill. He'll always be that way, Gregorius. You'll never change him.'

'I'm not sure that I really want to,' the coach admitted. 'He's one of a kind. He breaks all the rules that the others have to follow, and he gets away with it.'

'He's a winner.'

'I know. I just hope I can keep him healthy until 1940.'

'You will.' Anton reached for his wine and they clinked mugs together. 'The Olympics. *Prosit.*'

'*Prosit.*' They drank. 'A touch more?'

Anton held out his mug to be filled. The mulled wine, the hot stove, the odours of the ski hut, and the novelty of speaking his native language all combined to lull him into relaxation. In that mood he decided that Gregorius wasn't such a bad fellow, and although he had noted the Bavarian accent, he asked, 'What part of Germany are you from?'

'Grainau, near Munich. Have you ever skied there?'

'Never.'

'The most beautiful mountains in the world.'

'That's the way I feel about the Arlberg.'

'Is that where you're from? I knew you were Austrian, but . . .'

He fell silent. They were both Americans now, but in other days they had been from opposite sides of a different border, and in this year of 1937 the possibility of *Anschluss* – the enforced union of Germany and Austria – was on everybody's mind.

'Tell me, do you think he'll do it?' asked Anton. There was no need to use a name; 'he' could only be Hitler.

'*Anschluss*? Yes, of course he'll do it. The bastard will walk into Austria just like he did with the Rhineland. And not one of your Austrian patriots will fire a shot to stop him, either. They'll be lined up ten deep on the Ringstrasse, waving and cheering.'

Anton thought of Otto and all the others like him. 'You may be right.'

'I know I am.'

'When did you leave?'

Gregorius made a sour face. 'Two years ago. The Nuremberg Laws. Suddenly I wasn't allowed to be married to my wife.'

'She's Jewish?'

'No, Chinese,' Gregorius said impatiently. 'I'm sorry, of course she's Jewish.'

'I'm sorry too,' said Anton, although he had nothing for which to apologize. At that moment it seemed proper for anyone speaking in German to be sorry for something.

'I understand. More wine?'

'No, thank you.' The *Gemütlichkeit* was gone from the room. The talk of *Anschluss,* the thought of an Austria forcibly absorbed into the Third Reich, the nightmarish concept of Otto and his gang triumphant in Vienna . . . all this had robbed the occasion of its cosiness. He wanted to get away now, and, despite his liking for Gregorius, he wanted very much to stop speaking German.

'I have to go,' he said. 'My son is waiting for me.'

That evening Anton took Digger and his date to Moriarity's where the two young people stuffed themselves with clam chowder, rare beef, and Boston cream pie in a joyous escape

250

from college food. The girl's name was Elena Montejo, and she impressed Anton with her quiet good looks and her respectful manner. He was further impressed when he learned that her father was the Argentine consul in New York City, and that Elena, although born in Buenos Aires, had been raised in Washington and New York. When he got back to Sedgewick Falls that night after a three-hour drive in the dark he was careful to relate this information to Elizabeth, who had waited up for him. Her hair plaited and her face creamed for the night, she received the news with pretended indifference.

'A foreigner, is she?' Anton was not sure if the word was supposed to refer to the girl's nationality or to the fact that she lived in New York. 'All slick and sophisticated. Well, thank God for small mercies, at least she'll know how to keep from getting pregnant.'

Had they heard those words, both Digger and Elena would have yelled *foul,* for in the collegiate jargon of the time the girl was a 'saver,' as in 'I'm saving it for the man I marry.' Chubby and lively, she was a fun-loving virgin who could play the banjo, do a terrific imitation of Eddie Cantor singing 'Whoopie,' dance the Argentine tango all night, and drink rye and ginger ale for hours without showing a stagger in her step. She was also an adept in providing nonconclusive sexual satisfaction, and when she and Digger started dating she laid down the ground rules clearly.

'I'll do almost anything,' she told him. Her Spanish accent was slight, but engaging. 'After all, I like a good time, too. But there are two things I won't do. I won't let you put it inside me and I won't take my clothes off. At least, not all of them.'

'Is it okay if I take *my* clothes off?'

'That's up to you, but you're going to look silly standing there naked all by yourself.'

'Standing?'

'Standing, sitting, or lying down, you're still going to look silly.'

So Elizabeth was right, but for the wrong reasons, and sophisticated Elena Montejo was in no danger of becoming pregnant. All during that freshman year Digger settled for her brand of second-class fulfilment, a marked change from his Saturday nights back home with the willing daughters of farmers and mill hands. Still, it did not seem to matter very much, for he was learning a lot just from being with Elena. The Argentine girl was his first window out of the tight little world of northern New England, the first female he knew who did not speak with a nasal twang and take it for granted that there would be beans on the table for breakfast. He had never before come across anyone, including his mother, who read *The New York Times* regularly, who listened to Toscanini on the Victrola, and who could speak knowledgeably about Picasso and Miró. From Elena he heard about tea dancing at the Plaza, cocktails at the Stork, and how to mix a Jack Rose. From her he learned about Cole Porter and Fats Waller, about Rodgers and Hart, Schiaparelli and Clifford Odets. He learned to listen to music, to look at paintings, to read a book as a pleasure, not a chore. She taught him when to light a lady's cigarette, when to hold her coat and open her door, all to be done with the dash of a cavalier. In certain areas of sophistication he learned more from Elena during that freshman year at Quincy than he would have absorbed in four years at Dartmouth. She supplied his first layer of worldliness, one which over the years would deepen to a rich patina, and if the price for that was a sex life somewhat less than perfect, it was a price he was willing to pay.

There was another price, however, and this one he paid reluctantly. Elena was totally uninterested in skiing. More, she considered it a trivial waste of time. Hers was a world of commitment to causes, and along with her lessons in sophisticated living came lectures on the NRA, the WPA, the Blue Eagle, the plight of the Okies, the sit-down strikes in Detroit, the Communist Party, the Scottsboro Boys, and the rising threat of Nazi Germany. That winter when they saw *My Man Godfrey* at the Quincy Orpheum, Digger laughed himself silly at the sight of William Powell as the onetime socialite reduced to working as a butler until Elena explained the social significance of the role reversal. To him the high point of *Easy Living* was when the millionaire threw the mink coat out the window, but to Elena it was Jean Arthur's scathing denunciation of a system that could condone such waste. Elena really believed, it was not a pose, and when Emile Zola defended Captain Dreyfus, declaiming, '*J'accuse,*' she cried real tears.

To such a girl, Digger's ongoing love affair with mountains could seem like nothing more than thoughtless decadence. She could see the positive aspects of it – plenty of fresh air, exercise, and a golden tan that never faded – but to her it seemed that all Digger did was go up the side of a mountain and then come down again. True, he came down with the grace of a ballet master and the speed of a runaway locomotive, but when you got right down to it there wasn't all that much involved, and she told him so.

'Maybe not,' he admitted, 'but it's what I like to do.'

'Like? My God, you're obsessed with it. Do you realize what you could accomplish if you channelled all that energy into something constructive?'

'That sounds familiar,' he said, grinning. 'That sounds just like my mother.'

'Well, good for her, and I'll tell her so when I get to meet her.'

Digger visualized a meeting between Elena and his mother and hastily pushed the thought aside. 'Look, skiing is just something that I've always done. I can't remember a time when I didn't ski.'

'But why?' she insisted. 'What do you get out of it besides a terrific tan?'

Digger squirmed. It was like being asked why he bothered to breathe. 'It's hard to explain. There's a feeling . . .'

'You mean like something religious?'

'No, God and I don't get along.'

'Maybe it's something sexual,' Elena said thoughtfully. 'Maybe you ski so much because you're trying to prove your masculinity.'

'I didn't think I had to prove anything like that. Especially not to you.'

'Oh, that. There's more than one kind of masculinity.'

'There's only one kind that counts.'

'Neanderthal,' she said cheerfully. 'All right, I'm sorry I asked, but I'm trying to understand what makes you tick. I guess you ski all the time because it's what you do best. You're just trying to show the world how good you are.'

'You're making me sound like a muscle-bound ape with no brains.'

'No, I know you're more than that,' she said tenderly, and then, with the wisdom of an eighteen-year-old woman she remembered that she was dealing with an eighteen-year-old boy.

'I think you can do just about anything you put your mind to. I'm just waiting to see what it's going to be.'

That was as far as the conversation went that day, but Elena had opened a door in Digger's mind. He had never before questioned why he skied, and now he puzzled over it but came up empty of answers. He put the question out of his mind, and having stopped looking for an answer it came to him late one afternoon as he stood astride a ridge high up on the side of Mount Van Buren, the valley and the town spread out below him and underneath his skis the satisfying crunch of corn snow. Beyond the tips of his skis the snowfield stretched in a dizzying fall to the timberline, where it broke into trails that ran in streaks through the trees. The sky above him was clear with only puffs of clouds for punctuation, and the sun was soft on his skin. Above the timberline, and thus above the whisper of wind in the branches, he was folded in silence. He was totally alone, and in that moment he knew that Elena had been partially right. It was close to being something spiritual, it was close to being something sexual, it was close to showing the world how good he was. But that wasn't all of it. He was alone. He was always alone on the mountain, no matter how many others dotted the slopes, and he knew then that he needed it so badly in his life precisely because of that solitary state. It was the one consuming action he could take unaided and unimpeded by any other living creature. He skied alone, untouched and untouchable, and that was why he loved it so much.

Chapter Sixteen

On a day early in January of 1938, Marta von Ulm wrote two letters. The first was to Franz Harz, who, two years after leaving Vienna, was still living in southern California and showing no signs of ever leaving there. In those two years he had prospered as a talent agent, had established himself firmly in the *mittel*-European community in Hollywood and, his sure touch with women undiminished at the age of fifty-two, was living with the film star Beverly Baines in her ice-cream-cake beach house in Malibu. Marta's letter, one of many over the years, was a pathetic and unashamed plea for a reconciliation with the only man she had ever loved. All her other letters had gone unanswered, and this one closed with a sadly worded warning.

'What do you do with my letters, Franz? Do you flip them away, unopened and unread like an unpaid bill? Or do you read them and laugh? . . . read them and weep? Whatever you do with them, I must tell you this. Unless I hear from you this time, unless you reply, I will take the one course of action left open to me. I will come to California and fight for you with all the weapons that a woman possesses. I will come crawling if I have to, or I will come scratching and clawing, but either way I will come. It is either that or surrender to your indifference, and that is something I can never do.'

The second letter was written to her brother Anton, and was mostly an account of conditions in Vienna.

'Are there any people,' she wrote, 'who are more attractive, more genial, more gifted in the enjoyment of life than the Viennese? And yet these people today are living in a state of constant fear, like chickens waiting for the axe to fall. The axe being *Anschluss,* of course. Everyone knows that it is going to happen, but when? All this past year our local Nazis, financed of course from Berlin, have mounted a campaign of terror. Every day you hear of a bombing in some part of the country, and back home in the Tirol there have been violent demonstrations organized, I am told, by our charming older brother, who has now reached the exalted rank of *Gauleiter* in that congregation of thugs. Oh yes, it's going to happen all right. Dieter has it on good authority that the police have uncovered a Nazi plot to murder Chancellor Schuschnigg just as they did Dollfuss, and also that on the twenty-fifth the police raided the underground headquarters of the Nazi Party and found plans for an open revolt in the springtime. He says that Hitler will then send in troops *to prevent German blood being shed by Germans.* What a farce! A sad, sad comedy. And all we can do is wait for it to happen. Dieter says that we will not have long to wait.'

In a sudden shift of mood she then went on to describe the highlights of the current opera season, the roles she had sung and the triumphs she had scored. Almost as an afterthought she mentioned that Otto's younger son, Kurt, would soon be coming to America.

'He will be travelling with an Austrian ski team, not the national team but a group of collegians, and they will be racing in New England. No doubt he and your son will be getting together. He came to visit with me when his team was here in Vienna (afternoon tea in the English style, not a proper Viennese *Jaus*), and when the subject of the *Anschluss* came up (who talks about anything else these days?) he seemed truly embarrassed by the political position that his father and brother have taken. He is a loyal young Austrian patriot, the sort of engaging fool that I thought had died out with the Empire. He spoke touchingly of seeing Digger again.'

Kurt and Digger stood with their arms around each other's shoulders, faces red and sweating, their free hands gripping bottles of White Elk ale. Elena, sitting at the table, looked up at them admiringly. Beside her, Janet Newall, recruited to be Kurt's date for the Winter Carnival Week, looked more doubtful than admiring as she stared at the two young men whose eyes were bright and whose foreheads almost touched as they bent close together in song. A small-town girl from northern New Hampshire, she was unaccustomed to boisterous men bawling songs in bars.

> '*Boola-boola, boola-boola,*
> *Boola-boola, boola-boola,*
> *Boola-boola, boola-baaaaay.*'

Their voices rose to a screech. They sounded awful, but nobody seemed to mind. Not many people even heard them. The noise in Moriarity's was overwhelming, the taproom jammed with students, skiers, and alumni all in town for Carnival Week and everyone shouting to be heard above the din. Around the room other people were singing: at one table the Maine fight song, 'Cayuga's Waters' at another, 'On Wisconsin' at a third. At a far table the other members of the Austrian Ski team were chanting '*Ach du Lieber Augustine.*' It was a circus that Moriarity's survived annually, a relaxation of all the rules and a solid wink at the local liquor laws.

Outside the inn the scene was just as frantic as crowds pressed through the streets of the town and overflowed onto the snow-covered lawns along Main Street. The snow on the ground was

256

solidly packed, and more of it fell lightly through the chill evening air. Main Street had been lit with flares and torches, and now, closed to general traffic, it was the site of impromptu races between horse-drawn sleighs, the drivers cracking their whips wildly as they sped up the avenue. The college buildings all were decorated with strings of coloured lights, and on the lawns in front of them groups gathered to speculate on the ice sculptures erected there. The statues were masked by curtains of burlap that allowed no more than a hint of the figures represented, and the screens would be removed only just before the judging of the contest. The theme this year was 'Peace on Earth,' and all of the residency 'colleges' had entries, as did clubs such as the English-Speaking Union, the German-American Friendship Society, the Thespians, and the Quincy Choristers. Sturdy young men guarded the shrouded statues, for sabotage was not unknown. Carnival time at Quincy was a week of no classes and few restraints, and it would not be over until after the Inferno race at Mount Washington on Sunday.

'Boola-boola, boola-boola . . . '

Inside Moriarity's, layers of smoke hung in the low-ceilinged room along with the odours of wet wool, sweat, and beer. At eight in the evening the orderly system at the bar was totally broken down and now the waitresses simply circulated from table to table with pitchers of draught beer and bottles of White Elk ale, serving and collecting payment on the spot. One of them passed by Kurt, who disengaged himself from Digger's grasp long enough to snag four bottles and scatter a handful of change on the girl's tray. He set the bottles on the table next to a plate of sausages long gone cold.

'Hey, you two, sit down and be quiet,' Elena called cheerfully. 'You sound like a couple of cats on a fence.'

'Katzen?' Kurt rolled his eyes comically. 'A couple of Carusos, that's what we are.'

'You said it,' said Digger. 'Prince and Prinz, the skiing nightingales. You want to hear us yodel? We can do that, too.'

'Definitely not,' said Elena. 'Sit.'

'Are they drunk?' Janet whispered to her. 'I don't like it when boys get drunk.'

'For God's sake, all they've had is two beers apiece,' Elena said disgustedly. 'This is Carnival Week. Why don't you take off your girdle and relax a little?'

257

'I'm not wearing . . .' Janet stopped and pursed her lips primly. 'I don't know why you have to talk that way.'

'Because you're as much fun on a party as a rubber crutch, that's why.'

Kurt slid into his seat with a mock groan. 'Boy, this tour is getting to be hard work. Not the skiing, that's easy, but the parties, oh boy.'

'Easy skiing?' Digger sat down next to him. 'I beat you all at Franconia, I beat you all on Suicide Six, and I beat you all at Mansfield.' He punched his cousin lightly on the arm to emphasize each point. 'And Sunday I'm going to beat you all on the Inferno. You call that easy skiing?'

Kurt punched him back, and not so lightly. 'I didn't say the winning was easy, just the skiing. I don't have to win to have fun. That's the difference between you and me. With me the fun comes first.'

Digger and Elena looked at each other, unconvinced by Kurt's easy-going façade. Over the past weeks they both had seen changes in him as the news coming out of Austria became worse and worse. Every evening the members of the Austrian ski team gathered at the nearest radio to listen to the static-spattered broadcasts by William L. Shirer and the other correspondents in Vienna and Berlin. On February 12 the reports were that the Austrian Chancellor Schuschnigg had met with Hitler at Berchtesgaden and had been presented with an ultimatum which, if accepted, would have turned the Austrian government over to the Nazis within one week. The ban on the Austrian Nazi Party was to be lifted, all Nazis in jail were to be released, and Dr. Seyss-Inquart, a pro-Nazi Viennese, was to be made Minister of the Interior with authority over police and internal security. Another Nazi was to be appointed Minister of War, and preparations were to be made for the assimilation of Austria into the German economy. It meant the end of an independent Austria, but the alternative was a German invasion, and Schuschnigg had finally caved in and signed.

That night Digger and Elena had sat with Kurt in his room at Moriarity's Inn, and it had been like sitting up after a death in the family. Digger had brought along a flat pint of Mount Vernon rye whisky and had solemnly poured them all drinks, but no one had much of a taste for it that night. The drinks were left untouched as they sat in silence, and then Kurt said slowly:

'It's the end of everything, isn't it? It's the end for us and it's the beginning of the end for the rest of the world. I hope you never know what it's like, to see your country go down without a shot being fired. I'm not a fighter, and God knows I'm not a hero, but somebody should have fired just one stinking shot. If I had been there . . . who knows? Maybe I would have fired that shot, maybe not, but I'll never know because I'm not there. I'm here. Will somebody please tell me what I'm doing here skiing while my neighbour is burning down my house?'

Elena put her hand on his arm. 'It's not your fault that you're here. You can't help that.'

'Sure, I know, but somebody from my family should have done something. My father, my brother . . . they'll be celebrating tonight.'

Digger said quietly. 'The rest of your team will be celebrating, too.'

'The team.' Kurt laughed, and it was not a happy sound. The other Austrian skiers had accepted the hospitality of the college's German-American Friendship Society and were staying at its clubhouse on Main Street. Only Kurt had taken a room at Moriarity's. 'The bastards, Nazis, all of them, more German than the Germans. The whole country is going that way. There are times when I think that I'm the last Austrian left in the world. I dream about that sometimes. Just me, wandering up and down the mountains, looking for my country.'

He turned his head aside then, because tears were coming. Digger looked away, embarrassed, but Elena moved to Kurt's side, put her arms around him, and pulled his head down to her shoulder. When Digger frowned she returned the look with defiant eyes and continued to hold Kurt gently. Digger shook his head and stared at the floor. They all sat that way, frozen in place, until the time seemed right to move again.

But once back in Austria, Schuschnigg regained some of his courage and, with the support of President Miklas, renounced several of the concessions he had made at Berchtesgaden. Hitler's response was troop manoeuvres along the border and a fiery radio speech that set off massive Nazi demonstrations throughout Austria. At that point Schuschnigg decided on a final, desperate gambit: a plebiscite of the Austrian people

259

asking if they approved of a 'free, independent, social, Christian, and united Austria – *Ja oder Nein.*' It was a vote he seemed certain to win, and now, two days before the date set for the plebiscite, the same date as the Inferno run on Mount Washington, Kurt's spirits were high enough again to join in the festivities of Carnival Week at Quincy. Across the room at Moriarity's his Austrian teammates had finished singing about Augustine and had started in on '*Deutschland über Alles,*' but even that failed to dampen his spirits.

'They're like you,' he told Digger, nodding towards the Austrian table. 'They like to win all the time.' He laughed. 'But so far you haven't let them.'

'Not even some of the time,' Elena pointed out.

Kurt was still laughing. 'No, they don't like Digger very much. But for me, it's enough that I ski and enjoy myself. Like now.'

Elena said, 'I wish Digger could be that way, not so juvenile about having to win all the time.'

'Jesus, what kind of crap is that?' said Digger. 'You don't know what the hell you're talking about.' He stood up and plunged into the crowd, heading for the men's room.

'Did I say something awful?' asked Elena.

'Not awful,' Kurt assured her. 'But you really shouldn't compare Digger to anyone else when it comes to skiing. It's almost like robbing him.'

'Robbing him of what?'

'You have to understand that as far as Digger is concerned he owns all these mountains. He owns the rocks, the trees, and the snow. He lets the rest of us come by and ski on the mountains only because he's a nice guy, but they're still his mountains, and when he skis on them he expects to win because they're his. When someone else wins it's like somebody robbed him.'

Janet said, 'I thought these mountains were all owned by the state.'

'Go back to sleep,' Elena told her. 'We'll wake you up in time for breakfast.'

'Well, they are.'

'Are what?' asked Digger, appearing out of the crowd.

Kurt looked at his watch and jumped to his feet. 'It's getting late and we have business to attend to.'

'I'm ready when you are,' said Digger.

'What about the diversion?'

260

Digger said to Elena, 'Give us half an hour, then you know what to do.'

'Don't worry, I'll be there,' she said, and then nodded at Janet. 'What do I do with little Miss Prim over here?'

'Take her along. She can help carry the beer.'

'What beer?' asked Janet. 'Where are you going and what are you talking about?' She seemed alarmed.

'Take it easy, I'll explain as we go along,' Elena told her. To Digger she said, 'You'll be careful, won't you?'

'Smooth as silk.'

'What *is* all this?' Janet asked as Kurt and Digger left. 'What are you getting me into?'

'Don't snap your garters, all you have to do is carry a stein of beer and do a little flirting.'

Janet laughed uncertainly. 'Flirting? I'm not sure I know how.'

'Just be your own sweet natural self and don't promise anything you can't deliver.'

'Honestly, the way you talk sometimes.'

Outside Moriarity's, Kurt and Digger grinned at each other and began to ease their way through the throngs on Main Street. Once at the corner and away from the crowd, they trotted down the side street and turned up the avenue parallel to Main. The back yards of the residency 'colleges' and the social clubs abutted there, fenced-off portions of woodlots filled with fir and spruce. Digger counted the houses as they passed by and stopped at the back of the German-American Friendship Society, popularly known as the Bund House. A quick look up and down the street to ensure privacy, and then he swung himself over the fence, Kurt following at once. In the wooded yard they crawled on their bellies over the cover of freshly fallen snow, working over bumps and around trees until they came to a small shed half buried in drifts. Two shovels were propped against the shed. Digger took one and handed the other to Kurt.

'No noise,' he warned as they started to dig, scooping away the fresh snow, and then the ice and the dirt underneath. It took them fifteen minutes to uncover a thick, burlap-wrapped cylinder of ice more than six feet long.

'A big baby,' grunted Kurt as he lifted his end of the cylinder. 'Just the way we grow them in the Tirol.'

'In Vermont we'd call this one just fair to middling,' said Digger, but he also grunted as he lifted his end.

The construction of the ice cylinder, and its burial behind the Bund House, had taken them three days of hard and surreptitious work, and now they silently lugged it around to the front of the building and crouched in the shadows at the top of the lawn. Halfway down the lawn was the Bund's entry in the ice-sculpting contest, which, like those in front of the other houses, was still curtained by burlap sacking. Although Main Street itself was brightly lit and alive with people, the section directly in front of the house was dark and would stay that way until the judging began. Only the two guards stood near the burlap curtain.

'Hey, where's Elena?' whispered Kurt.

'Give her time, she'll be here,' Digger assured him.

Moments later they spotted Elena moving through the crowd with a reluctant Janet in tow. Each girl carried an oversized stein of beer, and as they approached the edge of the lawn, Elena called out to the guards, 'Hey, you two, want some beer?'

The guards looked at each other, looked at the girls, and shrugged.

'Come and get it,' Elena said. 'We brought it just for you.'

Janet held the stein high in the air and shouted, 'Yeah, come and get it, big boy.'

'Jesus,' Digger murmured. ' "Big boy." Who told her to say that?'

'She's trying,' Kurt said sympathetically, 'but she's not very good at it.'

The two guards had not moved. Elena turned and started to move away from the lawn. Then she looked over her shoulder, and her round little rump, encased in ski pants, seemed to tremble with a will of its own. 'Last chance,' she called. 'If you don't want it I'll bring it over to Exeter House.'

'Hey, don't do that,' said one of the guards. 'That's a waste of good beer.' They both started down the lawn towards the sidewalk.

'Now,' muttered Digger, and he and Kurt darted forward, crouched over with the cylinder under their arms. They covered the ground in a few quick strides, and then they were behind the burlap curtain with their burden, safe from view. They stayed there for only a minute, and then they were sprinting

262

back the way they had come, empty-handed and making for the shadows at the top of the lawn. Once they were there they turned around in time to see Elena and Janet melting back into the crowd and the two guards with their faces buried in the flowing steins.

'*Phantastisch*,' said Kurt, clapping Digger on the shoulder. 'Like clockwork.'

'Let's get out in front. I don't want to miss the judging.'

Minutes later, after a race around the block, they joined the girls at the back of the crowd assembled for the judging of the sculptures. The awards committee, composed of six respected members of the Quincy faculty, had been drawn in a sleigh to the front of Exeter House, the first on Main Street, and the signal had been given. Spotlights flooded the Exeter lawn, the burlap curtain fell away, and the entry was revealed: a glistening globe of the world twenty feet in diameter and adorned with a sculpted dove to symbolize the theme of *Peace on Earth*. There were murmurs of appreciation from the crowd, and then a round of applause as the judges descended from the sleigh to examine the entry more closely. After making their notes they returned to the sleigh to be drawn up the street to the next house. In that fashion they would proceed up Main Street, and at the end of the road their decisions would be made and the awards announced.

'If they get that far,' Digger noted. He was trying for nonchalance, but his eyes were bright and he was having trouble holding in a grin.

'I wish somebody would tell me what's going on,' said Janet. 'Moriarity is going to want those steins back, and I bet we'll have to pay for them.'

Kurt whispered to Elena, 'What about her? Will she keep quiet?'

Janet, overhearing, complained, 'How can I help but keep quiet? I don't know anything yet.'

'She'll be good.' Elena's voice was tight and fierce. 'I'll personally disembowel her if she isn't.'

Digger put a hand on her shoulder. 'Don't be so tough with her, she'll be okay.'

'I'm not worried for myself,' Kurt explained. 'You're the ones who could be expelled.'

'Expelled!' Janet's voice broke on the word. She might have

said more, but her voice was buried by the crowd's roar of appreciation for the entry of the English-Speaking Union just revealed, the figures of Uncle Sam and John Bull with arms outstretched and fingers touching to symbolize *Hands Across the Sea*. There was a round of applause joined by all save the tight group standing in front of the Bund House, which included most of the Austrian ski team.

'Bastards,' said Kurt, and spat on the snow.

'Take it easy,' Digger warned him. 'Don't show it.'

The sleigh with the judges moved on to St John's House, where the entry was titled *Beat Your Swords into Ploughshares*, and was revealed to be massive but unimaginative renderings of those two instruments. There was little applause, and the sleigh moved on to St Hilda's, a woman's house, where the curtain came up on a giant cornucopia from which flowed the fruits of the earth under a banner proclaiming *Peace Through Agriculture*. Next was Merton House, where the theme of *The Brotherhood of Man* was represented by a grouping of men of all races, although in glistening ice it was difficult to distinguish between the African, the Oriental, and the American Indian. Still, the effort was applauded as the judges' sleigh moved on to stop in front of the Bund House.

'The next entry,' came the announcement, 'is by the German-American Friendship Society, and is entitled' – a quick look at the list – '*Germany Extends the Hand of Friendship to the World*.'

'Nobody laughs,' Digger said out of the corner of his mouth. 'Straight faces.'

A twitch of a cord and the burlap curtain fell away; spotlights clicked on and the Bund House lawn was awash with light. There was total silence in the street.

Germany's hand of friendship was ten feet long and lay palm-up on the snow, all five fingers extended and slightly curled in a welcoming fashion. It was clearly a female hand, delicately made, the fingers tapered and the thumb arched with exquisite precision. It was, indeed, the perfect hand of friendship, and across it, lovingly placed there only minutes before, lay a six-foot-long, glistening, rampant, carefully circumcised cock. It lay there as if it belonged there, destined from birth for that place. At the tip of the icy cock flew the Austrian flag of red-white-red, and below it a sign that said:

The ripple of laughter started with those in the crowd who were
closest to the lawn and then spread outward and back, up and
down the street. What started as a ripple grew to a wave, and
then a roar as more and more people realized what was lying
on the Bund House lawn, and as the sign was read and the
words passed back. Along with the laughter came the applause,
spontaneous at first and then settling into a rhythmic clapping
that went on and on. There were some whistles and catcalls,
but it was mainly a note of approval bolstered by a laughter in
which everyone joined except the Bund House boys. After the
shock of discovery they frantically tried to replace the curtain
and hide the offending member, scurrying around and slipping
on the ices as they tugged at the burlap.

'Straight faces,' Digger repeated, but by then he and Kurt
and Elena were past that and smiling broadly. His remark was
meant for Janet, and her reaction surprised them all. As soon
as the curtain was whisked away and she realized what she was
looking at she burst into laughter as loud as anyone else's in the
crowd. She doubled over from the force of it, her face contorted
and her breathing broken into gasps.

Digger looked at her with alarm and asked Elena, 'What's
with Miss Prim? That's the last thing I expected.'

'Hysteria,' said Elena, and began to whack the other girl on
the back with the flat of her hand. 'She's in a state of shock.
The sight of that thing was too much for her.'

'Wish fulfilment,' Kurt agreed.

'I am not in a state of shock,' Janet managed to say. She
straightened up and she was still laughing with tears rolling
down her cheeks, but her breathing had slowed. 'I just want to
know whose it is.'

'Whose what?' Elena asked, whacking her back again.

'Stop that, it hurts. Whose . . . thing, that's what.'

Up on the lawn the Bund House boys had given up on the
attempt to reraise the curtain, and now they were trying to prise
the frozen penis free from the hand of friendship. Kurt and
Digger watched the procedure judiciously.

'What do you think, Herr Doktor?' asked Kurt. 'Is such a
removal possible?'

265

'Never, my dear colleague. They will have to operate.'

'Whose thing?' said Janet. 'That's all I want to know.'

'Make sense,' said Elena. 'What are you talking about?'

Janet's laughter had subsided into a series of giggles. 'To make something like that you have to have a model. I want to know which one of them posed for it, Digger or Kurt?'

Elena looked at her with new interest. 'I was wondering if you'd ever wake up.' To Digger, 'It's a good question. Whose is it?'

'Actually, we worked mostly from memory.'

'In this kind of weather,' Kurt added, 'it had to be that way.'

Janet tugged at Kurt's sleeve. 'Herr Doktor, the surgery is about to begin.'

The Bund House boys had decided that self-destruction was preferable to ridicule and had sent for axes. Blades flashed and chunks of ice flew as the hand of friendship and its unwelcome guest were hacked to pieces. What had taken days to build was levelled in minutes, and chunks of ice began to fly back and forth between the Bund House and the crowd. One of them landed at Elena's feet.

'Let's get out of here,' said Digger. 'We did our part.'

'I hope we don't have to pay for those steins,' said Janet.

They strolled arm in arm back to Moriarity's, where they did, indeed, have to pay for the steins. Nobody really minded that, not even Janet. It was part of the fun of the evening, and it was still fun when they sat themselves before the open fire with fresh mugs at hand, ready to retell the adventures of the day. They were full of their own cleverness and daring, eager for bigger battles, and then somebody turned the radio on and the fun faded quickly.

Over the static came the rhythmic 'Sieg Heil, Sieg Heil,' and over the chant came the voice from Vienna announcing that Schuschnigg had resigned and that the Nazi Seyss-Inquart was the new Chancellor. Sunday's plebiscite was cancelled, German troops were on the march at the border, and the Austrian army had been ordered not to resist. The occupation of the country was expected to be complete within twenty-four hours, and Hitler would arrive in Vienna the following day for a triumphal entrance into the city.

It was Anschluss, final and irrevocable. Austria was now a

part of the Third Reich, and down on Main Street the kids were still throwing ice at each other.

'I was right,' Kurt said after a while. 'It isn't a dream any more. I really am the last Austrian.'

Two days later Digger raced the Inferno Run on Mount Washington and in the space of six minutes and twenty-nine seconds he became a living legend in American skiing. In later years fortune would come to him in different ways. He would win many races, attract vast wealth and the most desirable of women. He would fight, kill, love, marry, and raise up sons. His government would honour him with medals and glory. For what he did both on and off the mountains his name and face would become familiar to many. But nothing that Digger ever did later on would mark him as did the Inferno of 1938. After that day he was as much a myth as a man.

Kurt Prinz was there to see it happen, but not as a competitor. The day before he had told his teammates that it would be inappropriate, and even frivolous, for any Austrian to race on the day that Hitler was scheduled to enter Vienna. He would stay for the race, he told them, as a mark of courtesy to their hosts, but he would not participate, and that evening he would take the train to New York on the first leg of the journey homeward. He urged them all to do the same, but his suggestions were met with cold contempt. The team, he was told, would be proud to race under such circumstances for the greater glory of the Fatherland and the Third Reich.

'Did you really think they wouldn't race?' Digger asked him.

'No, but I had to try.'

'All packed and ready to go?'

Kurt nodded. 'I'll leave just as soon as you beat the shit out of these bastards.'

Digger was silent for a moment, then said, 'It's funny, but in a way I wish I were going with you.'

'I know. But things don't work that way.'

They stood at the top of Mount Washington at midday under a cloud-packed sky, the wind whipping up glinting particles of ice and snow. Below them was the short stretch from the top of the mountain that quickly dropped away into the Headwall of Tuckerman's Ravine. Along the sides of the slope they could see some of the skiers still making the climb to the six-thousand-foot level, for there were no lifts on the mountain. The Inferno was the premier race of its kind in New England, calling for a combination of guts and stamina, and a touch of insanity. First the skiers made the climb, and then they ran the course that took them onto the awesome Headwall, a pitch a thousand feet high with a sixty-degree incline at the top, and finished up at the end of the zigzag Sherburne Trail four miles down the mountain. Conventional wisdom called for a couple of high-speed, swinging turns at the top of the Headwall in order to cut down speed. It was the only way to run the Inferno and survive.

Digger set a can of Sterno on a flat rock that protruded above the snow, lit it, and reached for the battered pot of wax in his knapsack. Kurt took it from him and said, 'Let me. I'll get it started.'

They crouched together over the fire, Kurt shaking the pot gently until the wax began to melt. Then Digger laid out his skis on the snow, bottoms up, and they each began to apply the wax, brushing it on in long, even strokes. Once the wax had dried in the frigid air they went to work on it with rubbing corks, removing all the excess. Then they exchanged skis and started the process over again. Around them, also crouching in the snow, the other racers were doing the same.

'Vell, vot's dis? Friendly enemies?' Martin Gregorius stood over them. To Kurt, he said in German, 'I was hoping to see you ski today, Prinz, but I respect your decision. As a German, I have to say . . . what I mean is . . .'

'I understand.' Kurt held up his hand to prevent further embarrassment.

'Thank you.' Gregorius crouched down beside them and said softly, 'I understand that you are going back.'

'I'm leaving on the train tonight,' said Kurt. 'If I'm lucky I'll be home in two weeks.'

'I don't call that lucky. Do you know what it's going to be like with the Nazis there? Not very nice, I can tell you.'

'I know.'

'Not the way I do. I lived through it in Germany.'

Kurt kept his head down, applying the wax in even layers. He said nothing.

'You feel you have to go?'

His head still down, Kurt murmured, 'I have no choice.'

'I understand. You have your family there, your university.

268

And you probably have no money.' Gregorius hesitated. 'I can't make this a promise, but if you wanted to stay I might be able to arrange something here at the college. Some sort of a scholarship, perhaps.'

'Kurt . . .' Digger's mouth was open to say more, but he closed it when he saw the look on his cousin's face.

Kurt shook his head sadly. 'I didn't mean my family, and I didn't mean money, and I didn't mean school.'

'I see.'

'It's my home.'

'Yes.'

'I belong there. Right now that's where I have to be.'

Gregorius rocked back on his heels, and then forward again, teetering like a solid little toy. 'Two years ago I had to make the same decision, I had to decide where I belonged.' He stabbed a finger into the snow. 'And I decided that I belonged here. Right here. Perhaps it's age. Perhaps at my age I had to leave my home, and at your age you have to go back to it.'

'Perhaps,' Kurt said politely.

Gregorius turned to Digger, switching to English. 'Und you? Are you ready?'

'I'm okay. Ready to roll.'

'How many checks do you make on the Headwall today? Two? Three?'

'I don't know yet.' Digger gave elaborate attention to the ski he was working on. 'It depends on how fast I'm going when I get there.'

'I'm telling all der other boys, three checks on der Headwall, no less. Remember dot, Digger. Any less und you're going too fast. You hear me vot I say?'

'I heard you, coach.'

'So I see you at der shtart gate.' Gregorius stood up, and before he walked away he touched Kurt lightly on the shoulder and said, '*Glück,* Prinz.'

When the coach was out of hearing, Digger muttered, in a passable imitation of Gregorius's accent, 'Remember dot, Digger. Any less und you're going too fast.' He chuckled. 'I thought going fast was the whole idea.'

'How often do you usually check on the Headwall?'

'In training? Two or three times.'

'And today?'

269

'How would you run it?'

'That's a sixty-degree hill there. I'd take three, maybe four sharp turns to slow me down. But I'm not you. How many?'

Digger looked at him blandly. 'Like I told the coach, I'll know when I get there.'

Kurt absorbed the look, nodding slowly. Over the past few weeks he had got to know his cousin as well as he knew anyone else in the world. There was a question that had to be asked, but he could not ask it. Instead, he made it a statement.

'Digger, nobody has ever schussed the Headwall of Tuckerman's Ravine. Not in a race. It can't be done.'

'That's right, it can't,' Digger agreed with the same bland look.

'It would be crazy to try.'

'Crazy.'

'Suicide.'

'Right.'

'Digger . . .'

'What?'

'Nothing.'

It was time to get ready. First they 'married' the skis to the snow, pressing the freshly waxed bottoms into the powder and rubbing them back and forth. Then, while Kurt carried the skis and the bamboo poles over to the starting area, Digger knelt to relace his boots, wriggling his toes inside the silk dress socks that he wore under the heavy woollen ones. Long-handled red flannel underwear, loosly cut ski pants, a shirt, a sweater, and a short, lightweight jacket completed his outfit. He tied a peaked cap with earflaps under his chin, pulled on his leather gloves, and strode over to where Kurt was waiting with the skis laid out on the snow. He stepped into the beartrap bindings and snapped them shut. Then he carefully wound the long, thin leather straps around boot and ankle, effectively binding each foot to the ski. He accepted the poles from Kurt and adjusted a pair of battered aviator's goggles above the peak of his cap. Kurt reached into his pocket, took out a piece of silver, and flipped it into the air. Digger caught it and looked at it.

'Saint Bernard?'

'For luck.'

Kurt poked a thumb in the air as a salute and moved off to the side, where his own skis were parked in a snowbank. Around him his Austrian teammates followed him with their eyes, but he looked straight ahead. He strapped on his skis and slid sideways down the hill until he was level with the lip of the Headwall. From there he could see the starting gate, the opening stretch, and then the precipitous drop down into the ravine. The sky was lighter now, the clouds spread thin, and the starting gate lay in a patch of sunlight. The first racer moved into the gate and hung there waiting for the signal.

'*Go!*'

The racer lunged forward and down the top of the course, went over the lip of the Headwall, and at once went into a swinging turn across the fall line to cut his speed. Another turn back the other way, another and another, four in all, and then he went scooting down the Headwall into the ravine and out of sight. The next racer ran the course the same way, as did the third and the fourth, some taking three and some taking four of those speed-cutting turns.

Kurt watched as Digger, starting fifth, moved into the gate, watched as he stamped his skis in the snow and slid them back and forth while twin plumes of steam rose up from his nostrils in the icy air. He was only freeing ice from the bottoms of his skis, but the motion was that of a highly strung horse snorting and pawing the earth in anticipation. In that moment Kurt knew what was coming next.

In the years to come the story of how Digger Prince schussed the Headwall at Tuckerman's Ravine would be told and retold, embellished and expanded into a contemporary legend, but the simple facts are more eloquent than the stories that grew up around them. Digger came out of the gate and went over the lip of the Headwall. He made no move to turn; he had never intended to. He schussed the wall hitting eighty-five miles an hour as his skis chattered over the icy snow, shattering the surface. The strain on his legs was intense; at that speed a fall was unthinkable. Wind pressure dragged at his cheeks and sucked at his breath. He locked his ankles and knees, and let it happen to him. He was skiing blind, gloriously out of control, and his heart lifted up with the speed of it. At the timberline he came onto the Sherburne Trail riding a built-up head of speed that hurled him downhill. There was no way that he could stay up, but he did as he navigated the S-turns through the trees, digging deep, scrambling, lurching, miraculously still on his feet. One last tree came rushing towards him, and he fought for the

271

control to wrench himself away from it. He felt his skis skid, hold, felt the sting of branches on his face, and then he was out of the trees and skittering down the final stretch to the finish.

He covered the four-mile course in 6:29.4, which was one full minute faster than the man who finished second, Dick Durrance. It was the largest winning margin in the history of American skiing. It still is.

After it was all over, after the congratulations, after the awards ceremony, after Gregorius's garbled, screaming lecture on suicidal skiing and the prideful bear hug that cancelled out the words; after all of that there was the ride back to Quincy on the bus that bounced down rutted roads and crawled through covered bridges. It was a silent ride for Kurt and Digger, unmoved by the excited chatter around them. The seed of the legend had been planted and already the stories were sprouting, but Digger was down in the bottom loop of the curve that came after achievement. Washed out from the race and saddened by the thought of Kurt's leaving, he sat slumped in his seat, his eyes on the muddy floor of the bus. Somebody passed around a basket of apples, and he took one without thinking, bit into it, and then looked in surprise at the unwanted fruit in his hand. He nudged Kurt, and offered it to him. Kurt shook his head, his eyes fixed on the window and the grey landscape rolling by.

'What time is your train?' Digger asked.

'Ten-oh-five.'

'Plenty of time.'

'Yes.'

'Time for a beer.'

'Yes.'

'You knew I was going to do it, didn't you?'

'Yes.'

'And I did it.'

'Yes, you did.'

'Cheerful, aren't you?'

Kurt dragged his eyes away from the window. They were round and sad. 'No, I'm not cheerful at all.' His eyes went back to the window.

Digger sighed, looked around for a place to put the apple, and, finding none, rode all the way back to Quincy with it clutched in his hand. Elena was waiting for the bus in front of Moriarity's. She was wearing a dress under her coat instead of

272

the usual tweed skirt and sweater. She greeted Digger with a kiss on the cheek.

'I heard what you did,' she said.

'I buried them.'

'Yes, that's what I heard.' She turned to Kurt. 'Did you see it?'

'I saw it,' he said. 'It was the finest piece of skiing I've ever seen.'

They went into the inn, and Digger led them towards the taproom. Elena said, 'Kurt, you'd better go up and get your bags now. Digger and I will meet you in the bar.'

Kurt shook his head. His face was suddenly pale. 'No,' he said, 'I'll go in and sit down with you now.'

'It would be better the other way,' she said firmly.

'I'd prefer it my way.'

'Kurt . . . please.'

He looked at her pleadingly. Then he looked at Digger. Then he turned and went quickly up the stairs.

'What is this?' Digger asked. She did not answer. She brushed past him and went into the bar. He followed her to a table and sat opposite her. She folded her hands in her lap and looked down at them. The radio behind the bar was on, Edward R. Murrow reporting from Vienna.

'*It's now nearly two-thirty in the morning and Herr Hitler has not yet arrived. No one seems to know just when he will get here, but most people expect him some time after ten o'clock tomorrow morning. It's, of course, obvious after one glance at Vienna that a tremendous reception is being prepared.*'

Digger repeated, 'What is this?'

She lifted her eyes and looked at him squarely. 'I'm going away with Kurt. Tonight, on the train.'

The words registered slowly. At first they had no meaning, then suddenly they did. 'Why?' he asked. He felt heat on his face, and on the backs of his hands.

'He needs me.'

'That's no reason. So do I.'

'No, you don't.'

'Son of a bitch.'

'You don't mean that.'

'I didn't mean him. Just everything.'

'*The crowds are courteous as they've always been, but many people are in a holiday mood. They lift the right arm a little*

273

higher here than in Berlin and the "Heil Hitler" is said a little more loudly.'

'Kurt wanted to tell you himself, but it's better this way. He couldn't tell you before the race. You understand that, don't you?'

'Yes.' He looked around for a waitress, found one, and held up two fingers. 'Going away. Where and how?'

'I'm going to New York with him tonight. After that I don't know. If he wants me to go to Austria with him I'll do that too.'

'When did this all happen? How did it happen?'

'It just happened.'

'I didn't see it. I didn't see anything like it.'

She put her hand over his. 'Digger, let's try to do something very intelligent. Let's try not to make this bigger than it is. You and I never talked about love. We were having a good time, that's all. You're not really losing anything.'

'The hell I'm not. I'm losing plenty.'

'I'm sorry you feel that way.'

'Don't flatter yourself, I wasn't even fucking you. There are plenty of other cunts around.'

'You don't have to use words like that. Does it make you feel better to use those words?'

'There isn't a great deal of hilarity, but at the same time there doesn't seem to be much feeling of tension. Young storm troopers are riding about the streets, riding about in trucks and vehicles of all sorts, singing and tossing oranges out to the crowd.'

The waitress came with the bottles of White Elk. Digger picked one up, felt the cold glass, and put it down again. 'You don't understand. I'm losing a guy who could have been . . . that's what I'm losing.'

'It doesn't have to be that way.'

'Christ, that's a dumb thing to say. Of course it does.' In a different voice, he said, 'They'll kick you out of school if you miss more than a couple of days.'

'I'll have to handle that.'

'What about your parents?'

'I'll handle that too.'

'There are still huge crowds along the Ringstrasse, and people still stand outside the principal hotels. . . .'

'You've got everything figured out, don't you?' Digger stood up. 'Nothing for me to hang around for.'

274

'Don't go yet.' She reached for his arm, but he moved it away. 'He'll want to see you.'

'No.'

'Will you be at the station?'

'No.'

'Don't, Digger. You don't know what he's been going through.'

'I guess not. Whatever it was, I didn't know it included my girl.'

'Let's not start that again. I was never your girl, not really.'

'No, I guess you weren't, but now you're his, and you can't ask me to like it. You were right about one thing, anyway. He needs you, and I don't.'

'Everything is quiet in Vienna tonight. There's a certain air of expectancy about the city, everyone waiting and wondering where and at what time Herr Hitler will arrive.'

He left her sitting in the taproom without looking back. Going through the lobby he saw Kurt coming down the stairs, but he kept on going and he didn't look back then, either. He collected his skiing gear from the bus and walked up the street kicking snow.

Chapter Seventeen

BEVERLY HILLS HOTEL
LOS ANGELES

18 February 1939
Mr Franz Harz
c/o Beverly Baines
Casa Filigrana
Malibu

By messenger

My dearest Franz:
I trust that I have addressed this letter properly, that is, in care of Miss Baines, since it *is* her home in which you live. Equally,

I trust that you take no offence at my precision. You taught me long ago to be precise in all forms of address, just as you taught me about knives and forks, and how to handle servants. So, *cher maître,* the Baroness von Ulm acknowledges another obligation, and is pleased to address you in care of your current bitch in heat.

And having delivered myself of that thought, let me congratulate you on the manner in which you stage-managed the scene this afternoon, allowing me to stand there in the driveway in front of that ridiculous house, all globs of *Schlag* and Turkish taffy turrets, with the sun on my head and the taxi driver leering at me insolently and your two hired gorillas blocking the door with their arms folded across their chests like the harem eunuchs from *L'Italiana in Algeri.* . . Mr Harz ain't home, and he ain't gonna be home . . . all quite dramatic and amusing, and for a fleeting moment highly complimentary when I stopped to think of all the money you must have spent to keep me away from you. (Or is it her money, and her gorillas?) No matter, I was touched. And humiliated, of course. I cannot deny you the pleasure of knowing that. My first day in Los Angeles, my first attempt to see you, and you managed so effectively to strip me of my dignity. But how like you to be so excessive. Surely one gorilla would have been enough, or do Hollywood gorillas come only in pairs? May I suggest that next time you employ two baby baboons to swing from your palm trees and sing in duet . . . Mr Harz, he ain't home, lady, and he ain't gonna be. Less expensive, I should think, and far more picturesque.

So, you may sit back tonight in contentment, knowing that I was humiliated this afternoon in front of your flunkies, and in front of a cretinous taxi driver who apparently was born with a toothpick attached to his lower lip, and who occupied himself during the drive back from Malibu by trying to look up my skirt in the rear-view mirror. (I know, it's impossible, but he clearly tried. Perhaps he was trying to look down, not up.) Humiliated, yes, but strangely enough that was not the dominant emotion within me as I rode through the dreadful, sticky heat back to my hotel. For I knew when I embarked on this journey, which every person save one has called a hopeless venture, that I would be exposing myself to your anger, your scorn, and that humiliation would be only one of many courses in the meal I would eat every day.

I knew that, yet I came, for there was nothing left for me to do. End of the line for me, Franz, last stop, and if I cannot convince you that we must reshape our lives together and recapture what we had before, then like Butterfly I will have only two choices left. *Due cose potrei fare: tornare a divertire la gente col cantare oppur, meglio, morire.* Yes . . . *morire.* God, how many times have I sung those lines without a thought in my head except for the value of the notes, the tilt of my chin, the line of my bosom, and, of course, the projection to the highest balcony. Never a thought for the words themselves, but now I sing them to you, without song but in deadly earnest. For if we cannot be what once we were together then, like Butterfly abandoned, there are only two things I can do. Go back and sing and dance again, or else, better . . . *morire.* I do not use the word to frighten you. I know you too well for that. But still, the word remains.

So, humiliation yes, and resignation as well, but sitting in the back of that taxi with my skirts tucked firmly down I also had to wonder why God made me the kind of woman that I am. Other women love, and learn to live with despair, and then to love again. Why not me? Must I always follow my heart? And must I always, in the end, be spanked like a puppy for peeing at the wrong time and place? Dieter says yes. He says that such is my nature: to love only once in a lifetime, to love tenaciously, and like the untrained, untrainable puppy to be regularly smacked on the bottom with the rolled-up newspaper of my lover's neglect.

Despite this, it was he who urged me on this journey, insisting, in fact, that it had to be made, that I had to try just one more time to bring you to your senses. His words, not mine. He considers you senseless, since he cannot understand any sensible man rejecting the love I have to offer. He raises me too high, of course, but what woman could resist such flattery: to be urged by her husband to recapture her errant lover? Certainly not I, and so I have come to California on this capricious venture, disrupting my career and my family in the process. My performances all have been covered (at considerable expense I might add), Dieter has been left to fend for himself, and the twins have been given leave from the university and have been packed off to St Anton for a skiing holiday. They, at least, will show a profit from this madness. And all of this for you, Franz, all this

Sturm und Drang so that I might come to California to be humiliated with the noonday sun hot on my head. And in February, yet.

So you have had your initial triumph, but I warned you once that if I ever came to California I would come armed with all the weapons that a woman possesses. I said that I would fight, and I said that I would crawl, whichever suited my purpose best, and that is exactly what I will do. You *will* see me, and we *will* talk, and what comes after that will rest on God's fingertips. But you will *not* ignore me, I promise you that.

I know you so well. You want me to forget, don't you? How easy that would make everything. Forget it all and go on to something new. But I will not do this. To forget is to regret, and I regret nothing of the life we once shared. Pick something for me to forget, I dare you. Shall I forget that time in Berlin, the room at the Bristol and the smoked trout at Kempinski's afterwards? Dear God, I can still remember the dusky rose wallpaper and the bite of the horseradish that came with the fish. Shall I forget nights like that one, and shall I regret the world we built together? No, Franz, never. I have always followed my heart with you, and now I have followed you to this ugly place of heat, and grease and palm trees where gorillas bar your door to me, and where I promise you I will spend every night like a schoolgirl waiting for a call to come, a whisper in the dark, a word, just a word. . . .

The best of times came when Willi and Mimi were alone, and what they had was undiluted by the presence of strangers. Everyone, even Mamá and Papá, was in some way large or small a stranger who just by being nearby, seemed to weaken their bond. They had never defined that bond, they had never needed to, but they knew that it was something like a magnetic field held delicately in place, pole and antipole responding, and that the intrusion of any foreign object into that field resulted in a warp that weakened. This was their distinction, and they were convinced that it had only in part to do with being twins. They had known other twins, had come close enough to them to sniff their psychic air . . . and had smelled nothing like what they had. A bond, yes, a yoke and an intimate knowledge one of the other, even a communal identity . . . but not the single force, the unseamed oneness. These others did not read from a single book, paint with a single brush, sing with a single voice; and these others had no *threep* and warble, *pok,* whistle, click, and glottal gasp that formed their private native tongue. The book, the brush, the single voice were only tricks, they knew that, with no meaning beyond their ability to perform them. The tricks did nothing more than dramatize the oneness, symbolize it, but they were tricks the others did not have. From this they concluded that their bond only began with twinship, and that most of what they had would have been theirs even had they popped from different pods.

The worst of times came when they were forced to be with people, partly because at such times they felt their power to be weakened, and partly because they felt awkward and inept with others. At the age of nineteen they were social innocents. They could dine decently, make small talk, and dance, but these were chores that they hated, and it showed. They were sexual innocents as well. Not that they were unaware. No one could grow up in the Vienna of their childhood and be unaware of the luxuriant sensuality of the city. They heard all the stories, knew who was sleeping with whom, and why, and how. But it touched not their lives. No rampant passions burned in Willi's nineteen-year-old bones; no aches and yearnings plucked at Mimi's strings. Short and slight, black hair cut to a mutually acceptable length and framing pale, androgynous faces, they were a matched set marked only by the slight swell of Mimi's hips and breasts, the marginal broadness of Willi's shoulders. With childhood passed, they could no longer dress identically, but even in conventional clothing they managed to preserve that illusion. They were Mimi and Willi, as whole and as perfect as a single unfertilized egg.

If being alone was their ideal, being in St Anton to ski the high mountains was absolute Eden. Best of all was when the snow was so thick that the birds stopped singing, the brooks were still, the smoke from the chimneys in the valley rose up as straight as strings, the touring skiers stayed close to the fires, and all of their world was white, and clean and empty. Then they would fill their knapsacks with bread and cheese, pack their sleeping bags, and take to the high places for days at a time, sleeping in woodsmen's huts and in the hay cribs built in lonesome places. Those cribs, in particular, provided admirable retreats for the night, being stuffed with fragrant animal fodder grown during the summer on the Alpine meadows. The soil of those meadows was able to produce a crop only once every two years, and so it was the custom of many farmers to store their hay up high where it was cut and climb to the cribs from their farms to replenish supplies during the wintertime. For the twins, the trick was to enjoy these abodes at night, moving from one to the other daily to avoid being caught by a visiting farmer.

This made for a simple and idyllic way of living. During the day they would ski along the ridge lines where no one else ventured, and before the darkness came they would find their hayrick for the night, build their fire of dung chips and straw, bring it to a roar, and strip before it to bathe in the snow. Mugs of tea, bread and cheese to chew on like fastidious rodents, and then in the night they slept curled and content in their fleece-lined bags, dreaming, they knew, identical dreams. After a week of this they would descend to their grandfather's house to replenish supplies and then, knapsacks full, they were off again to the high and empty places.

This was the way it was when they went to St Anton while their mother was in California. They took at once to the high places in the mountains, the reaches that they thought of as their own, but they realized at once that this time they were not alone. They saw the signs in the woodsmen's huts and the hay cribs where they slept. Someone else was sleeping in those places, using the dry dung and straw to build fires, and leaving behind faint traces: the end of a crust, a sliver of rind, and once the mark of a boot in frozen slush. It was Mimi who saw the boot mark and pointed at it accusingly.

'Somebody else on our mountain,' she said. Actually, the sounds that she made were a series of clicks and whistles.

Willi nodded. He also thought of it as their mountain, at least at this time of the year. 'That's no farmer's boot, and it can't be a tourer, they don't come out this way.' The noise he really made was like the strum of a guitar in their private tongue, a reminder of their oneness.

Their arms went around each other and they pressed close, quivering. They stayed that way, protecting each other from whatever it was that had come to their mountain. They felt their blood flow and their one heart beat, they pressed even closer, and after a while they kicked at the boot mark until it was gone.

For the next few days they were aware of some other person

skiing nearby, sometimes above them, sometimes below, but always just out of sight; and at night in the hay cribs the signs of that presence were always there. Whoever it was kept hidden, not even a creak in the night, but no tracks were covered, either.

'He's playing a game,' said Willi. 'Cat and mouse, and he thinks we're the mice.'

'I'd rather be the cat,' said Mimi.

'He'll have to show himself eventually. Then we'll see who's what.'

He showed himself the next morning, a trim young man dressed all in black and skiing effortlessly along a ridge above them. He waved to them once, then dropped over the ridge and was gone. They saw him again the next day, and the next, always too far away to hail or to chase, never in sight longer than it took to wave a salute. That night they slept in the empty hut of Jakob the woodcutter, and in the morning they climbed partway up the Gamskar Spitze and then skied along the arête that led to the Graff Hütte hundreds of metres below. They were stopped for a breath in the lee of the ridge when Mimi suddenly made her sound for alarm deep in her throat.

'*Pok?*' said Willi.

'There,' she said, pointing.

He stood below them on the slope, sideways to the fall line and motionless on his skis. He was still dressed in black, and with his goggles down they could see only the lower part of his face. He raised his arm in the salute now familiar, but this time he beckoned with his hand. When they did not move he beckoned again.

'He wants us to come down,' said Willi.

'He still thinks he's the cat.'

Again the figure waved, more urgently this time, and without consultation they slowly began to sideslip down the hill, ready to edge the slip into a traverse and scoot away if the cat showed claws. Inch by inch, foot by foot, they eased their way down towards the motionless figure, and when they were close enough he raised his goggles in a gesture of welcome. Now they could see all of his face, could see that he was smiling and that it was a gentle smile.

'*Grüss Gott,*' he said in a voice that was equally gentle, and that was how they met Wolf Karsh.

*

. . . so again my apologies, darling Dieter, for the foolishness of the long-distance call, but last night it seemed imperative to hear your voice and listen to your words of comfort. Such an expense, Los Angeles to Vienna, and for what? So much static I could hardly hear your voice. Do forgive me for waking you at such a ridiculous hour and all, but I was feeling so depressed . . . no, no apologies between us, you understand.

So, to repeat what I tried to say last night, my adventure does not go very well at all. In the past week I have tried telephoning the wretched man three times a day, each time being told that Mr Harz is not at home, and each time leaving a message to be called. With no results, of course. I have also written three letters, each hand-delivered, but with no reply forthcoming. (Actually I'm surprised that he accepts the letters. A good sign, don't you think? He is clearly curious.) I also tried to see him at his studio, beard the lion in his lair, but that did not work, either. It seems he has had me barred from the MGM lot. Can you imagine? Actually, it makes one feel rather distinguished. I did not think he had that kind of power here. Just figure that, our Franzie barring people from a place like MGM. It almost makes one proud.

I also wanted to tell you that I saw Eddie Gottlieb. You remember him, of course, from the Théâtre Royale in Vienna, but here he is a booking agent, one of the biggest, and so I paid him a visit at his offices yesterday afternoon. (A reception room the size of the Prater and a private office big enough to hold a ball in.) Dear Eddie, I felt that I had to give him some reason for being in California, and so I told him that I was listening to some offers from the studios. I need not have bothered. He gave me one of those shrewd yiddische looks, and I shall do my best to reproduce what he said.

'Marta, sweetie, if you was talking to any studio, believe me I wudda heard about it half an hour later. No, I tell a lie, make that fifteen minutes, tops. So don't give me the studio *narashkeit,* bubbelah. This is a small town, smaller and nastier than Vienna, and half the people in the industry know why you're here. Don't you read the columns? Louella had it yesterday, something about Marta Prinz in town to rekindle the old flame from Vienna. Nice, huh? Makes you look great. You think nobody knows how you tried to crash the house at Malibu? You think it's a secret that you been barred from the MGM lot? Just nobody printed it yet, that's all. You're making yourself look bad all over, sweetie, but that's your business. Just don't tell me from studios. Personally, I wish you luck with Franz, although I never knew what you saw in that *alta putz*. But I gotta tell you if this was a horserace I wouldn't bet a nickel on your chances. The great Mr Harz, he's got himself a sweetheart of a situation with Beverly and it's gonna take a hell of a lot more than you singing two hearts in three-quarter time to blast him out of it. He won't even show you his face. Believe me, you've got as much chance of getting to Franz as you do of crashing Beverly's party next week, and for that one I hear she's got goons from the sheriff's office guarding the gates.'

He went on that way and all I could do was smile, rather weakly, I'm afraid. I knew nothing about the gossip columns, and I'm sure he exaggerates when he says half the industry, but still . . . ! Then, to my surprise, he turned rather brusque and businesslike and said that if I were really 'on the Coast' for 'business purposes' he could probably 'get something lined up.' (His words, where indicated.) What he apparently had in mind was a radio programme, paid for by a soap company, which features a repertoire of light opera with the occasional war-horse added in for 'cultural' purposes. I do believe he was thinking of something from Carmen for me, which shows how silly people can get when they come to this place. Eddie knows that I've never sung Carmen and never could, but that did not stop him from making the suggestion. He was also careful to point out that I wasn't Grace, and I wasn't Lili, but he could still get me 'top dollar.' How sweet. I said no, of course, but he asked me to think it over and it seemed simpler at the time to agree rather than be firm. He also said something about the Hollywood Bowl, but that sounded more like icing on the cake than anything else.

When I left Eddie I took a taxi back to my hotel. But that statement deserves an explanation.

You recall in my last letter that I mentioned the taxi driver who drove me out to Malibu on my first day here, an oaf of a fellow, clearly a criminal type. Well, imagine my surprise that morning on the way to Eddie's office when the doorman at the hotel put me into my taxi and there was the selfsame driver at the wheel. I was halfway into the machine when I realized who he was, in an awkward position with one foot still on the kerb, and I stopped. He turned around to look at me, this twisted, leering face that seemed to say: 'Well, well, I've got her again.' I did not know at all what to do and so, as usual, came down on the side of not making a fuss. I got into the cab, seated myself (with skirts pulled firmly down), and gave him the address of Eddie's office in a no-nonsense voice. As I had feared, his eyes were on me in the rear-vision mirror all the way, but I managed to ignore that and the trip was uneventful.

So much for that, but when I left Eddie's office to go back to the hotel, there he was again, parked at the kerb. When he saw me he jumped out of the car and opened the door. I was astounded, and could only say, rather stupidly: 'What is this? Were you waiting here for me?' He said nothing, just grinned at me insolently, the inevitable toothpick bobbing on his lips. Of course, I at once turned on my heel, went back inside to Eddie's office, and had one of his people telephone for another taxi. When it arrived, the first one had gone.

I tell you this story not to alarm you but, on the contrary, to assure you that I am being most cautious in this topsy-turvy place where everything seems slightly out of focus. We both have heard the California stories that people parrot foolishly. Most of them are told by those who have failed here and now feel compelled to parody the place. But I tell you, Dieter, once you are here you realize that in California parody is understatement. This business with the taxi driver is a perfect example of the local lunacy, and I have decided to do away with the problem by hiring a car and driver. Something I should have done in the first place . . .

Wolf Karsh was a twenty-two-year-old law student, a Viennese and a Jew. He had been in Vienna at the time of the *Anschluss*, had seen Hitler's triumphal entrance into the city, and had seen how the mass of the Austrian people had welcomed him with hysterical enthusiasm. He had also seen the first fruits of the *Anschluss*: hundreds of Jewish men and women rounded up and put to work scrubbing the streets on their hands and knees under the eyes of the storm troopers while the ordinary citizens of the city, those easygoing, fun-loving Viennese, gathered around to yell taunts and insults. Hundreds of other Jews were conscripted to clean the latrines of the barracks where the storm troopers were quartered, and tens of thousands of others were jailed and their possessions confiscated. That was only the beginning. During the first weeks after the *Anschluss* a sprawling concentration camp was constructed at Mauthausen, on the north bank of the Danube near Enns, and the 'Office for Jewish Emigration' was established under the authority of Karl Adolf Eichmann. All this while Vienna alternately cheered and yawned.

Wolf's grandfather was his only living relative, a retired dentist who had raised him since the death of his parents. The old man, a fragile seventy-five with parchmentlike skin and an undependable heart, was one of the first to be imprisoned as an 'enemy of the state,' and he lasted less than a month. The notice of his death came to the apartment in the Plosslgasse in the form of a black-bordered postal card. It came less than twenty-four hours before a third Nazi roundup of Vienna's Jews, one which Wolf evaded by abandoning the apartment and taking to the streets. With the university closed to him, as to all Jews now, he survived the summer and autumn of 1938 by living in the shadows, sleeping in any one of Vienna's many parks, and depending on the generosity of a few gentile friends. It was a night-to-night existence that lengthened into weeks and months, but when the first cold winds began to whistle down the streets of the Inner City it was one of those gentile friends who pointed out that his luck could not last much longer.

'It's one thing to sleep in the parks in September,' he was told. 'It's something different in January. That's what the SS is counting on. Once the weather turns bitter there will be another roundup, the final one. You've got to get out of Vienna, Wolf.'

Getting out of the city in the autumn of 1938 was difficult, but not impossible. The movement of Jews attempting to leave the country was closely controlled by the Office for Jewish Emigration, where the going rate for escape and freedom was beyond the means of a young law student. (The rumour was that Baron Louis de Rothschild himself had managed to buy his way out by turning over his steel mills to the Hermann Goering Works.) But movement within Austria still was possible for a young and active man willing to take risks. All that was required was a cool head and the ability to hike around checkpoints. As soon as the first snow fell on Vienna, Wolf left the city outfitted by his friends as a touring skier on his way to the Tirol.

'After that it was easy,' he explained to Willi and Mimi.

'Outside Vienna everybody skis. You put a pair of skis over your shoulder and it's like having a new set of identity papers.'

Once out of Vienna he made his way west, and when he came to the Tirol he took to the high places where few ever ventured. Working along the ridges from point to point and sleeping in hayricks just as Willi and Mimi did, his plan was to wait out the winter and at the first sign that the mountain passes were clear to cross over into Switzerland at the Bieler Höhe above Piz Buin. So far he had managed to keep himself hidden, and on the few occasions when he had been seen skittering along some faraway face he had been ignored by the superstitious peasants as just another mountain gnome. His needs were few and easily satisfied: there was always clean snow to boil for water, an occasional winter hare, a farmer's chicken here and there, a loaf of bread lifted lightly in the night. Nothing to cause alarm in the farms and villages. The only staple that he truly missed, he admitted, was tea. He had been without tea for two months. The moment he said that Willi reached into his knapsack for a pot, scooped up fresh snow, and put it over the fire while Mimi got out the screwed-up piece of paper that held the last of their tea.

'Is that why you showed yourself to us?' she asked lightly. 'Because you wanted some tea?'

Wolf shook his head. 'I don't really know why I took the chance. I watched the two of you for days before I decided. I can't say why, but I got the feeling that you weren't dangerous, that I would be safe if I showed myself.'

This was the night of the day that they met, and the three of them had returned to the hayrick of Jakob the woodcutter. At first there was silence as the fire was built and the bodies were warmed, but once Wolf started to speak, the story of his days since the *Anschluss* came rolling out. For the last two months he had spoken to no one but himself. He told them everything, knowing that he was putting his safety in their hands, but apparently unconcerned by the risk he was taking. The fire grew higher and light from the flames flickered across his lean, dark face. He spoke with his eyes on the fire, his voice a monotone. While the tea water boiled Mimi sliced bread and cheese for all of them. Wolf nodded his thanks and spoke on as he chewed, and when the tea was ready he gulped it down eagerly.

Grinning, he held out his cup for more. 'The tea is wonderful, but it wasn't that. I just felt I could trust you.'

Willi and Mimi looked at each other silently. There was no need to speak, not even in their private tongue. They were both aware that Wolf was the first person they had ever met who had entered into their field without weakening or warping it. If anything, he seemed to lend it strength. This novelty, in itself, should have been alarming, but even that could not disturb the peace they felt in his presence, for never before had they met anyone so close to being a candidate into their circumscribed world. Mimi left it to Willi to put into words.

'You were right, you're safe with us,' he said. 'That's the last of the tea, but we'll get some more tomorrow.'

After a week in southern California, Marta was convinced that Los Angeles was the devil's playground. Both the people and the architecture were demented, the food was insipid, and the hot and sticky air left a grime that lay over everything she touched. She knew that she was biased, that her attitude was coloured by her reason for being there, but still she hated the place. To the sufferer, she told herself, a psychosomatic pain is just as difficult to bear as the real thing.

Then, the morning after her visit with Eddie Gottlieb, she awoke to the rare California morning that justifies every local enthusiasm. The sky was clear, a westerly breeze brought scents from faraway islands, the very air seemed to sparkle, and the fruit that she had for her breakfast was the fullest and sweetest she had ever tasted. With that sort of start to the day she decided that she was entitled to a vacation from her obsession. There would be no thoughts of Franz today, just some leisurely shopping, a decent lunch somewhere near the water, and in the afternoon, perhaps, a dip in the hotel's pool. Refreshed in body and spirit, she ordered her newly rented car brought around and went down to meet it. The machine waiting in front of the hotel was a maroon Packard, and the driver standing beside the open door was the same leering, insolent cabbie of the days before, dressed now in ill-fitting livery.

She stopped and stared at him, then said, 'Now this is really impossible. What are you doing here dressed like that?'

His eyes on the ground, he said, 'I drive the car. That's what I do.'

'Yes, I know you do,' she said bitingly, 'but why does it always have to be my car? Yesterday you were a taxi driver, today you are a chauffeur. What *are* you?'

'I drive all kinds of cars,' he muttered. 'I'm a good driver.'

'You haven't answered my question.'

'At the garage they said to bring the Packard over here this morning. That's all I know. You want another driver, I got to call the garage and tell them.'

He looked up for the first time, and his eyes were soft and pleading. For the first time she realized that he was Mexican, that what she had taken for a leer was a scar that gave a permanent twist to his lips, and that he was closer to sixty than forty. She hesitated, then asked, 'If I want another driver will there be a delay?'

'Maybe half an hour.'

'Very well, call the garage. I shall wait in the lobby.'

He mumbled something she did not hear.

'What was that?'

'Means I don't get paid today.'

'I see.' Again, she hesitated.

'*Baronesa,* please.'

'Oh? How did you know to call me that?'

'At the garage they say to call you *la baronesa*. Please . . . this man Harz, the one you want to see? The one who lives out at Malibu?'

She was suddenly stiff. Half of the industry? Half of Los Angeles, it seemed. She forced herself to say, 'Yes?'

'Every Thursday he has lunch at Quasimodo's down by El Segundo. Every Thursday, one o'clock, never fails. Today is Thursday.'

'How do you know this?'

'You hear things when you drive the cars. Monday they always go by Musso Frank's, Tuesday the Derby, Wednesday Chasen's, Friday the Lounge. But Thursday always Quasimodo's, him and Miss Baines.'

'Every Thursday.' She tapped her lower lip with a glossy fingernail. A decision half made, she asked, '*¿Cómo te llama, tú?*'

'*Antonio, baronesa, a sus órdenes.*'

Antonio, like her brother, Anton. A sign of safety? Feeling half a fool, Marta completed her decision. 'Very well, Antonio, you will drive for me today. First I want to do some shopping, and then luncheon at . . . Quasimodo's, was it?'

She spent enough time shopping to be sure that she arrived at Quasimodo's slightly after one o'clock. Most of the tables were outside under trellises, positioned on a hill that led from the lower roadway to the restaurant's main building at the top. The best tables were on the hump of the hill, where the view was magnificent and the trellises were covered with brilliant bougainvillea. Franz's table was on the hump, naturally, and even from the bottom of the hill Marta could spot him by his crest of silver hair, sitting with a woman in a flame-coloured dress who could only be Beverly Baines. Peering out of the car window and up the hill, she saw the man she loved for the first time in two years and was so affected by the sight that she made an immediate tactical error. There were two ways she could have approached Franz's table: on foot from the bottom by ascending the flight of stairs laid into the side of the hill, or by driving around and up to the main building and descending those stairs to the hump. She chose the second option, ordering Antonio up the zigzag of streets that led to the top, where she left the car, brushed past an indignant maître d'hôtel, broke through a cordon of waiters, put down her head, and made her descent to the hump past tables full of startled diners.

Her approach was fast and loud, enough to alert Franz. His head came up, and when he saw her his face froze. He jumped to his feet, looked around for an exit, and said something quickly to Beverly Baines. Then, as Marta came charging down the hill, he skipped nimbly over to the outdoor stairway and raced down the steps to the bottom road, where his car was parked. By the time Marta reached his table he was in the car and heading north on the boulevard.

'You blew it,' said Beverly Baines in a friendly voice. 'You should have checked it out. He always parks down there.'

'I just wanted to talk to him,' said Marta, her eyes still on Franz's car growing smaller in the distance. 'That's all, just a little chat.'

'I know, but that's what he's afraid of.' Beverly looked up, shading her eyes with her hand. She was trying hard not to smile. 'You should have made your approach from the bottom of the hill. That way he wouldn't have been able to run.'

'I can see that,' Marta agreed. 'You see, I'm used to chasing him in Vienna. It's a different game over here.'

'Don't blame yourself, it takes a while to get used to California. You should have seen his face when you came charging down the hill. He turned white.'

'There was a time when he would have turned purple with passion.'

'Well, there you are, time is the killer. Sit down and have something to eat. Take Franz's salad. He only just started on it.'

Beverly stretched her arms above her head and grinned. It was a careless motion, but one of her hands still held a glass of wine, and with her legs asprawl the gesture became one of carefree abandon. Stretched that way every line of her body showed through the thin fabric of her dress, and it was clear to anyone interested that the dress and her shoes were all that she wore. Marta looked down at the fine-boned, yet good-humoured, face of the movie star smiling at her. It had been said of Beverly Baines that as an actress she was capable of registering two emotions: rapture and indigestion. The statement, although close to being accurate, was unimportant. A beauty herself, Marta knew that she was in the presence of one of those magnificent animals whose entire talent was compressed into physical expression. Her own beauty, by comparison, was a candle in the sun.

'Sit down,' Beverly prompted. 'There's no sense chasing after him now.'

The invitation was put too pleasingly to be refused. She sat down in Franz's place, looked at the plate in front of her, and asked, 'What is it?'

'Quasimodo's A-line salad. Abalone, avocado, and apple.'

'I know about apples, but not the rest.'

'California. Try it.'

Marta took one hesitant taste, and then tucked into the salad heartily. Beverly watched her eat with approval, then called for another glass, and wine to be poured. 'You've got a good appetite,' she said. 'I do, too, but if I ate like that I'd turn into a horse.'

'I've always been able to eat this way,' Marta confided between mouthfuls. 'It's my peasant background.'

'What peasant? I thought you were a baroness.'

'That, too. My husband is a baron, so that makes me a baroness, but it doesn't change who my parents were. Everybody in my family eats this way.' She speared a slice of abalone and chewed on it thoughtfully. 'I'm beginning to change my mind about California. So far, everything today has been lovely. I don't even mind that Franz got away.'

'He moves fast.'

'I'll get him tomorrow. Or the next day. Right now I'm just glad that he left his salad. What happened to the gorillas today? Why aren't they with you?'

'The which?'

'Those two thugs at your house who stopped me from seeing Franz.' She broke a seeded roll in two and inserted a chunk of butter the size of a walnut.

'Oh, those two,' Beverly said, laughing. 'They go with the house, they don't travel with us.' She looked around for a waiter to pour more wine, muttered something about fucking incompetents, and poured it herself. 'I read what you wrote Franz about using baboons instead. I liked that. As a matter of fact, I like *you*. I didn't think I would, but I do. And, of course, I adore your voice. I have every record you've ever made.'

Marta had a fairly good idea of how true that was, but she smiled graciously. She rarely went to the cinema, but she said, 'I don't think I've ever missed one of your films. You're the most beautiful woman in pictures today.'

Beverly accepted that with equal grace. 'Compliments exchanged, that makes us even.'

'Not quite.' Marta fished for a last piece of avocado, underneath a lettuce leaf. 'At the moment you happen to have my man.'

'Some moment. Two years is more than a moment.'

'I know,' Marta agreed. 'That's why I'm here, to straighten things out.'

'What's to straighten? If you want him, take him. That is, if he'll go. I don't think he will.'

Marta put down her fork and stared. 'You mean that? If I want him, just take him? You wouldn't try to hold him?'

'What's to hold? If a man wants to go, he goes. Who's going to stop him? Who would want to?'

'I would,' Marta said firmly. 'Do you think we could have some more wine?'

291

'Sure.' Beverly raised a finger and wiggled it. White jackets stirred. 'Yeah, Franzie told me how it is with you. He says you kept him on a short leash for years in Vienna. I could never do that. Too humiliating.'

'It's just the way I am.' Marta buttered another roll, jabbing at it with her knife. 'My husband says that it's part of my nature to love only once in a lifetime, and to love tenaciously.'

'Is that how he got to be a baron, saying things like that? Frankly, sweetie, your husband sounds like a shmuck, if you'll pardon my French.'

Marta giggled. 'He really isn't. He's really very sweet.'

'So he's a sweet shmuck, the world is full of them. If he's so sweet what are you doing chasing around the world after a bum like Franz Harz?'

'Because I love the bum. And he isn't one, not really. If he were, you wouldn't be holding on to him the way you are.'

'Listen, you keep saying that, but I'm not holding on to anybody. Let me explain about Franzie and me. First of all, he *is* a bum. He's a coldhearted son of a bitch who doesn't give a damn about anybody but himself. But I adore the guy, maybe because he's that way. All I know is that he's good for me. He's old enough to play Papa, if you know what I mean, and still young enough to bounce around the bedroom. So he's important to me, but if he ever said that he wanted to leave I'd never try to stop him. Hell, I'd pack sandwiches for him, I'd buy his bus ticket. Who wants a man around the house who wants to be somewhere else? Not me.'

Marta said wistfully, 'I wish I could believe that.'

'You can, because I just said it. The trouble with you is, you're kidding yourself. You think that all you have to do is sit down with Franz and talk sweet reason to him and he'll come running back home to Mama. Well, he won't, and you're a fool if you think that he will.'

'You may be right,' said Marta with dignity, 'but it's something I have to do. I have to speak with him. Face to face.'

'And that's all you really want? Just to talk to him?'

'Yes.'

'Well, you're certainly entitled to that much.'

'I am?'

'Sure you are, sweetie. Who the hell does he think he is, after all those years with you? Fair is fair.'

292

'Thank you. I wish he felt that way. You see how he is, he refuses to see me, much less talk.'

'Oh, him, I told you he's a coldhearted son of a bitch. But he'll see you. We just have to plan it right.'

'We?'

'Sure, we. We should be able to think of something.' Her face lit up as a spark was kindled. 'As a matter of fact, I know exactly how we're going to do it. Next week is my party, and you're invited.'

Antonio absently rubbed the right front fender of the Packard with a chamois cloth. The fender was glossy, and needed no rubbing. From where he stood, in the hilltop parking lot of Quasimodo's, Antonio could see the restaurant, the tables on the hump, and the boulevard below. Thus he had witnessed Marta's charge down the hill and Franz's flight, and now he could clearly see *la baronesa* sitting at the table with Beverly Baines, the two women apparently chatting as amiably as school-girl chums. The sight offended him. He realized that among the *anglos* it was sometimes necessary to socialize with your enemy before you killed him, but it was foreign to his temperament, and annoying. Not that he doubted that when the proper time came *la baronesa* would kill both Harz and the Baines woman. *La voz divina* was too much woman not to do so, and when she had made her charge down the hill he had fully expected her to shoot the *cabrón* with the pistol he assumed she carried in her handbag. Indeed, he had been ready to back her play with the stubby Colt that rested under his jacket. But the bastard Harz had run, and now the divine one sat with that Malibu *puta* drinking wine as if they were sisters, not enemies to the knife. He sighed as he moved his chamois over the fender. He had been twenty years north of the Rio Bravo and he still did not understand the workings of the *gringo* mind.

It was clear that the woman had been wronged: her man of many years had left her for another. This was a known fact, mentioned in the gossip columns of the *anglo* newspapers and discussed in the back seats of the taxis and the limousines that he drove. The news was official – both Hedda and Louella had consoled her in print. Clearly, therefore, her name had been cheapened and her honour had been damaged. By his standards only blood could right such a wrong, preferably blood spilled

293

by the woman's protector. But this woman stood alone. True, she had a husband somewhere far away, but she had come to California by herself to seek her satisfaction. In most women he would have seen this as a sign of helplessness, but not in the case of *la voz divina*. As far as he was concerned she had no weaknesses, and he was sure that when the time came she would do what had to be done.

Marta had been wrong about Antonio's age. He was only forty-seven, but it was a Mexican forty-seven with every day on loan and the interest collected annually. A father at seventeen and a widower at thirty, he had lived for the past twelve years in the back bedroom of his brother-in-law's house on Alvarado Street. For the use of that room, and for his share of the tortillas and beans consumed at the family table, he paid his dead wife's brother nine dollars each week. At that rate he felt himself to be mildly victimized but he valued the privacy that the money bought him, for in the *barrio* he was known as an eccentric, a loner without a woman and without friends. The son he had sired long ago was back in Mexico now, and his solitary state was complete. He preferred it that way.

His needs were few and his possessions meagre. Aside from well-worn clothing he owned only a guitar and a flute, the snub-nosed Colt, a washing pot, a set of good wrenches, and an almost new Philco combination radio and phonograph. He also owned over four hundred phonograph records, the storage of which took up all of the wall space in his tiny room. The records were mostly Victor Red Seals with a sprinkling of HMVs, EMIs, Deutsche Grammophons, and other foreign labels, and each had cost between seventy-five cents and two dollars when purchased new. This was a considerable capital asset in the *barrio,* but Antonio was considered an eccentric by his neighbours not because of the money that he spent on his records but because of the kind of music that he played late into each night behind the pulled-down shades of that back bedroom window. He owned not a single copy of *Cielito Lindo,* or *La Virgen de la Macarena,* or *Malagueña Salerosa.* Antonio was an opera buff. Over the years he had pieced together complete album sets of *Don Giovanni, La Bohème, Aida, Tosca,* and every other war-horse in the non-Wagnerian repertory. There were places of honour on one wall of shelves for the recordings of Caruso, Schipa, Pinza, Gigli, Tibbet, and Chaliapin; and on another wall was a mixture of Pons, Jeritza, Ponselle, Rethberg, Jepson, and Galli-Curci. But the third wall was his particular pride, reserved exclusively for the work of the one artist he idolized above all others: Marta Prinz, *la baronesa* von Ulm. Unlike Beverly Baines, who had used the phrase as a pleasantry, he literally owned every recording she had ever made.

Antonio folded the chamois cloth and carefully replaced it in the glove compartment of the Packard. The sun was high and hot, but he stood in it patiently. He could have taken refuge in the shade at the rear of the restaurant, but he preferred to stay where he could keep his eyes on *la baronesa*, now huddled in intimate conversation with the Baines woman. That was the job he had assigned himself all week, keeping an eye on her, and it had cost him most of his pay in trading jobs with the other drivers. He considered the money well spent. The time was coming close when *la divina* would have to strike at those who had wronged her, and when she did he would be right behind her to see that justice was done.

The next day Willi and Mimi went to get the tea for their new friend. They made Wolf promise to stay close to the hayrick of Jakob the woodcutter while they made the trip down to the Prinz farm. The trip took them most of the day, as they circled wide to conceal the direction from which they were coming, climbing ridges and skiing along unfamiliar valleys in order to approach the farm from the west. There they endured the attentions of their grandparents while they loaded their knapsacks with bread, cheese, slabs of chocolate, the crusty butt of a baked ham, and as much tea as they could stuff into their pockets. Then they were off again, climbing, and it was close to dark by the time they arrived back at the hayrick.

There was no sign of anyone inside the gloomy, lofted rick, but when Willi whistled sharply, twice, a head appeared from out of a loosely bound bale, and then shoulders and arms as Wolf worked himself free from his hiding place. Mimi laughed delightedly as he appeared bit by bit.

'You look like a mole coming out of his hole,' she told him. 'You didn't have to do that. The farmers here aren't monsters. If they catch you, they just run you off. They wouldn't hurt you.'

Wolf brushed straw from his hair and shoulders. Quietly, he

said, 'Maybe that's all they would do to you. There are different rules for me.'

There was a moment of silent embarrassment; she had forgotten so quickly. 'I'm sorry,' she said. 'What would they do to you if they caught you?'

'There's a camp near Enns where they're sending all the Jews.'

'A camp? That doesn't sound so bad.'

'Not the kind of camp where you play tennis all day. Jews go into this camp, but they don't come out.'

'A concentration camp?'

'That's what they call it. At Mauthausen.'

She hugged her shoulders, and her head went back and forth. 'I'm sorry, I'm saying all the wrong things.'

'That's all right.'

'No, it isn't.' She looked to Willi for help, but he was silently unpacking the supplies and arranging them on a pile of clean straw. 'Willi, say something.'

He looked up, his face troubled. He chose his words slowly. 'What's to say? These things that are happening now . . . we've never paid much attention to what's going on in the world. It was never any of our business. We never thought about things like this. I'm sorry, but that's the way we are.'

'Don't apologize,' said Wolf. 'I understand.'

'No, you don't. You can't understand how it is with us. But I guess we'll have to start thinking differently now.' He shook his head as if to clear it, and looked down at the supplies on the straw. 'At least we got plenty of tea, all you can drink.'

'Wonderful. I'll get the fire going and you boil some water.'

'There are other things too,' said Mimi, suddenly anxious to please. 'Bread, and chocolate and meat.'

'Even better,' said Wolf, rubbing his hands. 'We'll have a regular feast.'

But before the tea and before the feast came the ritual of the twins' nightly bath. Once the fire was high enough they stripped off their layers of clothing and left the shelter of the rick to roll naked in the clean snow outside. Wolf watched, his eyes narrowed, as they unashamedly rubbed each other up and down with handfuls of snow, gasping with pleasure. When they came back in to warm themselves by the fire his eyes recorded Mimi's slim loveliness, the slight but provoking flare of hips and breasts,

and then he looked away. He had never before seen such unconcerned and naïve nudity.

'You should try it,' said Mimi, rubbing herself dry and
searching for a clean pair of socks. 'It makes you tingle all over.'

'Maybe tomorrow.' He kept his eyes on the pot over the fire,
waiting for the tea water to boil.

In a short time the enclosure in the rick was filled with the
odours of overboiled tea, toasting bread, and slices of ham
frying in a pan. Willi was in charge of the cooking. When he
judged the meat to be done he fished a slice of it out of the
pan, laid it on a piece of bread, and started to hand it to Wolf.
In the middle of the motion he stopped and pulled back his
head. He turned to Mimi with a stricken look on his face.

'We've been very stupid,' he said.

She nodded. 'We both forgot.'

'Forgot what?' asked Wolf.

'That you can't eat ham.'

'Who can't?' he roared. He grabbed the bread and meat from
Willi and took a bite of it, chewing rapidly.

Mimi said, 'I thought that Jews didn't eat ham.'

'Some do, some don't.' Wolf's lips were bright with grease.
'This one certainly does. Right now I'm so hungry I could take
a bite out of the archbishop of Vienna.'

'We didn't know that,' said Willi. 'I guess we've got a lot to
learn about Jews.'

'Ask me anything.' Wolf waved a hand in the air gaily. 'I'm
an expert on the subject.'

'We can teach each other a lot,' said Mimi, 'but you wouldn't
want to bite the bishop. He came to the house once and we had
to kiss his ring. His hand is all bony, not much meat. You're
better off with the ham.'

It wasn't much of a joke, either, but it was the first one she
had ever made, and the others respected the effort. They settled
down to their feast around the fire, content in their new
friendship.

Thus began the happy days. Willi and Mimi, the perfect egg,
had always lived in a time suspended from that of the rest of
the world. Things were . . . they never changed. Things were
the same now as they had been yesterday, and would be
tomorrow. Some days were better than others, but all were
essentially the same within the protection of the egg. Because

297

of their oneness they had never been lonely, because of their father they had never been hungry, because of their mother they had never felt fear. They dealt with the other basic emotions on the same level. They loved and they hated, they wanted and were satisfied, but all within the coolness of the egg. They knew that they were children of privilege, some of it social and more of it psychic, but they carried no guilt because of that. It was just the way life was: Either you were in the egg, or you were out of it. They were well aware of the life outside the egg, but it had never interested them much and they had done their best to ignore it.

The entrance of Wolf Karsh into their lives changed all that. His presence required a subtle shift of psychic weight within the egg, but once that was done they made him their own. In one stroke they acquired a friend to be cherished, a dependent to be protected, and an acolyte to be initiated into the mysteries of the egg. Over the next few weeks they revealed those mysteries to him slowly, showed him their oneness and at the same time showed him how he might, someday, become a part of it. Each evening by the fire they revealed another mystery. They sang songs to him in a single voice, they told him stories that only they knew, they drew charcoal pictures on hayrick walls, two hands working as one. They even taught him the basics of their private tongue of clicks and buzzes, and laughed with delight each time he was able to reproduce one of the sounds. Overnight they went from being one to being one plus something else, and the addition gave them a strength they never had before. With this newfound strength came the knowledge that what they had now would surely never come again, and that they must cherish these days and live them fully. For the next few weeks they devoted themselves to skiing the mountains by day, and in the evenings to sitting beside the fire and carefully reshaping the structure of the egg into a home for three, not two. It was a time of adventure and a time of contentment; it was the time of their lives.

Antonio eased the Packard a few feet up the driveway and stopped behind a silver-grey Bentley. The road up to Beverly's house was jammed with cars, the line moving around to the front entrance in irregular spasms. Burly men in the uniform of the Los Angeles County Sheriff's Office were spaced along the gravelled roadway in the dusk directing traffic with flashlights, but there was little they could do to speed the process of the arriving guests. It was stop and start, inching over the gravel. Beverly's annual costume party, even by the standards of the place and time, was one hell of a bash. Four hundred guests, the elite of the industry, had been invited, and perhaps fifty more would find a way to crash the gate and wander through the beach house converted for the occasion into a set designer's dream. Two orchestras played, one in the ballroom and the other in a pavilion set up on the beach. A champagne fountain flowed in the courtyard, liveried servants hovered everywhere, and at the point where the trees met the sand a barbecue pit had been dug big enough to hold the carcasses of half a dozen steers rotating over the coals. Three bars operated at full press, and buffet tables bordered the brightly lit pool area. The costumes on display were predictably magnificent, but lacking in variety, since the guests all had access to the same studio tailors and dressmakers. Among the women the clear favourite was the image of a southern belle in sausage curls and hoopskirts à la Miriam Hopkins, followed closely by flocks of Mata Haris, Juliets, and Cleopatras; while the men tended towards Hamlets, Tarzans, cowboys, and the dress uniforms of the better regiments of the British army. Only a few men had been radical enough to come dressed in nothing more exotic than dinner jackets, but they were all senior producers with their own distribution deals, and thus were entitled to the eccentricity.

Antonio let the car roll forward a few more feet. With the engine idling he glanced in the rear-view mirror at *la baronesa* in the back seat. She looked her loveliest, he decided, more lovely even than the photo of her he had pasted to his bedroom wall: Manon in a long and shimmering gown. Tonight her gown also shimmered, the Oriental garb of Madama Butterfly, but the lady shimmered as well, her eyes gleaming from behind the domino that masked the upper half of her face.

It would be better if she were calm, he thought. She looks like the tigress closing in for the kill, and that might be noticed. She has done well so far and she must not spoil it. I do not know how she managed the invitation to this *tontería,* but she is about to enter the fortress of her enemies in disguise. What could be better? Then the slaying will begin.

Only one aspect of the evening disturbed him. Once his

299

baronesa passed into the house she would be beyond the protection of his snub-nosed Colt. If there were only a way he could get inside . . . but with all the *policía* that was clearly impossible. Well, she had come this far alone and she would have to finish the course that way. No matter what else, he and the car would be waiting.

If Marta appeared excited to Antonio, she herself felt calm and resigned to whatever the evening might bring. One last roll of the dice, a quiet talk with Franz, and then if God was good to her the beginnings of a reconciliation. She did not expect the man to fall into her arms and beg to come back; she was too much of a realist for that. All she sought was a chance to hope, a chance for the future, and thanks to Beverly's fairness she was getting that chance. It was Beverly who had sent her the invitation in the name of a friend, and it was Beverly who had told her where to rent the Butterfly costume so that the two of them would be dressed exactly the same, complete to the white satin domino that masked her eyes. And it was Beverly who had told her precisely where in the house Franz would be before the party really took hold: in his study reading scripts.

She imagined how she would slip through the study door to stand half concealed in the shadows, waiting for him to raise that shaggy silver head and smile his welcome, taking her for Beverly. She could hear his voice.

'The perfect Cio-cio-san,' he would say. *'You look as if you just stepped out of a Japanese painting.'*

'No, Franz, just out of the past,' she would whisper as she lifted her mask, and she would see herself revealed in his eyes as he half rose from behind his desk, not quite believing . . .

The car jerked to a stop, and she lurched forward on the seat. They were finally at the entrance. Antonio came running around to open the door, and she stepped out into the cool evening.

'I don't know how long I shall be,' she said to the chauffeur. 'Perhaps not long at all. Make sure the car is ready.'

Antonio nodded understandingly. 'The car will be ready without problems, and so will I.'

He watched as she presented her invitation at the gate. Cars behind him sounded their horns. He ran back to the driver's seat and pulled the Packard away from the entrance, following the waving flashlights to a section of lawn on the south side of the house that had been set aside as a parking lot. There were

300

no *policía* on the lawn, only a couple of Mexican boys in charge of the cars. The boys had been dressed in someone's idea of a picturesque costume: twenty-gallon hats, serapes, and chaps that jingled with imitation silver dollars sewn into the linings. Antonio parked the Packard and strolled over to the nearest of the boys.

'*Mira, 'mano,*' he said to him. 'Talk to me a minute. I got some business for you.'

The boy gave him a brilliant smile. 'Got no time to talk, I got work to do.'

'Yeah, I see how hard you work. Come on over near the trees.'

The boy's eyes rolled. 'Hey, what you thinkin' about?'

'Don't talk stupid, *pendejo,* I said it was business.'

They went over to the trees. Minutes later the boy went back to work and Antonio strode across the open lawn with the twenty-gallon hat pulled low over his face, his chaps jingling with every step.

Marta passed into the courtyard, surrendering her printed invitation at the gate, and made her way around the champagne fountain and into the house. A passing waiter, whose costume gave him a mild resemblance to the late Franz Josef, offered her a glass of wine from a tray. She drank half of it thirstily, looking around her. It was after nine, and the party was beginning to hum. The younger men, mostly actors, were busy paying their compliments to the older women, mostly the wives of studio executives; the younger women were beginning to wonder why they had bothered to come at all; and the older men were gathered in business clumps passing the time before the high-stakes poker games that would begin after midnight. From the ballroom came the sound of the Lester Lanin orchestra playing 'You Must Have Been a Beautiful Baby' to the obbligato of the shrieks and splashes that came from the pool. For the moment she was surrounded by a sea of costumes as cowboys and Indians, Camilles and Roxannes, swirled around her. A portly man made up to look like Mussolini blocked her way for the moment, then moved aside to let her pass.

How odd, she thought. If someone came here dressed as Hitler he'd be torn to pieces by this crowd, yet they still think of Mussolini as a figure of fun.

Following Beverly's instructions, she found the hallway

301

leading off the ballroom and followed it, turned left to cross a veranda, and wound up in another corridor facing an oak door studded with brass strips. She stopped in front of it, touched the surface with her fingertips, then drew back her hand. She could feel the pounding of her heart, but she was breathing easily and her head was clear. It was a sensation not unlike the one that always came before a stage entrance. She adjusted her mask and smoothed the material of the Butterfly costume over her hips.

Nothing dramatic, she thought. No arias tonight, no *un bel di*. I came all this way just to hear his voice and see his face. That will be enough.

She knocked once on the door, lightly, then turned the knob and slipped into the room. The door clicked shut behind her. The scene was just as she had imagined it would be. The room was dark, only a pool of light at the desk where Franz sat, reading. His head came up with a silvery flash, and he smiled at her. The smile went through her, as it always had.

'*Guten Abend,* Marta,' he said. 'You always did make a magnificent Butterfly.'

Marta? She stood, frozen.

He gestured to the chair beside the desk. 'Come, sit down.'

She did not move.

'Nervous? There's nothing to be nervous about. You wanted to talk? So sit down and we'll talk.'

She found her voice. 'You were expecting me?'

'Of course.'

'She told you.'

'What did you expect?'

'So. Betrayal.'

Franz shook his head. 'Too big a word. Try reason. Try understanding. Try sanity. Much better words.'

'No, it's a betrayal, all right. I trusted her.'

Beverly stepped out of the shadows on the other side of the room, a duplicate Butterfly. She said, 'I gave you what you wanted, hon, a chance to talk. It's better this way. We'll all have an old-fashioned chat and get everything out in the open.'

'All of us?' Marta's eyes searched the room until she found what she was looking for: the two gorillas standing in the shadows near a set of French windows that opened out onto the

302

lawn.' She motioned towards them. 'Are they included in the conversation?'

Franz stood up and said impatiently, 'Stop talking foolishness. Mickey and Clyde are here for a very good reason. I don't want any fuss tonight, just a quiet conversation.'

'And they'll make sure that it's quiet?'

'They will if they have to.'

Beverly said, 'He's got a good point, hon, you got to admit it. You *have* been acting sort of nutsy, you know.'

Franz snorted. 'That's putting it mildly. Making a scene in front of the house, trying to crash the studio, and the other day at Quasimodo's . . . insane. I'm telling you, Marta, I won't take any more of this. I can't afford to.'

'He really can't,' said Beverly. 'Everybody in town knows what's going on. You don't know what Hollywood is like. Something like this could ruin him here.'

'Poor Franz,' Marta said softly. 'And all this time I thought that I was the one who was being embarrassed. All right, you can send the gorillas away. I won't make a fuss, I promise.'

'No, they'll stay. Just in case.'

'And you expect me to talk to you in front of them, and in front of this woman?'

'No, of course not.' Franz switched to German. 'We'll talk in our own language. The boys don't understand it and neither does she. Are you sure you won't sit down?'

She shook her head. 'I can see now why you agreed to this meeting. You're afraid, aren't you?'

'I'm afraid,' he said, nodding. 'You're doing me damage here. You could do me much more.'

'It didn't have to be that way. If you had seen me right away . . .'

'That's water under the bridge. Now that you're here, go ahead and talk.'

She shrugged helplessly. 'Not so easy under the circumstances. Besides, it all seems so pointless now.'

'Oh my God, pointless, she says.' He slapped his hands against his sides. 'For two weeks you've been driving me crazy and now you say that it's pointless? What the hell do you want from me, Marta?'

'I want you to come home,' she said simply.

'Now I know you're crazy. I *am* home.'

'No, I mean home to Vienna, home to the opera where you belong. Home to Sacher's, and Demel's and the Café Opern. Home to Dieter. Home to me.'

He sighed. 'That's impossible. That world doesn't exist any more.'

'I am a part of that world. Don't I exist any more?'

He hesitated. 'If you have to put it that way . . .'

'I do.'

'Then . . . no. No, you don't. Not that way.'

She felt something hollow open up within her, stretch wide, and swallow her. 'Is it possible, after all those years together, that there should be nothing left?'

His voice softened. 'I didn't say that. There are always the memories. Plenty of memories, little one, but times change, people change . . .'

'I don't change.'

'No, you don't. You're from a different world and a different time. You're faithful and you're loyal, and look what it's got you.'

'Love doesn't change either. You loved me once.'

'Yes.'

'But not now.'

'No.'

'And her? Do you love her?'

He looked around nervously.

'Speak freely, you said that she doesn't understand. Look at me, Franz, and tell me the truth for once. Do you love her?'

He smiled weakly, and shrugged. 'You know how it is.'

'Ah, yes, I know. She was right. You *are* a coldhearted bastard, aren't you?'

'I never claimed to be anything else.'

'Then I'll be going now, and you won't have to worry about me any more. I won't embarrass you again.'

'Before you go . . . there was something that you said in one of your letters that concerned me. It concerned me very much.'

'Oh, that.' She plucked at the sleeves of her costume. 'The lines from *Butterfly? Oppur, meglio, morire*?'

'Yes.'

'You needn't worry about that, either. There won't be any scandal. I may have felt that way then, but not now. I refuse to die for you, Franz. You're not worth it.'

304

'I'm glad you finally see that.' He inclined his head in a mocking bow and said in English, 'Clyde, Mickey, the baroness is leaving. Please see her to her car.'

Marta turned and walked to the door. Before she reached it, Franz said, 'No, not that way. The French doors lead to the lawn and the parking lot. It's shorter that way.'

She stopped and stared at him. 'I'll go out the way I came in. I told you I'd be good.'

'I prefer not to take the chance. Out the back way, boys.'

Beverly chimed in, 'It's really much shorter that way, honey.'

Marta's chin came up, and she snapped the one word, 'No.'

'Don't be difficult,' said Franz. 'You're not going to get the chance to embarrass me again. You're going out the back way whether you like it or not.' He nodded to Clyde and Mickey.

She looked at him curiously. 'Would you really let them put their hands on me? I can remember a time when you would have killed a man who tried to do that.'

Franz grimaced and said, 'Get her out of here.'

Clyde and Mickey came out of the shadows slowly and reluctantly. Marta took a step backward. They each took two quick steps forward and held her arms above the elbows: She looked from one to the other, then opened her mouth to scream. Mickey's hand came up to cover it.

'Let go of her, you sons of bitches.'

The French windows swung open with a crash, and Antonio walked into the room. He looked ridiculous in the twenty-gallon hat, the serape, and the jingling chaps, but there was nothing ridiculous about the snub-nosed Colt that he was holding in his hand.

The time of three making one, the time of growing, the happy time of learning to enlarge the egg, came to an end when the shadow of Gerhard Klausner fell across the entrance to the hayrick. The rick belonged to Klausner, and he had made the climb up from his farm, a journey of several hours, to replenish his supply of fodder. His means of transporting the bricks of hay was a sturdy A-frame which, when strapped to his back, would allow him to carry a load of over one hundred kilos. The loaded frame, however, made an unwieldy object that towered over the bearer and was the cause of more avalanches in the Arlberg than all the natural disasters combined. Leaning,

swaying, fighting for balance, the burdened farmer had to pick
his way down the winter mountainside with only a staff for
support, and he often did not make it all the way home. At
least once each winter some unfortunate, bent over double with
aching muscles, would lose the battle for balance and pitch
forward down the hillside. Once that happened he was gone.
The bouncing body picked up speed and snow, growing ever
larger into a massive ball, and then came the crack and the
whoosh as a slab of snow separated itself from the mountainside
and began the fatal race to the villages below. It happened at
least once every winter, but still the farmers made the climb
and packed their hay that way.

Willi, Mimi, and Wolf were resting at midday in the rick when
Klausner's shadow fell across the entranceway. They looked up,
saw the farmer, and scrambled to their feet.

'The Prinz kids,' Klausner grunted. Short and bandy-legged,
he farmed a small holding that barely supported his family. Willi
and Mimi had known him since childhood as dirty and foul-
tempered. 'Setting fires, are you? Stealing hay? I could report
you to the *Bürgermeister* for this.'

'We aren't kids any more and we aren't stealing anything,'
Mimi said coolly. 'All we use is the straw, not the hay, and the
dried dung. And it isn't the *Bürgermeister* any more, it's the
Gauleiter, who happens to be my Uncle Otto.'

'Well, this Hitler fellow will change all that,' said Klausner,
who had a sketchy idea of politics. He began to load his rack
with hay, but his eyes were on Wolf. 'And who's this one?
Never saw him around here before.'

'A friend.'

'A city friend from the looks of him. A friend from the city
poking around where he doesn't belong, is that it?'

'Just a friend, Herr Klausner,' said Mimi. 'And who are you
to be asking us questions?'

'My rick, isn't it?'

'Yes, and a smelly, filthy one it is, too.'

'Not so bad that you won't sleep in it, you and your city
friend.'

'We won't be staying here tonight,' said Willie. 'We'll leave
as soon as we have our tea.'

'Tea, is it?' Klausner wheezed from the exertion of loading

306

the hay. 'Fancy business from the city. Invite the Emperor up for tea next thing you know.'

'There isn't an Emperor any more,' Mimi pointed out.

'Yes, well, this Hitler fellow will fix all that.' When Klausner had finished loading the A-frame with hay, he looked sideways at Willi and said, 'Help me get this up on my back, will you?'

'Don't know why we should, the way you've been talking,' said Willi, but he and Mimi moved to help. Wolf stayed pressed into a corner of the rick, his eyes averted.

'Make sure you're out of here tonight, and no more fires,' said Klausner. He staggered under the load, steadied himself with his staff, and without another word started down the mountain.

They watched him go, and before he was out of sight the twins were clicking and buzzing away at each other so rapidly that Wolf was unable to follow them. He let them go on for a while, then raised his hand.

'Hold it,' he said. 'You're going too fast. What are you saying?'

'Trouble,' said Mimi.

'Bad trouble,' Willi confirmed. 'You saw the way he was looking at you. He'll report you as soon as he gets to the village.'

'For what? For being a stranger?'

'Even in the old days a stranger around here would have been unusual. The way things are today they'll send people up to find out who you are.'

'The SS?'

'The local police first. Just as bad in the long run.'

'Then I've got to get away from here. Far away.' Wolf began to collect his gear. Mimi made a series of sharp noises, followed by a puffball of air. Wolf, who understood that much, nodded, and said, 'I know, it means breaking up what we've done so far, but we've got no choice. I've got to run.'

Willi made a deep and mournful sound in his throat, an organ note gone wrong and prolonged beyond reason. Wolf said, 'I don't understand that. What does it mean?'

Mimi put it into words. 'It means that if Klausner doesn't get down the mountain we have nothing to worry about.' She explained how often the overburdened farmers fell to their deaths. 'No one would ever know. It happens all the time.'

'You could catch him easily on skis,' said Willi. 'One push and it's over with.'

They looked at each other, probing with their eyes. None of them wanted to abandon the structure of friendship and intimacy they had built so far. The structure was incomplete, but the chance to build that way would never come again to them. They knew that, and it seemed insupportable to lose the chance because of one dirty and irascible old man. And it would be so easy.

Willi asked the question. 'Well?'

'I couldn't do it,' said Wolf. 'Never. I'm sorry.'

'You wouldn't have to,' said Mimi. 'Willi would do it for you.'

'He would?' The two young men looked at each other. Willi nodded soberly.

'No, I can't let you do that. It would be the same as doing it myself.'

'Whatever you say,' said Willi, disappointed. There was a lot that Wolf had yet to learn about protecting the egg. 'Then you'll have to run. Where will you go?'

'Switzerland, the way I always planned it.'

'You planned it for the spring,' said Willi. 'You can't get across with snow in the passes.'

'I can get as far south as the Bieler Höhe. I'll hole up around there until the snow begins to melt.'

'There will be patrols at the border.'

'I'll have to chance that. What else can I do? I can't stay here now and I can't go back to Vienna. They're rounding up Jews there every day.'

'Then it's the end for us,' said Mimi. 'For what we had.'

'I'm sorry.' Wolf took her hand in his, then took Willi's hand as well. 'I love you, I love you both. I've never loved anybody this way and I never will again.' He held their hands in silent communion until Mimi broke the silence.

'We're wasting time,' she said practically. 'We should be making plans. First of all, I think we can stay here tonight. It's almost dark and they won't send anyone up until tomorrow. We'll leave early in the morning, ski down to the Jakobstal, and from there across to the Devil's Tongue. What do you think, Willi? He can start south from there, yes?'

Willi nodded his approval. 'He should take all the food he

308

can carry. And he'd better switch sleeping bags with me. Mine is newer.'

'And your gloves,' she said. 'His are in shreds.'

'Mine are too small for him.'

'Damn. Then give him your scarf, he can always use that.'

'And some spare socks, too.'

They spent the next hour tending to all the sad chores needed to send Wolf on his way. There was no need for speech of any sort. It was over, and that was all there was to it. When the darkness came they made the usual fire, but they omitted the ritual of the snow bath. It somehow seemed too joyous, out of place. They huddled together for the evening meal, but even that was grim and silent. At last, like dogs licking wounds, they crept to their sleeping bags and let the night take over.

Full night now, only faint embers of the fire glowing. Darkness in the rick, and beyond it the lunar silences of mountaintops. Mimi slept fully, deeply, as if nothing could ever wake her, but something did. Coming up softly from sleep she smiled as she smelled the odours of wool and chocolate, sweat and smoke in the folds of her sleeping bag, and just before waking felt the pressure beside her. Felt him, and knew him, and whispered his name.

'Wolf. What?'

No answer, only the steady pressure close to her, the warmth of his body next to hers, and then the heat of his lips on her neck. There were words to be said, the no no no of not this way, not now because this wasn't part of the oneness. This wasn't two or even three packed into the egg, but a broken shell with each one weak and all alone; and now the one and one joining to make two. She knew what two was, had always known that, but not with him and not this way with body heat building from the core of her, building so high and hot that numbers now were meaningless. Ones, and twos and threes, but there was only the heat and the press of him pushing, his hands at her hips and his lips on her shoulders and neck, and there was nothing more to do then than to slip from the bag and open her arms as she turned to him.

Her cries wakened Willi. They were soft and ragged puppy cries, puffs of breath expended, whispers so close to the calls of pain that Willi came out of sleep in immediate search, blindly looking to battle whatever intruder had come in the night. Clicks

309

and buzzes formed in his throat, calling to Mimi, and then his throat closed up as his eyes opened wide and he saw in silhouette, in the last of the ember glow, what she and Wolf were doing: her legs in the air, feet flying like flags. The puppy was happy, and nowhere near to pain.

He watched, then closed his eyes. Blind, he heard her cries again, and covered his ears. Deaf and blind, he matched her whimpers deep in his throat, felt his tears, licked the salt, liked what he licked, and felt a growing pleasure growing firm and hard as the root of him rose up to battle the intruder. Firm and hard, in disbelief he touched himself, and exploded.

The next morning they sipped lukewarm tea brewed in the ashes of the fire. They stared at their cups and sipped silently, each adjusting to a world now out of whack. If Willi could have had his way the silence would have lasted forever, but then Mimi said, 'I'm going with him.'

Willi would not look at her. He sipped his tea, and said, 'Yes.'

'And you?'

He knew what he wanted to say, but there was no chance of that any longer. 'Someone has to go back to Vienna, tell Mamá and Papá. That's me, I guess.'

'What will you tell them?'

'I'll tell them something, don't worry.'

It was time to leave then with grey light forming, and they gathered up their gear and skied away from the rick just as if it were any other morning and the world were still on track. Willi leading, Mimi following, and Wolf in the rear, they worked along the ridgeline that trailed south from the Gamskar Spitze until they were over the Jakobstal. The dawn grey never turned bright, the clouds were low and tucked against the peaks, and the wind was strong on their backs. They skied silently and steadily, and within an hour they had crossed the valley and climbed the rise to the ridge they called the Devil's Tongue. It stretched out ahead of them, a long and narrow arête that dropped away on either side to a pitch of unskiable scree, a steep drop of two hundred feet into a chasm of rock and ice. Beyond the Tongue the way was clear to the south.

At the top of the ridge they sheltered in the lee of a slab of stone to rest and smoke a cigarette, their backs to the stone as the wind whipped snow about their heads in glints of green and gold. Wolf tossed away his cigarette and shuffled his skis nervously. He said to Willi, 'I love you, too. You know that, don't you?'

'Yes.'

'It's not the same, we're not three any more, but I love you both.'

'Yes.'

'We'll be leaving you now.'

'No,' said Willi, 'I'll ski it with you. See you safely off.' He turned to his sister. 'Mimi, *du*.'

She looked at him, deep lines around her eyes, waiting.

'It's all right,' he said. 'Don't worry about it. Everything is all right.'

She smiled faintly at the reassuring words, but shook her head as if to say that nothing would ever be exactly right again. Then she shoved her goggles over her eyes and took off down the ridge.

They skied rapidly under the lowering sky, first Mimi, then Willi, then Wolf, skimming the ridge as the trail narrowed sharply, skirting the chasm below. Wind whistled and their tips planed up as they sped downhill in the last run they would have together, the last hard push from the peak. For just that tick of time they were one again, with themselves and with the mountain, and then they rounded a shoulder of ice, edges cutting deep. Mimi made the turn and went on. Willi went deep into his crouch and threw himself into a violent wrench that brought him to a stop and blocked the trail. Wolf came on, unable to stop, and Willi extended his arm and ski pole as gracefully as a matador addressing the bull.

Wolf cried out as the point of the pole took him in the chest, and then his hands came up to grab at the pole and tug, pulling Willi towards him. They collided, slamming into each other on the lip of the ravine, and then they were grappling with each other while the edges of their skis fought for purchase on the snow. Mimi stopped down the trail and looked back to see what was happening. She saw Willi and Wolf hanging together on the edge of the ravine, rocking back and forth. She opened her mouth, but nothing came out, sucked air in a soundless scream as they both went over, falling together in a desperate embrace as the ice and rocks rushed up to meet them.

Mimi's knees crumpled and she fell to the snow. She stared

at the spot where they had been, unwilling to believe the empty ridgeline. Clicks and buzzes blended on her lips: *You promised, you said it would be all right.* She could not rise. She dragged herself uphill to the spot where they had gone over, and looked down into the ravine. There was nothing to see. The bottom was too far down, and there were patches of fog in the low places. It did not matter; she knew what she would find there. After a very long while she got to her feet to begin the long and painful journey down.

'I said to take your hands off her.'

The two gorillas, Mickey and Clyde, released their holds on Marta; their arms dropped to their sides. They stared at the Mexican in his ludicrous costume framed by the French windows and tried to figure out how serious a threat he posed. Franz also stared at the invader, but haughtily, and Beverly seemed about to break into laughter. Only Marta was frightened, convinced that her driver had finally gone over the line.

'Okay, kill him,' said Antonio. 'Kill him now while I've got the other two covered.'

'What in the world are you talking about?' said Marta. 'Put that gun down.'

But Antonio was past hearing words like those. He tossed a sneer at the room and said to his *baronesa,* 'Go ahead, do it. Take out your pistol and do it.'

'Do what, you silly man?'

'*Mátalo,*' he screamed.

'Who?'

'Who? You ask me who? The one with the silver hair, who else?'

Franz said carefully, 'Marta, does this creature belong to you?'

'I'm afraid so.' She sighed and said, 'Antonio, this is absurd. Get the car and bring it around to the front. I'm leaving now.'

Mickey and Clyde had edged away from her slightly. Out of the corner of his mouth, Mickey said to his partner, 'You make a sort of distraction and I'll make a move on him.'

'Bullshit,' said Clyde.

'You'll do nothing of the sort,' Marta said to them both. 'This man doesn't know what he's doing. He's been acting strangely all week long.'

Antonio said with an odd sort of dignity, 'Forgive me, *baronesa*, but I know exactly what I'm doing. I'm holding a pistol on these people while I wait for you to do what you came here to do. Now, are you going to kill him or not?'

'Certainly not.'

'But why? You came all the way across the ocean and now you won't kill him? Isn't he the man who humiliated you and cheapened your name?'

Not unkindly, Marta said, 'Antonio, you surely don't expect me to discuss such matters with a servant, do you?'

'Brava, Marta, that's putting him in his place,' said Franz. 'Now see if you can get him to put down the gun.'

'Could he at least close the windows?' asked Beverly. 'It's getting chilly in here.'

Still wearing his dignity, Antonio said, 'And if I've been acting strangely this week it's because I've been worried about you. Do you know how much it cost me just to switch jobs and fares, just to be near you? Thirty-nine fifty so far, that's how much.'

'That was very sweet of you. I'm touched, truly I am. The money will be added to your salary at the end of the week.'

'I don't want your money, don't you understand?' The dignity was gone now, shredded, and his voice was shaking with excitement. 'I want you to act properly, like the *voz divina* that you are. I want you to kill this son of a bitch and then if you want to you can kill his whore too. But do it now. Take the pistol from your purse and do it.'

Marta made a helpless gesture with her hands. 'But I don't have a gun in my purse. Even if I did, I wouldn't know how to use it.'

Stunned, he said, 'You came here without a pistol?'

'I came here to have a chat with an old friend.'

'A knife?' he asked hopefully.

'Not even that.'

'Jesus Christ, I've never understood you people and I never will.'

'Put that gun away, Antonio, and get the car. It's late, and I want to go home.'

For one long moment he stood there as if saying goodbye to a dream, then he bowed his head and said, '*Sí, baronesa,* whatever you say.'

He turned and started out through the French windows, and as he did everything happened at once.

As soon as Antonio's back was turned, Mickey drew a flat automatic from under his jacket and took a wild shot at the Mexican. The bullet hit Antonio in the right thigh, and he went down sideways. On his way down he twisted around and fired twice. He killed Mickey with a lucky shot to the forehead and caught Clyde, still fumbling in his pocket, in the side of the neck. Mickey's pistol clattered across the floor. At the sound of the first shot Franz slid under the desk. Beverly dived for Mickey's gun, grabbed it, and brought it up pointed at Antonio. Marta screamed and leaped at the same time, coming down hard on top of Beverly. The two women struggled for the weapon. Antonio, down on one knee, and in pain, stared at the two identical, masked Butterflies rolling over and over on the floor, their legs flashing and their sashes unfurled. He pressed his fingers to his eyes to clear his vision, and peered again. As he did, one of the Butterflies came up from the floor with the pistol in her hand and a cry of triumph on her lips. Without hesitation, Antonio fired. The bullet caught her in the centre of the chest, exploded her heart, and stilled forever the divine voice of Marta Prinz.

Chapter Eighteen

From the Sedgewick Falls Monitor, 7 September 1939

LOCAL BOY NAMED TO OLYMPIC TEAM JOHN PRINCE A MEMBER

John 'Digger' Prince of Sedgewick Falls has been named as one of the skiers who will represent this country next year at the Winter Olympic Games in Sapporo, Japan. The list of athletes was made public today by the United States Olympic Committee in New York City. The games are scheduled to begin January 27, 1940, on Japan's northernmost island of Hokkaido.

The selection of Prince, son of the locally prominent Mr & Mrs Anton Prince, came as no surprise to those who follow the sport of skiing. Now in his junior year at Quincy College, young 'Digger' has, in the past two seasons, won every major skiing event in the East at least once and is considered, together with former Dartmouth star Richard Durrance, to be the best downhill and slalom skier that the United States has to offer in international competition. He is also renowned as the first, and so far the only racer ever to 'schuss' the awesome Headwall of Tuckerman's Ravine at Mount Washington.

Both Mr & Mrs Prince expressed their pride to a representative of the *Monitor* today, but the young athlete's mother cautioned against any premature celebration, since it is rumoured that the recently declared war in Europe may lead to a cancellation of the Games.

Other members of the team named today are, in alphabetical order: Merrill Barber, Walter Bietila, Robert Blatt, Wendall Cram, Richard Durrance, Alf Engen . . .

From the Journals of Elizabeth Chandler Prince

Monday, Christmas 1939

. . . a handsome stone marten cape from my husband, and from my son an edition of the poetry of Lord Byron (Potter & Greeves, London) so tastelessly bound and illustrated that once the holiday season is done it will at once be consigned to the darkest corner of the bookshelves. The thought was admirable, of course, but the boy has no taste in such things and should stay away from those areas in which his ignorance is so easily displayed. However, I showed no sign of this and his gift was cordially received when we gathered round the tree this morning. Our own gift to him (his father's choice, not mine) could not come as a surprise, since it has been sitting in the garage these past three days, but one hopes that the Oldsmobile will serve to lift his spirits. He has been in a state of absolute depression since the announcement of the cancellation of the Olympic Games. It is a sadness, of course, to work so hard, achieve the goal, and then have the prize snatched from one's hand. But it is a game, after all, a sport, and the agent of his discontent is a bloody, tragic war in which young men his age are being killed and maimed. Today it is Polish boys who are

315

falling before Mr Hitler's tanks. Whose turn will it be tomorrow, and does anyone really think that this cup will not come our way again? I've tried to get this across to him. It was not God, in His infinite wisdom, who decreed the cancellation of the Olympics, it was Mr Hitler and those of his ilk. Great forces are in motion throughout the world today, and matched against them the importance of his precious Olympics becomes meaningless. When I think of the people we know who have suffered truly tragic losses . . . poor Dieter losing both Marta and the boy within days of each other. And Lili, as well. I hold no brief for her husband, but now I hear that both of her sons, Hannes and Kurt, have been taken into the German army. Some elite corps of mountain specialists, the Alpinkorps they're called, but to me it sounds like just another fancy phrase for cannon fodder. And here sits Mr John Prince safe and sound in the United States of America, with a chicken in his pot and an Oldsmobile in the garage and his senior year in collge coming up, and all he can do is put on a long, sad face about those blessed Olympics.

It's positively indecent, but try telling him that. I tried, and for my pains I got a blank look and then I was told that I don't understand. (Mothers never do, of course.)

'You don't understand,' he told me. 'I'm the best, everybody says so. How would you feel if you were the best violinist in the world and they told you that you couldn't play the fiddle any more? Well, that's the way I feel now.'

Which goes to show how his mind works these days, for the comparison is both inexact and intellectually dishonest. In the first place, nobody is stopping him from sliding down a hill whenever he pleases; and in the second place, just imagine him comparing himself to Heifetz or Menuhin! Purely self-centred, I call it, but I suppose at that age a young man's horizon is right at the tip of his nose.

Tuesday, 3 June 1941

We are returned this day from Quincy, New Hampshire, where our son was graduated from the university there. No honours were involved, but none were expected. I must confess that during the past four years I have lived with the daily expectation of his dismissal for one reason or another, but he has stayed the course. I cannot help but feel that he has either been very lucky,

316

or his athletic ability has marked him for particular treatment. Whatever the reason, I cannot complain. I am pleased.

There now remains the question of his immediate future, although the question is academic, since he will be coming into the family business. I cannot help but wish this were not so. I made this business for my husband and no other, and besides, the boy lacks the will for hard work. But what else is he to do? Anton says that he will be an asset to the firm if only because of his reputation as a skier, but that remains to be seen. I have my forebodings.

In the meantime, we hear in the trade that Prinz Skis in Vienna is going 'great guns,' what with plentiful orders from the German army. That Alpinkorps business again. I have enough to do in my own backyard, but it makes my blood boil to think of how we were bilked. Our day will come, however. I have said that in other circumstances, and have not been disappointed.

Monday, 8 December 1941

This afternoon we listened on the radio as the President addressed the Congress and the nation. He is the President of all of us now, regardless of how we might have felt before. A day of infamy, indeed. What surprises me is that everyone is so surprised. I saw this coming a year ago, and more.

Our son was not with us as we listened to the broadcast. He was down at the post office along with just about every other able-bodied young man in town, offering his services to his country. His father is proud. I am pleased. I see nothing to be proud about in taking a course of action that is not only unquestionably proper, but also overwhelmingly popular.

He says that there is talk of establishing a mountain regiment similar to what the Germans have in the Alpinkorps. No doubt he will gravitate towards it. And no doubt they will want to buy skis.

The concept of an elite mountain unit for the US Army was the brainchild of Charles Minot Dole, who, in 1938, had formed the National Ski Patrol System, an organization dedicated to safety in the mountains. In 1940 he convinced Army Chief of Staff General George C Marshall of the need for such an outfit, and a year later the 87th Infantry Mountain Regiment was activated at Fort Lewis, Washington. The objective was to train men for mountain warfare in both winter and summer, and Dole's National Ski Patrol was hired by the War Department to recruit the men for the job. Dole's method was simple: He grabbed off virtually every topflight skier, climber, and instructor in America and shipped them out to Fort Lewis, where they became the cadre of what eventually would be the Tenth Mountain Division.

Private First Class Digger Prince arrived at Fort Lewis in March 1942 after completing his basic training, and reported to the officer of the day. The second lieutenant looked at his papers casually and turned him over to a sergeant who seemed equally unimpressed.

'You're in B Barracks,' the sergeant told him, and pointed the way. 'It's too late to draw gear today, you can do that tomorrow. Do you know how to ski?'

Digger controlled his surprise and kept his face straight. 'I can get around on them.'

'Good, then you can draw skis tomorrow too. Chow time in half an hour. Better get settled in.'

Puzzled by his reception, Digger shouldered his bag and strode through the muddy snow to the barracks door. Once inside, however, his puzzlement dropped away. The first two men he saw were Walter Prager and Gordon Wren, both ace ski instructors. Down the line was Peter Gabriel, onetime head of the Franconia Ski School, and farther along was Eldon Metzger, the mountain man from Seattle. He stood in the doorway taking in the scene. He recognized almost all the men in the room, the best skiers and climbers in the country.

'Hey, it's Digger Prince,' someone shouted.

'Jesus, it's the schussboomer himself.'

'Hooray, Quincy finally got into the war.'

'What took you so long, Digger? Get stuck on the Headwall?'

Within minutes he was surrounded by the men with whom he had skied for the past four years. He found an empty bunk, dropped his B-bag on it, and began to organize a footlocker while the others filled him in on the outfit. The general impression he got was that he had just joined up with the quickest, toughest gang of rock busters and ski breakers ever put together on one mountain, and as soon as they got their training done they were going to whip the shit out of the Alpinkorps and anyone else who stood in their way.

Bunny Holcombe, late of the Harvard ski team, gave him a

hand with the footlocker. 'It's a great outfit,' he told him. 'Plenty of spirit, and all the skiing you'd ever want.'

'What are the officers like?'

'Not bad, a little slow. It'll be better once they learn how to ski.'

'Say that again.'

Bunny laughed. 'You heard me right. The officers are all Regular Army people, from Colonel Rolfe on down. They've never been on skis before in their lives. *We're* teaching *them*.'

'You mean none of our guys are officers?'

'Look around you.'

Digger saw what he meant. Every man in the room, the best mountaineers in America, wore a single chevron on his sleeve. They were all PFCs. 'No sergeants, no corporals?' he asked.

'A single stripe is all we get,' said Bunny. 'Maybe it'll be different later, but right now the regulars run the outfit. We're just the hired help.'

'That explains it.' He told Bunny about the lieutenant and the sergeant who had checked him in. 'My name didn't mean a damn thing to them.'

'Impossible.' Bunny recoiled in mock horror. 'You mean they never heard of Digger Prince, king of the hill? Come on, Digger, tell us how you schussed the Headwall. Or did you tell us that one already?'

'Damn it, Bunny, the sergeant even asked me if I knew how to ski.'

'Do you?' Bunny asked seriously. 'If you don't, I can fix you up with a great instructor. Bend zee knees, five dollars, pleeze.'

Digger reached for a pillow to throw at him, then decided to laugh.

'It isn't as bad as it sounds,' Bunny told him. 'It's really a terrific outfit. You'll see after you've been here awhile.'

Over the next few months Digger found that Bunny was right. The regimental spirit was high, the nonskiers (officers and enlisted draftees alike) learned quickly, there was all the skiing in the world for those who wanted it, and by the time the snow was off the ground the 87th had become an efficient unit of potential fighting men.

The only trouble was they were still training, not fighting. During the rest of 1942, while Allied forces landed in North Africa and on Guadalcanal, while the battles of El Alamein and

Stalingrad were being fought, while the Army Air Corps was bombing Tokyo and the US Navy was triumphant at Midway and the Coral Sea, the 87th Infantry Mountain Regiment continued to train for a task that had yet to be defined. In the autumn the outfit was moved to Camp Hale, high astride the Continental Divide in Colorado, to be the premier regiment of the newly formed Tenth Mountain Division, but the training routine remained the same. To Digger, the outfit shaped up as a group of the most highly trained, and overtrained, specialists in the army. Their engineers could erect aerial tramways up mountains, their signalmen could lay wire on skis, their artillerymen were at home with the 75mm mountain howitzer, and their medical personnel were skilled at the mock evacuation of wounded from deep snow. They knew it all, but they had yet to use any of it.

On December eighth, with the war a year old, Digger complained to Bunny Holcombe, 'They can't keep this up. They've got to send us into action, even if we go as line troops.'

'Be a hell of a waste if they did,' Bunny noted, 'after all this training.'

'Better than sitting up here for the rest of the war. What am I going to tell my grandchildren when they ask me what I did in the war? That I took a holiday and went skiing?'

'If we ever have any grandchildren,' Bunny said sadly. 'Tell me the truth, Digger, when was the last time you got laid?'

'That's something else that's got to change. Damn it, Bunny, this is a great outfit, but I've got to get out of here.'

As if the gods had been listening, he was gone the next day. That afternoon he was called into Colonel Rolfe's office and handed orders detaching him from the 87th and ordering him to report to an address in Washington, DC. He read the orders in disbelief, then looked at the colonel.

'I don't know anything more than what it says right there,' said Rolfe. 'I don't even know the name of the outfit they're shipping you to, and I don't know why. But I do know one thing. I've been in the army long enough to know when an order isn't something routine. This one came through with muscle behind it. They want you there in three days, and that's when you'd better be there.'

Quick goodbyes to the men who had become his closest friends, and then it was three days and two nights of riding on comfortless trains, heading east. He reported to the Washington address on the afternoon of the third day, a nondescript building with no signs on the doors and no uniformed personnel in sight. His orders were accepted by someone who was obviously an army officer in civilian clothing, and then he was driven in a civilian automobile out of the city and south into the Virginia countryside. Less than an hour later he was delivered to a quiet farmhouse set in a stand of birch trees. It was dark, and there were no other houses in sight. He was asked to wait in a comfortable sitting room where a fire crackled in the hearth. After three days of travel he was weary and confused. He sank into a chair in front of the fire and promptly fell asleep. He was awakened by a light touch on his arm, opened his eyes, and looked up into the face of Martin Gregorius, his coach from Quincy. He was wearing an army uniform and there were oak leaves on his shoulders.

Gregorius laughed at the look on his face. 'No, not a dream, dot's really me.'

'Coach . . . uh, major.' Digger started to struggle to his feet, but Gregorius waved him down.

'Not even major,' he said. 'It's vot dey are calling a stimulated rank.'

Digger thought for a moment, then said, 'Simulated.'

'Ja, dot's better. I knew it vas close. I dink maybe vee talk in Cherman so vee don't make no mistakes. Okay?'

'Yes sir. Just go slow at first. It's been a while.'

'Good. First we'll get you something to eat and to drink, and then I'll tell you why you're here.'

Over thick ham sandwiches and bitter black coffee, Gregorius told him that the name of the organization was the Office of Strategic Services and that he had been attached to it since the beginning of the war when the call went out for Europeans with particular skills. The OSS, he explained, was an intelligence organization that also did odd jobs behind the enemy lines.

'If that sort of thing bothers you,' he told Digger, 'now is the time to stand up and walk out of here. The same car will take you back to Washington and you'll be back at Camp Hale three days from now.' He looked at Digger expectantly.

'That doesn't bother me, sir.'

'Good, then we continue. We asked for you because there is a particular job to be done and you're the one who can do it.

321

If you decide to do this job, and the choice is yours, it will involve a high degree of risk and no recognition when it's over. No cheers, and no medals, and you won't be able to tell anybody about it for years. Do you accept that so far?'

'So far.' Digger took a cautious sip of the hot coffee.

'Also, when the job is done you'll have your choice. You can either go back to your old outfit or stay on with us. Do you accept that part of it?'

'So far.'

'Then it's time for you to meet Colonel Olafson.' He stood up. 'You can take your coffee with you if you want to. We're rather informal here.'

Olafson was waiting for them in the next room, which had been fitted out as an office. A tall, sharp-faced man, he stood up and held out his hand to Digger. Gregorius said, 'We've been talking in German. Best to continue that way.'

Olafson nodded and waved them to seats. 'Speaking of that, how is his German?'

'Not too bad,' said Gregorius. 'Fluent enough, but a heavy American accent.'

'No harm there. He doesn't have to pass as a German, just communicate in the language.' He turned to Digger. 'What other languages do you have?'

'Bad French, and that's it. I never studied anything else, and the German comes from my father.'

'Yes. Well, I suppose it would have been too much to hope for Slovenian. Ever use a parachute?'

'No sir.'

'Explosives?'

'No sir.'

'What weapons have you handled?'

Digger went through the list of weapons that he had used both in basic training and with the 87th, then he said, 'Colonel, I know this is out of line, but I'm tired, I'm confused, and all these questions are just making me more of the same. So would you please tell me what the hell you want from me?'

'Fair enough. Just one question more. What do you know about the Alpinkorps?'

Digger answered automatically, repeating what he had heard at indoctrination lectures. 'An elite corps of mountain soldiers in the German army, highly dedicated, expert skiers and rock

322

climbers. Pretty much the same as my outfit. The difference is that the Germans have seen action, and so far we haven't.'

'Exactly, and one of the places where they've seen action is in the mountains of northern Yugoslavia against Tito's partisan forces. One of their crack regiments, the 156th, has been operating in that area for the past few months after taking over from the Italians.'

'Yes sir.' This was news to Digger.

'Three weeks ago the first battalion of the 156th ceased to exist, virtually destroyed in ambush by a band of partisans. It's the first time that Tito's people have been that effective against line units of the German army. During the operations the partisans took two prisoners. Does that signify anything to you?'

Digger shook his head. 'Only that it's unusual. I thought guerrillas didn't take prisoners. They can't afford to.'

'Quite right. Normally the partisans will milk a prisoner dry and then shoot him, but not this time. The two prisoners were both officers in the 156th, a captain and a lieutenant, and they've managed to convince the partisans that they have something valuable to offer. They claim that they were never Nazis, the usual garbage, and they want to come over to our side. They say that they can give us detailed information on the organization of the Alpinkorps. Order of battle, placement of units, status of reserves, that sort of thing. Do I have to tell you how important that could be to us?'

'Sir, all I've got is one stripe on my sleeve, but I guess it would be pretty important.'

'You're guessing right, and at the moment those two are sitting on top of a mountain in Yugoslavia, partisan prisoners.' Olafson paused to stuff a pipe with tobacco. 'Of course, it may all be nonsense. They may be spinning the partisans a story just to keep themselves alive, but we can't afford to let the chance go by. Someone has to go into Yugoslavia, get those people off that mountain, and bring them out. The job calls for a crack skier who can speak decent German, and has been trained as a mountain soldier.' Olafson pointed the pipe. 'You.'

Cowboy Karl Lang was a year short of fifty, but he felt like an old man. He knew that he looked like one, too. His hair was sparse, his middle was thick, and his nose was puffed out from too much brandy; but a surer sign of age was that nothing seemed to be fun any more. That troubled him because he remembered himself as a joyous youth, and even the years in Landeck Prison had failed to blunt his spirit. But sometime after that, during the years between the day he left prison and the day he went to work for the von Ulm family, the fun went out of it all and he seemed to grow old quickly. Suddenly he had no more horizons. He had only his job, his room over the garage, and Marta's family, which, more and more, he had come to think of as his own. That was all that he had, and the sad part was that it was all that he wanted.

His room over the garage was warm and comfortable, although furnished sparely. A bed, a chair, a table, an armoire, and a long bookcase left plenty of space unused, and the only adornments on the walls were the postcard-size pictures of American Indians sent to him years before by Anton Prince: Cochise, Crazy Horse, Red Cloud, Mangas Coloradas. But the bed was firm, the chair was easy, and the shelves were filled with a variety of books, including his boyhood favourites, the novels of the American West by Karl May. In wartime Vienna it was a lot just to be warm and comfortable.

He spent much of his time in the room, for there was little chauffeuring to be done these days. The shortage of gasoline meant nothing to the baron, none of the shortages seemed to affect him, but over the past few years the social life of the household had been severely restricted. Dieter rarely left the house these days, his nights of marathon card games a thing of the past, and most evenings Mimi was called for by any one of a great number of uniformed men who drove their own cars. Since Marta's bizarre death and Willi's tragedy four years before, the house on the Hadikgasse had become more like a mausoleum than a mansion.

He pulled his chair close to the window and stared out over the grounds. He found himself doing that often these days: sitting in his room in the evening with the light out and with unlit Vienna beyond the window, the last of the sun filtering through the haze that seemed to hang everywhere now. In a while he would go down to the baron's study, where Dieter would be waiting. They would have a brandy together, perhaps two, play a hand of cards, and talk in simple sentences before separating for their solitary meals. The years had done that as well, altering the distance between master and man. There was no true intimacy involved, no use of the *du,* no presumption of equality. Neither of them would have wanted that. What did exist was a tenuous link to the past through Marta, a grief that refused to fade and an unspoken desire to preserve what was left of the family, as a family.

And so I sit at the window and stare, and wait, he thought. For what? For the war to be over? For the world to turn again? For a piece of my life to be finished?

He shook his head in irritation. Again, these were an old man's thoughts and he was still short of fifty.

He stirred at the sound of an automobile engine and the crunch of gravel on the driveway. Through the trees, and through the haze, he saw the long snout of an Opel appear, and then the car was around the curve and pulling up in front of the entranceway. An official car, he saw at once, not military but party, with the insignia blazoned on the door. A uniformed driver jumped out and ran around to open the back door. Otto Prinz, in party uniform and favouring his bad leg, stepped out. He looked around at the house and the grounds and the trees before pulling himself erect and limping up the steps to the door.

Karl watched him enter the house, his face expressionless. It was the first time he had seen Otto since the day he had shot at him, but he had seen photographs of the *Gauleiter* in the newspapers and had recognized him at once. He nodded thoughtfully, as if in reply to some unasked question, then slipped quickly from his room and made his way through a back staircase to the main part of the house. Down one back hallway and partway up another brought him to a small room that abutted on the baron's study. The room was used only for storage, and the walls were thin. He pressed close to the wall and listened.

'You understand,' Otto was saying, 'that I've come to see you about this personally only because of our family connection. I could just as easily have turned this information over to the Office for Jewish Emigration, or the Gestapo.'

'I understand a blackmail scheme when I see one.' Dieter's voice was cool, biting. 'And a very crude scheme, I must say. Who dreamed up these fantastic charges?'

'There is no use taking that approach, Dieter – '

325

'Excuse me. You may be my brother-in-law, but I wasn't aware that we were using Christian names.'

'Hardly Christian in your case, Herr Weissberg.'

'You persist in that fantasy?'

'It isn't a fantasy when three trained investigators work more than six months to turn up the facts.'

'I'm flattered that you would spend so much time on me, but your facts are pipe dreams.'

'Facts,' Otto repeated. 'Ezra Weissberg, born in Bratislava the fifth son of Israel Weissberg, a contract tailor. Mother's name, Lena. Brothers' names . . . shall we skip all that? Left home at the age of fifteen to come to Vienna, lived by his wits as a runner for a gambling house, part-time pimp and shylock. At the age of twenty began using the name Dieter Ulm and three years later ennobled himself with a von. In 1910 . . . ah yes, here's the part I like best. And you have the nerve to call *me* a blackmailer. In 1910, apparently secured a large sum of money from a certain Count Podolski in return for the destruction of letters written by the count's wife. Used that money as capital for shylock activities and over the years became one of the most influential moneylenders in Vienna, specializing in financing gambling debts. Has always maintained a respectable façade claiming family investment in Silesian coalfields, which is obvious fiction. Personal wealth is estimated in millions of reichsmarks but exact figures impossible to obtain because of cash nature of his business. Maintains a palatial residence in the Hadikgasse, married to the opera singer the late Marta Prinz, father of two children, one of whom – '

'Enough,' said Dieter. 'There's no need for that part of it.'

'Then you admit the rest of it?'

There was silence, then Dieter said, 'There's no reason not to, I suppose. If you were going to give this over to the Gestapo, you wouldn't be sitting here talking to me now.'

'Then you admit it. You're nothing more than a yid moneylender, a shylock.'

'Your choice of words. My clients never thought of me that way.'

'Amazing. The best-kept secret in Vienna.'

'Not really so amazing,' Dieter said carelessly. 'The sort of people I deal with are noted for their discretion. It's really a

326

gentleman's game . . . but you wouldn't know anything about that.'

'Wouldn't I? That little remark is going to cost you something extra.'

'Now we're getting down to it. Your blackmail, not mine. How much is this going to cost me?'

'You realize what would happen if the Gestapo got involved in this? I'm doing this only because of the family, understand. There's your daughter to be considered, as well.'

'I'm touched by your family loyalty. How much?'

'One million Swiss francs.'

'Clever. Possession of foreign currency is illegal. If I pay you in francs you have something else to hold over my head. I may not be able to get that much together in francs.'

'You'll get it. Otherwise it's a long vacation at Mauthausen for you and your daughter.'

'What an amazing person you are. You're talking about your niece, you know.'

'Under the Nuremberg Laws she's just another Jewess. One million francs.'

'It will take time to arrange.'

'I can give you three days.'

'Not enough.'

'Three days,' Otto repeated. 'On Thursday night at nine o'clock my car will be parked on the Hauptallee alongside the Prater. Bring the money in a suitcase. Once I have it in my hands you get the dossier. If I were you, I'd burn it.'

Dieter said dryly, 'And it's the only copy, of course.'

'You'll have to trust me on that, won't you?' Otto's voice went soft and slick. 'Look, this is a business deal for me, and in business I keep my word. You'll have nothing else to worry about. Remember, it wouldn't look too good for me to have members of my family sent to the camps. Thursday night, at nine.'

There was the sound of the bell as the butler was called, and the clap of the door as Otto was shown out. Karl listened carefully, but no other sounds came from the other side of the wall. He opened the door that connected to the study and went in. Dieter sat slumped at his desk, his face grey. Karl went to the cabinet, took out a bottle, and poured two glasses of kirsch. He put one in front of Dieter.

'Drink it,' he said.

Dieter looked up. 'You heard?'

'Yes.'

'What am I going to do?'

'Pay him, of course. You have no choice.'

'I didn't mean that. I meant afterwards. Will he keep his word? Will this be the end of it?'

Karl gulped his drink and poured himself another, thinking: He wants to believe but he's fucked, and he knows it. That son of a bitch will take the money, then squeeze him again later on. No matter what he says now, he'll do it again and again. And then, when he's dry, he'll throw him to the Gestapo, you can bet on it. And the girl, too.

'It may be all right,' he said cautiously. 'He sounded as if he meant it.'

Dieter tried to smile, but it didn't work. 'We both know better than that.'

All because Kranski hit my arm, Karl thought. If he hadn't hit my arm Otto would be dead. Aloud, he asked, 'Is it true, all the things he said?'

'His dossier is remarkably accurate.' Sudden pain showed on Dieter's face. 'You may leave whenever you wish if my being a Jew offends you.'

'Please, I didn't mean that. I meant about the moneylending.'

Dieter shrugged.

'In a business like that you must have some . . . unusual connections.'

He shrugged again.

'With connections like that, could you get me a pistol?'

Dieter sighed. 'And what are you going to do, challenge him to a shootout on Main Street? This isn't the Wild West, Karl.'

'How about explosives? Could you get your hands on some?'

'Please, don't even think of it. This isn't one of your novels. All I can do is pay, and hope.'

And you'll wind up in Mauthausen, Karl thought. And so will the girl. A good man and a young girl, Marta's husband and her daughter, on the block and ready for the chop, and there's nothing that Cowboy Karl Lang can do about it. Some cowboy. I guess I've been reading the wrong kind of books.

While Karl and her father were mourning her future, Mimi lay flat on her back in a hotel bedroom, gazing at the ceiling

328

and listening idly to the sounds coming out of the bathroom: running water, an interminable gargle, a voice humming something off key, and then another surge of water. My God, she thought, he's going to drown himself in there. Does he want to make love or go swimming?

She rubbed herself against the sheets, caressing her skin with satin, and her eyes picked out the plaster *putti* that adorned the mouldings on the walls. How nice that he chose the Metropole; not many other hotels in Vienna still had satin sheets. What every young girl should know: satin sheets and cherubim, that's how we know it's the Metropole. How clever we are. Satin on the skin, *putti* on the walls, a wine bucket close beside the bed, and a Luftwaffe uniform carefully hung on the clothes tree. A neat one, for a change. Her own frock, and wisps of undergarments, lay crumpled on the carpeted floor. She rolled to the edge of the bed and inspected the wine bottle in the bucket. French, of course. No Gumpoldskirchner or Grinzinger for the conquering heros. Well, he could afford it, whatever his name was. Name? Klaus? Maybe.

'Hey,' she called, 'are you going to be all night in there?'

'Why?' came his muffled voice. 'If you can't wait, start without me.'

'I might just do that.' She made a face at the bathroom door.

'I'll just be a minute.'

Don't hurry, she thought, I have plenty of time. I have all of the time in the world.

She closed her eyes and let her thoughts drift, knowing that they would come to rest, like a weary Ark, on the top of a mountain. It was always a mountain at times like this, just before making love, the mountain of Willi and Wolf. And the accident. That's what they had called it, an accident, and nobody had argued the point. Like a simple car crash and she was the only survivor coming out of it knowing that now she was considerably less than half of the perfect egg she once had helped to form. Out of the crash and home to that other survivor who had lost both wife and son, rattling around the empty house together with memories for company; but father and daughter had rattled to different tunes. Dieter grieved, but Mimi questioned. Mamá was gone and there was grief from that, but deep down daughters know that someday mothers must go. If not, how would daughters ever get hold of the best china and silver?

But Wolf, and Willi, Willi and Wolf . . . why? For making love for the first time in her life? For wanting to stay with him?

Is that why it happened? Was it that much of a sin?

In those early days she had asked herself the questions, clicks and buzzes forming in a language that no one else in the world could now understand. Nobody answered, nobody could.

Is that the reason? She insisted on knowing. Or was it because he was a Jew?

The question had to be asked. All her life she had heard about pig Jews, and Jew dogs and kike swine, and now she had loved one, lain with him, felt him jolt and spurt within her.

Was that the sin?

She had to know, but who was there to ask? Nobody talked about Jews any more, not even in whispers, and the Jews themselves were gone . . . to where? Nobody knew, nobody cared, and there was nobody to ask.

Was that the sin? In time she came to believe it: She had lain with a Jew and had been punished for it. She was slightly mad with grief, of course. She knew that, but she also knew that she was logical within her madness and that it was a logical move to pin her sin on the hook of a Jew. The concept was too appealing to be rejected. She had sinned, she had been punished, and now she must be redeemed.

Her redemption took the form of a sexual express train so fast and far-ranging that it startled even jaded Vienna. The army, the Luftwaffe, the Foreign Office, the Chancellery, the SS, the young men of every service became meat for Mimi. She scrubbed herself with their flesh, scourging herself to wipe out the stain of her sin. Poland crumbled, and Mimi fucked. France fell, and Mimi fucked. London burned, the U-boats plundered, the Third Reich conquered half a world . . . and Mimi fucked.

Klaus finally came out of the bathroom, his hair slicked down and his skin gleaming. A waste; she would have preferred some grime and sweat. Already erect, he came to the bed and leaned over her. She stopped him with a finger against his chest.

'Not yet,' she said. 'First get your belt. I've been a bad girl and I have to be punished.'

A grin broke over his face. '*Liebchen,* why didn't you say so before?'

'I didn't know until just now how bad I'd been.'

*

330

Digger lay on his side on the cold metal deck of the Lancaster bomber and tried to sleep. He had been trying ever since takeoff from England, but without any luck. The din of the engines, the stench of motor oil, and, above all, the icy deck made sleep impossible. He shifted his body to rest his head on a parachute pack, and that placed his nose only inches away from the left leg of the waist gunner standing above him. He tried to figure out where they were and decided on somewhere over Belgium. The bomber droning through moonlit skies was part of a formation of twenty on the first leg of a course that would eventually bring them over Stuttgart in southern Germany. But this particular Lancaster was going farther than Stuttgart, much farther. Abandoning sleep, he sat up and went over the past week in his mind.

Having spent a year bucking up against the army way of doing things, he had been amazed to see how quickly and efficiently the organization could operate when the right people pulled the strings. Olafson was clearly one of those people. The day after Digger had arrived at the farmhouse he had been flown to Fort Benning, Georgia, for a condensed two-day course with a paratroop training unit, had made three jumps, and had returned to Virginia for a quick drill in specialized weapons, map reading, and signalling. That night he sat with Gregorius and Olafson in the farmhouse kitchen and went over the details of the operation. Olafson took the floor, speaking in German and referring to a map tacked to the wall.

'The partisans we have to reach,' he said, 'operate *here* in the Julian Alps, up in the northwest corner of Yugoslavia. That part of the country is called Slovenia and the language they speak is Slovenian, although a lot of people speak German there as well.' He rapped the map with a knuckle. 'Hard country there, truly mountainous. The partisans are holed up on Mount Krn, *here,* over two thousand metres high. Quite remote, almost inaccessible. The Germans have been trying to root them out for over a year now, without success. Our Red friends simply slip down the mountain under the cover of darkness, do their spot of raiding and pillage, and climb back up to safety before the Hun can react. The caves of Mount Krn, that's where they're keeping our prisoners.

'Phase one is getting you in, and the RAF has agreed to handle that part of the job. The Brits are bombing fairly regu-

331

larly in southern Germany now, and you will be aboard a bomber that will use such a raid as a diversion. Your particular aircraft will slip past the target and continue on over Austria and into Yugoslavia. We anticipate that you will reach the jump point just before dawn. If all goes well you will be on target, but from a practical point of view don't expect to be. There is no such thing as pinpoint accuracy, no matter what the flying fellows say. Expect to spend twenty-four to forty-eight hours locating the partisans and making contact with them.

'So much for phase one. Phase two is getting these people out, and the only practical way is by sea. That means that you're going to have to ski your way out of the mountains and then make it overland to the coast near Fiume. That's the Italian name for it; the locals call it Rijeka. The partisans should be able to help you along the way, and after that we've arranged with the navy, the Brits again, not ours, for a three-day submarine rendezvous off the Istrian coast. You'll be given the dates, the coordinates, and the recognition signals later on. Essentially, it should be a simple operation. Just flash the right combination of lights at the right time and the sub will send in a boat to pick you up. But remember that the contract with the Brits is good for three nights only. If you show up on the fourth night you've missed the bus.'

Over the drone of the Lancaster's engines came the pilot's voice in Digger's earphones, the tone laconic. 'Let's have your attention, please. We'll be coming up to the IP shortly and the rest of the squadron will be making the turn for the run to Stuttgart. As you know, we're not bombing tonight, we're in the delivery service, so we shan't be making the turn with the others. We'll be going straight on, solo, so let's have the eyes open all around. We're on our own from now on.'

The pilot's voice clicked off. The waist gunner looked down at Digger and gave him a grin that featured a collection of misshapen teeth. Over the engine noise, he yelled, 'Delivery service, and you're the prize package. Door to door, no extra charge.'

Digger grinned back and jabbed a thumb in the air. He closed his eyes and leaned against the parachute, his mind going back again to that night at the farmhouse. Olafson had then turned the floor over to Gregorius for an explanation of the terrain.

'It's going to be hard skiing,' the former coach had said. 'No

332

manicured *pistes,* no racecourse conditions. This is a wild and desolate place, and you're going to have to handle the worst conditions you've ever seen. But the only way out of there is on skis, so remember this. Speed won't be as important as safety; you won't be competing against a clock. Your job is to get these people out safely, you understand that? Safety first.'

'It sounds familiar. You preached that to me for four years at Quincy.'

'And you never paid a bit of attention to it. One thing more. You'll need rank to deal with the partisans, so we're sending you in as an officer. Effective at once you have the rank of captain.'

'Christ.' In his surprise Digger reverted to English. 'People out at Camp Hale are still bucking for corporal.'

'That's a general idea of the mission. The details will be filled in later. Now, if you have any questions, let's hear them.'

'Yeah, I have a couple.' Digger got to his feet and began to pace up and down the kitchen. The questions had been nagging at him for days. 'They may sound dumb to you, but remember that up until a few minutes ago I was a private first class in this man's army, and I haven't got any smarter since you made me a captain. Question number one, what if these guys are deadbeats? You said yourself that they could be spinning a story just to save their necks. What happens if I sit down with them and see that they've got nothing to offer? Do I risk my ass to bring out a couple of phonies?'

'You do not.' Olafson was emphatic. 'If, in your considered opinion, you think that the prisoners have no information of value, then you will notify the partisan command and let them take the appropriate action. Is that clear?'

'Clear enough. I'm not sure that I even have a considered opinion, as you call it, but I get what you mean. Kill them, right?'

Olafson frowned. 'I prefer "appropriate action." '

'Next question. You're sending one man in to take out two. That's assuming they're cooperative. What happens if they're not? Figure it this way. Once we're out of the mountains they decide to change sides again. What happens then?'

Olafson looked at him calmly. 'Then it will be your turn to take the appropriate action.'

'Uh-huh. You make it sound easy.'

333

'No, that's the one thing I never said it would be. But this is a one-man mission, it has to be, and you're the man.'

'So you say, and that brings me to my last question. Why me?'

'I thought we made that clear the day you arrived here.'

Digger waved that aside. He was pacing again. 'I know, you want an ace skier who can speak German and who's been trained as a mountain soldier, but there are plenty of people like that. What you really want is somebody with my qualifications, but who also speaks the local language, also knows the area, and also has some experience in this kind of an operation. I took my first jump the day before yesterday, I've never been in Yugoslavia, and I know nothing at all about partisan warfare. So I repeat, with all respect, why me?'

Olafson and Gregorius looked at each other silently. Olafson shrugged and said, 'You might as well tell him now. He has to know eventually.'

Digger said woodenly, 'Has to know what? What have you been holding out?'

'The prisoners,' Gregorius said slowly, 'are both named Prinz. Captain Hannes Prinz, and Lieutenant Kurt Prinz, both of the 156th Alpine.'

'Son of a bitch.'

'Your analysis was quite accurate – we have other people we could send, people with the qualifications you just mentioned. But we can't use them. You see, your cousins have asked for you personally, they've made it one of their conditions. They say you're the only one they can trust to get them out of there.'

'Pilot to waist gunner.' The voice crackled in his ears. 'Toby, get our guest up and ready, would you? We'll be over his jump point shortly.'

'That's you, mate, upsa-daisy,' said the gunner. He reached down a hand to help Digger to his feet. 'All ready, then?'

He watched critically as Digger worked himself into his gear: a chest-pack parachute, a backpack of equipment, and strapped across the pack, a stubby pair of skis. The gunner ran his hand over them and shook his head.

'I've done drops before,' he said, 'but I never saw a bloke jump with a rig like this one. You look like you're off to a bleedin' holiday in Scotland.'

'You guessed it,' Digger told him. 'I decided to try the mountains this year. The beaches get too crowded.'

'Some people have the luck, and in wartime, too.'

The gunner pulled at the hatch handle, and the section of metal slid open. A blast of air rushed in. Digger moved up into the hatchway, gripping the sides; the slipstream clawed at his face. All he could see in the faint moonlight were patches of clouds and the rolling shadows of valleys and hills. He remembered what Olafson had said about pinpoint accuracy, and he wondered how many of those hills he would have to climb before he found the right one.

'Steady,' said the gunner's voice in his ear. 'Red light on, green light coming. I'll give you the word.' A pause, and then, 'Enjoy yourself and send us a card. Go!'

He felt the slap on his shoulder, and he dived out into the night.

The suitcase was old and shabby, but well constructed. It had arrived at the house late in the afternoon, delivered by a man equally old and shabby who had insisted on giving it into the hands of Dieter personally. From this, Karl had assumed that the suitcase contained the money for Otto, a million Swiss francs accumulated from sources he could only imagine. Caches of cash tapped for the emergency, favours called in and liquidated, a premium paid for the foreign exchange; all of this conducted on the cutting edge of Vienna's black market. Even the shabby suitcase seemed a proper part of the transaction, a veteran of similar situations in the past. How many other ransoms had been delivered in it? How many bribes, how many dowries? The very leather had a furtive look, as if capable of containing great mysteries, and the single lock might once have turned on secrets still unknown. It was an object both foreign and familiar, attractive yet repellent, and faded from former glories. It was
. . .

Karl stopped the train of thought. He had been about to conclude that it was obviously a Jewish suitcase.

'It weighs a ton,' he said, picking it up and hefting it. He put it back on the floor.

'Don't do that,' Dieter said sharply, then eased the words with an uneasy smile. 'I'm the only one who should handle it. In case of fingerprints, you know.'

What fingerprints? thought Karl. What's he talking about?

But he said nothing. Dieter was nervous, and so was he, the two of them standing in the study drinking kirsch with half an hour to go before it would be time to start for the Prater and the payoff.

Trying to apologize, Dieter said, 'I only meant that we don't know what tricks Otto might have up his sleeve. Better not to take any chances.'

'All right.' He took a sip of his drink. 'Under the circumstances . . . would it be possible to ask a question?'

'Only one? Under the circumstances I should think you'd be bursting with a dozen or more. What is it?'

'Marta . . . the baroness. Did she know?'

'About my being Jewish? No, certainly not. I suppose I should have told her, but there never seemed any reason to. You see, I never really felt I was hiding anything. As far as I was concerned, I stopped being Jewish when I left Bratislava, and I was foolish enough to think that the rest of the world would see it the same way. And for a while it worked, but not any more. The gentiles decide who the Jews are, not the rabbis.'

'And your business?'

'No, she knew nothing about that either. Not that it would have shocked her, but she had no head for business. With all her talent, and all the sophistication that she acquired, she always stayed a country girl at heart. Your part of the country, at that.'

'Yes. It's a good country, too.'

A coincidence. He had thought often of the Tirol recently trying to recall the features of a land he had not seen in almost thirty years. Another sign of age, he decided, but at the same time wondered if he might not, someday, be able to go back. There was nothing to keep him from it now, no family to disgrace. Perhaps after this war was over there would be time to do all the things he should have done over the years. There was Anton in America, and maybe he should have taken him up on that offer, maybe he still could. Just for a visit, to see what it was really like outside the books. Yes, back to the Tirol and across the seas to Anton's America, and perhaps a pilgrimage south to those mountains where he had served as a young soldier. Back to the Julians where once he had been Cowboy Karl, the Korporal who made the best soup in the

336

regiment, always plenty of meat in it, and who took good care of his boys. Took good care. Shit.

'We should be going now,' said Dieter. 'You know what to do?'

'We drive to the Prater, I park the car, you make the exchange, come back, and home we go. Nothing for me to do except drive.'

'Is Mimi at home?'

'I'm afraid she left a while ago.'

'Some young man?'

'From the Waffen SS, I believe.'

Dieter sighed. 'She's young, she doesn't know.'

She knows plenty, thought Karl, and wondered how much her father knew about the sexual express train his daughter was riding. Probably nothing, although it was common knowledge. Fathers know what they want to know.

'I had wanted to see her before we go,' Dieter said, 'but she's never still these days.'

'Perhaps when we return.'

Dieter smiled thinly. 'Yes, perhaps.'

They drove slowly through the darkened streets, Dieter sitting up front next to Karl, the suitcase resting on his lap. They did not speak, each alone with his thoughts. They crossed the river over the Reichsbrücke and then on to the Lassallestrasse, around the circle and onto the Hauptallee with the Prater on their left and with the skeletal form of the darkened Ferris wheel, the Riesenrad, looming above them. The street was empty save for Otto's Opel parked against the kerb on the right-hand side. Even at that time of year they could smell the odours of fresh earth and trees on the breeze that came out of the park.

'Not too close,' said Dieter as Karl pulled in against the kerb. He parked several lengths behind the Opel. 'Still too close. Back up some more.'

Karl backed farther up the street until Dieter nodded his approval. Dieter opened the door on his side. Before he could get out, Karl put a hand on his arm.

'I have something to say, please. Don't get into any arguments with him. Just give him the suitcase, take the file, and leave. Don't say anything to make him angry. You understand?'

Dieter nodded. His eyes, fixed on Karl's, were deep, sorrowful, and suddenly Jewish eyes. 'Karl, you listen carefully,' he said. 'We both know what Otto is, and we don't know what could happen in the next few minutes. If something should go wrong, if anything should happen to me, I want you to promise that you'll look after Mimi.'

'Nothing is going to happen,' Karl said gruffly. 'You'll pay off the bastard, and that's the end of it.'

'I know, but just in case, promise.'

'Of course, whatever I can do.'

'Good. Now I'll go and get this over with. As soon as I'm out of the car, back up to the corner and wait for me there.'

'No need for that. I'll wait here.'

'No, you're still too close. If anything happens I don't want you connected with it. Wait at the corner.'

In that moment Karl's eyes turned as sad as Dieter's, and he realized that he was never going to see the Tirol again, or Anton's America or the Julian Alps of Korporal Lang and Feuerwerker Kranski. In that moment he knew that those were the makings of an old man's dreams, despite his age, and that he had waited a touch too long in the dreaming.

'Yes,' he said to Dieter, although no question had been asked. 'You didn't want me to handle the suitcase, and you want me to look after Mimi, and you want me up the street and out of the way. I think I'd like to look in that suitcase.' He reached out a hand. 'Will you open it for me?'

Dieter gripped the case protectively. 'We have no time.'

'Humour me. I'd like to see what a million Swiss francs looks like.'

Dieter shook his head.

'I'm going to have to insist.'

'And I'm going to have to refuse.' Dieter might have been smiling; Karl couldn't tell. 'This is a very unusual suitcase. It only opens once.'

'I thought so. You couldn't get any explosives for me, but you could get some for yourself.'

Dieter made a sudden move to scramble out of the car. Karl's right hand shot out to hold him. His left hand went into the side pocket on the door and came out with a wrench always kept there. He slapped the wrench against Dieter's temple, not quite hard enough. Another slap, and Dieter's eyes closed and his head slumped forward. Karl grunted and put the wrench back. He reached across Dieter to close the right-hand door.

338

He opened his own door, got out, and took the suitcase with him. He stood without moving for a moment, then reached into his breast pocket and took out the wallet with his identification papers in it. He tossed the wallet onto the front seat and closed the door. He picked up the suitcase and walked up the street to the Opel. The rear door on the kerb side swung open.

'Get in,' said Otto.

He climbed into the back seat of the car. In the darkness no faces could be seen.

'Who are you?' said Otto.

'The chauffeur. I was told to give you this and get something in return.' He passed the suitcase over. Otto laid it on his lap. Beside him on the seat was a grey file folder bound in tape. Karl said lightly, 'I suggest that you count it.'

'Don't worry. When a Jew gives me money I count every bill. Maybe I shouldn't have said that. Maybe you didn't know that your boss is a Jew.' He fumbled with the suitcase lock.

'I knew it,' said Karl. He looked out the window. He felt oddly relaxed. This was the way it was done. This was the way of the Apache and the Sioux, of Cochise and Geronimo, Red Cloud, Mangas Coloradas . . .

The explosion blew the Opel across the street and shredded the bodywork. The three men in it, including the driver, were killed instantly. The suitcase was destroyed, and so was the file folder. The fire that followed completed the destruction.

The explosion shocked Dieter into consciousness. He pulled himself up and stared at the scene. It looked just as he had been told it would, but he had not expected to see it. His hands were shaking and he willed them to stop, but he could not will away the tears in his eyes. He brushed his sleeve across his face and slid behind the wheel. It was years since he had driven a car himself, but he managed. He was well away from the scene and on his way home before the first of the fire engines arrived.

'I would have shot them on the spot,' said Ivan Canker. The partisan leader buried his nose in a mug of tea, and when he lifted his face his moustache was dripping. 'We don't take prisoners in this business. But they were lucky. There was a commissar with us that day, a representative from AVNOJ, the anti-Fascist council. He was the one who questioned them and he was the one they sold their story to. And he believed them, the fool. That's the only reason they're still alive. Me, I would have shot them.'

'We're glad that you didn't,' Digger said carefully. 'My government thinks they may have important information for us. That's why I'm here.'

'That's shit, pure shit. Governments don't think. You're here because that jackass from AVNOJ, that Comrade Kozina, sold the story to someone at Supreme Headquarters who got on to the radio and sold it to the British in Alexandria, and the British sold it to one of your people, who decided to send you halfway around the world to see if maybe, just maybe, there's one drop of truth in it. Which there isn't, and in the end we'll have to shoot them anyway.'

There had been no difficulty in finding the partisans. They had found him. He had landed in the middle of a swirling snowstorm, had carefully buried his parachute, adjusted his pack, strapped on his skis, and taken his compass bearings. And then had realized that there was no place to go. He was totally lost, all landmarks obscured by the storm. There was the feel of a mountain nearby, and he trusted that feeling. He had grown up with the feel of invisible mountains looming somewhere close, and had learned to follow the feeling. He was never wrong, the mountain was always there, but in these strange surroundings he was reluctant to test his luck. He had just about decided to dig himself a hole in a snowbank and wait out the storm when they came up silently and took him. It happened so quickly that he wasn't aware of being hit. One moment he was standing, and in the next he was flat on his back in the snow. There were two of them, bearded and dressed in layers of rags. One held a knife to his throat while the other went through his pockets. The second one found his papers; he couldn't read them but he knew what they were. He held them up and grinned.

'GI Joe,' he said.

'Close enough,' said Digger. 'Tell him to take the knife away.' And then he had repeated the one word he had been instructed to use for recognition. 'Cankar. Cankar.'

'Cankar, Cankar,' they agreed. It was the name of their commander. 'Come, we go now to Cankar.'

They went, but not before the two of them dug up the parachute he thought he had buried so carefully. They admired the

340

nylon and cut it into strips that they tied around their bodies from waist to armpits; and then they were ready to go, leading him out of the clearing in which he had landed, skimming along on skis even shorter than his. They went without looking back to see if he would follow, and neither of them offered to help with his equipment pack.

They skied over trackless terrain, through stands of snow-laden trees, and once along a ridge that was overhung with needles of ice. The snow never let up, and they moved through it blindly. When the terrain began to tip up they climbed for as long as they could with their skis strapped on, then took them off and kept on climbing up the mountain. The two partisans climbed effortlessly, and they did not offer to stop and rest. Digger climbed with them, never more than a step behind, but he felt it in his belly and legs. They climbed through most of the morning, and around noon the snow stopped and the storm lifted. With the air clear they could look down and see what they had left behind: a white world far below with the lines of a town and a river etched in. They kept on climbing until they came to an indentation in the mountainside about a mile across. It was a punchbowl with steep and icy slopes, and on the far side of it the north face rose up to form the dark peak that gave the mountain its name. Mount Krn . . . Krnberg . . . Montagna Nera. At the base of that peak was a ridge that was dotted with caves, and that was where the partisans had their camp.

They took him to the cave in which Cankar lived. That was not his real name. Like many in the partisan movement he had adopted a *nomme de guerre,* in his case the name of an early Slovenian playwright and patriot. This Cankar was a lean and leathery old man with broad moustaches that curled at the ends. He commanded a band of three dozen men and a handful of women. They were lightly armed, had two mules for transport and a radio that was their only link to the outside world. They also had dozens of cans of paint. It was ordinary house paint, and Cankar was using it in his idle time to paint pictures on the walls of the caves. That was how Digger saw him first: crouched with a brush in his hand, his nose up against the wall of the cave as he applied the paint to the seamed surface of rock. The picture was that of a young girl, her head covered with a black scarf. All the other paintings in the cave were also of people, members of the band.

'We captured the paint in an ambush,' Cankar explained. 'The same ambush in which we took your two prisoners. God only knows what the Germans were doing with so much paint. We took it not knowing what it was. It came in boxes and we thought it might be cans of food. We carried it all the way up the mountain, not knowing. Some of the men were angry when we opened the boxes and saw what it was, but I use it to pass the time. Unfortunately, the only colours they had were red and black and white, and so the paintings scream when you look at them.'

'They're very good,' Digger said politely. 'Were you a painter before the war?'

'A house painter, like Hitler. But I always knew I could do something like this if I had the time.'

He offered Digger a mug of tea, and it was then that he said that if the choice had been his he would have shot the prisoners.

'They're lying, of course,' he said as he worked black paint into the section of rock that formed the young girl's scarf. 'A captain and a lieutenant, what would they know of such value? Shall I tell you? Nothing, that's what they know, and I could have found that out in ten minutes if it hadn't been for Comrade Jackass from AVNOJ. But no, says Comrade Jackass, we don't touch these prisoners, we don't try to persuade them to tell us the truth. This is a matter for inter-allied cooperation.' The old man worked around the big words carefully. 'They are very strong for inter-allied cooperation at AVNOJ these days, and so they use the radio and from halfway around the world comes a young boy to find out what I could have told them after ten minutes with a sharp knife. I am a good Slovenian, and a good Yugoslav and a good Communist, and so I obey orders, but since I have been in these mountains I have not seen anything as stupid as this business with these prisoners.'

'Many stupid things happen in war,' said Digger. 'And sending me here may be one of them, but I am not a boy. Nor am I an old man who paints on walls. I am an officer in the United States Army, and we are also very strong for inter-allied cooperation.'

Cankar stepped back from the wall to admire his work. Casually, he said, 'On the other hand, I may kill them anyway.'

'Not until I talk with them.'

'And I may kill you, too.'

'Not until I eat.'

The old man turned to look at him curiously. 'You are hungry?'

'I'm starving. If you're going to shoot me, give me something to eat first.'

'Why should I waste food on someone I'm going to shoot? You're almost dead.'

'All of us are almost dead, but nobody is as hungry as I am right now.'

Cankar nodded his approval and pointed to the painting of the girl. 'You're right about that. She will be dead within a month. Tuberculosis. That's why I'm painting her now.' He waved a hand at the other paintings on the walls. 'All my people, and they will all soon be dead from one thing or another. A disease or a bullet, it makes no difference. We don't last long in these mountains. That's why I paint them, to leave something behind.'

'And what about me? Are you going to paint me before you shoot me, or are you going to starve me to death?'

The old man grinned. He had no teeth. 'No, I'll feed you first and then you may talk with the prisoners. They are related to you, yes?'

'How did you know that?'

'The names are almost the same, and they asked particularly for you.'

'They are cousins of mine. They are also enemy soldiers.'

'Well, talk to your cousins.' Cankar flapped his hand carelessly. 'You deserve that much after such a trip. Then, once you talk to them, maybe I'll shoot you all.'

'Maybe,' said Digger. He looked around the cave at the paintings. 'You're doing this all wrong. If all these people are going to die, then you should be painting German soldiers on the walls.'

'I never thought of that. Maybe they sent the right man after all.'

Chapter Nineteen

Cankar had one of his women get Digger a plate of beans and a chunk of bread, and when he was finished eating he was taken

343

to see the prisoners. They were in a small, separate cave with a guard at the mouth. They had a tiny fire and some goatskins, but no other comforts. They both were still wearing white camouflage sheets over their field uniforms, but the sheets weren't white any more, they were filthy. They were both filthy all over, and they stank. They had let themselves go badly. Later, Kurt explained that it came from living under the gun, not knowing each morning if they were going to be shot, not knowing if their scheme had worked, not knowing if Digger would ever show up.

Because it was a scheme all the way. Cankar was right, they had nothing of value to offer and they were lucky to be alive. They had been an inch away from the chop, a cocked hammer on a pistol, when Kurt had started spinning his fantasy. He created it on the spot, selling it as top-secret information: orders of battle, regimental dispositions, advanced training schedules, Alpinkorps troop movements in northern Italy, defence systems in Norway. He threw the whole package at them, inventing feverishly, and even threw in a new land mine that would cause avalanches to roll down on enemy positions. He didn't fool Cankar, but Comrade Kozina from the anti-Fascist council bought the pitch, and after that the bureaucracy took over. At that point the prisoners belonged to the council and nobody could lay a finger on them. The message went out, and everyone down the line bought it and passed it on until it landed in that farmhouse in Virginia.

But as Digger stepped into the cave he didn't know yet that the story was a phony. Kurt took one look at him and started grinning all over, but he didn't move. Hannes reacted the same way. Neither of them knew if he should come to attention and salute, or throw his arms around Digger and kiss him. Their problem was that they didn't know if they were supposed to recognize one another. Kurt had pulled off one scheme after another by getting them to send for Digger, but he hadn't mentioned the relationship. So the two of them stood there trying not to wag their tails like a pair of happy puppies, and Digger cleared up that part of it right away.

'At ease, gentlemen,' he said, although they weren't at attention. 'Comrade Cankar knows that we aren't exactly strangers.'

That was as far as he could go without being accused of fraternizing with the enemy. For all his kidding about shooting

344

people, the old man was perfectly capable of doing it. He didn't believe any part of Kurt's story, but his hands were tied by the council and his pride was bruised. All he needed was the smallest excuse to kill the deal, and at the same time kill every stranger in sight. They were all strangers to him, and enemies. The Germans, the Americans, the Italians, the British, even the people at the anti-Fascist council were enemies. Anyone who was not of his band or of his mountain was an enemy, and therefore disposable.

Now he said, 'Yes, a regular family reunion, isn't it? Well, *Offizier,* I'll leave you to your interrogation, and I will expect a report when you are finished.' They spoke in German, and when Digger had given him the comeback about being an officer in the US Army the old man had started calling him *Offizier.* For all the time that he stayed with the band he was never called anything else.

As soon as Cankar was out of the cave, Kurt let loose. He rushed over and threw his arms around Digger. He was singing something under his breath, and it took a moment to realize that it was 'Boola-boola, boola-boola.' Hannes let loose in a different way. He wiped the grin off his face, glared at Digger, and spat on the floor. Even under those circumstances he couldn't conceal his dislike for his cousin.

Digger got out of Kurt's grip and motioned them both to crouch down near the fire. He knelt next to them. In English, he said quietly, 'I don't think the old man speaks English and I'm pretty sure the guard doesn't, but let's make this quick. What the fuck is this all about?'

Kurt gripped his knee excitedly. 'You came, you made it. I knew you would. I prayed and I knew.'

Hannes asked, 'You'll get us out of here, Digger? You can do that, yes?'

'I'm not doing anything until I hear what you have to say. What's all this about secret information? What have you got to sell?'

Hannes said stiffly, 'That is something we can discuss only with your superiors. Your job is to get us out of here to safety. When do we leave?'

Digger turned to Kurt. 'Do you go along with that?'

Kurt was worried, and it showed. 'This is very sensitive infor-

345

mation that we have. It would be better to wait for a proper debriefing.'

'Also,' Hannes added, 'there is much that you would not understand.'

'Try me. Give me a sample.'

'No samples,' Hannes said firmly. 'Not until we have an understanding with your superiors.'

Digger almost laughed in his face. He sounded like a girl holding out for a wedding ring. Kurt knew it, and he tried to smooth it over.

'Please,' he said. 'Hannes is putting it strongly, but he's right. We can discuss details once we're safe, but the most important thing now is to get out of here quickly. These people aren't soldiers, they're animals. They could decide to shoot us anytime. Tonight, tomorrow, anytime.'

'Maybe even sooner than that,' Digger said, and stood up. He began to walk towards the mouth of the cave.

'Where are you going?' They said it together.

He turned to face them. 'My orders were to find out if you had any real information to offer. If the answer is yes I'm supposed to get you out of here. If the answer is no I'm supposed to advise Comrade Cankar to take the appropriate action.' He paused to let the words sink in. 'You've got nothing.'

Kurt's voice was low and urgent. 'Digger, please, come back and talk.'

'Talk about what? More secret information? What the hell would a captain and a lieutenant know? You want to blow some more smoke up my ass about Norwegian defences and troop movements in Italy? For Christ's sake, in my outfit they wouldn't even give you the keys to the office safe.' He turned to Kurt. 'And you, I expected more from you. Where the hell do you get off insulting my intelligence this way? Did you think this was going to be a family get-together, everybody have a schnapps and talk about old times? This is a war and we're wearing different-colour clothes. Now, unless you have something important to say, I'll make my report to Cankar.'

'Come back,' said Kurt. 'Yes, I have something important to say.'

He went back to the fire and crouched down. Kurt lowered his voice to a whisper. 'All right, we have nothing,' he said. 'We are ordinary soldiers, we have nothing to do with intelligence. When we were captured they questioned us briefly and then they were going to shoot us. Three other men were captured with us, enlisted men. We saw them shot, a bullet in the back of the neck, and then it was our turn. That's when I started talking. I never talked so much and so fast in my life. I said anything that came into my head. Hannes saw what I was doing and he picked it up. We were talking our guts out and it wasn't doing any good, but then we got lucky. One of their big shots from headquarters believed us. They threw us in here and we've been here ever since, not knowing what was going to happen.' He turned his hands palms up to show that he was empty. 'That's all there is. No information. The rest is up to you.'

'How the hell did I get involved?'

'That was Hannes's idea. We knew they'd have to send someone to check up on us, and that anyone they sent would see that we were faking it.'

'So we asked for the famous skier Digger Prince,' said Hannes. 'The only man who could get us off this mountain. Actually, it was quite a compliment, no?'

'And you figured that I'd back your play.'

'We figured we could trust you to get us out of here,' said Kurt. 'Whether we had any information or not.'

'And why would I want to do that?'

That startled Kurt. He looked from Hannes to Digger, and back again. He knew how Digger felt about his brother. Then he understood. 'You mean because of Elena? You'd hold that against me? Something like that? Now?'

'How is she? Where is she?'

'You want to talk about that *now*?'

'No, I guess I don't. We'll talk some other time. Right now I've got to make my report to Cankar.'

It was dead quiet in the cave. 'What are you going to say?'

'I'm going to tell him that your information seems legitimate, but that most of it is too technical for me and you'll have to be interrogated at a higher level.'

'You mean you're taking us out?'

'That's right.'

Kurt grinned broadly. Hannes shuddered like a foundering horse. Kurt said, 'Jesus, you sure made us sweat for it.'

They wanted to know the details of how he was going to do

it, but he told them that would have to wait. He went back to Cankar's cave. The old man was working on the painting of the young girl, rubbing shading into her eyes. They were sad-looking eyes, and the way he had painted the girl she looked more like a Madonna than a partisan fighter. He laid down his brush and looked at Digger questioningly.

'Well, *Offizier,* what have you discovered?'

Digger said what he had planned to say. The old man didn't seem surprised. 'So, you have decided to save your cousins' necks.'

'I'm taking them out.'

'I expected as much. Blood counts, always. They're lying, of course, and now you are lying too, and thanks to Comrade Jackass from AVNOJ there is nothing I can do about it.'

'Can I count on your cooperation?'

He made a face. 'I would rather shoot the three of you, but I have my orders. What will you need?'

Digger explained about the rendezvous at Rijeka. 'The submarine will be there for three nights starting the twentieth. How long will it take me to get there?'

'It isn't very far, but you will be travelling off the roads to avoid the patrols. Better allow for a full day, overnight. One of my people will guide you down the mountain as far as the river. After that you are on your own. Halfway between here and Rijeka I can give you a safe place to stay overnight. What else will you need? Food and water, that you can have. What else?'

'Nothing. I'm grateful for what you are doing.'

'Reluctantly, *Offizier,* very reluctantly. Not that I don't understand. Blood is blood, there's nothing you can do about it.' He twisted his moustache thoughtfully. 'Most young men find it difficult to take advice. Do you have that problem?'

'Sometimes. It depends on who is giving it. I'll be glad to hear whatever you have to suggest.'

'Your two cousins. I've had them for over a month now, and I have eyes. One is a lamb and the other is a wolf. Do you agree with me?'

'Yes.'

'Good, it saves time. My advice to you is to kill the wolf.'

'I don't understand.'

'You understand well enough. You are determined to go through with this crazy mission, and I cannot argue with you.

348

It's all wrong, but I cannot argue. The blood tie makes it right for you. But I'm telling you this. Save the lamb if you must, but kill the wolf. If there really is any important information, then bringing out the lamb will be enough. If there isn't, which I believe, then if you don't kill the wolf you may never reach Rijeka. Kill him here, or kill him on the way, but get rid of the wolf. That's my advice to you.'

'I thank you for it. It's something to think about.'

'Yes, it is. But you won't. At your age I wouldn't have, either.'

That day was the sixteenth, and they had to leave on the nineteenth in order to be at the rendezvous point on the first of the nights that the sub would be there. During the waiting time Digger wandered through the camp, poking his nose into the crowded caves. Nobody tried to stop him. Wherever he went he was invited to share what was bubbling in the pot. It was usually beans, but sometimes there was stew if a rabbit had been snared. The people were mostly countrymen, small farmers and woodsmen who had taken to the mountains in July of 1941 when the call had gone out for resistance to the invaders. Few of them were Communists, but they all supported the right of the party to direct the resistance. All of them detested the king, the government-in-exile in London, and the Chetnik guerrillas operating under Mihajlović. Even the young people felt that way, and the youngest of all were Cankar's grandchildren: Vlado, who would be the guide down the mountain, and Marina, the girl in the wall painting.

Vlado was sixteen, blond and sturdy. He had been on the ambush that had hit Kurt's outfit, and he had done his part of the job. He was a good skier and hunter, and it was he who snared the rabbits for the pot. He was still a boy, despite the roll of reddish beard along his chin, and if there had not been a war he would have been working on his father's farm, or learning a trade. But there was a war, and the farm was gone, and his parents were dead, and the only trade he knew was killing Italians and Germans whenever his grandfather ordered him to.

His cousin, Marina, was eighteen. She had dark hair, an oval face, and the shadowed eyes of the Madonna. She was one of the only three unattached women in the band, and her life was isolated. The partisans were prudish people, and the maidens

349

were often fenced off from the rest of them. That didn't apply to Digger. It wasn't so much that he was an honoured guest, but he was just passing through and so no one minded when the girl tagged after him. She was full of questions, the usual wide-eyed curiosity about America. Digger lied a lot and made Vermont sound like heaven. He was curious about the girl. Cankar had said something about tuberculosis, but she showed no sign of illness. She was active and lively, and it was fun feeding her stories about the land of milk and honey. There was nothing between them at that point. There was no way that there could be.

The prisoners were allowed outside the cave for an hour every morning under guard, and the first morning there Digger walked with them and laid out the plans. He told them everything they had to know, but he didn't tell them what would be waiting off the coast at Rijeka. He also gave them the ground rules of the game.

'If I were in your boots,' he said, 'I'd promise anything to get off this mountain and then I'd look to screw you. That's what I'm expecting you to try, so listen to the word. At the first sign that you're trying to pull anything, you're both dead. Not just the one who makes the move, but both of you. No threats, no warnings, just pop, pop, and it's all over. Just so you understand.'

'You're saving our lives,' said Kurt. 'I made a deal and I'll stick to it.'

'No, he is right to warn us,' said Hannes. 'He understands that it is a soldier's duty to try to escape.'

'Your duty, not mine,' said Kurt. They were walking along the ridge with a guard close by. 'I was never much of a soldier.'

'How did you get into the army at all?' Digger asked him. 'You were such a strong anti-Nazi. I figured you'd be in a prison camp by now, not a uniform.'

Kurt smiled sadly. 'That was exactly the choice I had. It was easy to sound like a hero when I was in America. Once I was back in Vienna it was easier to go along with what was happening. When my class was called up, I went with it. After that came the Alpinkorps, Hannes asked for me, and there we were. Do I disappoint you? I'm sorry if I do. It was this or a camp. I found out that I'm not as brave as I thought I was.'

Hannes frowned and moved away from them, unhappy with

350

such talk. He strode on ahead, waving his arms and slapping his sides to keep warm. When he was out of hearing, Digger said, 'Nobody knows what he'll do in a spot like that. I'm glad it's a decision I never had to make.'

Kurt nodded his thanks. 'You asked about Elena yesterday. Does that mean you never heard from her?'

'Never.'

'Then I should tell you what happened. She went that night with me to New York, and two days later I sailed for home. She wanted to come with me, but I couldn't let her. I knew what I was coming back to, but she didn't. All we had was a night on the train and two nights in New York. Not much of a romance.'

'It's more than some people get.'

'I suppose so. Once I was back in Vienna we wrote often. We made a lot of plans. Then the war came and there were no more plans to make.'

'Where is she now?'

'The last letter was from New York, but that was over a year ago. Maybe after the war . . .' He made a helpless gesture, kicked at a snowbank and sent up a spray. 'It wasn't right, what we did to you, but it happened. I'd like to think that you aren't angry about it any more.'

'It was a long time ago. By now she's probably married to some rich 4–F with a punctured eardrum.'

'You don't really think so, do you?'

'Who knows? You've got more important things to worry about.'

They looked up ahead to where Hannes was trotting in a small circle, keeping warm as he waited for them to catch up. 'Strange that I should wind up here,' said Kurt. 'My father served here in the last war.'

'Is this where he was wounded?'

'Yes.'

'Make sure it doesn't happen to you. If I have to go to take you out it won't be any wound.'

'I gave you my word and I'll keep it. I have no desire to go back to the army.'

'You're not the one I'm worried about. Remember, if Hannes tries it, you get it too.'

'I know,' Kurt said sadly. 'You've made that quite clear.'

Digger spent the next day getting his equipment together and going over the route down the mountain with Vlado. There was a small pack apiece for the brothers and for each a pair of the stubby skis that the partisans used. Vlado carried a Schmeisser machine pistol, the kind with the folding stock. The partisans had resupplied with weapons after the ambush of Kurt's outfit, and they had extras. Vlado offered one to Digger, but he turned it down. He was already carrying a carbine, a pistol, a mountain axe, and a foot-long Brent knife on his hip. Another weapon would have set him clanging.

There were no maps, but Vlado made a sketch of the way down the mountain. They would leave just after first light, skiing down through the punchbowl indentation in the hill, and then off onto the south face, keeping below the ridgeline until they came to where the timber began. Once within the trees they would be safe from direct observation, but below the trees was the tricky part. That was the farthest point to which the Germans pushed their patrols, and they would have to wait under cover until the slope was clear, then make a dash for it. They would be in the open for about half a mile, and then it was timber again until the river. There Vlado would show them the crossing and set them on their way to Rijeka. That was as far as he would go.

'We will travel in single file,' he told Digger. 'Forgive me for giving instructions, *Offizier,* but this is my responsibility. I will go first, then the two prisoners, then you. The commander has given me firm orders. If there is any trouble, I am to shoot the two prisoners at once. You understand that?'

'Without question.'

'It is not something that one wants to do, but those are the orders.'

'Mine as well.'

'Good, then we understand each other.'

After that there was nothing to do but wait for the morning. They slept, and when the morning came the fog came with it, greyish-white and thick. It filled the valleys, blanketed the highlands, and buried the peak as well. There was no visibility at all. To travel by foot would have been difficult, to ski a mountain impossible. Digger went to Cankar's cave to ask how long the fog usually lasted in those mountains. The old man was painting on the wall again. The portrait of Marina was finished,

352

and he had blocked out the figure of a man. It was only the outline, and he had just begun to fill in the details.

'The fog comes, the fog goes,' he said. 'Nobody knows.' He applied paint carefully, working in facial features.

'There has to be a pattern. There always is.'

'One day, maybe two. Never more than two at this time of the year.' He looked at Digger and squinted. 'Turn your head a little bit towards me.'

'What for?'

'So I can see the shape of your nose.'

'You bastard, you're not putting me up on that death wall.'

He laughed and held up his hand. 'Just a joke. Not you, somebody else.'

He went to tell Kurt and Hannes that they would not be travelling, and then settled down to wait out the day. He could wait one day, even two, but on the third day they would have to start for the rendezvous. Towards the end of the day the fog appeared to thin out, but that was illusory. In the night it thickened up again, and in the morning it was just as heavy as before. When Kurt came out for his exercise, Digger told him that they would not be travelling that day, either.

'What about tomorrow?' he asked anxiously. 'We have to go tomorrow, no matter what.'

'Don't worry, we'll go. Cankar says that two days is the limit.'

He went looking for Vlado and found him whittling pegs for rabbit traps. 'You won't be able to use those until the spring,' he said, crouching beside him.

'I like to have them ready early.'

'Do you think we can go tomorrow?'

'Hard to say with fog.'

'Cankar says that it never lasts more than two days.'

'Comrade Cankar is the commander. He would know.'

Vlado didn't sound confident about it. Digger said, 'If it weren't for the Germans we could use bells.' He told him how in Vermont when they were kids they would ski in the fog with bracelets of tiny bells on their wrists and a cow bell clanging from a ski pole. They would shake the bells on a downhill run to warn whoever was on the hill, and it was great fun until somebody came along who didn't know the rules. There was always someone who wasn't wearing bells and who came booming out of the whiteness, and then it stopped being fun. He told that to Vlado, and the young man smiled.

'I think I would like Vermont,' he said. 'Perhaps one day I will go there and ski with the bells on.'

The next morning Digger was up long before sunrise, waiting to see if there would be any dawn. He sat in the mouth of the cave and watched the darkness slowly turn into a cottonish sort of light. The fog was still there, but it was patchy. At times it shredded and then he could see clearly down the mountain, but the open patches came and went.

Vlado came by and asked, 'What do you think?'

'It isn't good, but we have to go.'

'It would be better to wait another day.'

'If we don't go today it's all over.'

He explained about the rendezvous with the submarine. Vlado was impressed. 'In that case we should certainly go. Nothing was said to me about a submarine.'

'It was not necessary for you to know. Now it is.'

'I will tell the commander that we are leaving.'

Digger got Kurt and Hannes out and gave them their packs and their skis. They looked around doubtfully; the fog had thickened again. Kurt didn't want to say anything, but Hannes came out with it.

'You expect us to ski in this?' he asked. 'Impossible.'

'It's either that or a bullet, take your choice.' Digger moved up close to him. 'Hannes, you don't mean a damn thing to me. You're just a tired old piece of dogshit who happens to have the same name as mine. I said that I would get you out of here, and I will, so keep your mouth shut and do as you're told. If you even cross your eyes the wrong way, you're finished. Now saddle up and let's get going.'

There were goodbyes to be said. Marina waved shyly from a distance. Now that Digger was leaving it would have been improper for her to have done more than that. Cankar looked worried as he shook hands. 'Bad weather, *Offizier*. I wish you didn't have to go.'

'You said it never lasted more than two days.'

'Sometimes three,' he admitted. 'The way it is you could ski right into a German patrol.'

'A chance we have to take.'

'Yes.' The old man raised a hand and Digger thought he was

354

about to be blessed, but all Cankar did was slap him on the shoulder and mutter, 'Remember what I said about the wolf.'

They left the ridge and skied down into the punchbowl, Vlado leading, then Hannes, Kurt, and Digger in the rear. The terrain was bad, but it could have been worse. It meant keeping his eyes on the surface and hopping, stepping, jumping around and over the obstacles, and swerving suddenly to avoid the stretches where the cover was gone. Since they were carrying weapons, Vlado and Digger skied without poles, but the brothers had theirs. The only problem was the fog. They ran in and out of it, and once they were inside a patch of it they had to trust to luck not to hit anything. Still, they made good time down the punchbowl, and before they turned onto the south face, Vlado signalled for a halt. He spoke directly to the Prinzes.

'We run this section below the ridgeline,' he said. 'As you two know, the ridge is under observation by your people. If either of you shows himself above the line, he will be shot. Understood?'

They both nodded, and the troop turned downhill again. The south face was easier to run. It was smoother than the punchbowl, and the cover was thicker. They came down it single file, well spaced, and with the singing of windblown snow in their ears. As they came to the timberline the fog closed in again. They made it into the trees, and then they had to stop. All they could see was white wool.

Vlado's voice came out of the fog. 'Everyone is to stay still. *Offizier,* please do not move. If I hear a sound of movement I will fire at the sound. This fog will pass quickly.'

The fog rolled on, and minutes later it was clear enough among the trees for them to see each other. Vlado led them down the slope to where the belt of timber ended. Below them was the open stretch that they would have to run before they came to the river. They lay on their sides at the edge of the trees and watched the slope. It was empty, no sign of patrols. The fog blew in patches across the hill, northeast to southwest, and the wind was brisk. Vlado humped himself over the snow until he was next to Digger and put his lips close to his ear.

'*Offizier,* here is where a decision must be made,' he whispered. 'Do we wait for the fog to clear entirely, or do we make a run now? A patrol could come at any time. I realize that I

355

am the guide and that it is my decision, but they are your prisoners and I wish your opinion.'

There was no question in Digger's mind. He said, 'We go. Let's do it.'

'We go,' Vlado said to the Prinzes. 'Same order. *Los.*'

He led them onto the slope, Hannes, then Kurt, then Digger running swiftly down the fall line crouched over their skis. The face of the hill was open to the river, a straight run. They ran through a light patch of fog, burst out into the sunlight, and ran into another. Out of that and into a third, and this one was thick. It was as bad as the stuff at the top had been. Digger checked from side to side, slowing. He was skiing blind, but Vlado's voice came floating uphill.

He called: 'Keep moving, don't stop, it will clear.'

Digger kept moving, skiing blindly in silence. All he could hear was the hiss of skis on snow. Then a sudden thump, a cry, and the pop, pop, pop of Vlado's Schmeisser firing. He jammed on the brakes. The firing stopped and there was silence again.

He called, 'Vlado.' There was no answer. He called again into the blankness. 'Vlado?' Silence. 'Hannes? Kurt?'

'I'm right here.' It was Kurt's voice. The fog was beginning to thin. He was below on the slope. He said, 'Digger, don't shoot. I know what you said, but don't.'

'What happened?'

'I don't know. I'm not moving. I'm not doing anything.'

The fog was thinner now, and Digger could see him. He was twenty feet downhill, facing up, his poles braced in the snow. His face was set with strain. Digger waited for the rest of the fog to clear. It went quickly, and when it was gone the slope was open. Fifty feet below Kurt, Vlado lay face down in the snow. The snow was red under him, and his Schmeisser was gone. There was no sign of Hannes. Digger skied down to where Kurt stood, his head swivelling, searching. The pocket of fog was gone, the slope was clear in all directions, and there hadn't been time for Hannes to ski to the bottom. He was still somewhere on the hill.

Digger said to Kurt: 'Ski down in front of me. Slowly. Stop next to Vlado.'

Vlado was dead. There were holes in his chest, and his eyes were already glazed. He had never had a chance in the fog with Hannes quickly up beside him. A grab for the Schmeisser, a

356

wrench, quick shots, and he was gone. To where? Digger cased the hill again. No sign.

Kurt looked at him pleadingly. He didn't know what was going to happen. Neither did Digger. What he was supposed to do now was to get rid of Kurt, forget about Hannes, and go back up to report to Cankar. There wasn't a mission any more. There never had been any information to pass, his try at getting his cousins out was blown, and a good kid was dead. That's what he should have done. What he wanted to do was find the son of a bitch and kill him. He fought with himself, and then in no time at all the decision was made for him. He heard the popping of the Schmeisser, saw the puffs in the snow, felt the hot wire across his ribs, and then Hannes stood up from behind a snow-drifted slab of rock, still firing.

Digger fired, rolled, tumbled, fired again, and kept on rolling downhill. The tangle of his skis slowed him. He was bouncing down the slope as Hannes hosed the Schmeisser back and forth. He hit a rock, went up in the air, and came down on his back. He rolled over on his belly, edged in hard with his skis, and sighted in. Frozen in the frame of his eye was Hannes crouched behind the slab, aiming, and Kurt in a low tuck skiing towards him and screaming something. He fired, and Hannes took the shot full in his chest. He fell forward and lay still, the Schmeisser falling from his hands to lie half buried in the snow. Kurt skidded to a stop beside him.

'Keep away from that weapon,' Digger yelled. He was up on his skis.

Kurt threw him a disgusted look and bent over his brother. He rolled him over as Digger skied across the slope and stood over them. Hannes's face was covered with snow, his mouth was open and he was breathing. Blood bubbled from a wound in his chest. His eyes were open and he glared up at Digger. There was a world of hate in those eyes. His chest made sucking sounds, but his eyes never left Digger's face.

'We've got to do something for him,' said Kurt.

Digger shook his head. He could feel the blood flowing along his ribs and soaking into his clothing. He knew that he could never make it to the rendezvous, and his contract with the submarine was about to run out. Besides, he had a dead boy who had to be brought home to his grandfather.

'Digger, please.'

'Get out of here. Get going, now.'

'Going? Where?'

'Down the hill. Back to your own lines.'

'What about Rijeka?'

'That's finished now. Your only move is back to your own people, and my only move is back up the mountain. Do it now, while you can. That Schmeisser made enough noise to attract attention.'

'What about Hannes?'

'I'll take care of him. Move out.'

'What are you going to do! He needs help.'

'I'll help him. Get moving.'

'How are you going to help him?'

Digger yelled, 'What the hell do you think I'm going to do?' The sucking sounds from Hannes's chest were getting to him. 'There's only one thing to do.'

'No.'

Digger poked at Hannes's head with the carbine until one cheek rested on the snow. He put the muzzle an inch away from the temple and pulled the trigger. The head jerked. The one eye he could see still looked red and angry.

'I told you to get the hell out of here,' he said. 'Now will you go?'

He propped the carbine against the rock, unhitched the Brent knife from his belt, and got the axe out of his pack. Kurt still stood there, staring. His mind wasn't working and he couldn't see what had to be done. Digger had to bring Vlado's body up the mountain, and once he got there he would have to answer to Cankar. The old man would want to know what had happened, and there had been one lie told already. Tell him that he had killed one prisoner and that the other had escaped? Cankar would never believe that without proof, and the proof was lying here where the Germans patrolled regularly. The proof could vanish within the hour, and Digger knew that he couldn't carry two bodies up that mountain. He wasn't sure that he could carry one. He knelt beside Hannes's body and looked up at Kurt.

'Will you for Christ's sake fuck off? You don't want to see what comes next.'

Kurt didn't move. Digger turned his back to him and cut off Hannes's head. It wasn't easy, but anyone who had ever seen a hog butchered on a cold winter morning knew what had to be done. After it was done Digger's arms were soaked to the elbows. He emptied his knapsack and put the head in it, then washed his tools in the snow. He stood up and the nausea hit him. He told himself it was from the pain in his side. The pain hadn't been bad when he was kneeling, but once he stood up it started again.

He left his skis in the snow and hiked up to where Vlado's body lay. He knelt next to it, got a hitch on an arm and a leg, and worked it onto his shoulders. He tried to stand up and made it on the second try. He looked downhill. Kurt was still standing next to the headless body of his brother. He wasn't going to move, locked there by blood. Digger put Vlado's body down, unslung the carbine, and put a round in the snow at Kurt's feet. That did it. He looked up, startled. Digger waved downhill. Kurt waved back, and then he turned his skis into the fall line and ran away towards the bottom. He didn't stop, and he didn't look back.

Digger packed Vlado's body up the mountain. It took him the rest of the day climbing, stumbling, sometimes crawling, and he never made it all the way to the top. Sounds of the gunfire had floated up to the camp, and Cankar had sent down scouts in a cautious reconnoitre. They found Digger on his hands and knees tugging Vlado's body uphill. He was part-way out of his head by then, and he wouldn't let them take the body or the knapsack. He told them that it was his job to bring them both in, and he wouldn't let go. They had to send for Cankar. When he came down, Digger let him have the body and the head. He was babbling a lot, and he said something about owing the old man a grandson. It was a debt he never paid, but Cankar never held him to it.

Eventually Dieter had to tell his daughter that she was part Jewish, and the day on which he chose to tell her was April thirteenth, 1945. Hitler was trapped in his Berlin bunker, Vienna was afire, and the Red Army was pouring into town in search of whisky, watches, and women. Tales of rape preceded the army, and the sensible and virtuous young women of Vienna provided themselves with cyanide tablets just in case the worst presented itself. No one had accused Mimi von Ulm of being either sensible or virtuous for years, but nevertheless that day she allowed her father to immure her in an oversized wooden packing case in the basement of the house. That was Dieter's idea of protection, nailing her up in a box with cheese, bread, and bottles of water, and air holes carefully punched in the sides. The action was quietly ironic. There was nothing that the hordes of the East could have done to Mimi that had not been done many times before, and expertly. Still, rape is not only unwanted sex, it is a very special kind of theft, and no one was going to take anything from Mimi that she was not prepared to give freely. So she let her father nail her up in the box, and before he did so he told her the tale of Ezra Weissberg, the tailor's son from Bratislava, who became Vienna's own Baron Dieter von Ulm. It was time to tell her because time was short, the world was running out of breath, and as Dieter doggedly banged in the nails he told his daughter that her father was a Jew. And that she was half a Jew, too.

Mimi heard the story with growing horror, and said, 'Wait, stop banging in those nails. I can't be a Jew. I hate Jews.'

Dieter nodded understandingly. 'That's the way it is. If people didn't hate, there wouldn't be any Jews.'

'But I can't hate myself.'

'Why not? Most people do.'

'But I don't want to hate myself. I love myself.'

'Then you'll have to learn to love Jews, too.'

He went back to banging the nails, and she stopped him again. 'Wait,' she said. 'Don't do this to me. I don't want to be a Jew.'

'Then don't be.'

'I have a choice?'

'Everybody has a choice.'

'But how can I make a choice? I don't even know what a Jew is.'

'Who does?'

'Don't you?'

'I thought I did once, but actually all I knew was what people told me. It wasn't enough. Everybody has to find out for himself.'

'Did you?'

'I thought it over and decided against it. I didn't like the percentages.'

'But what about me?'

360

'You'll have to think it over too. It's up to you. Maybe you'll find out while you're in the box.'

He finished nailing up the box then and left her in the dark with her bread and cheese and water. Mimi took her father's advice, thought it over, and decided that, for her, being a Jew was a joke on a cosmic scale. She stayed inside the box for three days enjoying the joke. Outside the box the world she had known was going up and down in flames as the Red Army indulged itself. The women in Vienna were assaulted and some even bit their cyanide tablets, but inside the box there was only laughter. The sin, the awful sin of lying with a Jew. Mimi doubled over with mirth, stuffing her mouth with bread to keep the silence. All those years of scrubbing away at her so-called sin, whipping herself with the rods of God knows how many men, in search of redemption. And all that time . . . more bread to choke the giggles . . . all that time she was a Jew herself. Or part of one, it made no difference how much or which part, the thought of it was enough to send her off into another fit of hysterical laughter, purging herself with glee.

She stayed in the box for three days, savouring the cosmic joke, and on the third day, made impatient by sudden silence, she broke through a slatted side and emerged. Her father was gone, washed away somewhere by the final wave of the war, alive or dead she never knew, and she never saw or heard from him again. The city was silent, save for the wailing and the crackle of fires. She came out of the box far saner than she had been for years, badly battered and still confused, but able to grin. She came out of the box as a Jew.

Like most Viennese, Mimi spent the next year in simple survival, for Dieter's wealth had disappeared with him. She found a cheap place to live, got a job with the post office, queued for meagre supplies, and learned to build a future of bricks without mortar. Late in 1946 she went to work for the office of the Judge Advocate General of the US Army, and there met a young lawyer, a first lieutenant from the state of Colorado, named Henry Rosenzweig. Henry was the first American Jew she had ever met, and after a while, after the usual while of words and eyes, coffee and wine, gestures shared and completed, after all that while she let him know that she was Jewish, too.

'You're a rarity,' he told her. 'A survivor.'

361

'I know.'

'How did you manage to do it?'

'That's something I don't talk about.'

'I see. I understand.'

'No, you don't. You never could. I just won't talk about it.'

'I think you're wonderful to be so brave about it.'

'I'm not brave. I just want to forget the whole thing.'

'All right.'

'So please don't ask me again. I simply can't talk about it.'

'I'll never ask,' he promised, and he never did. Rosenzweig thought of himself as a simple and uncomplicated person. His friends back home thought of him as a good-natured shnook. Both opinions were accurate. He looked at Mimi and saw in her the representation of six million slain, a symbol of survival. Something inside of him melted, and he took her in his arms. When his tour of duty was over in April 1947 he applied for permission to marry her, and with the permission granted he took her over the ocean and across a continent to his home high in the mountains near Denver.

Volume 2

BOOK ONE

KELLY

Chapter One

I was ten years old when Digger first told me about Mount Krn and what happened there. That was in 1969, the year that Karl Schranz won the Arlberg-Kandahar, and we were in St Anton for the races: my father and I standing in the press area near the finish line of the downhill and giving out with the high-pitched *hup-hup-hup* just like everybody else did when their favourite skiers flashed under the banner. The old man was rooting for the Americans, but I didn't much care who won and so I cheered for everybody. I didn't care because I wasn't competing – I was a decade away from that kind of competition – and in those days if I couldn't win a particular piece of gold or silver or bronze I didn't give a damn who did. That was the kind of a kid I was. So I cheered all the racers as they cleared the *Kängaruh-sprung* and headed for home, and after it was all over I cheered for the winner even though Schranz was an Austrian. That got the old man sore, and got me a dirty look. He would do anything to beat an Austrian racer, or see one get beaten.

So I was down a point in my father's books by the time the race was over, and then I made it worse. I was ready to do some skiing of my own then, but there was a crowd of people around the old man asking him what he thought about Schranz's win, about the condition of the snow, about the chances of the Americans in the next Olympics, and all the other bullshit questions that people ask when they don't know what else to say. By that time I had got accustomed to the idea that my father was Digger Prince, a big name in American skiing even though he hadn't competed for years, and I was no longer surprised when people clustered around him. It wasn't that they really wanted to know what he thought, they just wanted to be able to go home and say, 'I was talking to Digger Prince in St Anton and he said that Schranz wouldn't have had a chance on drier snow.' Or something like that. It was meaningless and Digger knew it, but he liked that sort of attention and he wasn't in any hurry to break away from those people. Some of them were journalists, others were old-time skiers who remembered him from his glory days, and he was the centre of their attention. Watching him with them, I knew that he had forgotten that he had promised to go skiing with me on Rendel after the race.

It was my first time in St Anton, and, as usual, I wanted to ski every hill in sight. I particularly wanted to go down Rendel, because that was where the family farm had been all those long years ago before my grandfather left Austria to go to America. It wasn't the biggest thing in my ten-year-old life, but I had been looking forward to seeing the farm, and now Digger just stood there chatting away in three languages, giving his public the big grin, rocking back and forth on his boots and drawing on a long, thin cigar. He was enjoying himself hugely, but I wasn't. I was sore and getting sorer. If there had been anyone else to go with me I would have taken off right then, but my mother was busy holding a different kind of court in the bar of the Post Hotel, and that was the year that my brother Mike was in the Marine Corps learning, as he put it later, how to ski in Vietnam. That left no one but my father and I finally called out:

'Hey, Digger, how about it? Are we going up the hill or not?'

That brought heads swivelling around to look at me, and Digger frowned. He made a shushing motion with his hands, but one of the guys standing there was Tony Asher of *The New York Times,* and he said, 'Sorry, Digger, we didn't mean to keep you away from your family.'

'That's all right,' he said, and he would have gone right on talking, but Asher turned to me now.

'We'll let your father go in a minute, son. Going skiing, are you?'

'Actually, we have a date to play polo and our ponies are waiting for us up on the mountain.' I didn't really say that, I just nodded. Digger had clued me in early on that you didn't mess with media people that way. It's a no-win situation, you can never beat them, so all I did was nod. But Asher wouldn't leave it alone.

'You like to ski?' he asked.

I stayed safe with another nod.

'Are you any good at it?'

366

And another, but I was beginning to burn.

'As good as your father?'

I shook my head.

'But one of these day you will be, right?'

I shrugged. He was getting to me, but I didn't want to show it.

'Well, you'll have to go some to beat your old man. He was one of the best.' His voice was slick and sweet. 'Digger, let's get the younger generation's opinion on this burning subject. What do you think of the future of American skiing, son?'

'I think you're looking at it.' I had had enough of him.

'How's that?'

'The future of American skiing is me.'

He laughed. 'You think you're that good?'

'I will be.'

'You're pretty sure of yourself. Should I look for you in the next Olympics?'

'Not if you have any brains. I won't be old enough. Look me up when I'm twenty. That's my year to win an Olympic gold.'

'That would be around 1980. That's a long time to wait for a story.'

'It'll be worth it. And now, if you're finished asking stupid questions, my father and I have a date with a mountain.'

That broke up the session quick enough, and the old man hustled me away from there. He was sore as hell at me, but he didn't say anything as we carried our skis out past the ticket windows and the outdoor stands that sell the sausages and the beer. Then we had to wait at the railroad tracks for a train that was passing through, and he opened up on me.

'The only reason that I let you get away with murder is that you're so God damn bright and so God damn good on the hill,' he said. He stripped a cigar, lit it, and blew some smoke for punctuation. 'Sometimes I forget that you're just a ten-year-old kid with a big mouth and delusions of grandeur. What the hell got into you back there?'

'You said we were going up on Rendel.'

'I said that we would, and we will.'

'Come on, Digger, you forgot. The sun's almost gone.'

'There's still plenty of time.' He squinted at the sun. 'And that's no reason to talk to Tony Asher that way.'

'He was asking stupid questions.'

'Kelly, they all ask stupid questions, I've told you that over and over. The trick is not to let them get to you.'

'I know, I know.' He was right about that part of it, and it bothered me.

'Now he's got another stupid thing to write about. *Kelly Prince, Future Olympian*. Won't that look sweet in headlines?'

'I'm not important enough to write about.'

'That's for sure, but I am and you're my son. Believe me, he'll write it. You know that it's too early to talk about things like the Olympics.'

'I'm sorry. It only happened because I got sore.'

'At him, or at me?'

'You promised.'

'Get off my back, there's still plenty of time.'

He was still sore at me as we crossed the tracks and started down the road to the Gondelbahn at Rendel, but I knew then that it wasn't for breaking up his press conference. He wasn't even angry at me for mouthing off at Tony Asher. He was furious because I had spoken in public about something that belonged within the family. Telling Asher that 1980 would be my Olympic year might have sounded cocky, or dumb, or just plain laughable to anyone whose name wasn't Prince, but in the family there was nothing funny about it at all. Some fathers, when a son is born, will sit down and figure out what his graduating class in college will be, or what year he'll be old enough to run for President, or any other fantasy that suits the mind. In my case Digger had calculated that 1980 would be my year to win an Olympic gold at the age of twenty-one. The war had cost him his own chance, and he had given up on my brother, Mike, by then. I was the only hope, and there was nothing funny about it inside the family. Nineteen-eighty was Digger's goal, and I had been in training for it since the day I started to walk, but that wasn't something we were ready to advertise to the world. Not yet.

There wasn't any wait to get on the gondola going up to Rendel – more people were coming off the hill than going on it – and we rose up quickly over the mountain, skis and poles stacked in the corner of the car. The hill below us was rugged and white, dotted with coloured candy drops rolling down, and as we gained altitude I saw that there was plenty of sunlight left in the day. On the other side of the valley the sun had been

368

blocked by the mass of the Peischlkopf, but here on the south side the shadows were still short and I began to think that maybe Digger hadn't forgotten after all.

'Down there,' he said suddenly. 'Directly below us. That's where the Prinz farm used to be.'

'How can you tell?' I asked suspiciously. A ski slope is a ski slope, and you can't imagine it ever having been anything else. 'It all looks the same to me.'

'I know this hill the way you know Mount Mansfield.'

'Did you ever bring Mike up here?' It was a risky question. You never knew how he might react to my brother's name.

'Don't be stupid,' was all he said, and turned to stare out the window.

At Brandkreuz we shifted to the *Schlepplift* that took us up to Gamberg, which is as high as you can go on Rendel, and the air there was cold and thin. The snow was crunchy under my boots, and there was enough of a wind to blow a white plume off the peak of the Parseirspitze down the valley. I had thought that we would ski straight down and then across the slopes where the farm had been, but Digger started off to the left, running along the ridge above the slope. I wanted to ask him where the hell he was going, but you don't do that when you ski with Digger. He leads and you follow. I took off after him, skirting the top of the slope until the ridge fell away in the other direction, and then we were running easily along a narrow *piste* that led through a notch in the rocks. It was dark within the notch, and cold without the sun. White dusted rocks rose up on either side of us, and in the deeper shadows there were gleaming strips of ice. We came out of the notch into sunlight again, and Digger stopped at the edge of a lip that fell away sharply into a headwall. He motioned me up beside him, and when I looked down all I could think was: *Shit, this is what I get for opening my mouth.*

This was no handcrafted, manicured piece of recreational real estate, it was the ass end of the mountain. The angle of the wall beneath the tips of my skis had to be close to thirty degrees, dropping away to a chopped and rutted slope. A cutting wind whipped across the hill, chasing itself and raising storms of powder on the surface. Boulders studded the snow as far down as I could see, some of them bare and some of them drifted so high that they looked like the humps of bison asleep in a blizzard. The snow itself was boilerplate, hard and crusty, and in the shadows of the rocks it had frozen over into streaks of blue ice that reached out like fingers. The old man had brought me to the dark side of the moon.

I knew that he was watching for my reaction, and so I said what was expected from a certified ten-year-old wise-ass and *Wunderkind*. 'Are we supposed to ski this, or are we going to turn it into a Japanese rock garden?'

Digger rubbed his chin. 'Yeah, I guess it's a little bumpy, at that. Not exactly up to Olympic standards.'

'Come on, Digger, I already apologized for that.'

'Do you want to run it or not?'

I nodded. It wasn't the first time I had been given a hairy piece of mountain to ski either as a punishment or as a form of training. That regimen had been going on since I was six years old, and I knew how much good it would do to object.

When I nodded, Digger pulled down his goggles and said, 'Let's go.'

He dropped over the lip of the headwall, and I watched him run it. It was always a pleasure to watch him ski rough terrain: He made it look so easy. He was forty-nine that year, but he flowed over ruts and moguls the way lava flows downhill from the peak of a volcano: smoothly and inexorably powerful, always true to the gravity of the fall line. You were never aware of technique when you watched him; he made his own style.

I started down after him, picking my way around the naked rocks and scraping ice each time I passed one. Below me, Digger had stopped to watch me work, and when I pulled up next to him, he said, 'You ran that like a little old lady sitting in a rocking chair.'

All right, maybe I had been sort of standing up, but nobody was paying me to make time on that terrain, and nobody was handing out any medals for it, either. I wanted to tell him that, but you didn't talk that way to Digger on the hill. Or off it, for that matter.

'What's wrong?' he asked. 'The ice bothering you?'

'No.' That was about as nasty as he could get; he knew damn well that ice didn't bother me. He had taught me that one early: If you can't ski ice then you can't ski with the biggies.

He turned away and started down again, and this time I didn't just stand there and admire his work. I figured that he couldn't watch me and ski the hill at the same time, and so I took off right behind him, following him down. I stayed in his tracks, making his moves, checking whenever he did, and I was still right behind him when he put on the brakes and curled to a stop beside a snow-covered slab of rock. I thought I had been pretty cute, and as I slammed in beside him I tried not to grin.

He shook his head. 'You were still dogging it.'

'Then how come I got here right behind you?'

'Because I was dogging it too. I figured you'd pull something like that. You should have passed me.'

We started off again, Digger skiing beside me and whipping me with words: *Move your ass, get up over your boots, get your fists out.* I pulled up and perched myself at the side of the slope. Digger stopped next to me and made a fussy production of getting out a tube of balm and using it on his lips and the tip of his nose before he would even look at me.

'Getting tired?' he asked.

'Just taking a break.'

'From what? You haven't exactly been sweating out there.'

'I'm taking a break from the bullshit you've been handing out.'

'Are you really?' His voice was mild, but that didn't mean anything. 'Most of the time I have to sit on you to keep you from busting your ass, but not today. How come today you're skiing with the rag on? Christ, your brother could ski this hill better than that, and he can't ski worth shit.'

I could have let that one slide by, but I didn't. By then I had learned to take whatever Digger handed out, knowing that half of the harsh words he threw at me were well deserved and that the other half were only the growls of a rough sort of love. But not when he brought my brother into it. With Mike ten years my senior it seemed that my entire life had been spent as a witness to the battles between my father and my brother, battles in which I was a silent, but partisan, partner. There was nothing good that Mike could do in Digger's eyes, and if the old man gave me loving growls he saved his snarls for my brother. It had always been that way, but now Mike was in a place called Khe Sanh, and each night I asked the god in charge of saints and idiots to look after him and keep him from doing anything truly stupid. Saints and idiots, because he was a bit of both and not accountable in the terms that applied to the rest of the world.

So when Digger said that the anger rose up in my throat and I came close to swinging a pole at him. Instead, my poles stabbed down into that boilerplate crust, my skis swung up and out, and then I was tucked and racing downhill with the wind in my ears. I schussed that miserable excuse for a ski slope without a check, flat out and running from the growls and the snarls, flashing by boulders and skimming over ice. I heard Digger yell something, but the words didn't register. Nothing could have stopped me then, I was drunk on speed and working the hill for a run that I wanted to last forever. Time stretched, and it might have been forever, but on that impossible terrain it had to end badly. I caught an edge on a streak of ice, flipped into the air, turned over twice, hit snow, slid, and wound up draped around the uphill side of an embedded boulder.

Digger was down the hill and crouched beside me almost instantly. He ran his hands over my arms and legs, brushed snow from my face, and muttered something about wise-ass kids taking stupid chances. He sounded angry, but I knew that he was worried. I pushed his hands away and tried to stand, but I didn't have the wind for it yet.

'Deep breaths,' he ordered. 'Boy, that was horseshit skiing. You were totally out of control, do you know that?'

I was groggy, but I was able to say, 'Is that all you're worried about? My back may be broken.'

'You're all right. You can't hurt a fool, or a drunk or a kid, that way.' It was one of his sayings.

'Everything hurts.'

'Nothing hurts, you're just banged up a little.' He put his arm around me and pulled my head close to his chest. I buried my nose in his parka, inhaling the sharp and comforting odours of iced wool, cigars, and sweat. Those smells had been with me all of my life, signals of safety, and I decided then that there was nothing wrong with a ten-year-old crying once in a while.

He must have heard the sobbing, but he decided to ignore it. 'What a first-class wise-ass you are,' he said. 'What made you do a dumb thing like that?'

I got my voice under control and said, 'You got me sore again, that's all.'

'What I said about Mike?'

'Could you do me a favour? Could you keep your mouth shut

about Mike when I'm around? I know how it is with you two, but could you do that?'

'I said that he can't ski worth shit. Well, he can't, can he?'

'No.'

'So what are you getting excited about?'

'Jesus, Digger, there are other things in life besides skiing, aren't there?'

That was a mistake. It was like telling a priest that there are other things in life besides the Holy Trinity. Accurate, but irrelevant. He shook his head impatiently and said, 'Try to stand up.'

I tried, and this time I made it. My skis were off, dangling from the runaway straps, and my poles were somewhere downhill. I moved my arms and legs, checking, and flexed my back. I ached, but there were no sharp pains. Fools, drunks, and kids: All three bounce like rubber balls.

But not always. Nine years before it had been Mike's turn to bounce, and he had landed with a thud. He was eleven then and I was just a baby on that day in 1960 when Digger and his older son went up on KT–22. The wind was sharp on a cold, grey afternoon at Squaw Valley, but the hill was filled with skiers taking advantage of a fall of fresh powder. Digger and Mike were near the bottom of the mountain where the kids and the snow bunnies run, but they weren't doing any running. They were standing still and staring at each other as Mike refused to move. He was filled with fear, and Digger was disgusted with him.

The trouble with people like my father is that they forget what the rest of the world is like. They have lived for so long with excellence and fearlessness that they have forgotten that the aesthetic of skiing is based on a man's ability to overcome his fear of speed and high places. There are some who cannot deal with that fear, but for years Digger refused to admit to himself that Mike might be one of them. He preferred to believe that what he had was a moody, imaginative child who needed only a strong example to follow, but standing there on KT–22 that day he finally had to concede that the boy was scared stiff. The fear was too clear to ignore. Mike could control it up to a point, but then the terror took over and froze him on the mountainside. Which is where he now stood, unable to move, his anxious eyes staring down the slope.

Digger put a hand on his shoulder and said softly, 'Look, it's an easy run. Just take a long traverse towards those trees down there and then make a little stem turn. Then another traverse and another turn. Three turns, and then we'll stop and rest for a while. Okay?'

Mike shook his head, still staring downhill.

'It's not that tough. Give it a try.'

Almost inaudibly, 'I can't do it.'

'Sure you can.'

'I can't, really I can't. I'm cold and I'm tired and I can't do it.'

Digger crouched down beside him. 'Try to understand this. You have to do it. Everybody has to do it, one way or another. It's the only way you're going to get to the bottom, and the longer you stay here the colder you'll get. Come on, push off and get it over with. The worst that can happen is you'll take a fall.'

'I don't want to fall.'

'Everybody falls once in a while. You know how to fall if you have to.'

'I don't want to.' His face was screwed up tight, and he was whispering. 'Please. I want to take them off and walk down.'

'You know you can't do that.'

'I don't want to ski, I want to walk. Why can't I?'

'There are a couple of reasons.' Digger's voice was tight with suppressed anger. 'The first is that your name is Prince, and people named Prince don't take off their skis until they get to the bottom of the hill. The second reason is that there are people watching, people who will see if you take them off and walk. Those are two good reasons, but there's a third one that is even more important. You're going to ski down this hill because it's the most important thing you'll ever do in your life. Because if you don't ski it, if you take them off and walk, no matter what else you do from here on in you'll never be worth a damn as a boy or a man.' He was truly angry now, self-induced, and his voice whipped along with the wind. 'Now push off and go. *Move.*'

Mike looked up at him with those hollow, haunted eyes, and time hung. Then he nodded, closed his eyes, and pushed himself forward with his poles. He sank into a crouch the way he'd been taught, but within ten feet he was out of control, off the easy traverse and schussing down the fall line like a rock dropping into a well. Halfway down he ran a rutted bump that sent him spinning in a windmill of arms and legs. He landed on his face, and he did not move. It could have been worse. Only his nose was broken.

So they don't always bounce like rubber balls, and perhaps the trouble between Mike and the old man was there from the beginning, fated to be, but I prefer to think that it crystallized that day on KT–22. All families have frameworks on which its men are made or broken. For Digger the mountain was the only measure of the man, and when Mike failed to measure up he was written off as an unredeemable investment. Not that Mike stopped trying. He still went up on the hills, and after a fashion he managed to ski them. Throughout the teen years he brought his minor triumphs home the way a cat will proudly present a half a mouse or the wing of a bird, hoping to light fires in Digger's eyes, but it was too late by then. Digger never forgave him for that day at Squaw Valley. It was bad enough that he had frozen on the hill and had wanted to walk down, but breaking his nose had been unforgivable. He really made the old man look bad with that one.

Later on we ate the chocolate. That was another part of the Digger Prince tradition: He never went up on the mountain without a slab of Swiss chocolate double-wrapped in silver foil and stashed in the side pocket of his parka, and about halfway down any particular hill he was likely to call for a chocolate break. He did it after we got off that desolate stretch of Rendel and onto the right side of the mountain, skiing off it on a trail that brought us out near the restaurant at the top of the Gondelbahn. From there we skied the upper part of the Brand-kreuz run until we were just below the timber, and then Digger called a halt by pumping his left fist twice in the air.

'This is it,' he said. 'The farm.' He bent over to bury the silver-wrapped chocolate in the snow. Despite the wrapping it always softened from the heat of his body, but a few minutes under snow firmed it up again.

It was easier to accept the existence of the farm at ground level – I could see open spaces where buildings might have stood – but it still was hard to believe that people, my people, once had lived and laboured there. My skis were edged in firmly against the slope to hold me in place and an easing of pressure would have sent me sliding, but men had worked this land and drawn from it, cattle had grazed here, children had scrambled with kites and balls, and women had slaved in the usual ways. Now it showed none of that, being simply a tilted saucer barely indented into the mountain and indistinguishable from any other part of the snow-covered countryside.

'When did they tear it all down?' I asked. 'The buildings, I mean.'

'Long before you were born. Wasn't much to tear down. The house, the barn, the carpentry shop, that's all. Fences, things like that.'

He dug up the chocolate then, and the two of us stood there munching. A gaggle of skiers came flying down from Brandkreuz, whooping to each other and passing within a dozen yards of us. Digger turned his head to watch them down the slope, his lips set and his eyes disapproving. At first I thought it was the whooping that had bothered him, but then I realized that, just for the moment, he was glaring at people who were skiing on his property.

'Digger?'

'Um?' The whooping had faded, and he turned back to me.

'Thanks for bringing me here.'

A grunt of pleasure. 'Everybody should know where they come from.'

We heard the hiss and scrape of skis again, and we swivelled around expecting more whoopers, but the sounds had been made by three sedate skiers, a man and two women, who had stopped on the hill about twenty feet away. The man was wearing goggles, and he stared at us. He raised the goggles to get a better look. We stood there that way, staring at each other, and then Digger raised his hand in a sort of greeting. There was no response from the man, not even a nod. He snapped his goggles down, said something to his women, and then they were off and skiing down the hill again.

Digger looked after them, shook his head, and said, 'God damn stubborn fool.'

'Do you know him?'

'Oh yeah, I know him all right. That was your Uncle Kurt. I guess he had the same idea about seeing the farm.'

Which meant that the women were my Aunt Elena and my

cousin, Anna. We had heard that they were in town for the races and staying at the Schwarze Adler. I had never seen them before, although I had heard some of the family stories.

'He didn't seem very friendly,' I said.

'That's putting it mildly. The damn fool hasn't spoken to me in . . . Christ, it's too many years to count.'

'I know that. I mean, I've heard it, but I really don't know why.' I took the chocolate out of his hand and broke off another piece. 'Do you think maybe I'm old enough for you to tell me about it, or would it be too much for my childish mind to handle?'

'Wise-ass,' he said. 'No, you're old enough, it's just that I don't know how to explain it. It goes all the way back to the war.'

'Try me. I'm bright for my age.'

'Bright? I wish that's all it was. You're not bright, you're some kind of a monster.'

'So try. Does it have anything to do with cutting off somebody's head?'

As soon as I said the words I knew it was bad and I wanted them back. It was a mistake, and it wasn't one of my certified *Wunderkind* wisecracks that I could wriggle out of. It was serious. Digger looked at me as if he couldn't believe what he had heard, and his face turned cold.

'Where did you hear that?' he asked.

I didn't answer.

'There's only one place you could have, and that's your brother.'

I didn't say anything to that, either.

'Well, did you? I'm asking you a direct question.'

That was making it tough for me. According to the house rules a direct question had to be answered. Also, according to the rules, we never lied to each other. Never. But there was another house rule that had to do with tattling.

'Digger, if I answer that question I'm squealing.'

'The no-squealing rule is hereby suspended effective immediately. Was it Mike?'

'Yes sir.'

'Exactly what did he tell you?'

'Do I have to say? I don't want to get Mike into any trouble. He's got enough trouble with you.'

'There won't be any trouble, I promise. Just tell me what he said.'

There wasn't any way around it. I let it come out slowly. 'He said that during the war you cut off somebody's head. He said that you killed him, and then you cut off his head. That's what he said.'

'What else? Any details?'

'No sir, that's all.'

'When did he tell you this?'

'Just before he joined the Marines. He told me about it, and then he said that the Marines were tough but he didn't think he could ever do anything like that.'

'He was right, he couldn't. And the Marines aren't all that tough, they just have good publicity. Well, what about it? Do you think it's true?'

'I don't know what to think.'

'Your brother has a pretty vivid imagination.'

That was an understatement. When I was real little Mike could read me a bedtime story and make it sound like the six-o'clock news. Despite that, I said, 'I don't think he would make up something like that.'

'You're wrong, he might. But you're right, he didn't.'

'Then it's true?' It was a direct question.

'Yes.'

'Is that all you're going to say?'

He let that sit. He unwrapped another square of chocolate, took a bite, and said, 'No, I guess you're entitled to the rest of it now.'

He told me then what had happened on Mount Krn, but he told me more than that. He went back to the beginning and told me how it had been between Anton and Otto, and how the hate had passed on to the next generation. He told me how it had been with Hannes. He told me how it had been, and still was, with his mother. He told me how close he once had been with Kurt, and how his cousin had refused to speak to him for over twenty years. He told it all to me, as best he could tell it to a kid my age, and he made it sound sad. He made the part about Kurt sound the saddest.

'He knew I had to do it,' he said. 'There was no other way. But he's never been able to forgive me for it.'

He looked downhill in the direction that Kurt had taken. He looked as if he wanted to call him back somehow.

'It's a hell of a family, Kelly. We never seem to learn from our mistakes.'

I thought about that and decided he was right. He hadn't said anything about how it was between Mike and him, and I wasn't about to mention it.

Chapter Two

There were gaps in the story that Digger told me that day in St Anton, lapses that he felt were allowable when telling a tale to a ten-year-old. He didn't go into his actual relationship with Cankar's granddaughter, Marina, and he sort of slid around the fact that my Aunt Elena had been his college sweetheart.

His private life aside, there was still more to the story than what he told me that day, but the parts he left out were tales I had heard told round the house for years, and some that I had read in books about World War Two. You don't know what it's like to read a history book and see your father's name mentioned. Life around the breakfast table can never be the same again. Not that the books always have it right. One thing that they never mention is Digger's intense pride in once having belonged to the Tenth Mountain Division. The men of the Tenth finally got their chance to fight in Italy in 1945, and almost a thousand of them were killed there. Their motto was *Vires montesque vincimus*, 'We conquer mountains and men,' and they lived up to it. If he had not jumped into Yugoslavia, Digger would have been with them. Another thing that the books always get wrong is when they say that Digger defied orders from the OSS when he decided to stay on in Slovenia and fight along with Cankar's partisans. Not that he wasn't capable of defying orders, but there was never any need for it. He made the request through radio channels, and the request came back approved, along with his permanent rank of captain. I guess they figured it was easier to leave him there than to try to get him out again now that they knew that the mission was a washout. So they made him a liaison officer to the Yugoslav partisans, and for the next two years he did his best to be a grandson to Cankar, learning the ways of the partisan band and raiding with them throughout that part of Slovenia. They raised all kinds of hell with the Germans by severing lines of communication, blowing up ammo dumps, and derailing trains. They would sweep down from the mountaintop camp on skis, strike quickly, and then scamper up like mountain goats to the safety of the heights. In the warm weather they stole horses and raided into Italy and up along the border. Those were good years for Digger, the best, he later said. He was doing what he had been born to do: ski, climb, and lead men in the mountains. He became Cankar's right hand, and after a while the old man restricted himself to planning and left the actual operations to his new grandson.

During those two years promotions came through the radio channels making Digger first a major, and then a light colonel in order to give him the rank he needed to deal with the other partisan leaders. The decorations came, too. He collected the DSC and the Silver Star for what he did at the battles of Neretva and Sutjeska, plus some bits and pieces from the Yugoslavs, the British, and the French, but during all that time he never wore a uniform or any kind of insignia of rank. He was the thorough partisan, and to his men he was known only as the *Offizier,* although the people close to him also called him 'Canker's grandson.' By the end of the war he was part of the folklore of the country, the only American to fight with the Yugoslav partisan forces, and today there are statues of him in Ljubljana and Zagreb, and there are streets named after him in small towns in Slovenia. All that was part of the public persona of my father, and thus familiar to me, but I had never heard the story about the head until my brother Mike threw it at me, and later when Digger explained how it had happened.

After he finished telling me the story we skied down to St Anton with the last of the sunlight streaming through the valley. The last run of the day has always been the best for me, with the promise of a fire and food to come, and so I didn't work the hill, just let it carry me home. At the bottom we lugged our skis up the street to the Post Hotel and I told Digger that I would take them down to the equipment room in the basement. He nodded his thanks; he was anxious to get inside to the Jack Daniel's, but I stopped him with his hand on the door. I knew that once he got into the hotel he'd head straight for the bar where my mother was waiting and that would be the end of our conversation. That was standard with those old-time skiers: As soon as they got off the hill they made straight for the bar. No shower, no fresh clothes, just a change into soft boots and then the boozing began. Before it did, there was something I wanted to know, and so I put my hand on Digger's arm before he went inside.

'A question,' I said.

'You have time for exactly one. Your mother and Mr Daniel await us impatiently.'

'How badly was Hannes wounded?'

'Bad enough. Sucking wound in the chest. Not much chance.'

'Is that why you killed him? Because it was the humane thing to do?'

'Is that how you've got it figured out?'

'I don't know. That's why I'm asking.'

He pulled out a cigar, his way of stalling. That's another thing about those old-time jocks, so many of them smoked tobacco, and you have to wonder what kind of racing times they would have turned in if they hadn't. Anyway, Digger fired up one of those long, thin Spanish jobs made of Canary Islands tobacco while he thought the question over. He blew smoke, stared at the coal, then said:

'I killed the son of a bitch because he was a low-life prick who needed killing. And that's the only reason I did it.' He gave me a knuckle job on the back of the neck. 'Go get yourself a shower and relax, and don't think too much about what I told you today. It was wartime, and things like that happen in the war.'

After I had showered I put on fresh clothes and soft boots and went down to the rathskeller to wrestle with Herr Czermy for an hour. Bobby – my mother – was convinced that every day of practice that I missed meant five more days of getting the rust out of my fingers, and one of her conditions when we travelled was that a piano had to be available to me. The only piano in the hotel was in the basement beerhall, and in the early evening the place was empty and the piano was mine.

I went through the exercises until my fingers were loose, then got to work on the Liszt nocturne that Kershkowitz, my teacher in New York, had assigned to me as a project for the trip. At that age I was just beginning to get serious about my music, practice was no longer a chore, and I worked with my head down in concentration. The hour was almost gone when I heard the door open in the back of the hall and, turning around, saw that some people had come in. Practice is a private business, and so I slipped out of the Liszt and into Charley Patton's 'High Sheriff Blues,' the one that goes, 'It takes boozey, booze, Lord, to carry me through.' I just rocked along with it nice and slow, and after a while the people in the back came up to the piano and stood around it. They were three young men and two girls, and one of the girls was my cousin Anna.

She was seventeen that year of 1969, and I knew nothing about her save that she was Kurt and Elena's daughter, but in later years I would come to worship her. Nothing strange about that, a young boy with a crush on an older cousin, but Anna was in no way a beauty. She was rounded and womanly but more than a little chubby. Her face was too broad, her eyes seemed never to be focused quite right, she wore her hair drawn back severely, and she dressed for comfort, not style. Despite this, I smiled whenever I saw her, and the smile started deep. She never failed to make me feel good. She made me want to touch her, hug her, talk to her, and not in the way you might think. As I grew older I had plenty of the other kind of fantasies about girls, but how I felt about Anna was nothing like that. She was a peaceful person, and she made me feel that I could share that peace.

But that was later on. Right then I knew nothing about her, and I closed my eyes and segued into 'Salty Dog.' I do that sometimes when I'm playing the blues, just close my eyes and pretend that I'm Hoagy Carmichael or one of those other old-time piano players just a-sittin' and a-rockin' in some waterfront saloon with a cigarette pasted in the corner of my mouth, singing the blues and not caring. When I finished 'Salty Dog' I opened my eyes and they all applauded. They were Austrian kids, all about Anna's age, and they were out celebrating Schranz's win. They had thought that the rathskeller would be open, had found it dark, and now they wanted me to play for them. I played some more blues, just noodling around, and the other girl stood close to me with her hand on my shoulder. She was standing too close, moving in time to the music, and once in a while the softness of her hip bumped into my shoulder. I wanted to tell her to move away, but I didn't want to seem rude. I kept on playing and she kept on bumping, and the three guys thought that was funny. One of them told her not to get the little fellow too excited, and for that she gave me an extra bump with her hip. I stopped playing, closed the piano, and picked up my exercise book.

'That's all for me,' I said. 'If you want music, play it yourself.'

The girl with the soft hips picked up my accent and squealed, 'Oh, a little American. How cute.'

'Listen, sonny, don't go yet,' said one of the guys. 'Play us some more jazz.'

'Sorry, but I might get too excited,' I told him. 'And it isn't jazz, it's blues.'

I walked out on them then, but Anna came after me and caught me at the door. 'Don't go away angry,' she said. 'They didn't mean anything.'

'Maybe not, but they're idiots.'

'No, just jejune. They thought they were being funny.'

Calling them jejune was just the right touch, and I wasn't angry any more. I didn't know it then, but that touch was typical of her.

'Come back and play some more,' she coaxed. 'It was such fun listening to you.'

'No, I have to go now, anyway. I'm not sore, but no more music.'

'All right.' She hesitated. 'Do you know who I am?'

'Sure, my second cousin, or something like that. I saw you on the hill this afternoon, and my father told me.'

'An odd way to meet a relative, no? I'm sorry for how my father acted this afternoon. He can be stubborn that way. He should at least have said hello. It was very embarrassing for my mother and me.'

'All fathers are stubborn, it goes with the job. Where I come from they have to pass a stubborn test before they're allowed to have children.' That got me a smile. 'Don't worry about what happened on the hill – there's nothing you can do about it. From what I understand it's been going on for years.'

'That's what makes it so stupid. Not to speak for all those years, and just because of something that happened in the war.'

'You're not being fair to your father. My old man killed his brother. That's something to stay sore about.'

383

That had been meant to rock her a bit in my best wise-ass way, but she didn't rock. She said gravely, 'Imagine your knowing about that. What an unusual young man you are.'

'Thanks, I'll settle for unusual, and gladly. Most people say strange, and some go as far as weird.'

'No, not weird, but definitely unusual. Look, our fathers may not speak, but that doesn't mean we can't be friends. Would you like to come skiing with me tomorrow? I hear you're terrific. All my friends will envy me.'

'Where did you hear that?'

'Oh, one hears things. Will you?'

'I can't promise,' I told her, 'but I'll be around the base of the Kandaharbahn at noontime. Look for me there.'

'Wonderful. *Wiedersehen*.' She touched my arm lightly with her fingers and went back to join her friends.

It was a date I had no intention of keeping, any more than I would have played music for her friends. Not that I wouldn't have enjoyed doing both, but I had learned by then that those things didn't work out. It was one of the paybacks for being a ten-year-old wise-ass and *Wunderkind*. Because no matter how wise and wonderful you are, you are still only ten years old and there is absolutely nothing you can do with, do for, or do to a seventeen-year-old girl with soft hips and a sense of rhythm. Sure, you can play the piano, juggle the words, show off your skiing, but once you do that you turn into a pet to be fussed over. It isn't worth it; I had learned that by then.

I had something to eat in the dining room, and then went looking for Bobby and Digger. They were still in the bar, my mother looking long and elegant, and more than a little bored. She was wearing a black one-piece jump suit with velvet boots and a chain-link belt. A single sapphire flashed at her throat and another gleamed on a finger. She hadn't modelled in twenty years, but she still looked the part. When she saw me in the doorway she smiled and blew a kiss, wiggled her fingers, and motioned for me to join them. I shook my head and leaned against the wall just inside the door. The old man was doing his act again, and I wasn't about to risk spoiling it twice in one day.

Digger was Vermont-born and- raised, but most of the time you would never know it to look at him and listen to him speak. Tall, tanned, and smooth, and with a carefully cultivated transatlantic accent, he looked and sounded the part of the war hero and ski champ who had in turn become a high-powered businessman and a world-class collector of desirable women. He was all of that, but underneath the layers of acquired polish he was also a smalltown Green Mountain boy, and when the mood was on him he wasn't ashamed to let people know it. Now he stood with a cigar in one hand and a glass in the other, entertaining a collection of the wellborn and the well-heeled with stories of his childhood in Vermont. Wherever we went the people my parents knew were much the same: powerful and respectable, with too much money and too little wit. To most of them Vermont meant Stowe and Sugarbush, Snow Valley, Mad River Glen, Terry's Club, the Lodge at Smuggler's Notch, the Green Mountain Inn, the Sazarac, and places like that. When Digger spoke of Vermont he preferred to talk about bitter winters and empty bellies, rocky fields and beans for breakfast, hardscrabble farmers and local humour.

'Yankee humour has a certain bite to it,' he was saying, 'an economy of language that makes it something special. You take old Jack Perkins when I was a boy back in Sedgewick Falls, Vermont. One day my father saw him walking down the street looking pretty glum, and so he said, "Jack, what's wrong?" Jack answered, "Feeling poorly, Anton. I had to shoot my dog." "Was he mad?" my father asked, and Jack said, "Well, he wasn't so danged pleased about it." '

There was a murmur of appreciative laughter around the room, but my mother's voice cut through it. 'The man was lucky to have a dog at all. When I was a little girl in Belfast only the Prods had pets. I don't suppose your Jack Perkins was a Roman Catholic, was he?'

'Hell, no. Just a plain old Yankee.'

'No Catholic Yankees?'

'Contradiction in terms in those days. The only Catholics in town were the Canucks if you left us out of it. My father was born one, but he never practised it after he left home, and my mother was as Yankee as Calvin Coolidge.'

'And you grew up in a white house with a green lawn and a picket fence.' She said to the others, 'You should see that house. When I was a girl in Belfast a house like that would have done nicely for the entire Kelly clan, aunts, uncles, and goats included.'

'Look, Bobby, let's not make comparisons, okay? You grew

up in the city and I grew up in the country, but that doesn't mean we had it easy. Do you know that if you took the entire state of Vermont and squooshed it down flat it would spread out to the size of Texas? And do you know what that means? That means rocks, the curse of Vermont. Land o' Goshen, when I was a boy there were farms around that threw a fresh crop of boulders every spring at ploughing time. You'd blast 'em out, haul 'em away, clear the land once and for all, and then the next spring there they were again. Toe-stubbers, plough-smashers, rocks that broke a man's hoe and his spirit at the same time. By God, we had rocks, we did. Rocks and beans, and sometimes that's all we had.'

'Attention, please, now he's going to tell you about the beans,' Bobby said, and explained, 'The poor darling claims that he was forced to eat masses of beans as a child. I should have been so lucky. Where I came from beans were a bloody luxury, like pets and bicycles.'

She was an expert at playing the game of who-had-it-tougher-as-a-kid. To my mother this was the highest form of sophistication, a reverse snobbery that fell just short of *nostalgie de boue*. She had no need to impress her friends with her money. They all knew that she had it, and most of them knew how she had got it. Born Barbara Kelly in Belfast's grime, she now had enough last names to fill the door of a Wall Street law firm. She was Bobby d'Kuyper Braun Frangetti Lindholm Prince, the onetime fashion model who had batted around with the Middle Eastern royalty of her day. She was also a whilom countess (the d'Kuyper name), the ex-wife of a Davis Cup tennis player (the Braun name), of an Italian industrialist (the Frangetti name), of a Swedish diplomat (Lindholm), and for the past twenty years she had been happily joined in tandem to Digger Prince. From a son's adoring point of view she was still long and leggy with a model's body gone pleasingly to flesh. The marriages had all taken place over a period of ten years starting when she was fifteen years old, and during those years she had acquired several million dollars (even Digger didn't know exactly how much) from her various friends and husbands together with a worldly-wise veneer that could not be cracked. Despite this, she was never that far removed from her Belfast origins to forget the gamine in raggedy skirts who had rushed the growler for her father at the local pub. Over the years I have heard my mother called a variety of names, but no one ever called her a phony.

'Bobby has it wrong, as usual,' Digger said happily. He could play the game as well as she. 'I never said that I *had* to eat beans. I loved them, still do. Anyways, I don't reckon we had beans for a meal more than ten or a dozen times a week when I was a kid. Breakfast, of course, always had beans for breakfast, and most times for supper as well. You people know what supper is, don't you? No, madam, it is not a lobster mousse and champagne at midnight. Suppertime is six-o'clock bean time in Vermont. Dinner is noontime, and we never had beans for dinner unless there was nothing else around. When that happened it was beans three times a day.'

Bobby broke in. 'You're proving my point. I never had *anything* three times a day.'

'That's not the point at all.' Digger's voice insisted on attention. 'It's not how many times a day you eat, it's how long the food stays with you. Now during the war, and I refer to *the* war, the big Deuce, I spent some time goofing off in the mountains of Yugoslavia dodging my draft board, and the staple diet there was also beans. But what a difference. Those Slovenian beans just didn't stick to the ribs. You ate a plate of them at six and your stomach was yelling bloody murder again at eight. But Vermont beans? I tell you when I was a kid a mess of those beans was solid fuel in your belly, lit a six-hour fire to keep you going, which comes in handy when it's wintertime in Vermont. Which it is most of the time. The best of all was Saturday night when the fresh crock came out of the oven, just a chunk of fatback in it and some cider vinegar for seasoning. Homemade cornbread to go with it and that was Saturday-night supper. Beans and beans and more beans, a real Vermonter never gets tired of them. I tell you, when I got out of the army I sat down to my first meal in my mother's house and after just one taste of those ambrosial beans I knew that for better or for worse I was back in Vermont.'

I sat silent as a ten-year-old mouse, marvelling at the banter of those golden folks of mine, wondering at the ease with which they slighted themselves and each other, and in the slighting built themselves up to be bigger than ever. Those word cascades, so richly spent. Did other boys have such magical parents, I wondered, a mother so casually at home with her beauty, a father so accustomed to casual command? That was the way I saw them then, and even now, fourteen years later when I know so much more and so much better, the aura still lingers about them. I know now what Bobby was and is, what Digger was and forever will be, and I love them not one whit less for the knowledge that they were something less than golden. And in the knowledge of now, not then, I must wonder at the images we have of our parents, and how much we are affected by them. Not what they are, but what we perceive them to be. The golden folk of all our childhoods, how far they skew our lives. And by extension, must they not have been twisted in their own turn by the idols of their younger days? Witness Digger, with his autocratic mother and his easygoing dad. Witness Kurt, with the vision of Otto as a cracked ba'al on a crumbling altar always before him. Witness Mimi, she of the bogus baron and the nightingale mother forever flitting, and finally flown. All of them grown . . . into what? All of them come home in those days from their various wars to their various mountains: Digger to his plate of beans in Vermont, Kurt to the Tirol, and Mimi to a haven on the eastern slopes of the Rockies.

Mimi took to Denver the way a carrier pigeon takes to a cosy coop after a long and wearying flight. For eight years, ever since the deaths of Willi and Wolf, she had been flying high and hard, and now she could fold her wings. The home that Hank Rosenzweig brought her to in the Cherry Hills section was a gem of glass and stone and brick, and a marvel of efficiency. With a machine to wash the clothes, another to dry them, and a third to do the dishes there was more practical luxury packed into that three-bedroom split-level than in all of the mansion at 72 Hadikgasse. There was more food on a single shelf in a single store than she had seen in a year, more cars than there were horses in Vienna, more smiles than a circus, more mountains, more skiing, more sky, more air, more of everything and more to come.

'It's like heaven,' she told Hank.

'Just Denver,' he assured her. 'A lot like heaven, only it costs a little more.'

'Your mother, she likes me?'

'She loves you.'

'You really think so, you're not just saying?'

'She adores you. All her friends adore you. Everybody thinks you're wonderful.'

'I'm glad. I want them to like me. For you.'

In fact, she had been thoroughly accepted and smothered with affection by the Rosenzweig family and their circle of friends in the Jewish community. Still, she faced two problems, and one of them had to do with that same community. To the Rosenzweigs and their friends she was an Austrian-Jewish refugee, a survivor of the Holocaust, and thus a form of heroine. No one in Denver suspected that she was a half-Jew who had never even known of her Judaism until the danger of being Jewish had passed. She knew that she should have set the record straight at once, but the explanation seemed so complex and wearisome that she let the original story stand even though it meant playing out a constant masquerade to keep from betraying her ignorance of Jewish customs and traditions.

Her second problem was sex. She was in love with Hank, committed to him, and she rejoiced in the ardour of their lovemaking for as far as it went. Which was not far enough. For years she had been accustomed to a variety of partners whose enthusiasm and expertise had kept her at a constant peak of sensual pleasure. The overstuffed orifice had become her norm, the fiery nerve end her goal, and the crisp touch of leather her favourite sexual condiment. There were things she longed for Hank to do to her that he couldn't even spell, much less imagine. All the high living had been replaced, willingly, by a love for one man, which did wonders for her soul, but which often left her aching and aquiver. So far she had not been tempted to go seeking after those familiar and forbidden fruits, but she feared that the day might come.

In the cramped corners of Mimi's brain the two problems fused into one that required a single solution. In order to secure her marriage she would have to become a proper Jewish housewife with a knowledge of the customs and traditions, and once having achieved that goal she would be safe from temptation, since, as everyone knew, Jewish wives led decorous lives. If this logic was less than impeccable, it was comfortable, and with such a solution in mind she sought out the rabbi of Temple Beth Israel and asked to be instructed in the tenets of the Jewish faith.

'What do you want to know?' the rabbi asked.

389

'Everything.'

'Don't be ridiculous, even I don't know everything.'

'Something, anything.'

'So give me a hint, what do you know already?'

'Nothing.'

'That's also ridiculous. How can a Jewish girl grow up knowing nothing? Didn't your mama teach you?'

'I used to know.' This was the story she had prepared. 'But I forgot.'

'Talk sense, you don't forget things like that.'

'I did,' Mimi insisted. 'It was during the war, and I forgot.'

'Amnesia?' the rabbi wondered out loud. 'Could it be?'

'I don't know. All I know is I forgot.'

'The *mamzahrem*,' muttered the rabbi, adding another war crime to the account that one day would have to be paid: the eradication of a cultural memory. He patted Mimi's hand gently. 'You did right to come to me. Today we'll just talk about the Jewish home, the Jewish family. The next time you come we'll start with simple things like benching *licht*.'

Mimi squeezed his hand gratefully and said, 'One other thing. Nobody must know.'

'Not even your husband?'

'Especially my husband. I'd be so . . . ashamed.'

'I understand, your secret is safe,' said the rabbi, and eased his hand away.

While Mimi was exploring the wonders of the new world, Kurt was back in the Tirol sifting through the ashes of the old. The war had virtually wiped him out. Aside from his mother he was a man without a family. His grandparents both had died during the war, his father and brother were gone, Dieter had disappeared, and his cousin Mimi was off somewhere in America. There was Digger, of course, but he tried not to think about Digger. Too much blood had obscured the memories of boola-boola and the giant cock in front of the Bund House. He knew that he owed his life to Digger, but still he could not think of him without reliving the horror of that day on Mount Krn.

In 1947 Austria was a divided country, split into Western and Soviet occupation zones. The year before, all the occupying powers had recognized the country's sovereignty, but the occupation continued as East and West failed to agree on the terms of reparations, and any economic recovery was hindered by the division of the nation into zones. Nobody in Austria had much in those days, but Kurt was luckier than most. He had the family farm, he had his mother, and he had a couple of dreams. Of all those assets, his mother was probably the most valuable, for Lili Prinz possessed a remarkable resiliency. She had survived an impossible marriage, a tragic war, the death of her husband and her elder son, and now she was determined that her younger boy would be a survivor, too. She gave him six months of moping around the farm, thinking too much and doing too little, and then she sat him down and demanded to know his plans for the future. He told her about the first of his dreams: to build Prinz Skis into a going concern again.

'Prinz Skis is a burned-out warehouse in Vienna and a stack of unpaid bills,' she reminded him. 'You'll have to start over from the beginning.'

'I'm willing to do that, but it will take some money to get started and I'll need a place to work.'

'There's the shop down in the village where your father started out. You can use that for a while. As for money, well, I can always sell some of the Wangenmann land.'

Kurt was impressed by this sign of faith. Austrian peasants did not sell land easily, particularly not land inherited directly from parents. He was so touched by what his mother was willing to do for him that he told her about his second dream: Elena Montejo.

'But you haven't seen the girl in years,' said Lili. 'She's probably married by now, and besides, you don't even know where she is.'

'I know all that, but I have to try. I just don't know how to go about it.'

It was Lili who went about it, getting in touch with the Argentine consulate in Vienna and bombarding the officials there with letter after letter requesting information on the whereabouts of Elena Montejo, daughter of Salvador Montejo, formerly of the Argentine diplomatic service in New York. It took months of harassment before the people in Vienna were able to report that Señorita Montejo had spent the war years with her family in Buenos Aires and had recently returned to New York, where she now resided. Her current address was enclosed.

'I've done as much as I can,' Lili told her son. 'The rest is up to you.'

The letter that Kurt wrote to Elena was composed and destroyed a dozen times before he was satisfied with the result. At first he tried a casual approach, then an attempt at humility, and then a reconnaissance in depth, and finally stated his case flatly. He told her that he loved her, that he had never loved anyone else, and that in the years since they had last seen each other he had never gone through a day without some thought of her crossing his mind. He closed by saying, *I don't know where you are in your life. I don't know if you are happy or sad. I don't know if you are alone, if you have a husband, or children. I don't know what you want for now, and for the future. I don't know anything about you at all except that I have never stopped loving you. I can offer you nothing more than that, but if that is enough, and you are free to come to me, then I beg you to do it, and quickly.*

Her answer came by cable:

> THANK GOD. WHEN I DIDN'T HEAR I THOUGHT YOU WERE
> DEAD. SAILING BERENGARIA FOURTEENTH. IS THAT QUICK
> ENOUGH? ALL MY LOVE. ELENA.

Digger also came home from the war with two ambitions: to qualify for the 1948 Winter Olympics at St Moritz, and to help build Prince Skis into a multimillion-dollar international corporation. He came back to an ideal situation. The postwar skiing boom in the United States brought a measure of prosperity to Prince Skis that his father had never envisioned, nor truly wanted. Anton would have been content to run a small, successful business out of his plant in Sedgewick Falls. But there it was, a surging interest in the sport sparked by new and easier access to the mountain areas, the proliferation of uphill transportation in the form of T-bars and chair lifts that eliminated the labour of climbing, and ironically, a load of military skiing equipment that the government dumped on the market as war surplus. Skiing, overnight, was changed from a sport for the knowing into a middle-class indulgence that rapidly assumed a set of middle-class values. A new generation of skiers wanted comfortable resort areas, labour-free pleasure, chic clothing to wear on the slopes, and, above all, skis that were easy to handle. The days were gone when a skier was willing to train all year round in order to be able to control the heavy pieces of lumber attached to his boots. The postwar skier wanted instant technique, and the ability to shift his skis as easily as he shifted his chewing gum. It was a time for growth and daring, a time when a young man could grab hold of things and mould his own future. Digger grabbed hold of his by suggesting to his father that they open a New York sales office with him in charge.

'It's what I do best,' he said. 'If I'm going to be of any help to the company it's going to be in sales, and New York is the market we have to crack if we're going to grow.'

'I never said that I wanted to grow,' Anton complained. 'What's wrong with the way things are now?'

'Plenty. If you don't grow you can't compete, and if you can't compete you're out of the ballgame. A lot of people are making skis now, like the big outfits, the sporting-goods companies. The same people who make the tennis racquets and the gym sneakers. You can't compete with those babies unless you have the volume to back it up.'

'Sales are up,' Anton pointed out. 'I'm not complaining.'

'Everybody's sales are up. The question is, are you getting your share? I don't think you are.'

'And you think a New York office is the answer?'

'It's one of the answers.'

'Maybe so, someday. But not now. Besides, in this business everybody starts at the bottom.'

The next day Digger went to work in the first of a series of the filthiest, most menial jobs that Prince Skis had to offer. He toiled in the wood lot clearing brush and trimming logs, he bucked timber in the sawmill, he nailed crates together in the factory shipping department and humped the finished products down to the railroad depot. The work was not unfamiliar to him. It entailed the same sort of odd jobs he had done as a teenager after school, helping out in the family business for pennies. He was being paid more than pennies now, but the work was the same. For six months he did it all cheerfully. He looked upon it as a form of initiation, and the physical effort was no hardship after the mountains of Yugoslavia. But when there was no sign of change after six months he went to his father and asked how much longer the game was going to continue.

'You can't run before you walk,' Anton told him. 'Besides, it's good experience, and the outdoor work keeps you in shape.'

'I don't need the exercise, Pop. I'm in great shape as it is.'

'Good. So how does it look for the Olympic team?'

'They announce the team in the autumn. Look, don't distract me, okay? When are you going to move me into the office?'

'Pretty soon. After a while.'

Digger shook his head. 'That's not good enough. It's Mom, isn't it?'

'What are you talking about?'

'She doesn't want me on the inside. She doesn't want me where the decisions are made.'

'I run things around here, not your mother,' said Anton, but he looked away as he said it.

'All right, have it your way, but do you realize how much talent you're wasting?'

'You have talent? You learned how to play the fiddle?'

'Not that kind of talent, Pop. Look, what do you think I did during the war? I ran a band of more than forty guerrillas, a bunch of cutthroats, outlaws. I got them to work together, to work with the other bands, to do things efficiently. I ran the most destructive bunch of thugs you'd ever want to meet, and I ran them damn well. Doesn't that mean anything to you?'

'I know you were a good soldier, Digger. But we're talking about business, not war.'

'We're talking about getting things done. That's my talent.'

'What things?'

'Anything. That's what I've been doing for the past few years, making sure that things got done right. It's not something that everybody can do. It's a talent, and I've got it, and I want to use it.'

'I see.' Anton fiddled with the papers on his desk, reached for his pipe, put it down, and looked out the window. Sunlight glinted on his glasses. 'Maybe you've got something I don't know about. I'm not saying no. But right now it's not so easy for me to make changes.'

'You mean she won't let you.'

'Don't sass me, you're not big enough, not yet. What I'm saying is I can't make any changes now. The outside work, okay, that's finished. You'll come into the office next Monday, but don't expect any more than that. New York? Maybe someday, but not now. Right now you just concentrate on learning the ropes and getting ready for St Moritz. The rest of it, using what you call your talent, that will have to come later.'

394

'It's not enough, Pop.'

'Maybe so, but that's the way it has to be.'

Digger felt his jaw clench, and he relaxed the muscles there. He was tempted to stand up, make one short, pungent announcement, and walk away from the situation. He knew that his father was the strongest, most dependable man he would ever know, yet his mother could run him like a trotting pony. Then he saw his father looking at him anxiously, as if he knew what was going through his mind, and he felt the warmth and love that flowed from the man.

'All right, Pop,' he said quietly. 'We'll do it your way. For a while.'

That autumn Digger was named to the Olympic Ski Team, and in the winter he and almost nine hundred other athletes gathered at St Moritz for the first postwar Winter Games. The Hero of Yugoslavia and the man who schussed the headwall of Tuckerman's Ravine drew the attention of the press, but he refused to make any predictions of victory. Privately he felt that at twenty-eight he lacked the last fraction of reflex, the tiny extra spurt of energy that a winner has to have. He was still a magnificent skier, but now there were other skiers equally capable, and they weren't twenty-eight years old.

'I might get lucky,' he told some of the reporters in confidence, 'but keep your eyes on this girl Gretchen Fraser. Her training times have been terrific, and she just might do it for our women.'

In the end he was right on both counts. Gretchen Fraser took gold in the women's slalom, the first American ever to win a medal in Alpine skiing, and Digger finished nowhere at all. Henri Oreiller of France and Edi Reinalter of Switzerland were the men's gold medallists, and the best American finisher was Jack Reddish, who came in seventh in the slalom. Digger finished twelfth in the slalom and ninth in the downhill, and on the last day of the Games he announced his retirement from competition to the reporters gathered in the lobby of the Hotel Belvedere.

'From now on I'm strictly a recreational skier,' he told them. 'During the week I'll help my father make skis, and on the weekends I'll wear out a pair or two. But no more racing.'

'Digger,' he was asked, 'do you feel bitter about not getting your chance back in 1940? You were a sure winner then.'

'There's no such thing as a sure winner in this sport,' he said. As he spoke his eyes roamed around the room. A small crowd had gathered to listen to the impromptu press conference. 'There are too many variables in skiing. But am I bitter? Hell, I don't know. Ever since I was a little kid my goal was an Olympic medal. I worked and trained for it, and sure, I had a good shot at it, but then the war came along and we all had more important things to worry about. Now? Well, we all saw what happened on the hill this week. It's a sport for kids, and I'm not a kid any more.'

Someone called, 'What are your plans now, Digger?'

'Wine, women, and song, and as I said before, the Prince Ski Company. That'll keep me busy for a while.' He paused for effect. 'Oh, and one other thing. I had my chance and I missed it, but that doesn't mean that someday there won't be a kid named Prince with a gold medal around his neck. You'll have to wait a while to see it happen, but when it does, remember that I called the shot.'

There was a buzz among the reporters, and one asked, 'Digger, does that mean that – '

'It means what you want it to mean,' said Digger, laughing, and the press conference was over. When the reporters had scattered he was approached by a tall, grey-haired man in his fifties, who introduced himself as Philip Lindholm. The name was familiar to Digger for two reasons. Lindholm was a Swedish diplomat and a distinguished mountaineer, a climber more than a skier. He was also renowned as the fourth husband of Barbara Kelly, the fashion model who occupied so much space in the gossip columns.

'My congratulations,' said Lindholm, 'on the end of an impressive career.'

'Not as impressive as it should have been, but thanks anyway.'

'No, Mr Prince, "impressive" is the word. You never won your medal, but you won't be soon forgotten. I wonder if I could persuade you to have a drink with my wife and me. She's sitting right over there and I'm sure she'd be pleased to meet you.'

'Thank you, you're very kind.'

A week later Digger was to say to Barbara d'Kuyper Braun Frangetti Lindholm, 'That first time we met I almost jumped you right there in the bar of the Belvedere. Christ, you looked so good, so full of juice. I almost did it right then and there.'

And she was to tell him, 'You *did* do it, you animal. You did it with your eyes. That's the first time I was ever fucked by somebody's eyes. I've seen men undress me with their eyes, but this was different. I actually came.'

'With Philip sitting right there and looking so bloody pompous and proud. As if he owned you.'

'Nobody owns me, sweetie.'

'Not even now?'

'Not now, and not ever, but the leasing terms are liberal.'

But that conversation was in the future. That afternoon in the Belvedere bar they stared at each other hungrily while Lindholm chattered on about mountaineering and Digger made absent replies. He could not take his eyes off her, and he was barely aware of it when Lindholm suggested that he come down to their chalet outside Sion for a few days of skiing and climbing. When the words finally registered, he started, and said, 'You mean now? Right away?'

'We're driving back in the morning if you'd care to come with us,' said Lindholm. 'I can't promise you anything exciting, but we should be able to get in a good climb or two. Might even do the Grünhorn if the weather is right.'

'Is that ski climbing?'

'Skis and skins, although it's a rope climb on the upper pitches.'

'Do say yes,' said Bobby. 'We'd love to have you.'

Digger looked at her carefully, searching for a sign, but her eyes were guileless. 'I don't know,' he said, 'I haven't done any climbing since the war. The past few years I've been going down the mountain, not up it.'

'It's not something one forgets,' said Lindholm. 'You needn't worry about equipment; we have everything you'd need.'

Bobby lifted her glass and looked at him over the rim as she took a sip. 'Come on, it should be exciting. That is, if you're as good at going up as you are at going down.'

Digger felt the surge inside him and fought to keep it from showing. 'Do you climb, too?' he asked.

'Of course she does,' said her husband. 'Quite adeptly.'

'Thank you, darling, but I just do what I have to do to get where I'm going.' Her eyes turned to Digger again, and this

397

time there was no mistaking her look. 'How about it, Mr Prince, are you coming along?'

'I wouldn't dream of saying no.'

The next morning they drove almost as far as Sion, and then south past Zina to where the Lindholms had their chalet: a classic structure of stone and timber with a batlike overhang. They rested during the afternoon and gathered at dinner to discuss the next day's climb up Grünhorn.

'It should make a pleasant little outing,' said Lindholm, his eyes on the decanter as he poured the wine. 'Nothing really strenuous. There's a four-man bivi where we can spend the night and then go on to the summit the next day. Not one of your luxury bivis, I'm afraid, just a humble hut. No guardian, either, so we'll have to cook our own dinner, but roughing it a bit shouldn't do us any harm.'

'I'm sure that Digger has roughed it before,' said Bobby. They were on first names by then.

'Yes . . . er . . . of course, Yugoslavia and all that. Well, shall we discuss the equipment?'

It was more a lecture than a discussion as Lindholm held forth on the relative merits of flexible Nordic skis versus the Alpine type, old-fashioned sealskins as opposed to plush, and *Harscheisen*, the little metal teeth that slid under the boot instead of the conventional crampons. Digger studied the couple as his host rambled on. Lindholm was at least twenty years older than his wife, fit for his age and distinguished in appearance, but not the sort of person one would expect to find married to the notorious Bobby Kelly. From the gossip columns and the magazine stories he knew that she was twenty-five and had been married to the first of her several husbands at the age of fifteen. Her marriages lasted for two years on the average, and no amount of legal formalities had kept her from occupying, at least in rumour, some of the fanciest beds in Western Europe. She had dressed for the evening in a long wool skirt of a smoky colour and a satin blouse that clung closely. She had the full and confident figure of a woman who knows that whatever the fad may be she will always be in fashion. He felt his throat close up with excitement and he wondered if the Lindholms shared the same bedroom. He decided that they did not, and at the same time decided that he would not do anything that might make him look foolish. Wait, he counselled himself. If she's so damn confident let her make the first move.

She made it in spectacular fashion. Early the next morning they took uphill transport as far as the ridge at Moran, and started the climb from there. It was not a good morning. There was no sun, the clouds were locked in solidly, and the air was wet and cottony with the feel of fog to come. They all felt it as they stood in the lee of a slatted snow fence, checking equipment before starting the climb. Philip snorted in huge scoops of air through his nose, letting it out slowly, tasing and sampling.

'It certainly smells like fog,' he said, frowning. 'I wonder if we should start up at all.'

'It's your mountain,' said Digger. 'Up to you.'

Bobby, adjusting a ski binding, looked up in annoyance. 'Did they forecast fog on the weather?'

'No mention of it.'

'Then what are you worried about? Let's go.'

Philip and Digger looked at each other, and Digger shrugged. 'Might as well make a start,' said Philip. 'If it comes up fog we can always come down.'

They started up on sealskin-covered skis, working away from the ridge at Moran and climbing to the first of the open snow meadows that rise there like steps. There is a rhythm to climbing on skis that starts with the swing of the thigh, the arc of the ankle, the gripping of skins on snow. Push, and pole and push. It is a relaxing rhythm timed to the beat of the heart, and the swing of the peaks that circle above in the sky like the masts of a ship at sea. Once learned, it remains, programmed into the flex of the muscle, the stretch of the skin, and Digger had not forgotten it. He climbed easily behind Bobby, with Philip leading. The smell and the taste of oncoming fog were clear now, and he tried to ignore it. It smelled and tasted much like the fog of that day on Mount Krn.

They climbed for an hour to the mountain brook at the twenty-five-hundred-metre line and rested there, eating chocolate. Digger cleared snow from a rock beside the run of black water that bubbled out of nowhere. They sat on the rock with their faces seeking the invisible sun. The wind was low, and beyond its murmur and the tinkle of the brook the silence was absolute. Bobby sat in a graceful sprawl, nibbling on a square of chocolate. She seemed to be waiting for something. Philip

shifted his position on the rock to stare downhill. He cupped
his chin in his hands, his eyes intent on the slopes below. He
nodded slowly, as if in answer to an unasked question.

'Yes, there it is, all right,' he said. 'Fog coming up. I was
afraid of that.'

Then they could see it, grey-white tentacles curling up from
the valley floor, sheets of it already slathered over the lower
reaches of the mountain. It was moving quickly, visibly, rising
up the hill like bathwater filling a tub. The air was suddenly
warmer, and Digger felt moisture slide along his skin.

'What a pity,' said Philip. 'I was looking forward to the climb.
We'd best start down before it gets much higher.'

'Do we really have to?' asked Bobby. 'What a bore.'

'Afraid so, darling. Wouldn't want to get caught in that stuff.'

'Couldn't we outclimb it?'

Philip took a critical look below. 'Might possibly, but I
wouldn't want to risk it. No, down we go.'

Bobby slammed her small fist on her knee. 'Damn, what a
stupid way to spend the day.'

'Sorry, darling.'

'But it's only two more hours to the bivi.' She looked at
Digger. 'Do you think we have to go down?'

The move was so unexpected that it was startling. There could
be only one leader on a climb, even a simple one such as this,
and his orders were to be followed without question. Digger
buried a grin. She wasn't being very delicate about it. He shook
his head and said, 'It's Philip's climb, Bobby. What he says
goes.'

'But it doesn't make any sense.' She was looking at him
fixedly, and he knew he was being tested. 'If we go down now
we'll be going down into the fog. What's so great about that?'

Philip shook his head impatiently. 'We shan't be in it for very
long and we'll be at a safer level. Digger, we'll descend in
reverse order, you leading.'

Digger didn't move. His mountain instincts told him that
Philip was probably right, but another instinct was riding him
now. 'Bobby has a point,' he said. 'We can be at the bivi in a
couple of hours and we'll be safe there.'

Philip looked at him in surprise, and his lips pursed up as if
he had bitten into something sour. 'Are you questioning my
judgement?'

'Not at all. Just pointing out the obvious.'

'And what do we do when we get there?'

'We can wait out the fog in the hut. Once it clears we can either go on to the top, or come down.'

'I've seen fog on this mountain that's lasted for days. No, it's out of the question. We're going down.'

Digger stood up and stretched. 'With all respect, Philip, I think I'll keep on climbing. It would be a shame to lose the day.'

'As you wish,' Philip said stiffly. 'Bobby, we'll be going now.'

'Darling, I think not,' she said. 'I rather agree with Digger. I'll keep climbing, too.'

Philip's face went blank. He was silent for a long moment before he said, 'Are you sure that you know what you're doing?'

'Oh dear, so dramatic. Yes, I'm quite sure, Philip. Now be a lamb and don't worry about me. I'll be perfectly safe with Digger.'

Philip stood without moving. He clearly wanted to change his mind and continue the climb, but there was no way that he could do that gracefully, and grace was one of the pillars that supported him. He picked up his rucksack and hesitated. For the first time his face reflected his age.

'Very well,' he said. He slipped on his pack and bent to strip the sealskins from his skis. He straightened up and looked at Bobby again. She stared back coolly. 'Very well.'

They watched as he skied away from the brook and down into the lap of the snow meadow below. They watched until he had crested the ridge there and dropped out of sight. Then Digger turned to Bobby and said, 'If you ever did that to me I'd kill you.'

She smiled at him sweetly. 'No, you wouldn't. You wouldn't do what Philip just did, but you wouldn't kill me, either. I know exactly what you'd do.'

'And what's that?'

She told him clinically, and in detail, exactly what he was going to do to her in just about two hours up at the hut, adding, 'Figuring that we start climbing right now.'

He let that sit for the beat of three, then jerked his head sideways and said, 'Lead off.'

They made the climb to the bivi hut in less than two hours, working up across the northeast face until the snow was too thin to use skis. They went the rest of the way with the skis on their backs and the *Harscheisen* under their boots, roping up at the end for a long pitch covered with scree. They cleared the ridge below the hut just before noon and shuffled the last few yards in a suddenly stiffening wind. They unloaded their gear against the side of the hut and turned to face the way they had come.

'Just made it,' said Digger.

They stood as if on an island. Fog filled the valleys below, and they were perched above a sea of rolling white. Other islands circled around them, the peaks of lower mountains poking through the surface of the fog. They were alone, and in silence.

'It will be up here in another hour,' Bobby said happily. 'Then we're locked in tight.'

'You sound as if you planned it that way.'

She gave him the grin of a little girl, not at all sophisticated. 'No, I'm not that good,' she said, 'but I certainly hoped it that way.'

The interior of the hut was one large room with four beds, a table and chairs, and an elementary kitchen. The sanitary facilities were out the back, and primitive. They brought their gear inside, and while Bobby unloaded her rucksack, Digger made a fire in the hearth with logs so precious that gnomelike porters would have to be hired to haul replacements up.

'Bloody hell,' said Bobby. He turned to see her staring into her open rucksack propped on the table. 'What rotten luck. All the food was in Philip's pack. There was a chicken, a pâté, and a cheese.'

'Great planning. What's in yours?'

She peered into the pack. 'It appears to be two bottles of bubbly and my diaphragm.'

'Christ.'

'What's wrong? Not enough champagne?'

'I wasn't very hungry anyway.' He came over to her and put his arms around her. She smelled of clean sweat, soap, and musk. She lifted her face to be kissed. After a moment, he said, 'I'll pop the cork if you'll pop . . . no, that doesn't work out, does it? I'll open the wine if you'll close the . . . no, that's no good either. What I'm trying to say is that I'll handle the wine if you'll handle the rest of it.'

'You brute,' she said, giggling. 'No preliminaries?'

'I kissed you once and I made you laugh twice. Aren't those preliminaries?'

'Close enough. Open the wine and turn your back.'

When she said that he could turn around again she was in the bed closest to the fire with the cover pulled up to her chin. He found cups in which to pour the champagne and brought them over to the bed. Her hand snaked out from under the covers, and he gave one to her. She took a sip, then another, and put the cup on the floor. She threw back the blankets and stretched herself out for him to see.

'You're right,' she said. 'Enough with the preliminaries.'

They spent the afternoon sipping champagne, making love and telling each other what extraordinarily fine folk they were, he so this and she so that, and both of them so well together. Mutual discoveries and compliments, the pride of healthy animals. They told each other that they could go on like this forever, and would if only the fog stayed put, but after a while they had to admit that they were hungry.

'Emergency rations,' said Digger. 'They must have something stashed away up here.'

'Stashed. Is that an American word?'

'I guess so.'

'I adore it. Sounds so lascivious. You stash me, and I'll stash you, and after that we'll both stash the butler.'

He poked her in the ribs. 'Start checking the cupboards.'

What they found was a blackened frying pan, some bent knives and forks, a can of Danish bacon, and six cans of beans. Bobby made a face when she saw the meagre supplies.

'Philip can be impossible at times,' she said. 'He must have known the food was in his pack. Beans, indeed.'

'You got something against beans?' Wearing a blanket as a toga, Digger was already at work opening cans and heating the pan on the butane stove.

'Not exactly one of my favourites.'

'Too plebeian for you?'

'I wouldn't put it quite that way.'

'Come on, admit it, beans are for the common people, right?'

A look of annoyance crossed her face. 'What on earth are you talking about?'

'I'm talking about culinary snobbery, that's what.' He was dicing bacon and shovelling it into the pan. 'Listen to me,

403

madam, where I come from the noble bean is the staple food of the diet, beloved by rich and poor alike for its delicate taste and meaty texture. Strong men exist on beans, striplings thrive on them, and ancient gaffers happily gum them into a palatable mush. I ask you, where would we be without the bean today, the innocent fruit that fuels the entrails of a nation, provides the energy that chops the wood, turns the mills and makes the railroads run on time? Aha, you have no answer to that, do you? The common bean – '

'What is this, some sort of a joke?'

'Up home in Vermont we don't joke about beans.' He brandished a spoon. 'The bean is our staff of life, our mother's milk, the bread of both our blessings and our afflictions. Why, when I was a boy I had beans three times a day and I was happy to get them, something that might be difficult for the landed gentry, the aristocracy, to understand. . . .'

'Landed gentry, my Irish arse.' Bobby jumped out of bed and looked around for some sort of cover. She pulled a blanket from another bed and draped it over herself. 'Who the bloody hell do you think you're talking to about the aristocracy?'

'You were a countess, weren't you?'

'You poor demented man, do you think I was born one? When I was a girl my meal was a potato, skin and all, and I'm talking about a black, lumpy, frost-bitten specimen of potato, not one of your American Idahos stuffed with sour cream and chives. And don't talk to me about eating three times a day, either.'

And they were off and at it, arguing for the first time, but certainly not the last, about who had it rougher as a kid. Half serious, half joking, it was the first in a series of debates that would continue down through the years until the act was as smooth as a stand-up comic's routine, coming full circle to that night in the bar of the Post Hotel where I sat just as still as a ten-year-old mouse and listened to them toss the words around one more time. I had heard it so often before, but I never tired of Bobby and Digger, the golden sitcom of my childhood. Their routine was family folklore, and from it came this reconstruction of how they came together in that hut on the foggy mountain. Their original physical collision, the bones of the story, are fact . . . Lindholm, the cabin, the fog . . . but the flesh of it has been supplied by an imagination which, I admit, is fevered at the moment. Still, that was essentially how it happened, and although I have supplied the flesh to clothe the bones, I now might wish for a gentler vision than the one I have constructed. A touch of romance, and not quite so much of the animal rutting. Some handholding, sweet words whispered, promises made and sworn to. They are, after all, my parents, and I should like to think that the union that eventually led to my being began with something more profound than Digger's rampant lust and Bobby's penchant for athletic young men. I'd like to think that there was more to it than *hey, let's make it,* and *oh, you gorgeous hunk.* I'd like to think that no matter what attracted them to each other in the first place, some lasting bond was formed right then and there. Not later on when they decided to marry, but right at the start mixed in with the lust and the raunchy curiosity. I'd like to think that after they finished their bacon and beans they sat before the fire in easy companionship, and after a while, she murmured:

'Well, I'm waiting. When are you going to ask the question?'

'And what question might that be?'

'There's only one question for you to ask me right now. You want to know if I've ever done anything like this before.'

A laugh from Digger, a snort of disbelief.

And from Bobby an impatient toss of her curls. 'No, I didn't mean this, what we're doing right here. I mean what I did to Philip today. Cutting off his balls that way.'

'Yes. I see. All right, the question is asked. Have you?'

'No, I never have, not to any man, and right now I'm beginning to feel deeply sorry that I did it to him.'

'Are you trying to make me feel guilty?'

'No, I've got room enough for all the guilt involved. I just wish I hadn't done it.'

'Then this wouldn't have happened.'

'That's the problem. I said I'm feeling sorry. I didn't say that I wouldn't do it all over again. For this. This something very special.'

'You're telling me something, aren't you?'

'I hope I am.'

Neat? Highlights her much better, doesn't it? Or roll it back a bit and try it this way:

'No, I've got room enough for all the guilt involved. But it had to be this way. If all I wanted was a quick romp in the hay

405

I would have smuggled you into my bedroom last night. I wanted something more than that. I wanted to be with you, really with you. Like this.'

'You're telling me something, aren't you?'

'I hope I am.'

That isn't much to ask for, is it? A touch of decency mixed with the desire? And having gone that far, let's go all the way and take it over from the top, *da capo*, Digger asking:

'And what question might that be?'

'Men always want to know about the other men in my life. Most of them want to know why I've married so often.'

'It's a question you won't hear from me. I'm not interested in the other men, and I'm not interested in your so-called marriages.'

'What the hell do you mean, so-called? They were legal, every one.'

'Sure they were legal, but were they marriages? A year here, two years there. Aside from the money, I don't know why you bothered with the legalities. Do you call what you have with Philip a marriage?'

'It's as close as I've ever come to one.'

'Then you're kidding yourself. All you're doing is running away from Belfast as fast as you can, still running after ten years. Hiding from Belfast in what you call marriages. It won't work, Bobby. One of these days you're going to have to wake up and find yourself someone you can live with for the rest of your life.'

A slap in the face, and small fists beating on his chest in anger. 'Damn you, don't you think I know that? Do you think it's so easy to find someone . . . anyone . . . someone like a lifetime? You bloody foolish man, why do you think you're here? Because I had to find out, had to try . . . to see.'

A silence, and then, 'You're telling me something, aren't you?'

'I hope I am.'

And then the ultimate variation. Twist it around entirely, *da capo* again, but this time it's Bobby who has a question to ask as they sit before the fire, filled with beans, saying:

'Something I'm curious about. The other day at your press conference you said something about somebody else named

406

Prince with a gold medal around his neck. Someday. You meant a son, didn't you?'

'Sure, what else? Substitute one ambition for another. I had some bad luck, I missed my chance. I'm going to make damn sure he doesn't miss his.'

'You sound awfully confident for a man without any children.'

'The ambition comes first, the details come later.'

'A woman isn't a detail, chum. Do you know who she is?'

'I know what she is. What she will be.'

'A goddess, no doubt.'

'Hell no, it's too tough to paper-train a goddess. Do you really want to hear this?'

'Yes, I think I do.'

Only the crackle of the fire, and then, 'She will have to be a special sort of woman, special in a way that goes beyond beauty, and compassion, and loyalty, and all the other qualities that men look for. She will have to be special in her strength. She will have to be as strong as I am to keep me in balance. She will have to be strong enough to raise the boy up into a man without weakening him with a woman's fears, yet strong enough to insist that he learn part of his manhood from a woman's grace. She will have to be strong enough to have gone through fires and come out tempered, strong enough to live in the mountains of my mind. She will have to be some of the things that my mother is, and all of the things that she never could be. She will have to be . . . fine.'

And this time it is she who says, 'You're telling me something, aren't you?'

And he who answers, 'I hope I am.'

Chapter Three

Mimi Rosenzweig struggled with the clasp of her pearl necklace, her hands behind her neck as she tried to snap it shut. As she fingered the clasp she looked at herself in the dressing-table mirror, and was pleased with what she saw. Looking at her out of the glass was an attractive young matron with upswept hair wearing an evening gown of black moiré silk with bouffant sleeves and a bodice cut a trifle too low for Denver, but allowable in view of the grandeur of the evening. On her bosom lay a double strand of cultured pearls, a gift from an adoring husband, and on her cheeks lay a gentle flush brought on by her efforts to close the clasp.

'Let me,' said Hank, standing behind her. His fingers took the clasp from hers and snapped it shut. He bent to kiss the back of her neck. She smiled at him gratefully, noting his appearance with approval. Like most slim young men he could wear a dinner jacket as easily as a football sweater.

'Will you be ready soon?' he asked.

'Soon enough,' she said with the serenity of a happy woman. 'Mama will have a fit if we're late.'

'We won't be,' she assured him, inspecting her makeup for flaws. She was far too shrewd to offend her mother-in-law that way. She had come too far in too short a time to risk it all on a social gaffe.

Mimi's campaign to educate herself in the ways of Judaism, and thus pass undetected in her husband's society, had been successful beyond her dreams. Her regular sessions with the rabbi had, over a period of six months, produced a woman wholly conversant with the laws of *kashruth,* the historical meaning of each of the holy days, and the cultural origins and concerns of her people. Her education was limited. The rabbi had drawn the line at teaching her even the elements of Hebrew or allowing her to delve into the mysteries of the Torah, holding those subjects unnecessary for a woman to study. In fact, what she knew was nothing more than what any properly brought-up Jewish woman would be expected to know, but in her case this was a considerable accomplishment. She could speak easily with other women about fasting on Yom Kippur or preparing a seder meal at Passover time, and even her mother-in-law admitted that when Mimi lit the *shabbas* candles on Friday night she imbued the ceremony with a particular grace. The campaign had been successful and the rabbi had kept his word. No one knew how quickly, and with what effort, she had become a proper Jewish matron.

And with the acquisition of that propriety, her second problem had solved itself. There were no more sexual temptations in her life, no more longings for overfulfilment, or for the tingle of the lash. Her nerve ends were insulated now, and her contentment with her husband complete. Somehow, by adorning herself with what her community recognized as the outward symbols of respectability, she had transformed herself inwardly as well. She had made herself into a proper Jewish housewife, and such women were beyond temptation. This she believed, and, believing it, she became it.

Not that there still weren't problems. She might be respectable and untouchable, but that didn't keep the men from sniffing around. All sorts of men, from the tennis pro at the country club to the mechanic at the gas station, the insurance agent, the cop on the corner, and all the way up to the senior partner at Hank's law firm. They circled around her like dogs on the scent, as if instinctively aware of what she once had been. Leo Epstein, Hank's senior at work was particularly difficult, the kind of gross and stupid man who pawed at her under tables and backed her into corners with the crudest suggestions. *Listen, Mimi baby, when are we gonna make it, huh? When do I get to shtup it?* She handled Leo the same way she handled all the others who, while not so blatant, leered and ogled, sidled close to sniff. She handled them the way she thought any other Jewish matron would have handled them: with an amusement just short of contempt.

Fingers to her hair for a final pat, Mimi stood up, ready for the evening. It was a gala night for Denver, the appearance of the new young coloratura Bridget Hollaman in a concert performance at Red Rocks, the outdoor arena theatre in the mountains west of the city. The Swedish-born soprano had recently sung with the Metropolitan in New York and at London's Covent Garden, and her appearance in Denver was the highlight of a patchwork season. It was a triumph as well for Frieda Rosenzweig, Hank's mother, who, as president of the Denver Opera League, had been instrumental in arranging the concert. A reception for Miss Hollaman would be held at her home after the performance, and a good part of musical Denver would be there.

Mimi found the performance disappointing. Ever since its opening in 1941, Red Rocks had been plagued with acoustical problems, and recently Wolfgang Wagner, son of the composer, had visited there to suggest improvements that might allow Wagnerian opera to be performed effectively. The improvements had been minimal, and besides, Mimi found La Hollaman's voice insipid. She knew that she was being unfair – she had been raised in the household of one of the great coloraturas of a generation and her standard of comparison was impossibly high – but she was bored by both the woman's voice and her programme: the usual weary war-horses interspersed with favourites from Foster and Gershwin. The typical mish-mash designed for a provincial audience, and it left Mimi cold. She did her best to conceal her feelings, just as she had concealed so much of her family background. She had never told Hank that she was the daughter of Vienna's favourite, Marta Prinz, and had given her maiden name as Ulm, without the gentile and telltale von. Whenever music was discussed in her mother-in-law's household, she retreated from the conversation by pretending an ignorance that served to mask her irritation at the true ignorance she heard being spouted around her. It was the same way tonight. She listened to Hollaman doggedly plough her way through a programme for the simpleminded, and when it was over she applauded just as enthusiastically as anyone else in the arena. Driving back to town, and to her mother-in-law's home for the reception, she managed to endure Hank's mindless comments on the singer and the songs, and at one point even complimented him on his musical perception. It was all part of the game she was playing, and a small price to pay for the security he had given her.

The Rosenzweig house was jammed with people by the time they got there. More than a hundred had been invited, and most of them were already in place at the bar which had been set up in the living room and at the long buffet in the dining room loaded with platters of meat, fish, and salads. Hank and Mimi worked their way through the crowd to a corner of the living room which the hostess had made her own, explaining to her close family and friends that the star of the evening would arrive any moment.

'The poor darling, she has to change her clothes first and everything,' said Frieda, and lowered her voice. 'You wouldn't believe, she told me after a performance she perspires so much her gown is soaked. Absolutely soaked. Would you believe?'

'I believe,' said Leo Epstein. He rolled his eyes comically, and smacked his lips. 'I wouldn't mind making her sweat a little, myself.'

Jerome Rosenzweig, Hank's father, was a short and mild-mannered man. He sighed and said, 'Leo, just for a change tonight, could we do without the dirty talk?'

'Dirty? What did I say dirty? I should maybe say perspire instead of sweat? Excuse it, please.'

'Children!' Frieda saw Hank and Mimi approaching and opened her arms to them. 'She'll be here any minute. What did you think? Wasn't she marvellous?'

'Marvellous,' said Hank, kissing his mother's cheek.

'Mimi? A voice like an angel? Am I right?'

'Like an angel,' Mimi agreed, also kissing. 'You look lovely tonight, Momma Frieda.'

'What's to look at my age? You, that's something to look at with that tiny figure. That dress you didn't buy in Denver, that I can tell.'

'San Francisco. Last month when Hank and I were there.'

'Lovely, but a little . . . you know? In the front?'

'Do you really think so?' Mimi looked down at herself. 'I don't think so, Momma Frieda, not really.'

'Hmmm . . . maybe not.'

Leo said, 'Why doesn't somebody ask me what I think?'

'Because everybody knows,' said Hank, laughing. 'Your mind is an open book.'

'An open sewer is more like it,' said his father. 'Leo, why don't you do us all a favour and go get yourself a drink?'

'I already got.'

'Mimi?' Hank asked. 'Get you something?'

'Some iced tea, please, if they have it.'

'For what I'm paying them they'll have it,' said her father-in-law, patting her fondly on the arm. 'And if they don't have it, for you they'll make it. Come on, Henry, I'll go with you and make sure.'

'Excuse me, darling,' said Frieda, 'I have to run and take a look at the buffet.'

As soon as the three Rosenzweigs moved off, Leo whispered in her ear, 'Don't pay any attention to what she says. Tits like yours, you should show 'em off, believe me.'

'Leo, don't you ever stop?'

'What's to stop? I haven't even got started yet. And once I get started you won't want me to stop.'

'Uh-huh.' Bored, she looked away. There was a stir of people at the door.

411

'You don't think so?' His voice was a harsh whisper. 'If you won't believe it, why don't you try it?'

She did not answer. She was staring at the doorway.

'Believe me, bubbele, you give me a half an hour and I'll have you seeing skyrockets. Red, white, and blue, like the Fourth of July . . .'

She wasn't aware of him any more; his voice was a meaningless blur. The rest of the room seemed frozen, all sound and motion fixed. She continued to stare, her eyes locked in place. In the doorway stood the star of the evening, Bridget Hollaman, poised there professionally before making an entrance. She looked fresh and confident. Beside her, a protective hand on her elbow, stood an old man in a rumpled dinner jacket. His leonine hair was thinner now, and more white than silver, but she knew at once who he was. His lips twisted in a characteristic grimace as he glared around the room. Franz Harz was sneering at Denver.

Mimi looked around for a place to hide, but she was stuck in the middle of a crowded room. She saw her mother-in-law rush to the side of the guest of honour with Hank and his father in tow, and the first round of introductions began. Frieda put her hand on the singer's other elbow and began to move the knot of people across the room, stopping only to allow a brief remark with a favoured friend, a gracious nod of the Hollaman head, a compliment offered up and accepted, and then the group moved inexorably on. In only one direction. Mimi saw that they were heading for her. She stood fixed, fascinated by what was happening. Even if there had been somewhere to go she could not have moved.

'That's some knockout,' said Leo, beside her. 'But you could give her cards and spades, kid, believe me.'

Then they were upon her, Momma Frieda beaming, her husband and son a respectful step behind, as she propelled the guest of honour and her companion forward to be introduced. Frieda, riding a crest of social glory, burbled, 'Miss Hollaman, let me present to you my daughter-in-law, Mrs Henry Rosenzweig. A great admirer of yours, a great admirer. And Mr Harz . . . Mrs Rosenzweig.'

Mimi managed to incline her head, and got the same in return from La Hollaman, but her eyes were on Franz. She knew that she should be saying something, but her throat choked. She saw Franz staring at her curiously, and she tried to signal him with

her eyes, flicking them back and forth and pleading, *no, no, no.*
Hank was staring at her, too, confused by her silence. She
gathered herself to say something, anything, and then she saw
the recognition flash in Franz's eyes. She almost screamed then,
but before she could Franz dropped his hand from the singer's
arm and bellowed:

'Good God in heaven, Mimi, what the devil are you doing
here?'

'What do you mean, what am I doing here?' said Franz. 'I
manage the bitch, so I go where she goes. The question is, what
are *you* doing here?'

'I didn't think you would recognize me,' said Mimi. 'I was
hoping you wouldn't. The last time you saw me I was only
sixteen.'

'Hoping? What, are you hiding from something?' He tilted
his head to look at her. 'No, you look about the same. Better,
fuller, but about the same.'

They sat together on a couch in a corner of the room, their
privacy arranged by Frieda, whose curiosity was all-consuming,
but who bowed to the wishes of the distinguished Mr Harz who
wanted some time alone with the daughter of an old friend from
Vienna. The reception went on around them, but Frieda was
not the only curious one, and eyes slid towards them constantly.
Hank, in particular, tossed looks across the room, more puzzled
than concerned. They sat with their heads close together, Mimi's
iced tea abandoned on a table, Franz with a very dark highball
in his hand.

'Not exactly hiding, Uncle Franz,' said Mimi, then hesitated.
She wasn't at all sure about the uncle part of it, although that
was what she had called him as a child. She wasn't sure he was
a friend.

Franz read her hesitation correctly and said, 'If you're
thinking about your mother, it had nothing to do with me. It
happened in my house, but that's all. A crazy Mexican shot her.
I don't care if you believe me or not, but that's how it happened.
He just went berserk and shot her.' At that point in his memory
Franz truly believed that was the way it had happened.

'All right, Uncle Franz. It was a long time ago, anyway. You
know about my brother?'

'I heard something. I'm sorry.'

413

'My father is gone, too.'

'Again, I'm sorry.'

'That's when it all started.' She stopped. 'I'm not making any sense.'

'No, you're not.' He lowered his voice. 'You still haven't told me what you're doing in Denver married to a kike lawyer.'

'That's a strange word for you to use. As I recall you had a lot of Jewish friends in Vienna.'

'And I have a lot of Jewish friends in Los Angeles, too. What's the matter with you? It's only a word.'

'A very unpleasant word.'

'You're right, excuse me. It was stupid to say when you're married to one of them.'

'I'm more than that. I *am* one of them.'

'You converted?' He seemed amused. 'You must really love him.'

'There was nothing to convert. I've always been Jewish. I just didn't know it.'

She enjoyed the confusion on his face, and she would have prolonged it, but she could see that her mother-in-law, across the room, was beginning to look impatient. Quickly and briefly, she told Franz about those last days of the war in Vienna, about the packing case in the basement, and about the confession that Dieter von Ulm, born Ezra Weissberg, had made to his daughter. Finishing it off, she said urgently, 'My husband and his family don't know anything about that, or anything else about my family. All they know is that I'm a Jewish girl from Vienna who somehow managed to survive the Holocaust. I want to keep it that way, Uncle Franz. You won't say anything, will you?'

'No, of course not. I won't spoil things for you.' Franz was laughing silently. 'That Dieter, what a guy. I knew about the moneylending, of course, but I never dreamed he was a Jew. What a con man he turned out to be. But why did he have to tell you all about it? He could have left you in peace.'

'You don't know what it was like in Vienna then. You didn't know from one day to another what was going to be. He wanted to tell me before it was too late.'

'Too late for what? It had nothing to do with you.'

'Of course it did. It meant that I was half Jewish, and he wanted me to know that.'

414

Franz started to grin, then thought better of it. 'Are you serious?'

'Of course I am.'

'By God, I think you are.' He finished off his drink and put the glass on the table. 'Mimi, you know, of course, that your mother and I were lovers.'

'Half of Vienna knew that.'

'So?'

'So what?'

'My God, girl, do I have to spell it out for you?'

'Now wait a minute, you don't mean that . . .' She put a hand to her mouth.

'That's exactly what I mean.'

'But you don't know. I mean, nobody can tell.'

They had been speaking softly, but he lowered his voice even further. 'Listen to me, Mimi. It was a holiday in Vienna every time Dieter von Ulm had an erection. They flew the flags and they fired off the guns. That's how often it happened.'

'You don't know that for sure. How could you?'

'How else? From your mother.'

'And you're telling me . . .'

'I'm telling you what your mother told me, and what half of Vienna knew. That I'm your father. You and poor Willi.'

'I don't believe it.'

He shrugged. 'Suit yourself. It's not something I'm particularly proud of, it just happened that way. The only reason I'm telling you now is because of this Jewish business. That's stupid. You're no more Jewish than I am.'

Struck dumb, she just stared at him, and in that moment she believed him.

'We'd better cut this short – your mother-in-law is coming over.' He patted her hand. 'Don't worry, I won't embarrass you. You've got a nice life here and I hope you'll be happy. But get this other business out of your head. If you're a Jew, then Donald Duck is a Christmas turkey.'

'Mimi, darling, I think you've monopolized Mr Harz long enough.' Frieda was standing over them. 'There are so many people who want to meet him.'

Franz got to his feet. 'Quite right, Mrs Rosenzweig, time to circulate.' He bowed to Mimi. 'A pleasure having this little chat about old Vienna. Thank you for spending the time with an old man and his memories.' He winked at her.

To her astonishment, she found herself winking back.

'Mimi, are you all right?' Frieda asked. 'You look kind of odd.'

'I'm fine, Momma Frieda. I just need a little air, it's so close in here.'

She looked for Hank and saw him deep in conversation with a group of men in the dining room. She went out on the porch and stood by the railing. It was a clear night of stars. She drew in crisp air gratefully. Then she began to laugh. She laughed silently, but so strongly that she felt it in the muscles of her abdomen. There wasn't the slightest doubt in her mind that Franz had been telling the truth.

She went back inside. Hank was still occupied in the dining room. She looked for Leo and saw him standing alone near the piano. When she went over to him he rolled his eyes and said, 'Mimi, baby, when are you going to give me a break? I'm dying for it.'

'Five minutes from now,' she said quietly. 'The upstairs bathroom, the one down the hall. Don't follow me up right away.'

His eyes narrowed. 'What is this?'

'What you've been waiting for. Five minutes.'

When he let himself into the bathroom exactly five minutes later he found her sitting on top of the washbasin, her gown up around her waist and her panties off. He locked the door and stared at her crotch. 'Christ, you really meant it,' he said.

She spread her legs and let them hang over the edge of the basin. 'Are you going to stare all night, or are you going to do something about it?'

'Take off your dress.'

'No.'

'Take it off before I fucking rip it off.'

He lifted her down from the basin and got her out of her gown. He turned her around, placed her over the edge of the bathtub, and took her from behind. When he was finished he cleaned himself off with a hand towel.

'Well, was it worth waiting for?' she asked him.

He handed her the towel. 'What the hell got into you?'

'You just did, and somebody else is about to. Paul Moskowitz is outside on the porch. Go down and send him up.'

Leo grinned widely. 'Oh, brother.'

'And don't go spreading it around. I'll decide who I want. Your job is to keep Hank occupied. Keep him talking, tell him you're going to make him a partner or something like that. Keep him busy.'

'I'll talk his ear off,' Leo promised, zipping his fly.

During the next hour Mimi had Paul Moskowitz, George Sterne, Sam Levin, and Jacky Blumberg. She then went downstairs and told Hank that she had a headache and wanted to go home. Mimi Prinz was back in business, and the next day she set out to reproduce in Denver the life she had led in wartime Vienna. The only difference between the two cities was that in Vienna she had been flamboyant, while in Denver she was reasonably circumspect. She did her best to keep Hank ignorant of the sexual parade marching straight down the centre of their marriage, and she would have got away with it, too, if it hadn't been for Senator Estes Kefauver of Tennessee.

Towards the end of 1950, and well into 1951, the best buy on daytime television was the hearings of the Senate Committee on Organized Crime. The chairman of the committee, Senator Kefauver, treated the viewers of America to a display of the nation's underworld royalty as the top leaders of the Mafia were called to be questioned. Nobody said very much, most of the mobsters invoking Constitutional protection, but everyone showed up for his day in front of the cameras. Everyone except Stiff Albert D'Abruzzi, head of a unique organization known as the D'Abruzzi Service. As morticians to the underworld, the service made a business of disposing of those unwanted corpses that are the inevitable by-product of criminal competition. Also, demonstrating fine impartiality, D'Abruzzi provided a similar service for those local law-enforcement agencies that often found themselves with one body too many and no way to get rid of it. Thus, Stiff Albert would have made a spectacular witness for the Senate committee, since he literally knew where the bodies were buried, but once served with a subpoena he dropped out of sight, and no one knew where he had gone.

There were speculations. Some of the wise money said that Albert was in Ischia, riding out the heat. Others said knowingly that he was playing ball with the feds, stashed away somewhere and giving all he knew to the FBI. Another opinion had it that Stiff Albert had been removed from temptation by a friend of

417

the family and was now an integral part of the new macadamized road that ran between Perth Amboy and Metuchen, New Jersey. All the wise guys were wrong. While Frank Costello nervously drummed his fingers on a Senate table top, and Virginia Hill posed prettily in a picture hat, Stiff Albert D'Abruzzi was holed up in a mountain lodge outside of Denver, where he spent several afternoons each week screwing Mimi Rosenzweig.

By this time Mimi was known to just about everyone except her husband as the owner of the roundest pair of heels in Denver. After her opening night at Frieda's house there had been a series of quickies with some of Hank's other friends and then, once the word got around, an accumulation of truck drivers, cops, firemen, and delivery boys. After this blue-collar warmup she raised her sights to include the business, professional, and political leaders of the City, and over a two-year period she worked her way through the male population of Denver in much the same way as she had conquered Vienna years before. She did it methodically, and only twice during that time did she call a halt. The first time came when Hank declared his desire for a family. Determined not to repeat her mother's mistake, Mimi did not wander from the marital bed until she was securely pregnant. She then resumed her activities until her increasing bulk and eventual confinement kept her close to home. Her daughter, Jennifer, was born in the summer of 1950, just before the first series of hearings by the Senate Committee on Organized Crime.

When Stiff Albert received his subpoena he dropped out of sight not because he was afraid to face his questioners; he could have taken the Fifth just like everyone else. Nor had he any reason to fear his underworld clients; the families had known and trusted the service for two generations. The people Stiff Albert feared, and who drove him into hiding, were on the side of law and order: the state and local police departments whose business he had been handling for years. He knew too much about them, and, unlike his other customers, they were not bound to him by ties of culture or tradition. It was time to disappear, and to a D'Abruzzi from New Jersey the state of Colorado seemed to be one of the farthest corners of the earth. With two of his close associates he rented a rickety old ski lodge at Berthoud Pass, some forty miles outside Denver, put in a stock of groceries, started to grow a beard, and settled down to wait out the heat.

That was where Mimi found him, two months after her baby was born. Quiet, generous, loving Hank had provided her with a nurse for the baby and had urged her to spend several days each week skiing at Berthoud Pass to refresh and retune herself after the confinement. The skiing was just what she needed for refreshment, and Stiff Albert took care of the retuning. He was exactly what she needed after a few months of enforced fidelity, and soon she was making the round trip from Denver daily in order to spend as much time as possible with her new lover and, for occasional variety, with his two associates. The regimen did wonders for her, and Hank was pleased to see his wife blossoming again so soon after childbirth.

Mimi never connected her lover with the celebrated undertaker of Kefauver Committee fame. She knew him only as Al, just as she knew his two friends as Vito and Jimmy. She knew by instinct that all three were difficult and dangerous men, but that was all she knew. Their bodies were all the credentials she required, and she used them recklessly just as she was used in turn. Weekends she spent with her family, but weekdays found her at Berthoud Pass, even on Thursdays, which was the nurse's day off. On Thursdays the baby went with her, warmly wrapped and cosy in a folding carriage, happy to sleep away the day in front of an open fire while Mommy cavorted with Al, and Vito and Jimmy.

It was on one of those Thursdays that Stiff Albert's fears materialized in the form of three men who had patiently tracked him across the country. These were no Mafia hit men, nor were they agents of the FBI. They were three deputies from Calhoun County, Georgia, whose sheriff had regularly employed the services of the D'Abruzzi organization and now wanted to close the account permanently. The deputies found Jimmy and Vito sitting in their undershirts at the kitchen table playing two-handed pinochle. They found Mimi and Albert resting from their labours in the bedroom. They found the baby asleep in her carriage with the nipple of her nursing bottle brushing her lips. One of the deputies took care of Vito and Jimmy with single shots in the back of the head. The other two moved into the bedroom. Albert and Mimi stared up at the sight of them.

'Hey no, don't do it,' shouted Albert.

Mimi shouted something too, but in a language of clicks and buzzes that no one in the world had understood for a dozen years.

The deputies sewed them together with neat stitches from an old-fashioned Thompson submachine gun working up and down each spine, and left them dead in bed. The noise of the shooting awakened the baby, and one of the deputies picked her up to shush her gently. As long as she was up he finished her feeding, burped her, and left her sleeping in the carriage before fleeing with the others in the gathering dusk.

Late that night a Denver police car drove Hank out to Berthoud Pass, and then drove him home again with his daughter in his arms. Numb with shock, he knew what had happened but he did not understand it. He had never understood much of it anyway, but he made sure that Mimi had a proper Jewish funeral.

Chapter Four

A fair day today on the island of Ibiza, a day of dry and friendly sunshine rare in this summer of 1983. It was a lovely day until the letter came from the Ski Team. Once each week I blast myself out of the family museum I have created for myself and go into town for supplies, driving down the rutted road through terraced fields of rusty earth, past crowded orchards, down through the layers of dust and into the dusty village. This morning only Justine and I made the trip; my cousin Anna stayed at home. Anna mostly stays at home these days, most times sitting out the days on the roof. Not as goofy as it sounds. The roof is ideal for sitting, partly tiled and offering a view of all of the valley from the crossroads to the sea. A good place to sit and try to figure things out. So far Anna hasn't figured anything out, but still she sits.

The first stop in town was at the bank to cash a cheque and pick up the mail. My mail these days is rarely more than a dreary accumulation of envelopes designed to be shuffled, cut, and dealt away as quickly as possible, but this batch was spiced by the red-white-and-blue logo of the US Ski Team lying on top of the pile. Out of the bank and up the streets towards the *ayuntamiento*, turning right at the tiny plaza and into the Black Horse Bar. Through the cool cave of the actual bar and out the back to the garden, a bottle of San Miguel for Justine and an orange drink for me as we sat at the tree-stump table with the bougainvillea all around. I slit open the envelope and read the letter from Coach Jim Casey. It was the fourth such letter I had received since the end of the season. He wanted to know my plans for the coming Olympic year. He wanted to know if I would be joining the team. I had already told him that I was finished, that I would not be at Sarajevo, but the letters kept coming.

I passed it over to Justine. She scanned it quickly and said, 'He doesn't give up easily.'

'He doesn't understand.'

'How could he? You haven't told him anything, just that you're quitting. Why don't you lay it out for him, tell him how you feel? At least it would stop the letters.'

How do I do that? I wondered. How do I tell my coach that just the thought of putting on a pair of skis gives me the shakes? How do I tell him that I'm too scared to ski?

'I couldn't do that,' I said.

Justine covered my hand with her own. 'You told me.'

'That was like telling myself. It's not the same as announcing it to the world. No, we'll let Casey write his letters. We'll watch the Olympics on television.'

Justine tried to play it light. 'What television? We don't even have electricity.'

'We'll go to Barcelona and watch it there. We'll buy popcorn and beer and sit in a hotel room and root for Philip and Steven and Billy Johnson.'

'And Christin and Tamara.'

'And boo all the Austrians.'

'Especially Klammer.'

We stopped it there. It was meant to be funny, but we had gone too far, taken it over the line. It was still too soon for that kind of fun. There's nothing funny about kicking a dream in the teeth. It had never been my dream, always Digger's, but it had been so closely woven into the fabric of my life that even now, having made the decision, it was hard to believe that it was over.

And once again I was struck by how little we learn from those who come before us. I had learned nothing at all from my father about fear, and how to live with it. If there was anything that Digger could have taught me, it was that. Every move he made was a demonstration of it. Yet I had learned nothing. None of us ever did. Digger said it himself that day in St Anton when I was ten. *In this family nobody learns from the mistakes of the past.* Certainly he never did, not when it came to dealing with my brother. That's something I still can't understand. My father spent a lifetime complaining about how he had been treated by his mother, and then he turned around and handled Mike the same way. He never learned either, never learned a thing from his mother's boilerplate conviction that he wasn't worth a hair from Anton's head. Later on, when it was important, he never remembered how it was on that day when he and Bobby came down the mountain from their overnight romp in the fogbound hut and found that while they had been gone the world had moved up a notch.

In the morning, when the fog lifted, they decided not to go on to the summit. They made the descent on skis, and when they got back to the chalet Lindholm was gone. He had left a note saying that he was returning to Stockholm, and that Bobby could follow whenever she wished.

'Cold,' said Digger, reading the note over her shoulder.

'That's blazing hot for him. He is very upset.'

'What are you going to do about it?'

'First off, I'm going to have an overdue bath, a much-needed breakfast, and then I think a stretch in bed is called for.'

'I was thinking just about the same.'

'Excellent. Shall we do it together? So much more chummy that way.'

'Right, and after that we'll stash the butler.'

They stayed in bed through that afternoon and night, and the next morning Digger took his own skis and went for a hike along the lower ridge of the mountain, down into the valley towards Sion, and back up again. He was gone for almost three hours, and when he got back to the house he knew at once that something was wrong. Bobby, stern-faced, met him at the door, took him into the sitting room, and sat him down before the fire. She sank to the carpeted floor beside his chair.

'What is it?' he asked. 'You look like death.'

422

She nodded. 'Look, lad, there's been some bad news. Your hotel in St Moritz called. They had a cablegram for you. I had them read it to me.'

He did not have to ask her what the message was, only which one was gone. There were seconds before the question had to be asked, seconds in which a choice was made in a silent scream. *Let it be her,* he screamed. *Let him be safe.* Then he cleared his throat and asked, 'Who died?'

'Your father. I'm sorry.'

'Christ.' He put his head in his hands. She did not speak. When he raised his head, he said, 'He couldn't have been more than . . . fifty-four? . . . fifty-five? What did the cable say?'

Bobby looked at a slip of paper in her hand. ' "Your father taken from us swiftly this day. Funeral Friday. When will you be home? Mother." When they say swiftly they usually mean a heart attack. At least, that's the convention I've encountered.'

'Funeral Friday?'

'That's today.'

'Pop. Jesus, Pop.'

She went away from him for a moment and came back with a pony of brandy. She put it into his hand.

'What's this, booze? It isn't even lunchtime.'

'Drink it, boyo. Medicine.'

He took a sip and set it aside. 'I can't believe it. Pop. It's like hearing that the Rock of Gibraltar died.'

She pushed the brandy back at him and ordered, 'Put that down in one piece. You're going to need it.'

He swallowed it without thinking. 'I can't get my head going. I know there are things I should be doing, but . . .'

'Telephone?'

'Yes, that first. I have to call home.'

'Give me the details and I'll get it started for you. I've learned to cope with these Swiss operators. After that, what?'

'Travel. I've missed the funeral but I've got to get home soon as I can.'

'I thought that might be it. The first step is to drive to Bern. I've called ahead and there's a flight to London this evening. From there we go to Shannon, then to Gander, then New York. After that you'll have to do the leading to Vermont.'

He almost missed the pronoun. 'We?'

'Do you want me along?'

'I don't know. Damn, I'm sorry, I know that doesn't sound right, but I really don't know. I can't think straight. Do you want to come along? I guess you do, you just said so, but why?'

'Do I need a reason? All right, let's say that I don't feel like facing Philip just yet. Let's also say that you may need a friendly shoulder in the next few days.' She broke the solemn mood with a quick grin. 'And for clinchers, let's say that I've just got to know you and I'm not quite ready to have you walk away. How are those for reasons?'

'Is there any more of this hooch?'

She pointed silently at the bottle on the sideboard. He poured another drink and sipped this one slowly. He had known her for only a matter of days, intimately for one, but he knew that their sense of union was already deep. Still, from what he had read about her in the press she had a reputation as a casual person, taking men and discarding them on whim. What she was now suggesting, going home with him to Vermont at a time like this, was either something entirely whimsical, and thus in keeping with her character, or the start of something uncharacteristically serious. Either alternative disturbed him. But when he looked at the elegant lines of her face, now formed into a mask of concern, and the graceful body poised for his answer, he knew that, like her, he was not quite ready to have her walk away.

'Let's get packing,' he said. 'They're going to love you in Sedgewick Falls.'

In the event, nobody got to love her in Sedgewick Falls, not even Digger, for they were in town for less than a day. The trip from Bern to Vermont, a nightmare of delays and missed connections, took three days. When the Colonial Airlines flight from New York eventually deposited them in Montpelier, they took a taxi to Sedgewick Falls, where Digger registered Bobby into the Palmer House.

'All I can do is ask you to wait for me here,' he told her. 'I'll be in touch as soon as I can.'

'I understand. Do what you have to do.' She looked around the rustic lobby of the hotel, smiled, and kissed his cheek. 'I'll be fine here.'

Outside the hotel he found a local taxi driven by Eddie Boyce, who had played guard behind his forward on the high school basketball team. Eddie reached back to unlatch the rear door and said, 'Where to, Digger? Home?'

'Home it is, Eddie.'

'I was sorry to hear about your father. He was a fine man. Everybody said so.'

'Thanks, Eddie.'

When he got there the house was empty. He walked through the rooms looking for his mother, looking for anybody, but the house squeaked of silence. He left his bags in the front hall and went out again. The taxi was still parked in front of the house.

'Where to?' asked Eddie. 'The factory?'

'Right.'

They drove out to Brush Hollow Road in silence. Inside the plant, Digger went at once to his father's office, a small room in the rear of the building. The girl sitting at the desk outside the office was Ethel Bowman, who had also gone to high school with him. Weeks ago, when he had left for Switzerland, she had been a clerk in the bookkeeping department. She had always been a bright and pleasant girl, a bit on the fluffy side. Now she wore a severely tailored suit and her hair was pulled back in a bun.

'I'm sorry, but you can't go in, Digger,' she told him. 'Your mother is in conference.'

The sign on his father's office door read: *Elizabeth Chandler Prince, President.*

'What's this? My father never had a secretary.'

'Mrs Prince figured she needed one.'

'Who are you trying to look like, Ethel? Myrna Loy?'

'Don't you like it? I think it's great.' She ran a finger along a grey flannel sleeve. 'You never had much taste in clothes anyway. Or in girls, for that matter.'

'I never knew you were after my body, Ethel. You should have told me. Now you're really coming up in the world, sassing the boss's son and everything.'

She reached into a desk drawer and handed him an envelope. 'Your mother said to give you this when you showed up. If you showed up.'

The first thing he saw when he opened the envelope was a company cheque for five thousand dollars. It was signed by his mother. He pulled out the letter and read it standing over Ethel Bowman, conscious of the amused look on her face.

425

Dear John:

I have always believed that a young man should make his own way in the world. Your father did. He travelled thousands of miles to a strange country where, against all odds, he made a success of himself. Now he is gone and no one can take his place. No one. Nor should one try.

As you no doubt know, for years I have functioned as the Richelieu to your father's Louis in the direction of this company. Now that he is gone I intend to continue that direction in my own right. It is clear to me that were you to continue with Prince Skis the result would be inevitable friction between us, and eventual conflict. I propose to avoid all that. Enclosed you will find a cheque for five thousand dollars which you are to consider partly as severance pay and partly as a gift to start you off in any new venture that may come to your hand. You should also consider it as your patrimony, since I am the sole legatee of your father's estate.

I think that upon reflection you will agree with this course of action. I am not an insensible woman. I have the normal desires of a mother to do well by her son. If this action seems harsh at first, I am convinced that in the end it will be best for us both.

Your loving mother

Digger folded the letter and slipped it into his pocket with the cheque. He nodded towards the door. 'I don't suppose it would do me any good to wait, would it?'

'No good at all,' said Ethel. 'She's going to be busy all day. Do you really think I look like Myrna Loy?'

'Asta, Ethel. More like Asta.'

When he went outside, Eddie Boyce's taxi was still parked in front of the building. He got into the back seat and said, 'You knew all along, didn't you?'

Eddie shrugged. 'Small town, Digger. Where to now?'

'The cemetery. Then back home. Then to the Palmer House.'

He stood for a while beside his father's grave, but there was nothing there for him. His father was still alive to him, not buried under that mound, and standing there made him feel silly. He knelt beside the grave, patted it once the way he would have patted a friendly old dog, and went back to the taxi. At the house he collected his luggage and his skis, packed another bag with odds and ends, and stuffed it all into the trunk of

426

Eddie's taxi. He went back inside, called the Palmer House, and asked to be connected to Bobby's room.

'Have you unpacked yet?' he asked her.

'I'm just about to. I bathed first.'

'Don't bother, we're leaving town. Check out and have them bring your bags down. I'm on my way over.'

Down through the years he never forgot that all she said then was, 'Right-o, lad. I'll be waiting in the lobby.'

They packed her luggage into the trunk of the taxi along with his, and when they were settled in the back, Eddie Boyce asked the usual question. 'Where to, Digger?'

'I'll be damned if I know. Anywhere but here.'

'I know even less than you do,' said Bobby, 'but it seems to me that New York would be a logical destination.'

'New York it is.'

'Now that's a problem,' said Eddie Boyce. He twisted around on the front seat to look back at them. 'No sense taking you down to the depot, 'cause there ain't no southbound train tonight. Same thing with Montpelier – you done missed the evening flight. So like I said, where to?'

'Anywhere,' said Digger. 'I'm not spending the night in this God damn town.'

Bobby leaned forward and gave the driver her full attention. 'Pardon me Mister. . . . ah?'

'Me? Boyce, ma'am, Eddie Boyce.'

'Mister Boyce, I wonder if you would consider driving us to New York.'

'Me? In this heap?' Eddie grinned at her. 'Lady, you ask me nice enough and I'd drive you to hell and back, but I don't know about New York. Trip like that would take seven, maybe eight hours, and to tell you the truth I ain't never been south of Brattleboro in my whole natural life.'

'But surely there must be maps.'

'Oh yeah, I got one of them.' He scratched his chin. 'I reckon if I just head south on Route 7 and don't take no for an answer I could fetch us up somewhere close.'

'I thought as much. And would you consider two hundred dollars an adequate fee?'

'Adequate? Lady, that's more than this whole dang taxi is worth.'

'Then we have a deal?'

'Well, I reckon we do.' Eddie hesitated. 'That all right with you, Digger?'

'You heard the lady, Mr Boyce. On to New York.'

They rolled south out of town, and the trip took six hours. During the first hour Digger showed Bobby the letter from his mother and tried to tell her what it meant. He didn't do a very good job of it; too many emotions got in the way. During the second hour she asked him questions about his family, drawing him out, and it didn't take her long to get the picture. She found it hard to understand, coming as she did from a large and humble family where affection was the only negotiable commodity available. She thought about what Digger's mother had done as Eddie Boyce's taxi bounced down Route 7, and somewhere in the middle of Massachusetts, she said:

'Do you mean that she wouldn't even speak to you? Your own mother?'

'She's an unusual person. I guess she didn't want any arguments. There would have been some.'

'Too bloody true. Well, it looks like you're on your own, me lad. What are you going to do with yourself?'

'There's only one thing I know a lot about. Skis and skiing. That's the business for me.'

'Can you get a job doing that?'

'I'm not looking for a job. I'm looking to go into business for myself.'

'On five thousand dollars?'

'I'll need investors.'

'Do you know any?'

He grinned at her. 'Not yet.'

'Oh.' She let it sit that way until they were over the border and into Connecticut. Then she asked, 'Would you be interested in a partner?'

'You?'

'I've got it, you know. Bags of it.'

'How would Philip feel about that?'

'Screw Philip. I'm talking about my own money.'

'We're moving pretty fast, aren't we?'

'Faster than I had thought we would,' she admitted. 'What your mother did today rather speeded things up.'

'Are you feeling maternal? You make it sound as if you have to take over where she left off.'

428

Bobby drew her legs up and turned on the seat so that she was facing Digger directly. 'Now you listen to me, Digger Prince. I'm feeling anything but maternal towards you. Quite the contrary, I was thinking of something more than a business partnership. Bloody hell, I don't want to go into business with you. If you want the money, I'll lend it to you. It's the other kind of partnership I'm interested in.'

'Now we *are* moving fast. Are you getting all this, Eddie?'

Boyce shifted uneasily in the front seat and said, 'There's nothing much I can do about it, Digger. Lessen you people want to whisper, I'm bound to hear what you're saying. That don't mean I'm enjoying it. I don't want to know your private business.'

'That's quite all right, Mr Boyce,' said Bobby. 'It can't be helped. We'll try to think of you as a doctor or a lawyer.'

'Ma'am?'

'Professional secrecy. Your lips are sealed.'

'Oh, sure,' Eddie said happily. 'You can count on me. Just call me Dr Boyce.'

But there were no more secrets to be told on that trip. They lowered their voices, fell silent, and thought about what had been said so far. In the space of a few days they had sped through months of preliminaries and now they were close to planning a future together. Nothing more was said as they sped through Connecticut and over the border into Westchester County, but the seeds were planted. It would take some time for the seeds to sprout and grow, almost a year, but from those seeds would come the Royal Ski Company formed with Bobby's money and Digger's know-how, a marriage, two sons; and you'd think that something would have been learned that day, something that would stick with a man and illuminate his judgement through the years. But Digger never learned a thing from what happened that day in Vermont, and he proved it twenty years later on that Sunday night in St Anton after the Arlberg-Kandahar races. The year that I was ten, and the night that we heard about what had happened to Mike.

That part of the night began with Digger gravely requesting the menu and the wine list. *'Die Speisekarte, bitte, und die Weinkarte.'* I remember him saying it in a royal voice made grander by the bourbon that deepened its tone.

The words were addressed to the waiter who had come

429

hurrying over to us as soon as we were seated in the dining room of the Hotel Post, I for the second time that night. Cocktail time had run its course, the old man had made his daily dent in Austria's supply of Jack Daniel's, and the Bobby & Digger Show had come to its usual conclusion. Who had it rougher as a kid? They had rung all the changes on the subject, touched all the bases, entertained the people who passed as their peers, and in the end the beans of Vermont had finished in a dead heat with the boiled potatoes of Belfast. Bobby had finally extracted him from the bar. She was sophisticated enough to dine at nine, but not a moment later. That moment was now, and so the Princes dined *tête-à-tête,* with me as the extra ten-year-old *tête* tagging along in hopes of a second dessert before being sent up to bed.

'*Möchten Sie einen Aperitif?*' asked the waiter.

'Definitely nix,' Bobby told him. 'Das aperitifen vee haff gedrunken geplenty. Vun more machen der hole in der head.'

Digger stared at her indignantly, but he didn't make an argument out of it. He took the card from the waiter and asked me, 'What did you have for dinner?'

'Roast veal.'

'Any good?' That was to show me that my opinion counted.

'Too lean for you, but I liked it fine.'

'Any dessert?'

'I just had some strawberries.'

He didn't pick that up, but Bobby did. '*Just,*' she said. 'Does that mean you could handle some ice cream if it were offered?'

'Chocolate chip,' I said, and gave her the grin.

'He eats enough sweets,' Digger grumbled. 'He's supposed to be in training.'

'Training, my arse, a ten-year-old boy.'

'He's an athlete,' Digger said, but he turned back to the card. It was a fixed menu, but that didn't apply to Digger Prince. He ordered oysters, and then brook trout for them both, a bottle of Johannisberger '64, and he didn't forget my *Eis.* While he was ordering his hand wandered absently over the table, searching for a glass. His fingers opened and closed on empty air. He wasn't drunk, or anything like it, but he was accustomed to having a glass in his hand at that time of the evening.

'I saw my cousin Anna today,' I announced. 'Not that time on the hill, I mean later.'

'Where was that?' Digger asked, interested.

I told him what had happened in the rathskeller, and then, of course, he had to explain to Bobby what had happened on the mountain. Bobby liked the part about Anna putting down her friends by calling them jejune.

'She sounds as if she's grown into a pleasant child,' she said. 'Pleasant' was pretty high for Bobby.

'More than a child,' I said. 'She's seventeen.'

'How could you tell?' asked Digger. 'Was she wearing a sign?'

'For Pete's sake, I can tell a seventeen-year-old girl when I see one.'

'More than I can, not any more. These days they seem to jump from twelve to twenty-two.'

'Depends on who's doing the jumping,' Bobby pointed out.

He ignored that one. 'Say, do you think there was a reason why she came by here? I mean, do you think Kurt might have sent her?'

Bobby asked, 'Why in the world would he do that?'

'Well, you know. After what happened on the hill today. Like a peace offering?'

'A seventeen-year-old peace offering. Well, it shows imagination.' She turned to me. 'Kelly, did she look like a peace offering to you?'

I shook my head. 'I'm not going to joke about her. I like her.'

'Good for you. Digger, I don't think so. If Kurt wanted to send over a peace offering he'd send Elena, wouldn't he?'

'That isn't even close to being funny. Look, all I meant was that after what happened he might have felt like making some sort of a friendly gesture.'

'After all these years? You're getting soft in the squash, old dear. That man will go to his grave hating you.'

'You never can tell. People change.' He wanted very badly to believe that.

The wine steward brought the Johannisberger then and poured it for Digger to taste. He gave it a sip and a nod. He felt better now with a glass in his hand. Looked better, too, more contented. The look didn't last long. The hotel concierge came into the dining room from the lobby, looked around, and came directly to our table. He leaned over Digger and said quietly:

'Excuse me, Mr Prince, there is a telephone call for you from New York. A Mr Tully. Would you care to take it in the lobby booth?'

Digger's head came up, and he frowned. Joe Tulley was the manager of his New York office, and he would not have been calling for some trivial reason. My mother put her hand on his arm. I suppose we all thought of it at once: Mike. Anything to do with my brother, any communication from the Marine Corps, would come first to New York, where Tully would field it and pass it on to wherever Digger might be. He stood up at once, tossed his napkin on the table, and excused himself to my mother; but she was also on her feet.

'I'll go with you,' she said. Then she realized that that would leave me sitting there alone, and she hesitated.

'Go ahead, don't worry about me,' I said, and gave her a lordly wave of the hand. 'I'll sit here and keep up appearances while you two panic.'

But I was close to panic myself as they hurried out of the dining room. At that age I was having a tough time with God, trying hard not to believe and failing whenever crunches came along that left me in need of something to lean on. This was one of those times, and against my will I found myself silently praying for a simple wound, something that would leave him with nothing worse than a slight limp, or a scar on his shoulder or a trick knee that would pop out every time the weather went bad. Then I remembered that on the really bad ones they sent along a marine officer to notify the next of kin, and there were no dress blues in sight, but that was stupid because the notice was in New York, not here, and I started feeling bad again, but then my folks came back and I knew that everything was all right. Bobby was actually smiling, although Digger looked mad as hell. They sat down and Digger reached for his glass like a serpent striking.

'It's all right,' Bobby said quickly. 'He's perfectly fine.'

'Where was he wounded?'

'He wasn't. I told you, he's fine.'

'Fine, my ass,' Digger growled.

'Then what happened?'

Bobby reached around to put her arm across my shoulders. 'Darling, the important thing is that he's all right.'

'All right, my ass.' From Digger.

432

Bobby squeezed my shoulders. 'This other business is probably just a misunderstanding.'

'Misunderstanding, my ass.'

'What business?' I was close to screaming. 'Will somebody please tell me what the hell you're talking about?'

'Your brother,' said Digger, 'has managed to get himself courtmartialled.'

Bobby said soothingly, 'I'm sure it's all a mistake.'

'Mistake, my ass. The charges are "abandonment of government property" and "refusal to bear arms in the face of the enemy". What kind of a fucking mistake is that?'

Those were the charges, and they sounded impressive, but as we later found out the offence was quite understandable to anyone who knew my brother. All he had done was discard his M–16 and purchase a lookalike copy of the weapon, a Mattel toy that anyone could buy in the shops of Saigon. He carried that toy in combat for three months before they caught him and brought him up on charges. The wording of the offence was technically accurate, but what they really should have charged him with was learning how to ski in Vietnam.

It started when he decided to cover Vietnam with snow. He figured it would look better that way. He had seen as much as he wanted to see of rib-etched children and childlike whores, blackened skulls, ashen bones, jellied brains, body bags, burned-out hooches, burned-in eyes, and the multicoloured splendour of spilled intestines. He had smelled as much as he wanted to smell of putrescent corpses and fungus-ridden feet, steaming vegetation and roasted flesh, fish heads and sour cabbage, buffalo shit and rotting jungle. He had heard enough of the grumpy coughs of mortars and the burp of grenades, the insane giggle of MG fire in the night. There was no question in his mind that the sights, sounds, and smells of Vietnam would be greatly improved if he covered the entire country from the DMZ to the delta with a mantle of pristine, skiable snow.

Once he had covered Vietnam with snow the war became more bearable. Now he could lie awake at night and ski the clean country, schussing the shorelines and the jungle's maze, skimming down from the Central Highlands to the back streets of Saigon seeing only the deep powder, smelling only the tang of fir and pine, hearing only the whistle of snow in the wind.

He built his own mountain in Southeast Asia, and standing at its summit, he saw the places where the fear should be and the places where it could be ignored. He saw the integral relationship between man and mountain, saw where the mountain had to be accommodated and, beyond that point, where the man could fly free. Doing it that way it all seemed so easy, and he marvelled at the memory of the child who had frozen in fear on the side of the hill. Every night he retreated to the mountains of his mind and ran the steepest trails through to the dawn. It was a hell of a way to fight a war, but it was a great way to learn how to ski.

Having learned how to ski in the mountains of his mind, Mike then looked around for a field in which to test his newfound skill. He needed a practical area in which to test himself, and he found it in that toy shop in Saigon. For three months he carried his toy weapon into combat, aimed it wherever the situation demanded, pulled the toy trigger, and yelled, 'Bang, bang, you're dead,' at whoever was firing real bullets at him. He did it whenever he could to measure himself as a man, and he got away with it for as long as he did because he was only one of many flakes in his outfit. Around that time in Khe Sanh all sorts of people were doing all sorts of strange things, and if Mad Mike Prince wanted to play marine with a toy weapon nobody was going to put him down for it. It was his gig, and part of his karma, but it took only one unimaginative officer to spoil the game. That was the one who filed the charges, and on 15 February, 1969 Mike was brought before a court at Cam Ranh Bay and found guilty of abandoning government property and refusing to bear arms in the presence of the enemy. He was sentenced to the brig time already served and dishonourably discharged from the Corps.

He didn't much care. He had accomplished what he had set out to do. He had learned how to ski in Vietnam. He had done it by skiing the snow-covered jungle by night and carrying a toy weapon by day, and once he had done that he knew that there wasn't a mountain in the world that could ever again freeze him with fear.

But on that night in St Anton we knew nothing about that part of it. All we knew were the charges. Even those might have passed unnoticed, but one of the Associated Press people in Saigon had figured out that Lance Corporal Michael Prince was the son of the Hero of Yugoslavia, and that made it news. The AP man had gone after the story and had interviewed Mike and some of the other men in his outfit. The only statement Mike would make was that he didn't know what all the fuss was about, adding, 'All I was trying to do was learn how to ski in Vietnam.' But the other marines had said plenty, and after the story had gone out over the wires the news media people in New York had gone looking for Digger to get his reaction to it. When they couldn't find him one enterprising soul had thought to call my grandmother in Sedgewick Falls and ask her for a comment. What he got was vintage Elizabeth Prince. At seventy-six, her statement was crisp and clear: 'I don't know this particular grandson very well but from what I've heard he's always been a bad piece of work. Unreliable, as his father was when he was a boy. If he's guilty he should be punished to the full extent of the law. In my day they hung people for less.' It was then that someone had called Joe Tully and he had got on the phone to St Anton.

'Tully's been talking to the lawyers,' said Digger. 'Apparently, in a case like this Mike is entitled to civilian counsel, and we're getting him the best there is. We don't know what the specific charges are yet, but our people say we might come out all right on it.'

I noticed the pronoun. We were going to come out all right.

My mother said in a very small voice, 'Does that mean he won't have to go to jail?'

'Now Bobby, we don't know the details yet, but we're doing the best we can,' said Digger. 'Learning how to ski in Vietnam. Now what the hell is that supposed to mean? Is he deliberately trying to embarrass me?'

'That doesn't mean anything, that's just Mike talking,' I said. My ice cream came. It was a small scoop, but I didn't care. I didn't much care about anything right then, I was feeling so good. Digger was taking it like a tragedy, but it was more like a miracle to me. 'You know how he gets, Digger. Sometimes he says things just to fill in the spaces.'

'What I don't understand is your mother,' said Bobby. 'What a terrible thing for her to say.'

'Damn that woman.' The old man was staring at his oysters as if they were the cause of all his discontents. 'You notice that she didn't miss the chance to take a slap at me at the same time.'

He was feeling pretty miserable. It was a job for the certified wise-ass. I took a lick of my ice cream and said casually, 'I don't know why you're so surprised at what she said. Everybody's known for years that she's a silly old cunt who will say just about anything.'

Digger looked around and decided to swallow an oyster. Bobby leaned close to me. Light touches of her scent seemed to blend with the gleam of the stone at her throat.

'How many times,' she whispered, 'have you been told that you're not supposed to say "cunt" in front of a lady?'

'I'm sorry, Bobby, but . . .'

'But still . . .'

'Yeah, I know, but she really is.'

'You don't know that, you're just repeating what other people say. And even if it's true, there are other ways of saying it.'

'Like what?'

'You could call her a silly old bitch. That would be accurate enough.'

'Do you really think so?' I licked the last of the ice cream from my spoon. 'Look, would you answer this, please? Who knows more about skiing and making skis than anyone else in the world?'

'Your father,' she said promptly.

'And who's the most respected man in the skiing industry today?'

'Your father.'

'And who built Royal Skis into what it is now?'

'Once again, your father. The one and only Digger Prince.'

'But twenty years ago Grandma threw him out of Prince Skis, right?'

'Right,' said Bobby. 'That's when we founded Royal.'

'Which you financed, and which has made you a small fortune.'

'Well . . . yes.'

'Which makes you one hell of a good businesswoman.'

'Thank you.'

'But what does it make Grandma?'

'Oh, dear.' She sighed. 'I see what you mean. I'm afraid it makes her a silly old cunt.'

436

'I rest my case, judge.'

'Wise-ass,' Digger said affectionately. For the moment he had forgotten about Mike. 'How about some more ice cream?'

Chapter Five

After I finished my second scoop of ice cream I was sent up to bed, but not before I had a chance to meet Karl Schranz. He looked into the room, saw Digger, and came over to sit with us. Having just won the Arlberg-Kandahar that day it took him some time to cross the room – fervent handshakes, pats on the back, scraps of paper extended for autographs – but he finally made it to our table. Austrians take their Alpine skiing more seriously than Pittsburgh takes the Steelers or Los Angeles the Dodgers, and even then Schranz was close to being a national hero. He had won everything in sight except the Olympics, something he would never win, but there was a solid mass of opinion in Austria that he had been robbed of a gold at the Games at Grenoble the year before. That was the year when Jean-Claude Killy won all three golds, but there were still plenty of people who thought that the medal in the slalom should have gone to Schranz. He had the fastest combined time for the two heats, but they said he missed a gate on the second run and they gave it to Killy. It was a popular decision in France, but even today there are parts of Austria where you can start an argument by bringing up the subject.

Now he sat and chatted quietly with Digger about the race that day, but I could see that the old man's mind wasn't on it. He was still trying to absorb the news about Mike, but he nodded politely and kept up his end of the conversation. Bobby, too, was distracted, but not in the same way that Digger was. Like me, she was relieved that the news had not been worse. She had always had a realistic attitude about Mike, realizing early on that her older son was a lovable freak who could not be judged by ordinary standards. She had never expected conventional accomplishments from him, and anything he did that came out short of a disaster was a triumph to her. Thus, to her way of thinking Mike had once again come through in

437

style. He wasn't dead and he wasn't hurt. He was just in trouble, a situation too ordinary to be a cause of immediate concern.

While Digger and Schranz were deep in conversation she gave me one of those time-for-bed looks, which I let float by. I was trying to follow what the two men were talking about in a mixture of German and English. Most of it was technical talk about ski and boot construction. The year before, the first of the plastic boots had come on the market, and also the cracked steel edge for slalom skis. The French racers had taken advantage of the new rigid boots and the elasticity of the fibreglass skis and had developed a new technique for the slalom by learning to accelerate off the tails of their skis. The technique had transformed the sport, and every racer wanted to know more about it. I wanted to know too, and so I listened carefully, but after a while they got away from construction and started talking about the Olympics of the year before, the one in which Schranz supposedly missed a gate. Digger had been at Grenoble and had spoken to the officials after the race. His private opinion was that Schranz had really missed it, but he was too diplomatic to say that to his face. Instead, he switched the conversation to the American team which had done so poorly in the Games of 1968. Diplomacy again. The women, in particular, had had rotten luck. They had posted some of the top times in the first run of the slalom, and then all of them had been disqualified by falls or missed gates in the second heat. Schranz ticked off their names: Wendy Allen, Kiki Cutter, Rosie Fortna, and Judy Ann Nagel.

'There was another one,' he said. 'Quick as a cat, and when she came down the hill her pigtail stuck out straight behind her. She never got to compete. There was some sort of scandal.'

Digger said sourly, 'That was Jenny Rosenzweig. My niece.'

'Really? I didn't know that.'

'Not actually my niece, the daughter of my cousin.'

'Well, the blood always shows, doesn't it? She looked very good in the training runs. Too bad she never competed.'

'Yes.'

'Something political, wasn't it? Something to do with an East German boy?'

'That's right.'

'How did it all come out?'

'I really don't know. After the fuss blew over she dropped out of sight.'

He knew, but he didn't want to talk about it. Jenny Rosenzweig was the daughter of Mimi and Hank, the infant survivor of the killings at Berthoud Pass in 1950. She was nineteen years old now, holed up on an island in the Mediterranean with a stateless political defector from the DDR, and Digger felt responsible for much of what had happened to her.

Hank Rosenzweig never remarried after Mimi's death. He devoted himself to the raising of his daughter, and as she grew older a part of her education was the constant reminder that her mother had died in the arms of an eastern gangster and that her grandmother had been shot to death in a sordid episode in Hollywood. It was part of Hank's preaching that it was up to Jenny to prove that blood did not necessarily tell, and the eventual result was a reclusive child whose only interest outside her studies was the skiing that her father reluctantly allowed her. He would have preferred to keep her from it entirely, but in a place like Denver that was next to impossible. When Jenny was on the mountain she was wind-quick and nimble, with searching eyes and lips that were eager to laugh, but when she took her skis off she turned at once into a grave and troubled child.

'She's like two different kids,' Digger reported to Bobby after a quick trip to Denver. He had rediscovered that branch of the family when Mimi's death had made headlines, and he touched base in Denver whenever he could to see how the girl was growing up. 'Her father has got her believing all that crap about tainted blood and the sins of the mother being passed down, yea verily, even unto the third generation. Now where the hell does he get off telling a young kid things like that? Jews don't believe that shit, do they?'

'It doesn't sound very Jewish to me,' Bobby agreed. 'Sounds more like a man who never got over his grief. Any man, any religion.'

'And this business about skiing. If that jerk had his way he'd keep the kid off the mountain entirely. He's got skiing down as one of the original sins. Evil and immoral. He doesn't dare say it, not to me, but you can see that he thinks it.'

'Ida Gaitskill.'

'How's that?'

'Ida Gaitskill,' Bobby repeated thoughtfully. 'Her husband played golf every Thursday for twenty years. Harry was a golf nut. It was the only sport he enjoyed, and Ida never gave him a hard time about it. He worked hard and she figured he was entitled. Every Thursday morning he would kiss her on the cheek, throw his expensive bag of clubs in the back of the car, and go off to play golf. Then one Thursday he had himself a massive coronary and it wasn't on the golf course, it was in some cutie's apartment. That's when Ida found out that Harry never once in his life played a game of golf, never even pulled one of those expensive clubs out of the bag. Thursday was Harry's screwing day, and golf was his cover. Every Thursday when Ida thought he was out playing golf he was balling his girlfriend. Not the same girlfriend, not for twenty years, but Thursday was ass day for Harry. After she found that out Ida never again trusted a man who played golf. It was an occupation for idle, worthless husbands, and a golf club was the tool of the devil. She really believed it, she still does. Now, our Hank has the Ida Gaitskill syndrome, only with him it's skiing. Mimi used skiing as a cover when she was screwing that gangster, and that's what Hank remembers about it. Ergo, skiing is evil, and he doesn't want his daughter stained by it.'

'Snow doesn't stain.'

'Darling, that's an aphorism.'

'It's a God damn shame,' Digger said angrily. 'That kid is a sweetheart on the mountain. She's got the rhythm of a born slalom skier. Quick feet, quick change on the edges, and you should see the way the shoulder goes out in front of the turn. She's a natural, and I'm not going to let that loony spoil it for her.'

'What do you intend doing about it?'

'I'm going to take her over.'

'Will he let you?'

'He can be handled. That girl is only eight years old. There's plenty of time to work with her, train her properly. If she develops the way she's heading now she can be a world-class slalom skier by the time she's eighteen.'

'Eighteen, and she's eight . . . now let me do my sums. My, my, how convenient, just in time for the 1968 Olympics. You're going to get your gold medal one way or the other, aren't you?'

'I'm doing this for the girl, not for me.'

440

She ignored that. 'You're giving up on Michael, aren't you?'

'There's nothing to give up on. Mike will never make it, there's something missing, something . . . damn it, I don't know how to say it. He's my son, but I look at him and I see a loser, a washout. I don't see one fucking thing that reminds me of me.'

'I'd like to remind *you* that you're talking about a nine-year-old child, not a toy that was put on earth for you to play with.'

'Bobby, don't smother me with words. A father raises up his son, and that's not playing with toys. Jenny is a child, too, almost exactly the same age. She has it. My boy doesn't.'

'Damn it, why does it have to be so important to you?'

'It always has been. You knew that when you married me. It always will be.'

'What you're really saying is that you want another child, aren't you? Toss the first one on the ash heap and start over.'

That stopped him for a moment. He said slowly, 'That's a bitchy way to put it. I'm not tossing anybody away. He's my son, and I love him and I'll always take care of him. But as far as having another child . . . yes. I admit it, yes. If we were both a couple of years younger I would ask you to consider it seriously.'

'A couple of years, my royal Irish butt. I'm only thirty-six. Dr Kay says that I could carry to term without a care in the world. Piece of cake, he says.'

'He does, does he? And what have you been doing talking to Dr Kay?'

'Checking the lay of the land, so to speak. Digger, are you ready to talk deal with me? I'm serious. A gloves-off, hard-nosed, no-fucking-around deal. Are you?'

His eyes narrowed. 'What's your proposition?'

'Do you really want another child? No bullshit, now. Short and sweet.'

'Yes.'

'All right then, I'll have it for you. For you and for me, but mostly for you. And boy or girl you can raise it up to be your champion.'

He nodded. 'And what's your end of the bargain?'

'I want you to leave Michael alone. I don't want any more pressure on him. I don't want you to demand things from him that he can't deliver. Just leave him alone.'

'I haven't been that hard on the boy.'

'Hard? You've been impossible. Will you promise me that? Will you leave him alone?'

'Of course. I love him just as much as you do.'

'You don't, but we'll let that go. Just promise.'

'I do.'

'Then we've got a deal. You may commence the baby-making whenever it suits your fancy, m'lord.' She grinned at him. 'My, my, ten years between babies. Not exactly according to Spock, but it has a certain flair to it, don't you think?'

Thus the creation of Kelly Prince, the deal struck, consummated and delivered on time, but the fact that Digger was about to become a father again did not keep him from working with Jenny. At first he put her to work with a coach he trusted in Colorado Springs, but after a while, and after I was born, she began to spend part of each winter with us working with the old man. I don't remember seeing her. That period in her life lasted for only a few years, and by the time I was five and she was fourteen Digger had her racing around the country during the season. The following year, in 1965, the US Ski Association began a full-time programme for Alpine racing, the first ever in America, and Jenny was on her way. She qualified for the programme, and in 1968, right on Digger's schedule, she qualified for the team to compete at the Winter Olympics at Grenoble, France. She was eighteen years old, and although nobody expected a medal from her first time around, she was an acknowledged presence on the mountain. She was also the only girl in her high school graduating class who had never tasted hard liquor, never smoked a joint, never cuddled with a guy in the back seat of a Chevy, or anywhere else. On the mountain she was a picture of confidence and daring, but once she took her skis off she was little Jenny Rosenzweig again, afraid and unsure of the world around her.

After the worst of it was over and she and H-H were safe for the moment in Barcelona, she tried to write to her father about what had happened. She tried to show him, for the first time in her life, exactly who she was: child, girl, and woman; and how her life so far had been a progression of events that had led, inexorably, to what she had done at Grenoble. She tried to tell him about H-H, tried to explain what it was like to be eighteen years old and unloved, untouched, unsure even of what the words truly meant. To be loved, to be touched . . . the words frightened her. She had been taught to fear them all her life. Bad enough that fear, worse than that the fear that the love and the touch would never come, that they weren't hers to hope for and that what stretched ahead was a loveless, touchless life from which the only escape was the mountain. Only on the hill was she complete . . . loved, and touched and warmed . . . and how difficult it was sometimes to take off the skis at the end of the day and descend to that same grey life again. She tried to tell that to her father, and how that all had been changed by one kind and gentle person. Now the loving and the touching were hers without fear and she wanted him to know that. She covered several sheets of paper trying to tell him these things, but in the end she tore them up. She knew that he would not understand, and suddenly she wanted to write him a different sort of letter entirely. She wanted to tell him what she thought of a father who would raise a daughter in fear of sin where there was no sin, in fear of the touch which she now found a blessing, in fear of even seeing her own body naked in a misty bathroom mirror. She wanted to tell him what she thought about stories of tainted blood and faithless mothers, nightmare-makers that had frozen her youth in horror. She wanted to tell him that she was free of that now, the fearful frog turned into the fearless princess by the gentlest of kisses. But she did not write that letter either. It was another one he would not understand. Instead she sent a cablegram giving him her love, asking his forgiveness, and asking him as well to close out her account at the Rocky Mountain Savings and Loan and send her the $560 on deposit there. She did not say when she would be home.

Hans-Heinz Stengler was twenty-three, a cross-country skier from Karl-Marx-Stadt in the DDR. He was tall and angular, with the spare build of the *Langlaufer*. He had red hair, white teeth, an easy grin, and a consuming desire to defect to the West. His motives for defecting were more materialistic than ideological, more social than political. Hans-Heinz did not feel oppressed in the DDR, he felt bored. He loved the good things in life, or at least he knew that he would love them once he got his hands on them. He saw himself as an entrepreneur mistakenly set down in the midst of a socialist society. He was determined to correct that accident of geography, and he came

443

to the Olympics prepared to ski his way to freedom. All he needed was a cooperative westerner, preferably female and preferably American, to help him elude the security agents who accompanied the East German athletes wherever they went. On the opening day of the Games he settled on Jenny Rosenzweig, friendless, defenceless, and a long way from home. It took him only three days to set her spinning and to keep her that way.

On the first day he sat down at her table in the cafeteria of the Olympic Village and asked if he could practise his English with her. He traded his apple for her pear, told her how much he dug the Beatles, made her laugh, and later walked with her back to her dormitory. On the second day, after training, they strolled together holding hands, and on the evening of the third day they sat in a corner of the central lounge with their heads together, whispering intently.

None of this escaped the notice of Gerhard Steinbrenner, chief of the security service attached to the East German team. Nor did it cause him concern. He tried to keep his athletes isolated from the corruption of western influences, but he was realistic enough to expect that healthy young men and women would seek out companionship regardless of nationality. His attitude towards Stengler, in fact, was one of guarded approval tinged with masculine envy. If the young man was getting a bit of American ass, then more power to him. What Steinbrenner did not realize was that American ass was only second on Stengler's list of priorities. In fact, he and Jenny had done little more than furtively kiss, and hold hands. First on his list was defection to the West. He knew exactly how he was going to do it, and exactly how Jenny was going to help him spring loose from his guardians.

'Even now they're watching,' he said, his head close to hers. 'I don't think they ever sleep.'

'Where?' Jenny barely mouthed the word.

'Over there.' A jerk of the head. 'In the corner, with the magazine.'

Actually, he was not at all sure that there were any DDR politicals in the lounge, but it seemed better to say that there were, and so he nodded at an innocuous speed skater engrossed in the latest *Der Spiegel*. The surveillance was real enough and tight enough at times when it counted, and this was a minor exaggeration. Even if one of the 'sweethearts', the ones who were supposed never to leave your side, were in the room he would have been lost in the crowd. The lounge was full of athletes from all nations recounting the events of the day. They sat in large circles like Indians around a campfire. There were few small groups, fewer couples. They tended to gather first by nationality, then by sport: bobsledders, lugers, skiers all clotted together. The central fireplace was heaped high with logs and coals, and there was the comforting aroma of drying wool in the air, spiced by the tang of heated leather. The snow fell gently outside.

Jenny shivered with two kinds of excitement. The first came from sitting so close to Hans-Heinz, knowing that anytime she wished she could reach out and touch her fingertips to his cheek. The skin there looked so soft and smooth, but she knew how rough it could feel when he slid his cheek against hers. She knew, and had known since yesterday when it had happened for the first time. But not the last, she promised herself. Later, when we walk back to the dorms. She shivered again, this time from the knowledge that the man in the corner was watching them. Perhaps not at that very moment, for he seemed awfully interested in his magazine, but he was there to observe and report. It was like something out of a spy thriller, but she did not find it strange or unbelievable. Just about everything she was doing these days was tinged with the fantastic. Just to be here in France, seeing strange people and eating strange foods . . . and then meeting H-H and everything that had happened since. Not that *that* had happened, not yet, but she promised herself that it would just as soon as they were off by themselves. The thought made her shiver again, and H-H smiled when he saw her shoulders move.

'Don't look at me that way,' she said.

'What way?' The smile grew broader. He knew exactly the effect that he had on her.

'You keep it up and you're going to melt me right down to a puddle. I wouldn't be much good to you that way.' She couldn't help herself. She touched his cheek quickly and pulled her fingers away. 'Tell me again. Once it's over, if we get away with it, we'll be staying together, right?'

He looked at her reproachfully. 'I've already told you that. You know how I feel about you.'

'H-H, I'm a dumb little bunny about a lot of things, I've told

445

you that. I've never been involved like this before. You could fool me very easily if you wanted to.'

'Then why ask me? I could be fooling you now.'

'I know,' she said, and shook her head, puzzled with herself. 'I guess I just want to hear you say it again. Tell me about the rabbits, George. One more time.'

'Rabbits?'

'Didn't you ever read *Of Mice and Men*? Where the big dumb guy, Lenny, keeps asking George what it's going to be like when they settle down on the farm and raise rabbits. That's me, big dumb Lenny. So tell me about the rabbits, George.'

H-H remembered *Of Mice and Men*, it had been on the approved list at school, but he didn't remember the part about the rabbits. 'We stay together,' he said firmly. 'Once I get out of here I get political asylum from the French and then we head down to the south of Spain, where it's cheap to live. There are plenty of things I can do in the West, and not just skiing. I have a lot of talent, Jenny, talent that I've never been able to use. All I need is the right chance, the break, and you'll see. But whatever I do, we're staying together.'

'Thanks, George, thanks for the rabbits. Boy, what a dope I am. You could be feeding me the oldest line in the world and I wouldn't know it. How could I? Nobody ever tried it before.'

'That is hard to believe.'

'I know, I know. You think that every American girl is some kind of a swinger. You've got one gorgeous surprise coming to you, buster.' She lowered her voice even further. 'Have you decided . . . you know . . . when?'

He nodded lazily. 'Not here. Let's go for a walk.'

They walked aimlessly around the village grounds in the falling snow, keeping to the shadowed places where they could stop and kiss whenever they wished. At one of those places he held her close and whispered, 'It has to be during the fifty-K. The shorter races don't give me enough time.'

She nodded. He had already told her his basic plan, the only question being which race he would use as a cover for his defection. She agreed with his choice. The fifteen-kilometre and the thirty-kilometre would not give him enough time to manoeuvre. It had to be the fifty.

'It's a shame,' she said. 'The fifty is your best event. You might have won it.'

'I don't think so, but thanks. The Norway boys, they're too strong. Besides, I didn't come here to win a medal. I guess I'm the only one who didn't. I came here to make a new life for myself. And now, with you.'

'Yes,' she said in a tiny voice.

'You'll have to be ready to move fast.'

'There isn't much for me to do.'

'The car?'

'Taken care of. All I have to do is pick it up. What day is the fifty-K?'

He looked at her sharply. He did not answer.

She understood. She moaned as she said, 'Thursday?'

He nodded. 'I thought you understood that.'

'The same day as the slalom.'

'Yes.'

'Oh Lord.' She would not be able to race. Just for the moment she flashed the image of Digger's face, and then she shut it out.

'I thought you knew.'

'I haven't been thinking straight about anything the past few days. I'll have to say I'm ill. H-H, does it have to be Thursday?'

He put his hands on her shoulders. 'We just decided that. Jenny, there's still time to back out, you know. I'm not going to hold you to anything you said.'

'Ten years of training. Just like that, gone.'

'I know. It's the same for me.' He looked at her anxiously, then relaxed. He saw that she was going to do it. 'The same for me, but different. I'm getting something out of this. Something big.'

'So am I.' She pressed herself close to him. 'So am I.'

'Then you'll do it?'

'You know I will.' She rubbed her cheek against his, savouring the roughness. 'You're going to have to take good care of me, you know that? You're going to have to love me lots, and treat me right, and make me happy for a hundred years at least. You realize that, don't you?'

'I do. And I will,' he promised, and he was surprised to realize that, for the moment at least, he meant it.

His plan was simple, but effective. The East German athletes were so closely watched by Steinbrenner's security people that there was no possible chance of escape from within the Olympic compound. The only time that the athletes were unencumbered

447

by their guards was during competition. This was a meaningless freedom to a downhill racer, a jumper, a bobsledder, or a figure skater, but it gave a cross-country skier considerable room in which to manoeuvre. Stengler made his break for freedom during the fifty-kilometre race, which was laid out in the required fashion of one-third uphill, one-third downhill, and one-third on the flat. The racers ran on tracks, one for each ski, set in the snow by machines, and they started off at thirty-second intervals. They stayed in the tracks unless they were forced to yield to an overtaking skier, who had the right of way at all times.

Stengler ran the first twenty kilometres of the race in the steady thrusting style of the *Langlaufer,* covering ground economically and conserving his strength. His split times along the way were good, but not exciting. The excitement came at the twenty-kilometre mark when he suddenly jumped the tracks and skied off the course, sliding through a stand of trees that dropped away to a ridge, and then an open meadow of snow. Behind him he heard the shouts of surprise of the coaches and timers stationed along the track. He crossed the meadow in a burst of speed, burning the strength he had husbanded. The meadow ended at another ridge that overhung a narrow, rutted country road. He came off the ridge tucked in like a downhill racer, landed on the road, teetered on a rut, recovered, and scooted around a curve to where Jenny was waiting in a rented Fiat. The motor was running. She flung open a door.

'Hurry,' she called.

He stripped off his skis and looked for a place to stow them on the car. There was no ski rack on the roof. 'Where the hell is the rack?' he shouted.

'They didn't have one left.'

'You got a car without a ski rack? God damn stupid. . . .'

'I told you, they didn't have one. Leave the skis here. Let's go.'

'I'm not going to throw away a perfectly good pair of skis.'

'Yes you are, damn you.' It was the first time she had ever damned anyone. 'They don't belong to you, anyway, they belong to the state. If you take them with you that's theft, and they can charge you with it. Then what happens to your political asylum?'

'Holy . . .' He stared at the skis, then flung them from him

448

onto the road. He jumped into the car. 'You're right, I never thought of that. By God, you've got a good head.'

'Damn right I do.' The word came easier the second time. She flashed him a grin as she shoved the car into gear. Wheels spun on ice. She twisted the Fiat out of a rut, picked up speed, and less than ten minutes after H-H had dropped out of the race they were heading south for Marseille on the E-4 highway. They were well on their way by the time Steinbrenner's security forces were notified that one of their skiers was missing.

There was both good and bad news waiting in Marseille. The French were willing to give H-H temporary asylum and temporary papers, but as a political concession to the East Germans they would not allow him to stay in France. His reception at the United States consulate was worse. By then the news of his attempted defection was on the radio and television, and the American position was that he was an economic, not a political, defector. They wanted nothing to do with him. They had to move on, and that night they drove the Fiat down the coast to Perpignan and over the border into Spain, where they were given an enthusiastic welcome by the representatives of the Franco regime, ever willing to take a poke at a Communist government. The Spaniards stamped Jenny's American passport, provided H-H with travel documents, and allowed them to go on to Barcelona, where they got rid of the Fiat and checked into the Hotel Manila.

It was there, that night, that the touching and the loving began in a deep and dusty feather bed. His touch was as gentle as the feathers beneath her, his kiss both a promise and a caress, and when he entered her he took her swiftly to heights beyond the peaks of her dreams, exploding with her there before tumbling down the hill again. He led her up that mountain twice again in the night, and in the morning she awoke to write the letter to her father that she eventually destroyed. Sitting by the window overlooking the Ramblas, wearing her Olympic sweater as a robe, she thought of writing to Digger to excuse herself for destroying a dream. It was yet another letter she was unable to write, although in later years she was able to say the words to him directly.

With no letter written she sent the cable to Denver asking for her money, and for the next few days she and H-H wandered through the streets of Barcelona like curious children. They

449

slept late in the mornings, ate in the cheap *mariscarías* along the port, and read each edition of the *Paris Herald-Tribune* for the latest accounts of his dramatic escape and her dismissal from the American team for her part in it. They also brought themselves up to date on the results of the Games. H-H had been right about the fifty-kilometre cross-country; a Norwegian named Ellefsaeter had won it, while Marielle Goitschel of France had taken Jenny's slalom. She told herself that it did not matter, that she had gained more than she had lost. She was eighteen years old, and it was time to stop playing games. She wondered when she would ever ski again.

The money from Denver took a week to arrive, and when it did Jenny saw that her father had added a thousand dollars to it. He also sent a cablegram begging her to come home. She read the cable with sadness. Somewhere a stranger was trying to make his troubles her own. The next day they left Barcelona on the overnight boat that took them to the Mediterranean island of Ibiza, where, everyone said, the good life came cheap.

The island to which Hans-Heinz and Jenny came in 1968 was a fly-speck on the map of the Mediterranean only twenty-three miles long and eight miles wide, the home of a society of agrarian Spaniards overlaid with a foreign population of writers, painters, and various drifters. Among those foreigners the serious artists were few, outnumbered by the boat bums passing through, the would-be smugglers, the remittance men, the pot farmers, the social and political refugees, and the casually curious, all of whom found the place to be a congenial haven. The island to them was an arena in which one could work while living cheaply in a beneficent climate, a refuge in which to raise children free from the strictures of western civilization, a safe place far removed from a world in which none of them could live, a war which none of them had made, and a system in which none of them could have survived. It was a highly private place in which most shades of behaviour were accepted without question, and a highly public place in which everyone knew his neighbour's business. It was a society of individuals that prized personal ambition, but it was also a communal society in which money was loaned without conditions, shirts were given freely to the shirtless, and food and drink were dispensed by those who had them with a hospitality worthy of a bedouin prince. The motto

450

of the island was *la isla madre de la vida padre,* which translated best as 'the birthplace of the life of Riley,' and unlike most mottos it came close to being accurate.

Jenny and H-H came to Ibiza in the last of the golden years of the island, at a time when the living was still cheap and the natural beauty of the place was undiminished. During their first weeks there they slept late, bathed in the sea, made friends in the bars and cafés, sat far into the night smoking dope as a punctuation to extravagant conversation, and the next day awoke to do it all over again without the slightest feeling of time wasted or expectations unfulfilled. They felt as if they had found a home and more, for life in Ibiza then was a combination of summer camp and a trip to the moon. For H-H those first few weeks were the fruits of the dreams of the West he had cherished for years. He had no idea that Ibiza was as representative of western society as Disneyland might be, and if someone had tried to set him straight he would not have believed him. H-H knew the value of a permanent dream, and knew how to preserve one. Jenny, who should have known better, held hands with his dream and walked with it softly, careful not to shatter the illusion.

The house in which they eventually came to live was set on top of a hill overlooking a wide valley of orchards and fields. It was a very old farmhouse which had lasted well. The exterior walls were five feet thick and tapered to three feet where they joined the ceilings. The floors were of terra-cotta tile, and the ceilings were high and beamed. The main structure was a simple rectangle that held a spacious *sala,* a kitchen, a sitting room, a dining room, a bedroom, and a bath. Attached to the house, but without interior access, was an ell which once had been roofed-over *corrales* for sheep and goats and which now had been divided into another bedroom, a studio, and another bath. Trees of fig, carob, and almond surrounded the house. There was no electricity; everything worked on either butane gas, kerosene, or batteries. The water was stored in a cistern and was pumped to the roof tanks by a Briggs & Stratton putt-putt that always started on the first stroke. Or the second. The water itself was trucked up from the valley monthly by a farmer with the only tractor small enough to negotiate the winding roads, and towards the end of each month the pump sucked up a fine grey clay from the cistern bottom that left a gritty film. The water was the only true problem with the house, but despite that it was a simple and comfortable place in which to live.

It still is. It is where I live now. Anna, and Justine and me.

There is no terrace behind the house, but chairs can be put in the ankle-high grass, and at the end of the day Justine and I sit there and watch the procession of clouds on their evening parade down Morna Valley to the sea, their underbellies burnished by the last of the sun. The fields below us are silent, and the rising air brings odours of oranges, and mouldering earth and the cumin that grows wild among the uncleared trees. Justine drinks her vodka-tonic, and I my Trinaranjus, a bottled soft drink that calls for an acquired taste. The first of the *petroleo* lamps blooms a butterfly of light in the kitchen window as Anna goes to work on dinner, and after a while she comes out to join us dragging the bottle of kitchen sherry with her the way a weary soldier drags his rifle. It is a precious time of day for us, usually a time of silence, but this evening there are words that have to be said.

We sit silently at first, and then I begin to speak, the words drawn out of me reluctantly, but I know that I must say them. They are the words that I will put to paper in the morning, difficult words for me to say. Both Justine and Anna understand this and recognize my need to say the words aloud before committing them to paper. Unspoken, the words are unreal; once uttered, they cannot be recalled. Thus the need, and so both women listen attentively, but with their eyes directed at distant places as if to give me an isolated space from which to speak, a privacy to hedge my discomfort. I close my own eyes to make it easier, let the words flow loosely, and I am once again that ten-year-old wise-ass and *Wunderkind* in St Anton who thought he knew it all. Wise beyond his years, and who knew so little of the ways of the world, the ways of men and women, the ways of love, and the roads that a marriage can take.

The long-established marriage rules between Digger and Bobby stated that he was allowed to play around with two types of women. Bobby called them bits of fluff and sisters under the skin. By her definition a bit of fluff was someone unimportant whom Digger might be tempted to tumble for a night during a business trip or a weekend away from home. A sister under the skin was someone from their own social gang, generally a cool and experienced piece of machinery who knew that the rules prohibited permanent poaching. Both types were safe and unthreatening.

On the other hand, it was understood that Bobby's interests lay solely with equally unthreatening young men whose only assets were their hard, lean bodies, their vigour, and, on rare and joyous occasions, an innocence ready to be breached. Peter, the part-time taxi driver *cum* ski instructor, had no innocence worth speaking of, but he qualified on the other counts. At least, he seemed to. He lived in a tiny room in the basement of the Schwartze Adler close by the storage area and workshop where the guests of the hotel left their skis. It was there that Bobby had spent the afternoon while Digger and I were skiing on Rendl and examining the family farm, and she was there the next afternoon as well while I was skiing with Anna and while Digger spent hours on the telephone calling halfway round the world to see what could be done about solving Mike's problems with the Marine Corps.

Yes, I kept that date with Anna, although I had sworn to myself that I wouldn't, and I was glad that I did. She wasn't much of a skier but she was fun to be with, and we took the *K-bahn* up to Gampen and skied down from there on the runs she could handle. So I was zipping down the mountain without a care at just about the same time that Bobby was kneeling over Peter the taxi driver in his basement room, trying to develop his erection. Pity poor Peter, he was having trouble coming out of his corner for Round Two, and Bobby had been working on him for what seemed like an eternity. He lay there on his back with his eyes on the ceiling, his hands resting lightly on the back of her head, willing something to happen. But nothing did. Not that Bobby was complaining, not my easygoing mom. She was a good sport that way, sympathetic to the frailties of man, and so she knelt over Peter with her rump in the air and her breasts brushing his knees, working with fingers and tongue to arouse his flaccid interest. Way to go, Mom, a little farther to the left and use a longer stroke, use your finger there, right, now use your tongue, that's it, around the crown and down . . .

Peter should have been enjoying all this attention, but he wasn't. He was embarrassed, resentful, and as his frustration mounted so did his anger. Nothing was happening down there, despite what she was doing. It all came from screwing these older women, he decided. He never had a problem like this with girls his own age. Even with a woman like this one where you could see that she must have been a beauty once, her flesh still firm and her skin still clear, but she was still . . . older. Not young. Not what made his guts growl with desire, but still he was expected to perform like a machine, snap your fingers for an instant erection, you bitch, and if nothing happens it's all my fault, isn't it? God damn tourists with their God damn money and their million-dollar bodies held together by God knows what, and it isn't as if they ever laid any honest-to-God *Geld* on you, always a cute little gift when it was all over. Pair of cufflinks, a watch, pair of silver-backed brushes, and Christ, I'll be bald before I get to use all the brushes I've got, and what the hell is she doing now? Good try, lady, but nothing is going to work today, except maybe if we change your forty into two twenties. That might do it, but nothing else. All you're doing is rubbing me raw and making me feel like a fool lying here like this with no strength at all and nothing I can do about it. Nothing, nothing, nothing . . .

And then Bobby looked up from what she was doing and grinned at him. It was a friendly gesture, designed to encourage, meant to say, 'Hang in there, old sport, don't worry about a thing, we'll make it, got a couple of tricks I haven't even tried yet, so just relax and let me get back to work.' That's how she meant it, but that wasn't how he took it. She was laughing at him, amused by his limpness, his weakness. She had tried everything, and nothing had worked, and now she was laughing.

'You slut,' he said, 'you bitch. You think it's funny? Try this and tell me if it's funny.'

He reached down and slapped her across the face. The grin disappeared. It was an open-handed blow, not hard, but it felt so good to him that he did it again with the back of his hand, and that felt good too. His anger broke in him then. He jumped out of bed, pushed her over on the mattress, and began to punch her face with his closed fists. She tried to roll away from him, but he jumped on top of her, gripped her with his knees, and swung his fists back and forth.

Bobby knew at once that it was going to be bad. When he jumped on top of her she tried to cover her breasts with her arms, but he wasn't hitting her there, he was pounding her face. She raised her hands, but he tore them away and kept punching.

She felt her nose crush in, and one of her eyes was shut. She tried to scream, but there was blood in her throat and the scream came out as a burble. She spat out the blood and screamed again. This time she heard it echo in the room.

Kurt heard the screaming as he came through the basement from the ski room, his equipment over his shoulder. The sound bounced off the concrete walls, startled him, and stopped him in his tracks. He laid his skis against the wall and looked around; there was only the one door. He banged on it with his fist, but the screaming continued. He banged again with no response. The door was locked; he kicked it in. He saw a bed with a naked man on top of a naked woman, punching at her face. There was blood on the bed and the wall.

He pulled the man off the bed and pushed him against the wall. He held him there with one heavy forearm locked under his chin. With his free hand he slapped Peter's face sharply. The slaps sounded like boards of wood coming together. Peter's eyes rolled.

Kurt left him propped against the wall and went to the bed. Bobby stared up at him out of one open eye. The other eye was hammered shut, and her nose was clearly broken. Her face was bloody and beginning to turn colour, and her lips were twisted with pain. He pulled a sheet from the foot of the bed and covered her with it. He did not know who she was until she said his name.

'Kurt.' She could barely speak it. 'Kurt.'

He knew her then, and stared. 'Bobby?'

'Kurt. Digger.'

His mind turned over. He did not know if she wanted Digger, or if she wanted to keep him from seeing her. She solved that for him in a whisper. 'Get Digger. Please.'

He heard a scrambling sound behind him. Peter had grabbed some clothing and was out of the room. Kurt let him go. He bent over to listen to Bobby's breathing. It was regular, but with a rattling noise. 'It's going to be all right,' he said. 'Try to breathe easily while I get hold of Digger and a doctor.'

'No doctor,' she said with difficulty.

'You have to. Your nose is broken.'

'Ask Digger. No doctor, no press.' She was choosing the shortest words possible.

Kurt shook his head impatiently. 'Don't worry about that. The doctor is someone I can trust. Just rest now while I do this.'

There was a telephone on the table beside the bed. He got through to Digger at the Post Hotel and spoke in short, quick sentences, hung up and called Dr Mannheim at his office. He gave the doctor careful instructions, including the need for discretion. Then he pulled a chair up to the bed and sat down beside Bobby to wait. He shook his head at the sight of her ruined face.

It took Digger seven minutes to get there. He came into the room, nodded briefly at Kurt, and knelt beside the bed. Bobby's one good eye was open.

He said, 'Jesus, kid, who did this to you?'

She shook her head, a tiny motion.

'Who did it? I'll kill the bastard, I swear I will.'

'Not important,' she whispered. 'Let me tell you something, pal. No more sailors for me. I'm getting out of this neighbourhood, moving uptown.' She closed the one eye.

Dr Mannheim came bustling in then, a short, bearded man with an imperious manner. He ordered Kurt and Digger out of the room while he made a superficial examination. Digger wanted to stay, but Kurt took his arm and led him outside. They stood in the basement awkwardly, not knowing what to say to each other. Finally, Digger muttered, 'What happened here, Kurt?'

Kurt told him. Digger asked, 'Do you know the guy who did it?'

'I've seen him around. He gives lessons once in a while, drives a taxi the rest of the time. You know the type.'

'Christ, she had to pick one of those. I want his ass.'

'Let's take care of Bobby first. As she said, he's not important right now. He'll be here when we want him.'

'He could have killed her.'

'Yes. He was out of his head about something.'

'And you stopped it. I'm in your debt.'

Kurt shrugged. 'How can there be any debt? You saved my life once.'

'That was a long time ago.'

'It's still on the books.'

'In that case so is Hannes. On the other side of the ledger. And now this. It's all on the books.'

Kurt jammed his hands into his pockets and hunched his shoulders unhappily. 'It sounds stupid when you put it that way. Life isn't double-entry bookkeeping. I owe you, and you owe me. Very stupid.'

'It's been stupid for years. Ever since that business with Hannes.'

'Maybe stupid, but no matter what else, he was my brother.'

'He was also a miserable excuse for a man. Killing him was something that had to be done. It was our bad luck, yours and mine, that I was the one who had to do it.'

Kurt stood tensed for a long moment, accepting that. It had taken him twenty-five years to get that far, and a moment more was all it took. He eased off, and said, 'Yes, it was bad luck. Hannes has been on the books for too long. Nobody would carry a business loss for twenty-five years, they'd write it off.'

'Is that what you want to do? Write it off? Close the books?'

'I think it's time. Yes, as far as I'm concerned, they're closed. Nobody owes anything. We're even.'

'Even,' Digger repeated. He started to reach out a hand to seal the deal, but drew it back. It wasn't needed. Their eyes met and locked, and that was enough.

The doctor came out then and said that Bobby should be hospitalized at once. 'She's in no danger, you understand, but she should have immediate attention. I suggest Innsbruck. Our local ambulance could take her there.'

'Whatever you say,' said Digger, but he looked concerned. 'Couldn't she go by car?'

'The ambulance would be better.'

'Let me handle this,' said Kurt. He took the doctor aside and spoke to him quietly. The doctor nodded, said something else, and then left, hurrying across the basement to the stairs that led to the street.

'He's going to take care of things,' Kurt explained. 'I told him that you didn't want the ambulance pulling up here, wouldn't look good. We'll take her in my car as far as St Jakob. The ambulance will meet us there and we'll change over.'

'Thank you, Kurt.'

'He'll be back in a few minutes. You get some clothes on her while I move my car around. And don't look so sad – give her a smile when you go inside. It's bad, but it could have been worse.'

*

457

'I guess it could have been worse,' I said, 'although it didn't seem that way to me, not at the time.'

Full darkness now in the valley, the parade of clouds completed once more. Justine stirred beside me and asked, 'Did you know what had happened?'

'Not right away. They wouldn't let me go to Innsbruck to see her for two days. They said she had had an accident, but they wouldn't say what. Digger stayed with her in Innsbruck, and Anna took care of me. Kurt and Elena went back to Vienna, but Anna stayed with me. Not like a mother, not even an older sister. Like a friend.'

'It was nothing.' Anna's voice came out of the darkness. 'You weren't any trouble taking care of. You could take care of yourself by then, you little wise-ass.'

'That was all on the surface, not inside,' I told Justine. 'I couldn't have made it without Anna. Inside I was going crazy. They tried to keep things quiet, but after a while the word started to get around. Even the kids knew. That's how I found out that Bobby had got the crap beaten out of her for no good reason. All she did was give the guy the same highclass blow job she had been delivering for years without a single complaint. The son of a bitch never knew how lucky he was.'

There was silence. Neither of the women wanted to comment on that.

'On the third day they took me to Innsbruck and let me see her. They had set the nose, but she still looked awful. Skin all discoloured and the eye still shut, and one of her cheeks had a dent in it. I guess I cried a little when I first saw her, and then to show her that things were okay I gave her the Jack Dempsey routine. I said, "Hey, champ, what happened?" And she said, "Honey, I just forgot to duck." And then we both laughed to make each other happy, and Digger was there and he laughed too. Right after that they flew her to Zurich for the plastic surgery.'

'She was very lucky,' said Anna. 'The doctors did a wonderful job. After the surgery nothing showed on her face, nothing at all.'

'Maybe not to you,' I said.

Chapter Six

Jenny grew up in Ibiza. She grew up fast and hard, condensing years into months, and as she grew she learned a lot about herself. She learned that she wasn't nearly as much in love with H-H as she had thought she was, that the physical need she felt for him could be satisfied by others, and that if she was ever going to get anywhere in the world she would have to do it by herself, because no man she knew was about to do it for her. She also learned that she was not at all the dumb bunny she once had pretended to be. She was simply young, and untrained for anything except slalom skiing. She didn't know what she was going to do about that, formal education was clearly not the answer for her, and she decided that she would simply have to keep her eyes open and take advantage of whatever situations came her way.

She learned how she felt about H-H when she realized what a lout she was living with. She was too bright not to recognize what he was, and too honest to allow her emotions to blind her to it. In the Olympic Village he had overwhelmed her with what appeared to be a style of flashing wit and sophistication. In Ibiza, placed in the company of eager young writers and painters striving to express their art in new and daring ways, his conversation turned flat, his sophistication was exposed as a cheap cynicism, and his once acidulous wit became the carpings of a malcontent. He was still full of plans for his future. He was going to organize a rock band composed of local musicians, he was going to sell himself to the US Olympic organization as an expert on East German sports medicine, he was going to write a book about his defection at Grenoble. In fact, he was going to do nothing at all. Like Jenny, he had been trained to excel only on snow, and he was a long way from the nearest snowflake. Unlike Jenny, he didn't know what to do about it. He spent most of his time in the cafés along the port drinking the local *hierbas* and juggling his grand plans in front of anyone willing to listen to him. When Jenny realized that he was going nowhere, spinning his wheels in tropical sand, he began to bore her. The physical spark between them remained bright, but Jenny knew that it wasn't enough.

Just about that time she learned that H-H wasn't the only man who could fan that spark into a flame, found out the hard way when her lover ran in a ringer on her. He did it smoothly, half a dozen of the café regulars sitting late after dinner over wine, glasses of *hierbas* later at the Caballo Negro, and then up to the house on the hill to smoke some dope. Jenny was out of it by then, wine-weary and ready for bed. Left them all, boys and girls together, in a puffing arc around her fireplace, and tumbled into the bedroom and under the blankets. Quick release into sleep so deep that at first she did not feel H-H come slipping in beside her, feel his touch and caress in the dark. And then she felt it, felt all of him pressing and part of him probing, and happily turned to him. And to that now so sweet and familiar ride up the mountain climbing higher and higher right up to the peak and the pop; and then came tumbling down aware of something not quite right. Not right at all, indeed. Rolled out from under breathing hard, and not from pàssion spent.

'Speak, you son of a bitch,' she said in the darkness. 'Who the hell are you?'

No answer, not even a stirring beside her. She rolled again and reached for a match to light the lamp beside the bed, struck it, and before it even hit the wick she saw the grinning face of one of the café regulars. Ralph Something, always grinning, but his grin fading quickly now as he saw the look on her face.

'Hey listen, hey wait, hey don't get sore,' he said. 'H-H said it would be okay.'

What now? she wondered. Anger? Indignation? Screams of outrage? Knee to the groin? Why bother? It wasn't going to change anything, and, besides, it had felt sort of nice.

'Out,' she said wearily. 'Out of my bed and don't come back. I've got to get some sleep.'

The next morning, sipping coffee in the kitchen, she laid it on H-H, and he denied it flatly. 'You must have been dreaming,' he said.

'H-H, I may be the new girl in town but I know the difference between getting laid and a wet dream. Besides, he said he cooled it with you first.'

Trapped, H-H spread his hands disarmingly. 'Look; take it

460

as a compliment. Everybody was high, you know how it is. Ralph's had a thing about you ever since he met you.'

'And so you let him have me, just like lending him your umbrella.'

'Come on, it wasn't so terrible, was it?'

'As a matter of fact, it was damn good.' She had hoped to hurt him with that, and when it bounced right off him she grew suspicious. A thought peeked into her mind, withdrew, and peeked again. She tried it. 'How much did you get?'

He looked at her carefully. She was wearing an easy smile. He relaxed and said, 'Five hundred pesetas. I mean, why not?'

Five hundred. About eight dollars. The smile vanished as she threw the coffee cup at him. It missed, but it sent him scurrying from the kitchen. 'If you ever do that again,' she called after him, 'I'll cut your heart out. I mean it, Herr Hans-Heinz Stengler, I'll take a little knife and I'll cut out your little heart.'

But she was smiling faintly as she said it, remembering Ralph Something and how he had felt in the middle of the night. Only later did she realize that she should have demamnded part of the five hundred from H-H, and that pointed up another of her problems. They were slowly running out of money, for even in Ibiza fifteen hundred dollars had a limited lifetime. The bankroll, which she guarded carefully, was down to slightly over five hundred, and by this time she knew better than to expect any contributions from H-H. Over the next few weeks she tried her hand at several odd jobs: running up skirts for Dorita, the dressmaker; selling hamburgers at the stand on the port; baby-sitting for a family of seven. The jobs were odd and short-lived. She had no special skills, and there were too many others like her in the market. After the baby-sitting job ran out she sat down with H-H and told him that he was going to have to bring in some bread.

'I've got some plans,' he told her.

'We need money, not plans. Pepe Tur is hiring people.'

'Construction? Me?'

'Why not? You're built like a bull.'

'I meant it when I said I had plans. I'm going to make a run.'

'Oh, shit.'

In the back of her head she had always known that someday it would come down to running dope into France. From what she had heard, it always did. It was the only way of scoring big, and the chances of success were decent if you knew what you were doing. There were three ways of going about it. The worst way was to try to fly it into France on a commercial flight using any one of a number of devices: stuffed dolls, rolled scarves, a dummy suitcase. The failure rate was high, and so were the penalties. The best way was to run it up the coast by sea past Perpignon and land it on any of the deserted beaches there, but that required a boat and a knowledge of seamanship. Without a boat, the best way was to take the stuff in overland, crossing the Pyrenees through the smugglers' passes near Andorra. That was a good-weather operation. In the wintertime the passes were blocked with snow, and it was January.

'That's what I'm counting on,' H-H told her. 'This time of year those border posts are practically closed down. They figure nobody can get through in this weather, not even on skis.'

'Can you do it?'

'Any good *Langlaufer* could, and I'm one of the best.'

'I might as well hear all of it. What's the carry?'

'Fifty keys of Afghani Red. Some people I met on the port. They'll pay me a thousand dollars to bring it into France. That's all I have to do. They pick it up on the other side.'

'I'd rather see you working for Pepe Tur.'

He brushed that aside. 'I'll need to buy some things in Barcelona. Skis, boots, some clothes.'

'How much?'

'Two hundred dollars? We get it back five for one. Come on, Jenny, what do you say?'

Jenny made her calculations quickly, and the method by which she made them showed how quickly she had grown up in Ibiza. Two hundred dollars was almost half of what she had left, but there were other factors to be considered. Feeding H-H and paying his *cuentas* at the cafés were the heaviest drains on their budget; her own expenses were small. If he got away with the run and came back with a thousand they would be in good shape for a while. If he didn't make it, or if he made it and didn't come back, she would be rid, at the same time, of a financial burden and a lover who was beginning to bore her.

'I can give you a hundred and fifty,' she said. 'And don't try to talk me into more. I can't afford it.'

'Jenny!'

'You can pick up an old pair of slats in Barcelona. You're only going to use them once.'

'I should never have thrown away those skis in Grenoble,' he said, but he kissed her happily.

Three days later he took the boat to Barcelona, bought his equipment, collected his cargo, and took the bus up into the mountains along with dozens of other skiers on holiday. He stayed overnight at an inn, and the next morning he began his climb with fifty kilos of Afghani Red packed into his rucksack. He made his border crossing at the pass below Puigmal, and was busted before he got a hundred metres into France. The French border police, who were just as alert in January as they were in June, turned him over to the Spanish authorities, who gave him a bad beating, a quick trial, and seven years. Jenny never saw him again.

She was saddened, but relieved. For the next two months she enjoyed the comforts of the simple, single life, and then took into the house an English artist named Gerry Devine who did chicken-feather and barbed-wire collages on slabs of balsa wood. Gerry stayed around until a long-awaited inheritance called him back to England and out of her life and she then hooked up with a Spanish poet named Jorge Medina. Jorge left in the autumn and was replaced by an Italian painter, a retired South African wine merchant, and then a beguiling Irishman whose family paid him the classic monthly remittance of one pound sterling for every mile he kept between himself and Dublin.

When the Irishman left her to go to Tangiers for the winter, Jenny found herself alone for the first time in almost three years. She took a long look at herself and counted up the score. Since leaving Denver, and not counting casual encounters, she had lived with six different men. The number depressed her, and reminded her vaguely of her mother. Six men, and what profit could she show? The sex had been good with some, boring with others, and bad only with the wine merchant. Each of the men had been interesting in his own way, but none had saddened her with his departure. Was this all there was? Was this all there would ever be? There had to be something else, something she had missed so far, and she began to wonder if her mother, too, had been searching for it. She remembered her father's warnings and the lectures of her childhood, and she saw herself about to wander down a familiar and pathetic path when she met Sammy Wyatt and fell instantly in love with him.

Soft-hearted Sammy Wyatt was a slight, wispy Englishman, as friendly as a puppy and the most inefficient smuggler in the western Mediterranean. Until he met Jenny he lived aboard his thirty-foot cutter, the *Cromwell*, and he was the best-known, most admired, most sought-after smuggler between Sicily and Gibraltar. But despite his popularity he was a failure in business. Part of this came from his refusal to carry any sort of drugs or dope.

'I'm just an old-fashioned smuggler,' he would say. Although he was not yet thirty he even sounded old-fashioned. 'Whisky and cigarettes, that's all I carry. That way I get to sleep at night.'

The other reason for his failure was his method of doing business. Every other smuggler in the Balearic Islands bought English or American cigarettes under ship's bond in Gibraltar for twenty pesetas a pack, ran them into the islands, and resold them at forty pesetas each. Not soft-hearted Sammy. He bought them at twenty just like the others, but he sold them at twelve because his friends, the writers and painters, couldn't afford the higher prices. This made Sammy the most popular smuggler around, and he never seemed bothered by the inescapable fact that he was losing eight pesetas everytime he sold a pack of cigarettes. He was a man performing a public service, and he was proud of that. Also, he somehow always managed to make enough money to keep on going.

'I don't know how, God's truth I don't,' he told Jenny. 'I should have gone broke long ago, but somehow there's always enough to fill up on fuel and keep the old *Cromwell* in proper nick.'

By then he was living with her whenever he wasn't at sea. His presence in the house made things run smoothly: The water taps didn't dare to drip, the cistern pump behaved, the butane tanks were changed regularly, and Jenny's ancient Volkswagen purred.

'You just keep on doing things your way,' she told him. 'Everybody loves you and somehow we manage.'

They managed that way until the big-league smugglers from Mallorca told Sammy he was out of business. His hit-or-miss operation was bad for trade. They did it smoothly, the big-bellied *contrabandistas* from the provincial capital. Like everyone else, they genuinely liked Sammy and they wished him no harm. They took him to dinner, flattered him, and over coffee and *coñac* they told him that he was out of business.

'But I'm too young to retire,' he protested.

'You're too young not to,' they told him. 'Not if you want to get old. You're a good kid, Sammy, but you're inefficient. You're out of business in the Balearic Islands.'

'Right, I'm out of business.' Sammy knew that there was no argument available to him, but he seized on the phrasing. 'What about outside the islands? Places east, Corsica, Sardinia, places like that?'

There were glances around the table, and shrugs. Someone said, 'You do whatever you want outside our waters, but be careful, Sammy. Talk to the local people before you make a move in that direction. Those people over there can be very difficult.'

'I will keep it in mind.'

He came home to Jenny filled with anger and defeat and told her what had happened. That night she rubbed him with oil and massaged his back and buttocks, and the nape of his neck. When she tried to go further he pushed her hands away.

'Can't think about that,' he said. 'Got to think about my future.'

She lay beside him quietly. 'What are you going to do?'

'I've been thinking about Corsica. I could make a run of it. Pick up the merchandise in Skikda and carry it up to Ajaccio. They make a decent pack of Chesterfields in Skikda, very realistic, and people seem to believe their Johnny Walker Red. Yes, Corsica might do me nicely.'

'What about the people there?'

He pursed his lips judiciously. 'Certain arrangements would have to be made. I would have to set things up in advance.'

'Sammy, I would rather see you doing something else.' She had a flash of saying the same words to H-H.

'What else am I going to do? I'm a smuggler, that's all I know.'

He was gone for a week getting things set up in Ajaccio and Skikda, and when he came back he told her that everything was set. The Corsican customs had a proud history of cooperation with free-lance smugglers, and the manufacturers in Skikda, all of whom had heard of soft-hearted Sammy, were willing to supply merchandise on consignment for the first run. The only difficulties had come with the syndicate people, short old men in dusty black suits, but a word from Sammy's Mallorcan friends had taken care of that.

'The only thing is I'll need two men to crew,' Sammy told her. 'We'll be doing our own humping. Merchandise on, merchandise off. I'll need me a couple of beasts of burden.'

'Only one,' Jenny said. 'We can save one share if I crew.'

'No way. You can't go humping cases of scotch.'

'I'm a lot stronger than I look. You're talking to a trained Olympic athlete.'

'They don't hump cases of scotch in the fucking Olympics.'

'All right, I can't do as much as one of your animals, but I could help. And I could stand watch, and I could do the cooking too. Please, Sammy, we could use the extra money, and I don't feel like sitting here alone all summer.'

In the end he said yes, and hired only one man to work the summer with them. Angel Luzon was young and tough, and he had worked on boats all his life. When he heard that Jenny would be on board he grinned with very good teeth and the muscles rippled under his black T-shirt.

All that summer and into the autumn they picked up the stuff at Skikda ran it up to Corsica, and in the darkness brought the *Cromwell* directly into Ajaccio harbour. Sammy had the local people well organized. He even had a cop of his own to stand guard while he and Angel unloaded the cases of phony Johnny Walker Red and the imitation Chesterfields onto the parapet. Jenny didn't have to help with the cases. Coming directly into the harbour that way there were always some dock kids ready to lend a hand for a couple of francs. She stood her watches, did the cooking, and her only problem was keeping out of the way of Angel's quick fingers.

'You're the skipper, you tell him to keep his hands to himself,' she complained to Sammy. 'The man is an animal.'

'I'll talk to him.' He pretended to study her critically. 'It might help if you dressed a bit different.'

'What's wrong with the way I'm dressed?' She was wearing a bikini bottom and a transparent plastic raincoat to keep off the spray.

'Cover it up a bit, love. You don't throw meat in front of the animals.'

After that she wore an anorak instead of the raincoat, but still she seemed to find Angel's fingers waiting round each corner.

They got hit on a night late in October, and they never knew who did the hitting. They were lying off Ajaccio harbour with the darkness just setting in, the water stippled by paintbox colours left behind by the sun, waiting for the fullness of night. Whoever it was came at them in a quick dart around the cape, two small power launches swinging out from behind the headland. They were painted white and they flew the flag, which was the only reason that they got as close as they did. Sammy figured them for customs boats, which meant a shakedown, and he shook his head sadly as they drew closer.

'Somebody is getting greedy,' he said. 'You wouldn't believe the money I pay those people.'

'Do we have to take it?' Angel asked. 'We could lose them in the dark.'

Sammy looked at the sky, figuring. It would be close to full dark before the launches were down on them. He played with the idea, then shook his head. 'No, they're the law. I can't do business without them.'

'Maybe Jenny should get below.'

'Doesn't make any difference if they see her.'

'Up to you, but it doesn't look good.'

'Maybe,' said Sammy.

He called to Jenny, and she came forward bracing herself against the roll of the swell. She was carrying Sammy's Winchester cradled in the crook of her arm. Sammy took it away from her and gave it to Angel. He kissed the tip of her nose.

'What's the cannon for, shooting seagulls?'

'Is there going to be trouble?'

'No trouble, just some business,' said Angel.

'You better get below for a while,' Sammy told her.

She wrinkled her nose, but she went below quickly enough. As soon as her head disappeared below the combing, Angel punched the starter and got the engine going. It coughed, stalled, coughed again, and finally settled into a chugging mutter. That was what saved them. He had no idea of moving the *Cromwell*, but he knew what it would be like for Jenny down below with them wallowing in the chop, and he wanted to save her a tossing around. He gave the engine just enough gas to turn the bows into the sea and hold her steady there.

Sammy saw what he was doing and nodded his approval. He held up a thumb and a forefinger spaced an inch apart to tell him to hold it just like that, then turned to go aft.

They opened up just as Sammy turned, one man up forward in each of the launches firing automatic weapons. The light, rattling sound came across the water. Sammy went down from the first blast. The second stitched forward along the decking, tearing jagged holes. Angel threw himself flat on the deck beneath the wheel with the metal post of the binnacle for shelter. As he went down he slammed the throttle full forward. If he had had to start the boat from scratch they would have been dead in the water. As it was she bucked up on her sternboards and shot ahead slamming down on the swell and shuddering all along her ancient joints. Angel kept his head down. He could still hear that light, rattling sound and the occasional *tic* of a hit in the planking. He reached up one hand to hold the bottom of the wheel steady and fumbled along the deck for the Winchester with the other. At the same time he yelled as loud as he could for Jenny to get behind something solid below. He didn't know Jenny that well. Her head popped up above the level of the hatch. Lying on the deck as he was, they were face to face.

'Where's Sammy?' she said.

'Down.'

'How bad?'

'Don't know.'

She started to come up out of the hatch, and he pushed her back with his free hand. There was another burst of firing, but none of the *tic-toc* sounds of hits in the hull. He twisted around to see what was going on behind him. Sammy was flat on the deck, not moving. The two launches were keeping pace, but not getting any closer. The *Cromwell* was bucketing along at about eight knots, which was all she could do flat out. The launches couldn't do any more, but they could do it for longer.

Jenny banged a fist on the combing. 'Go get Sammy. You can't just leave him there.'

'Hell I can't,' he muttered, but he let go of the wheel and swung himself around to face aft. The two launches lay off either quarter, not closing. A quick glance showed that they were running almost due north, Ajaccio harbour behind them and the dark mass of the coast to starboard. They were in good shape unless the engine decided to throw a rod, or blow a gasket, or expire from the sheer excitement of doing eight knots flat out.

'Come up here,' he said. He gave Jenny the wheel. 'Keep her on zero-two-zero. Don't let her drift.'

'Oh-two-oh. Take care of Sammy.'

He slipped a clip into the Winchester, put a half-dozen more in various pockets, and dropped to the deck, crawling aft. When he came to Sammy he checked him over. He was dead. He looked back at Jenny; she was staring at him. He shook his head. She closed her eyes for a moment, then turned back to the wheel. He worked his way to the stern, laid the Winchester over the transom, and opened up on the nearer of the two launches. He didn't expect to hit anything, but he wasn't going to run without throwing something back.

They ran that way for almost three hours under a hazy quarter-moon that gave just enough light to mark the coast to starboard. At times one of the launches would pull close enough to try a burst, but neither ever got within proper range. Angel was luckier; he put a few into the portside launch, heard glass tinkle, and a shout. That was his only triumph. He spent the rest of the time sprawled across the transom pumping random fire into the night.

After a while he crept back to the cockpit to see how Jenny was holding the course. They were running against a northwest set and it would have been easy to slip off to port, but she was holding it close enough to keep the coast at a friendly distance.

'Is he really dead?' she asked.

'Dumb question.'

'Yes. Do you know who they are?'

'No, and I don't think we'll ever know. Could be anybody. Somebody Sammy forgot to fix.'

'Are they going to catch us?'

'Not if this bucket holds up.'

They gave up just after that, the two launches swinging around trailing wakes of green phosphorescence and heading south again. Angel stood up to watch them go, then hung the Winchester in the rack beside the wheel. 'They're gone,' he said. 'I'll take it now.'

She gave up the wheel gladly, the muscles in her thighs and forearms quivering once the strain was off them. She started to sink to the deck, then straightened up and went aft to where Sammy's body lay. She crouched down beside it.

While she was back there Angel cut the speed and tried to figure their position. The finger of land extending out from the coast had to be Calvi Point, and beyond it the bay and the town. If Sammy were alive it would figure to run for Calvi. Sammy had friends there, and he had the local police organized. With Sammy alive they could have scooted into Calvi and holed up, but Calvi was useless with Sammy dead. Angel couldn't see himself bringing Sammy's body into port on a shot-up boat full of contraband whisky and tobacco. Which meant that everything had to go: the boat, the cargo, the body, everything. He told that to Jenny when she came forward to the cockpit. She didn't like it.

'It seems like such a waste,' she said. 'Isn't there any other way?'

'Maybe, but I don't see it. Take the wheel while I get my stuff together.'

She took over while he went below. He was gone for only a few minutes, and when he came topside he was carrying his seabag. They switched at the wheel while Jenny went below. She changed into jeans and a shirt and packed what she had on board into a canvas bag. She stood on Sammy's bunk and reached behind the break in the bulkhead to where he kept his money box. The box was there. She pulled it out. It was empty. The last time she looked there had been just over seven thousand dollars in it. She shivered, but her face was blank. She went up top and told Angel she was ready.

When they were close enough to the point, Angel cut the engine and lowered the dinghy over the side with their bags in it. Jenny clambered down and got the oars shipped while Angel went below and opened the sea cocks. He came back up through the aft hatch, stowed Sammy's body below, and secured the hatch firmly.

'Better hurry,' said Jenny.

'No rush – she won't go down that fast.'

But she did, settling rapidly at the stern where the first burst of gunfire had caught her just above the waterline. Angel dropped lightly into the dinghy and pulled off to wait. The *Cromwell* went down stern first, the bows tipping up and over in a pathetic salute. Once she was gone, Angel began the long pull for shore, the dinghy bobbing merrily as if pleased to be one of the survivors.

It was just past three in the morning when they beached the dinghy, pulled it up to dry sand, and careened it for a shelter. The beach was deserted, and it smelled of wild thyme and honey. It was close enough to dawn so that a ground fog had already formed. Angel sat on the sand and pulled off his deck shoes.

'Nobody'll be looking for us in Ajaccio,' he said thoughtfully. 'Nobody really knows us there. We'll get a ride down in the morning and catch the first plane out to anywhere.'

'Whatever you say. You're the boss now.'

'Whatever I say?'

'That's right.'

He stood up and stripped off his jeans; they were all he was wearing. He touched himself lightly, and he was hard. He said, 'Take off your clothes.'

She stared at him without moving.

'Don't be stupid,' he said. 'It's gonna happen. Make it easy.'

She took off her jeans and shrugged out of her shirt. She folded the jeans and put them under her hips to keep out the sand. He lay down on top of her, entered her at once, and took her quickly. She moaned and thrashed under him. When he was finished, he flopped over beside her. They lay together silently, breathing deeply. She touched his arm with light fingers.

'That was good,' she said. 'That was the best.'

He grunted with satisfaction.

'I never had a thing that big inside of me before.'

He chuckled. 'That's gambling size. You can always bet on it.'

She moved closer to him. 'You going to take care of me now that Sammy is gone?'

'Don't worry about it. You stick with Angel, you'll be okay.'

'I'll stick,' she said eagerly. 'I'm the kind of girl, I need a man to take care of me. I always have. But you won't be sorry, I promise you.'

'Sure,' he said lazily. 'You're okay. Better get some sleep now.'

'Aren't we going to do it again?'

'You really dig it, huh? In the morning.'

471

'Okay, but I want that thing of yours again.' She moved away from him and stood up.

'Where you going?'

'Have to pee.'

She took a few steps down the beach in the dark to where the spare oar from the dinghy lay in the sand. She picked it up, and in one fluid motion whirled and brought it down on Angel's head. The oar made the sound of a fish being slapped against a flat rock. She brought it up to swing again, then saw that she didn't have to. His scalp was laid open and his eyes were rolled back so that only the whites showed. His breath came heavily.

'That was my money you stole,' she told him. 'And just for the record, you're not all that big.'

She went down to the water and washed away what was left of Angel, then came back and put on her clothes. She went through his seabag and found the money in two wads, wrapped up in socks. She put them in her own bag and sat down to wait for the dawn. She kept the oar close by in case Angel came around, but he never moved. He was still breathing heavily. She didn't know how badly he was hurt, and she didn't care. She thought of loading him into the dinghy and pushing it down the beach and out to sea, but she knew that she didn't have the strength for it. She thought of killing him, but she knew that she couldn't do that either. She sat beside him until the first light showed, and then she walked up the beach to the main road that ran between Calvi and Ajaccio. She kept looking behind her, half expecting to see him stumbling after her along the sand, but the beach was empty. She waited beside the road until the autobus came by. It was filled with workmen, farmers, and a sprinkling of sleepy schoolkids. She found a seat with the kids and slept all the way into Ajaccio.

At the airport she found that the first flight out was to Milan; the ones to Nice and Toulon were later. She would have preferred to go to Nice, but she was still looking over her shoulder. She bought a ticket for the Milan flight, and an hour later she was in Italy.

She could have gone back to Ibiza then, but she didn't. Later on, after she had met up with Anna, they both agreed that the fates had decreed otherwise in order that the two of them could meet. It was one of those half-serious jokes that people who care for each other make with each other, and so they half

472

believed it. In fact, Jenny came very close to going back to the island. When she landed at Milan's Malpensa airport she went directly to the Pan American counter prepared to buy a ticket for Barcelona, and then to Ibiza. Fortunately, there was a long line at the counter, and before she reached the front of it she stepped away and sat down to think. She knew then that she wasn't ready to go back to the hilltop house without Sammy, but more than that she wasn't ready to pick up the strings of a life that was missing a central, vital part. That part wasn't Sammy, nor was it any other man she had ever met. She didn't know what was missing, whether it was a person, a thing, or an abstract concept, but this much she knew: There was an emptiness at the core of her being that had never been filled, and until she found out what it was she would never be content to live as she had before. Something was missing, and she would find it only by seeking it out, not by retreating to her island haven.

Armed with that thought, and with Sammy's money still wrapped in Angel's socks, she took a taxi into Milan, checked into the Sheraton there, and gave herself two weeks of doing nothing at all. She slept a lot, ate regular meals, bought some warm clothing, and let her thoughts drift idly. Sometimes she thought about Sammy lying crumpled on the deck of the *Cromwell,* and sometimes she thought of Angel lying in the sand with his eyes rolled back, but most of the time she tried to think in basic terms of what she wanted for her life. And most of the time she came up empty. November rolled by as she thought of these things, and the weather had turned to sharp frost and wool when she read in the *Rome Daily American* that the first World Cup race of the season would be held on December fourth at St Moritz. The race was part of the preliminaries that would lead to the Winter Olympics in Sapporo, Japan, but the news, in itself, was only mildly interesting to her. She knew that racing was permanently gone from her life, and over the past four years whenever she had thought of skiing it had been in terms of sheer pleasure rather than competition. She had lived on the flat for those four years, but the feel for the mountains had never left her, and reading that newspaper story in Milan she decided that one of the factors that she wanted back in her life was the feel of her edges carving snow. Two days later she was in St Moritz.

The place had not changed much. As always in St Moritz, some people skied and some dressed for skiing. The streets and the terraces of the hotels were filled with bright, excited people who seemed to have known and adored each other since childhood. Even so early in the season the hotels were solidly booked, and Jenny had to settle for a room in a guest house. She did not mind. It was enough to be back with familiar odours teasing her nostrils, the familiar crunch of snow underfoot, and the familiar bite of the wind on her cheek. The stylish people did not bother her. The mountains around St Moritz – Piz Corvatsch, Piz Nair, Diavolezza – were never in or out of fashion. She strolled the streets with her hands jammed into her unfashionable pockets, and wandered through the ski shops marvelling at the prices and the profusion of the merchandise being offered. So much had changed in four years. Skiing had always been so black and white, and now it had blossomed into a technicolour extravaganza. There were stacks of glossy skis with pastel logos, apricot stretch pants and cerise parkas, vividly coloured boots that were plastic shells with a forward lean built into them. She indulged herself in an orgy of shopping, including a pair of Royals out of a half-forgotten loyalty to Digger, and when her bindings had been mounted she took her treasures back to her room on try on and play with like a child with new toys.

She approached the mountain cautiously, unsure of unused skills. The first day she did nothing more than walk on her skis and let her body remember itself. On the morning of the second day she climbed gentle slopes, let herself slip, then climbed again; and in the afternoon she let herself run downhill. Only on the third day did she actually ski the lower reaches of Piz Nair, and when the day was finished she knew what she could do. The next day she attacked the mountain, skiing it easily and revelling in all the old freedoms of speed and style and grace. She had lost little. She would never again be a racer, but she knew that she could ski wherever she pleased, and that was enough for now. She finished the last run of the day flushed and contented, kicked her skis free, and was bending to pick them up when a voice behind her said:

'Excuse me, but you're Jenny Rosenzweig, aren't you?'

She straightened up and turned. The question came from a woman about her own age, chubby and plain but with a warm smile and understanding eyes. She hesitated to answer. She had nothing to hide, but still she hesitated.

'Of course you are,' said the woman. 'I recognized you at once on the hill.' The smile broadened. 'You don't remember me, but that's all right. It's been years.'

'I recognize you now. You're Anna Prinz. We're sort of cousins.'

'Sort of. I knew it was you up there when I saw that pigtail flying straight out behind, just like when you were a girl. Where in the world have you been the past few years?'

'That's a question and a half. It would take me hours to answer that one.'

'That sounds ominous. Is it? Do you want to tell me? I have plenty of time to listen.'

'It's not all that interesting. You'd be bored.'

'I don't think so.' Anna cocked her head to one side, contemplating. 'I don't think so at all. Let's go someplace where we can talk.'

'All right, I'd like some coffee. One of the cafés?'

'Oh goodness, we can do better than that. I have a house here for the week. We'll light a fire and have coffee with *Mohntorte*. That's poppyseed cake, and there's a bakery on the way. Shall we do that?'

'It sounds wonderful.'

The house was a large and well-furnished chalet. They lit the fire, drank the coffee, ate the cake, talked through the evening and then through the night. Jenny did most of the talking. To her surprise she found herself at once at ease with this stranger of a cousin. There was a warmth and a strength to Anna that prompted confidences. Without any reluctance she found herself talking about the early days with H-H, the succession of lovers that followed him, and the final sweet romance with Sammy Wyatt. She told it all, leaving out nothing, not even the night on the beach with Angel. Anna's face showed sadness when she heard of Sammy's death, and anger when she heard about Angel.

'Do you think you killed him?' she asked.

'I don't know. Probably. I don't care. Does that shock you?'

'No. He sounds like someone that God forgot.'

'Not that bad, but bad enough. A real miserable bastard.'

'I've never met anyone like that.'

'You're lucky.'

'Actually, I've never met anyone like you, either. We're almost the same age, but you've done so much more than I have.'

Jenny laughed shortly. 'I could have done without half of it.'

'I live a very quiet life by comparison, very dull.'

'Not so dull if it gives you a house like this one.'

Anna made a depreciating motion with her hands. 'Just part of my job. I work for my father, for Prinz Skis. During the season I move around the ski areas checking out the shops, making sure our products are displayed properly, handling complaints, things like that. Wherever I go there's a house like this waiting for me. It's an odd sort of life, no stability. This time next week I'll be in Cortina.'

'That doesn't sound dull to me, it sounds exciting. Plenty of chances to meet people.'

'I'm afraid I'm not a very social person.'

'No boyfriends? I can't believe that.'

Anna got up to poke the fire. Her face was hidden as she jabbed at the logs. When she turned back her cheeks were flushed from the heat. 'No, no boyfriends. I've never attracted men that way. Just one. . . .' Her voice trailed off.

'Tell me about him.'

'Not a happy story.'

'What I told you wasn't exactly a barrel of laughs.'

'No, it wasn't.' She laid down the poker and stretched herself in front of the fire. The reflections of the flames flickered over her glasses and obscured her eyes. 'It seems so long ago, but it was only last year. That's why I'm doing this work for my father. To get away from Vienna. To get away from . . . him.'

She told the story quickly; there wasn't much to tell. He was older, he was a professor at the university, he was married. They had almost a year together of stolen hours, evenings, even several weekends. She did not complain, she loved him too much for that. She was happy with what she got and she did not ask for more. She was willing to have it go on that way forever, but forever only lasted until the day he told her that his wife was pregnant.

'The bastard,' Jenny muttered.

'No,' Anna protested, 'it wasn't anything like that. He never promised me anything. It was something that always could have

476

happened, and it did. After that I couldn't stay in Vienna, so here I am, telling you about my one big love affair. My first and my last.'

'You're too young to talk that way.'

'Young? I haven't felt young since I left Vienna.' She shook herself, shaking off memories. She looked at her watch. 'My God, the time, we've been talking all night. Look, you don't have to go back to that room of yours. Stay here tonight and move in tomorrow. Why waste money when I have the room here?'

'I'd like that,' said Jenny without pretence. 'I'd like that very much.'

For the next three days Jenny accompanied Anna when she made her rounds of the ski shops in the mornings. In the afternoons they skied, and they spent the evenings in front of the fire. They stayed away from the cafés and bars; they did not need them. They knew at once that they suited each other as friends, and they spent those days finding out exactly how much. It was a time of quiet contentment as they got to know each other, the learning process advancing with each shared confidence, each gentle joke, each demonstration of strength or weakness. As the days went by they found themselves in tune with each other, and in no way the same, but each one completing the other like pieces in a jigsaw puzzle. They were amazed at how quickly this sense of completeness came to them. It was as if they had been that way for years.

They learned the little things about each other, all the quirks. Jenny could not eat hard-boiled eggs; Anna was allergic to citrus fruits. Jenny could drink alcohol all night long without effect, but she rarely touched it; Anna loved the stuff but got fuzzy after two drinks. Jenny, the athlete, was an indifferent dancer, while Anna, the awkward one, turned light as a feather on the dance floor. It went on that way, the learning process, down to the daily details. Anna found relaxation in washing her hair, while Jenny found it a bore.

'I hate it,' she said. 'There's so much of it. One of these days I'm going to cut it short.'

'Don't you dare,' Anna protested. 'That lovely hair. Here, let me wash it for you. No, really, I'd like to. I'm good at it.'

Anna's strong fingers, the warm water, and the sudsy shampoo lulled Jenny into a gentle torpor. Wrapped in a terry-cloth robe, her head over the basin, she felt calm and relaxed, not just on the surface of her body but all the way down to the core of it. She closed her eyes and leaned back her head as Anna applied a herbal conditioner. The scent of it floated and lifted her. She opened her eyes and looked up into Anna's kindly face. She smiled, and got a smile in return. She tried to remember the last time she had felt so peaceful.

'One minute for the conditioner to set,' said Anna, 'and then we rinse again.'

'The man in Vienna, your lover,' said Jenny. 'It wasn't a man, was it?'

'How clever of you to guess. Under we go.' She pushed Jenny's head towards the basin and began the rinse. 'No, she was the professor's wife. Her name was Maria and she had long, thick hair just like yours. I used to wash it for her. She cried all afternoon the day she told me she was pregnant. Poor Maria, she wanted the baby so much, and she knew that it would kill what we had. She was so happy and so sad.'

Jenny's head came up streaming water. 'Your only love?'

'Yes.'

'No men?' She towelled her hair roughly.

'Never. I just don't feel that way.'

'You could have told me.' She reached for the dryer. 'You didn't have to say it was a man.'

'It seemed better at the time. Now I don't care that you know. Here, let me do that.' She took the dryer from Jenny and began to work on her hair. They both were silent, thinking. When the drying was done, Anna leaned over and kissed Jenny lightly on the lips. 'There, all finished until the next time. That's what my mother used to say to me.'

Jenny said in a small voice, 'Thank you. I never had a mother. You made me feel like a little girl, and I liked that. Hey, what did I say?'

There were tears in Anna's eyes. She shook her head. 'It's nothing. It's just that I've been trying so hard not to do anything to frighten you, and now I go and kiss you, just like that.'

'You didn't frighten me.' Jenny stood up and the terry-cloth robe fell open. She did not bother to close it. 'I'm glad you did it.'

'You are?' Wonderment in Anna's eyes.

478

'Nobody ever kissed me that way before, so gently. Not even Sammy.'

They stood only inches apart, looking into each other's eyes. Anna broke the silence. 'What are you telling me?'

'I'm telling you that I've never been with a woman. I don't know anything about it. I don't even know how to begin. What are you telling me?'

'That I think that I love you. That there was only Maria, and so I don't know much more than you do. That I'm frightened.'

'Don't be.' Jenny's eyes sparkled. 'We're two little innocents, aren't we? I guess we'll have to find out what to do together. We'll have to teach each other.'

'Yes.' Anna took her hand. 'Let's teach each other, right now.'

They spent the rest of the evening teaching each other, learning how fine they were together, and in the morning they woke with the prayer that what they had found would last beyond that night and that day. It lasted long enough for them to go together to Cortina the following week, and to Val d'Isère the week after that, to Davos, and Innsbruck and on and on through the winter. It lasted when the season was over and they went down to Ibiza to the house on the hill. It lasted through the warm weather and into the cold again, lasting and growing stronger, and as the months turned into years and it seemed everlasting, they came to the conclusion that they were, indeed, living happily ever after.

Chapter Seven

From the Journals of Elizabeth Chandler Prince
Friday, 11 April 1975

> *Age, I make light of it,*
> *Fear not the sight of it,*
> *Time's but our playmate, whose toys are divine.*
> THOMAS WENTWORTH HIGGINSON
> (1823–1911)

A considerable choice of epigraphs present themselves on one's eightieth birthday. I eschew the obvious and take the above for mine. Does it accurately reflect my feelings? Not totally. I'm afraid I'm not all that jaunty about being eighty. Wish I were, but these words will do. Certainly they're more to my mind than some rubbish about custom staling my infinite varieties. Never had many of those, any in fact, and I don't know as how I'd want them if they came free with the breeze. Infinite varieties, my foot. Fifty-seven did fine for Mr Heinz, and just one of me is more than enough for the world to worry about.

Not that anyone is doing much fretting about Elizabeth Chandler Prince these days, unless one includes the sort of worrying that goes naturally with advanced age and a sizeable estate. Well, let them bite their fingernails. I'm not going anywhere for a while yet.

Suppose I should set down some words of wisdom for the occasion. Trouble is, I can't think of any. Can't imagine where the concept got started that sagacity is one of the functions of age. Some doddering old Lear-like fool trying to pretend that his brain wasn't slowly turning to mush. As they all must do eventually. Can't be denied. Even a first-class mind has to go, same as how you can't expect even a Rolls-Royce to roll on forever. I've never denied, at least within the sanctity of these pages, that I am possessed of a superior brain, but even that exquisite organ is beginning to show signs of wear. Not the same snap to me any more, don't have the instant ability to learn new material and retain it in memory. Language is partly to blame for that. I grew up in a time when the English language was static and without much variation. (The vocabulary, that is, not the orthography, God wot.) New words came into the language in a trickle then, new phrases and combinations were few. But now? Dozens every day, most of them spawned by a self-intoxicated technology that invents something 'new' with each blink of the eye and instantly demands a linguistic label to stick on it. I see enough of it every day in the office. Had some overeducated jackass the other day talking to me about 'S-glass and pre-preg,' which I knew had something to do with the fibreglass we use in making the skis, but I must confess that I had no idea as to the actual meaning of the words. (Sound vaguely obstetrical, if you ask me.)

Well, I've seen it all, I suppose, starting back when my

beloved Anton would shape a ski on his workbench out of a single piece of hickory. Then the laminated wood, and then the metals. Oh my, those metals. Suddenly had to learn a whole new vocabulary. Flex curve, torsion factors, snake effect, and similar charming constructions. But what a difference those metals made to the business. Thousands and thousands of new skiers who wanted the fun without the work. It was a bonanza, and God bless Howard Head, I say. Should have been us, might have been if my Anton had lived long enough, but we were right behind the first ones, and right in front of them after a while. Now everything is fibreglass, of course. Just when I thought I had my vocabulary straight along came polyesters and epoxy resins, air-channelled okume and aluminium-honeycomb cores, and now they are experimenting with graphite and boron fibres. Those aren't words, those are formulae. *The morn is up again, the dewy morn, With breath all incense.* Those are words. But air-channelled okume?

But in the long run it has to be that way, doesn't it? I hear them complain about the so-called generation gap, and I wonder what they're bellyaching about. Of course there's a gap, there has to be. When I was a girl I didn't expect my elders to understand me, and I don't expect to understand my juniors today. Can't be done, different values. Heaven preserve me from those 'senior citizens' who are 'hip' and 'with it,' and who claim to understand the aches and passions that move people fifty years younger than they are. Senile nonsense, that's what it is, the bleatings of those who fear the sight of age, and fight it with bold talk and miniskirts. That first-rate brain of mine may be softening around the edges, but so far it has preserved me from that variety of folly. Who would dare to call me a senior citizen? I am known far and wide as a crotchety old woman, and that's good enough for me.

But age serves youth, and that's the rub of it. Should be the other way around, but it isn't. We exist to perpetuate, to extend the line, and that does not mean only in a biological sense. It means, as well, an orderly succession to pride and place, and . . . bite the bullet . . . fortune. Which in plain English means that it's time to make another, final, change in my will, and won't the lawyers love that, the hovering vultures? I have fiddled with that dratted instrument so often over the years that the very paper must be worn from handling. Yet it must be done.

I have a flourishing business founded with my capital and expanded, after Anton's death, into what it is today by virtue of my energy and wit. Shall that all crumble with me? I have a son and two grandsons, and I must choose.

And what a collection the three of them make. The Hero of Yugoslavia, his older son the *idiot savant,* and that monster of precocity who seems, finally, to be growing up into a fairly normal young man. As for Digger, let honesty reign and bias seek the shadows. He had done extraordinarily well with Royal Skis. Of course, he needed that trollop's money for funding, but who am I to carp at that? I did the same for my husband, and the dollar of a virtuous woman is worth the same at the bank as that of the harlot. No, I must admit that my son has done well. He is an able businessman, so able in fact that when last I looked Royal was outgrossing us worldwide by about nine percent. Net value per share is something else again, since I am sure he is milking out a small fortune in perks and side deals, but that is his business and more power to him if he can get away with it. Still, I do not regret my original decision. It would have been impossible for the two of us to float in the same boat. One of us would have gone overboard, and it would not have been me.

As for Michael . . . what a conundrum he is. He's cracked, of course, not certifiably, but at least ten degrees to windward of acceptable norms. Aside from that insanity in Vietnam (which at least had a smack of holiness to it), I am told that he is now a confirmed drug-taker and risk-taker, the sort of young man we have today who delights in living on the very edge of danger. Yet for all of his looniness, there is a touch of genius in him, too. The genius of madness, and if he is ever able to saddle his devils and ride them into a lather there is no telling what he might accomplish. For himself, and for others. As I said, a conundrum to be puzzled at, and I wonder. . . .

Which leaves Kelly, and I suppose I should be popping my buttons with pride over that one. Good-looking lad in a clean way, smart as a whip, and sound enough in wind and limb to ski with the best of them. Promising material, but badly flawed (from my admittedly restricted point of view) by a blinding adoration of his father. 'Slavish' is the word for it. Honour thy father, indeed, but this is worship at the clay feet of an idol, and one has to wonder if any boy has ever truly grown to

482

manhood in a kneeling position. If his grandfather were alive . . . now there would have been a man for him to emulate. But as it is we must wait and see.

Trouble is, I'm running out of waiting room. Three men, and if only one of them had been born clef instead of crested I would know exactly what to do. Oh yes, indeed I would, no matter what the lack of logic. She might be the most vapid cow ever calved, yet still I would . . . but there we are, the choice does not exist. As always, man proposeth, God disposeth, and we women take what's left.

By the time I was seventeen I thought that Digger was God. I wasn't alone. A lot of other people felt that way. If there was ever a God of American skiing, it was Digger, the *Soldier on Skis,* the Hero of Yugoslavia, the man who had schussed the headwall at Tuckerman's Ravine. That year when I was seventeen I raced with the US Ski Team, and God was my full-time coach and racer-chaser. This made for some awkward situations. As a member of the team I was under the control of the coaching staff, but nobody there was going to argue with God when he told them that he was in charge of my training. So I travelled with the team, ate and slept with them, but I had little to do with the coaches. Digger supervised my training and planned my races. This didn't make me very popular with the other kids, and Digger's working on my skis made it worse. A racer-chaser is a representative of the ski manufacturer who follows the competitors around the racing circuit to service the athletes who used his company's products. He waxes the skis, sharpens the edges, takes care of the flat filing and all the repair work, leaving the skier free to concentrate on the race. Having God for a racer-chaser gave me a clear edge over the other kids on the squad.

'Don't let it bother you,' Digger told me. 'You take every edge you can get, because you'll need it. Most of those people are fully grown, but your body is still changing. When that happens a skier loses some coordination, and he has to work like hell to get it back.'

I figured that he was speaking from experience, but when I asked him if it had happened that way to him as a boy he shook his head impatiently. Things like that don't happen to God. They didn't happen to me, either, but I never told him that.

That winter I started out strong with top-ten finishes at Courmayeur, Parpen, and Wengen. I was skiing all three events, but after Wengen Digger pulled me out of the slalom and the GS and had me concentrate on downhill only. I don't know why he did it. He never intended me to be a single-discipline skier, and in some of his more feverish fantasies he saw three golds at Lake Placid in 1980, not just one. Perhaps he saw something that was robbing me of speed, perhaps it was only a hunch, but whatever it was, in those days his word was the law. And it worked. The next week at Val Gardena I came in first by thirty-six hundredths over Paolo Monteleone, who was the hometown favourite, and won again six days later at Innsbruck. With two aces back to back I was on a roll and feeling good about it, but at Val d'Isère I crashed and did a job on my left knee. I came back strong at Garmisch with a good-looking third, placed second at Bad Wiessee, and came back to the States looking for a win at Aspen to finish off the season.

Digger left Europe a few days before me and met me out in Colorado. He had been doings things like that all season, popping away for a few days and meeting me at the next stop on the circuit. He must have flown transatlantic half a dozen times that winter. He said that it was business that he had to take care of in New York, but that didn't sound right to me. He had been taking care of business on the road for years, and if he needed an office there was always the plant in Bern. Whatever it was that was taking up his time, it was obvious that he didn't want me to know about it, and I decided to let it go at that. I had the racing to think about, and anything else would have to wait until the season was over. Still, I didn't like it, and I didn't like the way he looked. Whatever was keeping him busy was beginning to show in his face: weary eyes and lines I had never seen before. They were lines of strain on a face that once had seemed ageless, and when I met him in Aspen I was pleased to see that the lines were gone, at least for the moment.

'You're looking good,' I told him.

'Let's get a win here and I'll look even better.'

On the morning of the race Digger was up early on the mountain checking the snow temperature, the air temperature, the crystallization, and the weather forecast. All those factors influence what wax you use on your skis, and a mistake in waxing can cost you the race. Everyone has horror stories about waxing mistakes: skis that stopped dead in the snow and refused to move, and others that ran away with the hill but left the skier behind. Once Digger had all the information together he came back to the ski room of the lodge where all the equipment was kept and went to work scraping down my number-one pair of r&r's. The room was noisy and busy with the racer-chasers from all the other outfits – Head, Rossignol, K–2 – working on skis and boots. A ski racer develops bone spurs on his feet, just like any other athlete, and his boots have to be modified constantly to accommodate them.

I asked Digger what wax he was going to use, and he looked around to see if he could be overheard. He trusted nobody, which was another reason why I wasn't too popular with my teammates. On the US Ski Team the racer-chasers and the coaches pooled their information and came up with a consensus wax for the day. Not Digger; he shared with no one, not even the rep from Royal Skis who serviced two of the other kids.

'S–11,' he said finally, which was not the name of a wax but our own code for a mixture of Ex-Elit Black and Swix Polar. From the tone of his voice he could have been passing on the secret of the MX missile system. 'There's some light powder on top, and it's as cold as my mother's heart up there.'

He was something remarkable to look at. All the other reps in the room were wage slaves working away in ragged jeans and T-shirts, and there was my old man stripping down a pair of skis with only a leather apron over his tailor-made pants and silk turtleneck, a star-sapphire ring on his little finger and a *claro* clenched between his teeth. He looked as out of place as a peacock at a barbecue, but he knew more about the work than anyone else in the room. He glared at me impatiently. He didn't like my hanging around the ski room on race days. Worrying about the equipment was his job.

'Get out of here and let me work,' he said. 'Get some air, get some rest, just get.'

I went outside and walked around for a while, and when I came back he was ironing the greenish-black wax onto the bottoms of my skis in long, steady strokes. I told him that the temperature outside had gone up a touch.

'Down here, but not up on top,' he said without looking up. 'It'll stay close to zero there.'

'Maybe we'd better wax up another pair with something

lower. S–9 or S–10, just in case.' I went to the rack to get another pair of my skis. On the road we travelled with three pair of r&r's, the rock-and-rollers that really move, and a pair of inspectors for looking over the course. That was only for the downhill. We carried three pair of discos for the slalom and three more for GS.

'You don't need another pair,' he said. 'I've got the right wax.'

I stopped with my hand on the rack. 'Come on, Digger, why take a chance?'

'Nobody's taking any chances. She'll stay cold.'

'I'm going to look pretty silly out there if she warms up later.'

He finally looked up at me. 'You're going to look pretty silly with this ski wrapped around your ass if you don't get out of here and let me finish this job.'

That was final enough for me. I got out of his way, killed an hour on the local newspapers, and then it was time to go to work. I rode the lift up to the top of the mountain with Jerry Donner, the two of us in our one-piece, skin-tight red-and-white racing suits, helmets on our knees. It was cold going up, with no sign of warming, and I knew that Digger had been right once again.

Donner was a slalom skier who was trying to make the switch to downhill, and he was quiet during the trip, thinking about the race. That was the reason he had never made it in the slalom: He was an imaginative kid who thought too much. Digger had taught me early on to tune out my mind on race days, but no one had ever told that to Donner, and it ruined him for slalom. It was a shame, because he was a natural skier with beautiful technique. His problem was that he couldn't finish races. He would turn in outstanding training runs, but on race day, almost always, he would disqualify by missing a gate. It happened with depressing frequency, and always at the beginning of the run. Somewhere around the third, fourth, or fifth gate he'd miss the turn and his race was over right there. The coaches called it a lack of concentration, but I couldn't see it that way.

'I could understand it if he blew out near the bottom,' I told Digger, 'or even halfway down the hill, but how much concentration does it take to ski the first five gates?'

'You don't understand that kid any more than the coaches

do,' he said. 'Donner is a hell of a skier, he just thinks too much. He's like a writer who knows exactly what he wants to say but he's too impatient to put the words down on paper one at a time. Maybe a better comparison would be a painter who wants the physical product of his inspiration slapped right on the canvas, just like that, without taking the time to do the actual painting. Not that the kid is lazy, he isn't. He just hasn't learned yet that you ski a slalom course one gate at a time. When Donner is standing in the starting gate his head has already crossed the finish line. He's already skied the perfect slalom. Then he gets the go and he tries to do it at once. One explosive moment, he tries to run the whole race top to bottom, and bango, he misses a gate and he's out. Has to be. Damn shame – he's got all the talent in the world.'

'Then what can he do about it?'

'Stop thinking,' said Digger. 'That's all, just stop thinking.'

But he couldn't stop thinking, and after a while he couldn't ski slalom any more. Now he was trying to make the switch to downhill, but that wasn't working out either. He was still thinking too much.

When I got to the top I went looking for Digger and found him talking to a couple of FIS officials who were friends of his from the old days. CBS Sports was covering the event, and some of those people were there too. I gave him a silent wave. I was starting first, which meant that I would go off in about half an hour, and it was time to do what Jerry Donner had never learned to do. I began the process of tuning out my mind.

I picked up a handful of snow and stared at it. That was the way that Digger had taught me to do it: to stare at the snow going deeper and deeper into it until I found, in the centre of my mind, one perfect crystal. Enter into the crystal, marking the precision of the angles and the edges, again delving deeper and deeper until I was one with the snow-flake, one with the snow, one with the snowy mountain; and everything else dropped away. Everything. The race, the racers, the cameras, the crowd. Everything except the snowflake, and me attuned to the perfection of the crystal.

I skied lazily around the flat near the starting gate, my poles in one hand, the snow in the other, my helmet pushed back and my head down as I stared at the crystal. Moving slowly with my eyes on the flakes in my hand, my mind was halfway into the crystal when I heard an ugly rasping noise and felt a shuddering under my skis. In my concentration I had run over a half-exposed conduit for a television cable. I took my skis off to look at the bottoms; almost all of the wax had been stripped away down to the base. I went looking for Digger to show them to him.

'My my, you did quite a job,' he said calmly, drawing on his cigar and letting the smoke go with his head tilted back. 'Well, you'll just have to use them the way they are. They're all we have with us.'

I was trying for calm, but it wasn't easy. 'If you'd listened to me we'd have another pair here.'

'With the wrong wax,' he pointed out.

'Better than no wax at all.'

'Forget the wax.' He took another expansive puff. 'You'll win anyway. I know this hill, it's made for you.'

That did it. There went the calm, the crystal shattered. 'God damn it, Digger, I'll be dead without wax and you know it. I mean, I can't believe what you're saying. You're telling me that I don't need wax? You're telling me to run this son of a bitch with a pair of dead skis? You're telling me that . . .'

He stopped me by yawning in my face, and my voice spluttered out. When he was finished yawning, he said, 'You worry too much about details, Kelly.'

'Details. No wax. That's a detail?'

'You know, you kids today don't know how lucky you are. When I was a boy my father used to rub my skis down with bear grease. Now stop worrying. Just get a good start and push hard. You've got this one made.'

'Bear grease, huh?'

'Bear grease,' he said solemnly.

It sounded funny, but I was burning. I didn't trust myself to say anything more. I skied over to the start hut to wait for race time.

When it came I got my good start and came out attacking the top of the hill. I knew that I had to make my time there, on my edges, because I wouldn't be able to glide worth a damn without wax down below. I got everything I could out of the top part of the course, and it was one of those days when things went right with the turns, the outside ski carving snow like Michelangelo. The glide wasn't too bad either, I can always glide no matter what, and I came in at 2:18.42, looking up at the flashing numbers on the board as I curled to a stop in the outrun area. Then I had my skis off and up with the Royal logo on them facing out for the cameras. That's part of the game, getting those skis with the brand name on them in front of the cameras as quickly as possible. That's why they pay you the money, and some of the Austrians have the quickest skis in the West that way. One of them reaches down for the release latch just as he crosses the finish line, and one of these days he's going to hit it too soon.

So I got the Royals off and up for the public to see, and then Frank Emory of CBS had the microphone in my face and was asking the usual questions. I was so pissed off that I was tempted to say something about skiing without wax, but I didn't. It's a game and you play it. I said what had to be said, and when the camera was off me I grabbed a walkie-talkie from one of the coaches and spoke to Digger at the top.

'Eighteen forty-two doesn't sound bad,' he said, his voice a crackle. 'Any pearls of wisdom for the guys?'

You're supposed to pass along any tips about the condition of the course for your teammates coming down after you, but I was still sore and all I could think of to say was, 'Yeah, tell them to use wax. Some wax, any wax. But definitely use wax. Over.'

'Over and out,' was all I got back.

I stood around and watched the rest of the world take a crack at my time, and when it was over I had won by twenty-nine hundredths. Digger was down at the bottom by then, and once the win was sure he breathed a deep sigh and told me how worried he had been.

'I figured you were screwed,' he admitted. 'I didn't think you'd be able to finish on those skis, much less win.'

'That wasn't how you sounded with all that talk about bear grease.'

'Question of confidence. Had to keep you believing.'

'Confidence, my ass, it was total bullshit.'

'Not total. Even without wax you're better than most of these people. And it worked, didn't it?'

That should have been the end of it; but it wasn't. I couldn't let it lie there. It wasn't just that I was angry. It was time for some changes that were long overdue. Maybe I should have waited until we got back to the lodge, maybe I should have let myself cool off, but I wanted it out in the open right there.

'Digger, you'd better listen up,' I said, 'because I'm too pissed off to say this more than once.'

'Oh?'

'Yeah. You're treating this like a joke, and it wasn't. It was an accident compounded by an error in judgement. I got careless and scraped my bottoms, but that can happen whenever there are television cables lying around. More important was that we didn't have a backup pair of skis.'

'We never carry a backup.'

'Up until now. From here on in we do.'

He looked at me with interest. 'You giving orders?'

'I'm stating a fact. I wanted you to wax a backup and you wouldn't. I don't want that happening again. If I want something like that, and I don't care what it is, I want it done.'

'Is that so? You running this show now?'

'No, but I'm telling you what I want.'

'I think maybe you'd better watch your mouth.'

'Come on, Digger, don't pull that shit with me. What are you going to do, turn me over your knee in front of all these people?'

'Don't tempt me. You're big for seventeen but I still could do it.'

'Maybe you could, that's not the point. Look, you're taking this the wrong way. You're my father, you're my coach, and you're a great skier. I respect you for all those reasons and plenty more besides. But there's one thing you're not. You're not the racer in this family. I am, and it's my ass that's on the line out there. I'm the one who has to do the winning, and I'm the one who has to take the lumps. So you're still in charge, but if I want something like a pair of backups, or any other little thing like that, I want to get it without any chickenshit arguments. I just want it done. And if we can't work that way together then maybe it's time to rethink this whole business of ski racing.'

'What the hell is that supposed to mean?'

'It means that you and I don't share all the same obsessions. I enjoy racing and I'm good at it, but it wouldn't be the end of my life if I quit.'

'You don't mean that.'

'Don't try me on it. I wouldn't mind getting a decent education instead of the mess I have now. I wouldn't mind getting off the road and living in one place for a while. I wouldn't mind meeting some people who have something to talk about besides skiing, and while we're talking about it I wouldn't mind skiing just for the fun of it. So don't try me, Digger, I mean it.'

He reached into a pocket for a cigar, didn't find one there, and let his fingers flutter. His eyes were suddenly weary, and the lines I had seen all winter were back on his face. 'All right, I won't call you on it,' he said. 'I still don't believe you mean it, but I won't.'

'Then we understand each other?'

'We do. Christ, that's all I needed today, a fucking declaration of independence.' He looked at his watch. 'I've got some phone calls to make. I'll see you back at the lodge.'

We could have gone back together, but I let that go. I should have felt some sort of triumph as I watched him walk away, but I didn't. All I could think of was that he had given in much too easily.

Chapter Eight

With the racing season over I went back to Europe to ski what was left of the spring snow with my brother, Mike. Digger wasn't wildly happy about that, since Mike was supposed to be a bad influence on me, and Bobby wasn't happy either, because I was supposed to have spent that time with a tutor, but neither of them tried to stop me. I flew to Milan and hooked up with Mike at Cortina d'Ampezzo, and it was the usual hair-raising experience. Skiing with Mike was fun, but it also was hard on your nerves. You kept waiting for something to happen. In the years since he had come home from Vietnam he had climbed every mountain he could find, he had tamed wild horses in Nevada, he had done his meditating soaring over California cliffs, and he had criss-crossed the deserts of Baja on his Yamaha; but when the cold weather came he turned to the serious business of skiing. He did all this with a brace of cameras strapped around him, and the photographs that he took made money. A lot of money, enough of it so that whenever Digger made his periodic suggestion about going to work for Royal Mike could turn down the offer without regret. He would have turned it down anyway – the thought of working for Digger was terrifying – but the money made it easier.

Every winter he covered the circuit from Squaw Valley to Aspen, to Alta, to Stowe, and then overseas to Val d'Isère, Chamonix, St Moritz, Kitz, Cortina, Kranjska Gora, and back again, never travelling with less than six pair of skis, a stash of coke secured in the hollowed-out handle of a ski pole, and any one of a series of ornamental but vacuous women. He was an instantly identifiable figure on the mountainside, the spiderlike body all arms and legs, crouched over his skis, the ridiculous red stocking cap pulled down over his ears, and the cackle of his wild laughter as he raced across the slope. He skied hard all day, partied all night, and was out on the mountain early the next morning to do it all over again. He skied that way every winter until he broke something, and then the winter was over for him. He always managed to break something. He had broken both legs, his right forearm, every finger of both hands, three of his ribs, and improbably enough, the toes of his left foot while doing a *Geländesprung* on breakable crust. Along the ski circuit in the Seventies he was a living legend, and those who knew him well privately wondered how long it would take him to kill himself. They wondered, but they didn't worry about it. The kind of friends he had didn't worry about anything.

I worried, of course, and I told him so that spring in Cortina after he broke a small bone in the back of his hand. The break itself was nothing, but he had done it stupidly, schussing the run down from Tondi without a check and then trying to jump a gully at that speed. He had misjudged the prejump and gone into the ditch, breaking the fall with his hand and breaking one of those tiny bones as well.

'It could have been your neck,' I told him after he had been to the first-aid station at Codivilla. 'You must have been stoned to do something dumb like that. Tell me the truth, were you stoned?'

Instead of an answer I got a hoot of wild laughter. He held up his hand to admire the airfoam cast. 'Amazing, the progress in orthopaedics,' he said. 'I can remember when a cast like this weighed a ton.'

'You *were* stoned, weren't you?'

'Me? On the hill? Certainly not.'

I didn't say anything; I just looked at him.

'Jesus, Kelly, you can be awfully stuffy sometimes.'

'I worry about you. If that's being stuffy, okay.'

'Shit, I didn't mean it that way.' The rough edge was gone from his voice. We were sitting in the lounge of the Cristallo, and it was almost empty. He took a sip of his beer, and said, 'I'm sorry, I mean I know that you worry, but . . . look, you just worry about yourself. Your job is to keep your ass in one piece for the greater glory of the family. That's the golden plan. My job is to break bones, your job is to get a medal in 1980.'

'Don't start with me on that. I get enough of the golden plan from the old man.'

He looked at me shrewdly. 'You want it, don't you?'

'Sure I want it, who wouldn't? But I'm not sure I want what goes with it.'

'Fame and fortune.' He made the words sound like the tolling of bells.

'Not for me, for the company.'

'It's all part of the golden plan. You cop a gold wearing a pair of Royal skis and the sales chart goes through the ceiling. Don't worry, you'll get your share of it.'

'Maybe I don't want my share.' I knew that the words sounded hard and stubborn, but I didn't care. 'Maybe that's not the way I see myself.'

'The piano?'

I nodded.

'Boy, you're gonna break your daddy's heart. You're gonna make me look like an angel.'

'Mike, you know me better than anybody. You know I'm never going to be any kind of a businessman.' I walked over to the piano at the side of the bar, sat down, and said, 'Give me a cigarette, will you?'

'When did you start smoking?'

'I don't. Just give it to me.'

He shook a Marlboro out of his pack and handed it over. I wet the filter end with my tongue, then rolled the cigarette around on my lips until it rested hanging from the corner of my mouth. I half-closed my eyes against imaginary smoke, tilted my head back, and began to play. My left hand pumped bass and my right hand, feather-soft, whispered 'Memphis Blues.'

As I played, I said, 'Now I'm going to tell you something, and if you laugh, just once, you and I are finished.'

I told him then about the Hoagy Carmichael fantasy, the old-time piano player in the broken-down saloon, how he just sits there and does his music, and every once in a while a customer sends him over a glass of beer, and every once in a while a pretty girl comes by and rubs the back of his neck. And he never stops playing, he just looks up and gives her a wink, and he goes on doing his music.

'And nobody hassles him,' I said. 'You know what I mean?'

'Yeah, I know,' he said wonderingly. 'It sounds like you want to be a bum just like me.'

'Maybe everybody wants to be some kind of a bum.' I shifted into 'Mood Indigo.' 'But that's the way I see myself, I don't know when, but somewhere up the line. Just sitting in some waterfront café, some dive where the air is full of smoke and the piano is flat, and all I have to do is play my music. Nothing fancy like Bobby Short at the Carlyle, just a joint where nobody bothers me, nobody expects me to win any medals, and every once in a while a pretty girl comes by to rub the back of my neck. It doesn't sound like much, but that's what I want. Pretty dumb, huh?'

'Dumb, my ass, it sounds eminently sane. It makes me wish I could play the piano.'

'You've got your own way of doing it, you don't need a piano.'

'You'll never get away with it, you know. He'll never let you.'

'I know, but that's what I want.'

'Yeah, that and a gold medal, too.'

'Not necessarily.'

'Don't bullshit me, brother. Your name is Prince, the same as mine, and that means you want it all.'

'I guess I do.' I let my fingers slip from the keys. 'I guess I want them both. It's a hell of a combination, isn't it?'

The broken bone in his hand wasn't enough to keep Mike from his usual routine of finishing up the season at Kranjska Gora, over the border in Yugoslavia. The easiest way to get there from Cortina was to drive down to Udine by way of Belluno, take the secondary road that crosses the Yugoslav border at Matajur, and head north into the Julian Alps from there. That made it a nasty piece of driving when the snow and the ice were still on the ground, but flying meant going first to Vienna, and the train connections were impossibly complicated. So we made the trip by car, Mike and his girl and me.

Unblushingly, I must now invent a name for that girl. In those days Mike's women were all so much alike that they were indistinguishable one from the other. They were all incredibly lovely with the kind of physical beauty that hurt, actually hurt you when you looked at them. Sleek tummies and tapering thighs, sweeping breasts, sculpted nostrils and eyes . . . you looked at one of them and first there was a sense of outrage at this unequal distribution of God's blessings, followed at once by a blow to the gut when you realized that she would never be yours. They were all that way, and they were all, without exception, unredeemably stupid women. I admired and disliked them with equal intensity, and I could never understand how Mike could put up with them for more than one night at a time.

I'll call this one Lacey. Most of his girls had names like that: Lacey, and Stacey, and Marcey, and Jaycee, except for the post-preps who called each other things like Muffy and Buffy and Bumps. Lacey was thrilled by the idea of driving over the border into Yugoslavia. She had never been in a Communist country before and it sounded romantic.

'I'm going to write to my mother and tell her that I'm going behind the Iron Curtain,' she decided. 'Just in case I get arrested for spying, or something.'

'It isn't the Iron Curtain,' Mike assured her, 'and you won't get arrested.'

'At least not for spying,' I said, thinking about that ski pole of his with the hollowed-out handle. He never went anywhere without his stash.

Mike cocked an eyebrow, something I could never do. 'What's that supposed to mean?'

'Just trying to keep your nose clean. What's left of it.'

He held up his hands, a horrified protest. 'I travel empty, I always do. Nothing crosses the border with me.'

'Not always.' He had taken a bust in Spain that had cost Digger ten big ones and a couple of favours called in.

'That was in my foolish youth. There won't be a speck in the car, Kelly, not a trace.'

'Look, I'm not being a moralist about this . . .'

'Sure you are, but that's all right.'

' . . . it's just that I'm not anxious to do any time for your habit.'

'Trust me.'

'I trust you.'

'Would I lie to you?'

'Only if it was absolutely necessary.'

He spread his hands and grinned like a lopsided scarecrow. 'So there you are.'

'Yeah, there I am.' It wasn't morality and I wasn't down on his drug, even though it wasn't mine. When the monsters come calling everybody picks his own weapon off the wall. I was worried for him because nobody else seemed to be. 'All right, deal me in.'

'Does that mean that he's coming too?' Lacey was clearly disappointed. 'I thought it was going to be just the two of us.'

'Are you kidding?' Mike looked at her in mock surprise. 'We can't go without Kelly. We'd be lost in Yugoslavia without him.'

'Why him?' She was staring at me, puzzled.

'You said it yourself, it's a Communist country.' He lowered his voice. 'Kelly knows the ropes in there. He's CIA. That's for your ears only, of course.'

'But he's only seventeen.'

'That's his deep cover. They recruit 'em early these days. How long have you been with the Company, kid?'

'Since I was eight years old. Full-time once I turned ten.'

'You see? He has to go along.'

'Well, if you say so.' She wasn't fully convinced.

'I say so.'

'I just thought that . . .'

'No, you didn't. And if you did, you shouldn't have.' He reached out a finger and ran it along her smooth forehead. 'Thinking causes worry lines, Lacey. You don't want to get worry lines, do you?'

'I never get anything,' she said happily. 'I think I'm immune.'

'You're a lucky girl.'

'Not even the clap. Half my friends have had the clap, but not me, knock wood.'

'Worry lines are worse than the clap, Lacey. Worry lines are forever, like herpes. Promise me you won't think, okay? You'd look awful with worry lines.'

496

'Actually, I'm thinking all the time. Do you want to know what I think about?'

'No,' he said quickly. 'Just don't think when I'm around. I don't want to see you get all wrinkled up like a prune.'

I said, 'I'll bet I know what you think about.'

'You do?' A touch of suspicion there.

'Sure. I'll bet you think about beautiful things. Sunsets and full moons. The way a sailboat skims across the lake. The smell of fresh-cut grass and crushed wild flowers. The sleek way a cat walks. The tangy taste of a winter apple. The way a happy baby smiles. Things like that.' I ignored Mike's almost inaudible groan. 'I'll bet you never think of anything ugly or unhappy. Just cool breezes on hot days, and toasty jammies on frosty nights. That's what you think about, the good things in life.'

'Wise-ass,' Mike muttered.

'But that's amazing,' said Lacey, her perfect lips formed in a perfect circle. 'How in the world did you know?'

'It's a trick they teach us in the CIA.'

'*Wunderkind.*'

'It's just unbelievable,' she squealed. 'Mike, he knows me inside out.'

'Nobody knows you inside out,' I assured her solemnly. 'Actually, you're a very complex person, Lacey.'

'Jesus.' Mike was thoroughly disgusted now. 'I think maybe we'll leave you here after all.'

But he didn't, of course. We left the next morning driving south on the S–51 in Mike's battered Buick station wagon, the back of the car a welter of skis and boots, poles, cameras, luggage, and a half-dozen of the round white boxes of Italian fruitcake which had become Lacey's passion. With all that gear in the back we had to sit three in the front, which was all right with me because that meant Lacey sat in the middle. It was dizzying just to sit next to her, to inhale her fragrance, to study the flawless line of her cheek and chin, and to feel the pressure of her thigh against mine on the right-hand turns. Yes, I still remember those right-hand turns.

Mike did all the driving despite the airfoam cast on his left hand. He didn't trust Lacey on the winter roads, and although I offered to share it he said no. He said it the right way, too, not like an older brother slapping down a kid. He just waited a moment, thinking it over, and then said quietly, 'No thanks, Kelly, I can handle it.'

It was snowing lightly when we left Cortina, but once we were out of the mountains it turned to rain and a dirty haze. The *autostrada* follows the Piave there, and we could see the fog rising up from the river to spread itself over the fields of cut-back vines and chestnut trees that were ready to bud on the first warm day. The fog eased up below Belluno and disappeared entirely once we were in the lowlands proper and heading east for Udine. With the road clear the Italian drivers began to pick up speed in their ritual dance with death, hooting us down as they flashed by. Mike ignored them and kept it to a respectable one hundred and twenty klicks, which was not his style. He usually drove the way he skied, with a lead foot, and it bothered me because I knew why he was doing it.

'Pick it up,' I said. 'You're embarrassing us.'

He shook his head. 'Not with the family jewels in the car.'

We stopped for a quick lunch outside Pordenone, massive sandwiches of breaded veal, and when we came out to the car it was snowing again. This was the real stuff, wet and heavy, not like the snow we had got earlier. I breathed in, closed my eyes and held my breath. It was in the air, all right, strong enough to taste, the smoky smells of burning wood and bonded bourbon that mean a long and heavy snowfall. I opened my eyes and looked at Mike. He had taught me how to smell for snow, and I wondered if there was enough left of the inside of his nose for him to do it any more.

As usual, he knew what I was thinking, and he grinned. 'Yeah, I got it, too. We'd better make some time.'

The snow thickened into a storm before we reached Udine, and the *autostrada* packed up with the stuff until all signs of lanes and order were gone and the cars were like iceboats skimming down a frozen river. The yellow warning lights came on along the side of the road and on the overheads, and even the Italians were driving slowly.

It would have made sense to stay the night in Udine, but there was the chance that the border roads would be closed if the storm kept up, and so Mike decided to go on. 'We should be able to get through,' he said, 'and if we get stuck we can always find a place to sleep along the road.' He made it sound very matter-of-fact, but it was another challenge to him and he was coming out to meet it, testing and pressing his luck.

It was dark by the time we got past Udine, and the road wound up into the mountains again. After Cividale it was twenty kilometres more to the border crossing at Matajur, and along that stretch the road lights were spaced far apart. We drove from point to point, from light to pool of light with the flakes coming out of the night at us like white bullets and the fir trees that lined the road leaning in on us under the weight of the darkness and the snow.

The border crossing at Matajur was set on the hump of a hill with the town itself off to the right and below. On the Italian side the control point was a low grey stone building with plenty of glass and chrome stripping, and a covered drive-through to keep out the weather while the inspectors did their work. Fifty yards down the road the Yugoslav control point was an older, smaller building set out in the open with only a swinging pole to control traffic. The Italian building was lit by floodlights buried behind snow-covered shrubs, but on the Yugoslav side there was only a single lamp over the door. It was snowing just as hard on either side.

The Italians let us through quickly. All they cared about was money going out of the country, and all our forms were right. We drove slowly down the road and stopped in front of the light on the Yugoslav side. A soldier in a greatcoat buttoned high against the snow and a fur hat with a red enamel star on it came out, collected our passports, and went inside again.

Lacey whispered, 'Did you see the red star on his hat? *Extreem.*'

Mike looked at her wearily. 'What did you expect him to be wearing, a dollar sign?'

'It's scary,' she said. 'It's just like the movies.'

'Careful, you're starting to think again.'

We waited with the motor running, the heater blasting, and the window misting up; and after we had waited twenty minutes I began not to like it. It didn't seem to bother Mike. He looked loose behind the wheel.

'He's sure taking his time,' I said.

'They like to keep you waiting, it goes with the job.' Our eyes met, and in that moment I knew that he had lied to me and he was carrying.

499

I said softly, 'I've got a very heavy feeling. If you can get rid of it now, do it.'

He stared at me without expression, then gave a tiny shake of his head. It could have meant that I was wrong, or it could have meant that there was nothing he could do about it. He looked away. The soldier came out of the building. He tapped on the window and Mike rolled it down.

'You follow me,' he said in heavily accented English. 'Fifty metres.'

We followed him down the road to a low, wide, garagelike building with roll-up doors. The doors were open and the lights were on inside. We drove into the building, and the doors rolled down behind us. There were two other soldiers there, one of them an officer. He bent over to speak through the window.

'Good evening, I am Major Arzim. Would you all please get out of the car.' His English had no accent, and he was smiling.

We eased out, stretching, and Mike said, 'What's it all about, major?'

'Routine inspection.' He held up our passports. 'Mr Michael Prince. You have a certain reputation.'

'Oh, Christ, not that again. Every customs man in the world wants to bust Mike Prince.'

'Your name is familiar to us,' the major admitted. 'Your father, of course, is a national hero here, but you, I'm afraid, are a naughty boy. We give special attention to naughty boys.'

'It's a waste of time, I have nothing to declare.'

The major thought that was funny. 'I didn't think you had.' He waved us over to a table against the wall. 'Your pockets first, gentlemen. Miss Cumberland, your bag.'

We emptied everything onto the table, and Arzim went through it all: keys, coins, billfolds, cigarettes, lipstick, even the crumpled tissues in the bottom of Lacey's bag. He opened my billfold, peeked inside, and did the same with Mike's. He saw the thick wad of bills.

'You carry a great deal of money, Mr Prince.'

'Yes,' said Mike, 'and I know exactly how much is there.'

Arzim flipped the billfold onto the table. 'We are not thieves here.'

They did the body search next. The two soldiers went over Mike and me, while Arzim took care of Lacey. 'My apologies,' he said to her, 'but I do not have a woman here to do this.'

'I can see that you're heartbroken,' she said. 'Go ahead, enjoy yourself.'

He gave her a polite going-over, not lingering, and she took it stiffly. When he was finished he stepped back and said, 'So much for routine, now for the car. Do sit down – this may take some time.'

We restuffed our pockets and watched as they took our luggage apart. They unloaded the car and went through our bags. They checked the skis, the boots, the cameras, and peeled the rubber off the rims of our goggles. Arzim checked the ski poles, tapping the shafts and twisting the grips. He did not seem surprised when one of the grips came off in his hand. He held it up to look inside. It was empty. Mike grinned.

They started in on the car itself. They removed the seat, went behind the dashboard, and took up the floor. They checked under the hood, under the frame, then took off all the tyres and wheels and examined them one by one. By the time they were finished the soldiers were covered with grease and the leakage of dirty ice. They found nothing. Arzim strode up and down in front of us, his bootheels tapping on the concrete floor. He was disappointed, and he wasn't smiling any more. His eyes fixed on Mike's hand and on the airfoam cast around it. He smiled briefly, and his own hand shut out to grab Mike by the wrist.

'Of course,' he said. 'How stupid of me.'

Mike tried to pull away, and Arzim pulled back. It was a tug-of-war until one of the soldiers came around and pinned Mike to the table. I started off the bench, but the other soldier got to me and slammed me down again.

Lacey gasped, and Mike said tightly, 'Kelly, stay put.' He looked up at Arzim, who still had a lock on his wrist. 'Major, there's a broken bone under that cast.'

'If you say so.' Arzim was smiling again. 'And something else, perhaps.'

They held Mike's hand to the table and cut off the cast with a pair of tin snips. There was nothing under the cast, and nothing in it, either. Arzim cut it to shreds. Still nothing. He flung the snips across the room, and they clattered along the floor. He picked them up and threw them again. They bounced off an empty oil drum. He said something over his shoulder to the soldiers. They let go of Mike and me and went to work on the car, putting it back together again.

501

As soon as the hands on my shoulders were gone I slipped off my belt, buckled it again, and passed it over to Mike. He looked at it, puzzled, then nodded and fixed the loop over his shoulder to form a rough sling for his hand.

'Hang in there, won't be long now,' he said softly. His face was pale, and he was sweating.

The soldiers made the car intact and reloaded it. Arzim slouched against the oil drum, his eyes fixed on the floor. When the car was ready he nodded wearily and said, 'You may go now.'

We started for the car. I figured that I would have to drive because of Mike's hand, and so I went around to the left side. I had my hand on the door when Arzim said, 'Mr Prince, one moment, please.'

Mike turned. Arzim was standing behind him, his hand extended. 'Before you go I'd like to see your billfold one more time.'

Mike looked disgusted. 'What was that you said about thieves?'

'The billfold, please.' Mike did not move. Arzim wiggled his fingers. 'Shall I have them hold you again while I take it?'

'How much?'

'Just the billfold, and now.'

Mike reached into his pocket, came out with the wallet, and handed it over. Arzim opened it, extracted the thick sheaf of bills, and rifled it with his thumb. He rifled it again, then took the stack over to the table and spread the bills out in a fan. He picked one at random, held it up to the light, and put it down again. He did the same with another, then another. He held the fourth bill up, grunted, then looked at Mike over his shoulder.

'How many are there like this one?' he asked.

Mike did not answer.

'Save us some time, Mr Prince.'

'Ten altogether,' Mike said casually. 'The last ten in the stack.'

'Thank you.'

Arzim separated nine more bills from the pile. With his fingernails he clipped the corner off one of them and tilted it over the table. A stream of white crystals ran out of the corner and made a tidy pile. It wasn't one bill, it was two of them sealed together perfectly to form a pouch hardly thicker than the bills themselves. The pouch was filled with a superior level of coke.

'Ingenious,' said Arzim. 'You deserve every bit of your reputation.'

Mike shrugged off the compliment. 'I'm not in business, that's just my personal stash. What happens now?'

'Now we deal.'

'That's what I figured.'

'If you'll come with me please?'

Arzim led the way to a door at the back of the building. He and Mike went into a small room there and the door clicked shut behind them. A few minutes later Mike came out alone. He walked over to where Lacey and I were leaning against the car. His face was set in lines.

'How much did it cost?' I asked.

'He wasn't kidding, he isn't a thief. He doesn't want any money.' He was looking at Lacey, not me.

She caught the look and said, 'Uh-oh.'

'Yep.'

'Me?'

'That's it.'

'Oh, Lordy, I knew he was a creep.'

'That's his game. If you do him we can walk.'

'If not?' she asked.

'Then it's a bust, a heavy one.'

'The bastard, the creepy bastard.'

Confused, I said, 'Wait a minute, what's going on here?'

Neither of them answered me; they were too busy with each other. This is the way we were standing: me leaning against the front door of the car with Lacey beside me leaning against the back door, and Mike facing her, looking down into her eyes. The grim look was gone from his face. He seemed calm now, almost peaceful, and he was looking at her with such a consuming tenderness that I felt like an intruder and had to move away. I gave them some space by sliding down the car as far as the fender. That was all I could give them. Whatever was happening involved me and I had to be part of it.

Mike put his hands on her shoulders and said, 'I'm not asking you to do it. You understand that, don't you?'

'Sure.'

'It's not something I'd ask anybody to do.'

'I know that too.' She frowned, that perfect underlip bowing

503

slightly. 'But you're going to have to ask me whether you want to or not.'

'What the hell for?'

'Mike, you're asking me right now, just standing there and staring at me that way. You're asking me to go into a dingy back room and ball a cop so that we won't have to take a bust. And I'm going to do it, too. But you'll have to ask me first.'

'I won't do that.'

'You'll have to. Otherwise you can go back there and tell him that it's no deal.'

'But why?'

'Because if you don't we're finished, the two of us.' That underlip was trembling now. 'Don't you see it? This is the closest I've ever come to whoring. A lot of banging around, but not whoring like this. All right, I'm going to do it, but if I have to do the whoring then you have to do the pimping. Otherwise we're not worth shit together, and we never will be. Do you see it now?'

He saw it, but he still couldn't say it. 'The hell with it, we'll take the bust. We'll handle it some way.'

'You know you don't mean that. Maybe you mean it for yourself, but not for me and certainly not for Kelly.'

It was time for me to say something. 'Just leave me out of this. They're not going to do anything to a kid my age.'

My voice may have cracked on the words, because they both turned to smile at me. They weren't putting me down, it was fondness showing.

'Just stay put,' Mike muttered.

'Screw that, I'm part of this too. Tell that bastard to fuck off and let me call Digger. He'll take care of it.'

I expected Mike to object, but it was Lacey who said it. 'He can't do that, Kelly. Not any more. He's too old for that now.' Her voice was soft and solemn.

I looked at Mike, and he nodded. 'She's right. I'd rather do the time than do that.'

'So?' Lacey leaned back, waiting.

'I have to?'

'Damn right.'

'How did I ever figure you for just another body?'

'You never looked past the body. I do a lot of thinking, and

I don't give a shit about worry lines.' She put a finger to his lips, then took it away. 'I'm waiting.'

'All right, I'm asking.'

'Not good enough. In words.'

He sighed, took a deep breath and said, 'Lacey, I am asking you to go back there and screw that son of a bitch so that we won't get busted for this incredibly stupid thing I did. Okay?'

'Sure,' she said, flipping the word. She kissed him lightly on the lips. 'I've never had a Yugoslav before, not that I know of. Start the car and keep the motor running.'

We sat in the car and waited, me behind the wheel and Mike slouched low in the seat against the other door. I didn't start the engine. I just sat there staring through the grimy windshield, my hands gripping the wheel to keep my fists from pounding on things. I guess I went a little crazy then. I was ready to kick ass, draw blood, raise hair, and run wild in the night. I could feel my heart beating, my blood pumping, my face growing hot, then cold. After a while I began to say words in a steady stream, meaningless words, all of them ugly, over and over. Mike put a hand on my knee to stop me.

'Cut it out,' he said. 'You're only making it worse.'

'Fuck you.'

'It's only a game, remember that. All of it, a game.'

'Fuck you.' It was all I could think of to say.

'A game.'

'I don't believe that.'

'You're taking it seriously. That's when they beat you, when you start to take it seriously.'

'You let her go back there. You sent her back there.'

He sighed. 'She went back there because it was part of her game. You're too old to have idols, Kelly. You'd better start getting rid of them.'

'Maybe I've started already,' I told him, and that was all we said until Lacey came back.

Nobody said anything when she got into the car. She slid in next to Mike on the far side, which for some stupid reason pleased me. I didn't want her next to me, not right then. One of the soldiers rolled up the door, and I drove out into the night. It was still snowing heavily as I headed north on the road away from the border. I drove slowly at first, getting the feel of the car and the road, and after a while I let it pick up speed. Mike let me drive without comment. He reached out, took Lacey's hand, and held it. She smiled and put her head back, leaning it against the cushioned rest.

'Well, you finally had yourself a Yugoslavian,' he said.

'The hell I did. He couldn't get it up.'

They both thought that was hilarious. They started to laugh and they kept on laughing as I manoeuvred the car up and around the s-curves leading higher into the Julian Alps. I didn't think it was funny. It had too many overtones of St Anton seven years before and Bobby's bruised, discoloured face. I let them do the laughing while I drove. They were still laughing, on and off, when we reached the next town up the road. That was as far as any of us wanted to go that night, and Mike found us rooms at a hotel across the street from the railroad station. We had something to eat, the two of them giggling like kids all through dinner, and when I was finished I went up to my room without saying goodnight. I was sore at them both. I knew that I had no right to be, but I was. I sat in the room without turning on the light and looked out onto the street in front of the hotel. The snow had turned it into a fairy-tale lane of spun-sugar houses and peppermint lampposts. The street was empty, a stage-struck set. Directly under my window was the railroad station, and on the front of the depot was a sign with the name of the town. It was called Kobarid. That was the Slovenian name, and underneath it, in brackets, was the Italian name: Caporetto. Which meant that Mount Krn was somewhere close by.

Chapter Nine

I had a hard time getting to sleep that night. There was too much boiling in me. I was still pissed off at Mike and Lacey, not so much for what had happened at the border as for their lighthearted attitude about it afterwards. Sex to me then was still a private mystery. Only louts laughed about sex, not sensitive men of conviction. I finally fell off to sleep, and when I woke in the night a few hours later I wasn't angry at anybody any more because I was staring at one of those how-the-hell-did-it-get-here-and-what-am-I-going-to-do-with-it erections that seem to stretch to the ceiling. Still half asleep, I started to laugh. I wasn't mad at Lacey because she had been willing to screw a cop to get us out of a jam, nor at Mike because he had been able to laugh about it later. I was angry for the oldest of teenage reasons. Everyone was getting it except Kelly. I stared at the erection wondering what to do about it, did the usual, and went back to sleep.

When I came down for breakfast in the morning, Mike was alone at a table shovelling in eggs, toast, and tea. I ordered my own and he looked at me slyly, saying, 'Are you still pissed off at me?'

'No.'

'You were last night.'

'Teenage romanticism. I still break out with it once in a while.'

He nodded gravely. 'The acne of the soul. It disappears in time.'

'Where's Lacey?'

'Sleeping off last night's wild orgy.'

'Don't start.'

'Sorry. Sleeping late, that's all. I'll get her up. We should move if we want to ski Kay-Gee today.'

'Kay-Gee can wait. I had something else in mind. You know what town this is?'

'Sure, Kobarid. Caporetto in Italian.'

'Mount Krn is close by.'

'Digger's mountain?'

'And Otto's a generation earlier. I thought we might take a look at it.'

'Just the two of us?'

'We'll need a guide.'

'Sounds good. Finish your breakfast while I make the arrangements.'

The hotel supplied us with a guide and a Land Rover. The guide's name was Darko, and he was young, enthusiastic, and stuffed full of guidebook lore. When he heard that he was going to guide the two sons of Digger Prince, the Hero of Yugoslavia, he was pleased and proud. We told him that we wanted to see the caves of the old partisan camp, and he suggested using the Land Rover to take us partway up the mountain. This was no ski resort with lifts and marked trails and snack bars. You climbed as high as your legs and lungs could take you, and then you skied down. The Land Rover kept the exertion to a bearable level.

The mountain was marked on the map as 2245 metres, and the Land Rover took us up a switchback road that once had been used for logging. It was abandoned now. The logging operation had dug grooves in the road and the weather had frozen them solid, but the snow had filled in the ruts and the going was easy until the terrain became too steep. We left the Land Rover with the wheels chocked in, left the road, and worked our way up on skis from there through stands of larch and pine. We came out of the woods into bright sunshine, standing on the edge of a slope that was part of the south face of the mountain. It was a steep expanse that dropped from a ridge above us, and it was covered with the snow that had fallen in the last few days. The cover sparkled in the sunlight. It was an open stretch without a break for a hundred yards across. Darko stopped us at the edge of the woods.

'Here we must traverse the slope,' he said. 'But we are doing it carefully, only one man at a time.'

I didn't like the way it looked, and I said so. 'Isn't there any other way up?'

'Not to the caves, sir. Not if you wish to visit the old partisan camp.'

'What's the matter?' Mike asked. 'Spooked?'

I nodded. That stretch of sparkling snow looked as inviting to me as a pit of quicksand. 'Fresh snow,' I said, 'and wet. South face, springtime, slope over thirty degrees. It's straight out of a textbook.'

Mike looked at Darko. 'What do you think?'

'Herr Prince is being quite correct about the conditions. However, the slope is being quite safe if proper precautions are taken.'

I shook my head and asked the old riddle. '*Was fliegt ohne Flügel, schlägt ohne Hand und sieht ohne Augen?*'

'*Das Lautier,*' Darko answered promptly. 'Quite right, the avalanche beast flies without wings, strikes without a hand, and sees without eyes. In my opinion the slope is being safe, but if Herr Prince is not wishing to cross then we are returning to the Land Rover without question, by golly. The client is always being right.'

'Come on,' said Mike. 'He says it's okay.'

'Have you had anything recently?' I asked Darko.

'Sir, as always at this time of the year we are having the *Grundlawinen,* same like every year, the same places. So far this year only one of the *Staublawinen,* and that one where there are no people living, by gum.'

He was using the old mountain terms for the two types of avalanches. The first was the *Grundlawine,* an enormous avalanche of wet snow that generally flowed slowly down well-known tracks and gullies. The second was the murderous *Staublawine,* a fast-moving cloud of airborne powder snow accompanied by a wind blast that levelled houses and forests and tossed trains from their tracks like toys. Either type could kill you just as dead, and the terms were outdated, since modern research had categorized avalanches into many different subdivisions. But the old terms told me what I wanted to know: There had been numerous ground avalanches of the wet-snow variety, and there we were without any protective equipment or devices, no rescue equipment, not even a collapsible sounding pole, and as far as I knew no rescue teams in the immediate area. And that slope looked ready to pop.

I grew up with a healthy respect for avalanches passed on to me from my Tirolean grandfather by way of Digger. I learned about them at the same time that I learned how to ski, and I learned to look for the signs: the wind-packed mass, the scarp below the cornice, the tension of the creep on a convex slope. And at the same time I had been taught the basic rule that the skier must follow if he is caught out in the open with a ground avalanche coming down from above. Time after time Digger drilled it into me, using the same words that his father had used with him. *When the Staublawine comes all you can do is pray, but when the Grundlawine comes thundering down the expert skier races from it and everyone else breaks to the side.* The theory was ancient and simple. The airborne avalanche develops speeds of up to two hundred miles an hour, leaving you no place to hide. But a ground avalanche rarely exceeds thirty miles an hour, and a topflight skier can outrun it. Downhill racers routinely go twice that fast. So the expert's best bet is to try to outrun the *Grundlawine,* while for everybody else the best chance is to break for the side in a traverse away from the path of the slide. It is not a decision that you can make on the spot, Digger had told me over and over.

'You won't have time,' he had said. 'To break downhill or to the side, that has to be part of your reflexes, and the actual decision has to be made long before you hear the slope go and you feel the snow shift under your skis. It has to be part of your bone and your muscle. You have to know in your heart which is the best bet for you personally, so that when the time comes, if it comes, you'll make the right move without thinking.' And then he had always added, 'For people like you and me, the right move is always the downhill schuss. We're good enough to outrun it. Most other people aren't.'

I thought about all of that as I stared at that innocent-looking expanse of glistening snow. Mike shuffled his skis impatiently and Darko waited, resting on his poles.

'Well, what's it going to be?' Mike asked.

'It's dumb,' I said.

'Then don't do it.'

'No, I'll do it, but it's still dumb. But only one man on the face at a time, and he goes slow. And quietly, no talking.'

'Exactly,' said Darko. '*Und willst du die schlafende Löwin nicht weken, So wandre durch die Strasse der Schrecken.*'

So we had a guide who knew Schiller, and who also knew that if you don't want to wake the sleeping avalanche you walk quietly along the road of fear. That expressed exactly how I felt about it, but when it came to it we made the crossing without incident: first Mike, then me, then Darko. I felt no sense of relief. It was still a dumb thing to have done.

Once on the other side of the slope we were able to climb to the ridge where the partisan camp had been. Below us we could see the town, the river and the bridges, and beyond the town the chequerboard of black and white that a winter landscape assumes when seen from above. Also below us, but to the right, was a deep indentation in the hillside: Otto's punchbowl with steep and icy slopes.

Darko and Mike went to investigate the caves and left me alone looking down at the slope we had traversed below. It hit me then and I began to shiver. I tried to stop it but I couldn't. It wasn't the sort of shiver that comes from being cold. It started deep inside of me and radiated outward like the sound of a bronze bell booming, and the boom of it held me and shook me. There was nothing I could do about it. I threw up then in one startled whoops. I couldn't believe what I had done, and I scraped snow over the mess to cover it up. I scooped up a handful of clean snow and stuffed it in my mouth, but the shaking continued.

Mike came skiing back, leaving Darko higher up along the ridge where the caves were. He said, 'He found the one we want,' and then he saw my face. 'Jesus, what's the matter, kid?'

'I'll be all right in a minute.'

'What is it?' He saw the shakes, and he put his arm around my shoulder. 'What happened?'

'Saw a ghost, that's all. My own.'

'That slope?' He was quick. 'Was it that bad?'

'I could see it coming apart. I could feel it breaking up. I didn't think it was going to pop, I *knew* it. And then it didn't. I still can't believe that it didn't.'

The shakes began to ease up then. He squeezed my shoulder. 'Take a few deep breaths and ride with it. It'll go away.'

'What will go away? Being scared?'

He laughed. 'That's not being scared, that's just avalanche nerves.'

'I was fucking scared. Did you see the way I was shaking?'

'Nerves,' he repeated. 'There's nothing on the mountain that can put you down.'

Which shows how little even Mike knew about me. I wanted to tell him how wrong he was, but I couldn't. I wanted to grab him, and shake him and make him listen. I wanted to say, Look, this is a family of skiers, right? Starting with Anton, Otto, and Marta, and the second generation of Hannes, Kurt, Digger, and the twins, and yea, verily, even unto the third generation of you, me, Anna, and Jenny. All of us skiers, and all of us pretty good. Some, like Hannes and Kurt, good enough to ski and fight with the Alpinkorps. Some, like Jenny and me, good enough to ski on the World Cup circuit. One, like Digger, good enough to set a standard for his generation. But here it comes, brother. For all of that, in three generations this family has managed to produce only two authentic skiers. Authentic? Define? Sure.

Someone who is at all times in tune with the mountain.

Someone who has made his private arrangements with the mountain and will never go back on them.

Someone who skis flat out, without reservations, every time he puts them on.

My definition of the authentic skier, the genuine article, the uncompromising pistol. My definition only. In other circles it's called insanity. It has nothing to do with technical ability. On that basis, sure, I'm the best right now, and what about Jenny, the way she used to move your heart when you saw her swinging through the slalom gates with her pigtail stretched out straight behind? Despite that, there have only been two authentic pistols in this family. And you know who they are?

Digger and Mike.

That's all, just two. Digger because he can't help being that way, and you, Mike, because you can't help wanting to be your father's son. But not me, not by those definitions. Because I just don't care enough. So don't talk to me about avalanche nerves. I was scared out of my wits.

All that I did not say, and perhaps I should have, perhaps it would have saved a lot of problems later on. But I didn't. All I said was, 'Let's take a look at those caves.'

Darko was standing at the entrance of the largest of the caves. He had swept the cave mouth free of overhanging icicles. He greeted us brightly and said, 'Before entering the caves it is customary that the guide is giving short lecture.'

'Carry on,' said Mike.

'Thank you. After the Fascist invasion it is being decided in May of 1941 that the Communist Party of Yugoslavia is being the only political force in the country capable of leading the peoples in the struggle for national liberation and a better future. Therefore the National Liberation Partisan Detachments is being established in June of that year with Josip Broz Tito as commander, and in July is breaking out the guerrilla warfare. Shortly after that is coming here to Mount Krn many partisan fighters seeking haven and refuge in these caves. One of these is being the partisan leader Ivan Cankar, and later on the American freedom fighter John Digger Prince. Together they are conducting successful operations against the invaders using these very caves as their headquarters. The paintings you are about to see are being created by Ivan Cankar and are considered to be classics in the naif form. We are now able to enter the caves.'

'Dark in there,' said Mike.

'Fear not. The tourist association is providing pine torches on the wall to facilitate a superior illumination.'

He stooped low through the entrance, and Mike and I followed. He lit up one of the torches, a length of wood dipped in sticky pine tar that gave off a fitful, spitting light. He lit a second, and a third, and the walls of the cave jumped out at us. As much as I had heard from Digger about the caves at Mount Krn, I was unprepared for what I saw.

We were surrounded. From one wall a life-size partisan fighter glared at us, crouched and ready to attack, a Chicago-style tommygun cradled in his arms. On the opposite wall was a woman, tall and broad, her left fist clenched and raised, a pistol in her right hand. Beside her a man with a bayonet poked through his belt strode towards us carrying a flag, seeming to step off the wall with his red-starred banner rippling in the breezeless air. Farther into the cave, beyond the reach of the torches, were the forms of other figures on the walls painted in shocking slashes of raw colour. Primary and primitive, every jaw firm, every eye flinty, every muscle bulging with resolution.

'Jesus,' Mike breathed.

'No,' said Darko. 'Socialist realism.'

Mike and I each took torches from the rough sconces on the walls and walked back through the cave, stopping before each painting to stare and absorb. An entire community was represented: bearded chiefs and fuzzy-faced boys, crones and maidens, fathers, children, mothers with babes; all with a single aspect in common. Each carried a weapon, everything from that Thompson to rifles, pistols, even a scythe.

I raised my torch high to look at the next one, and without thinking, said, 'Son of a bitch.' And again without thinking, 'Excuse me, I'm sorry.'

'You should be,' said Mike. 'It's like being in church.'

We were looking at a painting of a young woman different in every way from the others in the cave. Cankar had depicted her without the stern resolution of socialist realism, and without a weapon in her hand. He had painted a Madonna in rags, a girl of quiet beauty and serenity whose long black hair framed an oval face, and whose slim body was only hinted at under rough peasant garments. She smiled out at us sadly, and all the ills of a faulty world were forgiven in that smile.

'The Madonna of the Mountain,' said Darko behind us. 'An all-time favourite. People are coming from all over to see her.'

'Cankar's granddaughter,' I said. 'It has to be.'

'Yes. According to the story she is being your father's lover, but perhaps you know that?'

'He doesn't talk about it.'

'It is being a very sad story. She is only eighteen and she is soon to die. Tuberculosis. Sad.'

'So is this,' said Mike.

He had passed on to the next painting. I added the light of my torch to his. It was a man dressed in the smock and beret of the partisan fighter. His chin was up and his eyes were fixed on the future. In his right hand he carried a long knife the size of a Bowie. It wasn't a Bowie, it was a Brent; I had seen it many times. In his left hand he held a bloody, severed head, his fingers twisted into the hair for a grip. I threw down my torch and ran out of the cave.

I stood outside the cave mouth and drew in long draughts of air. I started to shiver again, but this time I was able to control it. I was all right by the time Mike and Darko came out. Mike looked at me, concerned.

'I'm not going to talk about that,' I said. 'Not one God damn word.'

'All right,' he said, 'all right.'

We skied down the way we had climbed up. When we came to the slope that had spooked me before we gathered at the edge and decided to run it the same way: one man at a time. Mike, then me, then Darko. Again I got that concerned look from Mike, but I shook it off. It was just another piece of mountain to me now.

Mike made his crossing carefully. As did I. And then Darko. As Darko came off the traverse and into the woods the slope behind him opened up. A crack appeared where the tracks of his skis had been, then widened into a yawning cleft. Below the cleft the snow cover began to move downhill slowly, heaving itself up into folds and forming waves and creases like a huge white carpet being pulled across a bumpy floor. We were safe where we stood. We stared as the carpet picked up speed, and then, with a rumble that grew to a roar, it broke away from the slope entirely and went rushing down in a boiling mass. The power of the slide was awesome. Nothing alive could have stood

514

in its way and survived. It lumbered downhill like a freight train, leaving behind a bare slope scored by the marks of boulders swept along, and the mountain trembled under our skis. The avalanche cleared half a mile of snow off the south face in less than a minute, piling it up on the rocks at the next ridge below. The thunder of its passing stayed in our ears, and the air around us was filled with powdered snow.

Darko couldn't take his eyes off the slope. He crossed himself repeatedly.

Mike was grinning wildly, his lips stretched tight. 'You were right,' he yelled. 'You were right all the way. Avalanche nerves, that's what it was.'

I nodded, but I turned away from the sight of that bare and scarred slope. I was starting to shiver again.

The next day we drove up through the Julians to Kranjska Gora, and when we got there I heard that my Grandma Liz was dead. We came in over the valley road with the mountains on our right . . . Mangart, Jalovec, Vitranc . . . and the Austrian border only a few miles off to the left; and when we got to the Hotel Larix there was a cablegram from Digger waiting for me at the reception desk. It read: GRANDMA DIED TODAY CALL ME SOONEST, with the Sedgewick Falls telephone number after the signature. I made the call from the booth in the lobby, and while I was placing it I saw that Mike and Lacey were checking in at the desk. I stuck my head out to stop them, but before I could say anything Digger answered the phone. It was just past sunrise time in Vermont, but he sounded as if he had been up for hours.

'Where are you?' he asked.

'Kay-Gee.' I wondered why he had to ask, and then realized that he must have sent cables all over. 'How did it happen?'

'A quick coronary. We should all go that way.'

'Are you all right?'

'Me?'

'Yeah, you.'

'Of course I'm all right,' he said indignantly. 'Why the hell shouldn't I be? Look, the funeral is tomorrow and I want you to be here for it.'

'I'll do my best. How's Bobby? Put her on, I want to say hello.'

He hesitated a beat. 'She's fine, she isn't here right now.' The

515

way he said it finessed me. It sounded as if she was out for a while doing some shopping or getting her hair done. 'What about the funeral?'

I told him that I'd try to make it in time, and he snapped, 'Don't give me that "try" bullshit, just be here.'

'Hey, slow down. First I have to get to where the big birds fly.'

'What's closest?'

'Zurich, maybe, or Vienna. I'm not sure.'

'What's wrong with Ljubljana?'

The only thing wrong with Ljubljana was that it meant flying Yugoslav Airlines back to the States, but it was only an hour away from Kranjska Gora. 'I guess that's the closest,' I admitted.

'Then get your ass into gear.' His voice softened. 'Kelly, I'll understand if you can't get here in time for the funeral, but I want you here sometime tomorrow, anyway. Do you think you can do that?'

'Like I said, I'll try, but I don't get it. If I can't make the funeral, then what's the hurry?'

'Christ, and you're supposed to be the bright one. After the funeral they read the will.'

'Oh.'

'Yeah.'

'Who did she . . . I mean, how . . . ?'

'We'll know when they read the will.'

'Digger, I don't want any part of this.'

'You don't have any choice, boy. I'll see you tomorrow.'

He hadn't said a word about my brother, but that didn't keep me from lying. I came out of the phone booth and told Mike, 'He wants us there for the funeral tomorrow. We'll have to get the next flight out of Ljubljana.'

'Us? We?' He gave me his crooked scarecrow's grin. 'What's this plural jazz? He never said us or we.'

'He did.'

The grin grew broader. 'You'd starve if you had to lie for a living.'

'He really did.'

'Never. Come on, I'll drive you to the airport.'

'We're both going.'

'Not me. This is your show, not mine.'

516

'She was your grandmother, too.'

'I'm not going, and that's it. If the old man wanted me there he would have said so.'

He gave their room key to Lacey and drove me down to the airport, making time on the snow-covered roads, but it was a wasted effort. There was no way I could have got to Vermont in time for the funeral. The next Stateside flight out of Ljubljana was at eight the following morning, and even that was quicker than making a connection at Zurich or Vienna. I cabled my ETA to Digger, stayed overnight at the airport motel, and flew to New York in the same clothes I had put on the day before in Caporetto. At Kennedy I transferred to a feeder flight that brought me into Montpelier in the early evening, Vermont time, and sure enough there was Digger waiting for me in the arrival lounge. In the next few minutes I got two quick jolts. The first was that he was alone, and the second was that he had a rental car waiting outside.

He gave me a hug and said what he always said when he hadn't seen me for a while. 'You look terrific, but you need a haircut.'

I sidestepped out of the hug. 'Where's Bobby?'

'Is that the way you say hello?'

'I'm sorry.' I took a first good look at him, and didn't like what I saw. His face was lined, he needed a shave, and his eyes were red and weary. 'Hello, you look terrific, too. Where's Bobby?'

'She isn't here.'

'Is she at the house?' I meant the one in Sedgewick Falls.

'She's home in New York. I'll explain in the car.'

That car was the second jolt. It was a perfectly acceptable Ford Fairmont fresh out of the Hertz garage, but it was wildly out of place for Digger Prince. He never drove himself, never travelled in anything but a company limousine, or when he was out of town in a limousine locally hired. That was what should have been waiting for us outside, not a Hertz rental. Digger took my bag, tossed it onto the back seat, and slid in under the wheel as if it were something he did every day. The apparent unconcern was a mistake, he should have said something, and right then I knew that I had come back to a world that was somehow out of whack.

It didn't get any better during the drive to Sedgewick Falls.

He tried to explain why my mother had stayed in New York, but it was all meaningless chatter about sparing her the ordeal of the funeral and the reading of the will. As an explanation it raised more questions than it answered, and it left me cold and confused. I asked him what the funeral had been like, and he was happy to be off the hook and talk about something else.

'Very dignified, good taste,' he said. 'A short service at the church and a few words at the graveside. The way it ought to be.'

'Much of a turnout?'

'It looked like half the town was there. I didn't think the old gal had that many friends. Or maybe I should say so few enemies.'

I slid down in the seat and put my feet up on the dashboard. It was only a rental car. 'I guess if you live long enough you run out of enemies. What happens next?'

'We get something to eat, get a good night's sleep, and tomorrow the lawyers read the will.'

'I thought that was today.'

'They waited as long as they could for you, then they put it off until tomorrow.'

'I couldn't make it any quicker, Digger, really.'

He nodded without looking at me. He wasn't used to driving, and he wouldn't take his eyes off the road for a second. 'I know that, I'm not blaming you. It's just that we have to be there to make it official.'

'I don't understand the rush. It seems indecent.'

'Indecent and barbaric, both.'

'I wish I could skip it all.'

'I wish you could too, but you can't. You've been playing wise-ass and *Wunderkind* too long to hide behind your age now. You can't have it both ways.'

'I know.'

Just outside of town he pulled into a shopping mall to pick up some food for dinner. That was another surprise. I had figured we would eat at the Wellington Inn or one of the other halfway decent restaurants in downtown Sedgewick, but Digger had parked the car and was into the Food Fair before I could say so. He grabbed a shopping cart, headed straight for the frozen foods, and started pulling cartons of TV dinners, french fries, waffles, and pies. He really didn't know what the hell he

518

was doing. I put all the junk back in the freezer, took him over to the fresh meat counter, and picked out two packages of good-looking shell steaks. He looked at the label on one of them and grimaced.

'Six dollars a pound. Did you know that shell steaks cost six dollars a pound?'

I shook my head. I didn't know any more about prices than he did. He put the steaks back in the case and hefted a two-pound package of ground chuck.

'Look at that, less than half the price.'

I didn't know where all the economy was coming from, but I drew the line at chuck. I found some ground round at an acceptable price and told him that we would need fresh vegetables as well. He looked so defeated that I let him go back to the frozen foods and get some green peas and potato puffs there. I didn't object when he threw in a package of waffles for breakfast.

As we came out of the supermarket he said, 'There's coffee and eggs and bread in the house, so we're okay on basics. Whoops, not quite. Got to pay a visit to old Doc Green.'

'Who?'

'State store.'

In the state liquor store he stood in line with everybody else and studied the printed list on the wall while he waited, comparing the prices of Jack Daniel's, Wild Turkey, and the other sour mashes and straight bourbons. When he got to the counter he asked for a quart of something called Uncle Ed's Double Rich Kentucky Cream, and when he paid for it he got change from a five-dollar bill.

My grandmother's house was dark and empty when we got there, but warm inside. Digger had sent Mrs Cutler, the hired woman, home earlier in the day, but she had left the thermostat set at sixty, and she hadn't forgotten to lay out cut wood and kindling in the parlour hearth. The fire went up with a single match, and with the lights on the place was just as I remembered it: overstuffed rooms filled with overstuffed furniture, the bare walls studded with family photographs and a set of hooked rugs. It had always been an old woman's house to me, a musty place with hints of lemon oil and furniture wax, dried apples, damp wood, and the vague scents that elderly women use to mask the smells of age. Now it was a dead woman's house, and it didn't smell of anything at all.

The first thing I did was to call Bobby in New York while Digger went to work in the kitchen, and as I dialled I could hear him breaking out ice for the first drink of the night. I decided that I wouldn't say anything to my mother about not coming up for the funeral. If she and Digger were having problems I wouldn't be doing them any good by talking about it. When she answered the phone I said the usual, and she said the usual, and then she asked me how my trip had been.

'Miserable. Eight hours on Yugoslav Airlines and all they had to drink was slivovitz or Coca-Cola.'

'Horrors, what a choice. I hope you opted for the slivovitz.'

'I drank a lot of water.'

'Did they at least feed you?'

'More or less. I'm still not sure what it was, but I ate some of it.'

'In that case make sure your father gives you a good meal tonight.'

'Don't worry, he's in the kitchen right now whipping up dinner.'

'He's cooking?'

'Hamburgers. It can't be any worse than the Yugoslavs. Do you want to talk to the chef?'

'I wouldn't dream of distracting him. How is he taking things?'

'He doesn't seem any different. It probably hasn't hit him yet.'

'It probably never will. He's one of the tough ones.' There was an edge to her voice that I didn't like.

'I wish it would. He'd be better off if he broke down and got it out of his system.'

'Nickel-and-dime psychology, sweets.'

'Maybe, but I read somewhere that grief needs an outlet.'

'I doubt that your father is grieving greatly. Grief is a luxury that the heartless can't afford.'

'Hey, what's that all about?'

'Sorry, it just slipped out. Don't put it up on the scoreboard.'

I had decided not to say anything, but it was an easy decision to break. 'Bobby, will you please tell me what's going on around here? I mean, it's pretty obvious that something is, but I don't know what, and it bothers me.'

'There's nothing to worry about, Kelly.'

'The hell there isn't. My father is acting like he's down to his last dime, and my mother is talking bitchy about him. I think that's plenty to worry about.'

'Sweets, this is no conversation for the telephone. You do what you have to do up there, and when you come home we'll have a chat.'

'You mean there's something important to talk about?'

'Yes, darling, I'm afraid there is.'

She said goodbye then, but before she hung up, she said, 'I take it that Mike isn't with you or you would have said so.'

'He didn't get invited to the dance.'

'Damn that man,' she said, and then she did hang up.

Dinner could have been worse. Digger followed the package directions for cooking the vegetables, and he didn't overdo the hamburgers. He made a big fuss about setting the table properly and bringing in the plates, and we talked our way through the meal, with me doing most of the eating and Digger concentrating on the Double Rich Kentucky Cream. We kept the conversation safe. Neither of us wanted to talk about what might be in the will.

The law offices of Cobb and Cobb were in a new complex of buildings opposite the Town Hall in downtown Sedgewick Falls. Harrison Cobb III was the local man, and waiting with him the next morning was a Mr Jellicoe from the New England Trust company in Boston. Cobb was Digger's age, but bald and chubby. They had been to school together, and he was cordial enough to us, but Jellicoe was tired and irritable, and he showed it. A joyless, cadaverous Yankee in a black suit, he resented the day he had wasted waiting for me and he was anxious to get things done with and head back for Boston. They took us into a room with a long table and walls full of books, and once we were seated Digger stripped down one of those Canary Islands heaters and fired it up with a grunt of satisfaction. Jellicoe coughed before any of the smoke could have got to him, and when Digger saw the disapproving look on his face he grinned and blew a perfect ring at the ceiling. He seemed completely at ease with the cigar gripped jauntily between his teeth, but to me it looked as phony as that rental car he was driving.

Cobb shuffled some papers and said, 'This is always an awkward occasion, but one that can't be avoided. Unless someone has something to say I'll get right to the reading of the will.'

Jellicoe raised a lazy finger. 'Before we start, we seem to be one short. According to my file the testatrix is survived by one son and two grandsons, Michael and Kelly.'

'Michael won't be here,' said Digger. 'We'll have to do without him.'

Jellicoe shrugged. 'As you wish.'

Cobb started to read from a blue-backed document, his voice a drone. He mentioned bequests to old servants and faithful employees, a thousand dollars to every worker with five years of seniority, two thousand for ten years, five thousand to a foreman named McKenna, five thousand to somebody else, and then the droning stopped.

'That concludes the minor bequests.' Cobb cleared his throat and looked up, his round lips pursed unhappily. He shrugged, looked down, and read, 'The balance of my estate, both real and personal, including, but not limited to, my stock and other equities in the Prince Ski Corporation and its subsidiaries and affiliates, I bequeath to my grandson, Kelly Prince . . .'

I couldn't move. I managed to shift my eyes sideways at Digger. He was smiling faintly and his eyes were fixed far away.

' . . . said estate to be held in trust for him by the trustees designated below until he shall attain the age of twenty-one years at which time the trust will be dissolved and full ownership invested in him. I make this bequest in the full confidence that he will prove to be a worthy successor to the founder of the company, my beloved Anton Prince. . . .' Cobb stopped and looked up again. He was clearly uncomfortable now. 'If you don't mind, I'll skip the rest. It's just window dressing. Digger, I'm sorry, but that's it as far as the bequests go.'

'Quite all right, Harry. I didn't expect anything, haven't for years. I always figured that she'd leave it to the boy. Kelly, you look like somebody just kicked you in the gut.'

'That's about how I feel,' I admitted. 'I'm sorry, Digger.'

'Not at all, not at all.' He was at his urbane best. He asked Cobb, 'Who did she name as trustee?'

'That would be me,' said Jellicoe. 'Or rather, the New England Trust Company as represented by me.'

Digger nodded complacently. He looked too calm to me. 'A fine outfit. Kelly, you're in good hands.'

'Thank you.' Jellicoe shifted his bulk in his chair. 'First of all, young man, my congratulations. Next, I want to be sure that you understand your position. You have just inherited the Prince Ski Company, along with the other assets of the estate. Do you know what assets are?'

I nodded. The first shock was fading and my mind was beginning to move.

'Good. From a practical point of view what this means is that the company will continue to operate under its present management with the trust controlling the assets and acting in a supervisory capacity. Do you understand that, or shall I break it down into simpler terms?'

I nodded again. I was beginning to dislike him.

'This is necessary because of your age, you see. Once you reach the age of twenty-one we turn the business over to you with our blessings. I'm sure you understand the need for this arrangement.' He showed me some teeth to prove that he had a sense of humour. 'The law doesn't expect a seventeen-year-old boy to run a multimillion-dollar corporation.'

Another nod. My mind was racing now, and I was sure I didn't like him.

'Struck speechless, are you? Very understandable under the circumstances. This must be quite a shock to you. And a responsibility, never forget that. A heavy responsibility.' He was packing papers into his briefcase. He was in one hell of a hurry to get back to Boston. 'Obviously this is neither the time nor the place to discuss the future of the company. What I suggest is that we wait a few weeks and let you get used to the situation. Then we can get together in Boston or New York and go over the facts and figures. Very dull stuff, you know. How does that sound to you?'

I looked over at Digger. His lips weren't smiling any more, but his eyes were. He looked expectant, as if he were waiting for me to do something. I had seen that look before on the tops of mountains with only minutes to go until race time. I didn't know what he wanted from me, but I had to start somewhere, and so I said, 'What happens to the profits?'

Jellicoe looked up from his packing. 'I beg your pardon?'

'The profits,' I repeated. 'I'm seventeen years old, which means that you people are going to have control of the company for almost four years. What happens to the profits during that time?'

'Why . . . we assign you an allowance and the balance of the profits are held in trust for you. That's the usual arrangement.'

'How much of the balance? One hundred percent?'

He was finished packing and he clicked the clasp shut. 'Do you really want to go into this right now?'

'I just flew seven thousand miles to go into it.'

'But considering the circumstances . . .'

'As you may have noticed, I'm not exactly overcome with grief. How much of the balance goes into trust?'

'Why, that's a difficult question to answer. Not a hundred percent, of course. There has to be some reinvestment of profits into the company, reserves for taxes, the trustees' fees . . .'

'How much will those fees amount to?'

That got him stiff all over. 'Our fees are determined by the court.'

'And what happens if you show a loss for a year? Do you waive your fees that year? Do you reimburse me for mismanagement?'

He stood up, unfolding himself piece by piece from the chair. 'I must say that I'm not very happy at the tone this conversation is taking. Young man, are you aware of what a trustee is?'

'Mr Jellicoe, I'm a minor, not a mental defective. A trustee is a natural or legal person to whom property is legally committed to be administered for the benefits of a beneficiary. Now I'll ask one. Do you know what a ski is?'

Digger was grinning again. Jellicoe wasn't. He was staring at me, and his mouth was open. Finally, he said, 'Everyone knows what a ski is.'

'Sure, but do you know how to make one? Do you know how to test one? Do you know how to market one? You just said that the present management would continue to operate the company, but if you knew anything about this business you'd know that my grandmother *was* the management. She ran everything, and now she's gone. You don't know a damn thing about skis, Jellicoe, and now you say you're going to be running my company for the next four years? Well, I don't think so, at least not by yourself. I can see that I'm going to need somebody to represent my interests here, somebody mature and experienced in the business.'

'I'm afraid that's out of the question. In a situation such as this the trustees have full control – '

524

'Not if the trustees can't tell a ski pole from a barber pole, and any court will back me in that. I want my own man in there.'

He let that sink in, looking at me quietly. 'Are you by any chance a law student, Mr Prince?'

'No, but I'm a certified wise-ass and *Wunderkind,* and I still want my man.'

'And who would that be?'

'Who else? The only man I could trust completely. My father.'

'I was afraid you were going to say that.' He was trying to sound reasonable. 'Can't you see that's also out of the question? If your grandmother had wanted your father in control she would have named him in the will. I could never agree to that.'

I looked at Digger, but he was giving me nothing, making it all my play. 'That was my grandmother's decision, and I respect it,' I said, 'but now the decision is mine, and I want Digger. I don't see how her wishes are binding on me.'

'Perhaps not legally, but I should think that morally – '

'Mr Jellicoe?'

'Yes?'

'Fuck morally.'

His mouth screwed up tight like a fish on a hook. He nodded abruptly. 'Very well, we'll ignore the moral issues and get back to legalities. There is one overriding legal reason why your father cannot represent you. You seem to forget that your father is now your competitor. He is the sole stockholder of Royal Skis, and – '

'Just for the record,' Digger interrupted mildly, 'I don't own a single share of Royal Skis, and I never have. Those shares belong to my wife.'

'I see.' Jellicoe thought for a moment. 'Not that it changes the situation. You are the president and chief operating officer of Royal Skis, and under these circumstances no court in the land would allow you to be involved in the operations of a rival company.' He slapped his hands on the table. 'Mr Cobb, Mr Prince, you both know I'm right on this. Perhaps you can convince this determined young man.'

I hadn't stopped to think of that, and it made sense. I looked at Cobb, who laced his fingers into a steeple and peered at me owlishly over them. 'He's right, Kelly. You and your dad are competitors now. No court would allow it.'

I looked at Digger. He took the cigar out of his mouth, contemplated the burning tip, and flashed me the big grin.

'Nice work,' he said. 'You've got the makings of a first-class hard-nosed prick.'

'Am I supposed to thank you for that?'

'You will someday. Don't worry, you made all the right moves, and the courts can't stop you. As of three days ago I ceased to be president and chief operating officer of Royal Skis. To put it bluntly, your mother fired me.'

He stuck the cigar between his teeth and clasped his hands behind his head. 'Gentlemen, you see before you a man in search of a job, and it looks like I just found one.'

Digger drove me to Montpelier in time to catch the afternoon plane to New York, and during the drive he refused to talk about what was going on in the family. As he waited for my flight to be called, all he would say was, 'It's a complicated situation. Ask your mother when you get home. She'll explain everything.'

'That's a big help. Don't you figure you owe me an explanation? That was an earthquake you just threw at me.'

'It had to be done that way. You had to work things out and make the decision yourself, and you came through like a champ. What's going on between your mother and me is something else again.'

'The hell it is, it's all hooked up together. Look, just tell me this. Are you and Bobby splitting up?'

'It's complicated,' he repeated. 'Ask your mother.'

That was all I could get out of him at the airport. I was flying down to New York, but he was staying on for a while in Vermont. He now had a letter from the trustee, pending a more formal document, naming him as temporary general manager of Prince Skis, and he wanted to take a look at the operation from the factory level. He said that he would stay on at my grandmother's house for a while, and then a funny look crossed his face.

'If that's all right with you,' he said. 'It's your house now.'

'Jesus, Digger, aren't things screwed up enough without saying things like that?'

'Sorry, forget I said it. There's one other thing we have to settle. How much is Prince Skis paying me?'

The easy answer would have been to tell him to name his own figure, but I could see by the look in his eyes that I was on the spot again. It was like taking a snap quiz in school, trying to guess the most likely answer. I thought about it, and said, 'The same as you were getting at Royal, provided we can afford it.'

He nodded his approval of the answer. 'I also had a bonus arrangement with Royal based on sales. How about that?'

That one was easy. 'No bonuses for anybody until I see what kind of shape we're in at the end of the year. When does our fiscal year end?'

'Probably September.'

'Plenty of time, we'll talk about it then.'

Another approving nod, and a few minutes later they called my flight. I was bone-weary by the time the plane landed at La Guardia, I had been on the merry-go-round since leaving Cortina, but I wasn't in a hurry to get home. I wanted to see Bobby, but I wasn't ready to ask all the questions that had to be answered. I gave the taxi driver the Fifth Avenue address, and as we were crossing the Triboro Bridge I fell asleep. I was really whipped. When the driver woke me we were parked in front of the apartment house, Central Park budding across the street.

I had a few surprises waiting for me upstairs. I tried to let myself into the apartment with my key, but the lock had been changed. I had to ring the bell, and the middle-aged woman who opened the door was a stranger to me.

'Good evening, sir, you must be Mr Kelly,' she said. 'I'm Mrs Trupin, the housekeeper.'

'What happened to Delahanty?'

'You've been away all winter,' she said with a smile. 'I've been here since December.'

'Is my mother home?'

'No sir, she's out for the evening, but she left you a note. It's on the table in your room.'

Bobby's note said that she would be at the Grantheims for dinner and to call her there if I wanted her. I didn't call. I got myself unpacked, took a bath, fell asleep in the tub, and woke up with the water lapping over my nose. Once I was dressed I walked around the apartment trying to get used to it again. As Mrs Trupin had said, I had been away all winter, and although nothing had been changed, everything looked smaller. It's funny how that works with a city apartment. You stay away for a couple of months and when you come back all the rooms seem cramped. It isn't easy to shrink a twelve-room duplex, but that's the way it felt to me that night. I was home, but there were half a dozen hotel rooms that had been more of a home to me that winter. I got something to eat from Mrs Trupin in the kitchen, and after that it was a relief to take the high dive off into sleep.

I didn't see Bobby in the morning, either. She must have got in late, because she didn't show at the breakfast table, and if she doesn't make it to breakfast she's usually out of circulation until noon. I spent some time going over a list of books I would need for summer school, and then went downstairs and across Fifth Avenue to say hello to the bears in the Central Park zoo. They were all old friends, and I always checked in with them whenever I came back to New York. Their cages didn't look any smaller, but then they hadn't been away all winter. I took the bus down to Eighteenth Street to buy the textbooks at Barnes & Noble, and by the time I got home Bobby was gone again.

'She said to tell you that she was lunching with Miss Shana Stein,' said Mrs Trupin, 'and after that they're going to Soho to look at antiques. Also, she'll be home around five, and if you feel like seeing a show tonight you're to call the broker and order tickets.'

I spent the afternoon anaesthetizing my brain with medieval French history, and at the same time wondering how Bobby was going to handle her entrance. She had two styles to choose from: a pale tristesse with shadowed eyes, breathy whispers, and one hand over the heart, or a hearty bubble of maternal cheer. I was betting on the bubble, and I was right. Just before five she came sweeping in on a wave of endearments, dropped two parcels on the couch, flung the mink stole after them, and actually ran across the room to haul me to my feet. She held me off to look at me, pulled me to her, and held me off again.

'Darling, you are absolutely huge,' she bubbled. 'It must be the shoulders, they're broader. Very impressive, sweets, and all those wins, all those stories in the papers. Everyone I know has been talking about you. I'll have to resign myself to it, I'm getting to be known as Kelly Prince's mother. Oh, Michael called yesterday before you got in. Said to tell you that the snow

528

is terrific at Kay-Gee and that he and Lacey will be in New York in a couple of weeks. Darling, who is Lacey?'

'This year's earth goddess.'

'Attractive?'

'Knockout.'

'Amazing how that boy pulls the good-looking birds. And he's so unprepossessing.'

'You're nuts, Mike is beautiful.'

'Yes, darling, I know he is. It's just that I'm always surprised when someone else sees it in him. Did you call for tickets? What are we seeing tonight?'

'Bobby . . .'

'Not that it makes any difference, it's the celebration that counts. The champ is home again. Poor baby, I heard about the will. I know I should congratulate you, but it seems like such a burden to put on someone your age. Still, it's another reason to celebrate. First we'll change, and then off we go to the Alamo House for a positively enormous steak, and after that the night is yours.'

'Bobby, look . . .'

'My God, those shoulders, you'd better try your dinner jacket on. Yes, I must show you off tonight. Shall we do it big, really swank it up? Let's do that, darling, somewhere very smart where we can knock them all on their butts . . .'

'Mother.'

That did it. The bubble burst and all the false cheer ran out of her. 'Oh dear, you always sound so cross when you call me that.'

'I'm not cross, but there are some questions that have to be answered. Why did you kick Digger out of Royal?'

She drew herself up. 'I'm not going to talk about that.'

'Yes, you are. You've been ducking me for twenty-four hours, but not any more.'

'I wasn't ducking, darling, I was busy.'

'You were avoiding me,' I said flatly. 'If you want to keep it up you can run off and hide, but we're not going out tonight and you're not showing me off. We're going to sit right here and you're going to tell me exactly what's happening to my family. Exactly, and with no bullshit.'

She was totally deflated now. 'All right, but I want to change first.'

'Go right ahead, but keep it simple and don't take an hour to do it. There's nobody here to impress except me, and you did that a long time ago.'

'You *are* cross, aren't you? I shan't be long.'

She was back in ten minutes dressed in brushed denims and a fluffy sweater. She went to the drinks cart and made herself a vodka and tonic. She perched herself cross-legged on the couch, and said, 'Go ahead, ask your questions.'

'For starters, who is she?'

'Figured that out, did you?'

'There's only one reason why you'd do this to Digger, and that's a woman.'

'Well, there you are, that's the problem. She's barely a woman, she's an eighteen-year-old girl. An actress.'

'So what else is new? Digger has been chasing eighteen-year-old actresses for as long as I can remember, and it never got him in trouble before. I thought you people had your arrangements, like with you and your weight-lifters.'

She was sensitive enough to colour slightly, lower her eyes, and murmur, 'There was only one weight-lifter, darling, and he didn't last very long.'

'I still don't get it. What's so different about this one?'

'Everything. I suppose I put it badly. One says the word "actress" and a certain image is projected. This young lady is just barely out of high school, and she really isn't even an actress. She's a drama student from Fort Wayne God Damn Indiana, come to New York to conquer Broadway. You know the type, Kelly, or at least you should. Pale good looks, very intense, dedicated to her art. Lives in a wretched studio flat on Columbus Avenue and shops at Alexander's. Does her own hair and wears sensible clothes. A serious young lady and, from what I hear, totally incorruptible.'

'Sounds dangerous.'

'You smile but she is to somebody your father's age. Do you think I'd make such a fuss about some casual piece of cheesecake? From all the information I have she seems to be a hardworking, thoroughly nice girl, and he claims to be madly in love with her.'

So there it was, Digger had broken the rules with a girl who was neither the traditional bit of fluff nor a sister under the skin who knew how the game was played. He had got serious about her, and, according to Bobby, for the first time in their marriage she had had to warn him off.

'I told him when I first heard about it back in the autumn,' she said, 'and I thought he had dropped her. Then I heard he was leaving you on the road and popping back to New York to see her.'

'So that's where he went.'

'Exactly. Now, darling, I'm not an insensitive woman, I can understand his needs. The man is fifty-six years old and he thinks this is his last chance to touch base with his youth. Well, fine, but he's gone and got serious about it, and I can't allow that. You understand, don't you?'

'Yes.'

'And so I told him when I caught him at it again. I told him flat out, either you give her up or you're out of Royal Skis on your royal arse.'

'And I take it he told you to fuck off?'

'Not in so many words, but the end result was the same. He didn't even try to hide the fact that he was still seeing her.' She took a sip of her drink and made a face. 'Kelly, he was making me look so foolish in front of my friends. My God, she's only a few months older than you are.'

'She sounds like a great kid. The sister I never had.'

'Very funny, but not for me. I had no choice. He *left* me no choice. I called a board meeting last week and terminated his contract.'

'And changed the locks here.'

'Yes. I'll have to get you new keys.'

'You keep on talking about information. Did you hire people?'

'*De rigueur* in these cases.'

'Nasty.'

'I'm not the one who broke the rules. Hold on just a sec.' She rose up from the couch and was gone from the room for a few minutes. She came back with a manila folder and tossed it on my lap. 'That's the complete file on her. Cost me enough.'

I opened the folder and paged through it idly. There wasn't much to it: several sheets of paper and a few portrait photos. I left it open on my lap. Bobby was building herself another drink.

'I know how awful this must be for you,' she said, 'but with any luck it won't be for long. Did you know that Digger never owned a single share of stock in Royal?'

'I found that out yesterday.'

'Well, he never did. All he had was a bloody good job, and his perks, and a fancy expense account. Now he doesn't even have that much. We'll see how long he can handle going second-class. He'll come to his senses.'

'And then what happens?'

'He knows my conditions. When he gives up the girl he's welcome back to this house and he's welcome back to Royal. All he has to do is follow the rules.'

I wished then that I had a taste for alcohol. I had a feeling that a drink would help. Without one, I said, 'I wouldn't count on that, Bobby.'

'I know your father, sweets. He'll see the light.'

'I wasn't talking about the girl. Even if he dumps her he won't be coming back to Royal. He's working for Prince now. I hired him yesterday.'

'You did *what?*'

'You fired him and I hired him. He's my general manager now. I've got the best ski man in the business, and I don't intend to let him go.'

'But you can't do that.'

'I've already done it.'

'You can't.' She looked truly stricken. 'This changes everything, don't you see?'

I saw it, all right. I had taken away the only hold she had on him. 'I'm sorry, but that's the way it's going to be,' I said. 'He's staying with Prince.'

'But . . . Kelly, please.'

I looked at her silently.

'Please?'

'No. Don't ask me again, Bobby. That's it.'

Her voice hardened. 'All right then, I'm not asking you, I'm telling you.'

'That's silly. Throwing orders at me doesn't work any more, you know that.'

'Damn it, I'm your mother.'

'And he's my father. I'm sorry, but I'm not taking sides in this. What I did was for business. You'll have to get him back on your own.'

She saw then that I meant it, and she said some things that I would rather forget. Actually, I didn't hear much of what she was saying. I was staring at the folder in my lap and the photo in it. The name on the folder was Justine Jones, but the face in the photo was the same face I had seen a few days before on the wall of the cave at Mount Krn. It wasn't something similar, it was the same face. Digger's girl was the living image of Cankar's painting of the Madonna of the mountains.

BOOK TWO

JUSTINE

Chapter Ten

The first winter that Digger spent with the partisan band on Mount Krn was the last winter of Marina's life. Cankar's granddaughter faded slowly through those winter months, in the springtime she was gone, and when she left she took with her Digger's first love. They were lovers in the only way they could be, a love of fingertip caresses and furtive kisses each as light as the breeze. It could never have been more than that. Marina's illness, and the strict morality of the band, prohibited a consummation, but they were content enough with what they had. It was more than either of them had expected.

That was the short end of the winter after the aborted attempt to bring out Hannes and Kurt – March through the false spring of April – and the band raided only twice in that time, each time coming off the mountain to blow the railway line below Tolmin. They cut that line whenever they could, and the Germans always managed to repair it. That was the sort of war it was. Aside from those two raids they stayed holed up in their caves and waited for the true spring of May, when they would be able to steal horses and go raiding across the Isonzo into Italy. There was little to do in that slack time of waiting, and during those days Marina and Digger were constantly together. At first they spent the days outside, despite the cold, seeking privacy from the crowded caves, but as Marina grew weaker they were forced inside again. There they sought out precious corners where they could half sit, half recline against the rocky walls, their heads close together and their feet towards the nearest fire. They spoke softly in a combination of pidgin German and the Slovenian that Digger was rapidly acquiring, and every conversation was punctuated by Marina's sharp and rasping cough. She was coughing constantly by then. Nobody knew exactly what was wrong with her, and although Cankar called it tuberculosis the word was only a convenient term to

537

apply. It could have been anything connected with the lungs, but whatever it was, it was killing her. In a community of wind-weathered faces hers was pale, the skin translucent, and each cough brought up blood. Everybody in the camp knew that she had no chance, Marina knew it as well, and knew that there was nothing to be done about it. They had no doctors, no medicines, and no place to turn for them. There was one desperate possibility, and Digger put it to Cankar. She could be taken down the mountain and left to make her way into town to seek help there. The Germans would have her then, but she would be no worse off than she already was.

'She would be a great deal worse off,' Cankar told him. 'The Fascists know her, know that she is kin to me. There is much that she could tell them under a certain kind of pressure. Besides, what could they do for her? She is past that kind of help, even assuming that they would give it.'

'Then what the hell do we do?'

'Nothing. In peacetime a doctor would prescribe a year in a sanitarium.' His leathery lips cracked into a mirthless grin. 'Clean cold air, that's what they'd give her. A year in the mountains.'

At that point Digger grieved more about the certainty of Marina's death than the girl did herself. She had accepted what was happening to her and had set her face to a future measured in weeks with a serenity that was beyond Digger's under-standing. He would have preferred to see her rage against her fate, but she refused to do battle with the inevitable. Woman-wise, she preferred to spend the time that was left to her in quiet conversation with Digger, and what she wanted most to talk about was how things might have been and what kind of a life she might have lived had there been life for her beyond eighteen. It was not a morbid curiosity, only a sad one.

'Look what I gain by dying young,' she told him as they huddled together in the corner of a cave. 'You see me now and I am beautiful for you. The beauty of youth, and that is the way you will remember me. Never old, never wrinkled. You will never get a chance to grow weary of me. And if I take any memories with me, and I think I will, they will be of a strong young man in love with me before he grew grey, and soft and indifferent.'

'Never indifferent,' Digger protested.

'Thank you, but it happens to other people and it could have happened to us. But not this way.'

'No, not this way.'

'Still, there are things that I will never know, and that is the unhappy part of it. I will never know what it would be like if we had truly been lovers. . . .'

'We are, as truly as possible.'

'I mean lovers in a time of houses with roofs, featherbeds, and fireplaces, soft nights and a lifetime before us.'

'A different time,' he admitted.

'Yes. In a time such as that you would first have called upon my father. That is, if my father were still alive, which he is not, but if he were alive we would still be living near Skofja Loka. Do you know where that is?'

'No.'

'Farming country north of Ljubljana. There the custom is still to call on the father, and you would bring a gift for me, *trniči.*' She looked at him expectantly.

He guessed, and said, 'Cheese?'

'Yes, but a special cheese that a young man gives to a young woman as a token of love. The outside of the cheese is decorated with pieces of wood, beautifully carved by the boy himself.'

'I could make you a beaut,' he said in English. 'You're talking to the original Yankee whittler.'

She ignored the words she did not understand. 'And after my father had approved there would be land to find, to farm and to build on.'

'I never figured to be a farmer. I've seen too many farmers defeated by rocks.'

'Right now you are a farmer, just for the moment, please? And since you are a farmer we would have to find you a strip of land. That is the way it is done with us. The land is owned in strips only fifty metres wide but stretching for thousands of metres out onto the Sora Plain, and at the head of each strip is the farmhouse. That is the big building and around it are the small buildings, and out in the fields are the *kozolci* to hold the drying hay. Do they have *kozolci* on the farms in Vermont?'

'No, the hay is dried in stacks in the open air.'

'Yes, that is the best way,' she agreed, 'but on the plains so close to the mountains we have too much rain and it is impossible to dry hay completely that way. We must hang it in the *kozolci* to finish the job. We would be lost without the *kozolci*.'

'And so would the boys and girls looking for a private place to meet.'

'That also,' she said with a faint smile. 'I have heard that said. But we would have no need of that. We would have our home, which you would build with your own hands.'

'First you make me a farmer, and now a builder.'

'Please, today you are many things and it costs you nothing at all. You would build our home in the style of our village, the first storey of brick with a wooden upper story bounded by the *gank*, which is both a corridor and a balcony protected by the overhang of the roof. Can you picture that?'

'Yes, and I can picture vines growing up the side of the house to flower and leaf along the *gank*, and give shade.'

'Yes, yes, that is just how it should look. And inside the house large vaulted rooms, and an open hearth in the kitchen.'

'To cook the soup.'

'And other things. I know how to cook more than soup. I would make you sausages, and chicken with paprika, and dumplings as big as your fist.'

'Enough. I'm hungry already.'

'And there would be a large clock on the wall, and in the bedroom a mattress with a mountain of goose feathers in it. A mountain, I tell you.'

'I like our house, it's comfortable.'

'It should be, you built it. Have you seen the garden yet?'

'How could I? I've been too busy hauling bricks from sunrise to sunset.'

'Never mind, you are young and strong, and while you've been building the house I've been planting the garden. Peas, and beans on poles, and onions and tomatoes.'

'No flowers?'

'This is a farmer's garden. The flowers come from the fields and the high places. Chickweed, and monkshood and gentian, a pot of them on every windowsill.'

'In Austria they make alcohol from the gentian.'

'No alcohol now. You need steady hands for building the beehives.'

'Am I a beekeeper also?'

'The keeping of bees has been done for hundreds of years in my country. It is something a man does.'

'I saw a bear go after wild honey once. After a while brother bear lost his sweet tooth.'

'It is something to learn, but the hive must be built. Unless, of course, there is a hollow stump of a tree, which will do just as well.'

'We'll make do with the stump. All you need to build a stump is an axe. All right, we have our strip of land, the *kozolci*, the house and the garden, and the beehive ready for the bees. What else do we need?'

'Why, nothing. Only ourselves, and the time to live our lives.'

'Yes.'

'And a child to make all the work worthwhile.'

'Yes. Many of them, three or four.'

'Of course, but right now one would be enough.'

'Yes.' It was suddenly over, and he knew that there would be no more pleasure in talking about it. He felt cheated and angry by the talk of land, and houses and children, and he said, 'We have no child, but we have some time left to us.'

'Yes, some weeks perhaps, and that is not a small thing to have. Still, I wish I could know what it could have been like to lie in a bed with you, to make a child, to bear it and raise it. I wish I could watch you grow old and wise. I would praise you when you were right in things, and scold you when you were wrong.'

'You would never scold me, you would not dare. I would beat you if you did.'

'You would not.' A smile. 'In America the men do not beat their women, even I know that. American men are kind lovers, just as you are. Even in a crowded cave on an icy mountain.'

'Without a featherbed or a fireplace.'

'And the only clock the melting snow.'

For a moment he could not see her; his eyes were blurred. He said, 'I have spent every winter of my life surrounded by snow, and I have never known a time when the snow did not melt. If just this once I could hold back the spring I would give . . .'

She stopped him with a finger to his lips. 'You have given,' she said. 'I thought I would have nothing, and look what the snows brought me. A love for my last winter. You have given me plenty.'

In that way they were lovers through the last days of winter and into that part of the year when the snow began to melt in the highest places, and with the melting of the snow Marina weakened quickly. The irony of her dying was that she faded as the flowers freshened and the odours of spring invaded the caves. By then she could only lie all day wrapped in blankets by the mouth of the cave, alert for the slight songs of birds and the touch of the breeze on her cheek. Digger sat by her during those days, fed her, cleaned her and tended to her in every way. Within the customs of the people these were not tasks for a man to perform, and at first the grandmother, Katya, objected.

'You are shaming her before the others,' she told Digger. 'I am the one who should tend to these things.'

'Grandmother, don't talk to me about shame. I don't have time for it. She is going away from me soon, and I will need all the memories I can gather. Even these.'

The old woman nodded, and after that she left them alone through the days.

On the night of one of those days Digger slipped down the mountain and into the town by himself, eluded the German sentries, and robbed the storeroom of the medical unit attached to the Alpinkorps there. He went without Cankar's approval, and he came back to face Cankar's anger. He brought with him a crate of totally useless jars of potassium permanganate.

'What are we supposed to do with this?' asked Cankar. 'Paint our faces purple to scare the Fascists?'

'I thought it was sulphur,' Digger admitted. 'I didn't have time to open the box and look.'

'The same stupidity all over again, just what I did when I stole the paint from the Germans. And even if it had been sulphur, what good would it do her? She's past that, man, she's dying.'

'I'll go down again tonight and see what else I can find.'

'You will not. I forbid you to leave the camp.'

But that night Digger slipped away again, down and into town, and, bucking the odds, robbed the same storeroom. This time he came back with a crate of gauze bandages and another filled with aspirin tablets.

'Better,' said Cankar. 'This stuff we can use, but for Marina it means nothing. Will you get it through your head that you cannot help her now?'

'It was all they had,' Digger said desperately. 'That and more permanganate. I'm going back again tonight, and this time I'll get her a doctor. The Germans must have one attached to that unit.'

'Bravo. You're going to kidnap a German doctor and pack him up the mountain on your back just to have him tell you that there is nothing he can do for my granddaughter?'

'There might be something he can do.'

'With what? Potassium permanganate? Then, of course, you will have to shoot the German because he will have seen too much. What a way to fight a war. We don't have to kill the Fascists, we just have to assassinate their doctors and they'll all die of disease.'

'I'm going.'

'You're not. There will be two men beside you all through the night to see that you don't.'

In the end, however, there was no need for the men to guard him. That night he sat beside Marina's makeshift bed, his hand on hers, and now even he had to admit that there was nothing to be done. She had wasted away to a fragile wisp and she could scarcely breathe. When she spoke he had to lean close to make out the words.

'Afterwards,' she said in his ear, 'do not let them say that I was some sort of saint. I hear the people talking.'

'The Madonna of the mountains.'

'But you know better. I was never a saint to you. I never had a chance to be much of a sinner, but I was never a saint.'

'I don't like all this talk about saints. Tonight I go to find a doctor for you.'

'No, enough,' she said faintly. 'The kind of man you are, you had to try for the medicines, but now enough. There is nothing a doctor can do. Let me go now, let me slip away.'

'I can't do that.'

'You must. You are all that is holding me here. I can feel it, your need, holding me. Let me go now, Digger. Please.'

'Don't ask me that.' His hands gripped hers, and if he could have he would have gripped her soul as tightly.

'You must. Listen, I'll make you a promise. Let me go now, just for a while, and someday I'll come back.' Her fevered lips

543

moved rapidly. 'I will, I swear it. I don't know when, but one day I'll come back to you and I'll be healthy and strong then, ready to love you and live with you all the rest of our lives together. That's my promise to you. I'll be back.'

He did not speak, he could not.

'Trust me, believe me. I won't leave you alone. I said I would come back, and I will. We'll find our land and build our house with the vines on the walls and the beans running wild in the garden, and in every window a pot of monkshood and gentian from the fields. Clocks on the walls and a mountain of feathers on which to rest, and a son to make the work worthwhile. I promise you that, the land, and the house and the son.' Her voice floated up to him faintly. 'But now you must let me go. Like a balloon on a string, just open your fingers. Let go. It's all right, really it is. I came through into the springtime from the winter of my love, and now it's time to go. But I'll be back someday, I promise you that.'

She said it over and over. She was raving now, her voice running out like thread from a spool, and as she made her promise again and again, lower and lower, he came to see that she was right. That their only hope was this faintest hope. That somehow there would be a way back to him from where she was going, and that she would find it. He let go of her then, felt her slip away, and in that moment she was gone. She rose out of his life like a balloon set free, drifting away forever, he thought, until she drifted back over thirty years later in the person of Justine Jones.

'At least, that's the way he sees it,' said Justine. 'Actually, my family is mixed Welsh and English, nothing else that we know of. Third-generation Americans, no connection at all with Yugoslavia. But Digger insists that I look like this girl that he knew over thirty years ago. He insits that I *am* this girl, and nothing seems to make any difference. He's convinced.'

'You do look exactly like her,' said Mike.

'You saw the painting in the cave?'

'We both did,' I told her. 'A few weeks ago in Slovenia.'

'And it really looks like me?'

'It *is* you.'

'But it isn't,' she said wearily. 'It's some girl who died in 1944.'

544

'We know that,' said Mike, soothing her. 'But the resemblance is remarkable. You look enough like her to be her twin.'

'Enough to knock Digger flat on his ass,' I said, and added, 'Enough so that he thinks he's twenty-four years old again.'

'I never tried to do that,' she said. 'I never played any tricks on him. I never tried to be anyone but myself.'

She frowned at me as she said it. I had been needling her ever since we got on the ferry, and it was getting to her. We stood on the open deck of the boat to Staten Island, just the three of us there with our noses poked into the wind. Gulls wheeled and screamed overhead on the draughts of a sharp spring afternoon. We were halfway across the harbour with the towers of Manhattan astern and the flat fifth wheel of the city up ahead. The meeting had been Digger's idea. He wanted his sons to meet Justine, and he intuitively felt that the first contact would go better without him. The place for the meeting had been Justine's choice. She had been in New York for almost a year and she had never ridden on the ferry. Now she leaned against the rail, facing forward. Her hands were jammed into the pockets of a worn tweed coat, its collar up, and she shivered inside of it pleasurably when the harbour breeze hit her. Mike looked at me over her head. He was dressed in one of his city disguises: a grey pinstripe suit under a charcoal topcoat, the homburg held firmly in his hand. You had to look closely to see Mad Mike Prince, but he was there. I returned his look with a shrug, as lost as he was. Neither of us had wanted this meeting, but Digger had insisted on it when he came back to New York from Vermont.

He had taken a suite at the Stanhope, and I saw him there. He explained to me that the suite was only temporary until he found a suitable apartment. I was puzzled by the vague note of apology in his voice until I realized that the hotel bill would be charged to the company. It was disquieting to hear, and I wondered how often he had used that tone of voice when Bobby had been paying the bills. I gave him a casual wave of the hand to show that I understood, and it was then that he said that he wanted Mike and me to meet Justine.

''It's important to me,' he said. 'I don't want you getting the wrong idea. I want you to see what kind of a person she is.'

'You really sure you want this?' I asked. 'It's sort of a delicate situation.'

'You mean because of her age?'

'I mean because you happen to be married to my mother.'

'You taking sides?' He seemed surprised. 'Did I raise you to be a moralist?'

'No, but you raised me to be a realist, and when I subtract eighteen from fifty-seven I get a lot of zeros left over.'

'Yeah, I figured you'd say something like that. Look, I want you to do this for me without a lot of wise-ass remarks. And Michael, too, I want him to meet her. Does he still have that girl with him? What's her name . . . Lacey?'

'He parked her in London.'

'Just as well. She's a little on the flashy side, if you know what I mean.'

'Who's talking like a moralist now? Where has your friend been living, in a cocoon?'

'Fort Wayne, Indiana. Same thing.'

'I got the impression she was a sophisticated actress.'

'Not at all, she's just a drama student.'

'Where, in a convent?'

He sighed. 'Take it easy, will you? She's studying and working at the Midtown Theatre Club. Bobby's a member there, and that's where I first saw her. They were doing something by Ibsen, something about a builder.'

'*The Master Builder?*'

'That's it. Justine was one of the women in the crowd. That's all, no lines.' He leaned back in his chair and closed his eyes. 'You have to imagine what it was like, seeing Marina's face after all those years. I couldn't believe it. When I told Bobby she said I was hallucinating.'

'You told her?'

He opened his eyes. 'Of course, she was with me. The next night I came back to the theatre alone to make sure that I *wasn't* hallucinating, and after the show I knew I had to see her.'

'Standing at the stage door, clutching a bunch of posies.'

'Accurate except for the flowers. I met her, took her somewhere for something to eat, and we talked halfway through the night. I told her about the war, about Yugoslavia, about the painting in the cave. I told her who she is. And who she was. She couldn't accept that part of it. She still can't. After that I took her home, and after that . . . things just seemed to happen.'

546

'They usually do. How long are they going to keep on happening?'

He lifted his hands and turned them palms up. It was a touchingly helpless gesture. 'Until she tells me to go away. I'm in it for as long as she'll have me.'

'You're throwing away thirty years of marriage.'

For the first time I saw concern on his face. Not for Bobby or himself, but for me. 'Are you going to hate me for that? I hope not. Killing the marriage is Bobby's idea, not mine.'

'You're laying too heavy a threat on her, you're not giving her any room to manoeuvre. You can't expect her to treat this like some quick roll in the hay.'

'Maybe not, but she's got to understand what this means to me.' His eyes were closed again. 'But she won't. And you won't. And nobody else will understand it, either. How could you? You don't know what it's like to be fifty-seven fucking years old and to have thirty-three of those years just go sliding away. Zing, just like that. You don't know what it's like to have the love of your youth back again. You can't.'

'No,' I agreed, 'I can't. Digger, are you telling me that you really believe that this Justine is the same girl you knew during the war?'

'Yes.'

'Then your eggs are scrambled, that's all there is to it.'

'Wait a minute, let me expand on that. Marina died back in 'forty-four, I know that. Dead is dead, and I've seen enough dead ones lying around to know one when I see one. So she died, and I helped bury her with these two hands. But she came back, just as she promised she would. Somehow she found a way to come back.'

'Like Christ on Easter?'

'Don't confuse me with religion. All I know is that she's back. She's just the same age as when she went away, and now she's come back and it's time for us to do all the things we never had a chance to do before. She was my first love, Kelly, and now she'll be my last.'

'You really believe that.' It wasn't a question. I could see that he did.

'I have to, don't you see? I loved her then and I love her now. How else could it be?' The same helpless gesture with the hands. 'That's why I want you to meet her, get to know her, see what kind of a woman she is. After that maybe you'll be able to understand at least a part of it. Will you do that for me?'

I said that I would, and that was what I was doing as the ferryboat clawed against the current to line itself up with the slip at St George. Bells rang and a grinding noise rose from the engine room as I watched her standing against the rail. She was slim and smooth, with the pale oval face and the long dark hair of the cave painting. Her eyes were dark and warm, and the line of her chin was sharp as she tilted her face to the breeze. The same breeze carried her scent to me: forest jasmine nestled in pine. She spoke softly, smiled gently, and seemed the owner of a natural calm. Tucked into the worn tweed coat with the collar up to her ears she looked like a little lost waif. The ferry eased into the slip, and the light traffic of a weekday afternoon began to disembark. Still hunched in her coat, she twisted her head to look up at Mike.

'What happens now?' she asked. 'Do we get off?'

He gave her a shocked look. 'Get off? Are you mad? The only people who get off are those who have to live here. Do you want to live in Staten Island?'

'Is it anything like Fort Wayne?'

'It is a great deal like Fort Wayne.'

'Then I don't want to get off.'

'A wise decision. You just enjoy the scenery, sniff the salt air, and cruise back and forth across the harbour like the *Flying Dutchman*. But do not get off at Staten Island. It would be the social gaffe of the century.'

'Yes sir.' A grin poked at the corners of her lips. 'I like the part about the *Flying Dutchman*. I've been wanting to do this ever since I first came to New York. I tried to get Digger to go with me, but he wouldn't. He said that he was too old to ride the ferry just for the hell of it.'

'There seems to be a flaw in his logic,' I said. They both turned their heads to me. 'He's also too old to be screwing teenage girls just for the hell of it.'

Justine turned away to lean on the rail and stare over the side. The look that Mike gave me was a mixture of indignation and amusement. To Justine's back, he said lightly, 'You mustn't mind him, he's the family menace. We've been overly indulgent with him and now he thinks he has a licence to be outrageous.'

When she did not respond to that, I said, 'I seem to have offended you, but I'm confused. Which word did you find objectionable? "Teenage" or "screwing"?'

She turned around. Her face was composed and her voice was more sad than angry. 'The words don't offend me, Kelly, but your attitude does. What I have with your father is something very special and precious to me, and I don't like to hear it cheapened. This meeting was Digger's idea, not mine. He had some idea that we might be friends, the three of us. I can see he was wrong.'

'A touch optimistic,' I agreed. 'I'm sorry that you don't like my attitude, but there are only two reasons why an eighteen-year-old girl takes up with a guy Digger's age. Either she's looking for a father figure or she's looking to improve her tax bracket. Which is it with you?'

The deck rumbled under our feet as the boat prepared to get under way again. Justine turned to Mike and asked, 'How long will it take us to get back to Manhattan? I want to go home.'

'Hey, don't take that stuff seriously. That's just Kelly doing his wise-ass thing.'

'I want to go home. This was a dumb idea.'

'You don't want to do that, that's letting him win. Come on, it's all part of his game.'

'What game?'

'Everybody has a game, this one is his. He pushes you to see how far he can go.'

Justine looked at him doubtfully. She leaned back with her elbows on the rail. 'Look, you two, this situation is tough enough for me without playing any games. It's none of your business, but for the record I've never taken a penny from your father. I've never accepted an expensive gift from him. I pay my own rent and I buy my own clothes. That's the way I want it and that's the way it's going to be. As far as father figures go, I've got a perfectly fine one back in Fort Wayne. My dad is a great guy and I don't need any substitutes.' She looked at me directly now. 'Also for the record, I don't like you, and I don't like games, and I still want to go home just as soon as we get off this *Flying Dutchman*.'

'You can't,' said Mike. He jammed the homburg onto his head at a jaunty angle. 'I mean you can get off the boat, but you can't go home yet. We have a party to go to.'

That was news to me. 'What party?'

'Eddie Hochman and his gang at First Philly. They closed an oil deal in Louisiana and the party's been rolling since Tuesday. We're invited.'

Eddie Hochman was one of the hot Wall Street underwriters of the moment, still under forty and head of the underwriting department at the First Philadelphia Corporation. The firm was young, fast, and smart, and with an instinct for knowing when a company was ripe for a merger or a takeover. Hochman's department handled the new stock offerings, the massive deals to promote the stock of private companies going public. Whenever one of those deals was closed it was party time at First Philly, which meant a small fleet of limousines, a couple of suites at a midtown hotel, and a dozen women from an escort service. Supplies were laid in . . . the bottled goods, a few ounces of coke, a roast pig and everything that went with it from Cremona's . . . and the party was on. According to Mike, who knew Hochman well, it could run for days.

I moved close to Mike and said quietly, 'Do you really want to take her to one of Hochman's bashes? From what I've heard, it really isn't her scene. As a matter of fact, it isn't mine, either.'

'Then go home,' he said pleasantly. 'You've been acting abominably anyway.'

'What are you trying to do, needle Digger? This is a sure way to do it.'

'Nonsense, it's a party, not an orgy. I think we owe her some entertainment after the way you've behaved.' He turned to Justine. 'What do you say? Shall we go?'

'Is there any reason why I shouldn't?' she asked.

'None that I know of.'

'Then sure, why not?'

That's all it took to turn her around. One minute she was dead set on going home and the next, because I was against it, she was all for the party. We hadn't known each other for much more than an hour but the lines were already drawn.

'I'm not really dressed for a party,' she said. She unbuttoned the old tweed coat and held it open. 'Do you think this will be all right?'

Mike had some trouble controlling his face. I didn't bother, I just stared. It wasn't the dress she was wearing, although that was perfectly fine. With her coat open she no longer looked like a little lost waif. She had been using it to cover a body of centrefold proportions: slim, yet full and sleek.

'I think that should do very nicely,' Mike managed to say.

'I'm glad.' She closed the coat. 'I don't have much of a wardrobe for a woman living in sin.'

'Nobody used words like that,' I said.

'Nobody had to.'

The party was in two adjoining suites at the Crestwood on East Fifty-sixth. It wasn't an orgy, but it wasn't a church social, either. The outside rooms were for drinking, and dancing and nibbling at Cremona's buffet. The inside rooms were for what couldn't be done in the outside rooms. There were a couple of dozen people moving around, some of them dancing to the piped-in music. Nobody was wearing nametags, but none of the women looked like anybody's wife or sister. As we came into the room, a man as broad as a door and with sandy hair and moustache hurried over and put out his hand.

'Michael, Michael,' he said, both of his hands covering one of Mike's. 'Now the party is official, Mad Mike Prince is here.'

Mike didn't try to rescue his hand. 'Eddie Hochman, Justine Jones. Eddie, this is my brother, Kelly.'

'Justine, a pleasure. Kelly, great to meet you, heard a lot about you. Come on, let's get rid of those coats and get you people something to drink.'

He led us over to the wet bar and got a scotch for Mike, a glass of white wine for Justine, and an off-season beer for me. The buffet table was set up next to the bar, and on it were the remains of a roast pig. It was mostly bones.

'Eddie, you're going to need a new pig,' Mike pointed out.

Hochman looked at the table thoughtfully. 'You're right, and that's the second one. This looks like a three-pig party. We never went through three before.'

He snapped his fingers and told someone named Tommy to call Cremona's for another pig. Considering the time of day and the state of the party, Tommy suggested ordering only a half. Eddie frowned and said, 'No, make it a whole pig. I don't deal in broken lots.'

He put a hand on Mike's shoulder. 'Mike, your drink okay? Justine? Kelly? Good. Michael, I think I see that certain light in your eye, and if I'm right you'll find what you're looking for right through that door in the next room.'

'Do you think so, Eddie? Do you think I really will?'

'I can guarantee it.' His hand on Mike's elbow, he moved him towards the door. 'Why don't you take Justine with you while Kelly and I stay out here with the health freaks and the clean livers.'

He had assumed that Mike and Justine were together, which was both irritating and amusing. What wasn't amusing was Justine wandering off into Noseland. I wasn't responsible for her, but if Digger found out about it I was the one who would get the heat. I watched them go unhappily.

'Lovely girl,' said Hochman. 'Mike can really pick 'em.'

'Uh-huh.' More irritation. The assumption was that a girl like that wouldn't be with a kid like me. 'She's an old friend of the family. I wouldn't want her to wander into the wrong kind of scene.'

He looked at me in surprise. 'Kelly, Kelly, what are you saying?'

'No offence, but from what I can see she's the only civilian in the house. I wouldn't want anyone to mistake her for one of the working girls.'

'Civilian?' He looked around the room at the girls from the escort service. 'Civilian, yes, I see what you mean. Please, there's really nothing to worry about. Take my word for it.'

'If you say so.'

'I do.' He gripped my arm as he said it. He did that a lot. 'Listen, I'm awfully glad you stopped by with Mike. I was hoping to get a chance to talk to you.'

'What about?'

He smiled. 'You're either very modest or very sophisticated. You've got to know that people are talking about you.'

I waved that one away. 'Thanks, I had a good season, but so did a lot of other guys.'

'Season? Oh, I see. Yes, you won quite a few races, didn't you? Actually, I was talking about what's been going on at Prince Skis since you took over.'

'I only took over a short while ago, Mr Hochman – '

'Call me Eddie, please.'

' – and there hasn't been time to do much of anything.'

'That so? Funny, the things you hear on the Street. I hear most of the talk, and all last week I heard talk about how a certain sporting goods manufacturer was maybe thinking of going public. Probably just talk, huh?'

It wasn't. That day in Sedgewick Falls when the will was read to me, nothing had been said about the taxes on the estate. That blow came later, and it was a heavy one. It could have been eased if it had been anticipated properly, but my grandmother, in her stubborn Yankee style, had refused to look past the day of her death and the effect it would have on the company. We were feeling that effect now: a need for cash not only to pay taxes but also to purchase the new equipment that a new technology demanded. One of the possible answers to the problem was to go public, selling off sixty percent of the corporation stock while maintaining control with the balance. It was a decision that Digger and I had not yet made, but we were leaning towards it. What puzzled me was how Hochman knew about it. It was strictly family business.

'Eddie, you're talking over my head,' I told him. 'If you've heard any talk about Prince Skis on the Street then you know that my father is running it for me. I don't know a damn thing about the business end, all I do is ski.'

'How's your beer? Get you another?'

'I'm okay, thanks.'

'Right, training. Kelly, you don't have to pull the dumb jock act with me. From what Mike tells me, you're slicker than pigshit, no matter how old you are, but . . .' He held up his hands. 'I can understand it if you don't want to talk about it.'

'I wouldn't know what to say.'

'Fair enough if that's the way you want to play it. Only keep this in mind, would you? When and if the time comes . . . and I'm saying *if* you decide to go public, no one will do a better job for you on the offering than First Philly. This party stuff, don't pay too much attention to that. The icing on the cake. Underneath the icing we're a solid outfit and we do a solid job.'

'You don't have to sell me on your reputation, Eddie. I know how good it is.'

'Fine, then you know that we've handled a good many public offerings in the past. Just keep us in mind.'

'I'll do that,' I said, but I wasn't paying much attention to what he was saying. One of the girls standing at the bar had just casually taken her dress off. She tossed the dress on a bar stool. Now all she was wearing was shoes. She walked across the room, coming down hard on her heels so that her breasts bounced wildly. As she walked she called out in a loud, clear voice, 'Corporate mergers, anyone? I'm available for a corporate merger, gentlemen. Is anybody interested in making a merger?'

Hochman grinned at me weakly. 'She's supposed to do that every half hour. The idea is, we do a lot of merger work and . . .' His voice trailed off. 'Oh shit.'

The last was because as the naked girl reached the door to the other room it opened and Justine came out. The two women stood face to face for a moment, then Justine nodded gravely in greeting. They passed each other and the door closed. Justine came over to us and said to Hochman, 'My congratulations to Cremona's. They got the third pig over here in record time.'

'Jesus, I'm sorry about that,' said Hochman.

'Don't be,' she told him. 'I've seen better bodies in my high school gym class. Actually, that one could use an apple in her mouth.'

'Mucho apologies, kids, really sorry.' Hochman excused himself and went hurrying into the next room after the girl.

'I think I'd better leave before someone makes me an offer I can't refuse,' said Justine. She was trying not to smile. 'Was that why you didn't want to bring me here?'

'That was one of the reasons. You saw the other one in the next room.'

The smile disappeared. 'Fort Wayne isn't the end of the world, I've seen people using drugs before. Just a bunch of glassy-eyed heads sitting around staring at a bowl of guacamole.'

'Is that how Mike is? Glassy-eyed?'

'Just a little high.'

'And you?'

She wrinkled her nose. 'I don't use it.'

'Is any of this going to get back to Digger?'

'Ho, ho, and I thought you were trying to shelter me from evil. You were worried about Mike all the time.'

'You haven't answered me.'

'Isn't your brother a little old to be sheltered?'

'He doesn't need any more problems with Digger.'

'He won't get them from me. You may not think very much of me, Kelly, but I'm not a snitch.'

'I thank you for that. If you're ready, I think we should go now.'

'All right.'

She lived in a brownstone on Eighty-seventh off Columbus, and if she really was paying her own rent Digger wasn't saving much. At that point the neighbourhood was still climbing back uphill, and the rough edges showed. I let the taxi go and stood with her at the foot of the brownstone steps. She thanked me for bringing her home.

'I won't pretend it was a pleasant afternoon,' she said. 'You seem determined not to like me.'

'It isn't you. The situation is impossible.'

'Mike seems to be able to handle it.'

'Mike doesn't care. That's why he always wins.'

'You worry a lot about him, don't you?'

'Yes. I always have.'

'I like him. I think he likes me.'

'They don't come any better than Mike,' I said. 'He could be a good friend to you.'

'And you couldn't?'

'I don't know. It's too soon to tell, but I doubt it. There's too much working against it.'

'You're probably right,' she said listlessly. A light drizzle started to fall then, just enough to colour the evening a delicate amber. The first drops hit and she said goodbye quickly, leaving me standing there.

I watched as she mounted the brownstone steps in a hurry and went into the house. She had said goodbye unhappily, and I was less than happy to see her go. It has always made me sad to see girls go home alone in the rain. As if I have failed them in some way. As if I owe them a crackling fire, a bottle of wine, and a jest to challenge the rattle of rain on the windows. A silly sadness, but that's what I felt as I watched her go.

I took the sadness home with me in a rain that grew thicker and finally sent me racing down the street in search of a taxi. I was wet through when I got home, and I was alone there. Bobby was out with friends, Mike was probably still at Hochman's party, and the housekeeper was gone on her Thursday night off. I carried that little bowl of sadness around with me as I changed into dry clothing, found something to eat, and then sat by the window overlooking the park. The other side of the park from

Justine. I kept seeing the flash of her legs as she ran up the stairs to get out of the rain. It was coming down in sheets now, and I hoped she had a crackling fire and a glass of wine to brave the night. I wondered how much she really believed about the link between her and that girl so long dead, how much of it she secretly laughed at and how much of it she accepted in wonderment. She was only my age and a long way from home in a town where it sometimes seemed as if the rain beat on the windows every night. No matter how hard I had ridden her, I knew that she was a sad girl in a sad situation. The whole deal stank of sadness, and I decided not to think about her any more.

That was what I decided, but I thought of her the next morning when I woke, and often during the day. The next day was the same, and the next after that. I kept thinking of those legs flashing up the stairs, running away from me. I did not stop to think of what she might be doing then, or whom she might be with. All I could see was those flashing legs. The next day I put them out of my mind in the oldest of ways, with a girl of my own and an exhausting night that was designed to obliterate memories. But the day after that the thoughts of her were back again in ways I did not welcome. I could not get her out of my mind. She was embedded there in the amber light of that evening when the raindrops hit and she ran from me up the brownstone stairs, running from me into sadness. That was the only way I thought of her, and I thought of her that way for over a week before I realized the kind of trouble I was in.

Chapter Eleven

'You weren't the only one who got into trouble that day,' said Justine. 'You should make that clear.'

She had read what I had written, and that was her comment on a hot and sticky night in Ibiza. The kind of night to get out of the house, and with the day's work done in the family museum I suggested a drive into town for a drink at Sandy's Bar and dinner at Sa Punta. The suggestion was firmly rejected both by Justine, who refused to face the drive down the bumpy road, and by Anna, who fusses over her foolishly. Besides, said Anna, she had planned a dinner of Austrian specialities. *Gefüllte Paprika*, the way they make it in the Burgenland, served with *Dickgekochter Maisgriess* on the side. The first being stuffed peppers, which I have always thought of as being a Hungarian dish, and the second being ordinary *polenta*, which many Austrians refuse to admit is Italian in origin. (*Polenta irredenta?*) So there was no arguing with Anna, and the question of where to dine was eliminated by a line squall that came racing in from the sea to bump its head against the hills and let loose a torrent. Thus the cocktail hour was removed from the grass to the little sitting room that is part of the kitchen, the *sala* being too big for the three of us. Cushioned banquettes around a small hearth with the smallest of fires designed to offset the drumming of the rain on the roof. Anna in the kitchen area with the sherry bottle close at hand, me with my Trinaranjus, and Justine at the bar mixing the one weak vodka-tonic she allows herself each evening. She made a face as she measured the vodka, then brought the drink over to the banquette, walking carefully, her natural grace only slightly diminished by the body swollen with child. Plumped herself down on a cushion with a sigh, belly out to here, or at least to there, her hands resting on top of the mass and clutching her glass. A single sip, then her chin came up and she pointed out that I was not the only one who had got into trouble that day.

'You seem reluctant to put certain things down on paper,' she went on, 'but you can't pussyfoot around it, darling. It has to be said, the way I felt about Digger and the way I felt about you. I may have been young, and inexperienced and overwhelmed by the man, but I was in love with him. You're going to have to use that word whether you like it or not. I was in love with him, and the fact that I could fall in love with you at the same time doesn't change how I felt about him. Is that what you find hard to say? That a woman can be in love with two men at the same time?'

I did not answer. Anna, standing at the stove, said, 'It can happen to anybody, man or woman. I've told you about Maria, the woman in Vienna who was married to my professor. She loved me and she loved her husband. Equally, she said, and I believed her. It can happen. Most people don't like to admit it, but it's true.' She peered into the pot she was stirring. 'Should

I make a sauce for the *Maisgriess*, or will it be enough with what comes with the peppers?'

'Make something with raisins,' I suggested.

She gave me an affectionate smile. 'It's the Austrian blood, you never lose it.'

Justine finished her drink in one long thirsty sip and said, 'Anna, do you think I could have another very, very weak one?'

'Certainly not.' Anna came marching over, filled her glass with plain tonic water, and handed it back. 'You want to have a drunken baby?'

'I want to have any kind of a baby, drunk or sober, just soon.'

'You will, you will,' Anna soothed. 'Before you know it we'll be going to Barcelona.'

A month before the baby is due we will pack up and move into an apartment there. Anna's idea, again. The event is too blessed to be entrusted to the local doctors. Nonsense, of course, the attitude of an old-time island dweller who remembers when conditions here were truly primitive. However, my opinion doesn't rate very high in these areas.

Justine reached for my hand. 'You're going to have to spell it out,' she said. 'It started for both of us at the same time. I remember it so well, standing in front of the house that first day. We both felt it, a sudden surge, and we swayed towards each other like two trees struck by lightning. Do you remember it that way?'

'Yes.'

'We swayed, and we caught ourselves, and then the rain came down and I had to run. And if I hadn't run we would have been in each other's arms, I know it.'

'Yes.'

'Then you're going to have to say it that way. If you're going to set it down properly and honestly, I mean everything that happened to us over the next few years, then you have to begin at the beginning for both of us. On the day that we swayed towards each other like two struck trees. It took a long time for those trees to fall, but that's when it began.'

That was the year before the Lake Placid Olympics, the year in which to get it all together. The training season for the ski team began in June with a dry-land session at Aspen, and then we flew down to Portillo in Chile for training on snow. After that it was on to Hintertux in Austria for more snow skiing, back to the States for another dry-land session, and up to Mount Hood in Oregon, where there is snow the year round on the Palmer field above the timberline. Digger did not come along; he had good reasons for staying in New York. He was too new in the saddle at Prince Skis to delegate authority yet, and there was the public offering of our stock to be attended to. The decision had been made to go public in the autumn, and the underwriting had been assigned not to Eddie Hochman's outfit but to an older, more conservative house. The sale would give us the capital we needed and leave me with one-third of the voting stock of the corporation, enough to assure control. Those were good reasons for him to stay in New York while I trained with the team, but the main reason he stayed was to be with Justine. He was spending all of his time with her now, still convinced that she was the love of his youth miraculously returned to him. He was making a jackass out of himself in front of everyone he knew, but he didn't seem to care.

That time of training was a blessing for me in that it got me out of New York and away from Justine. Before I left for Aspen I saw her several times, always in the company of Digger and Mike. The old man wanted badly to create a form of family subunit by welding his two sons and his girlfriend together. It was pathetic, the way he tried. He whipped up dinner parties, theatre parties, even a picnic just for the four of us. They were boring fiascos. We all saw what he was trying to do, but none of us was comfortable playing the roles assigned to us. In my case Digger was trying to get me to treat Justine as some sort of sister, which was furthest from my mind. Each time he called me to set up one of those sessions I swore that I would not go, but of course I did. It was the old push-me, pull-me game. I wanted desperately to see her, and each time I did I came away saddened and depressed. Mike saw what was happening. He could always do that with me.

'Pale cheeks, red eyes, trembling chin,' he noted. 'All the usual signs of infatuation. Are you sleeping well these days?'

'Piss off.'

'Started writing sonnets yet?'

'Michael, don't be a prick about this, please.'

'And does the lady return your affections?'

'The lady isn't aware of them.'

'Not very likely. You're about as obvious as a wounded water buffalo bellowing in a rice paddy.'

'That bad?' It was enough that Digger was making a fool of himself. Two of us doing it would change the farce into a burlesque.

'You have to expect that people will notice if you go around with your tongue hanging out. I'm surprised at you, Kelly. In this direction lies madness.'

'It isn't as if I have any control over it.'

'Have you tried the usual cure?'

'Are you kidding? I've been humping my brains out with three different girls.'

'Ah, perhaps that accounts for the pale cheeks and red eyes.'

'It hasn't done a damn bit of good.'

'May I suggest a more radical remedy?'

'Is there any way of stopping you?'

'Seriously. Try to imagine the two of them together, Digger and Justine locked in carnal embrace . . .'

'Jesus!'

' . . . the moonlight striping the sheets of her bed and her body slick with sweat in the golden glow of the lamp as the midnight radio plays a touch of *Eine Kleine Nachtmusik* to the obbligato of creaking springs . . .'

'Cut it out, will you?'

' . . . the old man labouring over her, gasping for breath and hoping that his heart will hold out just one more time . . .'

'Christ, are you trying to drive me nuts?'

'Just trying to help. Thought it might exorcize a demon or two. Don't worry, lad, it will get better. It will get worse first, but then it will get better.'

It didn't, but being out of town helped. In the middle of November the team disbanded for a three-week break before the opening races of the season at Val d'Isère and I went back to New York to consult with Digger and make some decisions. The first had to do with how I was going to race in the coming season. The year before, Digger had taken me out of the technical events – the slalom and giant slalom – and had had me concentrate on the downhill. The move had paid off, and now we had to decide whether or not to continue that way. The decision wasn't easy. I was considered a better-than-average technical racer, good enough to score top-ten finishes and pick up World Cup points that way, but my main strength was in the downhill, where there was a realistic chance for a gold at Lake Placid. The situation was complicated by the fact that the three finest technical skiers in the world that year were the Swede, Ingemar Stenmark, and the Mahre twins, Philip and Steven, from White Pass, Washington. In that pre-Olympic year whenever there was talk about an American man scoring a gold at Lake Placid, the talk was about the Mahre brothers, not about me.

The dream of an American man winning a gold medal in Alpine skiing faded after Digger's loss in 1948, and it wasn't until 1960 that another American, Buddy Werner, was conceded a chance to make it in the downhill. But Buddy broke a leg in training before the Games, and although two other Americans, Billy Kidd and Jimmy Heuga, took a silver and a bronze four years later at Innsbruck, that was the total medal production to date. The dream came alive again in 1976 when the Mahre twins, as teenagers, placed fifth and thirteenth in the giant slalom, and in the post-Olympic years they began to gather World Cup victories and placings in the slalom and GS. Now, in the year before Lake Placid, Philip Mahre was ranked as the second-best technical skier in the world behind Ingemar Stenmark.

That year Stenmark was the acknowledged master of the giant slalom, having won ten out of ten World Cup races the year before, but in the slalom he and the Mahre twins were considered equals. Equals in ability, but not in personality and technique. Stenmark was outwardly so unemotional that on the circuit we called him the Silent Swede, while the Mahre brothers skied with obvious delight as they came slashing down the mountainside. Stenmark carved his turns with ice-cold precision, while the Mahres skied hot, hurling themselves through the gates. There was a difference in style, as well.

'Ingemar makes long turns that go across the fall line,' was the way that Philip explained it. 'He makes a quick, tight-radius turn, releases, gets off the edge quickly, and then glides through the rest of the turn. He's quick that way. Where I'm quick is changing edges on the straight.'

They were quick in every way, all three of them, and Digger and I decided that they were too quick for me. Sure, on any given day I might beat one of them, but from that point on my emphasis would be on the downhill. I would ski slalom, but only when that did not conflict with a downhill.

The second decision to make was what skis I would use in competition. Until then I had been skiing on Royals specifically designed for me, but now, considering that I owned the outfit, I should have been skiing a Prince product. Trouble was, I had skied on Royals all my life, they were a part of me, and it would have taken months of testing to design a Prince to suit my needs. Trouble also was that Bobby now was Royal Skis personified, and my endorsement of her product was a valuable asset to her. The business situation in the family was almost as ridiculous as the marital mix-up. Royal and Prince were two of the biggest in the industry, and in any other family there would have been some sort of accommodation between the two firms, or even a merger. But not us, we did things the hard way. Bobby would have nothing to do with Digger until he got rid of Justine; and from the day I had hired him, although she was cool and correct with me, there was a distinct lack of maternal warmth in our relationship. She had made it clear that she still considered herself to be my loving mom and whenever I was in New York her home was still mine, but she had also made it clear that, at least for the moment, I was one of the men in her life who had done her wrong and she wasn't about to forget it. I could live with that, but I had to make a decision about the skis. If I switched to Prince I was slapping Bobby in the face, and if I continued to race on Royals I was penalizing my own product. A third alternative would have been to use the Royals but with the Prince Ski logo applied to the cosmetic face, something which is done by racers more often than most people realize. That would allow me to use my familiar skis and push the Prince name at the same time, but I knew how much it would hurt my mother.

'Command decision,' I told Digger. 'We stay with the Royals. That's the way it has to be.'

He wasn't happy about it. 'You realize how much that decision is going to cost us?'

'Can't be helped. I'm not going to lay anything more on Bobby right now. She's got enough to handle.'

'I'll go along with it for this year,' he said reluctantly, 'but we're going to have to reevaluate the situation before Lake Placid. I'm not going to hand her the Olympics on a platter.'

562

With those decisions made I had two weeks to myself in New York before joining the team in Val d'Isère, and my goal was to get through the days without trying to see Justine. It would have been easy enough just to set eyes on her. The Midtown Theatre Club was doing a Noel Coward series and she was playing Amanda in *Private Lives,* but I fought the temptation to go. It was the push-me, pull-me game again. I wanted to see her to the point of desperation, but I knew how rotten I would feel after I did. Instead, I lay low at home, determined to spend a quiet time by myself. Mike was in Baja California doing a photo story on sport fishing there, Digger's time was taken up with the nuts and bolts of the stock offering, and although I was staying at the Fifth Avenue apartment my contacts with Bobby were limited to polite nods whenever our paths crossed during the day. There were other people I could have seen, but I didn't call them. Like an animal nursing a wound, I preferred to lick it in private.

During that first week I worked out every morning at Digger's club, went to bed early each night, and tried to do as much reading as possible as a substitute for the education I wasn't getting. I was not alone in this. It was virtually impossible to be a member of the US Ski Team and get a normal education at the same time. The schedule was too demanding. In almost every other sport the national team is put together expressly for Olympic or World Championship competition, but the US Ski Team is one of only two American organizations (the Equestrian Team is the other) that compete internationally on an annual basis. It's an ongoing proposition, it never stops, and it leaves little time for schooling. Some of the kids on the team didn't care; they were stone jocks anyway. Others tried to keep up as part-time students, and still others simply postponed their education until their racing days were over. The best that I could do was to read voraciously and hope that some of it was sinking in. I did that for a week, and then one evening, without any conscious planning of it, I put away my books at seven-thirty, threw on a tie and a jacket, and took a taxi directly to the Midtown Theatre Club on Forty-seventh Street. A single ticket was easily available, and I slipped into my seat just before the curtain went up.

The double terrace of the French hotel appeared, and after the opening exchange between Sibyl and Elyot, Victor came on,

563

Amanda followed, and there she was. Wrapped in a negligee, she looked exactly as Coward described the actress for the part: with a gay face and a perfect figure. At the sight of her I took a deep breath, relaxed, and knew that I was smiling in the darkness. This was terrific. This was what I should have done a week ago, every night in fact. I could watch her, listen to her, almost breathe in the essence of her unobserved. I could get my fill of her without any twinges of guilt and without the need to hide behind the verbal nastiness. I settled down to enjoy myself, and I did for several minutes. I let her performance flow over me uncritically, but not for long. Love is a magnificent buffer, it masks a variety of defects in everyday life, but not on the stage. The medium is merciless. Against the odds of love I watched and listened to Justine deliver Coward's witty, brittle lines, and it didn't take me long to realize that she was awful. She had her lines down pat, but that was all she had. She was stiff in delivery, she moved woodenly from mark to mark, and she had no sense of timing. Instead of bubbling over the stage she turned Amanda into a trudging bore. Not only was it a bad performance, it was insulting to the other players. The Midtown Theatre Club wasn't Broadway, but it wasn't amateur night, either. The young people who worked and studied there were thorough professionals at the beginnings of their careers. But not Justine. She was totally out of place among them. I felt deeply embarrassed for her. It was like suddenly coming upon the woman you love standing naked in a public place. I wanted to take off my coat and throw it over her.

I suffered through the first act, and at the intermission I followed the crowd out of the auditorium and into a large, plain room at the other side of the house. There were tables, a bar, and theatrical posters on the wall. A short girl with frizzy hair worked behind the bar, racing about filling orders. There should have been at least two people there to handle the crowd, but she managed it cheerfully. She never stopped smiling. I waited in line to pay two dollars for a paper cup full of plain tonic water and a weary slice of lime, and found myself a corner to lean against. I was over my embarrassment at Justine's performance and I was feeling cheerful again. I didn't give a damn how good or bad an actress she was, I just wanted to know how she was getting away with it. When the warning bell rang the room cleared out quickly, but I stayed behind. I went back to the empty bar and asked the frizzy-haired girl for another tonic water.

'You'll have to drink it here,' she warned me. 'You can't take it to your seat.'

'That's all right, I'm not in a hurry to go back inside.'

'Be brave,' she said with that cheerful grin. 'It doesn't get any worse.'

'Does it get any better?'

She shrugged. 'It's a good company. You should catch us when we're doing something else.' She gave me my tonic. 'Two dollars, please. I know it's a rip-off but we really need the money.'

'Are you part of the company?'

'Oh, sure. We all take turns on the bar if we're not working. All except the princess, of course.'

'Except who?'

She started swabbing down the bar with a damp rag. She jerked her head towards the door to the orchestra. 'The enchanting Amanda in there who is busily dumping all over Noel Coward.'

'She's pretty bad.'

'Bad? You think that's bad? You should see her do Lady Windermere. Enough to drive Oscar wild.'

'If she's that bad, how does she get the parts?'

'Ah, sweet mystery of life,' she sang softly, polishing the bar. 'The ways of the world, 'twas ever thus.'

'Meaning?'

She shook her head, that's all she was saying. She had no objection if I wanted to stay in the bar through the second act, but there wouldn't be any more company gossip. I stayed and chatted. Her name was Arlene Brent, she was from Bradford, Pennsylvania, and she was particular friends with Murray Wald, the owner and manager of the theatre club. That was the real reason she was working the bar. The other actors were happy to take their turns, but Murray preferred it when she was in charge of the cash register.

'Not that anybody would . . . you know,' she said. 'It just makes him feel better.'

'He trusts you.'

'He should by now, considering everything. If I wanted to

clip him all I'd have to do is go through his wallet in the morning.'

I stayed in the bar through the second act and through the crush of the second intermission. After the second tonic I switched to Perrier water. I saw Arlene giving me quick looks as she wrestled with the crowd. When the bar was empty and the third act running, she began to clean up for the night. There wouldn't be any business after the final curtain.

'Last call for that firewater you're drinking,' she said.

'No, I've had my limit.' I put the soggy cup on the bar. 'You leaving after you close the bar?'

'Home, sweet home.'

'Let me buy you a cup of coffee or something.'

She straightened up and looked at me curiously. 'I just as good as told you that I'm living with Murray.'

'Is he here tonight?'

'No.'

'Look, I'm not making any move on you. I'm just looking for company.'

'Are you in the business, Mr, ah. . . . ?'

'The name is Kelly.'

'I should have said the profession.'

'No, I can't do you a damn bit of good. Like I said, I'm just passing the time.'

She hesitated, then said, 'All right, I'll need about ten minutes to finish up here.'

I took her down the street to Jack MacReady's and bought us a couple of his club steaks and those home fries with the crust on top. She had a rye and ginger ale to drink. She laughed when she saw the look on my face.

'I've been in New York for three years,' she said, 'and that's still all I drink. It's one part of Pennsylvania I'll never get rid of. Don't you drink at all?'

'A beer once in a while. It's a habit I never got into.'

'Unusual these days – most people take something. You get to see that behind a bar. Even the health freaks, they'll take a glass of white wine.' The grin lit up her face. 'What are you, some kind of an athlete or something?'

'Something like that.'

She looked up from her steak and stared. 'Yeah, sure you are. I thought your face was familiar, I've seen your picture

566

somewhere. All those straight white teeth. You're that . . . what is it?' She snapped her fingers. 'Ice skater, right?'

'Skier.'

'Close enough. But the name isn't right, you said Kelly.'

'That's my first name. The whole name is Kelly Prince.'

'Sure, that's it, now I remember. Skiing, all that snow and ice. Not for me.' She went back to her steak, and then it registered. She looked up again, her face stricken. 'Prince? Oh, you son of a bitch.'

'Take it easy.'

'I just figured out who your daddy has to be. Just passing the time, huh?'

'A little chat, that's all I want.'

'I'll bet. About Justine, right?'

'Among other things.'

Her knife and fork went down with a clatter. She reached for her bag. 'Thanks for nothing, and good night.'

I reached across the table and touched her wrist gently with a finger. 'You don't want to go yet. If you do then I'll have to talk to Murray instead. You've already told me too much. He won't be happy about that.'

'I didn't say anything.' It was a weak protest. She sat back in her seat.

'You told me that you're carrying an actress in the company who's so bad that she probably couldn't get a job anywhere else in town. You also told me that it has something to do with my father. That's enough for starters.'

'So what? Is there a law against it?'

'Of course not. I'm just looking for information.'

'You won't get it from me.'

'Then I'll get it from Murray and you're going to have one hell of an angry boyfriend. If I get it from you nobody has to know anything. It's up to you.'

'Why are you doing this to me? What are you, some kind of a monster?'

'Eat your food, don't let it get cold.'

She began to eat again mechanically. She finished the steak, and the home fries and a side order of creamed cauliflower. I ordered her another rye and ginger, and she finished that too. She sat back, patted her lips, and asked, 'Do you have a cigarette? No, you wouldn't, would you?'

567

I found a machine and bought her a pack. She lit one, took a long drag, and said, 'You promise you won't repeat this?'

'Believe it.'

It was the oldest Broadway story there is, as old as the first footlight and the first broken dream. That's the way Arlene saw it. As long as there are young and struggling actresses there will be older, wealthy men willing to help them along. The Midtown Theatre Club, under Murray Wald, barely covered its expenses, and it needed all the help it could get. Digger was supplying the help, and in return his protegée was a featured player in the company.

'How much help?' I asked.

'I don't know any details.'

'Sure you do. If Murray trusts you so much he probably has you taking care of the books.'

'What the hell, I guess it doesn't make any difference. Forty thousand so far. It's all very businesslike. He gives us a cheque and Murray gives him a note.'

'What kind of a note? Secured?'

'Are you kidding? We don't own anything except the sets and the props.'

'What kind of a cheque? Personal?'

'Business. That ski company. That's how I knew who you were when you told me your name. Prince Skis.'

'Does Justine know about the money?'

'Christ, no. That's part of the deal. The only people who know are Murray and me. And now you. Besides, if she knew she'd act different, you know what I mean? She never tries to throw her weight around or anything like that. I'm sorry about what I said before about tending bar. She's offered to take her turn, but Murray won't let her.'

'What about the other people in the company? They must know something's up.'

'Oh, sure they do, but they don't know what. It's just the way things work in the theatre. Nobody would really mind except that she's such a rotten actress. Personally, I like the kid. She's sweet, she's sensitive, she's dedicated. The only trouble is she can't act for beans. I don't know how much longer Murray can get away with using her.'

'You'd think she'd realize that herself.'

She thought that was funny. It was good to see her grin again.

'If you can say that then you really don't know much about the theatre. The power of self-deception is infinite.'

I paid the check then and told her I would take her home. She thanked me for the offer and suggested cab fare instead. She lived in Jackson Heights. I put her into a taxi on Eighth Avenue. Before she got in she made me promise again about keeping quiet. I promised.

'One more thing.' She put her hand on my arm. 'I don't know why you want to know all this, but don't be too hard on your father. A man his age, he's entitled to a little pleasure in life.'

'Not on my money, he isn't,' I said, but she was already in the taxi and she did not hear it.

The next morning I called Jellicoe, the trust officer in Boston. As trustee for my thirty percent of the stock it was his responsibility to review corporate expenditures. I asked him if he knew about the loans to the Midtown Theatre Club. He said that he did.

'May I remind you,' he said, 'that your instructions to me were quite clear. Your father was to be in complete operational control.'

'Since when is a forty-thousand-dollar loan to a half-ass theatre club part of the operations of a ski company?'

'The funds were listed as part of an advertising and promotional campaign. As you have mentioned in the past, I know very little about how skis are sold.'

He was bullshitting me, and we both knew it. He had never forgiven me for that day when the will had been read, and this was his payback. He had followed instructions to the letter. I told him in the future that no further expenditures were to be authorized.

'Very well,' he said politely. 'And may I ask if those instructions apply to similar expenditures not directly connected to the Midtown Theatre Club?'

'What expenditures are you talking about?'

'One moment, please. I shall need my files.' He was gone from the phone and back quickly. 'I refer to the following monthly bills paid in the name of a Miss Justine Jones. Item: eight hundred dollars to a drama coach by the name of Victor Marmaloff. Item: three hundred dollars for dance lessons to a firm called Bedford Studios. Item: three hundred and twenty-five dollars to one Dr George Loughry for speech instruction and therapy. I repeat, those are monthly charges.'

She was paying her own rent and buying her own clothes, but that was as far as her principles went. Or maybe her principles went out the window when it came to her art. Some art. All that money spent to produce a third-rate actress. I told Jellicoe to continue to authorize the monthly bills, but that there would be no more payments to the Midtown Theatre Club. From here on in she travelled on whatever talent she could scrape together.

'If my father objects,' I said, 'you can tell him that the orders came from me.'

'With distinct pleasure, sir. I imagine that you will be hearing from him shortly.'

I did hear from Digger that afternoon, but it had nothing to do with bills and payments. He called to tell me that I had a date the next night to take Justine to dinner and meet her parents.

She was using me as a beard. She couldn't write home to Fort Wayne about Digger, so she had been writing home about me. As far as her parents knew, her boyfriend's name was Kelly Prince.

She had come to the city at the age of eighteen, and from the very beginning she wrote home every week without fail. She had not left home in anger or rebellion, but only because she conceived of the leaving as a part of her destiny. Her family shared this belief. She was the youngest of four children and the only girl, the fair and gifted one who bore the hopes of all the rest. Something finer than what her parents and her brothers had was hers by birthright, and when she went forth to claim it their pride and their fears went with her. The letters she wrote home were meant to confirm the pride and dispel the fears, and they formed a conventional diary of a young girl new to the city. Sometimes the stories she told were her own, sometimes they were borrowed from other girls she knew, but the sum of them presented a fairly accurate picture of what it was like to be eighteen and living alone in New York.

Except for the men in her life. She couldn't write about them because after the first few weeks the only man in her life was Digger, who was substantially older than her father. There was a gap to be filled, and she filled it with me. I was the man in

570

her life. It was easier than inventing someone. This had been going on since before she even met me. For almost a year she had been filling her letters and telephone calls with stories about dear, sweet, sensitive, sophisticated Kelly. When I was racing in Europe she was devastated with loneliness, when I came back to the States she was filled with joy, when I won she cheered, when I lost she moaned, and, she assured them, when I touched her she tingled. She had been carrying on this comedy without a thought for what might happen if her parents came to New York, and now they were here. To Tom and Ellen Jones of Fort Wayne, the Midtown Theatre Club was only a step removed from Broadway, and nothing was going to keep them from seeing their daughter's first appearance on the Great White Way. And nothing was going to keep them from meeting Kelly Prince. All this Digger related to me over the telephone. Then he told me that I was scheduled to have dinner with the Joneses the following night.

'I want you to listen carefully,' I told him. 'You're going to hear a click. That will be me hanging up. Please don't call back.'

I hung up. After a moment the phone rang again. I picked it up and said, 'No way, Digger. It's the craziest thing I ever heard of.'

'Sure it is, but don't blame me. I first found out about it yesterday.'

'You mean she's been feeding her folks this baloney for a year and you never knew it?'

'She never gave me a clue.' He chuckled. 'Actually, it was pretty clever of her, don't you think? I guess she had to tell them something.'

'But why me?' I couldn't even feel flattered by the deception. She had started it before she ever met me. 'If she was going to do something like that why didn't she go all the way and make it John Travolta?'

'Because you're cuter than John Travolta, that's why.' He was laughing again. He really thought it was funny. 'Look, she's on the spot and we can't let her down.'

'Sure we can, it's easy. I left for Val d'Isère yesterday.'

'No good. It was in the papers that the team is leaving Monday.'

'So what? Nobody reads the ski news.'

'Her parents do. Remember, they're fans of yours now.' He was having a hard time keeping the laughter down.

'It's not funny, Digger. I don't like being used this way.' Actually, the idea was beginning to appeal to me.

'Come on, how often do I ask you to do me a favour? There's no performance tomorrow night, so all you have to do is have a leisurely dinner with the three of them and buy them a drink at Jimbo's afterwards. It's a piece of cake.'

We tossed it back and forth some more, but by then he knew that I was going to do it, and I knew it, too. The chance to spend a legitimate evening with Justine was too good to miss. I made one more protest to show that I couldn't be muscled into it, and then I gave in gracefully.

'Good boy,' said Digger. 'I knew I could count on you.'

I picked her up the next evening at six, hiking up the three flights to her apartment. It was the first time I had been there, and she was waiting for me with the door open. She was dressed in something sleek and silky, and she glowed. She smiled as I came bounding up the stairs.

'Nobody's ever done that before,' she said. 'The people that I know are huffing and puffing by the time they get up here.'

'So am I. Breathless at the sight of you.'

'Thank you, but you're not. You're disgustingly fit.'

'That's why they pay me the big bucks.'

'This is nice, calling for me. Most people here expect you to meet them in a bar somewhere. This is more like a date back home.'

'Right, what's it going to be tonight? The drive-in or the Bowl-O-Rama?'

'Don't be unkind to Fort Wayne. Come in for a minute.'

We went inside, but we did not sit down. She had something she wanted to say before we left, and she stumbled over getting it out. Although she said it badly it was a true apology for having used my name in her letters. I stopped her before she went too far with it.

'Enough,' I said. 'You shouldn't have done it, but it's done. Now clue me in about the past year.'

'What about it?'

'Look, I don't want to make a fool of myself in front of your folks. What have you told them? How far have we travelled along the twisted trail of romance?'

572

That threw her for a moment; she looked confused. 'Well, I told them that we've been . . . dating. You know?'

'No, I don't. What does dating mean in Fort Wayne? How am I supposed to act towards you? Will they assume that we've been sleeping together?'

'Oh Lord, I don't know. I guess parents always think that, and then decide not to think about it.'

'All right, we'll play it safe. I'll be attentive and affectionate, but I'll try not to look as if we just crawled out of bed.'

'Kind of you.'

'I'll take your coat, hold the door for you, light your cigarette . . .'

'I don't smoke.'

'Damn, I bought a lighter for the occasion.'

'Did you really?' She clapped her hands in delight. 'Mama smokes, you can light her cigarettes. She'll be terribly impressed.'

'I'll try to remember.'

'Kelly, one other thing. I told them that you're twenty-two.'

'What? Why the hell did you do that?'

'Well, you know, I thought it would look better if we weren't the same age.'

'Christ, Justine, anybody who knows anything about skiing know I'm – '

'That's all right. I told them that athletes always take a few years off their age to make themselves look younger.'

'And they believed that?'

'Oh, sure, they know I wouldn't lie to them.'

'You've been lying to them for a year,' I pointed out.

'That's different.' She really believed that.

I looked at my watch. 'We'd better get going.'

'In a minute.' There was a glass on a table, the end of a drink. She poured a splash of vodka in it and drank it quickly. 'Butterflies, just like curtain time. God, how I hate this, lying to them.'

'You're stuck with it. You might as well do a good job.'

'I know.' She was close to me. She put a hand on my arm and leaned towards me. She said softly, 'We have to act it out, that's all. We have to be the happy young lovers they think we are. We can do that, can't we?'

'Sure we can.' She was leaning against me, her softness pressing.

'We'll be lovers for tonight, all right?'

'Yes.'

'We'll let them see the love and they'll believe it, won't they?'

'Sure they will.'

'They'll see that we're happy and they'll be happy for me.'

'Yes.'

'Me with my fine young man.'

'And me with their darling daughter.'

'Yes. Thank you, Kelly. We'll make it happen that way.'

She raised up on her toes and kissed me lightly on the lips, still pressing against me. It shook me, even though I knew that she was acting. 'Just to get us in the mood,' she said.

I took her arm and said roughly, 'Let's get the hell out of here.'

Tom and Ellen Jones were decent, intelligent people, and I liked them at once. They had a blind spot about their daughter, but I couldn't fault them for that. I had one myself, although mine did not extend to her acting abilities. The Joneses had been in New York for three days and they had been to see *Private Lives* twice. They were convinced that Justine was the next Glenda Jackson or Diana Rigg. I said nothing to cloud that illusion. They were much too nice. Tom had a wholesale hardware business that his father had run before him and that his sons would run after him, and Ellen was a onetime high school history teacher who was thinking of going back to it now that her children were grown. They both were tall and spare, with gentle eyes, and they made me feel welcome in their company.

They were staying at the Grand Hyatt on Forty-second Street, and they met us in the lobby there. Tom had booked a table in one of the hotel restaurants, and he asked if that was all right with me. I told him it was fine. I had grown up as something of a snob about food and drink and I was just beginning to realize how stupid that was. Almost everything I knew about food was secondhand from Digger or Bobby, and although I could recommend an impeccable Château Margaux I had no idea what it tasted like, since I didn't drink alcohol. So I was beginning to shed my prejudices about dining and I was impressed with the way Tom ordered our meal: with a simple dignity, an absence of pretence, and a respect for what we were about to consume that amounted to an unspoken grace.

During dinner I played the game. I kept the wise-ass streak under control, listened attentively, and made only the sort of comments that were expected of me. I did not light any cigarettes. Every once in a while I let my hand rest lightly on Justine's, and when I did she turned and smiled at me. Her smile was reflected in her parents' eyes. They liked what they saw. I may not have been the boy next door, but I was scoring points and the game was going well. It was Justine's game to win, but it was mine to enjoy, and I was beginning to forget that it was a game at all. After a while it seemed quite real.

Eventually the conversation got around to skiing. They had been reading about me for a year and they wanted to know what life was like on the racing circuit. It wasn't casual curiosity. The way they saw it I was prospective family and I was in a risk-taking business. They wanted to know what the odds were on me. I told them a few racing stories, keeping it all low-key. I made it sound as dangerous as a table tennis tournament, and Tom objected to that mildly.

'You can't tell me that there isn't a lot of danger,' he said. 'I keep reading about broken arms and legs. And worse. There's this fellow over in Italy who's still in a coma.'

'There are injuries,' I admitted, 'but not as many as there used to be. The equipment is better today and the trails are safer. People get hurt in every sport. Skiing is no different.'

'Nonsense, of course it is,' said Ellen, squinting her eyes against the smoke from her cigarette. 'That's the same argument that people use when they defend boxing. They say that people also get hurt playing football and baseball, but the logic is false. The point they miss is that in football and baseball the primary purpose of the game is not to maim your opponent. It is in boxing.'

'It isn't in skiing,' I said politely. 'I don't see how that applies to what I do.'

'It's the same kind of false logic,' she said. 'You say that people get hurt in other sports, which is true, but I don't know of any other sport which obliges a man to throw himself off a mountain at sixty miles an hour.'

'Down the mountain,' I said. 'Not off it.'

'Sometimes off.' She looked at me intently. 'Right?'

575

'Right, but rarely.'

'But if it can happen at all, why do it?'

'Mama, please,' said Justine.

'No, that's all right,' I said. 'I'm sorry, Mrs Jones, but I don't know how to reply to that. It's a question that people in my family have been asking themselves for three generations, and we've never come up with a satisfactory answer.'

'Well, that's honest enough. I was afraid you were going to give me that Mallory nonsense about climbing a mountain just because it's there. That one never washed with me. It always sounded like the sort of thing that a man says when he's trying to keep the women quiet.'

'Ease off, Ellen,' said her husband. 'You're talking about Kelly's *raison d'être*.'

'Sorry, didn't mean to offend.'

'You didn't. Actually, I had a grandmother who felt pretty much the same way. She married a skier, and she admired the athletics of it, and she built one of the biggest ski companies in the country, but I think that deep down inside she always felt that it was nothing more than an excuse for little boys to show off.'

That eased the strain and got a laugh. Ellen said, 'And little girls too. Justine told us that you taught her to ski. Is she any good at it?'

That called for a fast pickup. So Digger had been giving her lessons. I nodded, and said, 'She was really getting into it last winter. She has the natural grace and rhythm for it.'

'Ballet lessons,' said Ellen. 'She took ballet from the time she was four. That's where the rhythm comes from.'

'Skiing.' Tom said it with a frown. 'None of us ever did anything like that before. All three of the boys played football and Ben was on the track team at Purdue, but I don't know about this skiing business. I'm not sure that I like the idea of my daughter tumbling down the mountainside like Jack and Jill.'

'You don't have to worry about that,' I assured him. 'She's not doing anything dangerous, just playing around in the snow.'

'Well, I guess you should know.' There was a faraway look in his eyes. 'They say that you have to let go after a while, and you know that they're right, but you're so used to taking care of them. Taking care of everything they do, and then one day you're not in charge any more. I had the same thing with the boys, but somehow that was different. Now I have it with the girl and I'm not in charge any more. Somebody else is, or somebody will be someday.' He smiled sadly. 'I guess when it comes to mountains, that means you, Kelly.'

Justine said quietly, 'I'm in charge of myself, Daddy.'

'Sure you are.' He covered her hands with his. 'But not when you're up on a mountain.'

'No,' she agreed, 'not on mountains, not yet. Someone else is in charge there, but there's really nothing to worry about.'

'All right then, I won't. I can see you're in good hands.'

'The best.'

He beamed at me. 'How about that? The best. I guess she knows what she's talking about.'

I beamed right back at him. She was talking about Digger, but he didn't know that.

That was the end of it. We sat longer at the table and there was talk about the theatre, and living in New York, and football at Purdue, but they had seen what they had come to see and they were satisfied. Now they wanted an early night; they had sightseeing planned for the next day. We parted in the lobby, and the handshakes from Tom and Ellen were as solid as stamps of approval.

Going home in the taxi, Justine said, 'You were wonderful, they loved you. You were smooth as silk.'

I didn't say anything. I wasn't too pleased with myself. I hadn't enjoyed deceiving them.

She rapped me playfully on the arm. 'And I'm not just fooling around in the snow. I'm doing stem turns already.'

'Great.'

'What's the matter? Are you down? You sound as if you are.'

I looked out the window.

'Don't be down. Please?'

'Take it easy, you got what you wanted. The evening is over, you don't have to act any more.'

'I'm not acting, and the evening isn't over yet.'

I wondered what that was supposed to mean. I found out as soon as we got back to her apartment. There was no question that I was coming up with her. She waited only until the door was closed and our coats were off, and then she came to me.

Her face was set and serious. She put her hands at the back of my neck, pulled me down to her, and kissed me.

'You seem to like doing that,' I said. 'What's it all about?'

'What does it feel like? You're my young love.'

'You've been acting all evening and you still are. You don't even know who I am.'

'I'm not, and I know who you are. You're the boy who was nice to my parents tonight. The young love.'

Since when? I wondered. 'How many loves do you have?'

'Right now only one. The young one.'

'Yeah, you're acting all right.'

'Maybe I am. Do you mind?'

'Yes.' My arms were around her.

'You don't. It doesn't make any difference to you.'

'You're wrong about that.'

'No, I know you. You want me.'

'Not this way.' I was kissing her now, breathing her in.

'Any way you can. The same way I want you.'

If she was acting she was doing a far better job than she did on the stage. Somehow there was a couch and somehow we were on it, locked together. My hand was at her breast and she was tugging at my belt. I pulled back and said, 'This is crazy. Don't you have a bed?'

'In a minute,' she said in my ear. 'First this, then bed.'

'Why? This is high school stuff. Two hot kids on a couch.' We were tearing at each other, ripping clothing. She wriggled under me, and her nipple came erect against my palm.

'Isn't that what we are?' she asked.

'Is that what you want it to be?'

'Yes, two hot kids on a couch. That's the way I want it. That's the way it has to be.' Her eyes were closed, her voice a singsong. 'Now do something nice to me, but don't make any noise. They're in the next room and we don't want them to hear.'

There wasn't any next room, just a tiny kitchen. She was really into it. I whispered, 'What about your other love?'

'That's a different world,' she whispered back. 'I can be Marina for him and I can be Justine for you. I can be both, really I can.'

That did it. I stood up and pulled her off the couch. She stumbled against me, her bare breasts pressing my chest. She had ripped the buttons off my shirt. I looked around.

578

'Where the hell is the God damn bed?'

Before she could answer I heard a key slide in the lock, and then a click. The front door swung open and Digger came in. He stood framed in the doorway, then he kicked the door shut. He stared at us with no expression on his face. He crossed the room to go to the kitchen. As he passed the couch, he said:

'You both look ridiculous. Kelly, get the hell out of here.'

I let go of Justine, and she slipped back on the couch. She lay there looking up at me. She made no move to cover herself. I heard Digger in the kitchen getting ice from the freezer, clunking the cubes into a glass. I stuffed in my shirt and buckled my belt. The shirt, without buttons, flapped open.

Digger's voice came from the kitchen. 'I meant what I said. It's time you went home.'

Justine said softly, 'I didn't know he was coming tonight. I really didn't.'

I couldn't look at her. I tried pulling my shirt together, then let it flap and looked around for my jacket. It was important to find the jacket quickly. I had to get out.

'You don't have to go,' said Justine. 'This is my house.'

Again, Digger's voice. 'Son, I'm going to take a couple of sips of this drink and then I'm coming in there. When I get there you'd better be gone.'

I had my jacket on and was reaching for my coat. My hands were trembling. I dropped it.

Justine said, 'Don't do it. Maybe you have to go, but don't let him chase you this way.'

She didn't understand. He wasn't her father. I moved for the door. I almost made it.

Digger came into the room with a glass in his hand. He looked at me wearily and said, 'I thought I told you to go home.' He came up to me and slapped me across the face with the palm of his hand, then came the other way and slapped me with the back of it. Both blows stung more than they hurt. 'Now get out.'

I turned to go. His voice stopped me.

'Something else, just to get things straight. I heard from Jellicoe today. Don't you ever go behind my back again. When I'm in charge I spend money the way I see fit. If you don't like it, then get yourself someone else. Is that what you want, someone else?'

'No.' I just managed to get the word out.

'Then no more of this horseshit with Jellicoe. I'm running Prince my way, understood?'

'Yes.'

'Good. Now, get going.'

'Digger . . . ?'

'No, Kelly. Out. Now.'

I went out the door and turned to close it. I saw Justine rise up from the couch to come to him. I shut the door, ran down the stairs, and went home. I stayed at home and saw no one until it was time to leave for Val d'Isère. I did not see Justine again for over a year.

Chapter Twelve

You ran.

It wasn't exactly running. . . .

He hit you and you ran.

Big deal. Fathers hit their kids every once in a while.

Fathers hit children, not men.

You don't understand.

Don't I? The old lion came padding into the den and caught you nibbling on one of his lady lions. He cuffed you around and tossed you out in the cold. And you didn't do a damn thing about it.

He didn't really hurt me, just a couple of slaps.

Worse yet. He treated you like a cub. He would have mauled a full-grown lion. All he had to do was box your ears and kick you down the stairs. And you took it.

What was I supposed to do? Take a swing at my own father?

Are you saying that you didn't out of respect for him?

No.

You didn't do anything because you couldn't do anything. You were scared shitless.

For God's sake, it was my *father*.

You ran.

It wasn't exactly running. . . .

You ran.

Yes.

Circular arguments inside the head spinning into the vortex that leads nowhere. And so you try to forget it. You put it out of your mind. You try to forget about the words, and the blows and the girl who was watching it all, her ripped dress and her still, sad face. You forget it all and you clamp on a pair of skis and go racing. With predictable results. You ski a little crazy.

Digger showed up in Val d'Isère two days after I did. He played it as if nothing had happened, and I played it the same way. It was either that or forget about the season. There were mountains to ski and races to win in the pre-Olympic year, and so we settled into the old routine. He was my father, he was my coach, he was the boss. We went on from there. Neither of us had forgotten anything, but by silent agreement, we weren't going to let it get in the way of what had to be done. The trouble was that I started off the season skiing like a wild man.

Val d'Isère is often the first stop on the World Cup racing circuit, because the slopes there remain skiable all year long, and the first big event of the season is the Criterium de la Première Neige. I have always looked forward to going there. It is Jean-Claude Killy's town, which makes it special, and the mountains there have always been good to me. This time, however, I came out fighting the mountain and the mountain fought back.

For once the conditions were not ideal: The snow was poor and there was fog on the mountain most mornings. On the first training run of the week I registered the fastest time over the course, but it wasn't fast enough for me. On the second training run I skidded wide on a turn, couldn't hold it, and went into a restraining barrier that shook me up but didn't do any damage. The next day, on the third training run, I promised myself that I would carve my way precisely through that turn, but by the time I came into it I was carrying a head of speed that blasted me off the course. Again I was lucky and wound up with bruises. At that point the officials decided that the conditions at Val d'Isère were too poor for competition; they sent the women's tour to Piancavallo in Italy, and they sent us over to Schladming in Austria. Schladming was a disaster for me. In the giant slalom I came out so hot that I missed a gate at the top of the hill, and in the downhill I skied so wildly that I caught an edge and went end over end for what seemed like a mile but was only a hundred yards down the hill. My head rang for an hour afterwards.

I skipped the slalom at Madonna di Campiglio, but it was more of the same at Val Gardena and at Kranjska Gora after that. I was crashing regularly, both in the training runs and in the races, reaching for impossible speeds. I expected Digger to say something about this, but he accepted it calmly. This was partly because he wasn't with me through most of each week. It was the same as the season before. He would show up the day before a race, go over the course with me, set up my equipment, and the day after the race he'd be gone again. I figured that he was spending the rest of the time with Justine, and I was right. He wouldn't bring her to where I was racing, but she was always somewhere close by. So he really didn't see what was going on during the rest of the week, and when I crashed on race days he attributed that only to an excess of daring. He had always skied that way himself, and he firmly believed that recklessness went with the downhill franchise. What he didn't realize was that I was skiing well beyond the line that divides daring from folly.

It took Mike to see what was going on. He showed up at Val Gardena, watched me there, followed the team to Kranjska Gora, and watched me there as well. He went to Digger and told him that I was skiing badly and that I was heading for trouble. Digger gave him the usual back of the hand.

'Michael, I guess you mean well,' he said, 'but you don't know what the hell you're talking about. He's having some trouble with control, that's all. He'll pull out of it.'

'He doesn't have *any* control, Digger, that's the problem. He's skiing like a kamikaze.'

'That's exactly the way he's supposed to ski. That's what wins races.'

'He could ease off a little until he gets his control back.'

'That's exactly what I don't want him to do.' Digger exploded. 'Look, Michael, you aren't a racer, you never were, and you don't know the first thing about it. So stay out of this, will you? And whatever you do, don't go talking to Kelly about it.'

But he did. I banged up a shoulder at Kay-Gee and they gave me a shot for it. After that, Mike and I sat in my room and he told me I was wasting my time.

'Why bother skiing?' he said. 'Why not get a gun and shoot yourself? It's quicker.'

'More fun this way. Guns are for sissies.'

'No, really. What the hell are you trying to do?'

'Win races.'

'On your back?'

'Any way I can.'

'Tell that to the mountain. Jesus, haven't you learned that yet? The mountain doesn't move, it doesn't bend, it doesn't give. It just stands there. You're the one who has to give. If you don't . . .' His voice trailed off.

'The mountain moves for *you*,' I said slowly. The shot was helping but the pain was still there. 'When you ski the mountain bends.'

'No, it doesn't, it just looks that way because I make a lot of noise. The mountain doesn't move for anybody.' He looked away, and the next words came softly. 'Besides, the mountain and me, we've got a deal. We do business together. You don't have a deal like that. You wouldn't want it.'

'No, I wouldn't. And I wish you didn't.'

'Yeah, sure. I know. But don't ever confuse yourself with me. We ski two different kinds of hills.' He looked back at me, and his eyes were angry. 'You've got to take the edge off it. You'll bust your ass if you don't.'

'I wish I could, but I don't know how.'

'Everybody knows how.'

'All right, I know how to do it in my head, but my feet don't know how. If I tried to ski any other way I'd get all tangled up.'

'You ski with your head, not your feet.'

'That's you, not me. You ski with your crazy head and I ski with my crazy feet. Right now, that's the only way I know.'

'Bullshit. You're trying to ski like Digger, that's all it is.'

I didn't say anything.

'That's it, isn't it? What are you trying to prove?'

I shook my head.

'You can't ski like Digger, nobody can. Even he can't ski that way any more.'

'Leave it alone, will you?'

He looked at me shrewdly. 'Something happened with the old man, didn't it? Something to do with Justine?'

'Just leave it alone.'

'Sure, anything you say.' He got out of his chair and came over to the bed where I was lying. 'Get some rest, let that shot go to work.'

'It's working already. Not much pain.'

'Good. And remember what I said.'

'I will.' I closed my eyes.

'And one other thing. Those new friends of yours. They're not helping your skiing, either.'

My eyes snapped open. 'Where did you hear about that?'

'People like Charles and Claudia, they live in my world. So I hear things.' He grinned as he went to the door. 'Just don't leave your races in the bedroom, kid.'

In order to understand people like Charles and Claudia de Trobriand you have to understand that in Europe the top Alpine racers have super-celebrity status both within their own countries and across the continent. The sport, so minor in America, is a national mania in the Alpine and Scandinavian countries, and the faces of the top skiers are as well known as the latest rock star's. Their private lives are public knowledge, their autographs are cherished, the young boys imitate them, the young girls melt when they walk by, and there is often heavy gambling on the outcomes of the races. For the top American skiers arriving in Europe there is always the shock of being transformed overnight into celebrities. Going the other way, it is always a relief to come home to the relative anonymity of American skiing.

Charles and Claudia were part of the crowd of ski buffs who followed the races from weekend to weekend. They were Swiss, with a home in Geneva and a chalet near Davos, and from either location they were close to the various stops on the World Cup circuit. In that crowd snagging a racer was a social triumph, and they worked hard at it. Charles was about forty, and into machine tools. Claudia was about thirty, and into anything that intrigued her. They had good bodies, good minds, good looks, and enough money to get whatever they wanted. That first week at Val d'Isère they decided that they wanted me, and I decided that I was available.

They had an apartment out at the Chalet Bazel in Le Fornet, and they invited me there one afternoon when fog on the mountain had cancelled the training runs. The preliminaries consisted of tea and an hour's worth of conversation about how great a skier I was. They had decided to call me Jean-Claude, a play on Killy's name and mine. I asked them not to, and they said I was being too modest. That was about as subtle as they got, and after a while Claudia slipped out of the room. Charles stretched in his deep chair, his eyes lively, and said:

'Claudia fancies you, you know.'

'Does she?' I kept my voice neutral.

'Oh yes, couldn't you tell?'

'Not really.'

'I could. Of course, I know her so well. Yes, she definitely fancies you.'

'I'm flattered.'

'You should be. What do you think of her?'

'Charming.'

'She excites you?'

I made a motion with my hand that could have meant anything, and looked out the window.

'She does not arouse you?'

'You're married to a lovely lady. You're a lucky man.'

He frowned. 'Most men find her highly attractive.'

'It would be ungallant to disagree.'

He didn't know what to say next. I wasn't playing it his way. He needed to hear me say the words; it was part of his game. He said, hesitantly, 'Sometimes when a woman is wearing ski clothes it is difficult to see how she really looks. If you wish . . .'

I raised a hand to stop him and put him at ease. 'Charles, if you need the words I'll be glad to say them. Claudia is an exciting, alluring, very sexy woman. She has a magnificent body, and it's been driving me wild all afternoon. I'm excited, my cock is hard, and if it's all right with you I'd like to spend the rest of the day fucking your wife. Is that enough, or do you want more?'

He murmured, 'Amazing for one so young.'

'Feel better now?'

'Thank you.'

'Good. Now you can go inside and tell Claudia that you talked me into it.'

While he was gone I took off my clothes. He brought her back into the room naked, holding her hand high, presenting her. Her body was lean and firm, no hips at all and small, high breasts. She looked as neat and as efficient as one of his machine

585

tools. He gave me her hand, making a little ceremony out of it. It was part of the kicks for him. As she took my hand, she said, 'Merci, Charles. You are very kind to me.'

That seemed like part of the ceremony too. It may have been exciting to them, but it was putting me off. I said, 'What am I supposed to do now? Light a candle? Throw you a rose?'

She smiled with tiny, even teeth. She looked down at me and said, 'I think you know precisely what to do now.'

I did, and I did it. Sliding into her was like coupling up with a highly sensitized erotic cat. She was cat-quick and cat-smooth; cat-wild when it was time to be. It lasted for quite a while, and we peaked together, crying out. We finished up lying in front of the fireplace on piles of pillows. The glow from the fire danced across her skin. After a while, she kissed the tip of my nose and asked:

'Do you always do that when you come?'

'Do what?'

She raised an eyebrow in surprise, hesitated, and dismissed the subject by kissing me again. Then she slid down the length of my body to go to work preparing me for the next encounter. With her head between my legs, I closed my eyes and leaned back. When I opened them, Charles was standing over us ready to join the party, as bare as we, and projecting.

I laced my fingers behind my head, looked up at him steadily, and said, 'I'm sorry, but if you have me in mind I don't swing that way.'

He made a face of disappointment. Claudia's head came up and she said, 'Don't be so difficult, chéri, nobody is asking you to do anything. Just lie back and let yourself be done.' She slid up until she was lying next to me again, half on top of me. She nibbled at my chest and ears with quick kisses and whispered, 'After all, what's the difference, one pair of lips or another?'

As if on signal another pair of lips began to work on me below. She was right, there was no difference. She kept me occupied while he got what he wanted, and when I came again she sighed happily. Then, of course, I had to watch while Charles made love to his wife to show me that he was really a regular fellow who liked girls too. More ritual.

Lying in front of the fire, I asked Claudia, 'Did I do it that time too?'

'Do what?' she murmured.

'What I did before. You said that I did something odd when I came.'

Her eyes widened. 'Ah, *mais non,* of course not. Not with Charles.'

'What is it I did?'

'You really do not know?' She looked at me closely. 'Perhaps not. You are in love with someone, yes?'

I waited a beat, then said, 'Yes. How did you know?'

'Well, my dear, when a man cries out a woman's name at the moment of the orgasm, and that name is not mine, then it is safe to assume that this man is in love. Don't you think?'

I nodded. I didn't have to ask the name.

After a while it was time for me to get back to the hotel where the team was staying. I got away with a lot because of Digger, but there were limits. Charles tried to get me to stay, he was so proud of his catch. They had plans for dinner at the Perdrix Blanche, and then on to Sagittaire. I told them it was impossible, and there were little cries of disappointment, kisses all around, and promises to meet the following week at Val Gardena. When I got back to the hotel I skipped dinner and went straight to bed. The next day was one of the training runs that I blew, but that had nothing to do with the party. I was just skiing wild.

The party picked up at Val Gardena, and after that at Kay-Gee. I belonged to them, and they weren't about to give me up. Nor was I running away from them. I was using them as much as they were using me. I had a lot that I wanted to put out of my mind, and burying myself in their warm and friendly flesh was the easiest way to do it.

About this time Digger began to worry about the way I was skiing. I was crashing almost every time I put them on. I hadn't won anything yet, hadn't even placed in the top ten, and all I had to show for the season was a collection of bangs and bruises. For the first time he saw what was happening as something more than an excess of daring, and after Kranjska Gora he sat me down and gave me the lecture. It was the basic rah-rah I had been getting all my life, adapted to the moment.

'You're skiing tough,' he said. 'That's the way I always skied and that's the way I taught you, but this is too much. You're skiing crazy.'

'I thought that was a virtue.'

'It is when you finish races. You haven't finished many recently. I want you to ease up on the turns. Make your speed on the glide but take it easy on the turns.'

'I can do both.'

'You can't. Nobody can, the way you're trying to do it.' His voice turned soft. 'Look, I've had this dream all my life, and you've had it all of yours. We've come so far, we've worked so hard for this. All those years. You've given up a lot for it, and so have I. The Olympics . . . it's so close now we can almost touch it.' He looked away from my eyes. 'Let's not screw up the dream just because you think you have something to prove to me.'

That was as far as he could go in talking about it. Even that much was a major concession for him to make, and it must have cost him a lot to make it. But it had come too late, and perhaps I should have told him that. Perhaps I should have told him that it was his dream, not mine. That it always had been, and that I was tired of living it for him. That I had dreams of my own and that whenever I reached out to touch one of them I found his dream blocking mine. He had it all. He had the dream and he had the girl. Perhaps I should have told him that, but I couldn't, not then. There was too much of the old Digger magic shining out of his eyes, willing me to dream his dream. The magic still worked on me up to a point, and so all I could do was nod and say that I would try.

'Just ease off a bit,' he said. 'That's all I ask.'

'All right.'

'Just enough to get you through the turns.'

'All right.'

'Get through those turns and then you can make your speed on the glide.'

'All right,' I said. 'All right.'

But it wasn't all right. It was the same the next week at Morzine and on the Lauberhorn after that. My skis had only two speeds: flat-out fast and sudden stop. The sudden stops were banging the hell out of me, but there was nothing I could do about it. I was skiing with less and less control as the season went on, and in the GS at Are, in Sweden, I lost what little control was left. I came busting down the hill, missed a gate, spun off the course, and wound up with my right leg doubled under me. They got me down to the bottom on a sled and took

588

me to the clinic in Oslo. The diagnosis was a lot of torn cartilage in the right knee. They said that I couldn't ski on it for a while, and that all that it needed was rest. It wasn't too bad, but it was bad enough to keep me out of the pre-Olympics at Lake Placid.

The year before each Winter Olympics the skiing facilities at the site of the Games are tested: The courses are evaluated, the bugs are all worked out, and the television people establish their camera points and angles. In that year of 1979 the pre-Olympics at Lake Placid were scheduled for the first week in March, and after that the World Cup races would finish up in North America and Japan. The doctors figured that I would have to miss Lake Placid and possibly Garibaldi after that, so I was in no hurry to get back to the States. Digger, however, had to be at Lake Placid to represent Prince Skis, and he left as soon as he knew that there was nothing permanently wrong with my knee. On his way to the airport he stopped at the clinic to say goodbye. He was disgusted with the situation, and he let me know about it. I had wasted a season, winning nothing, and now I was out of the pre-Olympics. I was skiing like a kamikaze pilot, and I was screwing up the dream. He was barely civil to me. I was the one who was lying there in pain, but he was the one who was sore.

'Get back to the States as soon as the leg feels strong enough,' he said. He stood over the bed, glaring down at me. 'You're enjoying this, aren't you? Rubbing my nose in it.'

'Lay off, Digger.'

'Showing me how tough you can be.'

'Easy on the jokes, it hurts my knee when I laugh.'

'Well, it isn't tough, it's just stupid. Asshole skiing all the way. You know what tough is? Tough is getting up and skiing on that knee. I've skied on worse.'

'So long, Digger. Have a good trip.'

'You think I haven't?'

'Sell lots of skis in Lake Placid.'

'You owe me for this. You owe both of us, and there's only one way to pay it back. Next year.'

I closed my eyes, and after a while he went away. The next day Charles and Claudia called to suggest that I fly down to Switzerland to recuperate at their chalet near Davos. Charles assured me that I would get the best of care, and Claudia promised to play nurse.

She said, 'I am very good with bad knees, *chéri*. I treat them just like any other joint. You won't believe the cure.'

So I sat out the pre-Olympics in the luxury of the de Trobriand chalet in the shadow of Piz d'Rel, surrounded by the usual crowd of charming, empty-headed ski buffs. It was a nonstop party for more than a week, fresh bodies shunting in and out of the lineup. They were all attentive to me, wouldn't let me put the slightest strain on my knee, and the only effort I expended outside of the bedroom was to play a little piano every night: some blues, some rag, some Mozart. It was fun playing that way, but it wasn't a part of the seedy café *cum* Hoagy Carmichael dream. No one thought to buy the piano player a beer, and no pretty girl came by once in a while to rub the back of my neck affectionately. The beer was on the house, and although there were plenty of pretty girls around they were more involved with passion than affection.

Lake Placid seemed far away, but on the day of the downhill we gathered in the salon to watch the race on television and I saw Peter Wirnsberger win what I once had thought would be mine. I watched it without sadness, resigned. I knew that even if I had not hurt my knee I would not have had a chance in the downhill. Not the way I had been skiing all season. Somewhere along the line I would have screwed it up and crashed.

Claudia, sitting beside me, squeezed my hand. 'Bad luck darling,' she said. 'This time next year you'll make up for it.'

'This time next year I'll wipe the hill with him.'

'You will, I know it.'

When they ran the giant slalom we gathered again to watch it on television, and the interest centred on Stenmark, the Swede, and my teammate Phil Mahre. Most of the people in the room – Austrians, Germans, and Swiss – were backing Stenmark, and some had bet on him heavily. We watched Philip waiting in the starting gate high on the side of Whiteface Mountain, below him the flagged gates that marked the course, and beyond the flags the countryside a chequerboard of black and white. He waited, tensed, held still by thrusting poles, his skis inclined to the plane of the slope, and then he exploded out of the gate in the Killy Start, his body extended and his boots the last to go over the line as he broke the wand that started the clock. Short, hard skating steps to build the speed, and then he dropped down the hill and into his tuck with the first of the gates rushing up to meet him.

Clickety-clack, he ran thirty-four of the fifty-six gates in his hard, aggressive style, taking, as always, the highest and fastest line. At the thirty-fifth gate he caught an edge, wobbled, straddled the blue-flagged pole, and fell, crashing into gate thirty-six before he came to rest. He lay there, not trying to move. He had broken bones before, and he knew what had happened to him. The first to reach him was Hank Tauber, the director of the team. Tauber bent over him, asked the question, and got the answer. Then he picked up his ski poles and angrily hurled them like lances deep into a snowbank. He signalled for the stretcher-sled.

The people all around me cheered. With Philip out of the race, Stenmark was a sure winner. They knew that Mahre was hurt, and hurt badly, but they were cheering. They didn't know how badly he was hurt. Later the team doctor, Dick Steadman, announced that he had suffered 'the ultimate broken ankle, a break of both the ankle and the lower leg with a complication of the weight-bearing surface of the joint.' No one knew if he would ever ski again, much less walk properly. The people in the room did not know that then, but they knew that it was bad, and they were cheering.

I got up, found a coat, and limped out onto the terrace. It was cold and silent there, and with the door shut I could not hear the noise from inside. I had been around skiing all my life and I had never before heard anyone cheer when a racer was injured. I leaned against the balustrade and looked up at the mountain. Piz d'Rel was not a friendly-looking peak. It was sharp and black, the profile of a savage face. Below the peak the snowfields stretched like a shifting sea, at rest but ready to roll. Wind whistled off the peak, raising plumes on the face. It was a mountain of substance, but it made me feel uneasy. I did not enjoy looking at it.

The door opened, and Claudia came out bundled up in a wolverine jacket. She stood next to me and slipped her arm through mine, the two of us staring out at the whiteness of the fields.

'I want you to go upstairs and take a nap,' she said. 'Get a

good rest. When you come down all those animals will be gone
I have told them that the party is over.'

'You didn't have to do that.'

'Oh yes I did. You don't know how much I did. What a
disgrace, I never heard of such a thing.'

'I guess it was just their way of cheering for their man.'

'You are too generous. That kind would cheer at the
Crucifixion. They probably did.'

'They're your friends.'

'Don't remind me. Right now they make me feel very sad.'

'I know.'

'This thing that just happened to your Philip Mahre, it
saddened you, no?'

'You don't like to see it happen.'

'No, more than that. It seems that you have so much sadness
in you. I don't understand it. Skiing saddens you, I know it
does. Making love saddens you too. So many things. I think
that if you drank you would be a very sad drunk.'

'Probably.'

She squeezed my arm tightly. 'You must get rid of this
sadness, chéri. This girl that you love, you should get her and
keep her, or forget her entirely.'

'Wise Claudia. The first is impossible, and I've been trying to
do the second, but without any luck.'

'Why impossible? Does she belong to someone else?'

'Do we still say that a woman belongs to someone?'

'A woman always belongs to someone,' she said firmly, 'no
matter what the fancy words they put on it. Does she?'

'Yes.'

'Then unless you can steal her you must forget about her. Get
up now and take your nap. Rest well, and we'll see how things
are when you come down.'

I went up to my room, and when I came down they were all
gone except Claudia. Even Charles was gone; she had sent him
back to Geneva. She had changed herself while I had slept,
changed the way she was dressed and the way that she looked.
She seemed softer, more glowing, less the highly polished sexual
tool.

'They're gone,' she said. 'Right now you don't need parties.'

'What do I need, doctor?'

'You need one woman, all your own. Me.'

'For how long?'

'For a while' She had fixed a plate of bread and cheeses, and had iced a bottle of champagne. She poured out two glasses. 'I know that you don't, but would you take a glass with me tonight? For the occasion?'

'Of course.'

We lifted glasses and drank. She looked at me impishly and asked, 'Is this the first time you have tasted champagne?'

'Yes,' I lied.

'If you say that the bubbles tickle your nose I shall assassinate you.'

'Only young girls are supposed to say that.'

'Indeed? And do they? The bubbles?'

'Definitely. Just like Coca-Cola.'

'You swine, I knew you would say something like that.' Laughing, she picked up a pillow and threw it at me. I threw it back and reached for her. The wine spilled as we wrestled with each other. We wound up on the rug in front of the fireplace, still laughing. I kissed her, and we lay there that way for a while, quietly and trying to think of nothing at all.

For a week after that we lived like young lovers, knowing each other in a deeper, gentler way than before, but in the end it did not work. Claudia gave it everything she could, but it wasn't enough. During that week we shared little joys and pleasures, and made a warm and legitimate game out of love, but underneath the warmth and the joy there was the sadness that she could not reach. She tried in every way she knew, without tricks, but with an outpouring of affection designed to swamp the sadness and sweep it out on the tide. It was a good try and I was grateful to her for it, but it did not work. Despite it all, there was still Justine.

At the end of the week Bobby showed up at Piz d'Rel to see how her younger son was managing on the road to recovery. She was on her way to Lucerne, she said, and the word among the knowing was that I was lazing around the Trobriand chalet with one leg up in the air, nibbling delicacies and being treated like a lord. This simply had to be seen, and there she was. She did not come alone. Her travelling companion was a muscular blond boy with full red lips and a perpetual frown on his face. His name was Harold Harmon, he was a few years out of Yale, and he was writing a play about Alexander VI, the Borgia pope.

'Of course, he really isn't,' Bobby confided, 'but I told him to say that. After all, one has to say something.'

'Why Alexander?' I asked. 'It's been done before.'

'Well, it isn't as if he's actually writing it.'

'Still, you could have been more inventive.'

'I know, darling, but I couldn't resist it. The old bastard was so delightfully sinful. Speaking of which, you seem to have a lovely setup here.'

'Why does Harold frown so much? Is he constipated?'

'How clever of you, I never thought of that. I must ask him. How is your poor knee?'

'Getting richer every day. I'll be skiing at Heavenly Valley on the eleventh.'

'All thanks to Madame de Trobriand. Is she making you comfortable? I mean, really.'

'Three square meals a day plus all I can eat.'

'A touch older, no?'

I laughed. 'My, my, listen to the kettle.'

'Well, at least you didn't call me the pot. How old *is* she actually?'

'I wouldn't know. My mother taught me never to count the rings on the trees.'

'I must have a chat with her, a private word between ladies. You and Harold amuse each other. Just don't talk about the Borgias, it makes him nervous.'

The two women went into another room, and they were gone for half an hour. I tried talking to Harold, but he wasn't much of a talker. Maybe that's why Bobby kept him around. We just slouched in our chairs and glared at each other until Claudia and Bobby came back. They made their entrance together, two pros posing for the barest moment before coming into the room. Bobby showed up well against the younger woman. There was a generation between them, but she didn't have to give away too many points.

'We've had the loveliest chat,' Bobby said, 'and we've decided that we adore each other. We know all the same people and we loathe every one of them.'

'Not quite all,' said Claudia. 'There are one or two barely worth saving.'

'Trouble is that we can't agree on the one or two.' Bobby bent over to kiss my cheek, and there was a quick flash of scent

594

to press old memories. 'You're in good hands, darling. Just don't make any problems for Claudia and be sure not to overtip the servants. I shall see you when I see you.'

Claudia offered lunch, Bobby declined, and then she and Harold were off. They had an appointment that evening in Lucerne. It hadn't been much of a visit. Nothing had been said about Digger, or Justine or the family situation. Nothing about me, for that matter: what I was doing and where I was heading. Just a couple of hugs, one kiss, and five minutes' worth of brittle conversation. It didn't seem like much. I hadn't seen her in five months.

'She wanted to see how you were getting along, and this was her way of doing it,' Claudia explained. 'Actually, she was quite concerned about you.'

'About my knee?'

'Among other things.'

'And she wanted to check you out.'

'Of course. Perfectly natural.'

'And she brought Harold along so that I could take a good long look in the mirror.'

She sighed. 'I'm afraid so. There's no comparison, of course, but it wasn't very subtle of her.'

'She made her point.'

'I suppose that means you'll be leaving now.'

'It was about time for me to go anyway.'

'Yes. I didn't do much good, did I?'

'You did as much as you could. It was a wonderful week.'

'Are we friends now, do you think? Really friends?'

'Yes. Much more than before.'

'Good, then I can say this to you. I worry about you. This sadness of yours, it's eating you up.'

'It comes and it goes. I can handle it.'

'I wonder. I couldn't handle it for you. I doubt if anyone can.'

'One person can, but she's not available.'

'That's what I mean. Shall I tell you what really worries me? Will you promise not to think me foolish?'

'Of course.'

'I worry that you race with this sadness inside of you. I don't think you should be racing right now. Is that very foolish?'

'No.'

'You understand?' I had surprised her.

'I've thought of it myself. But you see, I can't do that. I can't stop racing every time I feel . . . different. I wouldn't be worth anything then.'

'I don't believe that. I think that you want to stop, but you don't dare to.'

I thought about that, and said, 'I think we're saying the same thing in different words.'

'Yes, I suppose we are.'

I left the next day and took my sadness with me to Heavenly Valley and then to Furano, where I skied GS, finished poorly in both races but stayed on my feet for a change, and then the season was over. But that year there seemed to be no finish to the season, the end of one running into the beginning of the next. The summer went by in a blur of training, and suddenly I was at Val d'Isère again with the new season ready to roll and the Olympics only two months away. Seven races down the line was a better way to measure the time, seven downhills, and I could rattle off their names like a railroad conductor during rush hour. *This train will stop at Val d'Isère, Val Gardena, Schladming, Pra Loup, Kitzbühel, Wengen, Chamonix, and Lake Placid. Last stop Lake Placid, folks, change here for all other stations.*

No one was getting off the train, everyone was going all the way. According to the papers the Olympic downhill was up for grabs, no favourites. The three Canadians looked good: Read, Podborski, and Murray. The West Germans had Ferstl, and the heavy hitters for the Austrians were Wimsberger, Speiss, Grissman, and Stock. There was Burgler, the Swiss, Plank, the Italian, and Kelly Prince for the USA. Forget last year, folks, Prince was off his style and skiing wild, but in an Olympic year the top ones get it all together. It's crunch time, the year with no room for a backward glance.

At Val d'Isère Digger sat me down for the usual pep talk that opened each season, but this year it was a little different. The past was a bucket of melted snow, he said, and it was time to suck it up and go for it. The hungry man, the man who wanted it most, was the man who was going to take it. Inspiration? If you want inspiration take a look at Phil Mahre with a three-inch piece of metal in an ankle held together by screws. He was walking and skiing and aiming for Placid just like everybody else, and when you saw what he was doing you knew that this was the year of no excuses.

'None whatsoever,' he said. 'No more talk, just action. And no more rah-rah from me. I've been giving you the hype about this all your life, and now it's here. So we're going to forget about last year. The snow melts, new snow falls, and we start things fresh. We both know what happened last season, and it isn't going to happen again. You have all the equipment, physical and mental, to go all the way at Placid. I have every confidence that you are going to do exactly that.'

The amazing part was that he really believed it. Remember Arlene, the girl at the Midtown Theatre Club who said that actors have an infinite capacity for self-deception? To that she could have added fathers, coaches, and dreamers. As that year opened I was no more qualified for world-class skiing than I was for doing brain surgery. I knew it, many of the other racers knew it, and even the coaches on the ski team were beginning to suspect it. That sadness inside of me was as dead and as heavy as a stone, and I carried that stone with me down every course I skied. Sisyphus in reverse, forced to roll a boulder down the hill, not up, that boulder the boss as it pulled me down the mountain faster and faster. There may have been new snow on the slopes, but there was nothing new about the season for me. It was exactly the same as the season before. If anything, it was worse. It was over a year since I had last seen Justine, and on skis or off, I wasn't worth a damn without her.

The first few races weren't too bad; I kept them under some sort of control. I managed to finish at Val d'Isère and actually placed fourteenth at Val Gardena. I moved that up to eleventh at Schladming, and Digger began to see his dream unfold before his eyes. He saw things going according to plan, and he was sure that I was peaking.

'You're right on track,' he said after Schladming. 'We don't push it, we don't force it. Each week a little better. At the rate you're going you should peak just right for Placid.'

How blind can you get? Sure I was peaking, I was peaking for disaster, and it came two weeks later on the run at Kitzbühel. They call the run the *Streif*, and I streaked it all right. I came out hot and nailed the turns on the top, carving each one in a skittering line that held, and then I was tucked on the straight, the stone in my gut a counterweight to caution and dragging me

597

faster and faster as I hit the first of the humps, took air and wobbled there, recovered, landed, and tucked again in time for the next. Faster now, the wind a whistle and the track a blur, I came up off the rise and went high, too high and out of control, arms milling and fighting and losing as I came down hard and landed with all my weight on my right leg. And crumpled to the snow. It was like stepping out of a second-storey window.

It was the right knee, and at first I had no idea how bad it was. I could walk on it through the pain, and Digger said that it would ease off by itself. It began to stiffen up that night at the hotel, and he packed it with ice and tried to move it, packed it again and tried it again. He did that every half hour and at first I thought it was going to work, but then the knee swelled up so badly that the team trainer had to take ninety cubic centimetres of blood out of it. That was enough for him to put in a call to the team doctor at Lake Tahoe, and the next day they flew me there directly. Digger sat next to me during the trip, telling us both over and over that it was probably nothing at all, just a bad sprain, but he really didn't believe that, not after all that blood. I let him talk and didn't try to argue. The knee hurt like hell and it felt like a broken set of dishes.

The x-rays at Tahoe said that I was right. Landing so hard on one leg, I had fractured the right tibia, which then had been forced up into the meniscus. Everything was busted in there and floating around. They operated the next day. They made me a new meniscus by taking a V-shaped graft from my hip and inserting it in the knee, leaving room for fresh calcium to grow there. They did a terrific job, but that didn't change the fact that I was out of the Olympics and out for the rest of the season.

I was still coming out of the anaesthesia when Digger made his statement to the press. Not that the sporting media had rushed at once to Tahoe. If I had been a power forward or a tight end they would have been there, and if I had been an Austrian or a Swiss they would have been there too, but an American skier with a busted-up knee didn't rate that high in the national consciousness. Still, there were a couple of local people hanging around, and a stringer for *The Times*, and Digger made his statement to them. *The Times* put it on the wire, other papers picked it up, and the end result was almost as good as a major press conference. Digger said a lot of things, but what the press picked up was this:

'The accident was a terrible blow, coming as it did just before the Olympics, but my son is a resilient young man and I'm sure he'll bounce back from it. I have spoken to the doctors and they are confident that he will make a full recovery with full use of the knee in every way. That won't do us any good for 1980, but that leaves us four years before the next Olympics, and they will be four years of intensive training. Kelly Prince isn't giving up his quest for a gold medal, and I'm stating here and now that he will be in the starting gate at the Winter Olympics at Sarajevo, Yugoslavia, in 1984. I'm not only stating it, I'm backing it up. I'm going ten-to-one odds, and I'll cover any bet.'

I read the statement the next morning, the newspapers piled on my bed as I sat up having breakfast. Digger sat in a chair by the window flouting the hospital rules with a long, thin Canary Islands cigar. The sunlight coming through the window picked up the lines etched deep in his face and shone through his thinning hair. He was one week short of his sixtieth birthday and his Olympic year was forty years gone: the Games that never were. He looked worn and old, and I hated to do what came next.

I folded my paper and put it aside. 'You're going to have to make another statement to the press.'

He looked up from what he was reading. 'Why, did I miss something?'

'Only one thing. You forgot to consult me before you made the first one. You're going to have to retract it.'

His face hardened. 'What's that supposed to mean?'

'It means that I'm finished.'

'The hell you are.' He half rose out of his chair, then sank back glaring at me.

'No sense getting excited. I mean it. I'm bagging it, I'm hanging it up.'

He worked at controlling himself, and it showed. Finally, he said, 'You can't do it. We have a deal.'

'That deal was through 1980, no extensions. Don't waste your breath trying to talk me out of this, not now and not later. I'm finished.'

'You'll change your mind.'

'I won't.'

He looked at me hard and knew that I meant it. 'You're quitting.'

599

'That's right. I'm quitting because I want a normal life, I want to get off the road, I want to live in a house, I want to get some education. I want to live decently.'

'All that can come later. Are those things more important than an Olympic gold?'

I tried shifting around in bed. It wasn't easy; my leg was immobilized. The question wasn't easy, either. For years I had placed those values second to the chance for a medal, and, in truth, I still did. But there was more to it than that, and it was time that he knew it.

'No, the medal is more important,' I said. 'It has a value that can't be duplicated. It's something that you never lose once you get it. Nobody can ever take it away from you, and the way things are today that's saying a lot. I know the value of Olympic gold.'

'Then why?'

'Christ, Digger, are you totally blind? I'm quitting now because I'm never going to get that gold. I'd be lucky if I made it through another season, much less four, without wrecking myself.'

'You're exaggerating.'

'I'm not. You just don't want to face facts. You've seen the way I've been skiing the past two years. Like a loose cannon. And you know why, even though we don't talk about it. Well, maybe we have to talk now About Justine.'

After a moment, he said, 'What about her?'

'Just about everything that's wrong with me. I've got an emptiness inside of me that won't let me ski right, and now you're asking me to put in four more years of living with that emptiness. And I'm telling you that I can't do it. I'm alone. I've got you in a way, and I've got Bobby in another way, and I've got Mike in lots of ways, but I'm still alone without her. And I can't do it alone. Not what you're asking me to do. And so I'm quitting.'

He drew on the cigar, blew smoke towards the ceiling, then crushed out the coal in the ashtray. He turned to stare out the window. He stayed that way for a long time. He turned and said, 'Let me get this straight . . .'

'I'm saying that I can't do it alone. I can't do it without her.'

'Justine.'

'Yes.'

He nodded. His face showed me nothing. He got his coat

600

from the closet. It was the same coat he had worn at Kitz, and it was too heavy for Tahoe.

'Are you finished with breakfast?' he asked.

'Yes.'

'I'll tell them outside to pick up the tray.'

He left, and a little later they gave me some pills. I slept for hours, and they did not wake me to feed me food I did not want. I woke once with the midday sun banging on the blinds, woke again when the sun was fading, and when I woke for the third time in the early evening she was sitting beside the bed.

I awoke still groggy from the pills, and at first I could not believe that she was there. The room was dark, but she had turned on the bedside lamp; and I could see the angles of the shadows on her face. It was the face I remembered, the face I had never forgotten. I reached up to touch her cheek with a finger and felt a tear. Her hand closed over my finger and held it there.

'You're here,' I said. 'He sent you?'

'Yes.'

'Why?'

'To make a deal.'

'He would. How long can you stay?'

'For a while, but not forever. We have to decide what to do.'

'*And how long will it last, this ludicrous, overbearing love of ours?*'

She started at the words. 'What did you say?'

'*Private Lives.* I saw you in it. You were awful.'

'I wasn't,' she said automatically. 'My God, you're right. Amanda says it to Elyot. How did you know that?'

'It's all in the wrists.'

'Wise-ass and *Wunderkind,* you went out and memorized it. Because of me. *How long,*' she said in a wondering voice, repeating the line. '*How long will it last, this ludicrous, overbearing love of ours?*'

'*Who knows?*' I said, cueing her.

'*Shall we always want to bicker and fight?*'

'*No, that desire will fade, along with our passion.*'

'*Oh dear, shall we like that?*'

'*It all depends on how well we've played.*'

'Um hold it . . . yes . . . *What happens if one of us dies? Does the one that's left still laugh?*'

'Yes, yes, with all his might.'

'That's serious enough, isn't it?'

'No, no, it isn't. Death's very laughable, such a cunning little mystery. All done with mirrors.'

'Darling, I believe you're talking nonsense.'

It took me a moment to assemble the rest of it, then, 'So is everyone else in the long run. Let's be superficial and pity the poor philosophers. Let's blow trumpets and squeakers, and enjoy the party as much as we can, like very small, quite idiotic school children. Let's savour the delight of the moment. Come and kiss me, darling, before your body rots, and worms pop in and out of your eye sockets.'

'I never liked that part about the worms,' said Justine, dropping out of character. 'But I like the part about the kissing.'

She sat on the bed beside me. There was just enough room. She bent over me, and I reached up to her. We held each other that way, kissing. After a while she slid down a bit on the bed so that her head could rest on my shoulder. It wasn't very comfortable, but neither of us minded. It was the best we could do without moving my leg.

'Now comes the hard part,' I said. 'What kind of a deal?'

'Sometimes I'll be with him, and sometimes I'll be with you.'

'That's one hell of a deal. I don't want it that way.'

'It's the only way it can be. I told you that once before. I can be Marina to him, and Justine to you. Separate worlds, separate times. I can do it if you'll let me. But we all have to be very good about it. We have to be wise, and brave and understanding, and then with a little luck we all might manage to be happy.'

'What kind of a happiness is that?'

She stirred. 'If you don't want it . . .'

I pulled her closer. 'I didn't say that. I don't know if I can handle it.'

'It's all I can offer.'

'What would happen if I asked you to stay with me? Only me. Always.'

'Don't ask it. I'd have to say no.'

'He's an old man.'

'And I love him. You're a young man, and I love you.'

'Then this is your idea as much as his.'

'Does it matter? It's the only way it can be. Would you rather go back to nothing at all?'

I didn't answer; I didn't have to. Digger's deal, four more years in exchange for a half interest in the woman I loved. It was a rotten deal. It stank. Even in the sterilized atmosphere of the hospital I could smell it. I should have said no. I should have kicked and raged and damned them both. I should have tucked her under my arm and galloped off with her. I know that now. There were many things I should have done, but I did none of them. Because I was buying the deal. I knew it, and she knew it, too. As bad as it was, I was buying it.

'Trust me,' she murmured. 'I'll make it work.'

'I trust you,' I told her. 'But how long will it last, this ludicrous, overbearing love of ours?'

Chapter Thirteen

Our ludicrous and overbearing love, that phase of it, lasted three years, and during those years Justine divided her time equally between Digger and me. The rules were established, and there were only three of them. The first was that she would be with Digger during the warm months of the year, and when the weather turned cold she would come to me. The second rule was that we would never talk about the first rule. Instead we would lead a life contained within the world we had created. There was never to be a mention of what we did in the other half of the year, never a reproach, never a wish that our lives might be lived differently. We would be together from October to April, and by the rules of the game that was all I could ask for. Those were the first two rules. She told me about the third one on the first night that we spent together.

The division of winter and summer remained in force for three years, and it stamped its pattern onto our lives. One effect it had was to suspend Justine's career in the theatre. She was acting the most important role of her life, and she had no time for any other. A second effect was that Digger and I rarely saw each other any more. It had to be that way. When Justine was with me she was totally with me, and it worked the same when she was with him. Thus, because Justine went with me on the racing tour, Digger no longer could; and during the warm months he and Justine were away by themselves in a place of their own. The only times that Digger and I met were in the swing shifts of the seasons, the springtime and the autumn. We spoke by telephone, and messages between us flowed through the Prince Skis offices, but we became strangers to the sight of each other.

This warm-weather place of Digger's was in the Skofja Loka area of Slovenia, and from May to September during those years he worked at fulfilling the promise that he and Marina had made to each other just before she died. He was building the home that he and she had never had. Faithful to the letter of the promise, he was building it in her native Skofja Loka and he was building it with his own hands. It was a seal of faith on his belief that she truly had come back to him.

A slight exaggeration. He did not personally pour every bucket of cement, lay every brick, and trim every beam, but he did parts of all of it, working alongside the local masons and carpenters through the heat of each day, stripped down to shorts and canvas shoes. It was a formidable project for a man in his sixties, and there were difficulties all along the way. First there was the land to be obtained, and only because he was a hero of their war was this made possible by the authorities in Ljubljana. Then there was the style of the house, for he remembered so clearly the words of the dying girl describing the first storey made of brick and the wooden *gank* that ran above it. He found such a house in the nearby village of Puštal, a rare example of rural baroque design that had survived the war, and he found a builder who was willing to use the house as a model for his own. He had got that far with the project by the winter of 1980 when I banged up my knee, and the actual construction of the house was due to start in the spring. Ahead of him were three years of hard work in which Justine would share. There were the house, the gardens, and the *kozolci* to be reproduced, the vines that would climb to shade the *gank*, the bees in their hives, the clocks on the walls, the monkshood and gentian on the windowsills, the soup in the kitchen, and the mountain of goose feathers meant for a bed. It was more than a house that he was building. He remembered every rambling word that Marina had murmured before she died, and he was bent on bringing them to life.

All this Justine told me the first night we spent together.

604

Direct from hospital to hotel in a hired car, my leg extended, hippity-hop on a crutch indoors and up to the quiet room she had found for us. Apple-green and white walls, breezy curtains blowing, and the bed an inviting haven. I made for it, hopping and herding her along with the crutch. She laughed and moved away.

'What about your leg?' she asked.

'No problems, there are ways.'

'I have to unpack things first.'

'You don't.'

'I do. Things get wrinkled unless you unpack them right away.'

'Let them get wrinkled. Unpacking comes second, maybe third, maybe not at all.' I pulled her onto the bed with me. 'I've waited a long time, Amanda. I really don't want to wait any more.'

'Are you going to call me Amanda? From the play? Is that going to be a pet name?'

'It's as good as any other. Better than Sweetness, or Pumpkin, or Poochie.'

'You don't call a person Poochie. That's for a dog. If I'm going to be Amanda, are you going to be Elyot?'

'I'd just as soon not. The hell with Amanda. I'll call you Poochie and you can call me Rover.'

'I can do better than that. Here Prince, here Prince.'

'Better,' I admitted. My hands were working at her clothing, searching for buttons and zips, and I was doing a poor job of it.

'Wait,' she said. 'Give me a few minutes to get undressed.'

'I don't trust you. If I let you go you'll start unpacking things.'

'I promise not,' she said, and slipped away. She was gone for only a few minutes, and when she came back she stepped into a patch of sunlight by the bed, her body glowing. It was the first time I had seen her that way. I had imagined what she would look like, but she was so lovely that I could not speak. There was a thickness in my throat that would not go away.

She smiled down at me and said, 'You still have your clothes on.'

I cleared my throat. 'I'm sorry, but you're going to have to help me. My knee. There I was fumbling around with your dress, and I'm the one who can't get his pants off by himself.'

'No problem,' she said, bending to reach. 'It's a labour of love.'

It was all of that with my banged-up knee, but more love than labour. We made love through the afternoon, and it was evening before anything got unpacked. We ate in the room, made love again, and it was only when we were ready for sleep that she told me about the third rule by which we would live. She told me first about the house in Skofja Loka and the dream that Digger was trying to build. She told it to me in detail, and she made it seem real to me. Crazy, but real. It was an overwhelming vanity, this attempt to recapture youth by converting a memory into a reality, but it was a folly worthy of the man. Floating close to sleep, her voice came to me faintly as she recited the litany of Marina's dream house.

'Everything has to be just the way she said it. The house, the barn, the vines, the beans running wild in the garden. There have to be wild flowers on the windowsills, clocks on the walls, honey in the comb, a mountain of goose feathers stuffed for a bed, and after all of that, a child to make the work worthwhile. Just the way she said it. Are you listening? Do you hear what I'm saying?'

'Yes,' I said sleepily.

'Please, this is important.'

'I'm listening.' And I was. No excuses. I heard every word.

'What I just said. About a child?'

'Yes?'

'If there should ever be one. I'm saying if ever, someday. The child belongs to the dream. Do you understand that?'

'I'm not sure.' But I did.

'This is the only time I'm going to talk about this, so I'll say it again. If a child should ever come out of what we all have . . . you and me, Digger and me . . . the child is his. It belongs with the house and the dream. No matter who the father is. Now do you understand?'

'Yes.' Whispers of regret, but only whispers.

'It has to be that way. It's part of the deal.'

'All right.' It wasn't, but all right.

'And you agree?'

'Yes.'

'You're sure?'

606

'Enough,' I said. 'Don't talk it to death. I already said yes. Now leave it alone.'

We left it alone and turned to each other in the night.

We had five weeks before the swing of the seasonal pendulum would take her away from me, and we spent the time in Ibiza, staying with Anna and Jenny. My rehabilitation programme called for light walking, then swimming, jogging, hill running, and biking; a programme designed to prepare me gradually for snow skiing at the training camps in the autumn. Ibiza, with its low hills and miles of beaches, offered a pleasing setting for recuperation, and Anna and Jenny opened their home to us.

We arrived at the early start of a fat and fruitful spring. That year the fig trees near the house were black with heavy globes; the orderly rows of almond trees had already turned pink, then white, then green with pods; and at night huge lemons shone in the moonlight. The lambs and the kids were plentiful, the chicks all around a blanket of chirps, and offshore the honeycombs of rocks were filled with friendly fish. It was a peaceful time as well, with quiet nights disturbed by nothing more than the snoring of dogs, creaking timbers, and the rustle of grass as small animals passed on their way to water. In the days when we wandered through the valley below the house we breathed in smells from a world half forgotten: the acid odour of mouldering leather, the stink of sheep, the tang of peppers and *chorizo*, the light oil cooking in a farmer's kitchen, and the twisted ropes of garlic that hung by his door. It was the best of times to be there, and not the least of our comforts was the harmony of the household in which we stayed.

It was a happy home held in a balance, Anna's stolid good humour a counterweight to Jenny's exuberance. The two women were at peace with themselves, and with the world around them; their island world, not the world outside. They had given up on that outside world, venturing into it only to ski. Mountains were the one commodity that Ibiza could not offer them, and had there been a snowy peak down the road they never would have left the place. But there wasn't, and so once a year they went north to the Alps to get their fill of mountains and return. Aside from that one trip they needed nothing more than what they themselves, and their island, could provide. They had it all, the good and quiet life, and they had each other.

'You know what you are?' Justine said to them one morning. 'You're pacifiers. You spread peace like butter on bread. A person can't help feeling good just being around you.'

Anna tried not to look pleased. It was more than a compliment, it was an endorsement of a way of life. We sat outside the kitchen door balancing morning coffee cups, the sun climbing over the opposite ridge and the valley below us a pattern of green trees and rusty earth. Three of us sat in chairs, Justine sprawled beside me on the grass. I kept my bare legs up to get the sun on my knee. The scar there was a deep and ugly furrow.

Jenny looked up from a copy of *Time* that she was reading, and said, 'Peace, is that what you said? Maybe we're peaceful here in Ibiza, but when we go north to ski it's a battle every day.'

'You're exaggerating,' Anna protested. 'Maybe sometimes we have some little disagreement . . .'

Jenny let out a hoot. 'Wow, some disagreements. She gets furious whenever I want to go off and ski something tough.'

'Well, it's not so nice that you leave me alone skiing like some little old lady on the easy hills.'

'They aren't easy, they just aren't tough, and I don't do it that often.' Jenny appealed to me. 'Kelly, you know how it is. I used to be one of the best, and I'm still pretty good. Every once in a while I have to get me a hill with some steep in it. Wouldn't you?'

'Don't get me in the middle of this,' I said. 'I love you both.'

'That's okay. I have ways to get even,' said Anna. 'She does that to me and when we come back to the island I don't bake *Zimtsterne* or *Linzeraugen* for a month.'

Jenny made a face at her. 'That's no threat. I adore that stuff, but I have to watch it. She'd make me fat as a horse if I let her.'

She patted her belly. She was wearing a bikini, and I could see that she was just as trim and well muscled at thirty as she had been when she was competing. She paged through the copy of *Time,* and handed it to me. There was an Olympic roundup story in it with photos from Lake Placid. One of them showed Stock winning the downhill. I flipped by that one to a picture of Phil Mahre taking the silver in the slalom, only half a second

608

behind Sternmark, his skis canted up as he turned through a gate, the K–2 logo showing clearly on the bottoms.

'Un-bloody-believable,' said Jenny. 'A year ago they were saying that he might not ever ski again.'

I nodded, remembering the day at Piz d'Rel and the sound of those cheers when he fell. I passed the magazine to Justine. She turned back to the picture of Stock winning the downhill. She stared at it intently, then looked up. The way she was sitting, her head was level with my knee. She leaned over and kissed the scar lightly.

'Don't,' I said.

'I did that to you. If it hadn't been for me that would have been your picture in the magazine.'

'Don't talk that way.'

'I did. The way you were skiing, I made it happen.'

'Bullshit,' said Jenny. 'He crashed because he was skiing dumb.'

'She's right,' I told Justine. 'Nobody made that happen but me. And it won't happen again, the way we are now. Nothing can hurt us now that we're together.'

'Knock wood,' said Anna. She looked around for a piece, found the arm of her chair, and rapped it. 'That's no way to talk. You're not together, not really. You haven't accomplished anything yet. Your troubles are just beginning.' She stood up abruptly and flicked the dregs of her coffee onto the grass. 'Excuse me, emotion so early in the morning is bad for the digestion. And speaking of that knee, it's time for the exercise.'

The knee was improving steadily. I could swim without strain, and I could walk well enough with the help of the crutch. Every day I did a mile or so in one direction or another from the house, and I was about ready to throw that crutch away. I figured that after Justine left I would push the routine up and start the jogging. Jenny had appointed herself as my trainer, and she promised to keep me moving. Now she ducked into the house and came back dressed in shorts and a shirt.

'Let's go, Ace,' she said. 'Time to move the muscles.'

It was just a walk down the road, but it still was an effort for me. The important thing was to keep moving once I started and not give the knee a chance to stiffen up. With Jenny on one side of me and Justine on the other we went down the road that led to the shore, the two women adjusting their pace to my hobble. When we came to the main road we turned north. It was the first time I had gone that way; before it had always been south towards the village of Santa Eulalia.

'We'll go as far as the beach at Es Cana,' said Jenny. 'That should give you a little over a mile each way.'

'You're the coach,' I told her, 'but it doesn't seem like very much.'

'Little by little, Ace. A month from now I'll have you jogging twenty a week. And two months from now you'll think *that* was a picnic.'

'Why don't you two athletes go on ahead?' Justine suggested. 'I'll wait over there with a cold Coke while you torture yourselves. You can pick me up on the way back.'

She was looking at a low, battered building at the side of the road, a cement-block oblong with plaster that was grimy and pitted. A chicken-wire fence hedged it from the road, and the front yard was a litter of weeds and trash. The sign over the door read *Café Serra*.

'Not a chance,' I said. 'Part of the deal is that you suffer with me.'

'You wouldn't want to wait there anyway,' Jenny told her. 'It's a fishermen's bar, and it's filthy.'

By the time we reached the beach I was sweating freely and the knee felt loose, but my hip ached from the unnatural way I was moving. We turned around and started back at once to keep things flowing. By the time we passed the Café Serra again the ache in my hip was gone and I was beginning to feel close to normal, but Justine's face was bathed in sweat and her shoulders were down.

'Let's break for that Coke now,' I said to Jenny. 'We can all use something.'

'Better to finish it up. We'll have something to drink at home.'

'No, here.'

She shrugged and followed us inside. She had described the place accurately. It was a filthy fishermen's café. The bar was little more than a plank counter down one side of the room with a coffee machine on top of it. There were half a dozen tables with wire-backed chairs, and the only decorations were posters on the walls. The floor was sprinkled with shells of shrimp and clams, and the whole place smelled of ancient cooking oil. A four-bladed fan revolved slowly from the ceiling, moving stale air from one part of the room to another. A middle-aged man with sad moustaches and a huge belly lapping over his belt was making a casual pass at the floor with a broom. There was nobody else in the place. When we came in the man with the broom looked up and smiled hopefully.

'I'm sorry, you were right,' Justine said to Jenny. 'We'll wait until we get home.'

'No, we won't,' I said. 'This place looks just fine to me.'

Over in the corner was a sturdy, scarred upright piano. There was a hole in the top of it, and the stool looked wobbly. The keys were yellowed and some of the white ones were black. It looked awful, it looked beautiful, it looked like something out of a dream.

I said to Jenny: 'Translate for me. Tell the gentleman with the broom that I have some business to discuss with him.'

The gentleman's name was Jaime Serra, and for the next several months, until I left the island to join the ski team, I played that piano in his café every night for at least an hour. I played blues, I played rag, I played a mixed bag of ballads, and every evening was a new adventure. If the piano had ever been tuned it had been in another age, and so many keys were dead that each number called for split-second innovation. My efforts were largely unappreciated. The patrons of the Café Serra were fishermen relaxing after hours of heavy labour. They were short, dark men with knotted muscles and hands scarred from years of handling cordage. They sat at their tables playing dominoes and drinking coffee, *coñac,* and the local product, *hierbas.* They rarely smiled or raised their voices, and in the months that I played for them I never heard applause or saw a foot tap in time to my music. As far as those fishermen were concerned I was just another noise in the night, but their indifference never bothered me. It would not have bothered Hoagy Carmichael either. I played with my eyes half shut, an unlit cigarette dangling from my lips, and a San Miguel beer slowly going flat on top of the piano. The lazy fan revolved above me, the dead keys clicked and the live ones tinkled, and every once in a while Justine came by and affectionately rubbed the back of my neck. It was the realization of a pathetic little dream, and I loved every minute of it.

But it was my dream only. No one else understood it, or wanted to. The fishermen certainly didn't, and to Jaime Serra I

611

was just another crazy *estranjero* willing to pay for the privilege of making a fool of himself. (I was paying him a hundred pesetas a night, he certainly wasn't about to pay me anything.) Anna thought it was cute, Jenny thought of it as therapy, and only Justine was curious enough to question me closely.

'I can see how much you enjoy it,' she said. 'What I don't understand is why it means so much to you.'

'It's a dream I've had for years, something I've always wanted to do.'

'But why? What's so special about playing honky-tonk piano in a ratty place like that? You have so much else. You have the skiing, and the business, and the Olympics, and . . . everything.'

'What is "everything" supposed to mean? You? Are you everything?'

'I didn't mean it that way.'

'But you meant that I had you.'

'Yes.'

'But I don't, and I don't have the rest of it either. None of that stuff is mine. It all belongs to Digger, it always has.' I was close to breaking a rule, but I didn't care. 'The Olympic gold, Prince Skis, those are his dreams, not mine. And you're his too. All I've got there is a second mortgage on a dream. So what does that leave me? A piss-poor fantasy about pounding a piano in a run-down café. I know how sorry it sounds, but it's all I've got. I wish I had more, believe me I do. I wish I had some grand ambition I could show to you. But I can't because I don't. The grand ambitions are all gone. Somebody got there before me.'

'That's sad,' she said. 'You deserve a bigger dream.'

'Maybe I'll have one someday. Maybe when I've finished living out Digger's dreams for him I can start on some of my own.'

'I hope so. I really do.'

'It would be nice to think that if I ever do, that you would be a part of them.'

She reached up to take my face in her hands, her eyes on mine. 'I want to be a part of everything you do, no matter how big or how small. Whenever your dream is ready. I'll be ready too.'

She left the island in the second week of April. She did it the way she had said she would, slipping out silently and without any fuss. One day she said that she was leaving the next, and the next day she was gone. Jenny drove her to the airport; I stayed at home. I wanted no part of that sort of farewell. We would meet again in the autumn. She would know where I would be, and she would come to me. Until then I was without her.

I stayed in Ibiza through the summer. Both Anna and Jenny had there own ways of combating what they were sure was my abiding loneliness. Anna cooked tremendous meals for me to eat, and Jenny ran them off me. To Anna there was no problem in life so big that it could not be solved, or at least ameliorated, by a roast leg of pork with applesauce and *Spätzle*. To Jenny, enough roadwork and a good sweat made any particular problem insignificant. If you could still think about it, then you needed more laps.

True to her promise by the middle of June, first jogging and then running, she had me up to twenty miles a week. Then she started adding on the extras. First, a one-mile swim every day after roadwork. Next, one hundred sit-ups in sixty seconds. Next, one hundred pushups in the same time. Next, three hundred up-downs: running in place, hitting the turf, getting up to run again. All of this every day on a knee that was beginning to feel as sound as steel. All of this with Jenny doing every bit of it right alongside me.

'I am not trying out for the Green Bay Packers,' I reminded her one morning. 'I'm a skier, not a linebacker.'

'Oh, is that what you are? I thought you were some kind of a pussy dance instructor. You wanna quit, it's okay with me. You need this more than I do.'

'Nobody said anything about quitting. I'm just glad you ran out of surprises to throw at me.'

'Hah! That's what you think.' We were standing at the bottom of a low hill, drenched in sweat from the early run. She got behind me and said, 'Squat down.'

'Hey, what now?'

'Down you go.'

I squatted down. She swung her legs around my neck, and before I knew it she was sitting on my shoulders. I stood up. She rode there lightly without holding on.

'Up the hill, horsey,' she said. 'At the trot, and no slowing down.'

I looked up at the hill. It seemed a mile high, covered with brush and rocks. I grunted and said, 'How much do you weigh?'

'One twenty-two.'

I leaned forward, dumped her off, and said, 'It can't be done.'

'The Austrian ski team is doing it now, and when they do it the men carry each other up the hill. All you have to haul is a little girl like me.'

'Screw the Austrians, it still can't be done.'

'How much do you weigh?'

'One-eighty, even.'

She sighed and squatted down. 'Get on.'

I got on, for a joke. It wasn't any joke. She stood up and ran up the hill with me on her shoulders. Then she ran down again. She dumped me at the bottom and said, 'Well?'

I bowed. Then I squatted and said, 'Get on.'

I took her up and down that hill three times and then collapsed at the bottom, exhausted. We weren't far from the water. When my breath came back I got up and trotted down to the beach, Jenny following along. We stripped off our clothes and went into the water, wallowing around until we were cool, and then came out to lie on the beach and dry off. I rolled over on my side to look at her. There wasn't an extra ounce or inch visible. Trim and neat, with small, high breasts, she reminded me of Claudia. She saw the look and reached for her clothes to cover up.

'Relax,' I said, laughing. 'Your body is safe with me, pal. Just admiring the machinery.'

She leaned back and looked at me critically. 'Yeah, you're looking good yourself.' She wrinkled her nose at me. 'Back when I was straight you would have rated pretty high.'

'That's high-class flattery.' I closed my eyes against the sun.

After a moment, she said, 'Hey, Ace, you happy?'

'Too damn tired to be anything else.'

'No, I mean all the time. With this deal you've got with Justine.'

I opened my eyes and rolled over. She was on her belly, leaning on her elbows. 'How about you?' I asked. 'Are you happy with Anna?'

'I'm in love. Doesn't it show?'

'So am I. Doesn't it show?'

'That's different.'

614

'How? You and Anna are together all the time. You're luckier than we are. The way it looks, six months out of the year is all we're going to be able to manage. But that doesn't change the love.'

'That's a bullshit comparison. Justine is off with somebody else, not to mention who that somebody happens to be.'

'And if Anna wanted to spend some time with somebody else? Would that make you stop loving her?'

She frowned, thought about that for a while, then said, 'Did you know that I killed somebody once?'

'You hear stories, bits and pieces. You know how it is.'

'Let me tell you how it really was.' She told me then about Sammy the smuggler, about running the cigarettes into Corsica, and about what happened on the beach with Angel. Finishing up, she said, 'The thing to remember is this. I didn't slug Angel with that oar because he was a miserable excuse for a human being, and I didn't do it because he had just about raped me. I did it because he had taken something that was mine. That money belonged to Sammy and me. That made it mine, and nobody steals from me. Nobody.' Her eyes were hard and glistening. 'Does that answer your question?'

'Justine isn't cash. Justine isn't property. She's a woman.'

'Don't tell me what she is. I known damn well what she is. I'm a woman too, and I know what it is.' Her voice was high. She wasn't angry, but I had irritated her. 'For Chrissake, don't you even know when you're getting ripped off?'

I stood up and reached for my shorts. 'We'd better start back.'

'Yeah.'

She stood up, and without any warning she hit me in the belly with her fist. She hit hard. I had just enough warning to tighten the muscles. Her fist bounced, and she grinned, shaking her hand. 'You've got the body back, for sure. I just hope to hell you use it right.'

I left the island at the end of August with the understanding that I would meet up with Anna and Jenny for some spring skiing in Austria. I flew back to the States and on to Mount Hood in Oregon by way of Portland. I arrived at the Timberline Lodge two days before the Ski Team opened its slalom camp there. Mike was waiting for me with a load of Prince Ski equipment to be tested and adapted for me. With Digger unavailable he had agreed to work as my racer-chaser for the season. Digger had hit the roof when he heard about it. As usual, Mike could do no right. He wanted me to use someone from the factory, but I held out for my brother, and eventually Digger gave in. Mike wasn't too happy about it either. He was afraid of screwing up. He knew that if anything went wrong, *anything,* he was the one who would take the heat.

'Don't sweat it,' I told him. 'If anything comes up that you can't handle we'll work it out together.'

'Fair enough,' he said. 'Just clue me in on one thing. Are you skiing with your brains or your ass this year?'

'That's all over. I'm skiing hot, but smart.'

'What about the knee?'

'Good as new.'

'Justine gets amazing results. Listen, now that she's a family proposition, do you think you could work me in for two weeks around Easter?' He raised his hands in mock surrender. 'All right, all right, just a joke.'

I gave the knee its first workout on snow two days later when the camp opened. It was Labour Day, and down in the valleys people were splashing around in lakes and darting over tennis courts, but up at the eighty-five-hundred-foot level below the blown-out volcanic cone of Mount Hood's peak the Palmer snowfield fell in a sheer white drop that reached to the timberline three miles below. The central section of the snowfield was reserved for the use of the Ski Team, and it was studded with the bamboo poles of slalom gates set in combinations. The first day the team, as a whole, ran over a thousand gates as the coaches watched and made their notes. One of those coaches was ruddy-cheeked, amiable Jim Casey. He was the oldest of the coaches, had been around the longest, and because of that he got handed the chores that no one else wanted. That night he sat with me in the gallery of the lodge and gave me my warning. I was on the team, but I was also on probation.

'You looked terrific on the hill today,' he said. 'The knee looks like it's healed and your skiing is sharp.'

'Then why the probation?'

'Come on, Kelly,' he said. 'You know how bad you were skiing before you got hurt. You were a menace. We have to be sure that it isn't going to happen again.'

'It won't. I had some problems, but I've taken care of them. I'm all right now.'

'I hope so. You look okay, but you'll have to show us. I'm sorry, but that's the way it's got to be.'

I nodded my acceptance. There wasn't anything else I could do. I knew that he was right. Based on my performance over the past two years I was lucky to be on the team at all. Still, it was a strange position to be in.

Casey broke in on my thoughts. 'I understand that Digger won't be with you this year.'

'That's right. My brother, Mike, is taking his place.'

'Does that mean that you'll be living with the team? It might be better all around if you did. You were never really part of the team, travelling with Digger like you did. This way you'd get to be one of the boys.'

'Jim, I may be on probation, but don't give me the team crap, please. I'll never be one of the boys, and you know it. I might have been a couple of years ago, but it's too late for that now.'

'You could give it a try.'

'You asking or telling?'

He hesitated. Doing it the old way the team didn't have to pay my expenses. It was something to consider. He said, 'I'm asking.'

'In that case I'd rather keep it the way it was before. Mike and I will travel together and pay our own way. Sometimes there'll be the two of us, and sometimes somebody else. That okay with you?'

'Perfectly.' As long as the team wasn't paying it made no difference to him. If he had any idea who the extra person would be, he didn't let it show on his face.

'What will it take to get me off probation?'

'Just ski the way we know you can. You'll know when it happens. We won't even have to tell you.'

After the slalom camp there was a downhill training session at Hintertux, in Austria. On our way there Mike and I stayed overnight at the apartment in New York, just long enough for Bobby to crush me with the comment that my relationship with Justine was 'the sickest thing I ever heard of,' and then we flew out the next morning. Hintertux was a dream for me, I couldn't do anything wrong. I skied as well there as I ever had before: hot, but without the suicidal desperation that had sent me crashing for two years in a row. I was back to the best of my form, using my slalom skills to hold my line in the downhill turns and then making my speed in the straightaway glides. From the smiles that Casey threw my way I knew that probation was just a matter of time. All I needed was a few top-ten finishes once the season started to convince the coaches that my crazy years were over.

Claudia called me at Hintertux towards the end of our training camp. 'I was hoping to find you there,' she said. 'Will you have some time to yourself soon?'

'Camp closes tomorrow. After that I don't have to be anywhere for three weeks.'

'Would you like to come to Piz d'Rel?'

'I'd like that very much. What kind of a time did you have in mind? Party time or quiet relaxation?'

'Whichever you wish, my dear. The choice is yours.'

'I'd prefer to keep it quiet, actually.'

'I thought you might. From what I hear you've been *très sérieux* recently.'

'You hear everything, don't you?'

'Enough. Listen, Kelly, I must warn you. This won't be just a social visit. I have some business to talk with you. A favour.'

'Do you want to talk now?'

'No, face to face is better. When I see you.'

Mike went as far as Davos with me, dropped off to see friends, and I drove on to Piz d'Rel alone. It was evening when I arrived, driving the long and winding approach to the house in the dark, the terrace lights a beacon up ahead. Claudia was alone there. She had a chafing-dish meal and a blazing fire waiting for me in the sitting room. She looked as lovely as ever, but there were a few new lines around her eyes, and she seemed nervous. She fidgeted as she watched me eat the lamb curry and the rice from the chafing dishes, and apologized for not joining me.

'I had something earlier,' she said, and then changed that to 'Actually, to tell the truth, I'm much too nervous to eat.'

I looked around for the chutney and found it on the sideboard. 'Anything to do with this favour you want to ask?'

'Of course.'

'Talk.'

'When you have finished.'

I hurried through the meal while she drank a glass of wine. When I had finished I pushed the plates aside and said, 'Claudia,

618

let's make this easy for both of us. How much money do you need?'

She bowed her head, looked down at her hands. 'Ah, God, you do make it easy, don't you? Two hundred thousand.'

'Dollars or francs?'

She looked up at me in surprise. 'Dollars, of course.'

'Tell me about it.'

It was quickly told. Charles's machine-tool business was on the edge of going under, the banks had dried up on them and so had their friends. They needed a chunk of cash, and they needed it quickly. They wanted to sell me the chalet at Piz d'Rel.

'It's worth a good deal more, but we need the money now,' she said. 'If we put it on the market we might sell it for twice as much to some rich Arab, but it also might take months to get rid of it.'

'Surely you could borrow on it. Not for the whole amount, but for a good chunk of it.'

'And pay twenty percent for the money. No, you miss the point. Even if Charles manages to get through this *crise* we shan't be wanting a chalet like this for quite some time. The apartment in Geneva will have to go too. This is going to mean a total readjustment for us. Everything must go, and go quickly.' She held out her hands for me to see. Her fingers were bare. 'My jewellery went first.'

'I'm sorry.'

'Well, there you are, *c'est cela*. All part of the game when you live the way we do. But we must sell this place, and I thought at once of you. You seemed to like it here.'

I got up and walked around the room, thinking. She was right, I liked the house. It was a comfortable place, and it was located in the heart of some of the finest skiing country in the world. From what I knew about Swiss real estate her figures were right, and at any rate that could be checked by the lawyers. What intrigued me most was the idea of having a home of my own. Technically, my residence was Bobby's New York apartment, but in the past two years I had not spent two dozen nights under that roof. My home had been in hotels and ski lodges, hospitals and guest rooms. I was ready for a place of my own. The chalet at Piz d'Rel was more than I needed, but the time and place were right. The trouble was that I knew so little about my own finances that I did not know if I could afford it.

I saw that Claudia was watching me anxiously, and knew that I had to say something. 'I'm interested,' I told her. 'But I would have to make a telephone call before I could make a decision.'

Her shoulders slumped in relief, and she said, 'Yes, of course, I should have realized. Your money is all in trust, no?'

'Actually not. I turned twenty-one three weeks ago. But I still have to check with the people in Boston.'

Her face lit up and she clapped her hands. With all her problems she had time to be delighted for me. 'But that's wonderful, *chéri,* you are now of age. We should celebrate.'

'Not for something like that. I've been of age since I was eight. At least, it feels that way. It's only four o'clock in Boston now. Where's the telephone?'

'In the next room. Please, go right ahead.'

I got hold of Jellicoe in Boston and put the question to him. He was no longer my trustee, but no one knew my financial position better than he did. I expected a negative attitude, but I was wrong. Not only could I afford the purchase but the financing that he would arrange would provide a tax benefit. I told him that people from Geneva would be in touch with him, and thanked him for his time.

I went back to the sitting room and told Claudia that she had a deal. Charles had his two hundred kay and I had a chalet in the Alps. She took my hand and squeezed it, then sagged against me. I held her, and after a moment she straightened up.

'Sorry,' she murmured, 'but there has been . . . some strain. Please, if you will forgive me I must call Charles at once and tell him.'

She went into the next room to make her call, and when she came back she was more as I remembered. Her eyes sparkled and there was energy in her smile. 'A message from Charles,' she said. 'He says first to tell you his thanks, and that you are fine gentleman. Second, that you have got yourself one hell of a bargain. And third, he suggests that you spend the next several hours . . . how did he say it? . . . fucking my socks off. An Americanism, no?'

'Yes, but it doesn't mean a thing if you aren't wearing socks.'

'I told him that. I said, when do I ever wear socks? When I ski, that's when. Docs he want me to put on ski boots for the

620

occasion? Much too kinky, I told him.' She grinned wickedly. 'Besides, I told him, our young friend is *très sérieux* these days. He is under the spell of an enchantment. He is in love. Not so?'

'All of those things, but that doesn't mean I have to live like a monk.'

'Clearly. From what I hear the woman you love isn't living like a nun.'

'Far from it.'

'Well then, we are wasting time. To the bedroom.'

I stood up and reached for her. 'What's wrong with right here?'

'To the bedroom,' she insisted. 'That is where I keep the socks.'

It was, as always with Claudia, a bittersweet joy. So sweet in the giving, but with the bitter tang of knowing that whatever passed between us was, *au fond,* of no importance. Still, it was there, a friendly sexual handshake from an old chum, and later we lay in comradely silence, fingers laced, breathing in the afterodours of each other.

She was the first to speak in the darkness. 'I have surprised you today, have I not?'

I had an idea of where she was headed, but I didn't want to admit it. 'Explain.'

'I think you know what I mean. You did not expect me to be the sort of woman who would do what I am doing. Sticking it out with Charles this way. Selling my jewels. Starting over with him from the very beginning.'

'You had no choice.'

'Ah, but there's always a choice. I could have got out, I could have stayed clear of the disaster. I could have saved what was mine.'

'But you didn't.'

'No, and do you know why? Because I found, to my own surprise, that I am essentially a moral person.'

'I never doubted it.'

'I wonder. Most people today find it easier to redefine morality, give it a different name, than to admit that it exists at all. I've never been a reformist. I've always known that some of the things I do are good, and some are evil. I've never fooled myself about that. And by staying with Charles, by tying myself to his disaster, I know that I have done something morally admirable. It is a good feeling, not one I have had very often.'

'I'm pleased for you.'

'I wish I could say the same for you.'

'Bingo,' I said. 'I thought there might be a message for me in all that garbage about morality.'

'Not garbage, *chéri*. This may surprise you, coming from me, but I warn you. You are very close to shaking hands with the devil.'

'Two hundred kay is a high price to pay for a lecture on my sins.'

'That is unworthy of you.'

'Then I withdraw it, but I could do without the lecture.'

'Then that also is withdrawn, but try to remember where it came from. There is very little that I haven't done in the way of conventional sinning. In fact, I have done it all, and most of it twice. But this business of having your father's woman – not as a sexual accident, but as part of an organized plan – this, my friend, is an abomination. It brushes the skirts of pure evil, and I only hope that you do not have to pay for it someday.'

'I don't think I will. I don't believe in those things. But if I do, I'll pay up gladly.'

'Don't say that.' Her voice sharp.

'I mean it. You're a moralist and I'm a pragmatist. I believe in results, and what I'm doing, what I have with Justine, has changed my life in ways you'll never know.'

'Your skiing. Is that enough of a reason . . . ?'

'Much more than that. My sanity, my life, perhaps.'

'I find that hard to believe.'

'It's true. There's no way I can prove it to you, but it's true.' I smiled in the darkness. 'One small sign, perhaps you've noticed. I no longer have to call her name at the moment when I come with you. I didn't this time, did I?'

A moment, a heartbeat, and then she said, 'No, you didn't, but then you never did.'

'But you said it yourself, back when I first knew you. You said that I called out her name.'

'I said there was a name. I never said what name it was.'

'Not Justine?'

'No, never.'

'Then what?'

Another beat, and a quiet chuckle. 'Bobby.'

Ten days later the snow begins to fall as I stand on the terrace of my new home watching a car make its way up the winding road. Claudia is gone, the house is mine, with the details to be settled by the lawyers. I have called Prince Skis in New York to leave word where I am. Justine will find me. From the looks of that car she already has, and the time of waiting is almost done. We are coming into season once again, our season of the snows.

The snow falls thickly now, beginning to hold and to stick. Through the curtain of its falling I still can see the peak of Piz d'Rel. Unfriendly mountain, sharp and black, the never-changing profile of a savage face. A dusting of snow might soften that face, but never make it friendly. Some mountains act that way with snow, refusing the friendly embrace.

I am still an innocent about snow. Childlike, I still believe in its magic. The snows of childhood are gentle, each falling flake a benediction and an eyelid kiss. The stuff is no threat to the young. Flake on flake, layer on layer, it forms a mantle over nature's scars and man's mistakes. It decorates the child. Forget the impermanence, the melting days and the slush. It is enough for the child that now the day is white and bright with snow, each crystal signalling another delight: a snowball fight, an igloo to be made, a hill and a sled, and a fireplace-and-cocoa haven at the end of the day. Snow promises all of that to the child, and like any other child I still believe in snow that way.

The car draws closer; yes it's she, and now the snow is bringing me my love. This will be our winter of contentment. We will hold each other through the long, dark nights, and dare each day to last forever. I will race, and I will win, and she'll be with me while I do it. We'll laugh, and sing and brag; and with our good young teeth we will chew up the beef and spit out the bones. We will live like children in a world of snow, each flake a benediction, and when springtime comes I will give her up in the knowledge that the world will surely turn and that my time will come again in season.

Flickers of light from the car on the road: a signal, a greeting. Flickers of words from the months just past, all of them warnings. Anna's fears, Jenny's anger, Bobby's contempt, and Claudia's cool appraisal of evil. All of them women, and all of them warning me . . . of what? I don't know, and they don't, either. But being women they must warn the man against the wolves in the night, even in a peaceful forest. Warn the man and chide the child in him. I have had my warnings and I spit on them.

Below the terrace, the end of the winding road. The squeal of the brake, the slam of the door. She is here, and I am whole again.

Chapter Fourteen

During the next three years, Digger, Justine, and I lived our lives geared to the changes of the seasons, carefully observing the rules we had made for ourselves. They were good years for us all, not the best, not what we would have chosen, but given what we had elected for ourselves they were the best that we could expect. They were years of growth, years of age, years that led to the fulfilment of dreams. They were years that showed in our faces: Digger's gradually ageing, still strong and fierce, but fading; my own face firming up to manhood, the softness gone from the jaw; Justine's face a maturing bloom, the shine of the bud buffed away. I see those faces now as the medallions of those years, and I see the years themselves as they pass before me in memory.

In the first of those summers Digger worked on the home he was building at Skofja Loka, staking out the land close by a giant chestnut tree. It was time to lay the foundations, mix the cement, pour and shape. Four hired workmen laboured alongside him, much younger than he, but compared to theirs his body was still a muscular marvel. At the end of each day he straightened up to wipe the sweat from his face and smile at the sight of Justine laying food on a table under the trees. He called to the workmen to come to their meal, and they laid down their tools and took turns with a bucket of water and a towel before coming to the table. And later in the darkness with the workmen gone, they sat on a bench beneath the chestnut tree, Justine in the curve of Digger's arm, both of them content and dozing. The skeleton of their growing home, now well under way, cast eerie shadows on the land.

My own sweat matched Digger's that summer as I worked to capture his other dream for him. In Ibiza that year the training sessions with Jenny became a routine. Pushups, sit-ups, and then the run along the beach, along the rutted roads and up the hills. Sweat poured from us both, and sweat popped from my forehead each time I sat down to dinner and Anna lovingly laid a hot and heaping plate of food before me. And in the darkness of those Ibiza nights I sweated again lying with a girl on a beach, any girl on any beach, our bodies flashing moonlight, intertwined.

The seasons pivoted and the partners changed. Work on the house stopped as Digger went back to being a businessman in New York and Justine joined me at Piz d'Rel. The chalet was our winter home now whenever I was not racing, and Justine conformed it to her taste: fewer angles and edges, less glass and chrome, more depth and softness everywhere. Our time there was an unspoiled joy of rediscovery, always new, and then the cycle of the races began again: Laax, Adelboden, Wengen, and all the other mountains marching by in familiar procession as I exploded out of the starting gate poling fiercely, skidded a turn, floated a jump with fists up front and elbows in, tucked low over the skis with arms extended as I raced for the line, flashed over the finish and turned in a shower of ice and snow looking back over my shoulder at the electronic numbers flickering on the board. Settling into 1:42.10. Fourth place. Not good enough.

Another start, and this time I teetered on a turn, one ski up and then the other, and then I recovered with both skis working, zooming for the finish, over the line with the familiar curtain of ice that obscured the scoreboard just for the moment, and then dissolved to show the numbers. 1:40.60. Second place, and I could nod with satisfaction.

It happened again and again, racing and beginning to win again: a first, a fourth, another first. Mike backing me up, slaving away over the equipment in the ski room, and keeping me cool on the hill. Justine jumping excitedly at the finish as I came over the line, leading the cheering, and loving me fiercely through the long winter nights. The electronic numbers kept flashing that year: 1:38.42, 1:41.38. 1:40.22. First place. Third place. First place. Winning again, and then it was back to Piz d'Rel for the bittersweet time, a month or so of springtime skiing before it was time for Justine to leave. Jenny and Anna joined us then to ski beneath the savage face of Piz d'Rel, the four of us romping across the mountainside like kids on a backyard hill. Bittersweet, and then it was time for another pivot as Justine crossed to the other side of her life.

Life moved faster at Skofja Loka that second summer. The courses of bricks rose higher, the roof of the barn was raised, and the *kozolci* were hammered together in the fields. Justine worked in her garden, watering and weeding, and she gathered wild flowers to arrange in bowls. On luminescent evenings, Digger could gaze in satisfaction on what he had accomplished so far. The house at twilight rose up against the purple fields, the shell of the building complete. The neatly cobbled courtyard was in place, the walls of brick and above them the wooden *gank* with vines that would need another year before they could give shade. The house was dark, no one lived there. The dream was close, but incomplete.

Another summer passed for me as well, more days of sweating under the sun with Jenny pacing by my side, more evenings pounding ragtime at the Café Serra, more nights of casual encounters, fruitless writhings as I marked the time until the autumn. And after that the same mountains waited to be skied again. The numbers flashed on the board recording the triumphs of the season as I came back onto form. I was nailing them all, smoking every hill, and the boards flashed the triumphs of the team as well: Phil Mahre the World Cup champion again, Steve Mahre the winner of the World Championship GS at Schladming, Tamara McKinney only a year away from a championship of her own. The seasons rolled through another spring at Piz d'Rel, another separation, and at Skofja Loka that third summer one of the dreams approached its realization. All the structures were complete and only the details remained. Justine shopped for the huge black pot to hang in the hearth, for the clocks that would hang on the walls, and for the mountain of goose feathers to be transformed into a magic carpet of a bed. Together with Digger she wandered through the house, the two of them looking and touching, wondering at what they had wrought. They had recreated Marina's vision, taken the murmurings of a dying girl and made them real. They stood in the kitchen near the hearth, and Digger draped his arm across her shoulders. They were almost there, with only one more step to go. It was all so close, but now they had to part as the season turned again and the first snows dusted the peaks of the Karawanken Alps that rose above the plain.

That was the way we spent those three years, and in the autumn of the fourth all the traditional signs pointed to an early winter in the Alps, and a heavy one. Spotted weasels were found in the forests, migrating birds were massed against the skies, and knowing farmers noted that their horses were growing a thick and rough-haired undercoat. Other signs appeared: meteor showers, crimson sunsets, and the silver unicorn was seen at night, an unfailing herald of the coldest cold and the deepest snows. All over the Alpine country the farmers braced themselves, and waited.

And nothing happened. That year the signs were wrong. Early that winter the snow was bad wherever we went to race, and the officials juggled the schedule sending us from site to site in search of skiable courses. We bounced around from hill to hill, skiing wherever we could. About half of us figured that the winter was a washout and that the snow would never come, while the other half were sure that when it finally came it would bury us with generosity. We skied at Laax and Val d'Isère, Val Gardena and Parpan, and considering the conditions most of us were more concerned with getting down the hill in one piece than with posting the fastest times. We all wanted to win, but nobody wanted to wipe himself out so early in the year on pistes that showed patches of dirt and rocks against the white. That was the pre-Olympic year, with the competition to be held at Sarajevo on January 27. Nobody wanted to miss that one, and so some unfamiliar names turned up in the top tens during those early months: younger skiers looking to make a name and willing to risk a bad fall in order to post a score. It was an odd way to start off the season.

The season started off badly in another way. In the past Justine had always enjoyed riding the racing circuit with me, but this year she seemed to resent it. Nothing pleased her . . . the travel, the hotels, the food . . . and she complained constantly. I couldn't really blame her, it left a lot to be desired as a way of life, but it was the life she had chosen to share with me. I tried to make things easier for her, but all I did was make things worse, and after the first couple of weeks we were snapping at each other.

Mike's girl didn't help the situation. Her name was Jones, the same as Justine's, but she said it was her first name. She was from somewhere in Wyoming, painfully lovely and a crackerjack skier. Mike met her in Laax and she went on with us from there. The company should have been good for Justine, but it went the other way. She couldn't stand Jones, and she showed it. She didn't like the terrific way she skied and she didn't like the terrific way she looked. She was plainly envious. I had never seen her that way before. She fought with Jones constantly, nervous little battles over nothing. It soured the air, and by the time we got to Kitzbühel, Jones had had enough. She told Mike that she was going on to Arosa and asked him to come along. When he explained that he had to stay with me, she went anyway. He was so sore that he wouldn't speak to me.

'He'll get over it,' said Justine. 'He'll find another girl, he always does.'

'What did you have against this one?' I asked.

'She irritated me.'

'You did it to yourself. The girl couldn't help the way she looked and she couldn't help the way she skied.'

'You liked her, didn't you?'

'She was all right.'

'More than all right, I think. She really got to you, didn't she?'

'Don't build something. You're making a mistake.'

'Am I? I don't think so. You always did go for Mike's girls, didn't you? And Digger's girls, too. You like to keep it in the family, don't you?'

I couldn't believe that she had said it. She had never said anything like that before. I walked out of the hotel room without saying anything. I went down the street and sat in a coffee bar for an hour. I still couldn't believe that she had said it to me. I went back to the room, and when I opened the door I saw that the lights were out. I thought that she was sleeping, but then she was all over me, her arms around me, her lips on my neck and cheek, a stream of disconnected words in my ear.

'Never, never, never,' she was saying. 'Not to my love never. Never something like that never. Not me, really, never. Never I said it, never.'

She kept on with it over and over, and when she wasn't saying the words she was saying how much she loved me. I got loose

628

from her and flipped on the light switch. She had been crying, and she looked awful. I got her over to the bed, and she sat on the edge of it with her head down and her hands between her knees. She had stopped saying the words. I touched her chin with a finger, and she looked up.

'Are you ever going to forgive me for saying that?' she asked. Her eyes were dark and wide.

I didn't say anything.

'Do you know how much I love you?'

'Yes.'

'If you don't forgive me I'll kill myself.'

'No you won't. Don't talk that way.'

'I mean it, I will. You have to forgive me. You have to say it.'

'Shut up. I forgive you.'

She took a deep breath. 'I would have done it. If you hadn't said it I really would have killed myself.'

'All right.'

'I swear it.'

'All right, I believe you.'

She lay back on the bed, her eyes on the ceiling. 'I love you so much and I've been giving you such a rough time, haven't I?'

'Little bitchy, that's all.'

'To everybody. I don't know why I hated that girl, but I did. She scared me.'

'I know.'

'Did you really? That's terrible, that you knew.'

She started to cry again, and when that was over she said that she wanted to get off the road, away from the travel and the hotels. She wanted to go back to Piz d'Rel for a while. Anna and Jenny were there, skiing the mountain and living at the house.

'I could stay with them until I get my head straight,' she said. 'I'm not doing you any good the way I am. I'm supposed to be helping, but look what I'm doing to you. You'd be better off without me for a while.'

I knew that she was right, but I didn't like it. We had too little time together to waste any of it. I asked, 'How long would you stay there?'

629

'Ten days or so. I could meet you in St Anton for the Arlberg-Kandahar.'

'That means you'll miss Sarejevo.'

'Sarajevo is just another race this year. Next year it's important, not now. I don't mind missing it.' She had the idea fixed in her head now, and she liked it. 'Really, I think I should do it. I need the time to myself, and maybe you do too. I won't be alone, I'll have Anna and Jenny with me.'

'I don't like it. I don't like racing without you.'

'It's only for a week or so.'

'We never did it before.'

'I know that, but I think I should do it, don't you?'

'I don't know.'

'I think so, yes, I really do.'

I still didn't like it, but the way she put it made sense. I told myself that she knew what was best for both of us. I really believed that, and I wanted what was best. I told her yes, and she was happy. The next day she left for Piz d'Rel, and the day after that Mike and I flew with the team to Sarajevo for the pre-Olympic downhill.

We were at Sarajevo for four days, and the skiing was bad there too. There was plenty of snow on Bjelasnica mountain, but on race day there was also a hot sun, a balmy breeze, and a temperature of five degrees above freezing. It felt like the site of the Summer Olympics. Along the sides of the course the spectators peeled off their parkas and sweaters as the mountain melted away. Streaks of black and brown dirt appeared on the *piste,* rocks popped out from under the snow, and in the snack bars the cold sodas outsold the hot chocolate by ten to one. Up at the top we shuffled around in the slush and made jokes about the weather. The starting gate there was a joke, too. Under the Olympic rules a downhill course has to have a vertical drop of at least eight hundred metres, but when they measured Bjelasnica the mountain came up nine metres short. The local organizers solved the problem by building a restaurant on the mountaintop. It was four storeys high with a beer garden on the roof. The starting gate was in the beer garden, and a ramp ran down through the restaurant and out onto the course. That gave them the nine metres of vertical drop that they needed, and it made for some interesting starts. When you came down that ramp you had the feeling that you were going to hook somebody's beer stein with your ski. It was good for a laugh, and so we joked about the beer-garden start, we joked about the snow, we joked about the season, and after a two-hour wait they called off the race until the next day.

'This season is turning into a farce,' I told Mike. 'The year that there wasn't any snow.'

'It'll come,' he said, 'and when it comes you'll wish it hadn't.' He was one of the believers.

They called in the Yugoslav army, and for the rest of the day and into the night the soldiers collected fresh snow, dumped it onto the course, sprinkled it with chemicals, and tamped it down. By morning the mountain looked impressive, but as the sun rose the temperature rose with it and by noon the course was a mess again. Mike skied down along the side and came back up to report.

'It isn't any better than yesterday,' he said, 'but they'll probably run it. They'll have to.'

He was right. The television cameras were ready. Sarajevo had to have its pre-Olympic tryout, and they couldn't put it off any longer. There was a World Cup giant slalom scheduled for Kranjska Gora the next day, and all the teams were committed to be there. So they ran their race on a melting icicle of a mountain, and the times were unimpressive. Nobody was risking life and limb under those conditions. I finished out of the top ten and didn't care. The crowd didn't seem to care either. There weren't any high-pitched yips or clanging bells as the racers went by, and many of the spectators stretched out in the sun to improve their tans. It was a hell of a way to go racing. Two Austrians and a Canadian took the first three spots, and then we all ran for the airport to catch the plane to Kranjska Gora.

The weather was just as mild in northern Yugoslavia, and the hill at Kay-Gee was another joke. We knew they'd run the race anyway, television again, and I decided to bag it. I figured that if I skipped the races there I could go home to Piz d'Rel and spend the extra days with Justine before it was time to go to St Anton. I gave myself all the excuses I could think of. I was supposed to be concentrating on downhill, not slalom. The hill was a wreck and we should not have been racing on it anyway. I was worn out and needed the extra days of rest. They were all good excuses, but the only real reason for ducking out was that I missed Justine badly and I wanted to be with her. I asked Mike if he thought I could get away with it.

'Let me tap-dance it by Casey,' he said. 'Ace downhiller should not be risked skiing slalom under adverse conditions. Shit like that. He might buy it.'

He went over to talk to the coaches, and when he came back he gave me the thumbs-up sign and said, 'You're free. Let's get out of here before they change their minds.'

We flew to Innsbruck to pick up the car. It was snowing lightly when we landed, and it was snowing heavily by the time we had loaded up the skis and boots and started down the autobahn towards Landeck. Mike drove while I worked the radio for weather reports. The snow that we had been waiting for was finally coming, and there was going to be a ton of it. The Austrians had a storm watch on and the Swiss were talking blizzard. It didn't look like much at first, but the farther west we drove the thicker it got. We had figured on a three-hour drive from Innsbruck to the house, but by the time we reached Landeck we knew that it was going to take longer than that. It was dark by then and the snow was coming out of the night at us like white bullets, spattering against the windshield. After a while it began to build up on the road and Mike had to cut the speed. I told him to look for a place with a telephone. I wanted to tell Justine that I was on the way.

'Why bother?' he asked. 'She's not expecting you.'

'Just find me a phone, okay?'

He found a tourist office, one of those roadside places full of maps and telephones, and friendly people who will feed you coffee if you look the least bit drunk or tired. We didn't look either, but Mike negotiated some of the coffee while I called the house. Jenny answered the phone, and when I said who it was she let out a little shriek and then quickly lowered her voice, saying, 'Jesus, Ace, where the hell are you?'

'On the road, coming in.'

'You're supposed to be in Kay-Gee.'

'Let me speak to Justine.'

'Hold that a minute, we've got things going on here. First of all, we're snowed in. Can't turn a wheel, can't move an inch. We're socked in tight.'

'Shit. Put Justine on.'

'Hold it, there's more.' There was a crackling silence on the line. 'Your father is here.'

'Say that again.'

'Digger is here.'

Ice in the belly, a hard lump of it. 'What . . . I mean, what's happening? What's he doing there?'

'I don't know, I wish I did.' Her voice went even lower. 'He showed up a couple of hours ago. He went into a huddle with Justine, and then they tried to get out in his car. They got maybe a hundred yards down the road and that was it, *adios muchacho*. Solid snow. They had to hike back to the house on foot.'

'I want to talk to her.'

'I mean, we've got snow up over our ears.'

'Jenny, put her on.'

'Ace, I don't know if I can. She's up in the bedroom now with the door locked. Won't talk to anybody.'

'Give it a try.'

She was gone for a while, and when she came back, she said, 'No way. She won't talk through the door. She's just sitting in there.'

'Where's Digger?'

'In the sitting room staring at the fire like a brooding Viking. You want to talk to him?'

'Yes . . . hold it, no. You say nobody can get out of there?'

'Nobody who walks for a living.'

'Okay then, I don't want to talk to anybody. I'm coming in.'

'I just told you, you won't make it. The roads are stopped solid.'

'I'll make it. Jenny, do something for me. Put the terrace lights on and keep them on all night. Will you do that?'

'Sure, but you still won't make it.'

'Bet on it. You just sit tight. I'll be there.'

'Sit tight? Where the hell would I be going?'

I hung up and told Mike. Puzzled, he said, 'What's going on?'

'I'm not sure, but I think the old man is exercising the fine print in the contract.'

'You feel like explaining that?'

'Not now. First we have to get there. Tonight.'

He didn't ask any questions. He gulped down his coffee. 'Who drives?'

'You.' He was the best I knew for driving on snow.

It took us three hours to drive from Landeck to the Swiss border, inching along, feeling for purchase on the road. The storm was complete now, white all around us, and the headlights were good for only a few feet in front of us. The bulletins on the radio were warning motorists to stay off the roads, and we had the autobahn virtually to ourselves. The snowploughs were working to keep one lane open, and they managed for a while, but eventually the snow reclaimed the road. At regular intervals we passed the mound of an abandoned car. It was as bad a storm as I had ever seen.

At the Swiss border they warned us not to go on, but Mike concocted a fantasy about a family crisis that couldn't wait, and they let us through. We made better time on the Swiss side of the line, they had more ploughs working, but it was still a crawl. The wind was up now, and every time we came to an exposed stretch of the road it slammed into the car and rocked us back and forth. Mike drove with his shoulders hunched over the wheel and his eyes close to the glass. He was totally concentrated on what he was doing. It was something he did very well.

We turned off the main road at Zernez. The secondary road was unploughed, but it was bounded by a low stone wall on the left. The effect of the wind had created an open strip in the lee of the wall, and Mike was able to use it. We crept along looking for landmarks and counting kilometres. There was no use looking for signs, they were all buried. What I wanted to see was a blasted tree on the right side of the road. Lightning had hit it the year before and had split it into a V. The forestry service should have cut it down, but they hadn't got round to it. It was about thirty feet high, and it was opposite the turnoff that led up to the house.

'Over there,' I said when I saw it. 'We go left up the mountain here.'

Mike swung the car to the left so that the headlights pointed uphill. 'On what?' he asked.

There was no road, only a solid expanse of snow. I looked behind me, lining up with the tree. We were in the right place; the road was buried. The house was about a mile up the mountain. I couldn't see the lights of the terrace, but I knew that they were on. I reached in the back for my ski boots. Mike grinned and did the same. He was enjoying it all.

We got boots on and skis off the rack, and started uphill. I checked the time when we left and when we got there. The climb took sixty-eight minutes, and it was the hardest work I ever did on skis. They were the wrong skis for what we were trying to do, and we had no skins or anything else to give us traction. All the skis did was keep us from sinking into the snow, but that's all we really wanted from them. We put our heads down and bucked up the hill. It was dark, it was snowing heavily, and the wind was coming straight at us. It would have been easy to wander, but the road beneath the snow was bordered by trees still visible. The road switched back and forth as it rose uphill, and the trees followed it. The way we were climbing we were able to cut across the loops and take a straighter line.

We were more than halfway up when I saw the lights on the terrace. I pointed to them with a pole. Mike nodded wearily. The climb was taking it out of him. He stood with his chest heaving, his skis braced to hold him in place.

'One more push,' I told him.

'Shit.'

'I can always carry you.'

'Not that,' he managed to say. 'Just remembered. Forgot to lock the car.'

When we finished the climb we both were gasping. The front door was snowed in. We climbed to the terrace and took off our skis there. I banged on the terrace doors until somebody came to let us in. It was Jenny. She let out a whoop when she saw us, then caught herself and said nonchalantly, 'What took you so long?'

We came inside shaking and stamping. Anna came bustling in, and Jenny said to her, 'They're frozen. Get some coffee going.'

We unlatched our boots and took off our parkas. The parkas were stiff with ice. Anna took them and looked around for somewhere to put them.

'Anna, coffee,' said Jenny.

'I heard you the first time,' she said crossly. 'Always when something happens it's Anna make some coffee. Like in the movies they're always telling some woman to boil water. With me it's Anna make some coffee.'

'Where's Justine?' I asked.

'Still upstairs.'

I clumped out into the hallway. Digger was standing at the foot of the stairs as if he were guarding them. His face was set and stern. He didn't say hello. He said, 'Before you go up there – '

'Get out of my way.'

'She doesn't want to – '

'You're in my home and you're in my way. Move.'

He didn't move. I put my hand against his chest and shoved him aside. I shoved him harder than I meant to, and he went down on his butt. He looked up at me in surprise. Mike ran forward to help him to his feet. I went up the stairs to my bedroom, our room. The door was locked. I said through the door:

'Justine, it's me. Kelly. Open up.'

There was no answer. I waited, and said it again. Still no answer. I kicked the door in with one shot from a ski boot just above the lock. The door swung crazily on its hinges.

Justine sat in a chair by the window. It was after midnight, but she was dressed for travelling the way she must have been when the car got stuck: heavy trousers, sweater, boots. We stared at each other, and I felt a thickness in my throat. I knew that I was about to lose something, but I didn't know what, or how much.

'I skipped the slalom at Kay-Gee,' I said lamely. 'I missed you. I wanted to be here.'

Her hands fluttered, then were still. 'They said you wouldn't get through, but I knew you would.'

'Why was the door locked?'

'I didn't want to see you. I didn't want you to try to change my mind.'

'I'm going to try anyway. You were running away from me.'

'I had to.' For the first time I realized how pale she was. Her voice was low and shaky. 'I left you a note. Then the car got stuck and we had to come back. It's over there.'

The note was on the dressing table. I read it slowly. It was pretty much what I had expected.

Kelly dear,

A cowardly letter, but I don't have the courage to tell you this face to face. When I left you at Kitz, I thought I was pregnant. I came back here to see a doctor and find out. The tests say I

636

was right . . . two months. You know what this means. We had a deal, the three of us. If this happened the baby belonged to the dream, to the house, to Marina. And to Digger. I called him in New York as soon as I found out. I had to. That was also part of the deal. He's flying in today, he should be here this evening. As soon as he gets here we'll be leaving for Skofja Loka. We'll stay there until the baby is born. I don't know what will happen after that, but I know I owe him this much. It's something we all agreed on long ago.

I know how much this is going to hurt you. I love you both and I've tried to make you both happy, but it hasn't worked out, has it? In the long run someone always has to get hurt. Until now I thought that someone would be me. For three years I have been torn apart twice a year, and it has taken too much out of me. I thought I could handle it, but I can't, and before this happened I knew that it would have to stop. I knew that I would have to make a decision one way or the other, but now the decision has been made for me. If it's any comfort to you, if this hadn't happened the decision probably would have gone the other way.

But it *has* happened, and I must go with him. Because in some crazy way this crazy dream of his has become my dream too. Very slowly, over the years, it has become a part of me, and now the last part has come true. I'm carrying Marina's baby for her, and I have to finish the job.

I love you now just as much as ever, and I always will.

Justine

I put the note down and knelt beside her. I said, 'The most important question comes first. Are you happy being pregnant?'

'Oh, yes.' Just for a moment a smile bloomed, and just as quickly, faded.

'Then everything else will work out. This is my baby, isn't it?'

'I said in the note, I'm two months gone. I've been with you since October. Of course you're the father. But it isn't yours, it's his.'

'The hell with that.'

'That's easy to say. I made a deal.'

637

'That deal is bullshit, an old man's fantasy that he conned you with.'

'If it's a fantasy, it's my fantasy too. I said it all in the note. Don't make me say it again.'

'You're staying here with me.'

She put her hands over her face. 'Don't do this to me. Don't try to talk me out of it.'

'Do you really think that I'm going to let you walk away from here with my child? Our child.'

'You're doing it.' Her voice was weak. 'You're tearing me apart again.'

'You belong here with me.'

'Please, please don't do this.' She was sobbing behind her hands. 'I can't take any more of this, I can't. I promised him, and I can't back out.'

'I'm cancelling that promise. If he wants a child, let him make one of his own.'

'Oh, God, don't say things like that. You don't know what you're doing to me.' She began to weep deeply. 'You don't know what it's like to be this way, to love you both. Everything I do, every move I make, has to hurt someone. I can't do it any more.'

I rested my hand on her arm. 'I want you to do this. I want you to think about this some more before you make a final decision. Will you do that for me?'

'I've already done my thinking.'

'No, that wasn't thinking, that was reacting. That was doing something out of an obligation that doesn't exist. You're doing this because you think you have to, but you don't. You're free to make any decision you choose. All I'm asking you to do is think about it some more, take a good look at what you're doing. There's no hurry, nobody's getting out of here quickly. It will take at least a day before the ploughs get up here from town, so you have plenty of time. Will you at least think about it?'

She did not answer.

'Will you do that for me? For us?'

I waited, my breath tight in my chest. Very slowly, she nodded. I let my breath out.

'Fair enough,' I said. 'That's all I'm asking.'

I heard the scrape of feet behind me, and I turned. Anna was in the doorway, staring at the broken door.

'Like always, it's none of my business,' she said, 'so excuse me, but in Justine's condition I don't think she needs all this carrying on, all this yelling and breaking doors in the middle of the night.'

'What do you know about her condition?'

Her chin came up. 'I read the note she left you. While the car was getting stuck. What did you expect me to do?'

She glared at me defiantly. I wanted to laugh, but I couldn't. Justine sighed, and said, 'She's right, I really would like to rest for a while. I haven't had much sleep.' She hesitated. 'Kelly, do you mind? I'm putting you out of your own bedroom, but I'd rather be alone right now.'

'Sure.' I bent and kissed her cheek. 'I have some things to settle downstairs anyway.'

She looked alarmed. 'There isn't going to be any fighting, is there? Please?'

'Nothing like that, just some quiet conversation.'

I kissed her again as Anna came swooping down to help get her to bed. I could almost hear the clucking. I was feeling pretty good about things at that point. I had time on my side, and she had promised to think about it. As I clumped down the stairs I realized that I was still wearing ski boots. I sat on the bottom step, got them off, and left them there. I padded into the sitting room in stockinged feet.

The room in tableau as I entered: Jenny kneeling at the hearth, poking at the fire; Digger and Mike at the drinks cart with glasses in their hands; an urn of coffee and a plate of sandwiches on the table; and the windows banked high with snow. The room was warm and cosy, the aroma of coffee and pine nuts floating. Looking at my father and my brother standing side by side, chatting casually, I realized how rarely I ever saw them together, and how sad that was. Then Digger saw me standing in the doorway, and he gave me the big smile.

'We've been helping ourselves,' he said jovially, raising his glass. 'As you pointed out earlier, this is your house, but we didn't think you'd mind if we tapped the bar. Actually, I've been tapping it regularly since I got here. I must say that you keep a well-stocked cellar for a teetotal.'

I nodded to show that I didn't mind. This was vintage Digger:

639

no sign of enmity, no sign that I had just knocked him down, no sign that he knew what I was trying to do to him. He had the personality machine cranked up and running smoothly. I went to the table for coffee, and his voice followed me.

'Mike's been telling me how you got up here,' he was saying. 'It must have been a hell of a climb, I'm amazed the two of you made it. I doubt if I could have done it, even in my best days.'

He was really working at it, praising Mike as well as me. I couldn't remember the last time that had happened. I took a bite of a sandwich and turned to face them. Mike was glowing from the compliment. Digger looked at me expectantly through a stream of cigar smoke. I waited for words to come and chewed on the sandwich. It was liverwurst, and it was good. Jenny gave the fire a final poke and stood up with a tight little smile on her face.

'Where's Anna?' she asked.

'Upstairs with Justine.'

'I think I'll join them. I get the feeling that things are about to blow around here, and I don't want any part of it.' She went to the door, stopped, and said, 'Remember what I once said about letting people steal from you? I don't know how much longer you can keep on doing that, Ace.'

'Christ, did you read that letter too?'

She grinned at me and skipped out the door.

When she was gone, Digger made a gesture with his cigar and said, 'Well, are things going to blow around here?'

Mike said, 'Maybe I'd better leave too.'

'No, stay,' I told him. 'This won't take long, and nothing is going to blow. I promised Justine that there wouldn't be any fighting or shouting, and I meant it. So I'll say this nice and easy.' I turned to Digger. 'First of all, you're finished at Prince Skis, effective immediately. We'll settle your contract, but you're out.'

'You're just a touch late,' he said. His voice was as easy as mine. 'I left a letter of resignation in New York. Hell, I'm sixty-three, I was only going to give it another year or two anyway. My contract will cover my retirement, and I've got the house in Slovenia. I'll be all right.'

'I wasn't particularly concerned. Point number two. I've spoken to Justine, and she's agreed to think things over. Nothing is definite any more. She'll make up her own mind whether she

640

goes with you or stays with me. But it's still open, nothing set. I thought you should know that.'

He surprised me by taking that one in stride. 'Quite right, it was always her choice, anyway. I'm sure she'll make the right decision.'

'So am I.'

'Well, we shall see, won't we? Anything else?'

'Just this. I want her left alone. I don't want you bothering her. Let her do her thinking by herself. If you interfere, I promise you this. I'll break your fucking neck.'

He looked at me with interest. 'You know, I think you would, at that.' He jiggled the ice cubes in his empty glass. 'I'll just help myself to another, if you don't mind. Michael, join me?'

They fixed their drinks, I topped off my coffee, and we sat in front of the hearth: three men with their legs stretched to the fire. There was a quiet, comfortable feeling in the room, and in that moment we could have been any family from anywhere in the world on a skiing holiday in the Alps.

'It's not a night for sleep,' said Digger. 'Too late, and too much in the air. It's a night for sipping bourbon whisky and telling tales. Have you ever had nights like that?'

I shook my head. Mike said, 'Plenty of them. In Nam.'

'Yes, you would have. Then you know what I mean. Take a slug of your drink and tell us a tale.'

'Not me. I'm so tired I can't think straight.'

'Kelly?'

'I pass.'

'Then I have the floor, don't I?'

Without hesitation he began to talk about Vermont when he was a boy, and about his father. He didn't tell any tales. He just talked easily about what it was like to grow up with a world of mountains all your own and a father you could lean upon whenever the climb got rough or the hill grew steep. He didn't tell us anything that we hadn't heard before, but it was a finer, simpler time that he was talking about, and it was comforting to hear.

'My father was the soundest man I ever knew,' he said. 'I wish I could have been more like him, but I guess we can't control those things. Too much of my mother in me, much as I hate to admit it. Too much hardass, too much greed. Not like my father. His family came first for him, always.' He repeated the word. 'Always.'

Mike cleared his throat. 'Digger?'

'What?'

'Nothing.'

'Sure.'

The fire danced, the shadows shimmered, and I closed my eyes. I heard their voices as low monotones, heard the wind at the windows, the snap of a log, and without any trouble I slipped into sleep. When I woke it was close to four. The fire was down and my legs were cramped from the way I had been sleeping in the chair. Digger was asleep on the couch and Mike was curled up like a hound dog in front of the fireplace. So much for old soldiers sitting up through the night. I got up to stretch my legs and went to the window. The storm was over, the wind was down, and the skies were clear. It was white all around, and the setting moon made everything seem soft. I went back to the chair and went back to sleep. When I opened my eyes again it was morning, and Jenny was shaking me awake to tell me that Justine was gone.

'Gone?' I came up from sleep groggily. 'What do you mean, gone? There's no place to go.'

Jenny said patiently, 'Ace, her bed is empty, she's not in the house, and there are ski tracks leading from the terrace, heading for town.'

It took a while for that to mean anything, and then I sat up quickly. 'There's a metre of fresh powder out there. She can't ski that.'

'That's what I'm trying to tell you.' Jenny shook her head in exasperation. 'Now why would she go and do a dumb thing like that?'

It was an easy one to answer, but I kept the answer to myself. She wasn't hanging around to be torn apart any more. She had taken as much of that as she could. She was half out of her head with two kinds of love, and she was going some place where she could make up her mind by herself. She had picked a hell of a time to do it. I looked around. Digger and Mike were sitting up, eyes bleary, as Anna gave them the same story. It registered quickly with Digger. He frowned, looked at me, and asked:

'What do you think?'

'No good. She can't handle it. She may think she can, but she can't.'

'How long ago did she leave?' he asked Anna.

'Who knows? Fifteen minutes? Half an hour?'

'I'll need boots and skis.'

'In the room off the garage,' I told him. Then I was up and we were all moving at once.

The morning was clear and bright, sunny cold the way it can be when the wind whips the clouds away after a big one. The mountain was overhung with snow, the savage face of Piz d'Rel trailing a long white beard, and cornices curled from every ridge. We travelled in a line, Digger leading, then Jenny, me, Anna, and Mike. The tracks were easy to follow, the only marks on virgin snow. She had taken the way she knew best into town, a long traverse around the mountain instead of skiing down to the road and then along the flat. The way she was doing it was shorter, but it was taking her across too many open slopes. I tried not to look at those cornices up on the ridges as we hurried along. The snow was loose and fluffy, waist-high and windblown all around me. I rocked back on my skis to plane up the tips, and sat back with my arms high and my poles free. The snow crested over my waist and flowed around under my arms. I leaned back farther and the tips of my skis popped through the surface the way they will when the base below the powder is hard, and then I was riding a wave of snow, cutting a curving swath through it. There is nothing more enjoyable in skiing than running fresh powder, but you have to be in the mood for it, and I wasn't.

We followed her tracks across three open slopes, and we crossed them gingerly, space between us. None of us was happy with what we were doing. We were breaking every rule in the book. We should not have been on the mountain at all before the patrol cleared off those cornices, and we were travelling without the most basic equipment: avalanche cords and probing poles. We were doing everything wrong, but we had no choice. We had to follow her tracks.

We pushed on to the next slope and found her there. She was down and her skis were off, but she had dragged herself into the shelter of a massive projection of rock that split the slope in two. She waved when she saw us, pointed to her ankle, and called across the slope.

'I think it's only a sprain.' Her voice floated clearly in the cold air. 'But I can't move on it.'

Digger motioned to her to stay still and stay quiet. He didn't like what we had, and neither did I. We were strung out across an open slope, and what we were standing on could go at any time. The air was quiet, electric still, and I had the feeling that any move would make the mountain tremble. I called Digger's name softly, and he turned only his head to look back at me.

'This is no good,' I said. 'Too many people on the slope. We have to get off.'

He nodded. 'I'm closest. I'm going after her. The rest of you back off one by one, and clear out.'

Jenny, who was next in line to him, said, 'Don't be such a fucking hero. You can't get her out of there yourself. I'm going with you.'

I said, 'So am I.'

He grinned at us both. 'I *am* a fucking hero. I've been one all my life. I'll do this one myself.'

He started to move slowly across the slope. He almost made it. He was halfway there when the mountain came apart. We all heard the roar in the same moment and looked up to see the wall of snow descending. It was nightmare time, one which had haunted all of our dreams. The world turned in on us, and in that shred of time we each made a move laid down in decisions made long ago. Run for it, or break to the side? The tick of a heart to decide.

Digger dug down with his poles, came up on his tips, and turned downhill to run for it. He was sixty-three years old, but he had always been a mountain man and that was the way he chose to play it.

Jenny sideslipped gracefully into the fall line, following Digger. She was years away from her Olympic form, but she had been there once, and she was good enough to play it that way, too.

Mike yelled, 'Whoops,' and then he too had turned and was scooting downhill, trying to outrun the wall. He had never been a racer, but he knew where he belonged.

Anna did what she had to do. Every part of her wanted to turn downhill and follow Jenny, but she wasn't that good and she knew it. She broke left across the slope in a long traverse, straining for the projection of rock that sheltered Justine.

644

My play was the downhill run as well, and I made the turn in my mind. My brain gave my body commands for it, but my legs refused to obey. Instead, incredibly, I found myself dropped into a tuck and racing across the slope towards the shelter of the rock where Justine waited. It was the wrong move for me to make, but my body was in charge, not my brain.

The mountain belched and rumbled, tons of snow and ice cascading down, the formless mass growing in size as it came. Time hung, milliseconds dragging as we fled the rolling boil, three breaking downhill, two breaking left. Avalanche thunder: it filled the air, blocked the ears, and echoed down the ridgelines. I held my tuck, my eyes on Justine, straining to reach the shelter of the rock, and then I was at it, in it, and Anna came tumbling in after me. The wall of snow, split by the massive projection, rolled around us on either side and left us untouched.

The fist of the avalanche, the point of the V, caught Digger halfway down the hill, tossed him high and gathered him in. It came to Jenny farther down, plucked her gently, and pressed her to its bosom. Stretched out over his skis, his fists at the tips, Mike felt it coming, the force of its pressure building behind him. One glance over his shoulder, another downhill, and a cackle of wild laughter welled up as he saw that he wasn't going to make it. Still laughing, he flung himself around in a violent turn that left him facing uphill as the mountain came to meet him. He spread his arms wide to greet his old friend as the wall of snow rolled over him. The roar subsided as the avalanche reached the valley floor, grunted, humped, and finally rested. Up on the side of the mountain three people huddled, staring downhill dumbly. Anna leaned against a rock, turned her face away from me, and sobbed softly. Justine sighed and moved next to me; I put my arm around her. I kept my eyes on the downhill slope, trying to understand what had happened. I had skied it wrong to get to her, and because of that I had made it. The others had skied it right, and were gone. Along with the grief came the thought of how very unfair that was.

I sent Anna for help and tried to search, probing with my ski poles, but it was a fruitless effort. The patrols came and searched all day, but they didn't get the bodies out until just before dark. We took them down into town on sleds, and as we started down the hill the snow began again.

Chapter Fifteen

That was six months ago. We buried our dead and fled to Ibiza: Justine, Anna, and I. We holed up here, held hands, bowed our heads, and began to learn to live with the knowledge of what we had lost. It took a lot of learning, and the process is still incomplete. It took a lot of loving, and it took diversion too. Various forms of it. Justine had the baby she was carrying to fill her mind, keep the spectres at bay, and her days were spent marching to an inner beat. Anna had Justine to care for, to keep hand and heart busy with the need to mother the mother-to-be. And I had this chronicle to compose, seeking a semblance of myself as I rummaged through the past. I spent my days retelling the family tales, and in the nights I pounded the piano at the Café Serra as I tried to say goodbye to the dead.

Trouble is, the dead don't want to say goodbye. They're still alive inside my head. I still see Jenny beside me every morning when I run the road, her pigtail bouncing up and down. I still hear Mike's cheerful cackle in my ears, still see his scarecrow figure waving to me from some distant ridge. And I'm still sore at Digger, arguing with him in my head. I know that he's gone, but the battle goes on. Why did he have to leave so soon? We never finished fighting.

I say goodbye, but the voices hang around, and sometimes in the night I remember that other night, the last one, when Digger, Mike, and I sat stretched with our legs towards the fire. A night for sipping whisky and telling tales, Digger said, and he told us once again about his father and the mountains of Vermont in those simpler days. That was when I fell off to sleep, the voices of the two old soldiers a buzz in my ears, and sometimes now I think I hear them talking still, Digger's quiet chuckle, and then he says:

Hell of a night, hell of a storm, and it looks like your brother is sleeping. Kid can sleep anywhere, comes from all that clean living. Well, just you and me, Michael, and I'll tell you a tale that I've never told before. Nobody's ever heard this one, so listen up and I'll tell you the story of how your pappy schussed the headwall at Tuckerman's Ravine. Heard it before, have you? The hell you have. What you've heard are the skiing myths, and that myth is as good as a mile. What you're going to hear now is the straight poop, unadulterated. Digger Prince, the guy who schussed Mount Washington, and what nobody knows is that it was really an accident. God's truth, it was. Never meant to schuss that sucker. All the other racers were taking three, maybe four checks on the headwall to cut their speed, and I figured I'd be real gutsy and take only one or two. So I came over the lip, slammed down on the wall, shifted my weight . . . and nothing happened. I was, as they say, somewhat surprised. Tried it again with no results; skis wouldn't turn. They shifted a bit, but nothing really happened, had no traction there. Hell of a feeling going lickety-split down the side of the Empire State Building with no control over my skis. Well, sir, turned out that the bindings had sprung loose, big old beartrap bindings in those days, and it seems that when I came over the lip I slammed down so hard that both sets of screws popped their threads through the wood. They were just hanging in there, enough to keep my boots on the skis but not enough to give me any lateral control. Jesus H. Christ, what a feeling that was, and there was nothing I could do about it. Built up a hell of a head of speed by then, and all I could do was run it out. Which I did. Smoked that mother from top to bottom, greatest run of my life. That run made me, followed me around wherever I went, put me in business, in a sense. Digger Prince, the guy who schussed Tuckerman's. And all because of a couple of loose screws. But you keep that to yourself, understand? Private information, strictly in the family. Never told it to anyone before, and I never will again.

Voices in the night, Mike's incredulous: Jesus, Digger, is that really true?

Hell no, but it makes a good story for a stormy night, doesn't it?

Oh . . . well, yeah. I knew you were kidding all along.

Sure you did. Now it's your turn.

And slowly, hesitantly, Mike tells him how he learned to ski in Vietnam. How he covered the country with snow, and then at night could lie awake and schuss the shorelines and the jungle's maze, skimming down from the Central Highlands to

647

the back streets of Saigon seeing only the deep powder, smelling only the tang of fir and pine, hearing only the whisper of the wind.

Murmur of approval from Digger, and then, barely articulated: I've never told you how much I admire what you did in Vietnam. It was a courageous way to prove a point. I'm proud of you for it.

I did what I had to do.

Yes. I should have said this sooner. Years sooner. I'm sorry. I'm sorry for all the troubles I caused you.

I'm sorry for all the times I turned away.

I'm sorry, you're sorry, over and over their voices murmur in the night, reconstructing history, making things come out right. No, not right. They already came out wrong. But better.

Jim Casey came to the island the first week in September. Silver-haired, ruddy-cheeked, the coach with the soft voice, the coach who got the jobs that no one else wanted. Over the summer there had been four letters from the Ski Team, all asking about my plans for the coming season, all left unanswered. Now they sent Casey. He showed up late one afternoon, his rented Seat 600 raising dust as it chugged up the bumpy, tilted road to the house. He greeted Justine and Anna gravely, and asked if he and I could talk.

'Have dinner with us,' I said. 'We can talk all night if you want, but I can tell you right now that I'm not racing any more.'

'What's for dinner?' he asked, smiling easily.

He had a couple of beers and made Anna happy by going through two bowls of the fish stew that she makes with dill and cream. Lively and articulate, he kept a light chatter going through the meal, telling stories, that entertained Justine and had her laughing.

'No more jokes,' he said to her after a while. 'I don't want to be the cause of anything premature. When are you due?'

'In about five weeks,' she said. 'We'll be going to Barcelona soon.'

He worked the dates in his head. 'That comes out right. After the baby arrives, Kelly could join the team at Hintertux.'

She smiled and shook her head. 'You're pitching to the wrong person, Jim. Try that on Kelly, not me.'

648

'He's already told me that he's finished with racing. Is that what you want for him?'

'It's what he wants that counts. No, I have no objection if he wants to go racing, but it's up to him.'

After dinner Casey and I sat out under the stars while he smoked a cigar that reminded me of Digger. He tried the pitch one more time. I told him that I was flattered by all the attention.

'You don't need me at Sarajevo,' I said. 'The team is loaded. Phil and Steve will get you some medals, and Billy Johnson looks like he's ready. And the women, hell, they're dynamite. Tamara, Christin, Nellie, Debbie – any one of them could take a gold.'

'I'm not talking about the other people, I'm talking about you. You've been pointing towards this one season all your life. All that work, all that training. How can you just toss it away?'

'That was all Digger, Jim, not me. He was the one with the ambition, and now he's dead. The dream died with it.'

'I find that hard to believe.'

'That's the way it is.'

It was late and dark, and I offered him the spare room for the night. He accepted gladly, and asked what time I got up in the morning. I told him that roadwork started at five-thirty, and he was welcome to run off some of the beer with me. He groaned and made a face, but the next morning he was up and ready in baggy shorts and a sweatshirt.

We jogged down to the main road and then ran the four kilometres north towards San Carlos. He watched while I did my pushes and my sits at the side of the road, and then ran the four kilometres back to the beach with me. He was heaving a bit when we got to the beach, but he was in good shape for fifty. I pointed to the rock that was Rat Island, half a mile offshore.

'I go there and back now,' I said. 'Want to come along?'

'On your way, me lad, and don't be sassing your elders. I'll just paddle back and forth a bit.'

When I got back he was resting on the sand. I shook myself dry, put my shorts back on, and sat down next to him. He looked at me approvingly.

'You do this every day?' he asked.

'On rainy days I skip the swim.'

'You look to be in great shape. How come, if you're not competing any more?'

'Habit, I guess. You don't like to lose it.'

'On the contrary. I've seen hundreds of athletes hang it up, and the first thing that goes is the training. They turn into slobs.'

'Not me. I have the feeling that if I ever skipped training Jenny would come back and boot my ass.'

'Not good enough. You may have quit with your head, but not with your heart. If you can put yourself through this every day then you're still a racer.'

I said nothing. I looked out to sea.

'You want to tell me the real reason why you won't race?'

'It's pretty obvious, isn't it? I don't have it any more. I lost it that day on Piz d'Rel. Just the thought of putting skis on scares the shit out of me.'

He pushed a pile of sand together and started building a square. He worked quickly and carefully, his stubby fingers shaping the edges. As he did it, he said softly, 'I don't know how many hundreds of skiers I've coached, but there have been plenty. And the usual percentage didn't have what it takes for a high-risk sport. So they faded away, they dropped out. After a while you didn't see them around any more. But I never had a world-class racer come to me and say what you just said. That he was too scared to ski.'

'Well, now you've heard it.'

'Right, and I don't believe it. Anybody who has the guts to say what you just said has to have the guts to get back on skis and do what he does best.'

I told him then what it had been like after the patrols found the bodies. They took them down to the town on sleds. They needed a sled for Justine, too, because of her ankle. They took the bodies to the church, put duckboards over the altar, and laid them out there, covered with canvas. It was something that they did after an avalanche. The melting snow and ice dripped through the boards and made puddles on the floor. Covered in canvas the way they were, I could tell which was Jenny's, but I couldn't tell Mike's and Digger's apart, and for some reason that bothered me. The people from the town filed through the church to pay their respects. It was a small town, and everyone came. I sat through the night in the church. Justine slept at the doctor's house, and Anna stayed with her. The doctor sedated them both. I had no place to go. The road to the house was still blocked with snow, and so I stayed in the church. I tried to sleep, but whenever I closed my eyes I saw that wall of snow descending on me, and my eyes snapped open again. It was a long night. In the morning, when I came out into the daylight, I looked for my skis. I had left them propped against the church wall, but they were gone. Someone had lifted them, but I didn't care. I didn't care if I never saw another pair of skis again.

'All very understandable,' said Casey, 'considering what you'd been through. Things like that pass.'

'This hasn't. I just don't care any more.'

'You should give it a try. You owe yourself that much.'

'It wouldn't work.'

'Keep an open mind. The season opens at Kay-Gee on December second. When we get back to the house I'll give you a schedule of where we'll be training before then. You could join us at Hintertux if you want to. You'd be welcome.'

'Thanks, Jim. I appreciate what you're trying to do, but don't count on it. We'd better start back now.'

We never got back to the house, not that morning. As we were walking up the road a boil of dust came racing towards us. Anna at the wheel of the jeep, Justine slouched in the seat beside her, her face contorted. Anna stopped when she came up to us.

'Jump in,' she yelled. 'The baby decided not to wait for Barcelona.'

I got in behind Justine, Casey behind Anna. I put my hands behind Justine's neck to give her some support there. The jeep was bouncing crazily.

'Hang in there,' I said into Justine's ear. 'Fifteen minutes to the *clínica*, no more.'

She nodded. She had her teeth clenched and she did not want to speak.

'Concentrate,' I told her. 'Nobody has babies in cars any more.'

She managed a weak smile. Then the smile disappeared and she clenched her teeth again.

At the *clínica* they rushed her into a room, pushed me out while they prepared her, then let me back in for a minute. She held my hand. She looked awfully pale. She said, 'I'm glad you're here. Now get out and let me go to work.'

I waited with Anna and Casey in a tiled, high-ceilinged room that opened onto a tiny courtyard. The yard had a single palm tree and some bougainvillea growing on one wall. The doors to the yard were open, but the room smelled of antiseptic. Anna sat by herself on a straight-backed chair, her hands folded in her lap. She looked as if she wanted to check the corners of the room for dust and bacteria. Casey tried to make the waiting easier by telling me stories about his own three children. They were funny stories, but they didn't make anything easier.

'How old are your kids?' I asked.

'Twenty-six, twenty-two, and twenty.'

'Do they ski?'

'Oh sure, but they're not very good at it.'

'That doesn't bother you?'

'Why should it?' He seemed surprised. 'All three of them have got a million other things going for them. They don't need skiing.'

I tried to think of what I had going for me besides skiing and thirty percent of the stock of Prince. There wasn't much else.

An hour later a doctor in rumpled green came into the room, walked up to Casey, and said, 'Congratulations, Mr Prince. Your wife is in excellent health and you have a son, three point four kilos. Also quite healthy.'

'*Gott sei Danke,*' said Anna.

Casey burst out laughing. The doctor looked startled. I said, 'I'm the father.'

'Ah, very sorry. Again, congratulations. All is well. Would you like to see your son?'

'I'd like to see my wife.' I was calling her that now.

'In a while, she is resting now. Come, this way to the nursery.'

The three of us followed him down a hallway. I said to Casey, 'Tell me the truth, Jim, how much did you pay him to do that?'

He shook his head, still laughing silently.

They gave us masks and let us into the nursery. I don't know what I expected to see, certainly something different from the red and bawling scrap of flesh that greeted me. I must have looked disappointed, because Casey said, 'They all look that way. Actually, your boy is an above-average specimen.'

'He is adorable,' Anna breathed. Then she turned and ran out of the room.

'What are you going to call him?' Casey asked.

'Anton.'

'Tony Prince,' he said approvingly. 'Just the right size for a one-column headline in *The Times*. Let's see, he'll be twenty in 2004.' He said twenty-oh-four. 'The Nineteenth Winter Games.'

I shook my head. I could see that he was grinning through the mask. He said, 'Go ahead, tell me that you didn't figure that one out.'

'I didn't,' I said, but I was lying.

'How do you feel?'

'Terrific. I've never been drunk, but that's the way I feel.'

'Yeah, it hits you that way.'

'I feel bigger.'

'I know.'

'Wiser. I feel like a bloody genius.'

'I know.'

'He's really one hell of a good-looking kid, isn't he?'

'A rarity. One in a million.'

'At least.'

I looked down at my son. His fists were clenched tight, and he was smiling. I wanted a happy, open mind just then, but I couldn't help thinking of what he had caused so far. I thought of that drive through the storm with Mike hunched over the wheel. I thought of the climb to the house at Piz d'Rel, and what had happened there that night and what had happened the next day on the mountain. I thought of the church and the puddles of water under the altar. I thought of the worst of the nights when the wall of snow still came rolling down on me. I thought of all of that, and I said to my son, 'I hope to hell you're worth it.'

Casey heard me. I hadn't meant him to, but he did. He looked at me oddly and said, 'He will be. I only hope that you'll be worth it too.'

'I'll try to be.'

'How hard?'

'You're saying that I have to do it, aren't you? That I have to go back and race.'

'I don't see how you can avoid it. Not if you want to live with yourself, and with this boy of yours.'

'I'm still scared.'

'I know.'

'I don't know if it will work. I can't make any promises.'

653

'I'm not asking for any. Just that you give it a try. Will you?'

I hesitated. Casey's eyes were bright above the mask. I said, 'I still don't want to but . . . this changes things.'

'I know. You've never been a father before. You've always been a son.'

'Yes, it's different now.'

'Will you do it?'

'Yes.' It was easier to say than I had thought it would be.

'Will I see you at Hintertux?'

'Yes.' It was even easier the second time.

He hit my arm lightly. 'Good.'

We went back to the high-ceilinged room where Anna was waiting. Casey had a plane to catch, and she said that she would drive him to the house. He was still dressed in sweat-soaked shorts and shirt. So was I.

'I'll have time for a quick shower and change,' he said. He held out his hand. 'I'm sorry that I can't hang around. Give Justine my love and best wishes, and don't forget to tell her that the doctor took me for the father. I'm going to treasure that one.' Then he said in parting, the words he had said to me and to so many others many times before. 'I'll see you on the hill.'

When they let me in to see Justine she was half propped up in bed. A nurse had combed her hair and had put some colour in her cheeks. She looked awfully weary, but her smile was full. I sat beside the bed and took her hand.

'Have you seen him?' she asked. 'Isn't he lovely?'

'Not lovely. Awesome is the word.'

'He's lovely. What a fine job we did. I'm proud of us.'

'Yes.'

'We seem to be very good at this business of making babies. We must do it again, but not too soon.'

'Yes.'

'Just let me know when you're ready and we'll do it again, just like that.' She tried to snap her fingers, but it didn't work. 'Anyway, you know what I mean. But not too soon.'

'No.'

'I'm babbling, aren't I? They gave me something for the pain and it's making me babble. I really should sleep.'

'You're not babbling, you're doing fine. I can understand every word.'

'No, I am, but that's all right. We really did make a good job of it, didn't we?'

'The best.'

'That comes from loving your work. Or working your love. Does that makes sense? Anything to do with love makes sense. And how long will it last, this ludicrous, overbearing love of ours?'

'Who knows? It all depends on how well we've played.'

'You skipped a couple of lines,' she said drowsily.

'I know I did. Sometimes I cheat.'

'That's all right. So do I.' She smiled, closed her eyes, and was asleep.

I stayed beside the bed for a while, wondering what it would be like. I would join the team and go racing again; I would go to Sarajevo. I was certain of that much now. I would fight what had to be fought. And after that I would fight for something new, something of my own. I was finished with the past and everything in it. I had paid it all off and I owed nothing. I was finished with other men's dreams. It was time to say goodbye to dreams and to memories, goodbye to all the snow gods on the hills. Goodbye to what I was, and would never be again. Goodbye, little Jenny. Goodbye, older brother. Goodbye, my father.

I'll beat you yet.

Goodbye, goodbye, goodbye.